Sarah Harrison has written many bestselling novels
– *Life After Lunch*, *Flowers Won't Fax*, *That Was
Then*, *Heaven's on Hold* and *The Grass Memorial*
are all available from Hodder & Stoughton – as well
as children's books, short stories, articles and scripts.
She lives in Cambridgeshire.

Sarah Harrison

The Dreaming Stones

FLAME
Hodder & Stoughton

Copyright © 2003 by Sarah Harrison

First published in 2003 by Hodder & Stoughton
A division of Hodder Headline
First published in paperback in 2003 by Hodder & Stoughton
A Flame paperback

The right of Sarah Harrison to be identified as the Author of
the Work has been asserted by her in accordance with the
Copyright, Designs and Patents Act 1988.

1 3 5 7 9 10 8 6 4 2

A CIP catalogue record for this book is available from the
British Library

ISBN 0 340 83303 3

Typeset by Palimpsest Book Production Limited,
Polmont, Stirlingshire

Printed and bound by
Mackays of Chatham Ltd, Chatham, Kent

Hodder & Stoughton
A division of Hodder Headline
338 Euston Road
London NW1 3BH

For dearest Jean and Daddo

When I'd walked some way from the wood I stopped and looked back. High above the black treeline I could see the rooftops of the big house picked out by the slanting winter sun. The sight didn't, as it once had, fill me with longing and envy and a sense of my own ordinariness. It was only bricks, stones, timber, tiles, plaster: the repository of dreams, and the focus of many lives over many centuries, a burden, a passion. A house had no heart but that of the people who lived there.

It was getting colder. This, I thought, would be the first, last and only Christmas Eve when my grandson would allow us to sleep uninterrupted through the long night, and I was ambushed by the thought of all those unforeseen, incredible years to come . . . As I stood there the dog appeared, the wanderer, galloping across the billow of the hill, in and out of the brightness and the spreading pools of shadow, leaping and bounding over the scattered stones like a dolphin.

As I went on my way I wondered who the free, happy, fortunate dog belonged to. But when, a moment later, I glanced back, he'd disappeared. Gone home.

Evening

The night was cold and starless. But there was fire in the sky, and on the stage, and in the encampment that spread over the dark fields beyond. On the hills above, a cold dew was misting the grass, but down here tens of thousands of stamping feet had reduced the ground to mud, soft and warm. The crowd beat like a gigantic heart as the music drove through it. Its thrilling pulse shook Rags and vibrated deep in her stomach. Vapours – breath and smoke – churned in the fierce, fitful light above their heads.

The number was ending in a frenzy. Whips of sweat flew from the heads of the band. Guitars screamed and reared against a crashing avalanche of drums. The crowd surged upward and forward. Rags was lifted from the ground by its momentum. She was flying, high on sound and fury, floating for those few spaced-out seconds above her exhaustion and sadness. Flung back in time.

And then it was over. The number finished with an explosion of noise, and the crowd, too, seemed to explode. It rose, broke and crashed like a wave, no longer monolithic but a sea of roaring, random humanity.

Rags was close to the front. Hurled forward, she fought her way to the rope and ducked beneath it. As she swung one leg over the crash barrier she was barged from behind, lost her balance and lurched sideways into the ungentle entrance of the security team.

*   *   *

Claudia stepped outside and put her hands to her face as homesickness threatened to choke her. It was always at this time of day that it struck. Evening, when the light was uncertain and blurred the outlines of this island at the end of the world. They'd had no summer weather till now, but late September was being good to them, with days of hazy sunshine, crimson wallowing sunsets, and then these haunted, smoky dusks . . . It was almost possible to imagine oneself in Italy. But the notion was a chimera. The loud voices she could still hear from the convivial dining room had a solid, northern inflection; the music was the bagpipe, which Publius liked but she found wild and harsh like the sound of the wild geese that flew over the moors; the thick grass was cool and clammy round her ankles; the air was sharper, thinner — it made sound carry differently and put a cutting edge on the thin, drifting moon.

She walked slowly, away from the house and across the lawn, the hem of her dress quickly becoming heavy with dew. By the gate two servants were embracing tightly, a double-headed statue that divided and dispersed at her approach. As Claudia opened the gate the couple's smell still hung in the air, the fatty cooking odour of the youth from the kitchen mixing queasily with the girl's cheap scent: British smells. Even now, after ten years in this place, one whiff of thick green olive oil, of basil or thyme or garlic, the piercing sweetness of an orange, no matter how faded with travel, was enough to fill her mouth with saliva and her eyes with tears. It wasn't that they didn't have these things — what they couldn't grow they could import — but she was learning the truth of the saying that produce was never the same outside the place where it belonged. It was the sun-warmed skin of the fruit that she missed, the scent that rose from the crisp, hot herbs when you brushed against them, the flavour of a plant ripened luxuriously in steady heat and picked at the perfect moment.

She closed the gate behind her, and continued down the gentle slope beyond, drawn by instinct towards the temple. Childishly, she liked to imagine the deities standing together, talking softly, savouring the gentle evening and the darkening view, watching their patronal stars come out one by one, before sensing her approach and returning to their places to resume their benign, lofty expressions and gestures of frozen dignity.

The entrance was on the western side of the temple, approached by two shallow steps that were there for drainage more than architectural effect. The building was on a comfortable, domestic scale and in the style of the house, stone-built with a red-tiled roof and fronted by a covered veranda. In summer, swallows nested in the angle between the veranda uprights and its roof, and their recently vacated premises were a comfort to Claudia. The first swallows from this very place would be in Italy now, and in six months' time they'd be back, emissaries from home.

At the centre of the main temple roof was an open-sided turret containing a lantern. Its small yellow light bloomed softly into life as if to welcome her. This was a conceit of Publius', added to his specification when they'd moved into the villa. He'd liked the idea of creating a beacon above the western valley, even though it meant that one of the estate staff, usually young Luke who was tall, had to wobble precariously on a ladder to light the lantern with a candle on a pole at a time in the evening (she thought of the couple by the gate) when he would certainly have had more amusing things to do.

He emerged now and stood aside respectfully, ducking his head as Claudia passed. She didn't speak, and in the twilight he couldn't see her smile, so it was to all intents and purposes a formal encounter. She could well imagine Luke grousing about being checked up on – the slaves didn't hold her in quite the same affection and respect as they did her husband: their mistress was an unknown quantity.

On the finial above the door was another of their own additions, hers this time: a painting of Diana accompanied by her hound. The local man to whom they'd contracted the work had done a good job on the animal, modelling it as instructed on his clients' British hunting dog, Tiki. Publius

3

had chastised Claudia, not altogether seriously, about this being a bit of a liberty, but she said on the contrary: it showed how much they thought of the goddess that they were prepared to give her the best rabbiter in the province.

She crossed the veranda and entered the greenish semi-darkness. Luke always left his lighted candle in a bracket for the convenience of night-time visitors, and she didn't trouble to light another but went to the far side of the chamber and sat down on the ledge that protruded from the wall. Diana, Jupiter, Mercury and Minerva stood in their sconces, elegantly poised. She fancied she could detect the merest flicker of settling draperies, and wondered if the stolid Luke ever glanced down nervously from his step-ladder to see four pale, upturned faces clustered at its foot.

The noise of the uproarious dinner party was no longer audible, but the quiet of Claudia's surroundings magnified the small sounds of nightfall. She could hear the thin bleat of the sheep on the flank of the hill opposite . . . the rustle of bats in the eaves above her head . . . the patter of moths and leatherjackets against the warm glass of the lantern. In the morning there'd be a scatter of tiny corpses waiting to be swept from the face of the mosaic sun on the floor.

Now there was another sound, this time from the doorway, and Claudia saw that she had been followed.

Rags could see from the man's face that he didn't believe her, that he was caught between the twin embarrassments of proving either daft or wrong.

'Look!' she shouted, flipping up her lapel badge. 'Look, it's me – all right?'

He held the edge of the badge and drew his head back slightly to bring the image into focus. He may have been a hard man once, but middle age was kicking in.

'Okay?' repeated Rags.

'Yes, madam!' A second man came up and addressed her, but with a firm restraining hand on his colleague's arm. 'Sorry about that, but you were a bit unexpected.'

'I know. I'm the one who should apologise, you're only doing your job.'

The first man raked at his forehead with his thumb. It was a sheepish gesture, but even in the din that stormed round them, his voice grated with mortification. 'You want to have a care, madam.'

She gave him her best smile, gracious but warm and droll, what Fred called her milady smile. 'Oh, don't worry. After all, it's my party.'

They couldn't hear her properly over an announcement, but the smile had done it. They stepped forward to let her past, so she was able to walk along the corridor between them and the front of the stage. There was still some grass left here but it was matted and sodden, littered with fag ends, food packaging, roaches and drinks cans and – her feet slithered beneath her – God knew what else. As she reached the end of the stage and ducked through the canvas flap into the steel forest of girders and joists that led to the assembly area, a splintering explosion of sound and light behind her advertised the arrival of the next act.

No one took any notice of her here. Everyone was too busy being important, helmeted with headphones, tuned into mobiles, bristling with mikes and walkie-talkies, festooned with wires and identity discs. No one looked more than eighteen, but then that was how people looked these days, or maybe that was the perspective of a woman approaching her half-century. There was a strong, hot smell of sweat and alcohol. No tobacco – this was a no-smoking zone, another sign of the times: great lungs, lousy livers.

Most rock musicians in the early 1990s were muscular and drug-free, as likely to run a marathon as throw a TV out of a hotel window. Jagger went to test matches, Daltry was a country gent, Sting a model husband, father and friend of the rainforest. Way back when, even the idealists – *especially* the idealists – had had the decency to be rebels. Rags recalled them with tender mystification, the ravaged, attenuated pop heroes of her youth. How strangely androgynous they'd looked, ageless and sexually ambiguous, like the panda-eyed, heavy-fringed, Bambi-legged child-women they slept with, of whom she herself had been a paradigm. But for all that, the very air had been thick with sex, a pungent soup of the stuff in which they'd splashed and rolled without a care in the world, daughters of the Pill but abortion-happy, innocently promiscuous, oblivious to the cloud no bigger than a man's hand that was Aids.

She glanced up into the production unit as she passed, and saw a man she used to know, then slender and angelic as Brian Jones, now prosperous and paunchy, still getting off on the music business but from behind the scenes. Poor bastard, she thought. When he turned and squinted in her direction she whisked past, breaking out in a sweat of apprehension, not wanting to be recognised.

She emerged from behind the stage into the maze of roped-off parking areas for concert personnel. Rollers, BMWs and customised Ferraris rubbed shoulders with trailers, container lorries and state-of-the-art Winnebagoes. Two members of a well-known girl-band – famous for their flawless midriffs but now wearing parkas and pull-on hats – perched on the bonnet of a Ranchero with their boot-heels tucked over the bull-bar, ringed fingers curled round bottles of designer beer. Business as usual for them, waiting no doubt for the others and their driver in order to belt back down the motorway to London. Away to her left were the scattered lights and small fires of the campsite, like an army on the night before battle.

Before her, lying gracefully along the shoulder of the hill, was Ladycross, softly lit and elegant, gazing down her nose at the brutish steel towers and fitful glare of the concert platform. Ladycross, like a *grande horizontale*, observing with the benign sophistication of experience the posturings of a youthful hooker. Decorating the night sky above the house were stars, more than she had ever seen, larger and closer, as though they'd fled the light pollution in the valley and gathered where they could be seen to best advantage.

Rags longed to be back in the house. She was too old for this: was suddenly shattered, aware of the bruises and strains, and raw grazes inflicted by the crowd. She pulled the sleeves of her sweater down over her hands, the heavy cowl up around her face, and began to trudge up the slope towards home.

As she did so the wanderer appeared, materialising silently from the darkness as he always did, and walking alongside her at a distance of a few metres: not looking at her, or displaying any sign of recognition but still, unmistakably, bearing her company.

'Tiki?'

Claudia held out her hand and the dog advanced, pleased to see his mistress but a little uncertain of his ground – head low, ears down, tail swinging in a cautious greeting. Claudia took his head in her hands and looked down into his long, soulful face. 'Hallo, boy, what are you doing here? Did you follow me? What have you been up to?' Tiki allowed himself to be fondled for a moment, then set off more confidently, nosing around the floor, snuffling and sneezing at the dead insects, pausing for a thunderous scratch at the foot of Minerva. His coat was a light brindle, which could be hard to see against the bleached northern uplands when out hunting, but in here the pale barred pattern was visible even beyond the candelight.

Tiki wandered when and where he liked. Even in his old age he was a free spirit. Whoever he went out with – Publius and the men, Claudia, their son Gaius,(especially Gaius) – he accompanied them because he chose to do so. In this he was less like a dog than a cat. Claudia had no time for cats, considering them cold and opportunistic, but she did admire their independence. At home, thousands of skinny, feral cats roamed the city, colonising its great buildings and hunting through its narrow alleyways, the most free of all Rome's citizens.

Tiki returned to Claudia and lay down in front of her, his head resting on his muddy paws, pointing towards her like the arrow on a sundial.

'I think,' said Claudia, addressing the dog and herself, 'that I'd better go back to our guests.'

The dog's tail brushed the floor briefly. When Claudia rose, he did too, and walked at her heels as she crossed the temple floor, creating a slight draught that made the candle gutter and throw wild, wavering shadows against the far wall.

In the doorway, Claudia paused and looked over her shoulder. But the candle flame was motionless again, standing sentinel over the stone figures of the gods.

Rags went round the side of the house and in at the back door, still to the fierce pounding of the concert. She removed her mud-caked Nikes, left them on the flagstone floor of the outer passage, and padded through the utility room, where the twin Zanussis burbled with washing, the still room that smelt of pepper and silver polish, and negotiated the buckets of cut flowers and greenery awaiting her attention on the scullery floor.

Arriving in the warmth of the kitchen she adjusted the neck of her sweater and pushed the sleeves up. Phyllida was standing by the lighted cabinet of the microwave, a Grisham paperback in one hand and a glass of white wine in the other. Her finger, on the book's cover, tapped in time to the distant band. On the table was a tray laid for one. When she saw Rags Phyllida closed the book, eyes widening over her welcoming smile.

'Miranda, hi! Gosh, hope your ladyship doesn't mind my saying but you look knackered.'

'I am.' Rags retrieved her slippers from the box by the Aga and tugged them on. 'Too much fun, and much too loud.'

Phyllida lifted her glass. 'One of these? It was on offer at Waitrose. Cheeky but likeable.'

'Thanks. Why not?'

Phyllida got out another glass and filled it as the microwave pinged. 'Your homemade vichysoisse for Lord Stratton, his special request.'

'I'll take it up.'

Rags put the glass of wine on the tray and waited as Phyllida removed the covered bowl of soup from the microwave and placed it carefully on the matching Spode plate, between the silver spoon and the thick white napkin in its monogrammed ring.

'Will you be all right?' Phyllida asked. 'Okay, sorry. By the way, I took him up his Scotch at the appointed hour.'

'Thanks. Now, then,' Rags picked up the tray, 'why don't you knock off and go and listen to what passes for popular music with your generation?'

'Excuse me.' Phyllida pulled a face. 'I've seen what it did to you. Besides, my generation, not my taste. I like soul. So, if you're sure there's nothing else I can do here, I shall retire to my chamber with this fellow,' she indicated the Grisham, 'until the documentary on soldier ants.'

'Night, then.'

Rags left the kitchen, crossed behind the main staircase and went up the back stairs, expertly negotiating the connecting doors top and bottom. On the first floor she turned right in the west arm of the gallery and half-way along, put the tray down on the satin surface of the French card table. The hall below was enormous, the glow of the single lighted lamp driving the walls into obscurity, the foot of the stairs washed by darkness. As she opened the door of the red room she noticed that for some reason – the draught in the gallery, her tiredness, natural apprehension – the small hairs on her forearm were standing up.

Claudia did not immediately return to the dinner party, but went instead to take a look at her son. Tiki, anticipating her, went ahead and climbed on to the end of the bed, draping himself just beyond the boy's feet.

But Gaius was only foxing. He didn't move as his mother came to the side of the bed, but spoke up clearly. 'How am I supposed to sleep with that racket going on?' His hair stuck up in points, and his eyes were wide and bright.

Claudia sat down on the edge of the bed. 'Don't try. Shall I light the lamp?'

'Yes, please. Where did Tiki get to?'

She returned from the corridor with a small taper and lit the wick of the earthenware oil lamp. 'He was with me.'

'Why weren't you at the party?'

'I needed some fresh air. He must have heard me go out.'

'Father was singing. It was awful.'

'He's got a nice voice,' protested Claudia, but she was smiling.

'So why did he wait till you'd gone?'

'A very good point.'

Gaius laced his hands behind his head. 'Who's in there?'

'That you know? Let's see . . . Candidus, Flavia—'

'She's nice. Can she come and say goodnight to me?'

'I'll ask her. Who else? Tullio, the legate.'

'I thought you and Father didn't like him?'

'I never said that.'

'You did to Father. But he's here because he's important.'

Claudia was nettled. 'Not as important as he thinks he is,' she said, and realised at once that she'd given herself away. 'Anyway, he's amusing company, and if he's put up with your father's singing he can't be all bad.' She leaned over and kissed him. 'I must go back.'

'And you'll send Flavia?'

'I shan't send her, but I will ask if she wouldn't mind popping in to see you.'

'Thanks.'

'Don't stay awake for her, though, if you feel sleepy.'

'I shan't feel sleepy.'

'We'll see.'

By the time she reached the doorway and glanced back, Tiki was already lying alongside Gaius on the bed, his head resting on his shoulder. The boy's eyes were wide open, and his fingers plucked restlessly, distractedly, at the dog's coat.

In the dining room the music and singing had ended but the roistering was still in full swing. Claudia could tell by the slightly shocked smiles on the faces of the two young slaves, Minna and Alex, that everyone had been losing their inhibitions and there had been some indiscreet talk. When she came in the youngsters adjusted their expressions and bobbed their heads, but the group lounging around the dining tables were so busy celebrating their own wit and charm that they didn't instantly notice her. In the second before the wave of general conviviality broke over her she caught the eye of her husband and experienced again, for an instant, that dart of fierce, combative attraction that had got under her guard all those years ago and which, in spite of everything, kept her, if not in her place, then at least in this one.

His expressionless gaze moved at once to someone else: he wasn't going to be the first to welcome her back. But she could play that card too. Head high, smiling serenely, Claudia moved towards her guests. She would offer no excuse for her absence. Let him wonder where she'd been, her once-uxorious, tone-deaf lord and leader of men. Wonder, and worry.

'Evening, all.'

The red room was bright after the shady gallery and dark depths of the hall. Both the bedside lamps were on and the portable television emitted the banal chirrup of a game show. The trolley carrying the television had been pushed away, so that its cold light played unflatteringly on the porcelain complexion of Hortense, Lady Stratton, whose oval-framed portrait hung opposite.

Rags put the tray down on the adjustable table that stood beside the four-poster and put it down. She turned off the television, retrieved the remote control from the floor and placed it with the rest of the bedside clutter of empty whisky glass, portable radio, spectacles, clock, extra-strong mints and moisturised baby wipes. Then she pulled the special chair close to the bed and sat down.

'Thanks.' Lord Stratton was awake, just. His battery was so low these days that there was precious little difference between waking and sleeping, and the quality of both was desperately poor. His voice was a thread. 'What kept you?'

'I was down at the concert.'

'What were you doing?' He inhaled a thin, quivering breath. 'Brawling?'

She took one of the wet wipes and dabbed apologetically at her cheek. 'It was a bit lively.'

She didn't add anything because she could tell from his accelerated breathing and his forefinger rubbing the quilt cover that he had more to say.

'Who was—'

'A band called Diesel. Heavy metal.'

'No further forward . . . They make . . . a hell of a noise.'

'It's a different one now. Is it disturbing you? Because if it is I'll go down there and tell them to stop. There's only thirty thousand-odd in an ugly mood.'

His mouth twitched. 'You would too . . .'

'Come on.' She became practical, hooked one arm beneath his and gripped the edges of three pillows with the other hand. 'Up.'

'Oh, God, have I got to do something?'

'I've brought the soup you asked for,' she said pointedly. To cover his weak protest and her own desperate sadness she hoisted him up and adjusted the pillows behind him briskly. It was terrible how little he weighed, and how much the effort of being moved took out of him.

'Honestly, my darling, I don't . . .'

'I know, but let's make the effort, hm? For me.'

'Oh, darling . . .'

It was a groan of real despair. That was what she couldn't bear. Worse than his pain, worse than the indignity and incapacity of illness, worse even than the minute-by-minute dread of the inevitable was his awareness of it all. The minute spark that kept him hanging on was the same one that allowed him to see himself, both of them, as they now were. On the table at her side of the bed was a photograph taken in Barbados a year last winter. Incredible that such a short time ago they'd been warm and wet in their swimming things, drinking rum punch at a beach bar and smelling of coconut sun oil and sex.

She took the napkin from the tray, unfolded it and laid it across his chest, tucking it over his shoulders to keep it in place, shamefully glad of the excuse to cover the yellowing, waxy skin and staring collarbones.

As she stirred the soup, she said, 'That dog was on the loose again. He walked up the hill with me.' She tested the soup with her little finger and added, 'I'm surprised he wasn't scared of the noise. But I suppose he's used to fending for himself and there are plenty of pickings about, so maybe greed . . .' Neither getting nor expecting a response, she tailed away, spoon in hand. Looked at him pleadingly.

He gave a long, slow blink, steeling himself. 'Go on, then, woman . . .' His mouth opened like a scrawny baby bird's. 'I'm ready.' With a hand that scarcely shook at all, and without blinking, Lady Stratton, prepared to feed her dying husband.

CHAPTER ONE

―――――◆◇◇◆―――――

Miranda, 1960

She was being made an example of.

'This girl is to be expelled,' declared the head. She paused for the collective gasp of rapturous *schadenfreude* before adding, 'There is an old saying, "You can't make a silk purse out of a sow's ear." There is nothing that Queen's College can do with or for her, and we do not want her sort with us.'

The old bitch was loving it. Every word sung with a thin, pure hatred. Miranda was shocked not by the hatred itself but by the realisation of how long it had been suppressed and seething away, ready to hiss sulphurously forth at just such a moment.

'I am well aware,' continued Mrs Grace, cocking her permed head to survey the school in a manner both chickeny and threatening, 'that hers are the kind of antics which can arouse a misplaced admiration in the more impressionable among you. I can assure you that there is nothing clever, amusing or glamorous in what she has done. This squalid escapade has – sadly for her, fortunately for us – shown her in her true colours and for that we should all be grateful . . .'

And you in yours, thought Miranda. With her eyes fixed on *The Laughing Cavalier* at the far end of the hall she made a mental inventory of what those colours would be: sick-beige, spinach-green, scab-brown, pus-yellow—

'. . . always a sad day when this school, with its tradition of inculcating sound moral values, has to admit defeat, but in this

14

case we have no option but to do so, and to learn from the experience.' Mrs Grace turned towards Miranda with the air of someone obliged to handle a dead mouse. 'Let us hope, Miss Tattersall, that you will do the same.'

Miss Tattersall? Actually, Miranda rather cared for that – the evidence that she was no longer a pupil at this bloody horrible place. That she had outgrown it, sloughed it off, and could fly her 'true colours'. Shades of red, scarlet, crimson, vermilion, gules—

'. . . to await your departure. Matron will accompany you.' Mrs Grace turned away again, eyes closing momentarily to blot out the dismaying image of her school's failure. 'Thank you, Miss Parry-Jones.'

As PJ struck up with 'New Every Morning Is The Love', Miranda felt Matron's hand on her arm, heard the stiff rustle of her uniform and caught a whiff of her clean, soapy scent. A kind touch and an unthreatening smell. Nauseous with relief, but keeping her head high, she left the hall for the last time.

Neither spoke till they were back in the san. It was quiet and sunny. The fat, flu-flushed junior lay in her window bed reading *My Friend Flicka*. Her mouth was open to assist her phlegmy breathing, and she wound one greasy lock of hair round her finger as she read. As they came in she cast Miranda a fleeting, petrified glance over the top of the book.

Matron addressed the junior brightly: 'I'll be with you in a minute, Roberta dear,' and Miranda *sotto voce*, 'All right, Mandy, I'll come and tell you when your father's here.'

Matron was Jocelyn Menzies from Auckland, pretty, thirtyish and engaged to be married. She was universally acknowledged to be the sweetest member of staff and her gentle use of the diminutive reduced Miranda as Mrs Grace's harshness had not. 'Thank you, Matron . . .' Her voice wavered.

'Come on, chin up.'

'It's just so bloody—'

'Mandy.'

'Sorry, Matron.'

15

'Got a hankie? Here.' Matron produced a fistful of sweet-smelling tissues from her overall pocket. 'Hang on to them.'

'Thanks.'

Matron positioned herself thoughtfully between Miranda and the saucer-eyed junior, and spoke confidingly. 'Shall I tell you something?'

'Yes.'

'I'm not going to say anything more about your escapade, I think we've all heard enough about that, but one thing I do know. Ten years from now none of this will matter at all. In fact,' she leaned forward and lowered her voice even more, 'don't tell anyone I said so, but you're going to laugh about it.'

Miranda could appreciate the truth of this, although it was little present comfort. 'Maybe.'

'Absolutely definitely.' Matron's manner altered and became once more pleasantly official. 'Now, then, got everything? Something to read if you want to? Fine.' She placed a reddened hand over Miranda's and exerted a firm pressure. 'Not long.'

She sailed away, her crêpe soles whispering. In a place where everyone clumped about in their regulation shoes, or lacrosse boots, and where the clack of high heels provoked anything from mild anxiety to actual fear, Miss Menzies' movements made a summery sound, like a person walking through long grass – a sound that for the five years of her tenure had presaged comfort and laughter and gentleness. Sitting on the edge of the high bed, with its taped-on undersheet and folded grey blankets, Miranda watched as she ministered to the ailing Roberta – plumping her pillows, smoothing her lank hair and her rumpled sheets, touching her forehead with the back of her hand, slipping her a boiled sweet. She vowed that although she intended to expunge everything else about this hellhole from her memory, she would never forget Matron.

On the way out, Miss Menzies took something from her pocket and said, 'Catch!' It was a Nuttall's Minto. She gave Miranda a lovely, creased-up smile that was like a giant wink before shutting the door.

Miranda removed the wrapper and put the Minto in her mouth. The junior, embarrassed half to death at being alone

16

once more with the condemned, huddled beneath her bedding with her back to the room.

Miranda opened *Great Expectations* (a set book she intended to take with her) and stared at it. After a few minutes there was a timid tap on the door.

'Come in,' she said, as there was no one else to do so.

It was Rosamund Cotterill, a classmate of Roberta, a tall, solid girl with a shock of black hair. 'Oh, sorry,' she said, on seeing Miranda (although unlike her friend she didn't colour up), 'is it okay if I give something to Roberta?'

'Carry on, it's none of my business.'

'Thanks.' Rosamund scuttled across the room, there was a flurry of furtive whispering and a note changed hands. Then there was another 'Thanks!' as she whisked out and closed the door with scarcely a click.

The san was at the top of the front stairs, next to Matron's sitting room and immediately above Mrs Grace's study. In the carpeted hush of this end of the building it was possible even with the door closed to hear any comings and goings in the hall below.

It must have been at least an hour later – Miranda had finished the sweet, failed to retain a single word about Pip's London adventures, and twice crept, her bladder overflowing with anxiety, to the loo – when the car arrived. She knew it was her father's Daimler because no one else would have entered the drive so fast or braked so sharply on the sacred gravel. She heard the door slam smartly and his swift, crunching footsteps approaching the main entrance. There was a brass plate next to the front door which said, 'Please ring, enter and wait in hall,' but there was never the slightest chance that her father would comply with these instructions, especially this morning. The outer door was opened with a bang, then shut inconclusively as if under its own steam. Her skin prickled at the sound of her father's voice clashing rudely with that of Mrs Grace. But the head must have ushered him successfully into the study, for there was the sound of another door closing and the voices became more muffled.

The junior peeped fearfully over her bedclothes at Miranda, who felt that even at this late stage it was her responsibility to ease the tension. 'Don't worry, Bobby, I'll be gone soon.'

The reply was a mere croak. 'That's okay.'

'Still feeling vile?'

'Yes.'

'Poor you. Sorry about all this.'

The recipient of this apology – unprecedented in the hierarchical annals of Queen's College – turned a deeper scarlet with embarrassment. 'It's okay, honestly.'

The lengthy silence that followed was punctuated by the rise and fall of the voices below. It was evident that, after an initial passage of arms, the head was beginning to say more, and Miranda's father less. Miranda's desire to hear what was being said was tempered by the knowledge that if she heard it Roberta would too. The two of them pretended to read, in an atmosphere thick with apprehension, only dispelled by the susurration of Matron's approach. She entered at speed, with an air of quiet urgency, her cheeks rather pink.

'Mandy, your father's arrived.'

'Yes, I know, I heard him.'

'Ready for the fray?' Matron tweaked Miranda's tie and brushed her lapels, smiling sorrowfully. 'All this was never really you, was it?'

'No.'

'Anyway, I'll say bye-bye – oops!' The buzzer from downstairs issued its curt summons. 'There's Mrs Grace, I'll pop down and see what she wants.'

If ever a thing was beyond doubt, thought Miranda, as Matron's footsteps sighed away down the stairs, it was what Mrs Grace wanted. Time, thank God, to go.

Book closed now, she waited. With departure imminent, the wrath of Queen's College and its head assumed less importance, but the prospect of her father's reaction loomed large. Had his stormy entrance and raised voice been the product of outrage against the school or against her? As usual she couldn't prepare herself because she hadn't the faintest idea which way he would jump. During the whole of their interrupted relationship, Captain Gerald Tattersall had shown himself to be a man of few principles but many and volatile views, violently expressed.

The voices downstairs had gone quiet – probably Matron was speaking – and then, after a brief, soundless interval, as though she'd flown back up the stairs, Matron pushed open the door. 'Would you like to come down now, Mandy?'

Her voice was still kind and her smile warm, but something about her denoted a shift. Her exchange with the head, and with Miranda's father, had taken her back over the dividing line between staff and pupils, grown-ups and girls, which she usually bridged. This, of course, was why she'd said goodbye earlier. 'Crane's put your trunk in the car.'

Miranda picked up her suitcase, her Panama hat and her green gabardine mac, thinking with what pleasure she would stuff them into the dustbin at home. She looked over at the bed by the window. 'Goodbye. Get well soon.'

A faint murmur came from the heap of bedclothes. Roberta was dying for her to be gone.

They went down the curved staircase, Matron gliding swiftly on the outside, Miranda more awkward with her case, bumping the banisters as she went and to hell with the paintwork.

The door of the study was open and Mrs Grace and her father were standing face to face, almost confidingly, having apparently resolved their differences and reached one of those mysterious accommodations based on nothing more than mutual adult-hood. But when Matron tapped with one knuckle, both of them turned and subjected Miranda to the excoriating blast of their combined stares. The head's fat Persian cat, Cleo, trotted out and wove smarmily about her legs.

At least it was quick. Gerald Tattersall was not one to hang about once a decision had been made. 'There she is,' he said, in a tone Miranda couldn't begin to read. 'Go and jump in the car, will you, and I'll be with you in a tick.'

She went, not looking at him, or Mrs Grace, especially not at Matron. She did not say goodbye, although she thought she heard Matron murmur something as she passed.

Outside it was warm and sunny. Tennis coaching was in

progress on one of the grass courts. Crane, having stowed her trunk, was filing the edges of the lawn alongside the drive with a hoe. The fine-toothed rake lay nearby, ready to erase all signs of their departure. Crane was 'not all there' and was the embodiment of cowed discretion at the best of times (he had to be, since he cleaned the cloak-and changing rooms), and now his hunched shoulders proclaimed his abject desire to be invisible. He never even glanced up as she put her case, mac and hat on the back seat and got into the front.

Her father's smell overwhelmed Miranda. The leather of the car seats, the stale tobacco, the stuff he put on his thick hair, and the sweet, threatening odour of booze. She rolled down the window. The *pop-ping* of the tennis coaching and the scrape of Crane's hoe were like sounds from another world. She sat poised between that one and this. For a ridiculous moment she felt a pang for the one she was leaving. She had been caged, but at least in a cage one knew what it was one was trying to escape.

Too late, she had done it now.

Her father came out, leaving both doors open. His walk was an aggressive one, chest and stomach thrust out, arms held slightly away from his sides, feet splayed. As he got behind the wheel and turned on the engine Miranda caught a glimpse of Matron closing the inner door, her head bowed. They executed a swirling three-point turn. As they paused in the gateway before turning out, she looked in the wing mirror and saw Crane, head still bowed, patiently smoothing the gravel with long strokes of his rake. Erasing her departure.

Her father didn't speak, but he did drive fast, fiddling dangerously with his cigarette case, putting a cigarette into his mouth and lighting it with the car lighter, steering with his wrists, at one point even taking both hands off the wheel. He didn't have to do that, he was doing it to scare her. She'd learned to deal with his driving by willing herself into a trancelike state of passive acceptance. *If I'm going to die now*, she told herself, *I will. There's nothing I can do about it. It'll be over in a second.* She always tried not to add the childish *And then they'll be sorry*, but it was implicit, and the pleasure that gave her overrode her fear.

She managed – surreptitiously, so as not to incur her father's irritation – to wind down her window enough to let some of the smoke escape. In this as in everything else he was an exhibitionist, heedless of others, puffing and blowing like a dragon, flicking ash in all directions. Miranda's mother smoked too, but her habit was scrupulously contained, a swift, picky, practical matter between her and her ashtray.

They roared up the avenue, barely pausing at the junction, and accelerated sickeningly along the main road so that Miranda's head lurched back against her seat. But it was another ten miles (Lewes, she'd been counting) before he said, without looking at her, 'Well, well, well. What a stupid, selfish, common little guttersnipe my expensively educated daughter has turned out to be.'

She tried to tell herself it had been a triumph, albeit a ruinous one. She'd rated a full-length picture and two excitable columns inside the paper, and a teasing reference on the front page immediately below the masthead:

WE ASKED, CAN BRITAIN PRODUCE A BB? TODAY'S ANSWER'S ON PAGE FIVE!

And there she had been, curvaceous in her uplift bra and gingham sundress, with her bedroom eyes, mussed tumble of hair and bee-stung lips – a British Bardot complete in every particular.

'I'm sorry,' she said weakly.

'Oh!' He gave a thin, snarling laugh. 'Not half as sorry as you will be.'

She didn't know, and didn't dare guess, what he could possibly mean. Though she knew it would do no good, she continued to try to excuse herself. 'I never thought I'd win.'

The car veered on to the chalky downland verge and bounced to a halt.

'What?'

There was no point in pretending she had said something different: he had only asked in order to make her repeat it.

'I didn't think I'd win.'

'No?' His mouth and eyes were pale with rage, his sneer terrified her. 'Why not? Didn't think you'd look tarty enough?'

'It was just a joke, really.'

'That much at least is true. Look at you.' He did so, raking her up and down with his watery, yellowed eyes. 'Great lump. And don't they ever tell you to wash your hair in that place?'

She knew her hair was getting greasy, but she couldn't help it. 'They only allow us to wash it once a fortnight.'

'Ridiculous bloody nonsense.' He threw his cigarette end out of the window and slapped his free hands hard on the wheel so that she flinched. He had enormous, purple, swollen-looking hands, fleshy blunt instruments. 'Who took the photograph?'

'A friend.'

'Who?'

'You don't know him.'

'Him? Jesus wept, you got some wretched little self-abuser to take that ridiculous picture?'

'It was a joke, honestly. We were bored and he'd seen that thing in the paper and we were fooling about—'

'*He* wasn't bored. Take my word for it.'

The look he gave her was full of loathing. She hated and feared this attitude of his even more than his anger. It was more sinister because it was complicated; she had even less idea of how to deflect its implied threat.

'As for fooling about,' he went on, 'you went to rather a lot of trouble, didn't you? Messed about with your hair, covered your face in muck, climbed into that common little frock.' He waited, squeezing and releasing the wheel, staring at her. 'Hm?'

On these occasions she felt instinctively that it was better to keep talking, to say something. To play for time.

'I do my hair like that quite often, actually—'

'Dear God.'

'And the dress is an old one—'

'I could see you'd grown out of it.'

'The makeup was pretty awful but, then, I was pretending to be someone else.'

'"Britain's BB".' He spoke the words as if they were something revolting he was picking up between finger and thumb. Nothing she said was going to be right. She was at his mercy.

'Yes.'

He hadn't taken his eyes off her once. His big meaty hands still pumped the wheel without fully releasing it. 'Presumably,' he said, 'you were unable to see that you succeeded only in being yourself.'

This time she did remain silent, scorched, shrunk, by the heat of his contempt. He started the car, revved the engine noisily and swung back on to the road. Once they'd hit top gear he lit a cigarette in his usual death-defying manner. She was sweating. She could feel that her ampits were damp, in spite of Odorono, and hoped that he wouldn't notice and make some other vile comment.

But his focus, if not his mood, had changed. His attention had switched from her fall from grace to the dark place inside his head. His eyes flicked irritably over the road ahead and from time to time his lips moved as he spoke to himself, or to whoever he was thinking of. Once, hot ash fell from his cigarette on to his trouser leg and he swore and smacked it off, making the car swerve. Miranda stayed very still as the miles ticked by. With each one she was closer to home where, whatever the disapproval and distress of her mother, she would be safe. She had only to sit it out.

Well short of Haywards Heath he pulled over into the car park of a roadhouse. 'I need a break.'

'Okay.'

'I know it's bloody okay. Do you want something?'

'I don't mind . . .'

'Neither do I. You'd better come in and make your mind up. I'm not leaving you sitting here.' He nodded in the direction of her things on the back seat. 'Better bring those, we might stop over.'

Obediently, with a sinking heart, she got out, holding her

bag, and stood at a safe distance as he locked the car doors and walked past her towards the hotel with his exaggeratedly upright, duck-footed gait that was too arrogant to be comical. As she followed, he buttoned his blazer and she noted with bitter satisfaction that it was a shade tight over his bottom. He waited until just before they entered before taking her bag from her.

This was exactly the sort of place she associated with him and which she most disliked: a characterless pitstop for travelling businessmen, salesmen, reps and men otherwise on the loose.

He went straight up to the reception desk and asked, 'Where's the bar?'

'Through there, sir, but . . .' the man glanced pointedly at Miranda '. . . I'm afraid . . .'

'What is it?'

'The young lady's not allowed in there unless you're residents. May I ask if you're intending to stay with us?'

'Do you have a room?'

'Let's see . . . We do as it happens.'

'Then we are.'

'Two rooms is that, sir?'

She held her breath as her father threw her a testy, calculating glance. Exhaled with relief, as he said, 'I suppose it had better be.'

Sick with misery, Miranda waited as he signed the book and took charge of the keys. On his instructions she left her bag, hat and mac behind the desk before following him to the bar, which was deserted except for a group of youngish men in suits sitting in the corner. A loud, braying explosion of laughter burst from them as they entered and she felt humiliatingly vulnerable in her stupid, heat-stained school blouse and skirt.

'Take a seat.' She sank into one of the low-backed horseshoe-shaped armchairs. The red material, which looked shiny, felt gritty on the backs of her legs.

'Decided what you want?'

'An orange squash, please.' Even he couldn't take exception to that.

'Stay there. I'll get some nuts or something.'

His mood always improved immeasurably when he was

within striking distance of a drink. But the price to be paid was high: a night in this awful place, his beastliness tomorrow morning, and the delay in getting home. There was also the possibility that he might forget to tell her mother where they were and what they were doing, and that she'd worry and ring the school . . . Miranda pressed her lips together, swallowing tears.

He returned, carrying a glass of orange squash with a straw, and a packet of peanuts, which he put down on the table in front of her.

'There you are. I'm just going to sit at the bar for a moment.'

'Thanks – I say—'

'What?'

'Shall I ring home and say we're spending the night here?' She was gambling on this being a good moment.

'Might as well. There's a callbox in the lobby.'

'Can I – I don't have any change.'

He dragged a handful of coins from his pocket and sifted through them. 'That should do.'

'Thanks.'

She got up. She was half-way to the door and he on his way to the bar when he turned and said, loudly and rudely, 'Keep it short, and come straight back, won't you?'

'Yes.'

In the foyer she couldn't see a phone, and asked the man behind the desk. His attitude to her was in sharp contrast to the way he'd spoken to her father: he didn't deign to answer, but pointed to a corridor with a green neon 'Toilets/Telephone' sign over it, as if she were an idiot.

'Oh, yes, sorry – thank you.'

She couldn't help noticing that there was a copy of the *Daily Sketch* behind the desk. So, only three days ago this rude, jumped-up man would probably have been ogling the picture of Britain's BB. The thought, and the sense of power it gave her was some consolation.

Having located the phone she was by no means certain that her mother would be back from work, but after half a dozen rings there was a 'Hallo . . . hallo?' and she pressed button B.

'Mummy?'

'Darling – where are you?'

'In a horrible hotel. He wants to stay the night.'

'Oh, *no*. So, what time do you think . . . ?'

'I don't know. I've seen Haywards Heath on a sign, so it's not that far. I'm sure we'll be back by lunchtime.'

'All right, it can't be helped. I'll do my best to be here, I don't ask many favours.' There was a pause. 'How are you?'

'Miserable.'

'That was such a stupid thing you did.'

'I do know that.'

'But not wicked.'

'He thinks so.'

'Yes, well, he does pay the school fees . . . or did. I dare say when he's calmed down enough he'll appreciate the saving.'

Her voice had started to become high and harsh; now she collected herself. In the pause that followed Miranda heard her quick, anxious breathing. 'Look, I am terribly sorry about all this.'

'I'm sure you are, dear, I can scarcely begin to imagine what you've been through over the past couple of days. Anyway, one thing I can tell you now – I never liked that place.' The pips sounded. 'Time's up, I'll see you soon – see you soon! 'Bye!'

''Bye—'

They were cut off. For a moment Miranda hung on to the receiver, reluctant to return to the bar. Then she remembered the sign saying 'Toilets/Telephone', and walked purposefully down the corridor until she found the ladies'. The door on its spring hissed softly as it closed behind her. Sanctuary! Even the snake-eyed foreign attendant sitting in the corner couldn't spoil her relief at reaching this sequestered place.

She went into the cubicle furthest away from the woman and put plenty of paper down the bowl to muffle her torrent of pent-up pee. To her great relief two more women came into the cloakroom together, chatting and laughing, so she no longer felt conspicuous, and continued to sit there. If her mother's admission that she'd never liked the school had been intended as a comfort, it hadn't worked. Why, if she had disliked it, had she agreed to Miranda going there? Was she so scared of her ex-husband that she couldn't even express an opinion on a matter so vital as her daughter's education? Miranda's recollection was that her mother had not just endorsed the move but positively enthused about it, going on about how it was the sort of schooling that she herself had never had and always regretted, and how extraordinarily generous it was of Miranda's father still to want to go ahead with and pay for it, after the parting of the ways.

Well, he hadn't got to pay for it any more. Miranda pulled up her knickers, and adjusted her suspenders, the elastic of which was getting loose. No more having to feel grateful for a place and a process she despised. Maybe her mother had started something and they could all speak their minds at last. She pulled the plug and emerged.

One of the other women was in the loo, the other was combing her hair. This she did with short, careful strokes, her fingers following the comb, catching and crimping each strand of hair. Miranda fished an elastic band out of her blazer pocket and scraped her own hair up into a high ponytail, pulling it so that it flared out jauntily. The woman's eyes flicked briefly towards her reflection in the mirror as she did this but without much interest – she was no *Sketch* reader.

There were a few coppers left over from the phone call. Miranda had a lightning debate with herself over whom it would be best to placate, her father or the attendant, and without much difficulty chose to ignore the willow-pattern saucer with its handful of sixpences.

Back in the bar one of the young men from the corner table had fallen into conversation with Gerald while ordering more drinks. Miranda knew that it was only a matter of time before her father gravitated to the group, there to be the life and soul until they realised he was the kiss of death.

She walked boldly up to him. These were the circumstances in which, for reasons she was just beginning to understand, he would be nice to her.

'Daddy – here's your change.'

'Ah, here she is!' He swung round on his stool. 'My daughter. Mandy, this is Ken.'

'How do you do?'

Ken's hand was warm and moist. 'How do you do? Out for the day?'

She smiled and stayed quiet, allowing her father to answer: 'Yes, that's right – time off for good behaviour!'

Ken's eyes hadn't left her. 'Boarding school, is it?'

'Yes.'

'Bet you hate it.'

'I do, actually.'

He jerked his head towards her father. 'And I bet he says you'll thank him one day. Eh?'

'He does, yes.'

She was almost enjoying herself, because for once she held all the cards, was keeping their secret though it didn't matter to her either way. In fact, everything about Ken told her he'd have been thrilled to know of her escapade.

Captain Tattersall pocketed his change. 'Did you get through?'

'Yes. I said we'd be home before lunch tomorrow.'

'Sounds as though I've got my marching orders.'

Her father exchanged a man-to-man look with Ken, who said: 'I was just getting a round in – can I buy you a drink, Mandy?'

'I've got one, thanks.'

'She's too young anyway,' said her father. 'Believe it or not.'

'I'll have to take your word for it. Far be it from me to ask a lady's age.'

The drinks arrived and Miranda took this as her cue to leave. 'I'll go and sit over there.'

'Oh, Mandy,' Ken was becoming positively playful, 'won't you come and join us?'

'No, really, thanks.' She smiled as bashfully as she could. 'Please may I have the car keys so I can get my book?'

He shook his head. 'Brains and beauty, I don't know.'

Gerald handed over the keys. 'Don't drive off.'

'I won't.'

She felt them watching her as she left the room. She wasn't proud of herself for colluding with her father in his grubby little manufactured scenario of indulgent parent and sweet schoolgirl, but if it made for an easier life until tomorrow she was prepared to do it.

By the time she returned to the bar with *Great Expectations* and sat down at the table with her orange squash and peanuts, he had joined the others. He had his back to her and all might have been well had not Ken spotted her. From the corner of her eye she saw him petition her father, who glanced over his shoulder . . . the others joining in . . . her father's big hands thrown up in surrender . . . Ken's dreaded advance.

'Come on, young lady, we can't have you sitting over here all by yourself.'

'It's all right, I'm reading.'

'We shan't stop you.' He was so stupid. Insinuating and stupid. And he wasn't going to take no for an answer. Silently she stood up, and he picked up her glass. 'Allow me.'

Someone had placed a chair for her, and Ken introduced his friends – Steve, Stewart, Keith and Tony, 'partners in crime', as he put it.

'Are you sure you won't have a little dash of something stronger?' asked Ken. 'I'm quite sure your dad wouldn't object to a Babycham. Dubonnet and lemonade?'

He glanced at Gerald, who pulled a face that said these beverages were so utterly beyond the pale that they could scarcely be called drinks. Ken took this as acquiescence, and raised a playful finger. 'Don't go away. I'll get you something I know you'll like.'

You won't, she thought. You couldn't. Not in a million years.

What he brought was a snowball. She felt humiliated, and offended both by their stupid leching and their pathetic assumption of superiority. They thought they were men of the world, ogling her but treating her like a child, as if she didn't know her own power; as if she, not they, were stupid.

She thanked Ken for the snowball but pointedly left it

untouched while she sipped the orange squash. Her father was going on about his company, rapidly approaching that zone where the others would appreciate, too late, what a graceless, drunken bore he was. Not long after that they'd want him to go but her to stay, a dilemma with which she had no intention of helping them. They couldn't possibly imagine, the idiots, how hard he would be to shake off.

'. . . damn nearly the last profitable fleet of barges on the Thames,' he was saying to Stewart, 'but even so we're hanging on by the skin of our teeth. You chaps are too young to have fought in the war, and by the time you're my age you'll be lucky if there's a water-haulage business left in this country.'

Stewart looked baffled. 'We wouldn't want that.'

'Of course you wouldn't. One of the glories of England, our canal and river system. You think of it as veins and arteries, you'll get a sense of how important it is.'

Keith inclined his head towards Miranda. 'Remiss of me, Mandy, I didn't catch your surname.'

'Tattersall.'

'Tattersall's Barges – I know that name. I've seen them. Well, well.' He raised his voice to address her father. 'It says "Captain" on your card, sir – were you in the navy, then, during the war?'

Miranda played with her drinking straw. This was a hot potato for her father who liked to be taken for a former seafaring man, but whose bullshitting would be inhibited by her presence. Go on, then, she thought, let's hear how you get out of it this time.

He laughed heartily. 'No, no, no, I was one of the poor beggars on the firing line. And the inland waterways require a very different set of qualifications, mainly a sound head for commerce. Not something to be learned standing on the bridge of a destroyer. And it's Gerald, by the way.'

'My father was a merchant seaman,' said Tony. 'From what he's told me it was no picnic.'

'Good God, no, no, I wasn't for a moment implying that it was, those chaps did a terrific job, but you know there's an old rivalry between us grunts and the Royal Navy. In any event

30

that's all in the past. Fifteen years since that show was over and it seems like yesterday . . .'

He was off again. Ken turned his attention to Miranda. 'We're thinking of having some dinner here. Perhaps you and your father would like to join us?'

'I don't know . . . You'll have to ask Daddy.'

'I will, I definitely will. Captain Tattersall – Gerald – may I butt in?'

She sat watching demurely, listening to them all walk on to the punch. Her father, needless to say, was thrilled to bits at the prospect of a jolly dinner with an admiring audience of younger men (he was neither observant nor sensitive enough to see he'd lost them five minutes ago), and since he was still sober enough to realise that she was part of the meal ticket he was ready, if not keen, to include her.

'Oh, you needn't ask! She's been on hard tack in that school of hers for the past month, haven't you, Mandy? Not exactly Cordon Bleu, is it?'

No, she thought, it wasn't – when I haven't even been allowed in the dining hall for two days because I was an outcast and an untouchable, and how quickly you forgot about *that* when it suited you.

'So,' said Ken, slapping his hands together, 'you're going to let us treat you. What'll it be? A nice bit of pâté and toast, a steak, a slice of gateau with cream?'

'Actually,' she said, 'I'm not hungry. I think I'll just go up to my room.'

Gerald made a stupid, pop-eyed face of astonishment. 'Do my ears deceive me? Come along, young lady, don't be shy. It's not like you.'

There was a sting in the last remark, but in these circumstances she had the upper hand and they both knew it.

'Honestly, I'd rather not.'

'Not watching your figure, surely?' asked Ken.

'No.' She knew who was, though. Ignoring Ken's smirk she stood up, clasping her book to her midriff. 'Is that all right? Do you mind?'

'Of course I don't mind, why should I mind?' He flashed a

31

jovial glance around at the others. Heavy father, him? 'Look,' he fished in his breast pocket for his wallet, and took out two notes, 'there's thirty bob. If you get peckish order something from room service.'

'Are you sure?'

'Go on, don't be silly, take it.' He waggled the notes between his index and middle fingers. 'Off you go. Breakfast at eight.'

'Thanks.' She took the notes. 'I probably shan't—'

'Be off with you. Oh, room key.' He handed it to her. 'Good night.'

'Night.' She leaned forward, enjoying the split second of startlement before he did the same, acceding to a filial kiss. Then she included the rest of them in her diffident smile of farewell, and went.

In the foyer the young man on reception had been replaced by a cheery middle-aged woman, who gave her her things with a 'There you are, love', kind instructions on how to find the room, and the location of the nearest bathroom.

So as not to be wandering the corridor in her pyjamas she collected her towel from the bedroom and went with her bag straight to the bathroom. She undressed, had a quick bath, rinsed her hair in the basin, rubbed it dry and ran a comb through it, then cleaned her teeth and put her clothes back on.

Back in the bedroom she bolted the door, got into her wash-faded yellow pyjamas and slithered down between the stiff, tightly tucked-in sheets. Outside it was still broad daylight. Once more she felt entirely safe, at least for the next few hours. She picked up *Great Expectations*. The only thing she regretted was not having disinterred a clean blouse from her trunk. The room wasn't quite warm enough to risk rinsing out the blouse she'd been wearing. Her stomach yawned with hunger but she didn't like the idea of opening the door to whoever might bring up a tray, and then there was the question of a tip, so she didn't order anything.

Breakfast, bad temper, another hour and a half's drive, the potentially horrid and embarrassing exchange between her parents – and then it would be over. Or this stage of it, anyway.

32

It was nothing. By this time tomorrow, she told herself, the rest of her life would have begun.

By five to eight she was completely ready, had tidied her bed, unbolted the door and was sitting on the upright chair reading a magazine about the hotel. It was part of a chain. Anywhere you wandered, according to the magazine, anywhere you roamed, anywhere in Britain, you'd find a place like home. All she could say was, if the people who thought up the advertisement had homes like this she felt sorry for them.

There was no knock on the door. Eight and nine o'clock came and went, and nearly an hour later the chambermaid walked in unannounced.

'Oh, excuse me, madam. Did you know the room has to be vacated by ten for servicing?'

The 'madam' was not respectful, but intended to make her feel foolish.

'No, sorry, I'll go – I was just about to, anyway.'

She picked up her possessions and the chambermaid stood back to let her pass, holding her plastic basket of cleaning materials ostentatiously aloft and to one side.

A 'Do not disturb' sign hung on the door of her father's room, not that she would have dreamed of rousing him. There was nothing for it but to go down to the no man's land of the hotel foyer and await his appearance. She chose a chair angled slightly away from the reception desk (where the contemptuous man was once more on duty), which afforded her a view of the stairs, the closed door of the bar, and the open one of the breakfast room, from which the last, mostly male stragglers were emerging with a well-nourished air, carrying with them a torturing whiff of bacon and eggs.

She'd only just opened her book, her stomach growling, when a voice said: 'Good morning.'

It was Tony from the night before. She'd disliked him least, and he was on his own.

'Good morning.'

'Off soon?'

'Yes, I'm just waiting for my father.'

'Ah. He's probably having a lie-in.' The knowing snigger he was too polite to give lurked in his voice. 'Anyway,' he looked at his watch, 'time I wasn't here. Give my best to him, won't you, and I hope the rest of the term goes well.'

'It will,' she said, 'because I shan't be there.'

'Really? Leaving?' Her words had implied enough to pique his curiosity: she could tell there were questions he'd have liked to ask. 'Good luck anyway.'

'Thanks.'

The moment he'd gone, and the distraction ended, the hunger pangs returned with a vengeance, but just then a waitressy woman came out of the breakfast room carrying a tray.

'Excuse me!' To her own ears her voice sounded loud and shrill but the woman bustled over obligingly.

'Yes dear?'

'I don't suppose – I'm staying here but I missed breakfast—'

'We can do you coffee and biscuits out here if you'd like.'

'Thanks, that'd be lovely.'

'Room number?' She produced the key. 'Shan't be long,' said the woman.

She might well have been greased lightning but it availed Miranda nothing because the moment the waitress had gone her father flopped down the stairs, unshaven and puffy-eyed. Miranda remembered that he'd had no case, and if he'd drunk too much last night had probably slept in his clothes. She was both ashamed and wary of him.

'There you are. The maid said you'd left.'

'I had to, they wanted to clean.'

'Did you have breakfast?'

'No, I wasn't sure—'

'Why the hell not? Do you need your hand holding the whole time? Well, we've missed it now, I'll stop somewhere on the way.'

No, please, she thought, not more stops. 'Actually I did order some coffee and biscuits.'

'No time for that now, we need to hit the road. Bloody waste of money – breakfast was included, you realise?'

She stood up, mac over her arm, case at her feet, while he went to the desk and paid. She heard him explain, grumblingly, about the coffee. As they left, she saw the waitress return with the tray and gaze after them, shaking her head. She wanted to run back and tell the nice woman, who had seemed such a saviour at the time, that she was not a spoilt, capricious teenager but a victim of circumstances beyond her control.

In the car, he turned the heating on, and lit a cigarette. In spite – or because – of his hangover he was edgy and alert; she didn't dare open the window. He drove with angry carelessness, zooming and lurching so that her head was thrown back and her empty stomach churned. As a young child she'd suffered from travel sickness and he'd always been intolerant of it, only stopping when the threat to his upholstery was overwhelming, and even then not always in time, so that an even bigger unpleasantness had ensued. Now she was faced with a dilemma. Should she ask to stop now, and hope to see off the sickness with a minute or two of fresh air, with the possibility of not doing so and having to enrage him by asking again? Or hang on till the very last minute and get the whole thing out of the way, as it were, in one fell swoop? The second option carried the risk that the slightest delay on her father's part could spell disaster.

She felt awful. Her face and hands were cold and her stomach was sending its bitter, warning juices up the back of her throat.

'I'm sorry—'

'Mm?'

'Sorry about this, but I need to get out.'

He gave a short, grunting exhalation, was silent for a moment, then said: 'Are you asking me to stop?'

'Yes, I suppose so – yes, please.'

He glanced away from her out of the window, his hands squeezed the wheel. 'Then why don't you say so?'

'I know it's a nuisance.'

'Bloody right madam. We're late as it is.' Now, she thought, after I waited half the morning on an empty stomach for you to drag your hangover out of bed, *now* suddenly it's my fault that we're going to be late. She didn't answer.

35

He threw her a scornful, hate-filled look. 'Are you going to throw up?'

'I—' She had been going to say, 'I might,' but was obliged to put her hand over her mouth and nod.

'Jesus wept.' He swung violently into a farm gateway and bounced to a halt. 'Quick. Get on with it.'

She climbed unsteadily out of the car and took a few steps towards the back, to where he couldn't see her. For one awful moment she thought she might not be sick, that she was going to have to get back in and ask again, but – thank you, God! Cars went by, people must be staring and talking about her, but relief far outweighed shame. When it was over she wiped her mouth with her hankie and waited for a moment, one hand on the car, to see if there was going to be a second wave. When none was forthcoming she returned to the car.

'Thanks.'

'Don't mention it.' He started the engine. 'Open the window, would you?'

She did so. It was all right for him to stink the car out with his cigarettes, but the faintest trace of his daughter's humiliation was anathema to him. Still, the crisis was over and it was nice to have the fresh air on her face. And now the thought of food, solid and plain, was comforting: she began to think of what she might have when she got home – a sandwich of some sort, soup and bread, scrambled eggs on toast . . .

After a few minutes he asked her to close the window and announced his intention to stop somewhere where he could fill up with petrol and get a cup of coffee. There seemed to be no end to his perversity. She nursed her hatred of him, warmed her hands on it, reminded herself how much longer her future was than his, and how she would get her revenge by living riotously and well while he withered away . . . And then –! as for not speaking ill of the dead, she intended to do little else.

There were a couple of petrol pumps presided over by a man in a prefab, and a larger hut advertising 'Hot Drinks/Snax'. A handful of parked container lorries proclaimed the hut's clientele, but didn't prevent her father saying: 'Go on in and order me a coffee, will you? I don't suppose you want anything, but . . . I'll be in when I've filled her up.'

She went into the café. There were four men in there, two sitting together, one on his own, one on a stool at the counter. A fifth in a stained apron stood behind it, fishing large mugs out of a sink full of murky water and turning them upside down on a draining-board. The place smelt strongly of stale fat and the atmosphere was humid. Nothing on earth would have induced her to eat and drink anything at the chipped Formica tables with their grubby tin ashtrays. The floor felt sticky beneath her school shoes as she walked to the counter.

'Morning, miss, what can I do for you?'

'Can I have a cup of coffee, please?'

'You can have a cup of coffee.' Another joker, it was in his voice, and the other men were bound to be listening. 'How do you like it?'

'It's for my father. He has it black with sugar.'

'Coming right up.' He spooned brown powder out of a tin, left the spoon in the mug and held it under the hissing tap of the urn. 'Sugar's there.' He indicated a round glass object, its spout clogged with brown-stained sugar. 'Anything for yourself?'

'No thanks.'

'Sit wherever you like.'

She measured out two spoonfuls of sugar – it was an imprecise business because of the silted spout – and carried the mug to a table near the door, which bore crusted red swirls of imperfectly wiped ketchup. As she sat down she saw that one of the two men sitting together was looking at her over his shoulder; when he caught her eye he turned back to his friend and said something – she knew it was about her. Oh, no! she thought. Please, no! But then the other man glanced across, leaning ever so slightly to one side to get a better view.

For the second time in twenty-four hours – only the second time in her life, probably – she was pleased to see her father. For a man so intolerant of so many things, including his family, he seemed unconcerned about the dirty table, and dragged over the blackened ashtray with something approaching satisfaction.

'You not having anything?'

37

'No, thank you.'

'Probably right.' He took a deep draught from the mug. 'By the centre, that's more like it . . .'

He lit a cigarette, and stared with narrowed eyes out of the small window. Occasionally he took gulps of the coffee, exhaling wetly after each mouthful. The steam from the mug formed beads of condensation on his big nose with its open pores. The two men at the far table continued to look their way and exchange comments. To show she hadn't noticed and didn't care anyway, she made conversation. 'How much longer will we be?'

'Oh . . .' He glanced at his watch. 'An hour? Three-quarters, given a following wind.'

'Are you going to stay for lunch?' It was a point of information, but she tried to make it sound as if she wanted him to.

He wasn't so easily flannelled. 'Why?'

'I just wondered.'

'I bet you did. The answer is I'll stay for as long as it takes your mother and me to arrive at a decision about what's to be done. It's not a social call.'

'No. I know.'

He mistook her assumed meekness for calm, which seemed to infuriate him. 'Make no mistake, you've caused an unconscionable amount of trouble and inconvenience. And expense – this term's fees are paid and I'm almost certainly losing business as we speak.'

She kept quiet. It hadn't worked; all she had done was reactivate his ill-temper. When he'd finished the coffee, he announced that he was going to 'shake hands with an old friend', a phrase used without a trace of humour and which she found disgusting. She was left sitting there, entirely exposed, no book to read and no one to speak to. It seemed like for ever – what was he doing? But she didn't care to think about that.

To her enormous relief the two men got up, paid at the counter and made to leave, the second holding the door for the first. At the very last minute he leaned over his arm and said, very close, making her jump: 'Hallo, Brigitte. You can't fool us.'

'What?' she said, stupidly, because the last thing she wanted was for him to say it again.

His friend's grinning face reappeared. They knew they'd caught her. 'Saw your picture in the paper, and very nice too.'

'I don't know what you're talking about.'

'Suit yourself, darling. Only wanted to say congratulations.'

Gerald reappeared, running his thumbs round the waistband of his trousers. 'Anything I can do for you?'

'Not a thing, squire. Just saying well done to the little lady.'

Oh, no, thought Miranda, don't! Please don't!

'May I suggest,' said her father, 'that you get the hell out of here before I make you get out?'

'Calm down, no offence. This your niece?'

The choice of words was intended to insult, and succeeded. 'She's my daughter, and if you don't back off right now I'll make you wish you'd never been born.'

'We're going, we're going!' The man held up his hands, not taking it seriously. Both he and his friend were large and strong-looking and, if not young, at least a good deal younger than Gerald. 'You must be very proud, mate. She got our vote.'

What happened next was so exquisitely embarrassing that for years the mere memory of it had the power to make Miranda squirm.

'Right!' snarled Gerald. 'That does it!' He lunged at the nearest man with a stupid, awkward movement, his bottom sticking out and the shoulders of his blazer up round his ears. His intended victim simply stretched out an arm and pushed him away with the heel of one beefy hand. Gerald tottered backwards, arms windmilling, and crashed to the ground. Over the sound of his friend's laughter the man called to the one behind the counter: 'You saw it all, mate, I was defending myself!' They were still laughing as the door swung shut behind them.

The café owner and the other two customers rallied round, helping Gerald to his feet and on to a chair, bringing him sugary brown tea and telling him to take it easy. Miranda stood up and hovered at a safe distance, knowing they must think her a pretty poor sort of daughter, but also knowing how much he would hate to have her ministering to him.

'So, what was all that about, then?' asked the café-owner, when the others had gone back to their places. 'Not a very clever thing to do, was it?'

Miranda waited with interest to hear what her father would say. He looked awful: his face was blotchy yellow, grey and purple and he was mopping at it with his handkerchief. There was spittle at the corners of his mouth.

'The bastards . . .' he spluttered. 'The bastards were insulting my daughter.'

Now, she thought, I've heard everything.

The one good thing to come of the incident was that when they did get back on the road, twenty minutes later and against the café-owner's advice ('You want to call a taxi, mate'), her father for once didn't smoke. But his driving was even more erratic than usual, and he kept clearing his throat with a thick, bubbly sound. Once he rolled down the window and spat out of it. She was appalled. The hard carapace of his control was cracked: it was like treading on a snail and seeing all the slimy, sticky stuff that came out. If she had liked him even the tiniest bit she might have felt sorry for him. As it was she felt only revulsion.

When they reached home he got out, slammed the car door and marched straight into the kitchen at the side of the house. Miranda hated the way he still did this, and thought her mother should make a habit of leaving the latch on, but it was unreasonable to expect her to take this precaution on the off-chance that he might turn up. It would have been best if he'd realised of his own accord that such behaviour was no longer acceptable, that these days he came to the house as a visitor. Leaden with exhaustion, she followed him. She supposed it all came down to money – whatever he had a financial stake in he treated as his, and that included her, her mother and their home.

The kitchen smelt appetisingly of her mother's mild, sweetish chicken curry. As she entered, her mother appeared in the kitchen doorway, thin and wavery, stretched to tearing point between the dread of Gerald's arrival and delight at Miranda's.

'Mandy! Come on in – your father's just gone through, he looks awful, did you have a ghastly journey? Oh!' Marjorie Tattersall put her arms round Miranda. She was trembling with nervous energy and anxiety, and her brittle, permed hair tickled Miranda's face.

'It was fine, but he had a fall.'

'Ah.' She thought she understood, but of course she didn't and it couldn't all be gone into now. 'Let's go and see how he is.'

How he was, was in the living room, pouring himself a schooner of amontillado from the decanter on the sideboard. Both schooners and decanter were there for high days and holidays and he knew it. It would have been nice, thought Miranda, if having helped himself he had at least had the grace to offer her mother a drink, but instead he plonked himself down on the sofa and addressed Miranda: 'Right. Any ideas?'

'No.' She remained standing. Her mother perched on the very edge of an armchair as if poised for flight.

'Here's what I think,' he said. He waited for a reply, raising his eyebrows and pursing his lips grotesquely. 'Want to hear?'

They nodded. He looked at Miranda. 'I think it's pretty clear what you think of your mother and me, that our efforts on your behalf count for damn all.'

'That's not—'

'And,' he raised his voice threateningly, 'it's also very clear how you see yourself and where you believe your talents lie. If they can be called that. "Assets" is how they're usually referred to, aren't they, in the popular press of which you're so fond?'

'Gerald,' said her mother, almost indulgently as if he'd made a joke, 'it was a terribly silly thing to do but I'm quite sure Mandy didn't see it as anything but a bit of fun.'

'No, I'm damn sure she didn't, which goes to show that in spite of three years' infernally expensive education she's still stupid and has learned nothing.'

'She was doing well at Queen's,' said Marjorie. 'And she was

41

never stupid, Gerald, she's a bright girl, that's why you sent her there.'

'If she's that bright she'll do just fine at the place round the corner.' Gerald slammed his glass down on the coaster with its Redoute rose. 'And she'll have to, because I'm washing my hands of her.'

Miranda had wanted only to sit this exchange out, to keep still and let it wash round and over her so as to get him out of the house as quickly as possible, but at this point her resolve broke. 'Promise?' she said. 'Do you promise, faithfully?'

She must have learned it from him, the ability to wound, because once she'd decided, it was easy: she was good at it. He looked slightly surprised that she had spoken at all, and was sufficiently wrongfooted that he misread her intention.

'It's no good whining – I beg your pardon?'

'Do you *promise* to wash your hands of me?'

He stared at her truculently, temporarily stumped for a reply. She pressed her advantage. 'It's so sweet of you to do that. I really do appreciate you going away and being rude and drunk and disgusting somewhere else, as far away as possible.'

'Mandy . . .' Her mother was absolutely terrified, too scared even to be emphatic. Her voice was low and her manner conciliatory, she was hoping that by staying still and not making too much noise she could avert disaster. But Miranda was positively courting it now, she could feel all the vitality that had drained out of her over the past couple of days coursing back – her cheeks were warm, her muscles loosened, she could almost feel her hair growing, her ponytail springing out of her scalp like the plume on a helmet.

'I don't deserve you, I really don't. How did you know that all I wanted was never to see your ugly face again, or smell your breath, or listen to you ramble on, boring everyone to death?' He was sitting there transfixed. She turned to her mother, who was white as a sheet. 'When I said he fell over, you thought it was because he was drunk, didn't you? Actually he wasn't drunk, not then, he was hung-over from last night and he tried to punch a man in the café we stopped at, which wasn't very clever because the man was much younger and just pushed him over,' she looked back at Gerald, 'didn't he? Your bottom would be really sore now if it wasn't so fat. But at least we shan't have to watch it wobbling around any more. Thanks, Daddy.'

She took a couple of paces forward, leaned down and placed a kiss on his cheek. His skin was clammy under her lips and the sour smell of unwashed clothes, booze and stale tobacco rose off him. Why, she wondered, had she ever been scared of him? He was pathetic.

Nonetheless, she could see that he wanted to hit her, and would have done if he'd had the strength. He lurched to his feet, swore shockingly, and said, in a funny, high voice: 'I'm going to—' but didn't get any further because he staggered and his eyes rolled. Miranda would have let him fall over, and probably put her shoe on his face – she'd always wanted to do that – but her mother cried, 'Gerald!' and jumped up, catching him by the arm. Her knuckles were as white as her face with the effort of supporting him. Even so Miranda couldn't bring herself to help.

'Mandy!' gasped Marjorie. 'I think you'd better go upstairs!'

Miranda left the room, knowing that she owed her mother an apology for this, much more than for the BB competition. This had really torn it. And a *good thing too*, she reminded herself. That had been her whole purpose and intention. Except that it was her mother who was having to deal with it.

For some minutes it remained ominously quiet downstairs. She hoped he wouldn't take it out on her mother. He had never, as far as Miranda knew, struck his wife: his forte had always been verbal cruelty, treating the two of them like dirt – and now she was banking on him feeling too ill to do much. There was also a distinct possibility that her mother might, out of some misplaced sense of duty or guilt, press him to stay, to rest and be looked after by her until he was better. That would be the worst of all, giving him time to regroup, and put a spanner in the works of their fragile conspiracy against him.

But no, she heard her mother's voice in the hall, flittery and anxious, '. . . no excuse for . . . can't say how . . . phone in the next day or two?'

43

And her father's answering snarl, of which she caught only one word: '. . . nothing!'

The back door opened and she went to the small window next to the bed, which overlooked the door and the top of the driveway. He came out, without looking back, and got into the driver's seat. She saw his hands slap down heavily on the wheel, and could imagine the expression on his face. It was only after he'd started the car that she remembered her case and trunk were in the boot, but she wasn't worried – her mother would be sad to lose it all, but for herself, if she ever saw a pair of green over-knickers or an Aertex blouse again it would be too soon.

She needn't have worried. The car had only reversed a couple of yards when it stopped violently – she heard the groan of the handbrake being yanked on – and her father got out. He went to the back and she heard the boot being opened, the scrape and crash and cursing as he hauled her stuff out and dumped it unceremoniously on the ground. The effort must have been enormous in his weakened condition, and once he was back behind the wheel she saw him get out his wadded hankie to mop his face.

When he'd gone she opened her bedroom door and went downstairs. The front door stood open, and her mother appeared, staggering along with Miranda's suitcase, mac and hat.

She set them down heavily and said, without looking at her daughter: 'It'll need both of us for the trunk.'

Miranda went out with her and they grabbed a handle each. Between them, with difficulty and a couple of stops, they lugged it into the hall and let it go with a crash at the foot of the stairs.

'It'd be sensible to unpack it down here,' said her mother, 'rather than try to cart it up to your room with everything in it. Then we can put it straight in the loft.' She looked at Miranda with a worn-out expression, wiped of all emotion. 'Well,' she said, 'thanks to you, we're on our own now.'

CHAPTER TWO

————◆◇◆————

Claudia 130

Claudia had always expected to be married young to a man handsome enough not to be repugnant, clever enough to admire, and amusing enough to keep her entertained; and with him to bear a handful of spirited children in short order, so that while still young she might become the smartest and most sought-after hostess in Rome. She was a stubborn girl, a good catch if not a great beauty, with all the usual accomplishments and a mind of her own. She wanted whatever status and influence such a marriage could provide, and was fully prepared to do her part in its achievement and maintenance.

But Claudia was choosy, and it was only in her twentieth year that she threw in her lot with Publius, twelve years her senior, a career soldier with army-hardened ways and few immediately discernible social or artistic graces: the exact opposite, in fact, from what she'd always thought she wanted. There had been suitors, some of them quite personable, but when it came right down to it she found that for her the choice of a husband was a great deal more complicated than the ticking off of attributes on a list. Two had aroused her interest, but one had succumbed to a swamp fever contracted on active service on the North African frontier and the other, a charming and accomplished man, she had discovered to be effeminate. No parental pressure was applied to her – she was the apple of her father's eye and he would never have uttered or heeded a word against her – but if it had been it would have met with the fiercest resistance.

Everyone assumed that the marriage to Publius Coventinus was one of expedience, based on a measure of desperation and Publius' temerity in presenting himself at a time when she was in danger of becoming an old maid, in effect if not in essence. And everyone was right, except that she confounded the doubters and herself by gradually falling in love.

As a girl she would have laughed that 'gradually' to scorn: the fall into love was to be sudden, headlong and precipitate and not necessarily with one's husband. She was pragmatic enough to know that marriage was a contract to be sealed in a spirit of committed industry and goodwill. Fidelity might be its cornerstone, but that didn't preclude having passionate feelings for someone else. Indeed, many independent-minded women of the day took the view that a sound marriage was the best basis for enjoying romantic love elsewhere. What persuaded Claudia that marriage to Publius might be more than a solidly honoured partnership was the strength of their mutual physical attraction.

Even so, his proposal, if it could be called that, four weeks after their first meeting, was no declaration of tumultuous passion. Rather it was a speculative suggestion that they join forces. 'So, Claudia . . .' he'd said reflectively, as if rolling the idea around in his own head '. . . shall we be man and wife?'

'Who knows?' she replied. 'I see no reason why not. Yet.'

He hadn't exactly laughed but had given an appreciative grunt, as if surprised by a child's punch. 'Perfectly fair answer. In that case I'd better not give you time to find one.'

They were in the peristyle of her father's house in Rome, ostensibly left alone but undoubtedly overlooked from the surrounding rooms. The onlookers fell into two categories: there was her father Marianus, feigning paperwork in the tablinum of the main house at a time when he would normally have been enjoying a siesta. The carved wooden doors were not quite closed, and Claudia could imagine him perched, nod-headed on his folding stool, gazing at a page of figures but keeping the two of them in the corner of his eye . . . On either side of the enclosed garden were colonnades beyond which were respectively the summer dining room and loggias, and the kitchen and slaves' quarters. In the dining room one of the Spanish twins, the boy, was sweeping the floor with lazy, whispering strokes. From the kitchen came a desultory chink of pots, and the voices of the cook and his wife, not working but nosy, pretending activity for the sake of a little gentle spying. In the living quarters someone — Tasso, probably — was singing, with barely the energy to hold the tune, his sweet high voice occasionally dwindling into silence then re-emerging like a small stream: he knew what was going on.

The enclosed garden was to the south of the house, and on this early spring afternoon the sun was beginning to dip towards the roof of the western colonnade so that a broad blade of shadow bisected the courtyard. Among the shrubs now in shade Eusebor, stricken in years and bent double, shuffled about with a watering-can. The plants were supposed to be watered much later, at dusk, but Eusebor, preferring the comfort of servitude to the uncertainties of freedom, had granted himself a kind of private emancipation that enabled him to do as he liked. Besides which Marianus, out of good-heartedness, kept far too large a household so there wasn't enough for the servants to do and any occupation was welcome.

From all around, only slightly muffled by the thick outer walls of the house, came the clamour of the city, the shouts of teachers, buskers and tradesmen and the rumble of builders' traffic in the street immediately outside, blurring with distance into a dull roar that rose off the clogged thoroughfares and teeming, scuttling alleys — a roar punctuated by the occasional crash of falling masonry and loads being shed. It was a din that Claudia, an urban creature, would only have noticed in its absence; but which Publius, used to the contained bustle of a garrison from which it was possible to escape into birdsong, weather and wilderness, found oppressive

'Do you think this constitutes an agreement?' he asked.

'That's hard to say since you've asked me no direct question.'

'I'm doing so now.' She tilted her head prompting him. 'Will you agree to marriage?'

'Do you want to marry me?'

'I do.'

'Then I will.'

'Good.'

They sat in the bright half of the peristyle, Claudia on a wooden seat, Publius on the stone surround of the fountain, his back to the light.

What she saw was a man in early middle age, neither tall nor handsome, but formidable; with a skin weathered by campaigning and cheeks pocked by past illness; whose hair had turned grey when he was still young and was now the colour of pewter; whose eyes were dark and opaque, and blinked only rarely with a quick, impatient snap; whose right hand lacked a ring finger; who even when completely still seemed poised for violent activity, though whether at that moment it was flight or fight she couldn't have said. Later she came to realise that what she had perceived then was a worthy adversary, a man whose tough pugnacity it might be both her challenge and her pleasure to disarm.

'Very good,' he said again. Adding, without a smile: 'And so painless.'

For his part, Publius saw a woman who, even sitting with the cruel afternoon sun full on her face, radiated her own idiosyncratic brightness and energy: hair the colour of wet sand; tawny, slightly hooded eyes, which could seem humorous or haughty; a freckled skin not disguised by powder and paste; a broad mouth, strong jaw, graceful neck and square shoulders; a straight bearing and an open manner that made her seem taller than she was; large, capable hands that didn't fidget. A woman, he instinctively considered, worth taking on.

'Why shouldn't it be?' she replied. 'It's not a battle.'

But it might have been, thought Publius, as he left the house an hour later, having declined an invitation to dinner from his emotional future father-in-law. It might as well have been, because now that he was out here in the thickening semi-darkness, the uneasy crossing place between the rowdy commercial din of day and the equally noisy and far more nefarious night, now that he was outside her door he felt as if he'd spent the last hours in hand-to-hand combat with a tricky, dangerous enemy. His palms were sweating, his legs felt weak and heavy and his head hurt. Seeing a late wine-seller still unchaining his jars from the pillar outside his premises he bought a cupful and chugged it down, knowing that the price of improved morale would be an even worse head.

It was a mile and half's walk to his lodgings but he'd turned down Marianus' offer of a torch-bearer and didn't bother to hire one. As for the night-watchmen, he'd heard jokes at the bath-house about how they were like hen's teeth when you needed them, and quite likely to exploit their position by lightening your purse. These were circumstances in which he was perfectly confident of his ability to look after himself, and sure, too, that the confidence was its own protection. No, it was in there, trapped in that secluded garden with that young woman, that he was so infernally vulnerable and unsure. Not that she hadn't been straightforward with him – she had said yes, for gods' sake! – but with all her frankness she gave so little away. He'd thought to surround the fortress, to invest it, to take it by strategy and skill. Instead of which the gates had simply opened and he stood inside its walls, bewildered and uneasy. Now he had obtained Claudia (if that was what he had done) he was uncertain how to proceed with her.

He must be practical, he told himself. He had been lonely and now would no longer be. In the past year he'd found himself envying the companionship and support that many of his brother officers got from their wives. That was what he'd wanted: marriage was a sensible move for a man at his time of life and at this stage in his career. He had come to Rome, a centurion and *primus pilus*, to find a wife. He would return to the northern frontier, as camp commander and a married man. With his wife. He practised it. This is Claudia, my wife—

'Hey!' A youth barged him into another, he was thrown off-balance and felt the rough, urgent frisk of strange hands after his money. They found the hilt of his dagger first and hesitated for a split second, enabling him to drive his elbow into that boy's stomach and grab the privates of the one in front, nipping them with hard fingers. 'Forget it, or your mothers won't know you.'

They believed him and scampered off, yelping and blaming one another. No one took any notice of this all-too-common incident except a couple of tarts who tittered admiringly and offered business. They weren't bad looking in a highly coloured, over-decorated, big-city way but they couldn't hold a candle to Claudia and his expression must have told them as much.

'Ooh!' They were amiably beyond insult. 'Suit yourself!'

He realised that, however inscrutable his intended, he wanted her ferociously and that, surely, counted for something.

Betrothals, as Claudia had often heard her father say – perhaps as an excuse for her own lack of one – were two-a-penny in Rome these days and meant nothing. They carried about the same status as cheap jewellery taken on approval. Marianus himself was old enough to boast that *his* parents' marriage had been one of the last based on the old order – his mother given *in manu*, in an arranged union at the age of fourteen, and giving birth to the first of her family of four a year later. He was a widower now, but his own wholly conventional marriage to Claudia's mother had by all accounts been a model of *concordia*, the hallmark of conjugal happiness. These days, it was all freedom and independence and, he implied, far too much of both, and the result was a proliferation of unsuccessful and unproductive marriages in which true fidelity was considered almost naïve. A poor show, all round.

Of course, when it came to his own opinionated daughter getting betrothed Marianus was like a dog with two tails. 'He's a good man, an excellent man, you've made an admirable choice!' he declared, embracing her warmly after they'd told him of their decision, and Publius had left. 'Here, we must have some wine . . .'

Claudia loved her father, not least for his tolerance, but her conscience would not allow him to get away with this. 'The selection process wasn't arduous, Father. For some time suitors haven't exactly been fighting their way to my side.'

'No, no, well . . .' Marianus waggled a hand to show that this was neither here nor there. 'You intimidate them, sweet one. But you like him. You get on together. And he's a widower, so—'

'So he knows what he's looking for.'

'I didn't say that. Did I say that?'

'There's no shame in saying it, Father. We must be practical.'

He took her wine from her and set it down, did the same with his own, and took both her hands gently in his. 'Do I seem a very stupid old man?'

She smiled. 'Old? You?'

'Ah!' He gave his wheezy chuckle, kissed the palms of her hands, first one then the other in quick succession – it used to make her scream with laughter as a child, when his face had a sharper stubble than now. 'I walked into it! I should know better! But for all I drivel on about suitability, I want you to be as happy as we were, your mother and I. Scarcely a cross word in all the years we were together . . .' His eyes filled with the customary easy tears and he used her fingers to wipe them away. 'You do understand that, don't you, Daughter?'

'Father,' she kissed him, 'I do.'

It was true, she did understand. In all humility she knew she was his darling – the legacy of his love, his link with the past and his stake in the future. She was very like her mother, though judging from the paintings of Lucilla not as pretty. Handsome – on a good day she could be handsome, glamorous, even, but her features were too uncompromising for beauty. So, her father was allowed to be pleased in an old-fashioned way about the match she had made, no matter what her reasons for making it.

She scarcely knew Publius, bar a few plain facts. His own parents were long dead; there had been no children from his earlier marriage. He was a man alone and seeking female companionship. They had not so much courted one another as sized one another up, and now they moved quietly and undemonstratively through the pre-nuptial period, the tension between them like a bowstring. Claudia had little experience of men but her uncle, her mother's brother, had owned a farm in Brixia where she, her father and Tasso had often stayed, and the two children had taken it all in, appalled and giggling by turns. In this house there were plenty of pictures that showed what men and women did, and she was not afraid of it. She yearned for it. Since meeting Publius she found herself imagining what it would be like to do those things with him, how his skin would feel against hers, and what she might dare do to please him. But she couldn't say she loved him because she did not know him well enough.

They were wary as animals. Because each hoped the other would take the first step into intimacy, their conversations tended to be practical. He was an infantry officer with the twelfth legion on leave from Britain. His first tour had been in Colchester, which was, he explained, as British postings went, a soft one – in the south-east of the territory, largely administrative and surrounded by co-operative locals and decent farmland. But when he returned it would be to the northern frontier where he'd served as a young legionary, to one of the Hadrianic garrisons that gazed grimly over the great Wall to the unsubdued and largely hostile fastnesses beyond. Claudia took it as evidence of his respect for her that he did not withhold this information, or think it might deter her. He was right: she was resolved that if she were to be a soldier's wife she would be stoical, loyal and uncomplaining. Starting as she meant to go on, she'd asked him questions about Britain and the implications of living on the frontier.

'It's pretty civilised, if that's what you mean,' he told her. 'Any fighting these days is sporadic. It takes the form of skirmishes and is quite containable. We'll have a house to ourselves at the garrison, and depending on where we are the countryside around there is rather fine – what you can see of it,' he gave her his brief, dark smile, 'through the rain.'

'I ought to be prepared for that,' she said seriously. 'Is it cold?'

'No use pretending you won't find it cold to begin with. And when it's wet, it's very wet. But you'll adjust, as everyone does, and there's good locally made clothing available to keep the elements out. I wouldn't care to comment on the style, but it's extremely serviceable.'

From this Claudia inferred that the garments were awful. She who had never considered herself especially fashion-conscious now envisaged with gloom the hairy cloaks and heavy shawls dictated by a grim northern climate.

'Are there many other women at the garrison?'

'Too many, some say.' Catching her expression he added, without undue haste: 'Far be it from me.'

She'd let this pass, having learned to deal with his verbal prods by ignoring them. She suspected that, like her, he might be a person with a volcanic temper kept firmly and habitually under control, and that it would therefore be sensible not to tread near the edge of the crater. Time enough for arguments when they knew each other's strengths, and the worst they were capable of.

Claudia knew that there was another reason why Marianus has congratulated her on her sound choice: he had introduced them, so the congratulations were for himself as well. It had been at the dinner party of a friend, Tersissius Cotta, but she could tell from her father's manner when he performed the introduction that the choice of venue was merely a strategy, cooked up by the two of them so it wouldn't seem too obvious what he was up to.

So she was naturally on the defensive, and it was only Publius' corresponding reserve that stopped her immediately closing her mind to him. As it was, though their conversation had been stilted and sporadic, there had been even then, and unmistakably, that bristle of unspoken mutual curiosity.

And there had been a moment, insignificant in itself but telling in retrospect, when they had been gazing in silence across the room and seen Marianus and their host in animated conversation and suddenly both realised what the old men were talking about. Instantly, simultaneously, it had struck them as funny: the two of them standing awkwardly together over here, while over there – such high hopes! such gleeful expectation! They'd not even had to remark on it, but they'd both laughed, she out loud, he in that contained way of his, and the laughter had aligned them against the matchmakers, and satisfied just enough of the curiosity to start something between them.

Today was their betrothal party. Marianus had spared no expense and the house was packed, mostly with family friends and business acquaintances, some friends of Claudia's, few of Publius' because his life for the past several years had been overseas. You could tell at a glance who his friends were – a little older, the men in general rather less talkative, with a stern presence and something guarded in their manner as if they withheld endorsement of the engagement until they knew more. She considered that fair, even if it was uncomfortable: she felt the same herself.

It was a good party and the noise level rose. Marianus was a master contractor who had done well by the building trade and been repaid with interest. His house on the Via Aquila was known for its modernity and comfort, and the quality of its hospitality. For this evening's festivities there were lamps burning in all the sconces around the dining room, and thick candles twined with greenery on a low, round table in the centre of the room. The dining tables were laid not with the everyday red Samianware, but the best silver and bronze serving platters, all of them groaning with food, especially her father's favourite, pork in all its forms. The centrepiece was a suckling pig, its amber crackling oozing fat, served with a thick winy sauce flavoured with pepper, lovage, caraway and celery seeds, rue and olive oil. Huge racks of ribs, like edible armour, were studded with dried figs and olives, and glazed with honey. Hams had been baked in a flour and oil paste, and sow's udder mixed into a pâté with chicken, fish and delicate wild-bird meat. Secondary to this were rabbit joints and veal slices fried in a rich reduction of onions, wine, honey, raisins and vinegar, and pigeons – could there be any left out there? – stewed in a broth of barley and other grains. There were also cheeses made from sheep's, goat's and cow's milk, coarse crusty bread to mop up the meat liquor, elaborate towers of fruit, held together here and there by wooden pins, a trick of the chef's, and piles of stuffed dates, honey cakes, and wine buns with aniseed and lemon. The wine amphorae were kept full – Marianus hated the impression of parsimony conveyed by a jar's last trickle, even if it was to be replenished – so the slaves rushed to and from the kitchen like participants in some arcane sporting event. Even in the culture of social and gastronomic excess that those present were used to, they recognised lavish extravagance when they saw it.

Claudia knew there would be some gatecrashers in the house. Her father was a noted soft touch. She'd lost count of the number of times he'd returned from the baths with some creepy hanger-on who'd sponged an invitation to dinner; or, worse still, a couple of younger men who'd got his number and set out to do a spot of shameless freeloading, simply to amuse themselves and their friends, perhaps to win a bet. They'd guzzle down his food and wine, ogle her, pretend to flatter him, and leave with bellies distended and their napkins sodden with the juices of all the food they'd snaffled. He turned a blind eye, of course, excusing their dreadful manners by invoking their poverty, youth – or simply their charm, by which he meant their ability to fawn. She felt humiliated on his behalf, saw this open-handed indulgence as not kindness but a lack of dignity on Marianus' part but when she discreetly pointed this out he wouldn't accept it. 'I knew hard times once, and now that I'm comfortable I like to be generous.'

'But, Father, you could be more discriminating . . .'

'It amuses me to entertain strangers, easy come, easy go . . . Don't you nag me, Daughter, your mother never did!' This would always be accompanied by a disarming pat or a kiss.

Claudia had heard it said that women married men like their fathers. But it was hard to imagine Publius tolerating the sort of people her father found 'amusing'. He was having difficulty, even tonight.

Marianus caught her eye from the end of the table and beamed benignly, indicating with a small jerk of his head that she might talk to Cotta on her other side, a boring, bibulous man but an old family friend and a good customer. Publius had probably got the message too, for he rose and walked round to the table at the far side of the room. Dutifully, she turned to Cotta, who was gleaming with sweat and meat-grease, and had dribbled wine on his tunic.

'Wonderful spread as usual,' he said, waggling a large, dripping section of baked pigeon to emphasise his point, 'but, then, it would be, you're making your father a very happy man.'

'You mean he's getting rid of me at last.'

'Now, that's not fair. Did I say any such thing? Remember, it was in my house that you met! And anyway . . .' he leaned confidingly towards her and she could see the shreds of meat between his teeth '. . . Publius will be happy too, with such a lovely bride. And he deserves happiness.'

'I certainly want to make my husband happy, but does he deserve it more than the next man?' She was a touch astringent, because it nettled her to be treated solely as a source of other people's, notably men's, happiness.

Cotta's pouting, babyish face grew almost comically solemn. 'Yes, yes – oh, yes,' he declared, as if she might have missed the affirmative the first time. 'Such a tragic story about his first wife, do you not know?'

'No.'

'She was only a girl, no more than a child, and so tiny . . . She died in labour. And all her suffering was wasted – the infant died also,' he added, as a point of information.

Claudia wasn't sure she wished to be upstaged by past tragedy at her own betrothal party. 'Sadly, it's not such an uncommon story.'

Cotta shook his head mawkishly. 'No one thought he'd marry again . . .'

'Why? He imagined that in some way that it was his fault? That he inflicted the child on her?'

'No doubt about it. If her death wasn't precisely his fault, he was greatly to blame.'

For the first time in this particular conversation curiosity overcame her prickly resentment. She asked again: 'Why?'

'Dear oh dear, look at me, listen to me!' Cotta chortled,

showering her with pigeon-juice. 'What a subject for a girl's engagement party! I only meant to emphasise what a great occasion this is for celebration – and how well your father does it. There's always been a good party to be had in this house, and your mother – you have a look of her, it's quite uncanny – your mother was the sweetest, prettiest thing . . . She would have been in her element today, seeing you with your intended, and such a fine man, don't get me wrong, we've all done things we'd rather forget about – know I have!' He gave her arm an insinuating nudge. 'And I haven't the slightest doubt you'll redeem him as a good wife should!'

The notion of being her husband's redeemer wasn't one that had occurred to Claudia. While Cotta burbled on she looked across the room at Publius, contemplating him in this new and disturbing light. Like her, he was doing his social duty, listening to a gushing, garrulous middle-aged woman who must have been boring him to death. Whatever else he seemed, there was always a stern, tough steadiness about him. It was easy to imagine him being fierce in battle or before his troops, but much harder to picture him engaging in small personal cruelties, especially to a small, young girl, his child-wife.

As the eating, though not the drinking, began to slow down, she saw her father say something to one of the slaves, who bustled off, and returned a moment later with what she recognised as Marianus' most personal notebook. Personal to a certain point – it seemed disturbingly likely that he was going to recite. Ye gods, thought Claudia, stop him, please.

But this was Marianus' big moment. If the host of a large dinner party could exercise a right to entertain his guests as he chose, how much more could the father of a bride-to-be! It was a heaven-sent opportunity, to be milked for all it was worth. And although Claudia was hot with apprehension the guests, basking in a post-dinner glow, were sufficiently well disposed towards their benefactor as he rose to his feet to display nothing but pleasurable anticipation.

He already had their attention, but Marianus still raised a hand at once imperious and gracious. This was to be a performance with no half-measures.

'My friends,' he announced, 'now you've enjoyed your dinner – and I hope you *have* enjoyed your dinner –' as intended this provoked loud cheers, belchings, slappings of midriffs and raising of glasses '– now that you've enjoyed your dinner I ask your indulgence . . .'

He started with some verses of Catullus, an old and traditional favourite, but Claudia knew it wouldn't end there. Another of her father's benign pretensions was that of patron of the arts. When it came to the visual arts, perhaps because of his architectural and building expertise, he had a good eye, and one or two of his *protégés* had gone on to some commercial and critical success. But where writing was concerned he was, to put it charitably, less reliable. Lacking either training or aptitude he aspired to be something of a writer himself, and a judge of it in others. After the verses of Catullus, which shone down two hundred years with fresh-minted charm and delicacy, he embarked on a poem by one of his new-found talents, a clunkingly tedious piece, part-narrative part-panegyric, on an idealised Roman matron named Honoria – whom Claudia hoped was not based on a real person, or intended as an example to herself, for she sounded insufferable – whose fidelity to her husband extended to her ending both their lives when she found him to be suffering from an incurable disease. This behaviour seemed thoroughly wasteful to Claudia. Marianus' eyes filled with tears, while his audience's threatened to close.

Claudia looked across at her betrothed. Perhaps it was his military training that enabled him to remain quietly attentive, head bowed in concentration, eyes downcast but unblinking. His talkative neighbour, now visibly worse for wear after several glasses of her host's Optimian, inclined her head towards him and whispered something with a playful expression, to which he did not react. His manner made it clear that he was listening to the recitation. Claudia felt a twinge of something like tenderness for his stoical politeness. Was it possible that he had done something so patently wrong – wicked, even – that he 'deserved' the redemption of a happy marriage? He had not given away much about himself but, then, neither of them had. Her life might be an open book, having been shorter and less eventful, but she had kept her counsel on many things, believing instinctively that with Publius a degree of restraint would be found pleasing – you only had to look at his behaviour with that woman. Surely a man should be allowed to keep his secrets.

Publius glanced over at his bride. She was managing to look interested in her father's performance. He liked the fact that in this as in other ways she was a good daughter – she didn't want her father to make a fool of himself, but if it was his pleasure and privilege to do so then she would be loyal and betray no embarrassment. He trusted her to bring those qualities to their marriage. Once more he rested his head on his hand. It was no use pretending that his was a pragmatic choice. He had done that before and it had resulted in the deception and betrayal of a girl young enough to be his daughter – even, indirectly, her death. He wanted Claudia not for the duty, loyalty and fidelity she would undoubtedly give him – he had had that once, in abundance, it had not been enough – but for what he hoped, and sensed, they could share as equals.

'How terribly sweet,' whispered the woman next to him. 'Marianus has written something for the occasion!'

This, thought Claudia, was a test of character in its small way and, for her father's sake and her own self-respect, she was not going to fail it. The eyes of all present were on her, except those of Publius, which remained studiously shaded by his hand. She gazed steadily at her father.

'". . . close-kept treasure which I must soon give up
Into the keeping of another man;
Relinquishing also what he cannot know,
That other treasure which she, all unaware,
Carries in her eyes, her look, her smile,
And all the thousand things that make her days,
The days that till now –"

'I'm so sorry—'

Her father's eyes welled, there was a little answering sigh of sympathy from his audience. To her surprise Claudia felt her own eyes sting. But she kept her head up, and when he looked her way she sent him a slow blink of encouragement.

'"The days that till now we have shared:
The memory of her mother brought fresh to life—"'

Another murmur, rather more vocal: there were many here who remembered Lucilla. Claudia's approval and his listeners' responsiveness heartened him visibly, and when he went on it was with the strong voice of the born performer.

'"But we who have been blessed with married love
Know that there is no lasting loss in death
Nor even in departure's small farewell,
For all the space and time that lies between
Is but a single step for our true hearts to cross."'

'Thank you, dear friends.'

There was a moment's silence: perhaps people were taken by surprise by the poem's brevity, but then their applause was loud and genuine. It continued while Marianus came round to where Claudia was, took her hand to raise her to her feet, and embraced her, the tears pouring down his face.

'Thank you,' she said softly in his ear. 'That was lovely. Brave and calm, now.'

'I know, I know . . .' He patted her back. When he released her it was with a smile. He pressed the paper into her hand and folded her fingers round it. 'For you.'

'But you must keep it, Father, it's the best thing you've ever written.'

'Which is not saying much, eh?' He chuckled. 'Don't worry, I'm not so vain I don't know what people say . . . No, no, my darling, you take it, it's all up here.' He tapped his head. Then, with one arm still round her shoulders, he spread the other expansively. 'So there, I've said my piece, and you've been patient. Reward yourselves, eat and drink, listen to music – I insist, my house is yours!'

A warm babel of goodwill and enthusiasm rose off the guests, their party spirit thoroughly restored by this show of good honest sentiment. Tasso entered, with the flautist Marianus had hired for the occasion. The sounds of the flute and of the boy's pure voice spiralled sweetly above the noise, so that it abated a little, and the mood changed. Publius' attention seemed caught by the singing. He listened for a few moments, then rose, excusing himself to his neighbour, and went to Marianus' side, clasping his arm and exchanging a few words before coming to Claudia.

'That was splendid,' he said, keeping his voice low. 'Your father did you proud.'

'Yes, he did. I was—' Remorse stopped her short. 'I was pleased for him.'

'We shouldn't be surprised,' he said seriously. 'True feeling speaks for itself. I wonder, would you like to walk outside for a few minutes? Your father has no objection and it's a beautiful evening.'

'I would like to.'

'Who's the singer?'

'Tasso. He's been here as long as I remember. He and I grew up together.'

'He knows his business.'

They went out of the dining room and across the covered walk to the courtyard. One of the house slaves, an Egyptian, was sitting with his back against the wall, listening and dreaming, and jumped to his feet in confusion at their approach. She ignored him, and as they passed he settled back. Publius took his cue from her and made no comment except to say: 'You run a happy house here.'

'I think so. It's hard for me to say, since I've never known another.'

'You haven't, have you?' He paused and took her hand. 'Will you miss it?'

She didn't hesitate, because there was no point: no point in telling the man with whom she would be spending the rest of her life anything but the truth. 'Yes, of course. This place, and my father. But not for long, I'm sure.'

'I hope not.' He tapped the ring he'd given her, a circle of iron set in gold. 'This is rather plain – is it too plain?'

She recognised a career soldier's genuine uncertainty in matters of taste. 'Not at all. It's simple and strong.'

'Yes, good, I like that.' He gave his short, suppressed grunt of laughter. 'Very diplomatically put.'

'I am not diplomatic,' she said firmly, 'and I shall never be so with you.'

'Really?' They walked on. 'Is that a threat?'

'No, but it is a promise. I may remain silent from time to time but I shall never fob you off with half-truths.'

'I can see I'd better prepare myself for this life of pregnant silences and bracing honesty.'

They were now at the far end of the courtyard, protected by the warm darkness. Away from the light of the party and in the moon's shadow they could see one another but were invisible from the house. He took her in his arms and kissed her. They were the same height, thigh to thigh, breast to breast, mouth against mouth, in an equal embrace. Her eyes closed as her heart opened.

He drew back, his hands on her shoulders. His eyes were black. She was silent, knowing he could not read her expression in the darkness.

'Now,' he said, with a brusqueness she was starting to understand, 'might be the time for that diplomacy you so despise . . .'

In reply she returned his kiss. For a second only she felt him tremble, and understood her power.

The small room Publius was renting, off the least disreputable sub-tenant in an apartment block on the Via Antinus, was on the second floor overlooking the road. Unusually there had been a choice – the man had offered a slightly larger room at the back of the building – but as far as Publius was concerned this was the lesser of two evils. The larger room meant sharing, something he'd done enough of in the army, and it was rank and stuffy even by the standards of the *insulae* – the very walls reeked of the cooking, heating and bodily functions of the block's fifty or so other other occupants. The front room was equally smelly but at least the smells of the street brought with them the illusion of open air: they weren't odours laid down over years of cramped and squalid living. There was a rickety balcony hanging out over the road, on which were a couple of pots containing a tangle of desiccated roots. The pots were well past the point where there was any need to take them in at night, but during his stay Publius had discovered that while they might be safe from thieves they made an excellent target for small boys who would shy pebbles at them, yelp with glee at the satisfying *ping!* of each direct hit, then race away. He didn't waste his breath remonstrating with them: within seconds they were lost in the urban mêlée.

The chief price he had to pay for escaping the stifling atmosphere at the back of the building was the noise, which if it wasn't actually worse at night seemed so because a person was trying to sleep. The transport that was banned by day – driven cattle, supply wagons, carts and through traffic – took full advantage of the hours of darkness. Years of campaigning had accustomed him to sleep and wake quickly, in short snatches, and to keep one ear and an eye open for danger. He couldn't resign himself to this city-weariness, from which there was no easy escape.

He splashed his face, neck and hands – he'd been husbanding precious water as you had to up here, and was careful with it – then lay down. The bed was hard and narrow, no more than a shelf protruding from the wall, but that didn't bother him. It was the unceasing din . . .

He realised how used he had become to the long, cool northern nights, punctuated by no more than the bleat of far-off sheep, the occasional barking of dogs and the even more intermittent shouts of the sentries. The sounds of the British settlement outside the garrison walls only emphasised the relative seclusion of his quarters. Whereas this! He clamped his arms to his head as a herd of unhappy cattle surged past beneath his window, urged on by their vociferous provincial drovers. Rome was a city of which one half had no intention of sleeping at all, and the other, he'd discovered, had precious little chance.

But, then, how easy was it ever going to be to sleep tonight? He could stop his ears against the racket of the streets, but not close his mind's eye to the picture of Claudia. Soon to be his woman: but always, he suspected, her own.

When he did sleep, he had the nightmare and woke, with a shout of terror, in the deep dark before dawn.

Claudia, who always slept soundly, did so now.

She and Publius were married on a warm day in spring, in the fourteenth year of the Emperor Hadrian. All who came, or who turned out to watch the procession, said they had never seen a more arresting bride. In her flame-coloured wedding clothes of crimson, saffron and orange, with her leonine colouring and imposing bearing, she was more like a queen with her retinue than a woman who was (at least nominally) being passed from one man to another. Even now the most emancipated women tended to put on a show of maidenly submission for the occasion, but the impression given by this one was that she couldn't have done so if she tried. A handful, people suspected.

It amused the more gossipy among the onlookers to suggest, with much eyebrow-raising and lip-pursing, that this was a less than felicitous match, but others were emollient, pointing out that there had always been room for the attraction of opposites, and much to be said for the joining of complementary natures. Where the doom-mongers cheerily foresaw squalls and wrecks, the optimists predicted passion and lively but balanced debate. All enjoyed themselves immensely. You couldn't beat a good wedding.

Though Claudia may have looked regal, she was scared. And

the greater her fear the more queenly her bearing. The more her heart pattered and her stomach churned, the higher her chin rose and the steadier her gaze. It wasn't Publius she feared, nor even, exactly, the challenge of married life, but herself and her reactions. She was untested and she knew it. The confident manner for which she was well known was protective, she had learned to assume it at will. How would she react to a new life in a distant land with a man still largely strange to her? The thought of failure, through ignorance, immaturity, or some deep-seated but unforeseen character deficiency, was abhorrent to her.

And today she didn't even feel like herself. The scent of the wreath that held the crimson wedding veil in place – marjoram and orange blossom with a hint of verbena and myrtle for old times' sake – was sickly-sweet, not a scent she would have chosen but one imposed on her by tradition. The wedding dress and veil that suited her so well were, none the less, a uniform, one worn by every other bride, and she felt constrained by it.

What steadied her was the sense that Publius recognised and understood this. It was no more than a sense – how, after all, would he have framed such an observation? it wasn't yet within their emotional compass to have such an exchange – but she trusted it. At the ceremony at her father's house there had been that quietness about him, which had the effect of quietening her, too. If his natural restraint made him occasionally gruff it could also generate calm. During the ceremony at her father's house – the sacrifice of the pig, the offices of Cotta as *auspex*, reading the entrails and declaring the signs favourable, and their mutual exchange of vows before the witnesses – Publius' eyes remained downcast, or on her, so that even when he wasn't looking at her she felt he was thinking of her, or of the two of them together and what this meant for both of them.

But if she was nervous, and he unshowy, the others more than made up for it. Cotta was full of himself and his own importance, and Marianus was justifiably at his most emotional, with a hectic colour and hair on end. Beyond the group of eight witnesses gathered in the atrium Marianus had allowed those household servants who wished to attend to form a circle at a respectful distance. Claudia had sometimes felt that her father was too lenient with his staff, but if so she was reaping the reward in the form of their open affection for him and their pleasure in her wedding day. Their smiles, and a few tears, shone out of the cool shadows, a largely undeserved blessing since she herself had always been more reserved with them. There were no tears on Tasso's face, but he looked wide-eyed and shocked: she had seen that expression on the faces of slaves for sale in the market. She tried to send him a look of encouragement, but he had cauterised her treachery by cutting himself off from her.

After the sacrifice and the auguries, it was quiet. Encircled in the pool of light from above, and without the intrusive presence of Cotta and his bombastic drone, it was almost possible to believe that she and Publius were alone. They could hear the intimate flitter and rustle of small birds under the eaves.

He held out his hand to receive hers.

She gave it.

'*Ubi tu Publius, ego Publia.*'

Where you are, Publius, there shall I, Publia, be.

It was a simple declaration of fact, of intent, of resolve, which she'd often heard spoken by others. But to hear the words in her own mouth was moving. Their utterance made her part of something greater, the frail repository of timeless wifely aspirations. She was humbled. She wanted to do well.

His wife's hand rested lightly and coolly in Publius' own. Its lightness and coolness conveyed both independence and trust. Claudia did not cling, but looked openly to him for guidance and protection. He was overwhelmed. He would not let her down.

Red was the colour she remembered from that day. The red mist of her veil, the red of the sacrificial blood, of the old men's faces, and those of the party guests as they wined and dined and the temperature rose; the flickering red and gold of the five torches that lined her way to the house, which – for the purposes of this great day – Marianus had kept empty and told them to treat as theirs, and where Publius waited for her.

Chief of her three bridesmaids was Catia, sixteen years old, pretty and dark, and mad with envy. 'You're so solemn, Claudia!' she'd twitted, as they were preparing to leave the feast.

'Marriage is a serious business.'

'In that case you should be making the most of all this. Let your hair down, enjoy it, it might be the last chance you get!'

It was impossible to explain to Catia, on fire with the romance and glamour of it all, that enjoying her wedding ceremony and taking it seriously were not mutually exclusive. 'Perhaps,' she said, 'I'm expecting to have even more fun later.'

Catia gave a little shriek. This was more like it. 'Claudia!'

The half-dark through which the procession moved was lit with red, as though the crowded streets really were the thumping veins and arteries of the city. From far in front, beyond the torches, came the thin, flighty music of the flutes. According to tradition, she was led: each of her hands was held by a pageboy, the sons of friends, and a third walked just in front with the wedding brand of hawthorn twigs. The two on either side of her were stone-faced with self-consciousness, the hand of one was calloused, that of the other moist; the plump boy in front was enjoying every moment – from time to time he turned his face towards her with a round-eyed smile of sheer delight, star for a day. A crowd surged all around, some just gawping for a moment or two before falling back, others joining the procession, shouting the lewd suggestions and coarse comments that were part of the fun, but licensed by the need to scare off evil spirits. They accumulated a chattering rabble of children, lured by the music, the torches and the promise of the nuts that would be scattered when they reached their destination. All was noise and glare, and she the still centre of it, the excuse for all this merriment. Perhaps she should have smiled and waved as she'd seen other brides do, and as Catia would have recommended, but she couldn't bring herself to be so familiar with these grinning, yelling strangers.

When they reached the house, and the procession stopped,

the hubbub seemed to close around her. The children scampered and scuttled after the hail of nuts that were thrown to
them, symbol of the passing of the bridegroom's boyhood and
the fertility of his married state. The music, now they were
on top of it, was shrill and insistent, cutting the shouts of the
crowd. The smoke and smell of the stationary torches hung in
the air and black specks floated upwards through it to be lost
in the dark.

This was the moment when the redness ebbed away. The
doorway of the house was spread with white linen, scattered
with fresh green: a doorway from lewdness to purity; from
ribaldry to innocence; and to the end of innocence. Beyond
the entrance its spaces, though smaller than those of her father's
house, had the cool neutrality of a place as yet unoccupied –
no distinctive scent, or chosen objects, no fanciful decoration,
very few lamps – and she was glad of it. This was how they
should begin.

Some ritual still remained. In the quiet of the atrium Publius
was waiting. He was serious and practical, intent on getting
things right, offering her the copper bowl of water and the
lighted candle, tokens of ongoing life, which she accepted and
passed to her bridesmaids. Following Publius, Catia then led
her to the bedroom. Left her, with a squeeze of the hand, an
awed look, solemn too now under the spell of the occasion.
She closed the door.

They were alone.

She realised that it was the first time she had looked him
full in the face since the exchange of their vows many hours
earlier. The interminable party, the people, the procession,
all the well-wishing and the ruderies, the sounds, sights and
smells that had filled the day had come between them. They
had touched hands once, and been separated, till now.

They moved slowly, she out of shyness and he out of respect.
Piece by piece her wedding clothes were removed – the wreath,
the veil, the stole, the girdle and the jewellery; the elaborate
pads, coils and ornamentation of her bridal hairstyle. When it
was mostly done and she stood there in her tunic she was
painfully aware that her hair, which was strong and wiry,

would do strange things after its day in captivity. She didn't want to fuss, or appear vain, but he seemed to read her mind. Stepping close, he began to comb her hair gently through his fingers, smoothing it back from her face and over her shoulders with his hard soldier's hands. Where it was tangled he teased the strands apart with a mother's tender concentration, his eyes on his work. His hands did not touch her skin, but only her hair. When he stood behind her to attend to the back she remained still, neither turning nor tensing, her arms hanging by her sides: trusting him to do her this intimate service.

Another ritual. The room was so quiet that she could hear his breathing.

And now, another.

And when this was over, and they lay together face to face, she placed her hand over his pumping heart and said again the simple words that were no longer the words of the world, but of her deepest and most secret self: 'Where you are, Publius, there shall I be.'

CHAPTER THREE

<hr>

Bobby, 1992

In the place where I grew up, I was no longer welcome. I knew this, because the house echoed, throwing me back at myself like an unwanted offering. The rattle of the front door opening ricocheted like gunfire off bare walls and gibbered around exposed corners. As I walked across the hall the clack of my footsteps resounded loud and hard on the tiles. The jet of water from the kitchen tap hammered the metal sink with a furious snarl. Its cold spray spat at me.

By this time tomorrow I'd be gone. But the house wanted me out *now*.

Everything rebuked me. The small scars of hooks and nails, with their attendant dim haloes; the map of fading and scuffing on the rose-patterned rug in the drawing room; and the rectangles of fresh pile where furniture had stood; the blank sheaves of pictures with their faces to the wall; the items marked for other people with yellow post-its, like passengers on a death train; the cartons crammed with stifled books, and the others awaiting transportation to the charity-shop *gulag*, to do their bit for Macmillan Nurses and MIND; the brutal spaces left behind by items already despatched to the saleroom, the cut-price warehouse, the dump; the skeletal frames of lamps stripped of their shades; the cupboards gaping to reveal their emptiness. And then there were the many evidences of poor maintenance, a rash of minor disasters no longer camouflaged by the layered texture of family life – loose latches, cracked walls, chipped paintwork, stains, damp patches, window mould and sagging hinges.

None of these indoor matters had given the mortgage company surveyor pause, but outside it had been different. Here, the condition of the woodwork and of the roof – whose central gully had been an out-of-sight-out-of-mind area for the past decade – had attracted his attention and consequently that of the buyer, who had promptly adjusted his offer to take into account the work that needed doing.

No wonder the house was hostile. Built by my grandfather not long after the Great War, as a 'gentleman's residence' (I'd seen it so described in a back number of the local paper) where he and my grandmother could lead a life of blameless comfort and calm, it had since been occupied by two more generations of Govans, the second of which came in two waves: my younger brother and his family, then me.

It was difficult to say which of these last the General would have regarded with most disfavour: Jim and Sally with their raggle-taggle tribe (some children achieve tribe status at a relatively low figure) and unkempt pets – or me, a divorced, childless, middle-aged woman doggedly justifying her unsought independence and opening a bottle, unaccompanied, on the dot of six. In a gesture of defiance I poured myself a glass of Vouvray now. I liked to think that whatever Grandpa's views on the appropriateness of my lifestyle he would, as a professional soldier, have had some respect for what he might have seen as my pluck.

It was high summer and still light at ten o'clock. I opened the door and carried my glass, and the bottle, out into the loggia. I knew my purchaser had plans for the loggia, plans that almost certainly involved double-glazing, rattan blinds and cane furniture. But neither Jim nor I, nor our parents before us, had felt inclined to change it so it had remained almost as our grandparents had left it, with a deal table, four battered wood and canvas safari chairs, a cobwebby clutter of pots, trugs and urns against one wall, a tall, white, chipped enamel jug and bowl in the corner and a hurricane lamp hanging from the roof. I could remember being here on summer evenings during my grandparents' time when the floor would be littered with the incinerated corpses of moths, leatherjackets, and God knows what else that had been impelled to embrace a fiery death on the hurricane lamp. Now there were seldom any, because the insect world had grown not more savvy but smaller. The nightly panic of moths in the room when one was reading had all but gone. My father had been phobic about winged creatures and Jim and I used to hear him yelping and bumping in childish terror while my mother laid about her with a rolled-up copy of the *National Geographic*. These days, night after night and in the small hours – I was slightly insomniac – I sat up in bed with whichever book I was currently staring at, with the light on and the curtains drawn back, and was not disturbed by so much as a housefly.

I sat down on one of the safari chairs. The stained canvas felt cool and a little damp – a dew had already begun to fall. Jim and Sally's feral cat, Kev, was drifting across the grass, a darker shape on the grey. I had inherited the change-averse Kev on my arrival two years ago, and my purchasers would do the same. They had said they didn't mind a cat as long as it lived outdoors. I told them he'd be more than happy with that, not adding that a cat, given security of tenure, would set his own terms.

Kev and I had an understanding: we were not friends, but cohabitees. He took pains not to be mistaken for someone who gave a damn. Even so, he would normally have come to sit on the wall of the loggia as much as to say, 'Out here, are you? Don't mind if I do – just for a while, mind . . .' But on this occasion he stopped half-way across the lawn and sat there, surveying me with Ra-like inscrutability, giving my perfidiousness a wide berth. I raised my glass to him and he began at once to wash, showing me how little he cared whether I lived or died.

As a matter of fact I was with him on that. I had never been, nor did I expect to be, suicidal, nothing as dramatic as that. But I was pretty indifferent to life. It had become just a series of physical, professional and fiscal moves, including the one due to take place tomorrow. The moves were made, the shifts from here to there and from this mindset to that were managed, but their effect remained chiefly anaesthetic. The three events at the top of the stress scale had happened to me in fairly rapid succession, divorce, bereavement and moving house, and with each life-tremor I'd grown more numb, or so it seemed. I could see that as between my brother and me, Jim had not had the divorce and was still, on the face of it, a lot madder – but, then, who knew what strains were inherent in supporting Sally, a part-time psychotherapist, and the zoo? And maybe I was even now scheduled for a monster bout of post-traumatic stress disorder to everyone's general satisfaction. Who knew? And who, I asked myself, cared? I was not so much sorry for as bored by myself. I often thought how nice it would be not to have to lug around the dull, loveless low-achiever that was me, to have a fun, feisty *alter ego* that I could parade when occasion demanded.

I topped up my glass. Kev stalked off into the black rampart of the rhododendrons, fastidiously shaking each back leg in turn.

In the days when he still loved me in his fashion, Alan used to say: 'With you, what you see is what you get. That's a rare thing in a woman.' But being exactly what one seems is (a) rarely true and (b) not sexy. 'I love you, you do exactly what it says on the tin,' was another of his observations later on, when he was putting it about a bit but wasn't entirely sick of me, and we were affectionate, easy-going roommates. I knew that plenty of women would have been incandescent with outrage at these remarks, but I've never been someone who adopted a political agenda. Alan meant well when he said these things and I took them at their face value.

Also, because we'd known each other for so long, I'd been under the illusion that we were alike and that the amiable, unexciting mateship of our marriage was okay by both of us. I'd had a handful of brief, disappointing relationships before Alan, one of which ended traumatically and none of which suited me, and being with him was like coming home. I felt comfortable, relaxed – completely myself, as I'd come to know me. So I thought it must be love. I didn't know then that being in love means discovering not only another person but a new self, a heightened self that's like a gift, making you more alive than you've ever been. I didn't know, and I settled for what I had.

Not so Alan. If he didn't know to begin with he soon realised, and was unable to settle for less. You couldn't blame him, and I didn't. He was never a bad person. In the end I had a concrete reason to call a halt – Alison, a nice woman, but not the one he eventually married – and we did, with very little acrimony. Whether children would have provided the necessary incentive, glue, commitment, call it what you like, we'd never know: probably not. I was glad that we didn't have anyone else to inflict the damage on. As it was we cited irretrievable breakdown, and went our separate ways. I bought a nice twenties semi in the same neighbourhood and went on working as school secretary at Goss Street Junior. He rented a flat off the Holloway Road until he met Louise, when they sank their joint finances in a house nearby, and I reverted to my maiden name.

It was getting quite chilly now and I shivered, but I didn't want to go in. On one of the row of metal hooks was an ancient waxed jacket of my father's, which had always hung there. It was known as 'the gardening coat', for some reason, although he'd scarcely done any gardening and it was far too heavy to garden in. It had taken on a sculptural quality through age and long disuse. I got it down and put it on, pulling apart the stiff outer folds of fabric that were stuck together with damp, and watching the dead spiders rain on to the floor. To begin with the coat felt chilly and resistant, but its protective weight soon warmed the air pocket around me. I put down my cold wine glass and pushed my hands into the sleeves like a muff. I felt comforted; armoured.

If you had told me five, let alone fifteen years ago that I would wind up living at the Beacon again, on my own, for however short a period, I would have laughed the idea to scorn. Go back? Never! I might be a dull stick, but one thing I did know about was moving on.

Needless to say I operated a double standard where Sally and

Jim were concerned. They had a growing family, this was a large house, Jim's work was only an hour away. When my mother died and my father moved first to a garden flat in the town, then into sheltered accommodation, it seemed the perfect solution. With the younger Govans there, the family house stayed just that: my father could visit and feel that not all the ties had been severed and (as Alan had realistically observed) we could all hang on to a prime piece of real estate for a while longer.

Jim and Sally sold their place and spent some of the resulting equity on the Beacon, rehashing the drawing room, kitchen and main bathroom, before running out of steam. After eight years, what with the children's hormones kicking in and Sally wishing to return to part-time practice, they wanted to live in a town again, and I felt like moving out of one, so I found myself saying I'd go there. I rented out 55 Towcester Road to a nice Alan-type man in Alan-type circumstances (it's an ill wind) and did what I always said I'd never do: revisited my past.

But you can't step into the same river twice. Because the house had remained so unchanged, give or take the wear and tear of Sally and Jim's occupancy, returning to it was like being part of a controlled experiment. All the things that were the same highlighted what was different about me. And such things as had been altered were a shock, and somehow an irrelevance, as though the essence of the house, its spirit, had curled itself into a ball and refused to have anything to do with them.

I certainly wasn't about to add further indignities. When I moved in I didn't know how long I'd be there for: this was time in parenthesis, in brackets, set aside, though I didn't know what for. Kev and I drifted about the place, barely disturbing the air with our separate lives. He slept, supervised, and killed small creatures. I spent weekdays as an assistant dental receptionist — less demanding but a lot less fun than Goss Street Junior — and my evenings in contemplation.

Oddly, I had never in these past two years felt spooked. As a small child coming to stay with my paternal grandparents, I had always needed someone with me to go upstairs and along the corridor to my small bedroom, and a nightlight to keep me company. In my earliest memories of the place there had been a German live-in help, called Waltraut, who lived a secretive off-duty existence in the room at the very end of the corridor, and although I had no reason to think she was anything but a pleasant, stolid woman I was terrified by the thought that she might appear in my doorway, or in the passage when I crept to the loo in the night. There was something about knowing she was there, so silent, so self-contained, a dim presence behind that closed door . . . One of my first acts on returning to the house was to open the door, but of course there was nothing sinister behind it at all. All signs of Waltraut (if there had ever been any: I'd had visions of her dematerialising into a wisp of ectoplasm when off duty) had been expunged, and the room had since belonged to my youngest nephew Barney – there were scabs of Blue-tack and Sellotape on the walls, a Spiderman sticker on the window, and a pattern of grey fingerprints on the door of the painted wardrobe.

Then there had been the boiler room to revisit – a dingy cellar reached via the back door and outside steps, in which the black solid-fuel boiler crouched, demanding unceasing fuel and fealty in return for its reign of surly caprice. In my grandparents' day the gardener, Stone (I'm ashamed to say that if he had another name I never knew it) was in charge of this monster, and would be summoned from his home down the lane to feed and placate it on those not infrequent occasions when it went out at unsocial hours. But when, following my father's retirement from the army, my parents lived at the Beacon, the boiler became my father's sole province and specialist subject. True, Stone was stricken in years and fit only for a little desultory hoeing and digging, but I believe Dad actually enjoyed the boiler's waywardness, and may have been indulging some long-suppressed engine-driver fantasy with all that dust and grime, the coal heaving and shovelling, the satisfaction of getting things moving again when all was cold and dark. Unlike Grandpa, he was a bit lost without the army, and Managing the Boiler was nothing if not man's work.

But we had all decided that convenient and manageable central heating was essential, and had had oil-fired radiators installed just after my father died; my mother claimed not to understand them until her dying day, which was only three years later. Now the former coalhole was a utility room, and the outside stairs had been rerouted so you could go down without leaving the house. I remember at the time of the great conversion seeing the boiler standing outside the back door, waiting to be carted away, and thinking how small and grubby it looked, cut down to size by the march of progress.

Stone had still done the odd bit of grace-and-favour gardening for Jim and Sally, shaking his head and sucking his dentures over the state of things, and when they moved on he was pleased that I'd come to 'keep the old place going a bit longer'. He said this as though it would fall down if Govans weren't living there, when it didn't take a genius to see that the opposite was probably true. He was now impressively ancient, and I'd been down to see him a couple of times in his stifling, over-furnished sheltered accommodation, where the colour TV took the place of the coal fire he'd been used to, flickering away cheerily in the background.

'How is the old place, then?' he'd ask, and I'd reply, 'Oh, fine, thanks, you know . . .' resisting the urge to add something along the lines of 'Joints are playing up, but mustn't grumble.'

'Lot of work for you.'

'I've got a bit of help, don't worry. Not up to your standard, though.'

This would send him into a wheezy paroxysm of self-satisfied laughter. The help I had in the garden consisted of two lads and a vanload of equipment; they turned up every three weeks and put Mother Nature in her place with brutal efficiency. Sweet disorder was out of the question: this was damage limitation, at a price.

When all was said and done, I knew I was the last of the Govans to live here, and that I was preparing the Beacon for the market, and myself for – whatever came next.

Even now, the night before I moved to another house in another part of the country, I didn't know what that might be. I faced a brave new world of complete uncertainty.

This in itself was remarkable, since I had never been adventurous, but always a reactor to events, a responder to others; a follower, not a bucker, of trends. An accepter, not a refusenik, though I'd known some historic refuseniks in my time. If my between-worlds idyll at the Beacon had shown me anything, it was that I had to go out there and just for once see what happened – or what I could make happen.

I was absolutely terrified. The house with all its memories and associations might not have spooked me, but the wide open spaces of freedom scared me half to death. I was not tough, but stoical; not independent, but deserted. Isn't there a book, *Feel the Fear and Do It Anyway*? That was me.

As for the house, it reckoned I was a rat. The last of the line, deserting; handing it over to the people who'd made a killing in Chislehurst and were going to lavish their profits on every kind of enhancement.

I was leaving everything in the loggia, except for the gardening coat, to pay back Mrs Chislehurst for her cries of 'Oh, *fantastic*, I love it, it's a time warp, isn't it? Just like a set for one of those lovely white-flannels films . . .' Let them take the stuff to the dump, or to Merchant-Ivory productions, if they thought it so whimsical.

Still wearing the coat, I went indoors and closed the loggia door behind me, not bothering to lock it. I'd always been lax about security and something told me that the chances of being burgled on one's last night in a place were slim. I felt like a ghost anyway, lost and insubstantial, poised between this place and the next, belonging in neither.

The bed had gone to the charity warehouse, and the mattress lay on the floor, with a bare duvet and pillow. It was like being a child again, lying in what had been my parents' bedroom with the ceiling so far away. Through the uncurtained window I could see the stars. Somewhere out there Kev was hunting, unaware of the sea-change that was about to take place. Serve you right, I thought. As ye sow, so shall ye reap. Reap, you bastard, and don't expect to be praised for dropping eviscerated small rodents on her polished beechwood floors . . .

An enormous spider scampered over the duvet as if I wasn't there. I thought, If that had been my face, how horrible, I should be worried . . . But I slept.

★　　★　　★

The next day the house was no longer hostile. Accepting its fate it shrugged and submitted, properly house-like, to the indignities inflicted on it by J K Removals, whose representatives went through the obligatory if-you've-read-all-these-books-what-d'you-want-to-keep-them-for routine before warming, very slowly, to their task. Because so little in the house had been mine to begin with, and I'd got rid of so much of the rest, the job wasn't a long one and by two in the afternoon the van was loaded. I was going to the new house tonight, with a carload of support systems and a toothbrush, and JK Removals would overnight in a layby and reappear at the cottage in Northumberland at nine o'clock tomorrow morning. I didn't dare to think what their reaction would be to unloading my hundreds of imperfectly packed books into 2 Church Cottages, Witherburn. Sufficient unto the day was the grumpiness thereof.

When I'd waved them off, thinking what a huge act of faith it had been to entrust the whole material contents of one's life to three Philistines with an attitude problem, I went round the house once more, making sure I'd picked up all the keys to drop off at the estate agent's. The new people were also overnighting elsewhere, so there was no rush to leave.

I was not overwhelmed by strong emotions. The house seemed neutral – been there, done that . . . Waiting to be reinterpreted. Without the packed stuff standing around it was just a box, due for the kind of refurbishment that would have even the spiders running for cover. I could hear my mother's voice as she demonstrated the exquisite agony of eyebrow-plucking: '*Il faut souffrir pour être belle.*' This was where the Beacon would start suffering.

The phone rang, shockingly loud and resonant in the emptiness. I broke out in a sweat as I ran to answer it. 'Hallo?'

'Still there, then.'

'Jim . . . Yes, the van's gone, I was just having a last check round.'

'Everything go okay? We've been thinking of you.'

'Oh, yes, fine, thanks.'

'What sort of fine?'

'Fine-fine. No picnic, you know what it is, but no disasters either.'

'Kev all right?'

'You know him, fat, sleek and lord of all he surveys – till tomorrow at least.'

'They do know about him?'

'Of course they do.' I must have told him a dozen times.

Jim sighed, cleared his throat. Though he did sometimes leave work early on a Friday I guessed he was still in the office, because I could hear that he was smoking, an activity proscribed at home, *pour encourager les autres*.

'Bit of a sad day, I suppose,' he said. 'End of a chapter. End of an *era*.'

'Actually, I haven't found it sad. It's a new chapter too.'

He sighed. 'It's probably better for you doing it than for me thinking about it at a distance. Like childbirth. Although, come to think of it, I was there, but not doing it—'

'How's Sally? And the kids?'

'Okay when I last looked.' It was one of my brother's idiosyncrasies to talk about his family as though they were some weird and wonderful adjunct to his life whose presence he couldn't quite explain, like storks nesting on the roof.

'Did the stuff arrive safely with the haulier?'

'Yes, thanks for arranging that, it's all here, no loss, no damage, making itself at home . . . It's like living with a fucking Turner Prize installation. I seriously wonder . . . But it seems a shame to let this family stuff go.'

He sounded so unconvinced I felt it was my duty to reassure him. 'I don't think it is. If you've decided it's too big or you don't want it after all, get rid of it. Have a holiday on the proceeds –' he made a fat-chance sound, which I ignored 'but, for God's sake, don't feel you have to have it just because it's there.'

'I suppose you're right. As a matter of fact it's more Sally, she—'

'Jim.'

'What?'

'The stuff belonged to our parents. I'm damn sure they wouldn't want it to be cluttering up your place unnecessarily when there are other people out there who'd pay good money for it and love it to death. It's nice of Sally to be supportive,' I added diplomatically, 'but go ahead and make the decision. She'll thank you for it in the end.'

'Yes, well, I might. We'll see . . .' Yes, I thought, and Grandpa's mahogany tallboy will still be blocking the light on your landing five years from now.

'Anyway,' I said, 'I'd best be off. Thanks so much for ringing, Jim.'

'Not at all, and of course what I meant to say was good luck with the fresh fields and everything.'

'Thanks. I'm looking forward to it.'

'Are you?'

'Yes, I am.' Jim could never quite bring himself to believe that I really wanted to do anything. The fact that there was some truth in this made me doubly emphatic.

'If it's any consolation,' he went on, as though I'd admitted it was absolute hell, 'Sally's rather envious of you, free as air, brand new life, beginning again . . .'

'I'm only moving house.'

'If you say so.'

Jim had always been able, quite unintentionally, to infuriate me, and he was doing it now. 'Speaking of which. Give my love to everyone and I'll be in touch when I'm there.'

'Look forward. All the best, Bobs.'

'Thanks. 'Bye.'

I put the phone down and immediately felt remorseful. Jim was my closest kin, my dear younger brother who actually thought I was great but who worried about me, two things that had to be in the job description of any decent brother. The abrasive response he elicited from me was my defence against the blurry but accurate intuition of someone who knew me too well. He didn't even have to try to get under my guard, and would never have done so – he was under it already.

I resisted the urge to pick up the phone and call him back,

say sorry that I'd been brusque, it had been a trying day and so on. That second-thoughts reaction was common in our family: we called it 'doing a Govan'. Any kind of sensitive exchange was always followed immediately by a second, correcting the impression originally given. This applied particularly to the phone, where misinterpretation – or, at least, an interpretation counter to that desired – was most likely to happen. Speaking our minds was not our strong suit; we could all have done with some assertiveness training to get it right first time. I had an undeserved reputation for frankness, but only because I used a blunt manner to keep enquiry at bay.

Enough, already. I went out, shut the front door firmly and turned the key in the Chubb lock, put the keys in their designated Jiffy-bag, and got into the car. When I was out of the drive I got out again, leaving the engine running, to close the rusting metal gates behind me. As I did so Kev appeared from the shrubbery, a mouse dangling from his jaws. It was the first time I'd seen him all day, but he didn't spare me so much as a glance as he trotted purposefully over the gravel to deposit his kill in the porch. A nice welcome for the new owners.

That would amuse Jim.

The thing about having only your basic life-support systems with you, and the rest of your life somewhere in a lay-by on the A1, is that you realise you don't need the stuff that isn't there. Except the much-maligned books, of course.

On that first night in the cottage, I was sorely tempted to ring J K Removals on their mobile and say: 'Don't bother. Take the whole lot to the headquarters of some worthy cause and leave it there.' Most of it had been packed up for a fortnight, some of it since before I moved to the Beacon, and if I could do without something for that long, I reasoned, I could probably do without it for ever. The thought of all the slightly greasy kitchen implements, the musty curtains and cushions, the pictures freckled with damp and thunderflies, the pine chair that had always wobbled and the white-elephant-stall-worth of knick-knacks that I'd hitherto dignified with sentimental value but which I could now scarcely remember – it was utterly dismaying. God knows, even some of what I had with me wasn't what you'd call essential. Had I really meant to bring that half-packet of wholegrain rice whose use-by date was *today*? And the herbal teabags that were like desiccated lawn-mowings? And the bag of tights – when had I last worn the mulberry ribbed one-size? Let alone the sage green. In some distant past when I'd had a mulberry and sage-green pleated skirt, I supposed – a time best left undisturbed and unremembered. I tried to re-create my thought processes as I had singled out these items for preferential treatment and concluded that I must have envisaged myself turning into a fully herbal, wholegrain, ribbed sort of person the moment I got north of Doncaster.

Not that I was going to be in the sticks, exactly. Church Cottages comprised half a dozen early-Victorian dwellings built originally, I imagined, for local farm labourers. A communal path ran through the garden at the back. Opposite the terrace, set back from the road, was the church of St Mary's. It had a more sequestered air than most, which I attributed to the fact that it stood in the park of the local big house, and consequently in a special relationship to it, its occupants the Strattons and the rest of the parish. That the Strattons were toffs was not in doubt – they had their own path and gateway leading into the churchyard, a family pew and innumerable ancestors memorialised in the church itself and in the graveyard. This had been pointed out to me by the woman from the estate agent's with something of a flourish, as though I should be impressed by these picturesque feudal details.

I wasn't, but that was because my mind was focused on the cottage, second from the right, southern end of the row. This evening, I entered it with slight trepidation just in case, stripped, empty and a little grubby like the house I'd left, it had lost its charm. But I needn't have worried: it embraced me like an old friend.

Inside the front door was a tiny hall, enough to hang a coat and stand a pair of wellies, and then you turned left into the usual knocked-through living room, with its black iron fireplaces – they'd been retained in both halves – and a half-glazed door into the garden. Off the back room to the right was the kitchen, with a stable door to the garden. Upstairs were two bedrooms, a reasonable one and another that might politely have been called bijou, and the bathroom. At the back was what Purkiss and Rowe had been pleased to call a courtyard garden – a small patio, then two steps down to a path separating two borders. I didn't yet know what the gardens on either side were like, but I liked mine. Particularly because it *was* all mine. For the first time in my adult life I could say that I owned this place, outright, and owed no one either space, attention or money as part of the deal. Everything had been well done, and was plain and simple – a clean slate on which to write the next chapter of my life. With my new tendency to ascribe personalities to bricks and mortar, I perceived Number Two as a well-disposed house, ready and waiting to accommodate me, willing and able to make the necessary adjustments.

The stuff I'd brought with me in the car seemed about the right amount for the cottage – God knows where the rest was going to go. I dumped my sleeping-bag and pillow on the floor of the main bedroom, my case of clothes in the corner and my wash things in the bathroom. I unpacked the box of kitchen essentials and put them away, to the accompaniment of Classic FM. I switched on the immersion heater, checked that the phone was connected, and decided against calling Jim back that evening. Then I realised that for the first time in weeks there was nothing that I could or should be doing. For a little space, my life was on hold.

There seemed no option but to open the bottle of cheery red that stood on the side and drink my own health. I was trying to decide whether or not this was a good thing when there was a knock at the door. On the step, half turned away as if contemplating flight, stood a tall, thin young man in one of those patched army-surplus sweaters, balding beige cords and trainers. He had a waxen, blue-chinned complexion and longish black hair. Like a youthful David Essex without the cuddly charm. I'd always had a soft spot for David Essex.

'Evening,' he said. 'I saw your car.'

'Did you? Yes. I only moved in –' I looked at my watch – 'two hours ago.'

'I'm up the road.' He nodded to his left. 'We're kind of neighbours, so I thought I'd just sort of . . .'

'That's nice of you. How do you do? Roberta Govan.'

'Dan Mather.'

His handshake was very warm, vigorous and dry, at variance with his consumptive appearance.

'Why don't you come in?' I said. 'I was about to open a bottle of wine.'

'Won't, thanks, just wanted to introduce myself . . .' He took a step away, still slightly sideways on. For a man who'd come a-calling on a total stranger he seemed pathologically shy. 'Pleased with the house?'

'Very. Not quite sure how I'm going to fit everything in, but it's just what I want.'

'Good.' He added something, but since he was now looking in the opposite direction, it was inaudible.

'Sorry?'

'I did it – this cottage.'

'Really?'

'M-hm.' His pale face took on the look that went with blushing, without the colour. I was beginning to get his weight. The distance, the apparent vagueness – it was an affectation, a backing into the limelight.

I leaned on the doorjamb in what I hoped was an unthreatening manner. 'You restored it yourself?'

'It took me three years. Plumbing, electrics, floors, pointing, the lot.'

'Are you a – is that what you do for a living?'

'No, no.' He waved a hand to indicate the madness of such a suggestion. 'No, I do it so I can prat about making nice furniture. As a matter of fact it's about time I did over another one.'

I might have done reasonably well out of my sale and purchase, but it wasn't rocket science to calculate that Mr Mather must have done a lot better. I noticed a forest green Morgan with the top down, parked on the other side of the road by the church wall. 'So, you're a cabinet-maker.'

'Sounds great, doesn't it?' He gave another of his sheepish half-smiles. 'I'll leave you in peace.'

People always said that when they meant they wanted peace themselves, and he was already moving away, with one hand raised in farewell, as if to fend me off.

'It was nice to meet you,' I said. 'Thanks for calling.'

''Bye now.'

'And for doing such a good job on the house. If I need a dining table I'll know where to come!'

I watched as he climbed not into the Morgan but into the lived-in red Mini next to it. The rising snarl of a souped-up engine cut the stillness and the car bucketed off in a northerly direction, leaving a faint smudge of exhaust on the evening air.

This encounter had the effect of making me feel more at home. That was what such visits were for, of course, but it was nice to experience the effect so immediately. To be acknowledged as the new owner, to stand on one's own doorstep as of right, to extend an invitation even if it was declined – all these things *did* warm the house. And there was something nice about his wanting to know if I liked what he'd done to the place. I'd assumed that people in his position didn't care much – that it was a case of buy 'em cheap, do 'em up, flog 'em off and bank the proceeds, but he seemed to take a childlike pleasure in his handiwork and my appreciation of it.

I ate beans on toast washed down with two glasses of Chilean cabernet, soothed by chamber music. When I'd finished I went out into the garden. It was one of those evenings when, as the sun dropped, the sky grew clearer, revealing a three-quarter moon, standing quiet and almost transparent, in attendance above the horizon. The garden to my left was silent. From the one on the right I could hear low voices, the scrape of a chair, the clink of cutlery and glasses, a pause, a laugh: my neighbours, whom I should get to know, and who would get to know me, the new me, whoever that was going to be.

I conscientiously pocketed my keys and set out for a walk. Though I was tired, I was buoyed up by that elation which is part of a good, constructive tiredness, the sense of achievement pumping endorphins into the system, keeping it running on the reserve tank. The kind of elation that, I was reliably informed by

Sally, followed childbirth. 'There's a honeymoon period,' she said, 'when you're still feeling the difficult bit's over and haven't yet realised it's only just begun. It lasts about three hours, but if they could bottle it it'd be 'bye-bye post-partum blues.'

No blues for me. I'd moved on, as one was advised to do. I was free as air and light as a feather. The glum drudgery of the past weeks was forgotten. I had never felt so entirely in the present, without baggage, either real or emotional. The future was no longer ominous and uncertain, but bright with opportunity. I knew this perception wouldn't, couldn't last, but it was good enough to savour while it did, so for once I didn't argue myself out of it to avoid disappointment.

I had driven round Witherburn when I'd been up to view the cottage, but all I could remember was that if I turned right out of my front door and headed in the direction Dan Mather had taken, I was going away from the village and towards the fields with their drystone walls. I took this route now. In the cottage next door a small boy leaned his nose on the window while he ate crisps, quite a tricky manoeuvre. When I waved, he paused in his munching, the mouth that had been open for the next crisp staying open in bafflement beneath his squashed nose.

A young couple were coming out of their door and started walking in my direction. I said hallo, but didn't stop to introduce myself; they smiled back, taken up with each other, paying me no mind as if I'd been there all my life. I liked that.

Beyond the northern end of the terrace the road rose steeply. The air was wonderful – you could almost smell the high, open hills that lay ahead. There was a hawk stationed far above me, its small silhouette vibrating with fierce attention. On my side of the road were the fields, scattered with sheep; on the western side, uncropped grassland studded with rock, leading up to a stand of evening-black pines. Beyond and to the left of the wood was the great house of the Montclere family, lying along the top of the hill, a lovely, carelessly assured, romantic sprawl of castellations, chimneys and angled roofs, backlit by the westering sun.

I came to a break in the wall on my left, with a low wooden stile and a weather-bleached sign advertising a public footpath.

I crossed the road and climbed over. On the other side was a more businesslike notice, printed on white paper, laminated and nailed to a post. It was headed 'Ladycross Estate' and reminded walkers that this was private land, a fact that should be respected at all times, and that the public right of way should be adhered to.

I don't think I imagined it, or that my memory is affected by what I now know, but when I began to walk away from the road, and up the long slope of rocky turf towards the wood I was at once conscious of a numinous stillness, a kind of spell cast by my surroundings, as if I had stepped through an invisible curtain into – it sounds fanciful, I know – another dimension. It was eerie: not as though the place were haunted, rather that the ground itself was a sentient presence, and had a consciousness. That the thin, green turf, the half-submerged stones, the waiting trees were aware of me, and that I walked here by their leave, and under their scrutiny.

None of this was threatening. I felt trusting – and trusted – as I moved up towards the spreading evening shadows at the edge of the wood. Even when I saw a large, greyhound-like dog appear from the general direction of the house and disappear into the trees I wasn't worried, although I was generally nervous of dogs and this one must have belonged to the Stratton family and been within its rights to rush over, barking, to investigate. But it didn't spare me a glance. It seemed to have an objective and to know exactly where it was going.

When I reached the shadows I felt an instant drop in temperature, but they also seemed less dark now I was embraced by them, and I could clearly see the outlines of the trees and the course of the path between them. Daylight permitting, my instinct was to go through the wood and as far as I could up the side of the hill beyond. I thought that if I could look down on Witherburn, and my new home, it would enable me to put myself in context. If Daniel Mather's visit had established me in one way, this lofty perspective would do so in another.

The wood wasn't a large one but beneath the trees the quiet became profound. Not a silence – I could hear the measured whisper of my footsteps on pine needles – but a churchlike stillness. If the greyhound was somewhere near, burying things or sniffing out rabbits I wasn't aware of it.

When I saw the man walking towards me my first thought was: Of course, the dog's owner, a walker like me, it was his whistle or call that the dog had been obeying. But as he advanced, there was no sign either of the dog or – and this was what was so strange – that he had seen me at all. Admittedly he seemed preoccupied – his head was bowed, cap pulled down, and his hands were thrust into the pockets of his over-large corduroy jacket. I thought as he got closer that now he must notice me, but his unaltered gait and the angle of his head showed that he hadn't, and I even moved slightly to one side, because of the impression I had that if I didn't he might walk right into, or over me. I entertained the fleeting, mad idea that one of us might be a ghost, or the figment of the other's imagination.

As we drew level and passed one another, my 'Good evening' stopped in my throat as I noticed three things in a split second.

That this was a woman. That she was weeping.

And that I knew her.

CHAPTER FOUR

Miranda, 1960

The air in the house changed, the way it always did. The very moment he'd gone and they knew he wasn't coming back, it changed: the walls breathed easy, the furniture settled and spread, the fibres in the carpet unfurled. The fridge, which had held its breath, purred once more.

'You've done it this time,' said Marjorie, as they hit the early-evening sherry, her weak smile lopsided with anxiety.

'Yes,' replied Miranda, 'and aren't you glad?'

'Somebody has to be practical, Mandy. We're going to feel the pinch.'

'I can help. I'll get a job.'

'No, you won't, you have to finish your education.'

'Not necessarily.'

'You must!' said her mother, with two vertical lines like inverted commas digging in between her brows. 'Otherwise he'll be back in our lives like a shot.'

This remark told Miranda all she needed to know, which was that her mother's immediate concern rested more with Gerald's involvement than her schooling.

'Not if he doesn't know.'

'He's bound to.'

'Why? Who's going to tell him? You?'

'No, but that's not—'

'Well, I certainly won't! And as he's not going to be paying for anything any more it's none of his business.'

Her mother made a 'Huh!' gesture with her head. 'That won't stop him interfering, as you well know.'

Suddenly, Miranda had had enough of all this. If the air had changed, so had she. Her mother had been if not a saint, or even a brick, at least a survivor all these years, working hard, taking the flak, poised uneasily at the centre of a triangle comprising Gerald, Miranda and the wolf at the door. If there had been wolves of another kind she'd never mentioned or, as far as Miranda knew, encouraged them. Marjorie Tattersall's had been a life of much work, little play, thousands of cigarettes ('my one indulgence') and endless exhausting diplomacy. But if her mother was exhausted, Miranda was buoyed up.

'Maybe not, but we can stop him. And we will.'

'Oh, yes?'

'Yes! It's high time we did. We're free, Mummy, we can do as we like!'

Her mother smiled wearily. 'Nobody's free, dear.'

'*Everybody* is. If he turns up here, or rings, or anything at all, we'll tell him to get lost.'

'And he'll do exactly what we say, of course . . .'

'He might.' She had an idea. 'We could move house!'

'What with?'

'I don't know . . . With this one. Isn't that what people do? We could move into a smaller house, somewhere else.'

'What about my job?'

'It doesn't have to be miles away!' said Miranda, in exasperation. 'Just far enough that he can't find us.'

Her mother shook her head, gave a despairing, threadbare laugh. 'We could never be that far.'

'Then it doesn't matter, does it?' she declared triumphantly. 'But we ought to show we don't care about him!'

'Perhaps.'

So the balance changed, too. From that moment, though subtly at first, Miranda became the driving force in the household. It wasn't so much that she dictated what they would do and what their attitude should be, but she decided it in her head and behaved accordingly, and sooner or later, after a bit of token resistance, her mother would follow her lead with a slightly resigned air as if she were humouring her. But they both recognised that it was because Miranda had taken charge.

They didn't move house, but they did change the locks ('As if that would make any difference to him') and go ex-directory ('All he has to do is come round'); and Miranda got a job in the local electrical-goods shop, which also sold records ('If he sees you doing that he'll have forty fits').

Miranda didn't care twopence about that possibility – except in so far as even one decent fit would probably have seen off her father which was a cheering thought – but she loved the job, which brought in four pounds a week and the manager, Trevor, thought she was the bee's knees. 'I wish there were more like you around,' he'd say, gazing at her and shaking his head in wonderment as though she were a unicorn. 'You're a real asset.'

In all modesty she knew it was true. And what was especially gratifying was that she owed it to the Britain's BB competition. The well-spoken manner she had from her upbringing, and her looks were a gift from nature – but the spark of self-assurance lit by that picture in the paper, which the wrath of Queen's College had not only failed to extinguish but fanned to a flame, was standing her in good stead. She had something. She was an asset.

Whatever she and Dale Harper had expected when they sent the photo off, it wasn't that they'd actually win. Not that she was the only one – there were six, so that the *Sketch* could print a picture of a BB each day from Monday to Saturday. The readers were invited to vote for an overall winner but that was unimaginable.

Because she'd be back at school when the results were announced, they'd given Dale's address and phone number to the paper. His parents were famous for not giving a damn what he got up to, and wouldn't even be curious. It was his garden they'd taken the pictures in, on a dull, warm, suburban afternoon, sluggish with boredom. In spite of what her father thought, there was nothing between Dale and her, or not on her side, anyway. They'd hung around together since mixed infants, but he'd stayed local, gone to the boys' grammar and had the sort of 'teenage' social life that was not available to Miranda, and which her mother discouraged because her father considered it common, just as teenagers as a breed – their pop records, hairstyles, clothes and conversation – were common. It was a word he used often, just like Mrs Grace, but at least Mrs Grace, though a cow, was authentically posh, while anyone could see that Gerald Tattersall wasn't but would like to have been. Miranda realised that he was common himself, in the real, worst way – a jumped-up fraud, who thought that looking down on other people made him superior.

But that realisation hadn't fully dawned at the time the fateful photograph was taken. Then, she'd still pretty much toed the line drawn by her mother, which was that her father had to be appeased at all times because it was his hand on the purse strings.

Two weeks into term she'd received a postcard from Dale saying she had somehow or other to call him that afternoon between four and six. He could have had no idea how hard this would be for her: making a call from the phone box twenty yards up the road from Queen's College was an exercise akin to robbing the Bank of England, requiring exhaustive advance planning, complex subterfuge and the utmost stealth. She got Myra, a day-girl, to bring in a mac and headscarf and, thus disguised, went out during prep, having told the supervising prefect that she needed to get a book from the library. It was the oldest pretext there was, generally acknowledged to mean anything from a pressing need for the loo to having a smoke behind the gym or (though this was unlikely) actually going to the library. So there was some leeway, but the prefect certainly wouldn't have included leaving the college premises in that.

She scuttled up the avenue with her head down, praying that no one would be using the callbox already, that she had the right money and that Dale would be in. Her prayers were answered on the first two, but her heart sank when his mother answered the phone.

'Yes – hallo?'

The coins clattered down. 'Mrs Harper, it's Mandy Tattersall.'

'Oh, hallo, dear, all well?'

'Yes, thank you. Is Dale there?'

'He's just eating his tea.'

'I'm so sorry, but is there any chance I could talk to him for a second?'

'I don't see why not . . . Hang on.'

Miranda closed her eyes and pressed her lips together in an agony of impatience, the remaining coins (exchanged for two Crunchies and a packet of Craven A) growing sticky with perspiration in her hand. Come on, come on, you wanted me to ring, don't keep me hanging—

'Mandy?'

'Dale – what is it?'

His voice was low. 'Can't say much. The *Sketch* called, you're on their shortlist. They want to talk to you—'

'Oh, my God! Bloody hell, I don't believe it!'

'They want to know if you can go up to London and see them. I said I'd put you in touch with them.'

She let out a shriek.

'Can you write down a number?'

'No! Hang on – no, I haven't got anything with me. But, Dale – Dale?'

'Yes?' His voice remained stolid and even, for the benefit of those eating tea just out of earshot.

The pips went and she stuffed in some more coins, careless of cost, swearing under her breath as she waited. 'Dale?'

'Yes.'

'Anyway, I can't, I can't possibly!'

'Come on, Mandy, they want to interview you!'

'Oh, God, no . . .' She didn't know whether to laugh or cry, was in fact doing some of both.

'They're going to print the picture anyway. If their readers vote for you, the prize is a weekend for two in Paris.'

'And how would I do that?'

'With me, of course.'

'Da-ale! I couldn't – we couldn't – how could we?'

'Coming!' His voice rose as he replied to his mother's entreaties about cold shepherd's pie, then returned to her. 'All right, so what shall I do?'

'Say I'm really pleased but I can't do anything else. Explain that I'm going to be away or something.'

'You are away. Off with the fairies, if you ask me.'

'I'm *sorry*, Dale, honestly I am, don't be cross—'

'I'm not.' But she could tell he was, and bitterly disappointed, too. 'I'll make something up to tell them. But they're still going to print my picture.' So it was *his* picture, now. She was utterly crestfallen.

'Okay.'

'Got to go. 'Bye.'

She rushed back to school. A member of staff, the peripatetic Latin master Mr Porrit, was turning in at the back gate to the car park and she had to stop suddenly and loiter, pretending to rummage for something in the pockets of the mac. Her heart raced, her hands were clammy and her face cold. She was quite faint with exhilaration and terror.

She replaced the mac and scarf on Myra's peg in the gym passage and returned to class. She'd been longer than expected: the prefect had been replaced by another who said, without looking up, 'Did you find the book you wanted, Mandy?'

Damn and blast! In her hurry she'd come back empty-handed. 'No, it was out.'

'Bad luck.' The prefect put a full stop and turned to her, her chin resting on her fist. 'Did you not manage to find anything else?'

'No.' This was typical of prefects: they were drunk with power, they toyed with you. Staff might be sadistic cows but on the whole they were predictable. This one, Naomi, knew perfectly well that she hadn't been near the library, and knew that Miranda knew, but it was a toss-up which way she'd jump: she could let it pass with a supercilious not-worth-it air; or she could play cat-and-mouse and make life intolerable. The whole class, heads bowed, were listening.

'I see.' Naomi looked her up and down, publicly noting her dishevelment, her slight breathlessness, her hectic colour. 'You'd better sit down, then, and get on as best you can.'

Miranda sank into her seat, bathed in perspiration. There was no chance whatever of getting on: the text of Caesar's *Britannic Wars* danced in front of her eyes like a cloud of gnats. The enormity of what she'd done was like another more monstrous cloud, huge and dark, hovering above her, waiting to release its deluge. She was too shocked to contemplate the consequences of her actions, let alone prepare herself for them: she just knew they were going to be awful. *If* they were discovered . . . Her heart leaped – maybe they wouldn't be! Which of the staff would be a *Sketch* reader or, if they were, would admit to it? There might be the odd day-girl parent who'd see the photo, but surely it wasn't the sort of thing they'd notice, they wouldn't read every detail, they'd never put two and two together . . . She might go undetected!

Seconds after these heartening thoughts she was back in a galloping panic. Even if not a single parent, teacher or pupil saw the picture, there was the whole gossipy, hard-eyed army of ancillary workers to be considered, *Sketch* readers to a man, most of whom would relish the chance to seem like upright citizens for a change and spill the beans on Britain's BB.

She moaned, causing several heads to turn. But the end-of-prep bell rang at the same time so she escaped Naomi's censure.

That was a Friday. The picture was in the paper five days later under the heading 'Wednesday's BB' because, as the *Sketch*'s strapline excitedly put it, they had found 'an all-English dish for every day of the week!' Miranda had had no further communication with Dale, and didn't even know the picture had been published, let alone what it looked like, until she saw it lying on Mrs Grace's desk on Wednesday afternoon.

The summons came at tea-time. They were all in the dining room eating the prescribed slice of limp brown bread with white fat (a substance you could scarcely dignify with the name of margarine) and synthetic pink jam. Though there were strict place allocations at lunch and supper you could sit with whom you liked at tea, so she was beside Soraya Shamkhal, the arrogantly lovely daughter of a Persian millionaire. Soraya, also an outsider of sorts, was the closest Miranda had to a friend but still knew nothing of what had been going on. The dining room was thick with the characteristic odour of imperfectly washed after-games bodies, infrequently changed clothes and the ghosts of thousands of disgusting meals. The damp, greasy bread clung to the roof of Miranda's mouth like wallpaper paste – she could only shift it by swigging the stewed tea, the surface of which swirled with curds of on-the-turn milk.

'Uh-oh,' drawled Soraya, 'heaven help us, here comes Potter.'

The head's secretary Miss Porterfield had entered the dining room and was advancing on Miss Hanniford, the under-matron behind the teapot, with her peculiar gait that was between a shuffle and a glide, head held at a slight angle, eyes averted from the mob, a study in rigidly maintained discretion.

'Do you think she has a whole wardrobe of those fawn jumpers, or is it always the same one?' murmured Soraya, sipping black tea. She was on the 'special foods' list – by virtue of her father's stupendous wealth – which in her case meant not having to eat anything she didn't like the look of.

Alison Thorbury on the other side was a wag. 'She breeds beige rabbits, and they're all bald.'

Potter glided out, head tilted. Miss Hanniford rang her little bell and rose. Miranda's skin crawled.

'Miranda Tattersall?'

She put her hand up. 'Here, Miss Hanniford.'

'Could you come to me, please, I have a message for you.'

That, at least, was merciful, but it was common knowledge that to be singled out meant bad news.

'Good luck,' said Soraya. 'See you for a fag later.'

Miranda squeezed out between the chairs of their table and the next. As she walked towards Miss Hanniford everyone was talking again, but in a half-hearted, slippy-eyed way, hoping to catch what was going on.

'Miranda, Mrs Grace would like to see you in the drawing room.'

'Now, Miss Hanniford?' she asked stupidly.

'Yes, now, at once – oh, you'd better comb your hair first. Off you go.'

As she headed for the door there was a further lull in the conversation and she was conscious of everyone staring; as she closed the door after her the noise level rose once more, urgent with speculation.

The dining room opened on to the front hall, and the drawing room door was ajar. She didn't bother combing her hair but pulled her elasticated Alice-band down round her neck, and then replaced it, pushing her hair tightly back from her face in the approved manner. Then she knocked on the door.

'Come in.'

She entered. The room was full of sunshine. The comatose Cleo basked on the cushioned window-seat that overlooked the tennis courts. The games mistress was out there, measuring the net for tennis coaching. Mrs Grace stood by the mantelpiece. In front of the fireplace was a brass firescreen in the shape of a rising sun, its rays fanning out to a curved surround, like long, bared teeth. Mrs Grace pointed to a spot on the carpet (pale grey with pink roses) and Miranda stood there. The newspaper lay closed, facing her, on the coffee table from which all else had been cleared. It was a relief, in one way, to realise that This was It.

There wasn't the slightest doubt where attention was focused. All Mrs Grace needed to say was: 'Kindly turn to page five.'

She did so, leaning forward awkwardly to the low table. The first two pages rustled over . . . She was almost winded by a body-blow of mixed feelings. The picture was huge! Half a page at least and she looked really glamorous. There was a caption, from which she picked up the words 'sex-kitten', and a half-column of accompanying text including her name and Dale's, though what they could possibly have found to say about them she couldn't imagine. She was torn between the desire to read and the need to appease the head, but this conflict was resolved by Mrs Grace herself, who whisked the paper from under her nose, folded it with a double snap and tossed it on to the seat of the nearest Parker Knoll.

'There can be no possible excuse, of course, but I should be interested to hear any explanation you have to offer.'

'I haven't—'

'Speak up, please.'

'I haven't got one.'

'No.' Mrs Grace breathed audibly a couple of times, inhaling like a runner preparing for the hundred-yard dash. 'And do either your mother and father know about this?'

'Not unless they've seen the paper.'

'Don't try to be clever, Miranda.'

This was a favourite put-down of Mrs Grace and her staff, and it always struck Miranda as odd that, in an establishment which, in theory at least, existed to promote learning and excellence, 'trying to be clever' was a term of disparagement.

'I wasn't.'

'Be quiet. I have telephoned each of your parents. There is absolutely no question of your remaining at Queen's.'

She'd been told to be quiet, and a loud 'Hooray!' was anyway out of the question, so she said nothing.

'Never,' said Mrs Grace, '*never* in all my years of teaching and as head of this school have I encountered such a flagrant breach both of rules and of the common laws of decency and propriety. I am appalled, saddened and disgusted.' She paused for effect. Every word, every breath had been worked out in advance.

This time some kind of response seemed to be expected. 'Yes, Mrs Grace.'

'"Yes, Mrs Grace" . . .' The head heaved a long, quivering sigh of contempt.

'I'm sorry,' added Miranda. It was both an empty apology and one fated to fall on stony ground, but it was wrung from her anyway.

'I'm sure you are,' said Mrs Grace. 'I'm perfectly certain that you're sorry now, now that the damage has been done. Sorry for yourself.'

Miranda forebore to ask, What damage? And then suddenly, she knew what it was: Mrs Grace was jealous. She was a dried-up old bag with frizzy blue hair, a dewlap and hound's ears that hung over her waist, and that picture must have really rubbed it in. Miranda felt superior, if not forgiving. The head pressed the bell next to the mantelpiece.

There was a hiatus, during which neither of them spoke. From the dining room opposite came the dull roar of chairs being pushed back, then the sound of the door opening and the swift march of footsteps as the school filed out for ten minutes' association and gossip in the corridors and cloakrooms before prep.

Miss Porterfield slipped in and stood at a safe distance, head tilted away from Miranda as if avoiding infection.

'Yes?'

'Would you ask Matron to come down for a moment, please?'

'Of course.'

The door opened and closed again. Girls were still filing out of the dining room and would have caught a glimpse of the scene in here. Miranda could imagine the way it would be expanded and elaborated to enthralled listeners. She remembered Soraya's languid invitation to have 'a fag later' . . . with its implication that there would be a 'later' when whatever it was had been dealt with. Fat chance, she thought. It occurred to her that it was quite probable she would never see Soraya again.

There followed another hiatus, during which Mrs Grace studied the toe of her court shoe, turning it slightly from side to side. For want of anything better to do, Miranda also fixed her eyes on the toe of the shoe. It was navy leather with a pattern of punched holes. Mrs Grace stopped twiddling her foot and turned her attention to her rings. She had elegant hands with a cluster of rings on both annular fingers. The dining room door closed on the last of the girls and they could hear the rumble of the kitchen trolleys and the clatter and crash of melamine plates and cups being roughly stacked.

There was a knock and Matron rustled in, bringing with her her scent, which had the power to soothe.

'Matron, Miranda will be leaving us.'

'I see.'

'I have already contacted each of her parents and asked for her to be collected as soon as possible – this afternoon, or tomorrow at the latest.'

'Right you are,' said Matron, adding in a nice, practical way, 'So there's some packing to be done.'

'I wonder if you could see to that and then take this child and her overnight case to the sick room. I don't want a lot of silliness and hysterical behaviour in the dormitory.'

'Roberta Govan is in there at the moment,' demurred Matron. 'With the flu.'

'They don't have to be on top of one another.'

We'll do our best.' Matron was the one person who managed without a hint of disrespect to assume a certain equality with the head. 'Right. Well, then, Miranda, let's get on with it.'

Miranda was about to turn and follow her, when Mrs Grace stopped them in their tracks with an imperious 'Matron!'

'Yes?'

'Could I ask you to wait outside for one moment? I'll send Miranda out to you.'

'Of course.'

Matron rustled out, drew the door shut behind her. This was to be the *coup de grâce* and Miranda knew it, but nothing could have prepared her for its perfectly judged venom.

'There is one thing I want to make clear. Something you should be fully aware of before you leave here.'

A pause. 'Yes, Mrs Grace.'

'You are a plain child, Miranda. Your appearance is at best ordinary and your academic and sporting abilities merely average. It is characteristic of your sort of girl to seek attention in showy, vulgar ways.'

Another pause. This time Miranda said nothing. Her energies were consumed in staying dry-eyed, and not blinking.

Mrs Grace continued to wield her verbal scalpel in a curious dovelike, cooing tone, as if to indicate that it was all so terribly sad, but no longer, thankfully, her problem.

'I'm afraid such behaviour deceives no one. It serves only to show the person concerned in their true colours. Exhibitionism of the shabby kind in which you have indulged says more about you than you can possibly know. And as for beauty, well!' Mrs Grace rolled her eyes briefly to the heavens. 'True beauty is not for sale in Boots the Chemist. It cannot be painted on. It comes from within.'

For the first time Miranda looked the older woman directly in the eye. 'I know that, Mrs Grace.'

A flicker of pure understanding and hatred passed between them.

'Out of my sight. Go.'

What kept her going through the next twenty-four hours, the grim packing, the punitively downgraded food, the long sleepless night, was the knowledge that while Mrs Grace might be right about beauty (though who was she to talk?) she, Miranda, had something far more valuable and less tangible. Something that was anathema to Queen's College because its stealthy power could open doors, win hearts and influence events; something more precious than rubies and more powerful than beauty. Sex appeal.

And even now, in Trevor's electrical shop, long after such fuss as there was had died down, it was making a difference. Her hour in the sun of publicity might be over, but the heat and light it had ignited in her lingered on. She didn't have to do her BB impression – in fact, where Trevor and his customers were concerned the more she underplayed it the more effective it was. Now that she was living at home she could wash her hair, have a bath and change her underclothes every day, and her humble pay packet went a long way: she could wear fresh, cheap (though not in the way Mrs Grace would have meant it) scent, colourless nail polish and just a hint of coral lipstick. She quickly learned that an amused, self-deprecating approach towards her appearance in the press was the best way of handling it, and the one that people – men and women – found most attractive. But she could tell it intrigued the men that she could be two different people. She wondered how many of them had kept the picture from the *Sketch*, and how many said to their saloon-bar cronies, 'Do you realise that our very own Brigitte Bardot's behind the counter in AB Electrical?' with an avuncular chuckle to show that they had precious little interest in her themselves but that it might amuse others. She was beginning to understand men, and also to like them because the vast majority were not like her father. They became mildly jovial and flirtatious in the shop but her manner saw to it that none ever overstepped the bounds of propriety.

That was the older men. The younger ones, the boys and youths who came in to buy records, were trickier. If they hadn't seen the picture they'd heard about it, and read the follow-up piece in the local paper. Their attitude was a mixture of self-conscious curiosity and bravado. With them she was as cool as was consistent with being polite to customers.

Dale was still miffed with her for not having played the game. 'I'll never understand you, Mand, we could have got that holiday!'

'Don't be silly, the readers'd never have voted for me.'

'We'll never know, will we?' Dale stirred the foam in his Pyrex coffee cup grumpily.

'Well, sorry!'

'Tell you what, though,' he went on, 'I wouldn't mind going in for photography. That picture was pretty good, don't you think?'

She wanted to say, 'It was *me* that was pretty good,' but out of respect for his little-boy male ego, she said: 'Yes, it was really super.'

'Oh, super-dupah!'

Her boarding-school vocabulary always amused him, but she could tell he was mollified and pressed her advantage. 'I mean, they used it in the paper, and they're used to professional photographers, so . . .' She let the observation hang, as much as to say, 'The sky's the limit.'

'Hey, Mandy,' Dale's voice took on a wheedling tone, 'I don't suppose you'd let me take a few more?'

'No.'

'I mean, it could be useful for you as well to have a whatsit, a portfolio—'

'Dale, *no*.'

'Go on, be a sport!' He did his *Chalet School* impersonation again.

'I'm not being unsporting. I don't want to. I don't want a portfolio, I don't want any more problems, I just want to do my job and stay out of trouble.'

'It's too late for that. You've been expelled!' He leaned forward, teasing her. 'You're officially a bad girl now, so you might as well get on with it.'

She pushed her chair back and slung her bag over her shoulder. 'I'm off.'

'Do you want to go to the pictures on Friday? They've got *Doctor at Sea* at the Gaumont – Brigitte's in it.'

It was her turn to twit him. 'Oh, a *boy*'s film, no, thanks. Why don't you take a friend?'

She sailed out into the street, ponytail bobbing, bag swinging, buoyed up with the sense of her own power. Only some of what she'd said was true. She wouldn't mind having a portfolio – but not one taken by Dale. There was plenty of time.

Miranda and her mother couldn't afford a holiday, but they did give themselves a day out in September. It was heady stuff: they were like a couple of schoolgirls bunking off, not only because the schools had gone back and that didn't matter, but because they were free from Gerald, and no longer owed him anything. The cash they'd scrimped for the outing to London was all their own, the product of hard work and many nights on baked beans. Marjorie had even cut down on cigarettes, changing to a cheaper brand and smoking only twenty a day. Before, her intake of Rothman's had been one way of cocking a snook at her husband, a private form of conspicuous consumption at his expense. Now there was an incentive to economise.

They'd promised themselves some shopping in the morning – nothing extravagant, but a few things that it would be more fun to buy in London – and then lunch and a matinée, and perhaps tea in a hotel to get them past the worst of the rush-hour on the return journey.

In Derry and Toms, Miranda's mother caught her lingering over a pair of sky-blue matador pants, and bought them for her instead of the camel skirt she'd had her own eye on. But Miranda wasn't daft and knew that the pants had had to be at the expense of something else. 'Why don't you have a hairdo while we're here?'

The salon led off Ladies' Fashions and was only half full. It smelt warm and fragrant, with the slightly sulphurous under-tow of perming solution. Miranda could tell her mother was tempted. 'Go on, you've been wanting to for ages and there's plenty of room – much nicer than Marcelle.' She referred to the high-street shop her mother went to for her occasional trim and set.

'Oh, I don't know . . .' Marjorie glanced at her watch. 'What about the time? I mean, we're going to have lunch—'

'Don't let's worry about that. It's nice out, we can have a sandwich. And we can always go home for tea, so you can afford it – go on.'

'But what will you do?'

'We're in London, Mum!'

'That's what I mean.'

This was a gratuitous low blow, which Miranda chose to ignore. 'I'll look around and meet you here whenever they say you'll be ready. The show's not till two thirty.'

'Don't go far, will you?'

'Of course not.'

'Well, all right, I'll just go and ask.'

They told Miranda about an hour and a half, shrouded her mother in candy-striped nylon and whisked her away to a washing cubicle.

Miranda knew exactly what she wanted to do. She took the lift down two floors and went out into Kensington High Street. The air was warm – it was still late summer, not quite early autumn – and she soon turned off the main road. The area around here was beautiful: solid and graceful and confident. One street was flanked by tall red-brick apartment blocks with stone buttresses, bay windows, roofs and gables with fanciful Gothic decorations; another was an avenue of trees in full leaf, some of them just paling into yellow, with behind them the gleaming white façades of Georgian villas with steps, and window-boxes and sequestered rear gardens (she could imagine them) with more trees, red, green and silver grey, rustling their heads secretively together over hushed and dappled lawns . . . Here and there were side-roads with terraces of smaller houses in tempting sugared-almond colours, protected by little runs of black toy railings and front doors bright with brass. The whole neighbourhood was a vision of lives led amply by people at ease with themselves; of sunny, prosperous self-assurance and natural good taste lying languidly a stone's throw from the beat and bustle of the High Street. Miranda was enchanted. To live in a place like this was surely to be a different person.

When she looked at her watch it was half an hour since she'd left the shop, but she'd been wandering slowly and hadn't gone far. Moving more quickly she rounded one more corner and found herself in a square with a church in the centre of it. Unlike the modern one near them in Haywards Heath, and the grey-brick monstrosity they'd been marched to once a week from Queen's College, this had the tall, graceful lines of a mini-cathedral, and appeared to be set not in a churchyard but in a garden. There were no graves that she could see but plenty of trees, well-groomed paths and seats of the sort you got in parks. The doors of the church were wide open, and four people, two men and two women, were standing outside the porch talking and laughing. The men were in morning dress and the women were gorgeous, one in a floaty coat and a big satin hat with a pleated brim, the other chic in a tight-fitting blue suit. A wedding!

She glanced at her watch again: twenty to twelve. So the service was probably going to be at twelve. If she stayed for a while she could watch the guests arrive, maybe even the bride. Would that be cutting things too fine for her mother? Marjorie wasn't going to go anywhere without her and wouldn't worry, surely, for at least, ten minutes.

As she watched, cars and taxis began to glide up in numbers, disgorging people of unutterable beauty and sophistication. The women bloomed and fluttered forth from cars like flowers, or butterflies, or glossy birds, according to style. And the men in attendance, so severely elegant in their wedding uniform, sleek, virile and attentive. Miranda was swept with a sweet, rapturous longing, which many years later she would recognise as akin to falling in love.

It was a comfort not to be the only onlooker – the wedding had now attracted quite a few people, singly and in groups, drawn by the sense of a posh occasion, perhaps someone they would recognise. The presence of these others stopped her feeling too naked in her admiration.

'Why does everyone like it so much?'

The man's voice came from right beside her: it made her jump, stripping her of her anonymous privacy so that she blushed.

'A wedding,' he mused. 'What's the big attraction, I wonder?'

He wasn't looking at her, but towards the church. They might have been a couple of spectators at a sporting event. Which, in a way, they were.

'Everyone's looking their best,' she suggested. 'Everyone's happy.'

'Really?' He glanced down at her enquiringly from his great height. He was about her father's age, slim and bright-eyed, with a shimmer of energy like a fit, well-bred dog. 'Everyone? What makes you say that?'

'Well,' she said lamely, 'because it *is* a wedding . . .'

'What if I were to tell you that at this wedding *not* every-one's happy?'

'Gosh.' She could have bitten her tongue for that 'gosh'. But there seemed to be no rules to this exchange so she asked, 'Who?'

'Me, for a start.'

'But you're not –' she hesitated, dithered, slipping and sinking in a social quicksand '– are you? I mean—'

'I'm going over in a minute.'

Now she noticed the striped trousers under his terrible old mac.

'I'm not one of the principals, of course,' he went on, apparently happy to be telling her all this. 'But I should be.'

'Oh . . .'

He looked at her and laughed – not a chuckle, or a snigger or a polite ha-ha, but a full-blooded laugh as though he'd known her for ages and she really amused him. 'That's got you guessing!'

'I couldn't possibly.'

'No,' he agreed, 'you couldn't.' He spoke as if he were delighted, and very slightly baffled, by their conversation. Miranda was charmed.

'I give up.'

'Aha. Hey, hang on a tick, see those two?' He placed one hand on her elbow as if to steady her and pointed with the other at two men who'd appeared in the church doorway. One was looking at his watch, the other fiddling with his carnation, dusting his sleeves. 'See?'

'Yes.'

'Bridegroom and best man. Poor bastards.'

'Surely they're not. Not—'

'Poor bastards? Yes, they are. She'll be late. Very. She'll keep the whole pack of them waiting for hours. I'm well off out of it.'

She waited. But he was looking at her as though he was going to laugh again.

In for a penny in for a pound. 'How do you mean?' she asked.

'I should have been the groom!' he exclaimed. 'Damn nearly was! Just think,' he shook his head incredulously, 'I was *that* close.'

Emboldened by all these confidences, Miranda asked: 'Aren't you sad?'

'Sad,' he replied, 'is not for the word for it, my dear.'

With the last two words he opened a gulf between them which, for Miranda at least, was quite unbridgeable, and stopped her mouth.

He held out his hand and shook hers. 'It's been a pleasure. Into the fray.'

As she watched him go, Miranda realised two things: that

she would have liked to know his name; and that whatever the word was for what he *was* feeling, he hadn't told her.

Desperate now to see the tardy, jilting Jezebel of a bride, Miranda hung on, but after another twenty minutes had passed (during which the best man popped nervously in and out of the porch, attended by a calm vicar, used to such things), she realised she had to go.

She didn't like to run – although it would have been best – because her provincial instincts told her that running in smart London streets was not the thing to do. Perhaps if she'd lived here, been a *bona-fide* denizen of this glamorous neighbourhood, she might have felt entitled to do so, but as it was she strode along furiously, praying that her mother wouldn't do something embarrassing like report her missing. There had been a policeman outside the main entrance, and she could imagine all too clearly her mother's approach, the story catching light and her waxing dramatic in the warmth of the officer's manly, sympathetic gaze.

In her haste and perturbation she might have missed the bridal car except that when she was about to cross the road at a corner, she almost stepped into its path. Only its extremely stately progress and the iron nerve of the liveried chauffeur prevented a nasty accident. The Bentley paused and seemed to hover, collecting itself before streaming past. She caught a glimpse of the bride – a sharp, pure profile, sleek black hair in an Audrey Hepburn chignon, a floating miasma of fine organza veiling, a pale, delicate hand, a froth of flowers . . . In the background, the dark bulk and high complexion of a proud and prosperous father.

Miranda's heart snagged. She was unable for a moment to cross the road, but stood transfixed, watching the car glide away, carrying the fickle, beautiful bride to her destiny. Childishly, she could scarcely bear the knowledge that she was not part of the sophistication and romance of the occasion. Especially when, for a few minutes, she had been made to feel that she was.

Marjorie was perfectly happy as it turned out, browsing among the ladies' fashions as her daughter arrived, at the double and breathless. 'Sorry – I went a bit further than I meant to.'

'I was beginning to wonder if you'd got lost,' said Marjorie, who had clearly been wondering no such thing. 'What do you think of this?'

'Nice,' said Miranda. 'Try it on.'

But as she hung around outside the changing room she could only think, disloyally, of how much she did not want to be here, doing this, waiting to admire her mother in a ten-pound skirt, when out there, a few streets and light years away, was that other, infinitely desirable world.

Miranda was a pragmatic girl. The intensity of that envious, desolate longing did not last, though it left on her mind a stain like a bruise that never went away. For the rest of that day in London the longing possessed her, colouring everything, coming between her and her mother and even between her and herself. She became two people, the one she was obliged to be by circumstances beyond her control, and the one she was in spirit. Her only comparable experience had been the yearning for a pony when she was eight years old. Owning a pony had been her Eldorado, her Holy Grail, all she needed for sublime happiness and fulfilment. The thought that there were girls out there who actually did have their own ponies was too much to bear. For a year or more she had been eaten up by a despairing, broken-hearted jealousy that had made her life hell and her hell to live with. Everything her mother did to try to assuage the craving only made it worse – the few riding lessons that were too expensive to continue, the books about ponies, the ornaments and mugs decorated with ponies, the trip to the Horse of the Year show. If Miranda's ingratitude was sharper than a serpent's tooth that was only because she was in pain herself.

But she had been only a child then. So it was alarming to discover that she was now susceptible to even more agonising pangs. The day out became a torture-by-reality: the reality of her dim, dull life, circumscribed as much by upbringing as by financial limitations. She told herself that the man who had stood next to her outside the church and spoken so freely and charmingly of his involvement with the bride would simply not have been able to comprehend an existence as small and suburban as the Tattersalls', the bullying crassness of her father, her mother's industrious world-weariness, the endless making shift, the lack of vision and aspiration. She knew as she sat next to her mother in their upper-circle seats, beneath which lay the bag containing the blue matador pants and the ten-pound skirt, that these were shamefully disloyal thoughts, but she couldn't help them, any more than she could help her irritation with her mother and her dread of the train journey home and their return, with nothing to look forward to. Even the cheery musical couldn't lift her spirits, and the matinée audience, of which she and her mother were part, was depressingly predictable – people like them, mostly female, and provincial, and lacking in style.

When they emerged into a teeming Shaftesbury Avenue at five o'clock it was still bright and sunny and Marjorie, pink with enjoyment and the heat of the theatre, suggested they go for a walk down to the river before catching the tube or bus for Victoria. Miranda couldn't have cared less, but there was no option.

'What's the matter?' her mother asked her, as they threaded their way through the crowds of people with more interesting lives.

'Nothing.'

'You're very quiet. Do you feel all right?'

'Perfectly, thanks.'

'That's good.' Whatever her faults Marjorie Tattersall was no fool: her tone implied kindly but clearly that, in that case, Miranda might as well snap out of it.

She did try, for her mother's sake. And in fact when they reached the Embankment gardens and sat down on a seat in the sun away from the crowds, her mood eased a little. 'Sorry,' she said.

Marjorie waved a hand to indicate how little it mattered. 'Enjoy the show?'

'Yes – yes, it was good.'

'But not all that good, I agree,' said her mother, perspicaciously. 'Some pretty tunes but they talked a lot of rubbish.'

Miranda smiled. 'They did.'

'Still, I'm pleased with this,' Marjorie patted the department-store bag, 'and with this,' now she patted her hair, 'so I feel I'm going back a new woman.'

'I wish I did.' She couldn't help it, it slipped out, undoing all the good of her apology, but to her surprise her mother fished her cigarettes out of her bag and asked, in the manner of one ready to listen: 'What is it, Mandy?'

'I don't know, really.'

'The blues, they're horrible . . . It's all out there, isn't it, and you can't have it?' Further surprises.

'Yes.'

'M-hm.' Marjorie nodded through her first exhalation of smoke.

'It's stupid, I know.'

'No, it's not, it's natural. But it's only temporary, I promise.'

'You're going to tell me it'll look better in the morning.'

'Well – the fact is it probably will, but I wasn't going to say that. I meant you *can* have everything you want.'

Miranda sniffed a bit at this. 'I can't change who I am.'

'Of course you can. I didn't, but then you're not like me.'

This was said matter-of-factly, without self-pity, but something quite subtle seemed to be required in response, and it was suddenly important to Miranda to get it right. She sensed that although her mother would not exactly judge her on her reply, the balance and tenor of their relationship would be delicately and irrevocably altered by what she said.

'I am grateful to you, Mum. I can't imagine what it must have been like for you.' She thought: No, actually I can imagine, that's the trouble. Still, she could tell her mother was pleased.

'Oh, I've just got on with it,' said Marjorie, taking a drag. 'What else can you do?'

'But it must have been ghastly, all on your own.'

'No, it wasn't too bad. I had my job. And I had you.'

'Until –' She had been going to say, 'Until you sent me away,' but changed it to '– until I went away to school.'

'I'm sorry about that.'

'No, I didn't mean – and, anyway, it doesn't matter now.'

'It was mainly your father's idea.'

'I know.'

'And I didn't have the strength to argue with him.'

'I do understand, Mum.'

'Do you?' It was something between a comment and a question, a wondering-to-herself. Marjorie dropped her half-smoked cigarette and slowly screwed it into the ground with her foot. Miranda could remember no other previous occasion when they had been so intimate with each other. It made her realise that their relationship till recently had been based on Gerald-management – everything had been perceived, experienced and carried out in terms of his moods and his money. And if *she* felt that now, at this late stage, God knows how much worse it must have been for her mother, humiliated first by abandonment and then by years of crassly exacted obligation.

'We're going to be all right,' she said. 'Between us, we can make plenty of money.'

'Oh, Mandy!' Marjorie tipped her head back in a bitter, silent laugh. 'If it were only all about money.'

Miranda's remark had not been as simplistic or naïve as it sounded, and she wasn't sure it deserved to be laughed at, even affectionately. Remembering the people at the wedding she suspected that while it might not be *all* about money, a great deal of it was, and the bit that wasn't could be acquired if the right opportunities were funded. But she certainly didn't want to argue with her mother after their moment of closeness.

She sat in silence, gazing at the greasy shine of the river and marshalling her thoughts. Marjorie lit another cigarette. They didn't seem to be worrying about time any more: the pace and feel of the day had changed. They were in a kind of bubble where the usual rules and habits did not apply.

It was at this moment, with the westering sun making the buildings glow and the early-evening traffic swelling along the Embankment, that a barge came into view, passing beneath the bridge and moving from left to right in the direction of Battersea. On its side the words 'Tattersall's Barges' were arranged in an arc in yellow letters, some smaller words beneath.

'Sailing Ahead,' supplied Miranda's mother, from memory. 'I suppose we shouldn't be surprised.'

They watched the barge go by, Marjorie's eyes narrowed over her cigarette. For Miranda the appearance of the barge was a sign, a metaphor. As it disappeared up-river she seemed to feel, like the Ancient Mariner, the wedding guest at her shoulder. She was between two worlds.

She said: 'With more money, we could be more free.'

'Yes,' said her mother. 'I'll accept that.'

Because they'd left it late and the rush-hour was well advanced, the journey home was crowded and hot. They started by standing in the corridor of the train, but then Marjorie was offered a seat and sat by the open door of the jam-packed compartment, evening paper on her knee, fanning herself with her theatre programme.

The man who had given up his seat stood next to Miranda, leaning on the window bar, his stout hips swaying in time to the wheels. She knew from the moment he arrived that he was going to speak to her, though for the first five minutes he didn't even look her way. Every curve of his body, the small dark hairs on the backs of his plump fingers, the stubble-blackened pores on his cheeks advertised his awareness of her, and himself, and the connection to be established.

Miranda experienced the now-familiar sense of scorn and anxiety. Often, these days, she wished she had some practical experience with which to back up the former and dispel the latter. She knew her appearance belied her naïveté, and she knew that they knew, these strangers who sucked up to her. The power she was able to exercise in the safe, structured confines of the electrical shop, under the kindly auspices of Trevor, was not so easily managed elsewhere.

'It's a game this, isn't it?' He shook his head heavily with a world-weary smile, not looking at her but at the countryside trundling by – a man hardened and saddened by the rigours of commuting.

'Yes.'

He took a cigarette case from the inside pocket of his jacket and snapped it open. 'You?'

'No, thanks.' She had smoked all through her school days and still occasionally had the odd one, but didn't want to smoke in front of her mother – or, more importantly, seem to be joining in with him.

He placed a cigarette between his lips and clicked a silver lighter. The whole clichéd charade would have been comical, had he not been so horribly unattractive. Once again the image of the wedding swept through her mind like a sweet, warm wind from some distant sea, bearing the faint scents and sounds of another life. For once she was glad her mother was there, right behind her, even if she was now deep in the *Evening Standard*.

'You do this often?' the man asked, raising one eyebrow – a corny trick she could imagine him practising in front of his shaving mirror.

'No.'

'Lucky you. What, up to town for the day?'

'That's right.'

'Let me guess,' he pursed his lips teasingly, 'show, shopping?'

'Actually, no.' As if it was giving her her chance, the door of the compartment slid shut behind them. She didn't know what she was going to say until she said it, only that she wanted to shock him. 'Business.'

'Is that right?' He surveyed her with a look intended to be sexy and appraising but which contained the batsqueak of uncertainty she was after. 'Clever young lady. What line are you in?'

'I see clients.'

'About what?'

She was leaning back on the side of the compartment, arms folded. 'I look after them.'

'I bet you do.' His bottle nose was spotted with sweat, and he was struggling to maintain superiority in a conversation that had taken a disturbing turn. 'Do you mean what I think you mean?'

She shrugged. 'I'm not a mind-reader.'

He gestured at her with the cigarette held between thumb and forefinger. 'I . . . think . . . you . . . do . . . Well, I'll be—'

'You won't, you know,' she said, keeping her head to the front so that even if her mother did look up she couldn't guess what she was saying.

His man-of-the-world grin grew even less convincing, nibbled by uncertainty. 'So why's that?'

'Because,' she said, staring into his face, blanking him, blitzing him with beauty, 'you couldn't afford me.'

CHAPTER FIVE

Claudia, 131

As a soldier's wife, Claudia had been able to keep the spirit of her vow, but not the letter. It wasn't possible to be at her husband's side as she would have liked. The Roman army, the largest and most formidably successful in the world, tramped stolidly over the pretty butterfly of her good intentions, carrying Publius back to Britain and leaving her in Rome only three days after their wedding.

She was furious. 'Why can't I go with you?'

'Because I shall be travelling fast and uncomfortably with brother officers.'

'I wouldn't be a nuisance,' she said, not pleadingly but acidly. 'You wouldn't know I was there.'

'Yes, we would. Or *I* would . . . How could I not?' He gave her a quick, impatient look, admitting male weakness. 'And, anyway, you need time.'

'Only as much time as is available.'

'I want to make sure the quarters at the other end are acceptable.'

'I'm sure they're fine.'

'I don't share your optimism. Look, Claudia,' he took her right hand in his left and laid it firmly, almost brusquely, over his heart, so there could be no doubt of his honesty, 'I want you with me, as soon as it can be managed. In the meantime, arrange things this end. Spend a little time with your father – you owe him that, he's going to miss you.'

She felt patronised by this advice. 'I do know my duty.'

'And I know mine.'

'Publius—'

'Enough.'

He lowered her hand, exerting a slight pressure as he returned it to her – a pressure of farewell? of warning? she couldn't tell. He was still largely a mystery to her, and she wanted to shout at him: 'I barely know you! You are my husband and you are going away too soon, before we have had a chance to understand one another!'

But she didn't. The bounds were set, and she knew better than to overstep them – yet. The time would come when she would have the right to challenge him, but for now she had to accept his decision.

It was almost intolerable to her. In the tumultuous silence of their few nights together, their stroking was like speaking, their exploratory caresses leading to sudden, astonishing discoveries. On this level, they communicated as equals: when one dominated it was because that was what the other wished, for their mutual pleasure. In spite of her inexperience she had never once feared her heavy, taciturn, older husband with his battle-scarred skin and tired eyes; had never for one second held back. She had trusted him utterly and been repaid with delight, and the safety to rejoice in it freely.

But this freedom from constraint had not extended to their lives outside the marriage bed. Indeed, Claudia sometimes felt as though their profound, unspoken physical communication was a bar to talking openly, as if perhaps they – he – had given too much away, made himself vulnerable to her, and must regroup and redress the balance unless order should break down. She wanted to talk, to know everything about him and to tell him everything about herself – which was pitifully little, a poor exchange. She sensed in his lovemaking a longing to be unburdened. Once she had whispered to him, 'What? What . . . ?' And heard him catch his breath as though the unspoken words were sticking in his throat.

Afterwards she'd propped herself on her elbow and stroked his forehead, asking again, very softly: 'What . . . ?' But his eyes had remained closed, and his breathing steadied and deepened into sleep, shutting her out.

So Publius left, and Claudia remained, to make her farewells and comfort Marianus who, after his initial rapture, was beside himself at the imagined horrors she would be facing in the years ahead.

'But I have a good husband who loves me, and I love him,' she reminded her father (and, though he didn't know it, herself). 'Everything you wanted for me and I wished for myself.'

'I know, I know,' he moaned, 'but you will be a long way from home, and I'm no longer young . . .'

'You'll have to look after yourself and do your best to remain alive till I come back, won't you?' she said crisply. 'Go to bed early, and don't over-indulge.'

He looked even gloomier. 'I shall try, but it will be hard without you.'

'And do some more of your writing. I shall expect to find you've completed several more epics when next I see you.'

'Yes.' He nodded, brightening. An appeal to his vanity was generally successful. 'Yes, I shall immerse myself in my work. To write of sadness is to draw its sting. At least partly,' he added, in case she should assume that that made everything all right.

'I believe so,' said Claudia. 'I've heard that said by other writers.'

If she was sharp with her father it was because she didn't relish the prospect of saying goodbye, either. She would have liked to go at Publius' side, a wife with her husband, in a position of unassailable domestic virtue. All this hanging about, in spite of the packing, the guests, the visits and arrangements, served only to prolong the agony and to give Marianus time to wind himself up into a fine frenzy of woe and anxiety. Damn the army, she thought, each time she had cause to stiffen his spine and kiss away his tears before shedding her own of sheer frustration in private – damn the army, and damn orders, and damn Britain, that grey smudge on the northern horizon.

She had a similar exchange, though with a different outcome, with Tasso.

'What shall I do?' he asked, one afternoon as they sat together in the garden, she on a seat, he with his back against the fountain wall. 'I've never known this house without you.'

'No.' A sweet, sad wave of memories flowed over and between them. She tried to be firm. 'You will go on working for my father. He'll need you to sing to him. And to remind him of me.'

'But who will I have . . . ?'

Tasso's face was averted, but she knew from long experience the expression it wore – one of misery bound tight by a fierce scowl.

'Tasso. Look at me.' He didn't respond, so she leaned forward and touched his shoulder. 'Look at me.' He did so, grudgingly. 'I shall miss you, too. More than I can say. But I'm a married woman now. It will be a sacrifice for both of us.'

'Don't worry,' he said dully, 'I understand.' He got to his feet. Claudia wanted to catch one of his long, slender hands and press it to her cheek, but those days were gone. 'Is there something I can fetch for you?' he asked.

'No, thank you. Tasso—'

'Then may I go, please?'

'Of course.'

She was hurt and angered by his childish point-scoring, but she understood it. Besides, while he could wound her by playing the slave, he did so in the knowledge that she would never hit back by playing the mistress. In spite of their long friendship and the love between them, Tasso's was a position of helplessness that she herself would have found intolerable.

It was Marianus who came to the rescue, with one of those flashes of benign intuition that never failed to surprise her.

'Who will you be taking with you to Britain?' he asked one morning, looking up from his papers.

'I hadn't really thought. One of the girls . . . perhaps no one. Publius will have a household at the other end.'

'None of whom you'll know. A lady should have someone to take care of her on a long journey.'

'I shall be perfectly safe, Father.'

'I wasn't referring to safety, my dear, but to companionship. All those little things . . .' His eyes brimmed with tears again. 'I'm sorry . . .' He patted her hand. 'Take Tasso with you.'

She hesitated, torn. 'But, Father, surely you'll need him here?'

Marianus read the hesitation rather than the words. 'Please. For me. It will make me happy to know that he's with you.'

She was more grateful than she could say. But as they embraced, she felt her father's hand on her back, that little pat of understanding she knew so well.

Tasso, when she told him, was equally unable to put his pleasure into words.

'The Egyptian has a pretty voice,' he said. 'With a little coaching from me he won't offend the master.'

It was many weeks before she heard from Publius, and she had been ready and chafing for some time. The communication was the briefest of notes, inscribed with a stylus on a wooden tablet. He had made arrangements for her transport in Britain, north from the port, and was looking forward to her arrival. 'The house at the garrison is not luxurious,' he wrote, 'but since it's likely I shall serve out my time with the legion up here I am thinking of having one built nearby in due course. You would like that, wouldn't you?'

Without his voice as a guide, Claudia couldn't decipher the tone of this question. Was it a genuine query, to which a 'yes' or a 'no' was expected? And if so was it tentative or bullish? Or simply a courtesy, the coda to a foregone conclusion? She laboured long over the wording of her reply and opted for that which was entirely truthful but sidestepped the issue of the house, which she simply could not imagine, as she could not imagine the landscape, the light, the weather, the voices – anything at all about where she was going to go.

'. . . I'm sure the house will be nice,' she wrote, 'but what I look forward to is being with you, wherever that is.' She hoped this didn't sound meek when she'd intended it to be firm and forward-looking – it was so hard to convey feelings in a short written message.

She rarely thought of her mother as someone she missed, because she had never known her. But in her present situation she wished she had another woman with whom to compare herself.

On the day that she left her father surprised her with his composure, as if all the fussing and fretting of the past weeks had been a preparation for calm.

In fact, it was she whose throat was suddenly stopped with tears, and who had to hide her face in his neck as they embraced beneath the gaze of the household servants.

'Father . . .'

'There, there, child . . .' He patted her back. 'There, there, my sweetness. Be your brave self. Look after that husband of yours – the poor fellow has no idea how fortunate he is.'

Leaving Rome in the privacy of the comfortable carriage provided by Marianus, she wept in earnest, not just for her father, old and alone, but also for herself – no longer dreaming and longing but on her way to a new life of whose strangeness she could barely conceive. And during the long weeks of the journey north, with the skies, the light, the landscape and the temperature changing – not to mention the appearance and voices of the people – her father's words rang in her ears: 'Look after that husband of yours . . .'

Look after him? She knew, of course, that it was a turn of phrase, a figure of speech, but as the moment of her reunion with Publius drew nearer she realised that she had expected *he* would look after *her*. There were a hundred things she did not know how to do or which, where she knew a little, she would have to relearn in a foreign country. Her responsibilities stood before her like a row of stern, implacable matrons. There were many moments when only Tasso's presence and the need to maintain face prevented her giving way to childish panic.

Tasso proved the perfect travelling companion, happy and amenable, for the first half of the journey to the sea. But he was a creature of the sun, and as that became less reliable so did his mood. It might be late summer in Rome, but it was early autumn in northern Gaul, with overcast skies and chilly showers. No warnings had prepared him for this, and he took it as a personal affront, and sulked. Claudia might well have done the same, but the sight of Tasso's glum face, wan with self-pity, in the corner of the carriage, had a bracing effect on her.

'Come along,' she would say, as they left their overnight inn at dawn for the next day's travelling, 'worse things happen at sea.'

That much was true. On the sea-crossing, maddeningly, she was ill. She had seldom been on board ship before except for the merest summer-holiday pleasure-cruise in the bay off Ostia, and this was an entirely different experience. The ship pitched and rolled, wallowing in the troughs of foam-specked grey water and teetering on the crests. The wind blew cold across the decks, which were permanently awash, and the keening, yellow-eyed gulls hurtled and swooped, riding the air currents above them, jeering at their plight. The noise of the crossing became part and parcel of her nausea: the groan and squeal of the oars and the shouts of the oarsmen and the overseer; the hiss of the icy grey water sluicing across the deck; the boom of the swell around the wooden hull of the ship; the creak of the rigging and the slap of the sails; and the ceaseless moaning and retching of the passengers, of whom she was by no means the worst sufferer.

The passenger hold was no place for the squeamish. Tasso was not sick himself, but was far too fastidious to tolerate the company of those who were; he was driven to roost in whatever sheltered corners he could find, shrivelled with cold but safe from the afflicted. Once Claudia had recovered to the

123

point where she could make her way up the companionway she braved the leeward deck. Here, swathed tight in her cloak, with her hair whipped across her cheeks and one numb hand clutching the wooden rail, she encountered another woman, older and more experienced than herself, but with a Tasso-like intolerance to others' frailties.

'Ye gods,' wailed the weatherbeaten *matrona* coming alongside. 'My stomach can tolerate anything but the contents of other people's!' She leaned over the rail as Claudia looked away discreetly.

'I'm sorry, my dear.' She straightened up, wiping her mouth. 'Nothing left, really. I was a soldier's wife, and I've borne five healthy children and buried three dead ones. I've smelt rotten flesh, attended other women's labours and and dealt with any number of revolting childhood illnesses. But I'm not ashamed to say that that stinking hole full of complete strangers with no pride and less control is too much for me.'

Clauda was a little taken aback by this forthrightness but there was one area in which she could claim parity. 'I'm a soldier's wife, too,' she said. It was strange, like trying on a new dress. But this woman wasn't to know that.

'You are? Where are you going?'

'To the north.'

'To the Wall.'

'Yes.'

'M-hm,' said the woman, looking not at her but out to sea. 'I was there, years ago. Since my husband died I live down in the south, with my younger son and his family. They have a farm. It's all very quiet, couldn't be more different from what I was used to, but one adjusts.' Now she looked at her. 'As you will.'

Claudia did not think she was being over-sensitive in hearing an implied 'eventually' in this observation. A sudden fierce slash of wind and spray snatched her breath away for a moment before she could answer. 'I hope so.'

'Oh yes, you will!' The woman patted the back of her hand on the rail. 'Don't worry.' She looked up at the swirling purple sky, her eyes narrowed. 'All this,' she waved a hand as if batting away the gale, 'is a bit of a trial for the newly arrived.'

Claudia agreed that it must be.

'Are you from Rome? M-hm – you'll be in a minority. They all call themselves Romans, but a more mixed bag of people crowded together in one place would be hard to find. Garrison won't seem so very different from home, though. Noisy, smelly, especially in summer, but quite civilised, all the usual amenities. And when the sun *does* shine,' she raised her voice above another thunderous gust of wind, 'it's a real treat.'

The woman's name was Sullia. By the time they made landfall two days later, beneath grey-white cliffs that were like some massive fortification, she and Claudia were friends. Claudia recognised that this had been made possible by the instinctive bonding of army wives, her own anxiety, hope and ignorance eliciting the sympathy and support of the older woman, and while she was grateful for both, they begged the question, how much more did Sullia know that she did not choose to tell her?

They spent their last night at sea with the boat anchored in the bay, heaving and tugging on the swell, waiting for the tide, and for calmer weather. Most of the passengers had recovered from their sickness but it was frustrating to be delayed within hailing distance of their destination. Her long-awaited first sighting of Britain was not encouraging: that rampart of cliff, sliced by deep, dark hanging valleys, a grey beach below protected by a sprawl of tumbling black rocks through which the sea crashed and spouted furiously. Whatever the nature of the British countryside it was hidden by the cliffs and shrouded in low cloud. All that night it rained, and because they were at anchor the sound of it was different from the wild hiss of the storms at sea. It hammered down, nailing them in place, reminding Claudia of how far she was from home. Tasso had stopped speaking. His mournful eyes resting upon her were like a reproach.

But next morning the change in the light woke her from her shallow, uncomfortable shipboard sleep. She couldn't place at first what was different and then the realisation flooded her like warm wine – sun! Up on deck, colour had replaced grim monotone for the first time in days. The water was blue and green, shot with the black of submerged rocks. The cliffs gleamed white, their tops a brilliant green, and the gulls sparkled in a pristine sky, no longer mocking but soaring in celebration. The creak of the oars and rigging as the ship crept forward was like gentle early-morning breathing.

Tasso stood with her on deck, his face turned to the sun, eyes closed.

'Better?' she asked, and he nodded, wordless with relief.

As the ship rounded the headland and moved into the harbour of the adjoining bay, Sullia joined her, inhaling the warm, soft air. 'Aah, the sun . . . You can't beat an occasional visit from a dear old friend.'

'It's a different world!'

'It is.'

'I mean,' Claudia explained, because of some warning in the other's voice, 'that the sunshine makes it seem like one.'

'Yes.' Sullia stretched her arms high and let her head fall back. 'You don't realise how much you've missed the heat and the light until you've been deprived of them for a while.'

All day the weather was fine, the sky a thin, pure blue, the clearest Claudia had ever seen, with a swansdown drift of vapour on the horizon. As they went ashore in the rowboats at midday, the sun glittered on the smooth swell, and burned the pale skin at the base of Claudia's neck, above the collar of her tunic. Where the waves had fumed and leaped the day before, they were now no more than a saltwater kiss on the smooth pebbles. To the left of the bay was a stone-built breakwater and harbour and here they disembarked across a swaying gangplank on to a rickety ladder. As Claudia reached the top, an enormous arm came down and pulled her unceremoniously to ground level.

She had arrived.

Suddenly there was less comfort in the sun. The thin northern light, the voices and faces that surrounded her, even the stones beneath her feet were utterly foreign. The ship was riding serenely at anchor, wearing her furled sails like a *stola*. The dirt, the rats, the noise, the smell, the cold and discomfort of the voyage were forgotten and their memory superseded by something like homesickness, a longing, as a child longs, to turn back the clock and for it to be yesterday again.

'Goodbye, my dear.' Sullia took Claudia's hand in both of hers. 'Good luck.'

'Where are you going?'

'My son's here.' Claudia followed her nod and saw a large, bearded man holding the head of a shaggy pony between the shafts of a cart. 'We have a way to go.'

'Not as far as me.'

'No, but your husband will have arranged transport.'

'I hope so.'

'He's a Roman officer,' Sullia reminded her. 'Everything will be organised.'

And now Claudia could see the wagon, and the much-restored Tasso by its side, waving importantly.

'So,' Sullia said firmly, 'you're beginning your tour of duty.'

'May I ask you something?' Claudia would have said anything to detain her friend for a minute longer, but there was something she wanted to know.

'Of course. Can't promise to have the answer.'

'I just wondered why you went away – back to Rome.'

'A sad reason. My mother died. There were things to put in order.'

'I'm so sorry, I didn't mean to pry.'

'It's quite all right. She'd had a long and happy life.' She placed her rough palm against Claudia's face. 'Goodbye, my dear, and good luck.'

As Claudia was ushered through the quayside crowd by Tasso, she saw Sullia climbing awkwardly aboard the cart while her few bits of luggage were slung unceremoniously aboard by the burly son. She felt a squeeze of sadness; for Sullia, so proud and decided, but somewhat diminished by circumstances, reduced to an elderly and doubtless rather trying parent, a necessary burden on her family; and for her own father, for whom she might have to retrace the same melancholy journey at any time.

Publius' best endeavours had produced nothing like the elegant carriage that had carried them from Rome. The horse-drawn wagon to which Tasso handed her up had a covering,

127

drawn back in honour of the fine weather, though she could smell its musty odour. There was a bench down one side and a slightly wider one, with rugs, on the other. She hoped she wouldn't have to spend too many nights in there but, then, she had no idea what the alternative might be. The possessions she had anguished over and packed so carefully looked pitifully few for the adventure she was undertaking.

But in spite of her tiredness, her apprehensions and her craving – worse than hunger pangs – for a hot bath, her spirits lifted as the wagon, propelled by whip-cracks and shouts from the driver, rumbled through the harbour's crowds and its hinterland of ramshackle shops, small businesses and dwellings (she couldn't have dignified them with the term 'town') and began the climb up the valley between smooth, golden-green bluffs of downland pitted with chalky rabbit warrens. The road here was paved, and the wagon rattled along, jiggling in and out of the grooves ground into the stone by many wheels, the squat pony's head nodding heavily as he leaned into his task. In the grass at the side of the road she could see small hardy flowers, yellow, pink and purple, that grew in flat tussocks, but there was no sweet scent, just the smell of the sea.

At the first milestone from town the paving petered out and the road became a cart track. Their pace slowed accordingly, and when she looked back the way she'd come the boat that had taken and meted out so much punishment was like a wooden toy on the water.

The driver, perhaps used to passengers like Claudia, waved an arm to the right, without turning his head. 'Smart villa, lady . . .'

Politely, she and Tasso looked. He was clearly proud of the villa, a landmark and first evidence of Britain's ability to compete with anything on the other side of the water, but it was nothing much. A pleasant enough, solid, single-storey farmhouse on the brow of the hill with a row of trees planted on the coastal side but listing inland from the buffeting of the offshore breeze, a scattering of tiled outbuildings and a network of paddocks. Compared to their country house at home, it was small, plain and modest. Nothing wrong with that, she reminded herself, but it put into context the doubts Publius had voiced about the accommodation at the garrison, and his proposal to build a house. This might in theory be part of Rome, but in reality it was a strange, distant and wholly foreign island, to the far north of which she was bound, and its standards and climate were different.

'Look!'

Tasso's intake of breath alerted her to what was up ahead. And then she not only gasped too, but laughed out loud at the sheer brutal audacity of it.

For there in front of them, towering over the soft British downs, was a massive, modern arch gleaming in the sun, at its apex the Roman eagle poised in flight, at its base a scattering of sturdy, humbler buildings. For half a mile or so, beneath and beyond the arch, the road was once more paved to a high standard before reverting to twin chalk ruts where it headed, straight as an arrow, for the horizon.

Hearing Claudia's laugh Tasso glanced over his shoulder and smiled. For that moment it was like old times, they were reunited in understanding. They were still smiling as the rickety wagon continued on its way beneath the great concrete rainbow that was Rome.

There was plenty of traffic on the road, and precious little etiquette. Confronted by drovers with herds of cattle and pigs the wagon's driver adopted the simple but effective expedient of geeing up the pony and scattering stock in all directions. During these exercises neither man nor horse appeared anything but phlegmatic, the former remaining hunched even while yelling profanities, and the animal's ears only twitching slightly in response.

The herds and herdsmen seemed to be the commonest road-users, but there were also huntsmen with thin, arrow-faced, brindled dogs, travelling salesmen mounted and on foot, loaded with everything from cure-alls and cooking pots to souvenirs and scented oils. The salesmen were pushy and some of them, seeing a well-heeled young woman, newly arrived and correspondingly naïve, hung on to the sides of the wagon until batted away by the driver's whip, which he flailed from side to side rather as a horse does its tail to remove flies, with nonchalant efficiency. There were several passenger-wagons like theirs, displaying roughly the same degree of comfort and maintenance, and once a smart litter of the sort that were two a penny in Rome, its tooled leather blinds pulled back just far enough to reveal a glimpse of braceleted wrist and a pale face surmounted by smooth coils of hair.

They stopped to eat at a wayside smallholding in the late afternoon. It must have been by prior arrangement, for the driver hopped down and trudged round to the back, emerging later carrying something wrapped in a cloth that he slung on to the driving board next to Tasso, and a flat covered basket which he handed to Claudia. A very young girl who might have been the daughter of the house or its mistress, in a long green tunic and leather boots, her grey-brown hair in a loose plait, came and stood at a safe distance, subjecting Claudia to an unashamedly wide-eyed stare. Unsure of the social balance of the occasion, or its protocol, Claudia didn't offer a greeting, and tried to disguise her apprehension as she uncovered the food. She was ferociously hungry, but if she was going to have to eat in front of an audience she hoped it would be something appetising.

But the meal was plain and plentiful, containing nothing strange that she could see, and well enough cooked to dispel any fears she might have had about the rest of the journey. There was a kind of pie, or meat rolled in pastry, the former without herbs and largely unseasoned and the latter of a solid consistency; a bowl with some cooked vegetables she didn't recognise, and a heel of dense, fresh bread with which to eat them; nothing sweet, and nothing to drink, but the moment she paused from eating the girl – who might have been fifteen – came over with a mug and offered it to her.

'Thank you . . .' Again, Claudia didn't want to be seen to hesitate, sniff, or take too experimental a sip, and she was thirsty. Boldly, closing her eyes, she took a swig and was startled at the effect it had on her. This wasn't wine, but it was just as reviving and palatable – strong, and sweetish, for which she was grateful.

'Thank you,' she said again, this time with a smile, licking her upper lip to which a light sticky scum had attached itself. The girl didn't smile back, but gave a little nod of acknowledgement and dropped her eyes before withdrawing once more to her place near the house.

When Tasso and the driver had finished their provisions – which seemed to contain more bread and more to drink, though no pie – the driver clambered down again, tacitly gathered up the remains and handed the basket and cloths back to the girl. At a decent interval Claudia followed, hoping against hope that her mission would be understood. She needn't have worried, the girl gave another nod, this time of womanly complicity, and led her round to the back of the house. Here, two small boys were playing with a skinny black puppy, and the girl shooed boys and dog into the house – in a manner that clearly showed she was the children's mother – before indicating to Claudia that she should retire behind the thicket.

It was just as well she'd eaten before using these natural facilities because unlike the food they were very different from what she was used to. Whatever civilising influences Rome had exerted in Britain they had not extended to the lavatory arrangements in this place. It was no more than a shallow ditch behind the bushes, with a shovel stuck in the ground at one end, though in spite of this there was still ample evidence of general use. Praying that the little boys, not to mention the puppy, were safely out of the way, Claudia took a deep breath, held it, and hoisted her tunic. The blissful relief more than compensated for the conditions.

The girl and her sons – one carrying the puppy – came out of the house and accompanied Claudia back to the wagon. Tasso, conscious of his position and the necessity of reinforcing it, jumped down and gave her a hand up. He liked an audience. His soft, curled hair and perfectly enhanced complexion were as much a cause for curiosity as her own clothes, and he knew it. Playing along, she thanked him effusively.

As the pony leaned into the shafts and the wagon creaked in the direction of the road she looked back. The boys had lost interest and were once more running around after the puppy but their mother was gazing after the wagon with her hand shielding her eyes. Claudia waved, but there was no response.

Some time later, when the sun was low and the wagon and its occupants trailed a long, wavering shadow the driver pointed to a smear of dust on the horizon. Claudia had reached the conclusion that, though a man of few words, he saw himself as an *ad hoc* guide to those aspects of his country that would make a newcomer from Rome feel most at home. So when Tasso, peering, announced, 'Soldiers!' she wasn't surprised, but was still unprepared for the scale and majesty of the column that bore down on them.

And bear down it did – even if there had been the smallest question of whose right of way it was the cohorts could have decided it by sheer weight of numbers. The driver pulled over and kept going, at a slower pace, about fifty yards to the east of the road. They were in a shallow valley where the track had been solidly reinforced with logs. These gave an extra resonance to the thunderous tramp of the advancing legionaries, Claudia could scarcely imagine what the sound would be like on a fully metalled Roman highway. Neither the driver, still hunched and laconic, nor the travel-hardened pony paid the column any attention but she and Tasso watched spellbound as the world-conquering army in all its polyglot glory marched past. They threw up a cloud of chalky dust, which powdered their leather tunics and helmets to a pale grey. The only object to shine through it was the tall standard with its gleaming eagle bobbing and hovering far above the men's heads. Claudia, trying to imagine Publius marching like this at the head of his men, realised how little she knew of his life – perhaps he didn't march at all, was too important for that, or did he ride? He came from the old strain of equestrian class, Marianus had told her (the key word being 'old' – so much more dignified), but that did not mean he held a cavalry post. She remembered hearing him say to one of his colleagues at the wedding party that the cavalry were 'a trained-up rabble, but a useful one'.

It took them fully a quarter of an hour to leave the column

behind – or for it to leave them, for the soldiers marched far faster than the wagon could travel, by which time they, too, were coated with dust. The baggage train at the end of the column had been scarcely visible under a cloud of it, a great dirty wake pungent with the smells of sweat, leather and waste matter. Back on the road the marks of military might were plain to see, the ballast of logs chafed bare and in places shredded, and a scatter of debris – straw, horse dung from the pack animals, scraps of leather and metal, bits of foodstuffs – while a border fully a man's length on either side of the road was gouged and pitted like a dry riverbed by the pounding of a thousand marching men.

Looking up from this Claudia caught, for a split second, Tasso's head turned and his eyes resting on her. He immediately rolled it the other way and massaged his neck with one hand as though easing travel-stiffness, but she knew him too well. He was canny and perceptive, as these cultured slaves often were from a lifetime's onlooking, and perceived her anxieties only too well.

She drew herself up and sat straighter, in spite of her tiredness. She was an officer's wife, no longer young, and she would – must – assume the rank due to her.

The following morning was stifling, presaging thunder. The pure transparency of the previous day had given way to a heavy, low sky and air thick with humidity. Because of the earlier fine weather the driver had continued through the night, except for a couple of hours to rest and graze the horse, when he and Tasso had lain down beneath the wagon. The cover had been pulled over its struts to give her some privacy and she'd lain amongst the musty coverings on the bench, unable to sleep for the noise and discomfort when the wagon was in motion, and for the driver's bubbling snores and farts when they were stationary. She felt sorry for the fastidious Tasso, obliged to sleep on hard ground with that racket going on.

The result was that the heat affected her more than it might have done. She had a headache, her eyes itched and she felt soiled. They stopped for food in a settlement and were brought quantities of rough-ground bread, gritty with seeds, and a large jug of the local brew of which she drank more than was sensible, slaking her thirst but exacerbating the headache. Added to this and her tiredness the unaccustomed solid and fibrous food affected her usually strong stomach and she had the gripes. On no fewer than four occasions between their strange breakfast and noon she had to ask the driver to stop so that she could relieve herself. During these interludes Tasso sat with head bowed, suffering agonies on her behalf. Fortunately the character of the countryside had changed, so there was more cover available, but it was still a trial to her. She told herself that this was a test of character, not the first she had faced nor certainly, with all that lay ahead, the last.

By early afternoon when they stopped again to exchange the horse for a fresh one she had entered into an uneasy truce with her stomach, but its rebellion had left her weak and sweaty. The thought of many more days of this wretched journey was almost more than she could bear. She declined anything to eat but while the new horse was negotiated she walked some distance from the wagon and the cluster of wood and wattle cottages and sat on the ground. What she wanted was to lie down, but she was afraid that if she did so she'd never get up again.

Tasso came to a respectful distance and also sat down, plucking at the short grass between his feet. How ridiculous, she thought, that we two who share a common inheritance, a home, a past, everything, are here together in a strange land but too constrained by etiquette and tradition to speak.

'Tasso,' she said quietly, knowing he would hear, 'are you homesick?'

'Yes, a little.'

'I am too. Homesick as well as stomach-sick. What is that stuff they're giving us to drink?'

'Beer, the driver says. You don't like it?'

'I do rather, as a matter of fact. But it doesn't seem to like me.'

He plucked at the grass between his feet, then said softly: 'It seems very far away, doesn't it – Rome?'

'Yes. But it won't seem so far, I'm sure, when we get there.'

When we get there. She had wanted so much to travel well, to arrive strong and still energetic after the rigours of the journey, not like some wishy-washy novice. And until now she flattered herself she'd done so. The sea crossing had been her Rubicon, the point at which there had been no turning back, and since then she had felt herself more vulnerable, even though she was drawing ever closer to Publius.

The driver, following a long discussion, was leading the used pony away and there was still no sign of a replacement. The sky to the north was dark with bruise-coloured thunderheads, and a queasy, premonitory wind scuttled between the huts and raised goose pimples on her sweaty skin. She noticed for the first time that Tasso's delicate beauty was strained, that there were small spots round his mouth, and shadows under his eyes. His slim thighs and upper arms had a wasted appearance. She felt a pang of affection and pity for him.

'Tasso . . .'

'Lady?'

'Sing me something.'

'I believe I'm not in good voice.'

'Your standards are too high, I'll be the judge of that.' He made to stand. 'No need to get up, it's not a performance. Look on it as medicine for your mistress.'

'What shall I sing?'

'Something gentle, with a nice tune. Something my father liked.'

He tilted his face upward and began to sing, a little song she'd always known, and which she'd probably taught him when she was ten and he three or so, when they'd played in the garden together. A song about the pleasures of summer and holidays – birdsong, wine and food, friends, cool water and sea breezes. He had a sweet, high voice, very true and a little husky. A voice that had always enchanted Marianus, who had said often that if he closed his eyes it was like listening to his wife all over again.

The song's triteness, its lack of sophistication – it was scarcely more than a nursery rhyme, a list of simple pleasures rendered simply – conjured up home in an instant. She could see her father, hair standing on end, studying his papers, absentmindedly swatting at flies with one hand . . . hear the liquid chuckle of the fountain in the garden and smell the scent of the roses in the sun . . . see the cool, dark rooms that slept in the heat of the day and came to life in warm, vibrant colours in the evening when the lamps and candles were lit. She remembered that sense – one of which she had been scarcely aware at the time but which was now like a taste in her mouth – of the household softly ticking over in the long, hot days, the slaves going about their business in the background, soft voices, the susurration of footsteps on stone, gravel, marble, like a heartbeat. Marianus had run a happy, indulged, economically wasteful household, but a loyal one that made up in goodwill for what it lacked in efficiency. The house on the Via Aquila had been wrapped in contented indolence.

Tasso finished singing.

'Thank you,' she said, 'that was lovely.' His eyes were glistening, but she said nothing to comfort him. The moment of shared remembrance was over; words weren't necessary. In childhood she had been like his older sister, or even a little mother – bossy, affectionate and proprietary. Now that such a relationship was neither feasible nor appropriate, it still underscored their dealings with one another, a short-cut, she believed, to mutual understanding.

The new pony was a mulish creature with too much white around the eye and a long, bony head that it thrashed up and down, its ears flicking back and sideways suspiciously. Its stride was longer and less even than its predecessor's, so that the wagon rocked and rattled and any satisfaction to be had from covering the ground more rapidly was qualified by the likelihood of being shied overboard at any moment. Claudia could see Tasso's fingers blanched with fear where they clutched the driving-board. The driver allowed the animal to dictate the pace and showed no signs of consternation, bar the occasional snarling and smacking of the reins.

In the late afternoon, when the sky had been blue-black for nearly an hour and the scurrying wind made the pale grass race like shallow water over the hills, the thunderclouds discharged their load. The downpour was ferocious and sudden, beating on the wagon's cover like horses' hoofs. Giant prongs of lightning shot from sky to ground, stabbing the earth beneath the deafening onslaught of the thunder and rain.

The insistent violence of the storm, the abrupt drop in the temperature, the terrified squeals of the already unpredictable horse, the frailness of the wagon and her ignorance of what lay beyond it contributed to what Claudia knew was an irrational fear. This was only weather, she told herself, she had been in storms before – but never one where she had not had access to some safe haven. Surely there must be some nearby town, settlement, or even a farm where they could shelter?

She was shuddering with cold, and could scarcely imagine what it must be like for Tasso. When the thunder and lightning abated there was no relief, for the darkness of the storm was giving way to the dark of evening, and the wind found a new gear, screaming across their bows so that the wagon juddered and the icy rain began to seep in beneath the cover.

When the driver pulled up, she hoped it might be because they'd reached a place of warmth and safety, no matter how humble. She pulled back the intervening curtain and was immediately struck in the face by freezing water from every direction – from the roof, the curtain itself, from outside. The opaque darkness was scribbled and scratched with the hurtling rain.

'Where are we?' she shouted.

'. . . stop here!' bellowed the driver. '. . . sheltered!'

Claudia found this hard to believe, but these things were relative, she told herself. The driver got down and ploughed, head down to the front of the horse to uncouple it from the shafts. She looked up at Tasso, huddled in his sodden cloak and with another blanket (courtesy of the driver, she supposed) around his humped shoulders. He was rigid with misery, his face blue-white, the eyes dark holes rimmed with exhaustion, his beautiful hair a black, dripping slick, plastered to his skull. He looked close to death, a poor, bedraggled Mediterranean faun in this bullying northern tempest. She touched his frozen fingers where they clutched the edge of the blanket and realised what she'd already suspected, that he was too numb – and too far gone – even to feel her touch.

Enough! she thought. Time to use her rank of Roman matron and officer's wife, if only to get information. Stooping and stumbling she went to the back of the wagon and climbed down. Her breath was immediately snatched away by the gale, the rain smacked her in the face so she couldn't see and she rocked back on her heels and had to catch the side of the wagon to stay upright. Hanging on for dear life, hand over hand, she made her way along the leeward side of the wagon. With her eyes adjusting to the darkness she could make out hills, black with woodland, on either side of them: so, incredible though it had seemed, the driver was justified in claiming this was a sheltered spot.

At the moment he was tethering the horse a short distance away. Much as she disliked the animal she felt some sympathy for it as it fretted and circled, trying to protect itself from the maelstrom. When the driver plodded back she planted herself in front of him, and yelled, with as much dignity as she could muster: 'How long will we be here? Where are we?'

He pushed his head forward like a tortoise, peering at her, the rain pouring off the shaggy edge of the cloak that covered his head. She spread her arms wide.

'*Where are we?*'

Mimicking her, he flung out his own arm, pointing north-ward, eyes still on her face. 'River's not far! But too swollen . . . Stop here till sunrise!'

She wanted to ask something else, to demur, to assert herself a little if only for the sake of it. But the rain continued to lash the two of them as they stood glaring at one another, the ground beneath her feet was turning into a sucking quagmire, the wagon shuddered and groaned and the horse was tethered. Just now it appeared that the dictates of common sense and authority went hand in hand.

'Very well.'

The man made a disparaging snorting sound and took a couple of hides from the driving board, yanking the further one unceremoniously from beneath Tasso and nearly unseating him. He then began slowly and deliberately to drape these over the wheels to create a sort of tent beneath the vehicle where, presumably, he intended to sleep. Claudia fought her way to the back and climbed back in. In less than five minutes she had been soaked to the skin. Her next decision took less than a second.

'Tasso!' She shook his arm roughly. 'Tasso!'

He looked at her blankly. His lips were grey.

'Tasso, get in!' She pulled at him. 'Quickly, come on!'

Stiffly, responding like an animal to the pull and her tone of voice, he crept inside. She pushed him down on to the bench where she'd been sitting, spread one of the rugs and pushed him again, indicating that he should lie down. He did so, simply leaning to one side and collapsing, bonelessly, like a broken plant. His eyes closed at once. She lifted his feet up, and wrapped the sides of the blanket over him. It wasn't much but it was better than the alternative. By leaning very close she could just make out the flutter of breath on his lips, and the movement of his eyeballs beneath the near-transparent lids.

She heard the driver grunting and farting as he settled down (pig-like, she thought uncharitably) in the sludge beneath the wagon. She had other clothes in one of her bundles and now had the opportunity to put them on if she wished, but something told her it would be best to keep them in reserve. She swathed herself in the remaining rugs and pelts, trying to ignore their musty smell, and curled up on the bench, hoping the accumulated moisture in what she was wearing would warm up in time. With the rain still pounding on the roof and every joint complaining, she didn't expect sleep, but it fell on her like a hammer blow, bringing instant unconsciousness.

She awoke to a lurid half-light and the loud, uneven percussion of dripping water. She thought this was what had woken her, but then realised that someone was banging on the back of the wagon.

'Oy, Lady! We got problems!'

'Coming . . .' She struggled to her feet, feeling the cold air on her still-damp clothing, passing her hands over her matted hair.

'You there?'

'I'm coming!'

The driver was standing with his back to her as she parted the curtain at the end of the wagon and clambered awkwardly to the ground, dazzled by low sunlight reflecting off the sodden landscape.

'What is it?'

He turned, jerking his head. 'Horse has gone.'

'Gone?'

'That's what I said.'

The horse was certainly not there. Not even the metal tethering peg remained, just a circle of mud where he'd been stamping around in the night.

'What are we going to do?'

'Find another.' The man cleared his throat and spat. 'Shouldn't take too long now the rain's . . . You and him,' he nodded at the wagon behind her, 'stay . . . don't go away.'

'We won't,' she assured him, adding, in as cool a tone as she could muster, 'Is there anything we should know?'

He shrugged. '. . . heads down.'

Utterly helpless, she watched him plod away, his sacking bag over his shoulder. If he felt any sense of urgency he was not a man disposed to convey it.

But at least the night, and the storm, were over, and the sun was shining. The dingy inside of the wagon smelt acrid and she decided to try to take the cover down on her own. She had managed to push the sodden, resistant leather half-way back before she noticed two things, in quick succession.

Her wooden chest of valuables was open, and her jewellery bag – and Tasso – were gone.

CHAPTER SIX

Bobby, 1992

At the very last moment the woman's eyes slipped, unseeing, over my face, registering nothing. So far from recognising me, I was sure that later she wouldn't even remember that there had been someone else walking in the wood. If ever I had seen a person locked into a private world of grief it was her, on that beautiful summer's evening.

I was shocked, because at school she'd been famous for never crying. Her detractors (and they were legion) took the view that she was too concerned about her appearance to cry or, indeed, to get worked up about anything. Jealousy decreed that they disparaged her beauty, as people disparage nice handwriting, by saying it had 'no character', that anyone who looked like that must be superficial.

It didn't help that she was, if not exactly a rebel, a natural nonconformist. This was no pose: she didn't have to work at it. Things like the pecking order, school tradition, the divides between classes (in both senses), and between boarding and day girls, meant absolutely nothing to her. Like Kipling's cat, all places were alike to her, and that in itself was sufficiently unusual at Queen's to attract opprobrium or admiration, depending on your point of view.

In my case it was admiration. The boundless kind. Adoration would not be too strong a word. Miranda, like her name, was to be wondered at – or deserving of wonder, I've long since forgotten my gerunds and gerundives. Small, plain, junior tick that I was, I was in awe. I saw something in her that I don't believe I fully understood then, but which I have since defined as a kind of innocence. Miranda had been born with that face, that carriage, that air – it was a gift she carried all unawares, and simply. She hadn't yet taken responsibility for its use or management, in fact I swear that in those days she was scarcely aware of it.

The coterie of friends she did have were confident girls – nowadays that confidence would be defined as high self-esteem – who weren't put off their stroke by her looks or her manner. I remembered a glamorous Persian heiress who wore real pearl earrings with her mufti. I think what I perceived in some visceral way was that possessing beauty was like possessing wealth: it affected people's attitude towards you. No one, unless they, too, are beautiful, can react quite normally to a beauty.

We all knew Miranda Tattersall came from what was called 'a broken home'. These days, when divorce is practically the norm, it seems bizarre that we found this interesting at all, let alone shocking. Then it was all part of her mystique, as were her careworn and slightly common working mother, and her loud, florid, embarrassing father, both of whom (or each, for naturally they never visited together) she treated with equal and unreadable calm. The detractors took this as further evidence of her tainted character: she was the product of this disastrous pairing, so what would you expect? But I always felt, rather audaciously, that I understood her better, and that her manner towards her ghastly parents was the measure of her style and sophistication. My own mother and father, together after twenty blameless years, conventional, well-behaved, prosperous and devoted, could nonetheless reduce me to a state of squirming discomfiture with a single misplaced word or look. Indeed, this sense of one's family as a cringemaking liability was both pretty universal and unfair. In the Tattersalls' case it would have been fully justified but Miranda handled them with the utmost poise and aplomb.

Later that night in Witherburn I lay in my makeshift bed and remembered. Or called to mind, that's the phrase: summoned up the memories that had been buried under so many others in the intervening years. Like ancient treasures preserved in peat they emerged bright and clear, like new.

I remembered the first time I saw her, standing in the supper queue on the first day of the term we both began at Queen's – for she was that other strange thing, a late starter. She had the wrong sort of shirt, a white terylene schoolboy shirt instead of the approved cream cotton, and her thick stockings were several shades darker than the statutory bottle-green – almost black. The clothes police soon sorted out these parental oversights, but on that first occasion they added immeasurably to her allure. Her thumbs were hooked in the pockets of her blazer. She stood there balanced, patient, alert, waiting to see what happened. A wounded person, it seemed to me even then, but ready for anything. The sight of her caused me a sharp pang of complex emotion: envy, longing, a desire almost to *be* her or, failing that, to be as close to her as possible. With hindsight, I know that for many years this was the nearest I came to falling in love.

I ought to try to describe her, although beauty is always so much more than the sum of its parts. For one thing she had the kind of looks that would have been equally striking in a man. This was something that people commented on later when she was famous, when she was Rags, the face of this and that, the one who could sell anything to anyone. One particularly arresting photograph by Terry O'Neill showed her barefaced and rumpled in a man's suit, slouched over a desk, cigarette in hand, tie askew, like something out of *Hold the Front Page*. Its ambivalent sexiness caused a sensation.

What can I say? It's so hard to define. She was tall, square-shouldered and long-necked, well proportioned with athletic legs . . . had a very upright carriage, which could make her appear haughty . . . thick brown hair, and brown eyes too, always slightly shadowed, with strongly marked dark brows . . . pale, slightly freckled skin, a short, grooved upper lip, wide mouth and a determined jaw. Her strong face in repose could look quite forbidding; when she smiled it was a sunrise. She had a husky voice with a break in it when she laughed, which wasn't often. At one end-of-term concert she sang 'Unchained

Melody', an unheard-of departure among the nymphs and shepherds, and was predictably hauled off-stage and over the coals. I don't believe she was setting out to annoy, she just liked the song. And so did we. Those who claimed not to were only jealous.

She used to tie her hair back, we all had to if it was below a certain length, and the bunch was meant to be on the nape of the neck. Miranda's tended to creep up until on Saturday evenings (the only time when we could wear mufti) it was that frowned-upon thing, a ponytail. That ponytail – its angle, its fall, its jaunty bounce, its flicked-up end – was like two fingers raised to authority.

She wasn't a leading light in school events. All that was unusual about her ensured that she was deliberately over-looked, as though she were a spoilt child who needed keeping in its place. She didn't seem to resent this. She was *so* different.

Of course, she barely knew I existed. To her I was just another member of the herd, the mass to which, through no fault or intention of her own, she did not belong. I was painfully conventional and plodding, it was my sole wish to blend into the background and not be singled out in any way, and where Miranda was concerned I had succeeded triumphantly.

Lying gazing out of the uncurtained cottage window at the stars over Witherburn, my home now and apparently hers, too, I recalled the two brief occasions when we'd actually spoken to one another. Both of them when she'd been in trouble.

The first was just after the great 'Unchained Melody' furore. It was the penultimate day of term and I'd been sent on a ritual errand to the staff room to collect the holiday homework sheets, which would lie forgotten in assorted bureaux, shelves and top drawers all over the home counties for the next four weeks before being feverishly disinterred and attended to during trunk-packing.

While I stood waiting for the sheets to be produced, Miranda came out of the head's drawing room, and closed the door behind her. Whatever had gone on in there she looked exactly as she always did, the weekday ponytail was penitentially low. As she came by she pulled an empathetic face and said, 'Hi.'

Greatly daring, I replied in kind. 'Hi.'

'Are you in trouble?'

I wished she'd keep her voice down, and said in a hoarse whisper: 'No.'

'Lucky old you . . .'

That was it. But it's almost impossible to convey the startling, convention-busting nature of this small exchange. Not only had she been calm under fire, she'd treated me as an equal. This was entirely natural to her, but not to me. I was hidebound, steeped in the kind of fatuous lore and protocol that dictated everything from how you wore your tie to which slang terms you could use. Her entirely casual remarks had the heady impact of an unexpected bouquet. I was enslaved.

About eighteen months later I contracted a mysterious virus in the summer term. Looking back I can see that I was really quite ill and giving cause for concern to both Queen's and my parents, not least because my complaint (so far as I know) remained undiagnosed. The symptoms were a persistent high temperature – there was a period of days that I could not remember at all – a thumping sick headache and chronic debility that lasted for weeks afterwards, leaving me weak, dizzy and sweating after the least exertion. I went from my bed in the dormitory to the sick room, back to the dormitory, was returned to classes, passed out and was back in the sick room again. My parents came to visit, an event akin in seriousness to the last rites, and subsequently I was allowed to talk to them on the telephone, though this was probably a public-relations exercise by the school rather than for my benefit, because I didn't know what to say to them beyond that I was 'okay', a portmanteau word covering everything from rude health to swamp fever.

It was during my second convalescent period that the really big storm blew up. It all happened very quickly, and at the time I knew nothing about it, sequestered as I was in the sick room with nothing but *Lorna Doone* and Julius Caesar's *Britannic Wars* for company. I remember Matron took pity on me and lent me *My Friend Flicka*. I was allowed visits in the period between afternoon tea and prep, and my best friend Spud had been attending faithfully with news of the 'you missed-a-scripture-test-and-a-desk-inspection-you-lucky-pig-all-my-Dirk-Bogarde-pictures-got-confiscated' variety. But for two days – the days in question as I later found out – she didn't come, because she was a day girl and might have offended my invalid sensibilities with the juicy details. Heaven knows what they imagined she was doing down in school, surrounded by all those flapping ears and wagging tongues, craving gossip . . . It was a swiz, but as it turned out I was afforded a privileged insight that enhanced my *cachet* for months to come.

It must have been somewhere between four and half past, because I'd just finished my cup of strong tea and slice of privileged-status Battenburg cake. In fact, when I heard footsteps I thought it was probably Spud. Then when the door opened and I heard the rustle of Matron and her solicitous voice my heart sank – not another sickie, please! I was used to being in here on my own; now that I was feeling better the privacy was a rare luxury, more precious than rubies. Sharing the room with another girl, in all likelihood iller than me, probably from another form and ghastly, was not a cheery prospect. I was an unchristian little thing.

I rolled over and lay with my back to the door, my pony book in front of my face. I remember my hair smelt poochy and unwashed. I didn't see at first whoever it was that Matron ushered in and when I did steal a glance my reaction was a kind of thrilled panic: Oh, my God! Oh, my *God*!

The brief glance had told me Miranda wasn't ill – she was dressed and was carrying her mac, hat and suitcase. Matron said something to me, which I was too discombobulated to hear, and then the two of them talked for a moment in lowered voices. I couldn't catch any of it, though I strained every sinew.

Matron came over. I smelt her scent, she put a boiled sweet on the bedside locker and leaned over me, aware of and gentle with my awkwardness.

'How's little Bobby doing?'

'Okay, thanks, Matron.'

She stroked my hair back, felt my forehead, smoothed and tucked in the bedclothes. 'Miranda's going to spend the night here. She won't disturb you.'

'Okay.'

She touched the cover of my book with her finger. 'Enjoying *Flicka*?'

'Yes, thanks.'

She smiled at me, it was like a kiss, Matron was so sweet. Then she'd gone.

The still, sunny evening hummed with tension, and not only mine: Miranda went to the loo more than once. She asked me what I'd got, and when I said the flu it didn't really sound enough for someone who'd been in and out of the sick room for nearly a month. I felt pathetic. I wished my hair wasn't so greasy, that I was wearing my other pyjamas, and, treacherously, that I wasn't reading *My Friend Flicka*. That, given this heaven-sent opportunity, I was a different person altogether.

It would have been unthinkable to ask why she was there. And she didn't volunteer any information, though I could sense big trouble coming off her in waves. A lot of the time she sat on the bed with her feet up and her ankles crossed, staring at a book but not turning the pages. Her face was very white, and set. It occurred to me that one of her parents might have died and if so, no matter how vile they were, that would have been awful for her. She didn't seem to have been crying, but that, as I say, meant nothing: she never did. She got into her nightie early, and pulled the bedclothes round her ears. The next morning she went down to assembly with Matron and returned with two red patches on her cheeks. I remember she was given different food, but didn't eat it.

During the interminable, squirmy day that followed Spud came in. It was mid-afternoon, outside her allotted visiting hours, which was incredibly brave of her, and in view of the contents of her note she must have been appalled to find Miranda there.

What it said was: 'Miranda Tattersall's been sacked for sexy pic in the paper. It's going round the school and she looks super! XOXOXOXO Spud.'

After this I reached new levels of feverish discomfiture. But I was thrilled, too – I might be flu-bound, but I was at the eye of the storm.

An eternity later, Matron came back and told her her father had arrived. It was time for her to go, for ever. Miranda said goodbye, and told me to get well soon. My tongue clove to the roof of my mouth with the enormity of it all, but I stared, transfixed, over the bedclothes as she left.

And that was the last time I'd seen her in the flesh. Until this evening, more than three decades later, in the Ladycross woods.

The next day passed in a chaotic blur, as the truck-loading tape was reversed and the cottage filled up with my possessions.

They arrived at eight o'clock, and it was all orderly enough to begin with. I stood in the living room doorway as the men came in, and instructed them where to put things. But as the morning drew on and space, energy and good humour were used up, it was a case of telling them to dump the stuff wherever they could and I'd sort it out later. I told myself that I was being paranoid, that I only imagined the repressed gloating of J K Removals as all their worst predictions proved correct.

But paranoia or no, it was scarcely possible to move after they left at two o'clock. The euphoria of the day before gave way to headsplitting dismay at the scale of the task confronting me. Such furniture as I'd sprung from store and brought with me had been left in the appropriate rooms but was virtually invisible – and wholly inaccessible – beneath piles of boxes and bulging binbags. When I opened one or two and peered inside I didn't even recognise the contents. What was all this? Did I want it? Had I ever wanted it? I found myself longing for the blood-temperature familiarity of the Beacon, the things that had always been there and that were not my responsibility, where for all its disordered decrepitude everything fell readily to hand, and where no decisions had to be made.

I was in danger of becoming paralysed by panic and was actually quite glad when the phone rang and it was Jim. It was a Saturday, so he was at home.

'You're in, then!'

'And I may never get out. My bleached bones are likely to be found among those ruddy boxes three months from now.'

'Christ, it's hell, sis, you have my deepest sympathy.'

'Thanks.'

'But you still like it, do you? Glad you went up there?' I heard the self-interested anxiety in his voice.

'Don't worry, I'll settle. It's just the cardboard-carton blues.'

'Booze getatable?'

'What do you think?'

'Good. Have one. And remember you don't have to do it all now. It'll all be there tomorrow.'

'That's what bothers me.'

'Hang on, Sal wants a word.'

I braced myself.

'Bobby! How the devil are you?'

'As well as can be expected.'

'All moved in?'

Why did people ask these silly questions? 'Yes.'

'Great. You're awfully brave, I do admire you.'

'You wouldn't if you could see me right now. It's horrible.'

'Oh!' Sally moaned sympathetically. 'That's downsizing for you, horrible word . . . Never mind, chin up, it's going to be lovely. We can't wait to see it.'

'You must visit when the dust's settled.'

'Try to stop us! Look, lots of love, a card is winging its way, we'll be thinking of you. Here's your brother again.'

'Hallo,' said Jim, 'not much else to say, really, just wanted to know you were in safely.'

'It's nice to hear from you.'

'Neighbours okay, seen anything of them yet?'

'Not the next-doors, no . . .' I decided against mentioning Miranda: it was too complicated. 'I did meet the man who renovated this cottage.'

'A villainous property developer?'

'Far from it. He was rather nice, he actually came and knocked on the door.'

'I should have a care, sis, if I were you.'

'Sadly, he never laid a finger on me.'

'He's probably about to throw up a rash of red-brick starter homes on your pleasant rural outlook, that's why.'

I thought of Daniel Mather. 'I somehow don't think so.'

'O-*kay*,' said Jim, 'better go, time to get the kids to various improving activities with oaths and imprecations. Christ knows what it'll be like when GCSEs kick in . . . Keep in touch, won't you?'

'I will.'

'And look after yourself. Speak soon – 'bye, Bobs.'

I put the phone down. For the first time that day I looked out of the window and noticed, now that the light was no longer blocked by JK's behemoth, that it was golden sunshine out there. Grimly, I fought my way through the boxes to the shiraz, drank half a glass fairly rapidly, looked around me and thought: Right!

Drank the rest, took another look out of the window and thought: Sod it.

Sufficient unto the day was the shambles thereof. As Jim had observed, it would all still be there tomorrow when, given a following wind and a good night's sleep, I would attack it with fresh vigour.

Outside, the sun struck warm and sweet on my face and I paused for a moment, closing my eyes to drink it in. When I opened them I noticed that there were cars parked all along the street, as far as the eye could see. Big, shiny cars: there was a chauffeur sitting reading the *Sun* in a Daimler right in front of my door. The top of his window was open and I could hear the Lighthouse Family. When he saw me he buzzed the window down a bit further and turned off the music.

'Am I all right here? Not in your parking space, I hope?'

'No, mine's round at the back.' I looked up the street again. 'What's going on?'

'Big funeral at the church. It's due to finish –' he glanced at his watch '– in five minutes, then we'll all be gone. Matter of fact, here they come . . .'

He nodded and I glanced in the direction of the nod. The congregation, brightly clad, was starting to emerge from the south door and move round the end of the church to the graveside, following the black-suited coffin-bearers. Even those immediately behind the coffin were dressed in colourful summer clothes. One woman was all in white, like a bride: in fact, if I hadn't been told otherwise, or seen the coffin, I might have taken the occasion for a wedding.

'There are a lot of people,' I said. 'Do you know whose funeral it is?'

'Fred Montclere – Lord Stratton?' the man ventured. 'Local big house. Very nice man, I believe.'

That would make a good epitaph, I reflected, as I walked up the street. At school we'd been told never to use the adjective 'nice' in an essay, always to find something more interesting and specific. But used straightforwardly of a person as the chauffeur had just done, it spoke volumes – of integrity, warmth and kindness.

Further up the street, people were standing on the pavement, or in their doorways, watching. Opposite the church gate there was quite a crowd. They were quiet and attentive, some a little tearful, bearing out what the chauffeur had said. At my approach people stepped aside to let me through and one or two smiled. You could sense the unforced strength of feeling, the honest emotion that bound them together and which made them in some way more welcoming towards me, a stranger, as if we were all united and dignified by the man who had died.

Infected by the general mood, I stood with them. There must have been getting on for two hundred people in the churchyard; the gathering in the road was of those for whom there hadn't been room. The main congregation was now clustered round the grave. The only sounds were what reached us of the minister's voice and, once, the distant barking of a dog somewhere up on the hill.

Outside the gate were parked the hearse, and two more cars, a metallic grey Rolls with a dark-suited driver behind the wheel, and a black BMW convertible, top down. Along to the right, a couple of traffic policemen in fluorescent waistcoats stood in the road. Just beyond them, in a line of would-be through traffic, was the J K Removals lorry, becalmed. I calculated it must have been there for three-quarters of an hour. The nearside door of the cab was open to let some air circulate; a leg hung out. I doubted the atmosphere was as benign in there.

Ten minutes must have passed. I'm a passionately committed agnostic, but those minutes gave a new force to the song line 'He's got the whole world in his hand' . . . All of us – congregation, crowd, police, traffic, removals lorry, the whole village – seemed gently but firmly held, cradled in the moment. It was impressive: my skin prickled. I was moved, and not only because I was tired.

As the first people turned slowly and began to move away from the graveside the man next to me murmured, 'God bless him.'

We all remained there respectfully, and in my case curiously, to look at the faces of the mourners, perhaps to identify the principals. There was a bit of bustle in the road and for the first time I noticed a handful of press photographers getting into position, shepherded by the police.

Again like a wedding, the crowd in the churchyard parted to allow the mourners through. A couple in their thirties, more soberly dressed than most and accompanied by two children, came out of the gate. The woman and the children got into the Rolls, the man held open the door of the BMW for the woman in the white dress.

She placed her hand on his arm, said something, smiling, and went round to the driver's side. Her dress was crisp cotton, a long, button-through shirt with rolled-back sleeves, a brown leather belt. The woman's legs were thin and tanned and she wore sandals with criss-cross Roman ankle straps. She paused, unsmiling but gently composed, to let the photographers take pictures. There was nothing self-regarding in the pose, it was a cool, generous, professional response. Before getting into the car she said in her throaty voice, which because of the quiet she didn't need to raise: 'Fred and I really appreciate this – please, you must come up to the house.'

Even in this most conventional of settings, and bearing a terrible sadness, Miranda was, still, so different.

The man next to me said to the woman at his side, 'Shall we go up, then?'

'I don't know . . .'

'I reckon we should.'

She glanced around. 'But there's more than a hundred here. What if everyone goes? How will they cope?'

'It's not a three-bed semi, love, they'll have an industrial tea urn and a caterer . . . Come on.' Seeing her still hesitate, he added, 'Fred'd want us to.'

That seemed to settle it, and they began moving, with most of the rest of the crowd, across the road towards the church gate. I realised that all of these people were going to walk across the churchyard and up the hill path to Ladycross. Carried by the tide, I found myself moving with everyone else. She hadn't recognised me, there would be so many people, she'd meant what she said . . . and I did know her, after all; I was not a stranger . . .

'Hallo.'

It was Daniel Mather, marginally smarter in a balding pink cord suit, surely the fruit of a classic clothing shop, and a grey T-shirt.

'Going to Ladycross?' he asked.

'I thought I might, everyone seems to be . . . What about you?'

'I'll give it a miss. Too new to the place.'

'For goodness' sake, if you're too new where does that leave me?'

He shrugged sheepishly. 'Different profile.'

I thought it fair to clarify things. 'I used to know Miranda.'

'Did you? The Lady Stratton?'

'We were at school together.'

'Extraordinary . . . Does she know you're here?'

'No.'

'You ought to go.'

'Won't you come?'

'No.' He began backing away as he had before. 'Not my bag, I wouldn't be comfortable.'

This was so clearly the truth and not an implied criticism of me that I didn't demur. Behind us the traffic began to move again, and he broke into a loping run, threading between the cars to his Mini. With the strange pink suit, he was wearing truly terrible cheap black lace-up shoes. Both they and the suit looked as if they didn't belong to him. They certainly shouldn't have.

We queued politely to go through the lychgate; fanned out to cross the churchyard. Most people paused to look at the new grave and I did the same, mainly because I did not wish to be among the first to arrive.

A temporary plain white wooden cross bore only the words 'GEORGE FREDERICK HILAIRE MONTCLERE 1928–1992'. There were no flowers except a spray of lilies-of-the-valley, their stems tied with blue ribbon. No card.

Someone murmured, 'Poor Fred.'

I thought: Poor Miranda.

Hardly anyone spoke as we queued again to file through the kissing-gate on the far side of the churchyard. The gentle incline of the path after this point sorted the quicker from the slower walkers. I was stiff and tired after the day I'd had; it wasn't difficult to be near the back. When, about half-way up the hill, I looked over my shoulder Witherburn was deserted – the traffic, the police and the people all gone. With the stragglers meandering up the grassy slope in the afternoon sunshine, some of the women with small children by the hand, and the men with toddlers on their shoulders, an old couple hanging on to each other for support, it might have been a village picnic from decades ago. As if to reinforce this impression I seemed to hear, momentarily, a snatch of music.

The odd thing was that although the house could be seen from various points in the village, the hill was not a continuous gradual incline as it appeared from the street, but a series of undulating false crests, so that as we walked up, our objective disappeared from view. I suppose we'd been on Ladycross land from the moment we'd entered the churchyard. But as we drew closer there was a change in the air, a nuance, like the one I'd experienced in the wood the evening before. No wonder people were drawn to it. The house on the hill was a powerful presence. It cast a spell.

And there – I was certain this time – was the music again.

The narrow winding sheep-track of a path that we'd been following became wider and the grass on either side of it more lush, shepherding us so that we once more formed a kind of column. To our right and slightly below us was the wood where I'd seen Miranda the previous night. It looked smaller from up here, but still dense and secretive, keeping out the sunshine.

The path threaded through a scattered line of low, wind-warped moorland trees, which turned out to be the shield for some taller and more stately ones, beeches and oaks. The music was clearly audible now: I was no expert but recognised jazz, of that bubbling, conversational kind that lifts the spirits.

And then there was the house, and my first thought, a strange one under the circumstances, was that it was like the jazz, joyful: a thing of many parts amounting to more than the sum of those parts – random, raffish and elegant in its asymmetric harmony. Close to, it wasn't as grand or large as it appeared from the bottom of the hill, but its domestic detail and architectural contradictions made it, to my eye, more beautiful. Gables and tall chimneys surmounted a long, low, castellated frontage with an arched doorway standing open, surmounting a broad, curved step like an inviting lap. The predominant material was a rosy-grey stone but above the door and over the leaded windows in the older part of the house were finials in bright colours.

If the congregation might have been mistaken for wedding guests in the churchyard the impression was even stronger up here, where a large-scale thrash seemed to be in progress. People were scattered over the grass, most standing, some sitting on hay bales, talking and laughing. There was a table near the front door, which seemed to be dispensing tea (from the industrial urn, presumably) and cake, but everyone I could see was engaged in serious drinking. Thin, glamorous young people were distributing champagne, orange juice and *amuse-bouches* from salvers, with the haughtily unprofessional air of resting rock stars. It would have been hard to imagine a more festive scene.

My fellow walkers dissolved into the throng and became part of it by that proccess of social osmosis known as 'making oneself at home'. Indeed, from what I'd overheard maybe they did feel genuinely at home here. I found myself suddenly on the periphery, an outsider looking in.

The jazz band was on a large trailer at the edge of the trees. At the back of the trailer among the wires, bundled in gaffer tape, that headed off in the direction of the house was a brown plastic barrel packed with ice and cans of beer. An androgynous, monochrome teenager in the kind of tattered jeans that do not allow for underwear proffered a salver. I took a glass of champagne and sat down on the grass near the trailer.

The band were playing 'That Old Black Magic'. The five musicians were not young. They were probably all in their sixties, but not the type of men one would ever describe as elderly, let alone old. They struck me as the sort of charming, clever, eternally boyish individuals who might, when not entertaining at funeral teas, have been Radio Four panellists, Corinthian sportsmen, broadsheet columnists, Oxbridge dons or all four; the sort (I fantasised idly) who had sublimely happy but tolerant marriages to former toasts of the JCR, ladies who had their husbands' number and the self-confidence to deal with it. Men to lunch, laugh and love with. Good-time guys.

Sitting there on my own, but part of the company, I began to relax: to do as the others were doing and make myself at home. In fact, I did feel strangely at home, as if I'd found a place I had missed, without knowing it, all my life.

It was headily disorientating. I had come so far in forty-eight hours. Two days ago I'd been rattling around in the resentful, echoing, shabby rooms of the Beacon, surrounded by the last knockings of my then-life. This evening I was perched on a grassy hilltop four hundred miles away, my temporarily abandoned new home waiting for me down there in the lee of the church, my head full of music, laughter and champagne, honouring the memory of a man I'd never known. The only connection – and that a largely unacknowledged one – between then and now was Miranda.

As I thought of her she appeared, and the trumpeter held out his arm and practically lifted her on to the stage. Under the loose folds of the shirtwaister you could see she was terribly thin. Top models had to be like that, I reminded myself. But when I'd known her she hadn't been skinny. She'd been Britain's Brigitte Bardot.

She was laughing with the musicians, they were clustered around her, the arm of the trumpeter had slipped round her waist, you could see she was an adored member of the gang. The BB thing was even harder to imagine now than it had been then. I suppose she'd always had from nature that model's trick of thinking herself into whoever she wanted to be. Now, with her feathery short hair and cut-glass bone-structure, she was an archetypal English beauty in the Kristin Scott-Thomas mould.

Because Miranda was on the trailer, the focus of the gathering had shifted this way. Other people sat down on the grass around me, and more were gathering behind. The trombonist handed her a radio mike. The mood was expectant, was she going to say a few words?

No, she was going to sing. She gave us 'Stormy Weather'. She had – I remembered 'Unchained Melody' – not a great voice but a soulful one, sweet and low. She sang liltingly, not freighting the words with anything more than they already expressed, letting the song speak for her. Her voice didn't break and there were no tears in her eyes: it was a performance.

But if she kept her cool, most of us didn't. My own eyes prickled and my throat filled, and I hadn't even known Fred Montclere. The beauty of the day and the place, the warm conviviality of the occasion made the little song more poignant. As for 'Ole rocking chair'll get me . . .' it was unthinkable. Not her. Not Miranda.

When she finished singing, there was gentle applause and hear-hearing. She leaned towards the mike and said, 'You can carry on with whatever it was now,' which was greeted with rather louder cheers. Another squire stepped forward and she put her hand in his for support as she jumped down.

The moment was over. Sensing a natural break the band put down their instruments and picked up their beer. I clambered to my feet. Miranda was standing a few metres away, the white dress sparkled in my peripheral vision. I realised that what I did not want was for her to come over, to say hallo, wondering who I was, or perhaps (even worse) to recognise me at once. I wasn't ready for that, I couldn't face it.

I accepted another glass of champagne and walked across the grass in the direction of the house. In the narrow band of shade by the mullioned windows the under-employed tea ladies readied themselves and then, when I shook my head and raised my glass, returned to their gossip.

Through the open doors I could make out one or two other people in the broad, shadowed hall. I went in. There was a smell of roses. A black cord hung across the foot of the stairs which led up to a half-landing like a stage before dividing and continuing to join a gallery. The dappled light from arched, leaded windows somewhere high overhead gave me the impression of being in a forest, with the sun filtering down between branches.

The black cord, by discreetly prohibiting the first floor, implied permission to wander the rest. It surprised me, in this security-conscious age, that all and sundry were being given the run of a place which must be packed with treasures. I supposed it must also be full of elaborate and sensitive alarm systems, probably connected directly to the local police station.

There were large rooms on either side of the front door. One was a dining room – and there were the roses, a great golden explosion of them, spilling out of a silver jug in the middle of the table. Each flower was wide-faced, nearly overblown, showing its creamy heart; a scatter of petals lay on the highly polished surface: the scent seemed to rush out to meet me as I stood in the doorway. There was a smart elderly couple in the room, he in a blazer, she in a blue suit, and as I watched the woman leaned over the table and brushed the petals into her cupped hand. She looked around for somewhere to put them; her husband held open his blazer pocket and she tipped them in. All this was done quietly, almost reverently, without the need for comment – they were in tune with each other, if not entirely with the place, for I was sure the petals didn't matter.

Because the other room was empty, I went in there. It was a library. Here, too, there were roses – red this time – in a punchbowl in the hearth, but they were less advanced, the petals of each flower still cupped together, their curved edges forming a *moue* like a kiss. I noticed a small camera high in the far corner, like a watchful nesting bird between wall and ceiling. The room was formal. Over the fireplace was a large oil painting, showing a pop-eyed Georgian beauty in silver satin and lace, a half-open fan in one languid, boneless hand, a distant prospect of Ladycross, minus a couple of gables, in the background as though she had come all this distance to stand on a grassy knoll in her finery with – if the sky was to be believed – a thunderstorm threatening. There were half a dozen smaller paintings on either side of the door, spaniels with dead pheasants, horses, hounds and the like, and the rest of the walls were covered with books. Not all the books were ancient, valuable and leatherbound, there were plenty of recent hardbacks among the morocco and gold-leaf – Patricia Highsmith, Tom Wolfe, Wendy Cope, Robert Harris, Alans Bennett and Clark – an informal literary democracy, which appeared both cheeky and charming in such grand surroundings. The same applied to the drift of magazines on the long, low mahogany table in front of the fireplace. *Country Life* and *Horse and Hound* lay down with *Hello!*, *Private Eye* and *Harper's*. On a table in the window was a visitor's book, open, like almost everything in the house. I turned a few pages. The names, addresses and comments were mostly those of a warmly enthusiastic general public, spiked here and there with celebrities. Marylou and Evan Steen from Maryland ('Glorious and magical – a never-to-be-forgotten experience!') were followed by Charlie Watts (no address, no comment, three Xs); Mr and Mrs J. Pryke of Basingstoke ('Thank you for letting us see your lovely house') came hard on the heels of Princess Margaret (nothing).

I left the book open at the current page without making an entry. In the far corner of the room on the same side of the fireplace was another door, standing ajar. I put my head round. It was a small study or snug, with a Victorian rolltop desk to the right, beneath the single narrow window, an electric radiator, a couple of sagging armchairs; a fringed standard lamp, a chain-store Anglepoise; and assorted candles of various shapes and sizes each fixed to the stone window-sconce by a puddle of its own wax. Forming a background to this homely eclecticism was exquisite linenfold panelling and a magnificently antiquated threadbare Persian rug, its once-vibrant reds and blues dulled by wear. I surmised that the room might have originated as a small chapel or priest's hole.

There was no cord, or anything else to deter entry, so I went in, instinctively closing the door after me. It wasn't that I wished to pry. I had no desire to open the desk diary, or the Filofax, or the tangerine clam-shell laptop, least of all to look in any of the drawers. If I was an intruder that was only because I saw myself as one. For I did want to be alone here, like a child who's discovered a special place and calls it her den, peculiar to her. This was someone else's den, and I fancied that by simply standing here silently, absorbing its stillness, I might be vouchsafed an understanding of the rightful occupant.

I barely breathed. I folded my arms and turned slowly on the spot. Two things caught my attention: a framed pencil sketch on the wall facing the door, and a large photograph standing on the desk. The sketch was of Miranda, rather more as I remembered her, with shoulder-length hair and a heavy *farouche* fringe. The artist – a gifted amateur, I guessed, enchanted by his subject – had caught something about her that made his drawing instantly recognisable without having achieved a perfect likeness. Her expression was candid and unsmiling but not solemn: a look I thought of as typical of her.

The photograph on the desk showed a more recent, thinner, short-haired Miranda with a man who must have been her husband. They were on a terrace, with a balustrade behind them, and beyond that a turquoise holiday sea. He was older than her by perhaps ten or fifteen years, a tall, lanky, humorous-looking man with a charming smile that creased his face; a man from much the same mould as the boys in the band but exuding a *dégagé* patrician elegance. He had one arm round Miranda's shoulders, the other raised to flatten his wayward, thinning hair; in the raised hand was a floppy straw hat. The two of them together conveyed the same air as Ladycross itself – the harmonious whole amounting to far more than the sum of its complex and contradictory parts.

As I studied the photograph I heard soft sounds in the library beyond the door – the petal-tidiers, probably. Like an animal lying low, I stood stock-still and held my breath: I didn't want them to find this room, or not until I had left it.

They didn't. They were far too respectful to open a door that was actually closed. After a few minutes I breathed again.

There were a couple of large old military drums used as side-tables, and on one of these was a mini CD player and some discs – Mary Black, *Missa Luba*, a saxophone concerto, *I'm Sorry I Haven't a Clue* . . . I imagined Miranda in here late at night, or whenever her dying husband was asleep, recharging her batteries, escaping, perhaps, from the grandeur and history of the house she'd married along with the man.

I'd been secretive for long enough, and I left the little room, closing the door softly behind me.

As I emerged from the library, Miranda was coming in through the main door. Her arms were folded. We passed one another and she did flash me a quick, friendly smile, but she was coming in from bright sunlight and could scarcely have seen me. I had the impression that the smile, for all its apparent naturalness and warmth, was professional – the smile of the model, now the chatelaine.

I looked to see where she would go. She went into the library.

CHAPTER SEVEN

——◇◆◇◆◇——

Rags, 1962

'You're not our type,' said the gossamer blonde behind the desk. 'You know that.'

It wasn't a question, more of a reproof, so Miranda didn't answer. She hoped her silence appeared neutral rather than surly, though an air of surliness seemed pretty much *de rigueur* both in the offices of Face Value and, if the pictures on the walls were anything to go by, among their more successful clients.

The blonde riffled swiftly through her photographs again, like a bank clerk counting notes. 'I suppose we might give it a go . . .' she mused, in a way that warranted no comment. 'Do you mind waiting there for a minute.'

Once again it was not a request, since it was hardly likely that an aspiring model would leave without her portfolio. She scooped up the photographs in a haphazard way that made Miranda wince, and wafted across the open-plan office to the desk of a young man with a fringe and a bad complexion. She dumped the photographs in front of him and leaned on the desk so that their heads were together. He spread the pictures with his fingertips . . . She picked one up and waggled it, making some point . . . He sat back, then forward again . . . He seemed half asleep but perhaps this was like the surliness, a concomitant of being hip.

Miranda confined herself to not blinking. This was a small but handy gift, and one she had used to convince herself of her ascendancy over the establishment at school when in all other respects she was being taken apart. Although it came naturally to her, it appeared to others to be evidence of arrogance – self-control employed in the service of hauteur. Even – especially – her father at his overbearing worst could be discomfited by her unwavering and uninterrupted gaze upon him.

'And don't think you can stare me down!' he'd say, in his most sneering voice. 'It doesn't impress me.' He always put the accent on the last word as though he knew she spent her life attempting to put one over on people but *he* wasn't one of the impressionable herd. That it infuriated him was no surprise, since everything about her infuriated him, but the not-blinking made him uncomfortable, which was sweet indeed.

She didn't wish to discomfort the Face Value people, simply not to be cowed by them. The spotty young man and the woman glanced her way and then back at her photographs. They were talking about her. He produced Disque Bleu and they both lit up to aid the consultation process. Miranda continued not to blink, either actually or in her mind. If she was going to be a model she had to get used to this: to her appearance being a commodity; to separating her thoughts and feelings from her looks, just as they were doing. It was nothing personal, she told herself. If they turned her down, it was because she wasn't their type.

The blonde returned. She had a cigarette in one hand, and one of Miranda's photos in the other. 'May I ask who took this?'

Oddly, she had many of the verbal mannerisms of Mrs Grace – that ability to imbue the simplest words with a lofty disparagement.

The picture was one of Dale's, but since Miranda didn't know what the woman was going to say about it she thought it best not to be too specific.

'A local photographer, at home.'

'I thought so.' That tone again. 'Amateur?'

What was the point? 'Yes.'

'Friend?'

She hesitated, but that was enough.

'I thought so.' She looked across at her colleague on the other side of the room and gave a brief nod. 'Tell him not to give up the day job, it's a poor photograph. But it is interesting. Can you tell me something about it?'

'What would you like to know?'

The woman tapped her cigarette snappily, she prickled with impatience. 'Whatever you think it's worth telling me.'

'I was fifteen, I was still at boarding-school. My friend Dale Harper entered this picture for a Britain's Brigitte Bardot competition in one of the papers, and I won.'

'Really?' She sounded surprised rather than impressed. 'Which paper?'

'The *Sketch*.'

'M-hm.'

'Actually there were six of us – one for each day of the week.'

'I see . . .' The woman dropped the photo on the desk and narrowed her eyes at Miranda through her smoke. 'Because you don't look in the least like BB, do you?'

'I do in the picture,' she said.

'My point exactly. Did they print it?'

'Yes. I was expelled from school.'

This elicited a short, dry laugh. 'I bet. How old did you say you were now?'

'Eighteen.'

'And how old *are* you?'

'Eighteen in September.'

'Seventeen. Okay.' Abruptly, the woman stubbed out her cigarette, shuffled the pictures together and slotted them back into their folder before handing them to Miranda. 'We'll see what we can do.'

'Thanks – so—'

'Toni in Reception will give you a form. Fill it in correctly. We'll be in touch.'

'Thanks.'

'No promises, mind.'
'No.'

The first job, for the teenage section of a mail-order catalogue, came in within a week. She was nervous beforehand, but not in front of the camera, and it had gone well. Just the same, it wasn't until she was on her third booking, an autumn fashion shoot in Sussex for a women's magazine, that it dawned on her that, far from being a wild card for Face Value, they had snapped her up. All that 'not our type' and 'no promises' stuff had been bullshit, designed to keep her expectations low and her ego in its place. They must have realised from the first moment that their commission was safe with her but it would have been undignified and poor business sense to display too much enthusiasm.

Her view was confirmed by Katie, the magazine's stylist, entrusted with the task of making Miranda and her fellow model Noah appear cool, windswept and rain-freshened while wearing Donegal tweed and cashmere in the desert heat of the South Downs in August.

'You've got the look, haven't you?' she said, spraying and tweaking the side fronds of Miranda's chignon into breeze-blown chic. 'We always get interesting people from Face Value.'

'I don't know. Do you?'

'Oh, yes, always something different, something a bit thought-provoking . . .' Katie subjected the hair to a hurricane of lacquer, arresting it as it were in mid-gust. 'You don't mind my saying that?'

'Of course not.'

'You be sure not to lose it. Your uniqueness is the biggest thing you've got going for you.'

'Thanks, I'll try.'

'There.' Katie stepped back to indicate that she was done. 'You'll do. Stay one step ahead is my advice to you.'

A bit later when she and Noah were standing around with the hired horse, feeding it their sandwiches while having a fag, he put in his fourpenn'orth.

'You want my advice, Mandy, don't take on any old thing – be a bit choosy.'

Noah was a young man with the sexy, sculpted looks of a dissolute aristocrat. This impression could pass unchallenged until he opened his mouth when, like Eliza Doolittle, a tumble of glottal stops and missed aitches placed his Essex credentials beyond doubt. Not that he lived there any more, having made so much money out of his toffish features that he now owned a smart flat in Kensington. His was an opinion worth taking into account.

'I will be, don't worry.'

'No, I mean it,' he said, as if she'd argued. 'Your face is your fortune, darlin', like mine is, keep 'em hanging on a bit.'

'What happens if people get bored of hanging on and lose interest?'

'Doesn't work like that, sweetheart. It's like sex, same rules apply. You're like me, a bit surprising, a bit different. Not pretty, right?'

'I hope not.'

'That's the style!' He cuddled her shoulders. 'That *is* the style – you hang on to it. Don't let them suck you dry and wear you out or they will do before you're twenty. You want to be an icon.' He said this as one might have said, 'You want to change those trousers.'

She was doubtful. 'That's not really down to me, though, is it? I mean, I can't just say tomorrow, "I think I'll be an icon". Other people have to decide that I am one.'

'Listen to what I'm saying, Mand – people take you at your own valuation, yeah?'

At this point the horse, having had enough of Noah's philosophising and suspecting that he might have more sandwiches about his person, unbalanced him with a determined shove of its nose.

'Get lost, bastard!'

'Fall over in that lot,' yelled Katie, 'and I'll kill you!'

Miranda took Noah's advice to heart. What had started out as a way to make money, a simple exploitation of her natural assets (her father's horrible but apposite word), became more than that. If she was going to make a living posing for the camera, then it should not be as an anonymous face, least of all as some flash-in-the-pan lens fodder fit only for a quick glance before lining drawers and budgie cages. That would be proving Gerald Tattersall right. Noah was right: she must aspire to be one of the handful of models known by name to the public – like Fiona Campbell-Walter, or more recently the Shrimp. Then, like an author whose name came above the title, your identity superseded that of the product, or the publication, or the clothes you were selling.

Then, you were a star.

But being choosy at such an early stage was difficult. She didn't yet wish to lose the good offices of Face Value who, whatever their motives, had taken her on and given her a break. She needed to make regular money; and she was wary of becoming known as difficult.

Also, there was her mother's attitude, which was ambivalent to say the least. The money was welcome but there was little doubt that in her book modelling was only a whisker away from prostitution on the unsuitability scale. She wasn't so much straitlaced herself as concerned about what others might think, and the damage her daughter might be doing to what she insisted on calling her 'reputation'.

In vain did Miranda point out that she had no reputation.

'Then you don't want a bad one.'

'Mum! Britain's BB, expelled from top girls' school!'

'Don't remind me, Mandy, please.' Marjorie's brow furrowed in that familiar look of baffled, careworn dismay. She reached for her cigarettes.

'Can I have one of those?'

Her mother held out the packet. 'I don't approve.'

Miranda stayed her hand. 'You're offering me one or not?'

'You asked for one.'

'Yes, but do you want me to have it?'

'I don't exactly *want* you to have it, but you'll only do it somewhere else.'

'Fine. I'll go and get mine.'

'Mandy—'

But she was already in the doorway. 'It's okay!'

In her room she lit up, took a few deep breaths. She had to move out.

She loved her mother but without the bonding in adversity they'd enjoyed before, it was getting harder to rub along. When it had been the two of them against Gerald, it had all been straightforward. His behaviour was so immeasurably worse and his faults so much more glaring than any of theirs that they could overlook their own differences.

Not that this wasn't better in every other respect. The everyday pleasure of the freedom, the independence, the sheer, simple *peace*, was incalculable. But with these benefits came their first extended opportunity to examine and assess each other.

The trouble, as Miranda saw it, was that her mother couldn't lose the habit of duplicity, which Gerald had created. She was by nature an easy-going, affectionate woman whose approach to child-rearing, left to her own devices, would certainly have amounted to healthy neglect, or at least a woolly-liberal *laissez-faire*. But years of Gerald's piggish bullying had made her feel there were things she *should* disapprove of, and that she must have this disapproval minuted. Miranda knew very well that her mother, whatever her natural parental anxieties, would revel in having a photographic model for a daughter if she'd only let herself. And as for smoking, the 'doing it somewhere else' excuse was pathetic. They enjoyed having a fag together, but the ritual, martyred tutting had to be gone through every bloody time. It was as though the repulsive Gerald, like a diseased amputated limb, continued to make his presence felt *in absentia*.

She told Dale about her decision. He no longer harboured dreams of being a photographer, which was just as well, and had been more than good about it being the BB photograph that had decided it with Face Value.

'My picture, your face,' he conceded. 'You won.'

'Thanks anyway.'

'My pleasure. You ever want someone to land you in the shit again, I'm your man.'

'It may have been shit at the time, but it's turned out to be the best thing that ever happened, and I am grateful.'

Dale shrugged. They were having lunch in the greasy spoon near Office Solutions, where he was gofer and dogsbody. 'Just don't forget your old friends when you're a star.'

He was teasing and she told him to shut up. Then she said, 'I'm going to move out.'

'Your mum isn't going to like that.'

'She'll be fine once it's happened and she realises it's not the end of the world.'

'Where will you go?'

'I'll rent somewhere in London.'

'Just like that?'

'Why not? I'm earning pretty good money, these days. And I'll be saving on travelling up and down.'

'Bit of a difference . . .' he muttered, then cleared his throat and began again. 'Bit of a difference, these days, eh, between your life and mine.'

She could see he was downcast, and put her hand over his, giving it a little shake. 'No, there isn't. Not really.'

'Oh, yeah?'

'I mean, we're still the same people. We're mates, Dale. That won't change.'

He gave a glum, sceptical grunt.

'Dale, it won't!'

'Whatever you say. Who else will be in this flat, then?'

'I don't know, do I? Not yet. There are a couple of other girls with the agency who are all right, they might have a space. And I can always advertise—'

'Advertise? You don't know who you're getting, it could be some real nutcase.'

'But it won't be, because – I'll make sure it isn't.'

'The bigger the nutcase the more plausible,' observed Dale sententiously, but she could tell he felt better, fussing over her rather than feeling upstaged. The balance had been redressed.

'Tell you what,' she said, 'why don't you come up to

London with me on Saturday and we can have a look round together?'

'Get away,' said Dale, 'you don't want me along.'

They'd looked at ten places by four o'clock. Miranda had bought an *Exchange and Mart*, and a *Hot-Property Advertiser*, and made a number of calls from a phone box on Friday night.

It was depressing. They both felt it, but neither wanted to be the first to admit how they felt, she because of losing face and appearing to be defeated before she'd begun, he because he didn't want to put a dampener on things. But the parade of drab streets and dreary, under-maintained rooms, either cluttered and squalid or neat and bleak, was enough to make the sturdiest spirit wilt. It was shocking what you had to pay for the barest minimum.

When it came to rooms advertised in shared properties they were either so small that she couldn't imagine escaping into them, or they involved sharing the room with another girl. 'I'm not doing that,' she said firmly. 'After Queen's I'm never doing that again.'

There was one such flat, in Lexham Gardens, that seemed to offer everything – a decent-sized bedroom to herself, a balcony, and a reasonably leafy view from the window. The girls were well-spoken and had a bottle of sherry on the side. But there was a drawback.

'They don't like me,' she said to Dale, as they walked to the bus stop.

'Go on, they were fine.'

'They were okay. But if anyone else at all shows up with only one head, they'll give it to her.'

'You're paranoid.' He laughed and nudged her, but she was all bristly intuition and could hear his uncertainty.

'You know I'm right.'

'They weren't necessarily your type, but—' She raised her eyebrows and he admitted: 'Okay, if you insist.'

'Thank you.'

'I wouldn't take it anyway, if I were you.'

'I won't, don't worry.'

They were on the bus before Dale said, 'Want to know what it was?'

'Suit yourself.' But she knew he would tell her.

'They were scared of you.'

Now she looked at him in genuine astonishment. 'You *what*?'

'They liked you all right, but they wouldn't want you around all the time. You're far too good-looking.'

She looked hard at him. He lifted a shoulder, tilted a hand, as if to say, 'Don't blame me.' Knowing it was the truth, she looked away again.

'You'd better get used to it, Mand,' he said. 'It's human nature.'

'Yes,' she said. She'd had too much of bloody human nature already. As the bus rolled towards Victoria, she didn't blink.

The day spent looking with Dale, although fruitless, was a useful exercise. She could eliminate certain flats from her enquiries. She'd come to realise she'd rather have a modest place in a nice area, that she preferred north London to south, that she was unlikely to find a congenial share, although—

'You and I could share,' she suggested, on the way back on the train.

'You're not serious?'

'Why not?'

'For a start I've got a job where I am. For another thing, people would—'

'That doesn't matter.'

'People wouldn't like it. And, most of all, I couldn't do it.'

'Why not?'

'Mand . . .' He shook his head. 'When you say share, you mean chummy kind of thing, flatmates, like those girls only mixed.'

'That's right.'

'You might see it like that, but I couldn't.'

She saw that he couldn't, he really couldn't. His eyes pleaded for some kind of bargain, for her to surprise him, to shed a different light on things. But that was something *she* couldn't do.

'Okay,' she said. 'And you're right. No one would believe we weren't living in sin.'

The following weekend she found the perfect place. It was almost the shabbiest she'd seen, but it was on a steep road of tall, higgledy-piggledy houses clambering up towards Parliament Hill, with the windy spaces of the Heath at the top and a railway line, a bus terminus and a parade of shops at the bottom.

Eighteen Khartoum Road would once have been called a lodging-house: a warren of rooms with an assortment – or ill-assortment – of tenants, bizarre not in themselves but through unlikely juxtaposition. There were just two high-ceilinged clanking bathrooms, with hard cork bathmats and peeling enamel, where the narrow jet of water from the geyser steamed furiously, not because of its own heat but because of the icy air surrounding it.

The room that was advertised, and which Miranda took the moment she saw it, was on the top floor. From the window, even though the house wasn't at the top of the hill, you could make out the green billow of the Heath beyond the chimney pots on the other side of the road. The 'kitchenette', shared by both top-floor rooms, was nothing more than a large cupboard, also containing the header tank for the whole house, so condensation dripped permanently. Both rooms were shabby, but the nature of the house itself, and its situation, gave them a Bohemian charm.

Alaric Colquhoun, the landlord, lived in the ground-floor flat, which was below pavement level at the front but gave on to the garden at the back. Al let it be known that he was a writer, but not, as far as anyone could see, one who actually had to write. He was a handsome, charming, sprightly man of fifty or so, who managed to keep everyone happy by being so obviously happy himself. He made no bones about the fact that, being a creative, artistic sort of chap, he wouldn't dream of charging beastly high rents, but the unspoken deal was that he let out to as many people as possible and dealt with maintenance on a crisis-only basis.

There was something else about Al, something that greatly added to his appeal as a landlord where Miranda was concerned: he was an attractive man who did not appear to be attracted to her. This in spite of a stream of courtly compliments, which made her feel, for the first time in her life, like a lady.

'It's high time we had some youth and beauty about the place,' he told her; adding with a collusive twinkle that excepted present company: 'I like to think I run a happy ship, but we're not the most *elegant* crew in the world.'

'Now, then,' he went on, over tea and brandy snaps in the garden flat, 'I hate having to ask this sort of thing, but you will be able to manage the rent? I generally ask that it's paid weekly in advance, though there is always flexibility . . .'

She said there wouldn't be any problem.

Al sighed indulgently. 'So young and so independent . . . Would it be impertinent to ask what you do?'

'Photographic modelling.'

'Of course you do!' He was enchanted. 'I just knew there was something. I saw it, I *felt* it, the moment you walked in. Stay there.' He went to a bureau and came back with a leather bound notebook and a pencil. 'Where can I see your face?'

She gave him a list. 'And I've got a shoot for *Paris Elle* coming up soon.'

'And where's home?' enquired Al.

'Haywards Heath.'

'Your parents are going to miss you.'

She decided against getting into all of that now. 'Yes, but it's not all that far.'

'What made you choose this side of town, though?'

'This is the nicest place I've seen.'

'Hooray!'

'And it's nice to be high up,' she added.

'That's what I've always thought. It's very soothing to be elevated – to look out over London.'

173

It was agreed that she'd move in the following weekend. 'I'll have the room spring-cleaned for you,' he said. 'Mrs Falkirk will weave her magic.'

At the front door he shook hands with her and said, 'You will bring your parents to see us, won't you? I'm sure they'd like to know where you're living, and my cocktail cabinet's always open.'

'All right, thank you.'

She liked Al for saying that. On the way down the hill to the bus stop, she thought: This walk is soon going to be part of my life.

'Yes, well,' sighed Marjorie. 'I can see that it's probably best.'

Probably best? It was impossible to ignore the implied 'for both us'. After Al's kindly solicitude her mother's reaction came as something of a shock to Miranda.

'So you don't mind?'

'Well, naturally I'd prefer . . .' Marjorie let what she'd prefer remain unspoken. 'But in this new line of work I suppose it will be more convenient for you to be in London.'

'Yes – yes, it will be.'

There was a rather awkward pause, after which Marjorie seemed to think she should add something. 'Will you be able to afford it? I mean, afford the rent *and* have money for other things.'

'It should be fine, it's very reasonable.'

'That's the main thing.'

They were washing up the supper things, or at least Marjorie was washing up and Miranda was leaning on the draining-board holding a Happy Hastings tea-towel. She felt more flattened by her mother's apparent indifference than she would have been by opposition.

'It's nice,' she said. 'The room. I mean, it's not smart but it's a lovely big old house in a good area, right up by the Heath. You'd like it.'

Marjorie gave a short laugh intended to convey a multiplicity of meanings – scepticism, regret, doubt, envy – none of them especially positive. She rinsed a dish under the cold tap, splashing Miranda so that she took a step back.

'The landlord's really sweet,' she said, mopping at herself with the tea-towel. 'He's a writer – he lives in the ground-floor flat.'

'That's handy if you need anything doing. Is he married?'

'I don't think so. He may have been, but she's not around now.'

Her mother's mouth crimped. 'English?'

'Yes. Why?'

'I don't know . . . you hear such funny things . . .'

This was another of those odd remarks of her mother's, which was less than a warning but more than a mere observation. It implied that she suspected the worst but washed her hands of it. It left Miranda feeling not free, but confused and unprotected.

'I don't see what being English has got to do with anything.'

'I'm happier about it, that's all.'

'A lot of the tenants aren't.'

Marjorie emptied the bowl with a swoosh. 'What don't they like about him?'

'No, I mean they're not English.'

'Oh, well, it's the way of the modern world . . .'

A little later, raising her voice above Z Cars, Miranda said, 'Would you like to come and see it?'

Her mother didn't take her eyes off the screen. 'That's all right, dear, I trust you.'

Miranda thought this a bit rich, considering her mother's put-upon attitude to the modelling. 'But you don't, do you? That's the point. You don't trust me but you don't care either, so where does that leave me?'

Now Mrs Tattersall did turn towards her, eyebrows raised in an expression of pained surprise. 'I don't know how you can say that.'

'You just let things happen to you. I used to feel sorry for you, I wanted to rescue us from him – and I did – but you just sit there like a limp dishrag—'

'Mandy!'

'You're not in the least interested, in me or what I want to do. You don't even care where I live enough to come and take a look! I tell you what, the landlord was really sweet. He said I should bring my parents up to see where I was going to be. I bet he never dreamed my mother wouldn't give a toss!'

'Mandy . . .' Marjorie stubbed out her cigarette and began to cry. Miranda felt a brief stab, not of pity but of annoyance. She suspected the tears of being an escape route, a way of stopping the exchange in its tracks. Turning on the waterworks, she thought, before realising with horror that this had been an expression of her father's.

Shocked at herself, she said, with as much feeling as she could muster: 'Sorry, Mum.'

But Marjorie was already rallying. 'I do care – I worry about you all the time, I scarcely think about anything else, but what can I do?'

'I don't *want* you to worry, you mustn't worry, that's not the point. I only thought you might like to come and see where I'll be living, I don't know, so you can picture me there, so you can see Al hasn't got two heads and there aren't any rats . . .'

They laughed, grudgingly, in spite of themselves, and the awkwardness passed. But Marjorie never visited the house near the Heath and it was that conversation, rather than Miranda's actual departure a week later, which signalled their emotional separation. Gerald's leaving and the circumstances surrounding it had changed Miranda but not, it seemed, her mother. She had thought to witness a flowering, an expansion, an emergence of the real mother long suppressed by emotional tyranny, but now it appeared that Marjorie was, and probably always had been, this zestless and dispiriting person.

After the first disappointment, though, Miranda was liberated by this realisation. Once she'd got over feeling bleak and let-down, and vulnerable, she saw that here was something she no longer had to worry about. Her mother wasn't wicked, she wished her daughter well to the best of her ability, but she was emotionally lazy. That meant Miranda need not concern herself with the relationship any more. If not caring was the name of the game, she could do that too.

Dale hired a Mini van and took her and her possessions up to Khartoum Road. They spent an hour trudging back and forth up the four flights of stairs, getting progressively more out of breath. Dale made no secret of the fact that he was less enthusiastic than her.

'Does this bloke actually do anything for his money?' he asked, as he surveyed the dripping galley with its tank, oilcloth and silted-up gas rings.

'You mean Al?'

'Whatever his name is.'

'He fixes things and whatnot. I'm sure,' she added, because she was by no means sure.

Dale prodded the cracked lino. 'Not very often by the look of it.'

'It's fine! You don't have to live here.'

He went back into the bedroom. 'Is there any heating?'

She hadn't thought of this. 'I don't know – it's almost too hot up here.'

'That's attics for you – hot in summer, freezing in winter.'

'I'll get an electric fire.'

'Metered?'

She showed him. 'It takes half-crowns.'

'That'll cost you.'

'Yes, *me*, Dale, it'll cost *me*! Stop worrying about everything.'

'Somebody has to.'

This was rather sweet, and she took his arm, hugging it to her. 'I know . . . thanks, I appreciate it, honestly. But I will look after myself. And you must come and check up on me, often.'

As they went out into Khartoum Road to the van they encountered Al, striding down the road swinging a laden carrier-bag labelled Schwick's Delicatessen'.

'Hallo, my lovely, going so soon?'

'No, I just got everything moved in. Al, this is my friend Dale Harper who's been helping me all day.'

'A friend indeed.' Al held out his hand. 'Nice to meet you, Dale.'

'How do you do.'

'Care to come in for a drink, or are you dashing off?'

Dale opened the van door. 'Thanks, but I'd better get going.'

Al raised an eyebrow at Miranda. 'Can't you persuade him?'

'Yes, come on, it won't make any difference. And you ought to see Al's flat, it's gorgeous.'

Somewhat grudgingly, Dale allowed himself to be towed down the area steps, and to be bestowed – rather less grudgingly – with a glass of lager on the flowery rear patio.

'*Rus in urbe!*' exclaimed Al, leaning back in a canvas director's chair bearing his name. 'You can't beat it!'

They agreed, uncomprehendingly, that you couldn't.

'So how do you occupy yourself, Dale, when you're not helping charming young ladies move house?'

'Very boring, I'm afraid.'

'Stop! Never say that. Tell me what it is you do.'

'I'm a sort of glorified office boy.'

'You're an office manager.'

'No, I'm not.'

'I bet,' said Al, leaning forward over his glass, 'they couldn't manage without you, could they?'

'I don't—'

'Could they?'

'Well—'

'Think about it, Dale!'

'They'd certainly miss me,' Dale confessed, with a you-got-it-out-of-me smile.

'Then you're an office manager!' Al turned to Miranda. 'He'll be chairman of the board by the time he's thirty.'

They re-emerged an hour later, with Dale in a much-improved humour as he got into the van. 'I see what you mean, he's not a bad bloke.'

'He's sweet.'

'At least he didn't put his hand on my knee.'

She was mystified. 'How do you mean?'

He demonstrated from his place behind the wheel. 'Like that.'

'Okay!' She tweaked her knee away. 'But why would he?'

Dale shook his head in world-weary despair. 'And you're setting out to be a fashion model. You've led such a sheltered life, Mand.'

'I don't know what you're talking about.'

'He's queer as a three-pound note.'

Now she knew, though she did not really understand, what he meant. And she was shocked. 'But he's such a gentleman.'

'Course he is. He'll be your best friend.'

He closed the door, but she flapped at him to roll down the window.

'What?'

'Dale – don't tell my mother, will you?'

'What, about Al?'

'Yes. She thinks I'm living in a den of iniquity anyway.'

'Well, she's wrong. You may work in one, but you're safe as houses here.'

'Please.'

'Don't worry, I never see her anyway.'

When, later, Miranda came to look back on her time at the house in Khartoum Road, it was as others might on an idyllic childhood – happy, free, secure. But not, as in actual childhood, taken for granted, or powerless. She was still in that phase of her career where the work was steady and manageable – she could take on more and different jobs now that she was based in town, and the rent on her room was so far within her means that there was plenty left over for herself. It didn't take long for her to realise that she was probably the most affluent of Al's tenants. Mohan Singh worked in a clerical capacity for the Pru; Joan Marsh was a lab technician; Gay and Sally, the two jolly girls on the second floor, were secretaries, one on a women's magazine and the other at a Mercedes showroom in Piccadilly; Terry Budgit fulfilled some ill-defined role in a community centre in Kilburn; Lucien, a homesick Geordie infant teacher, occupied the ground-floor front.

And then there was Crystal.

Crystal lived in the other room on the top floor, crammed

with Miranda between the sidling pigeons, the groaning plumbing, and the damp and blackened shared cooking facilities. Whatever paid her rent occupied unsocial hours, and Miranda had been at Khartoum Road three days before encountering her.

She returned from an advertising shoot in a shed on an industrial estate in Willesden to find her neighbour making up a Betty Crocker cake mix in a bowl on top of the water tank. The empty packet, and shell of the token egg, lay on the oilskin next to her. There was a cigarette balanced on the edge of the tank, its ash teetering over the void. From the next-door from Jo Brown's 'Picture of You' warbled tinnily. The air was thick with the characteristic old-fat-and-carbon smell of the lighted gas stove, cigarette smoke, and something else that Miranda couldn't place.

Crystal glanced up briefly from her labours. 'Hi there.' Her deep voice crackled with phlegm. 'All right?' She coughed bone-shakingly; her hand trembled as she lifted the cigarette.

'Yes, thanks.' Miranda put down her bag. 'I'm Miranda.'

'That's what I assumed.'

'And you're Crystal?'

'All day.' She beat the mixture, her hand a blur; paused, frowning. 'Am I in the way?'

'No, not at all.'

'Want to put the kettle on?'

'It's okay.'

'I mean, why don't you? Shan't be long. Just get this into the oven and I'll be out of your hair.'

'Don't worry, please, take your time.'

There was water already in the kettle, so she switched it on, as much as a cover for her curiosity as for anything else.

'Mind the music?' enquired Crystal, scraping the freckled mixture into a tin.

'Of course not.'

She paused dreamily in her labours. 'I once fucked a Bruvver.'

This remark was arresting on so many levels that it effectively silenced any response Miranda might have made.

She later discovered that Crystal Madden was thirty-one, but on that first meeting she appeared like Rider Haggard's 'She', as old and alluring as time. Beneath her red sloppy joe and black skirt she had the pouchy, low-slung figure of a once-voluptuous woman now on hard times and short commons. Her hair was grey-blonde, straight and untrimmed, hanging in pointed mermaid fronds over her shoulders and down her back. Her heavy-featured face was scored with deep lines, its sensuality made harsh by exaggerated black eye makeup and thick, beige lipstick. There was a scattering of eruptions around her mouth. She had a pale skin, but her hands were thin and purplish with bitten nails, and rings on both index fingers and thumbs. On her grubby sandalled feet she wore rings on her long, bony big toes, too. Like a sexy zombie she smelt both sweet and sour, and exuded a perverse, eerie vitality.

Miranda experienced the powerful frisson of encountering someone who both drew and repelled her.

Crystal closed the oven door and came out of the galley, lighting another cigarette with the stub of the first. 'Sorry, want one?'

'It's okay, I've got my own.'

Crystal shook the crumpled packet at her. 'I should make the most of it, it doesn't happen often.'

'Thanks.'

She leaned forward to light Miranda's cigarette with hers, squashed the stub in the hearth then blew smoke in the direction of the oven. 'You can have a bit of cake when it's done.'

'Thanks.' The conversation seemed a bit one-sided so she added, 'I'm useless at cakes.'

'Me, too, angel-heart.' Crystal sank down on the divan, which clanked skeletally beneath its threadbare cushions. 'Je-sus, when will Al buy a few new sticks of furniture?'

'How long have you been here?'

'Long enough to know that he gets away with murder in this place.'

'That's because he's so nice, I suppose.'

'Nice. Nice?' Crystal tried out the word for size and found it lacking. 'I don't know about *nice*. He parades that hackneyed old lounge-lizard charm of his around the place quite effectively,

I suppose . . .' She coughed, and squinted at Miranda over her fist. 'He tells me you're a top model.'

'I'm a model who gets work.'

'I bet you do. You're very pretty. I could fancy you myself.'

Miranda didn't blink. Crystal gave a wheezy chuckle. 'Don't panic, petal, my troilism period's long gone. These days, it's just me under the covers, with a bikkie and a smutty book.'

'Good.'

'Good!' Crystal tipped her head back revealing a throat in which the bones stood out like stacked ashtrays. 'That's me put in my place. So, what kind of modelling do you do?'

'Anything, really. At the moment.'

'And where are you heading? What does it all lead to, modelling?'

'Nowhere much,' admitted Miranda, then added spiritedly, 'but the money's good.'

'And what does this money buy you? I mean,' Crystal cast a narrowed, disparaging glance at their surroundings, 'you're not exactly living high on the hog.'

'Freedom.' This had only just occurred to her, but the moment she'd said it she knew it was true. 'It buys you freedom.'

'Yes . . . doesn't it just?'

Miranda sensed that for the first time she'd struck an empathetic chord with the other woman, and was emboldened to ask a question of her own. 'What about you?'

'Oh, I mess around, you know . . . Help out a few groups, hang on to what's left of my glory days . . .' She closed her shadowed eyes for a moment, the smoke drifting past her face so that for a second it was like the vacant, ravaged face of a body on a battlefield. Then she said, 'Fuck that, I'm such a liar I can't tell the difference any more.' Miranda waited. Crystal opened her eyes and stabbed out the cigarette on the grate in front of the gas tap. 'Forget it, it's all shit. My glory days weren't that glorious and it's other people who are helping me out, not the other way round.'

Miranda pressed her advantages. 'You know Joe Brown?'

'Sure. And Elvis at the beginning. The Everleys. I knew

everyone, and they knew me. I was never as pretty as you but I could always pull 'em.'

Miranda was slightly nettled, and recognised that this was someone to whom one could speak one's mind. 'I can pull them, too. And I don't think I'm pretty. I want to be better than pretty.'

'Whatever you say, petal. But it's a distinction only a looker can make. I'm going to check the cake.'

She opened the oven door, admitting a warm blast of confused smells into the room, announced, 'Nearly there,' and returned to collapse once more on to the divan and fall asleep.

Twenty minutes later Miranda got the cake out of the oven. She ran a knife round the sides to loosen it, but was unable to prise it out of the tin, so left it standing on top of the stove. For reasons she couldn't quite explain she didn't wish to leave Crystal alone, so stood at the sink in the galley washing her smalls while the pigeons shuffled back and forth on the guttering outside the smeary window. From there she could just see the corner of the back garden and Al, in a Panama hat, attending to his border with a trowel. The Joe Brown E.P. had finished. From below came the sound of Eddie Cochrane and the chink of cups being carried across the landing. Footsteps creaked rapidly down the stairs, the front door rattled, there was a shout, a laugh . . . The house hummed with life.

She thought, I'm here. I've bought my freedom. I'm content.

CHAPTER EIGHT

Claudia, 131

For six hours Claudia waited, alone and feeling increasingly vulnerable. During those six hours there were sunshine and showers, both separately and together, accompanied by a spectacular double rainbow, and then the sky clouded over and a fretful wind made her wonder what on earth winter must be like.

She didn't know which was worse, the long periods when no one came by and she might have been the last person on earth, or the appearance of complete strangers in this strange land who might have been anyone or done anything. She was a foreign female, on her own, with no protection, no money or any means of transport. She damned the surly driver, who should never have left her, and herself for not having gone with him, when she was perfectly capable of walking any distance. Also plaguing her was the question of whether he'd come back at all, and what she would do if he didn't. Publius would be furious when she told him about this, but not half as furious as she was herself. She hated to feel so exposed and afraid. When travellers passed by she tried her best to appear purposeful, like a woman who owned the wagon and whose man might be inside it, or on some simple nearby errand.

Most of the passers-by ignored her. Once, a man in Roman dress riding on a mule came over to her as she sat on the driving-board. 'Excuse me, lady.'

She looked at him frostily without replying.

'Any idea how far it is to the coast from here?'

'It took us a full day to get this far.'

'Did it really? Oh, well. Better press on then before the next downpour.' But he made no move to go, adding, 'Taking a breather, are you?'

'That's right.'

'Think I might do the same.' He glanced around, impervious to her hostile glare. 'Not a bad spot, this.'

'No. My husband's collecting firewood.' Pretty lame but just plausible, she considered.

'Got a sound horse?'

'Yes.' She didn't enlarge on this for fear of displaying her ignorance.

'Lucky you. I'm making do with Big Ears here. Slow and uncomfortable but reliable, I'll say that.'

Claudia didn't answer. Just go away, you grinning, insinuating creep, she thought, find the coast and keep on going!

'Right. Onwards.' He turned the head of the mule back towards the path, then paused and nodded in the direction of the wagon. 'By the way, tell your husband that back axle's about to go. It's the damn mud, it puts a strain on everything.'

'He knows about it,' she lied, 'but thank you.'

'Go well.'

'And you.'

The minute he'd gone, his plump figure swaying above the mule's bony backside, Claudia considered she'd been churlish, treating the poor man like a potential criminal when he'd been trying only to be friendly.

When there was no one about, the isolation was far more disturbing than any imagined threat posed by fellow-travellers. The foreignness of her surroundings oppressed her: the capricious, ever-changing light and temperature, the whisper of the dark trees on the hillside, the creak and drip of the sodden wagon, the brackish smell of the air and the sharp calls of strange, distant birds made her jumpy. When the faulty axle gave an inch, causing the wagon to slip, she let out a shriek and felt her whole body tingle with shock.

She thought of Tasso, but without bitterness. Poor boy, dragged away from everything he knew and loved – frozen, sick, miserable and lost, driven to desperate measures. If he was still alive somewhere out there – and it seemed unlikely – his pangs of remorse would be far worse than anything she was suffering.

She knew him so well. Since childhood he'd been her playmate and her pet. There had been a time, when they'd both been less than ten years old, when they might have been said to be friends in the true and equal sense. In recent times he'd been her special servant, more of a companion, really, closer to her than any woman friend or lady's maid, sleeping at the door of her room, amusing her with his gossip, soothing her moods with his singing and playing, delighting her with his beauty. She was disappointed in his treachery, but not surprised. Though she would miss her jewellery, especially the pieces of her mother's given to her by Marianus, she would miss Tasso more. Secretly she hoped never to find him, so as to avoid the burden of having to impose some suitable punishment. Whatever a slave's special status, stealing *and* running away put him beyond the pale.

Claudia remembered well when Tasso had first arrived. She'd been tiny herself, it was one of her earliest memories. The child was one of her father's charity cases, the unwanted offspring of a house servant belonging to one of his business associates. As far as she was concerned he was a skinny, sallow cuckoo in the nest, living in the kitchen quarters where she herself most liked to spend her time, fed scraps like a kitten, passed around from hand to hand with a sort of weary amiability, tolerated and cared for because of the household's affection for Marianus. She'd been eaten up with jealousy. The sickly usurper had what she wanted – she'd have exchanged the indulgent servility with which she was treated for this rough acceptance any day.

But that state of affairs didn't last. As soon as Tasso was old enough he had to be put to work, and since she was the easiest to work for he was assigned to her. She began by bossing him about, but soon ran out of ideas for useful tasks – her needs weren't great – and used the bossiness to organise games. He was pretty, sweet and bright, well up to being anything from a horse to a general or an entertainer as the fancy took her. The understanding between them grew and when the complete equality of childhood was no longer possible she'd supposed – falsely, as it now appeared – that a special understanding still existed between them. The theft of her valuables and Tasso's disappearance proved otherwise, and yet she could not quite believe it. Wherever he was, she was sure he was suffering at least as much as her. He'd been ill, surely not in his right mind, and now he'd be roaming a strange country with not even the simplest skills, let alone the instinct for survival, like a pet songbird released from its cage, prey to the elements, to disease, to depredation from man and beast and its own kind. If it had been possible to do so Claudia would have sent him her forgiveness now, to alleviate at least some of his pain, the thought of which tortured her.

When the driver at last reappeared, leading a nodding, swaybacked farm horse, it took a considerable effort for Claudia not to fall on his neck with relief. The surly, incompetent and neglectful Briton had been elevated by her long hours alone to the status of saviour.

'. . . get going.' His mumbling way of speaking meant he might or might not have used some respectful form of address but she was disposed to give him the benefit of the doubt and summoned all her forces to greet him with ladylike composure.

'Did you have any difficulties?'

'Nothing to speak of . . .' He began harnessing the horse. 'Got lost, got robbed, got my teeth kicked in, half drowned in a flood . . . You?'

It took her a second to realise he was making some sort of joke. Responding to this unprecedented lift of mood, she said, 'Nothing, nothing at all!' before remembering that this account was no more true than his. An instinctive caution made her admit only to what he would find out anyway.

'I'm afraid my servant's gone.'

'Has he?' The driver ducked under the horse's head. 'Run off, did he?'

'He must have done, but I can't think he meant to desert me. He wasn't well last night, he was feverish.'

'Had a look round?'

'No.' Why hadn't she? 'I didn't like to leave the wagon unattended.'

The man grunted as he tightened a strap. '. . . could be lying around somewhere . . . Want me to . . . ?'

It took Claudia only a second to decide she couldn't bear to be left alone again. 'We mustn't waste any more time.'

'Right you are.'

'We might even come across him. We can ask people . . .'

He didn't reply. He had her number. Shamed by her own cowardice, she sat in silence as he completed his work with the horse and climbed, breathing sterterously, on to the driving-board.

The two brothers were in the wood, checking snares. They took long, crashing steps, trampling the tangle of low undergrowth. The older one already had three rabbits and a dormouse hanging from his belt. The younger one, well trained, followed at a respectful distance.

When they found a catch the bigger boy crouched down and finished the animal off briskly with a blow to the head before removing it and tying its back legs to the bunch at his waist. His brother watched. He was here not for amusement but to learn.

Although they were quite far in among the trees, they were still just within the band considered safe by the men of the village – the area from which you could escape quickly if you surprised something nasty. Wild pigs preferred to live and let live in peace, but those men who had got the wrong side of an angry boar had the scars to prove it and liked nothing better than to show them off to a wide-eyed audience.

Sometimes the younger boy's attention wandered. It didn't take long to lose your sense of direction among the trees and then he'd have to scamper, leaping and bounding, to catch up with his brother. He knew there'd be no heroics if he got into trouble through daydreaming. He was the youngest of six, at the bottom of the pecking order and not much use to anyone at present, as his mother frequently told him.

Once he called, in a hoarse whisper: 'Hey!'

'What is it?'

'I need a piss!'

'Have one, then.'

'Don't go too far!'

The older boy slid his back down the trunk of a tree and sat with his wrists resting on his scabby knees. The younger one hoisted his tunic and relieved himself with an exhalation of relief, eyes closed.

He opened his eyes again. Wraiths of steam curled up from where his urine had hit the ground. Beyond them, not a man's length from where he was standing, a pale, thin, figure rose ghostlike from the scrub and stood staring at him.

Paralysed, the boy gawped, one hand still resting protectively over his cock. The figure reeled, took a staggering step, reached out a trembling hand . . . The boy's jaw dropped in a silent scream. The figure took another step and uttered, its voice no more than a wheezy, broken whistle—

The boy found his voice, and let out a bellow of fear. His brother, who till then had noticed nothing, jumped to his feet, and only the tree behind him stopped both crashing to the ground as the boy cannoned into him.

'Steady on! What's up?'

The boy gibbered and pointed. 'Whoah!'

Now they both stared as the unearthly figure took another tottering step in their direction, its stained and tattered clothing catching on twigs, its face a mask of misery.

'Get away!' shouted the bigger boy. 'Get away, go on, get out of here!'

Not taking his eyes off the apparition he scrabbled with one hand for a stone and hurled it wildly, wide of the mark.

But his bravado bore results. The figure paused, wavered, made a last, desperate, gargling noise, and pitched forward on to its face on the forest floor.

*   *   *

Over the ensuing days, Claudia became of the opinion that the driver wasn't such a bad fellow after all. Since the night of the storm he had become noticeably chattier and more well disposed and she, more than ever appreciating her dependence on him, responded in kind.

He was also surprisingly sympathetic about Tasso, which did something to salve her guilt over not having searched for him.

'Bit more than a servant, was he?' he asked, as they set out one morning after a reasonably comfortable night in a way-house.

She would have been quick to detect any innuendo, but there was none.

'Yes. We've known each other since we were children. He was the only one I wanted to bring with me.'

'And now he's gone.' The driver sucked his teeth and shook his head. 'Shame . . . But you never know.'

'Whatever happens, my husband isn't likely to forgive him.'

'You have to respect that. Leaving you on your own in a strange country, not to mention the valuables. Still, he was only a lad.'

'He was. And not in the least able to look after himself.'

The driver flipped the reins. 'You'd be surprised.'

She would have let this rest, but curiosity got the better of her. 'How do you mean?'

'Nothing, lady, nothing at all. Just ways and means, you know. Smart boy, well spoken, sings a bit, got all the social graces . . .'

If there had been no innuendo before, there was now, and Claudia moved swiftly to put a stop to it.

'He's probably not even alive.'

'True. But who can say?' said the driver.

That night, only one day's drive from their destination, they stopped in a *vicus* where the British and Roman elements coexisted placidly enough without seeming to impinge on one another. The effect was curious; the clean lines of the brand-new Roman administrative and commercial buildings – the basilica, forum and surrounding arcade of stalls, small shops and food outlets – rose sharp and solid from the centre of the British settlement of round, rush-roofed huts, a firm declaration of status and intent that had not, as yet, taken root among the locals. But if the Roman buildings were not integrated neither did they appear beleaguered, and as the wagon trundled in among the British huts Claudia felt that the stares that greeted them were reserved rather than hostile.

There were a great many dogs of all shapes and sizes, far more than she'd seen before – small, bearded, yapping terriers and long, lean hunting dogs like those they'd seen on the busy port highway, sniffing at the wheels with their pointed muzzles, tails waving. There was other traffic too, mostly open carts of all sizes, and the occasional rider astride a long-maned pony, the man's feet dangling not far from the ground. In these narrow streets clogged with people and animals the driver reverted to type, brandishing his whip and snarling dire threats of which Claudia could make out the substance if not the fine detail.

The people who watched them pass were mostly of the same build and colouring as the young wife and mother who'd fed them on the first stage of their journey – tall, square-shouldered, pale-skinned and with brown or reddish hair and light eyes. She didn't yet appreciate that their appearance wasn't so different from her own and that but for her dress she might have been one of them. It was to be years before Claudia began to see the native British as distinct and individual and not simply a physically homogenous tribe.

She leaned forward to address the driver, but he couldn't hear her, so she tapped him on the shoulder. He started slightly.

'Yes?'

'I wondered where I was to sleep.'

He nodded in the direction they were going. 'Your husband's arranged a room.'

Thank you, Publius, thank you, gods.

'It's all paid for,' he added.

She considered this remark impertinent, with its suggestion that he understood her current position and wished to set her mind at rest.

'Of course,' she said crisply.

The room in question was over a fast-food shop on the forum colonnade. There was a dreamlike contradiction between the place's superficial similarity with home, and its utter foreignness.

She herself had never been in such a room in Rome, but she'd heard what they were like – Publius had been staying in one on that leave when they'd first met. This was newer, cleaner and more structurally sound than anything at home, and the terrace was only two storeys high so she was quite close to the bustle of the evening street. But once she'd parted from the driver and been taken to her lodgings, supplied with a plate of stew from the shop downstairs, it was the strangeness of her surroundings that affected her. The flat dialect Latin and the clunking inflections of the voices below, the smell rising from the plate in her hand, the sprawl of hunched and huddled thatched houses beyond the window – and the cold. A wind had got up and tiredness had tightened her joints so she shivered uncontrollably. She hadn't thought to ask whether there were baths nearby but even had it been appropriate she would have been too nervous to use them. She tried to imagine what the older officer's wife, the one who'd befriended her on the crossing, would have done: asked for what she wanted, no doubt, and got it. But who would she ask? Even some warm water would have been nice. The bland and fibrous stew went some way towards reviving her, but she didn't digest it properly and her stomach ached and complained. She needed sleep, and longed for it, but was fighting it, unable to relax for an instant. She was more jumpy here than when left alone in the wooded valley. There at least she was able to see anyone coming. Here she was surrounded by people all of whom were at best an unknown quantity, at worst hostile. It was not yet dark this far north, the light out of keeping with the temperature. She tried closing her eyes and felt panicky, as though blindfolded, stripped of a sense that she needed to protect herself.

She changed her clothes, wrapped herself in her cloak, and lay down on the narrow bed, prepared for a long night. Despite her exhaustion she took comfort from the fact that her husband had arranged this accommodation for her. She had at last crossed the no man's land between leaving her home and becoming part of his. It was his influence and protection that now stretched out to meet her, his care that she was under, no matter what the distance that divided them.

Ubi tu Publius, ego Publia . . .

The knock on the door made her jump, and she sat bolt upright, her skin prickling with apprehension. 'What is it?'

'Someone downstairs for you.' It was the wife of the stew-cook from the shop below.

'Who?'

There was no answer. The woman's footsteps clopped away.

Claudia debated with herself. Whoever it was, there would be other people around, and since she couldn't sleep anyway, some diversion would be welcome.

Her visitor was a shy, smooth-cheeked young official, prob-ably fresh from home like herself, despatched to see that she was all right.

'Tertius Favilus,' he introduced himself. 'Publius Roscius asked me to look out for you. I heard you had arrived and wondered if there was anything else you needed.'

'Sleep,' she said. Rather charmingly he blushed and she realised that this might have seemed like a criticism. 'But I do appreciate your concern.'

'Has the journey been good so far? As good as can be expected?'

This, she realised, was her opportunity to be frank. 'I didn't know what to expect. It's been long, and uncomfortable and expensive,' his blush deepened, 'because I lost my money and jewellery since arriving in this country.'

'But how awful for you. How did that happen?'

They were standing somewhat awkwardly at the back of the shop, with the business of the evening going on around them. Claudia said, 'I wonder if we could walk a little way?'

'Of course.'

He indicated which way they should go and fell into step on the street side of her.

'So – um – how unfortunate . . . I'm sure your husband

193

would want me to supply you with money for what's left of the journey.'

'Thank you. A little would be a comfort, I must say.'

'Of course, of course! But your jewellery is irreplaceable.'

'Yes.'

'You simply became parted from it?'

Tactful though he was, Claudia still shied away from telling him the truth. He was so keen and fresh and eager to please. The mere mention of thieving, let alone by a slave, might send him into administrative overdrive.

'I stupidly left it unattended in a town where we stopped, and when I came back, it was gone. Completely my own fault. The box may even have been picked up with other things by mistake.'

She sensed him weighing this up, deciding whether to be assertive or accepting. But she'd had her best Roman matron voice in play, and he decided on the latter.

'The jewellery must be distinctive,' he ventured. 'It may even be found.'

'I don't expect so,' she said, and added firmly, 'I take full responsibility.'

They were walking round the perimeter of the forum. It was gathering dusk now, with a nipping breeze that made the orange glow of lamps and cooking fires pulse unsteadily. There was the pervasive smell of smoke, and moisture – sodden cloth, damp thatch, the brackish odour of wet ground and sewage.

'Where do you live?' she asked.

'I have quarters on the other side. Not as smart as yours, pretty rough and ready, in fact. This is a brand-new development.'

'But there's a full administration here?'

'Not at present.' He looked rueful. 'You're looking at it.'

So they really were alone. She had to remind herself that all these people, whatever their differences, were Romans; that she should feel as at home here as anywhere else in the Empire; that Roman rule in Britain was successful and benign, free of violence since the rebellion a hundred years ago.

They came round to the north of the forum where there were fewer British homesteads. Tertius paused, to let her take in the view. He said, almost gently, 'North. Where you're going.'

Claudia stared. Away from the man-made lights it was still only twilight, the sky to the west washed by the setting sun's afterglow, and above them a frail sickle moon lying on its back. A single star shone, infinitely more distant but brighter than both.

But it was the land that silenced her. Beyond the colonnade and the road it spread before them like a grey sea, wave on wave of bleak hills, empty and still, rolling away to blend with the darkening horizon.

'How far . . . ?' she began, but her voice was a hoarse whisper. She cleared her throat and spoke again, with a more businesslike emphasis: 'How long should it take us?'

'A day, given the conditions. Two at most. Beyond the garrison,' he shrugged, 'more of the same.'

They walked on. Claudia kept her cloak wrapped tight around her, to disguise a shivering that was due not only to cold. Tertius, on the other hand, seemed to expand; he was taking a young man's pride in being the one in the know. 'Britain's not such a bad posting – it doesn't deserve the reputation it has at home. The people are mostly fine, and where I was before, further south, you could almost be in Rome. Weather apart.'

Right on cue she felt a handful of small raindrops on her face. 'What must it be like in winter?'

'Plenty of time before that's under way. And you'll find you learn to appreciate the sunshine more.'

Suddenly, Claudia was overwhelmed. She was glad of the soft rain, because tears of self-pity, shaming and unwilled, stung her eyes. To his credit, Tertius seemed to sense her mood, or at least realised that he had been too cavalier, for he added courteously, 'You must be tired. I'll take you back through the forum.'

The centre of the forum was not yet finished, still unoccupied and echoing. She sniffed – you could smell the building materials, sharp and raw, the fingerprint of Rome on the foreign air.

'How long before there are other people here?' she asked. 'I mean, a full administration.'

'Actually I was exaggerating slightly. They come and go all the time, sometimes the place is swarming with officials and contractors. And there are several good-looking villas outside town where the powers that be live. But they needed someone to be on site all the time while the work's being completed, and I drew the short straw.'

She asked directly, 'Are you lonely? Or just bored?'

'Fortunately I'm too busy for either. My day's one long round of petty management niggles and low-level diplomacy. When I next see my family, I shall take the domestic squabbling in my stride, believe me.'

She laughed. They were walking past the tall frontage of the basilica; she felt its solidity like a sheltering wing.

Tertius adopted an official tone again. 'Has the accommodation *en route* been satisfactory?'

It was an all-or-nothing question, and she didn't wish to add to his burdens. 'It's been fine. Some places better than others, but I wasn't expecting luxury.'

'And the room here is all right?'

'Perfectly. It's clean and the food was fine.'

'Good.'

They emerged from the forum, within a short distance from where they'd started. Real darkness had now fallen. A boy appeared, with an inexpertly assembled torch of twigs, emitting a small light and a great deal of smoke. 'Where to?' he asked.

'Up here.' Tertius pointed. 'The stew shop.'

'Follow me.'

'Keep your distance, the lady doesn't want to be asphyxiated.'

'Gotcher.'

'It's all right,' said Claudia.

'Not entirely his fault,' explained Tertius. 'The material's usually damp.'

When they reached the food-seller's he gave the boy a coin, saying, 'I'll make it up to you next time,' getting an openly rebellious glare in return.

'They think they should get the same whether it's a mile or a few yards,' he confided.

This exchange reminded Claudia of something. 'I wonder – should I report the loss of my valuables? And if so, who to?'

'Tell your husband when you arrive there, and he can pass the information on. There's no one here at the moment who could be much use to you. Was there anything particularly distinctive?'

'Some jewellery that was my mother's. One necklace in particular. It was gold with freshwater pearls, and a pendant with a woman's head engraved on it.'

'Your mother's portrait?'

'I think it was, but my father said it didn't do her justice and it could have been anyone – but it's very unusual, and would stand out anywhere.'

'I'll spread the word. Though I have to say,' he shook his head, 'that the chances of it turning up are pretty slim.'

'I accept that.'

'And you can't remember where you might have left it – at what stage in the journey?'

This time she didn't hesitate. 'No. But I know I had everything three days ago, because I checked.'

'We'll do our best. I hope everything goes smoothly from here, and that you arrive safe and sound.'

'Thank you.'

Just as he left, three drunks rolled up at the food counter. The proprietor and his wife, veterans of street commerce, squared up to them, the man exposing massive arms below rolled-up sleeves, his good lady holding a ladle the size of a hacking-sword.

But the drunks, though noisy, weren't looking for trouble. There was a lot of rowdy argy-bargy about who had the money to pay, accompanied by some amiable pushing and shoving, while the food-sellers looked on, stone-faced.

One of the men was familiar, and Claudia realised it was the driver. Instinctively she took a step back into the shadows of the hallway so she could observe him in this new light. With his hood thrown right back over his big shoulders, his hair standing on end and his face shiny with drink and bonhomie he seemed a different person, expanded in every way.

The pointless joshing about payment ended when one of the others, emphasising a point with his beefy fist, missed the counter and brought his hand down with a splash and a hiss into the boiling stew. His howls of pain were drowned by his friends' bellows of unsympathetic laughter.

At this point the proprietor, unamused, intervened: 'I'm charging you for that. So unless you want to pay full whack just for making a mess and spoiling my food you'd better order smartish.'

'All right, all right!' This was the driver. 'I'm in the chair. We'll have three portions of your finest and whatever you want for the inconvenience. Stop that racket, Col. Haven't you caused enough trouble already? You'll frighten the lady.'

Claudia knew it must be the shopkeeper's wife he was referring to, but the remark still made her jump. The driver's expansive behaviour shouldn't have come as a surprise: what else would he do on a night off but eat, drink and be merry? And yet it was a shock. She had believed she had his measure, and the balance between them, but she'd been wrong. As he and his friends took charge of their bowls of stew she realised he was younger, more volatile, altogether less predictable than she'd given him credit for.

He slapped the money down on the counter with a showy instruction to keep the change. For a split second, as he turned away, his bright unfocused eyes and self-satisfied grin seemed to flash over Claudia like a torch. She flinched, but he hadn't seen her.

She went to bed, this time to fall asleep at once. And had a dream in which she walked north, completely alone and carrying nothing, to a point where she stood on the crest of one of those broad hills and saw, as she turned a full circle, that there was no building or settlement anywhere, and that even the rough road she'd travelled had disappeared.

Next morning the wagon was beneath her window at the agreed time. It was the sort of of still, overcast day she was beginning to think of as peculiarly British – dour, secretive weather that kept you guessing about whatever it had up its sleeve: it would be too much to hope it would stay like this.

In keeping with conditions, and what must have been a raging hangover, the driver had reverted to his workaday self with a vengeance. He hauled her possessions aboard with wordless ill-grace, coughed and spat till he threw up, and walloped the wretched horse before it had had a chance to take a step.

Because she wouldn't have to put up with him much longer, Claudia couldn't resist teasing him a little. 'Did you manage to get a good night's sleep last night?'

'Not bad.'

'Where will you go when you've delivered me?'

'Back south.'

'Do you have a family there?'

'Wife . . . three kids.'

'They must miss you when you do these long-haul jobs.'

He sighed heavily, worn out by the interrogation, but she caught the words '. . . see the back of me.'

'On the return journey,' she said brightly, 'you must be sure to ask around for my jewellery. There'll definitely be a reward for anyone who finds it.'

'Hm . . .'

She left him in peace. A watery sun was coming out and long pale shafts of light penetrated the clouds and played over the heathy slopes all around them. Now that they were travelling through the landscape towards their objective it seemed less daunting. Here and there they passed small settlements and a handful of locals, mostly children, would come out and stare at them. Sometimes someone would wave and she'd wave back, sending the children scampering and shrieking in an ecstasy of embarrassed delight.

In the soft, changeable light she thought she might have imagined something on the horizon.

'What's that?' she asked, pointing.

'That's it,' said the driver, sounding more animated than he had all day. 'That's where we're going.'

★　　　★　　　★

She only wanted to see Publius. She was full of a nervous, passionate longing that superseded any reaction she might have had to the crowded clamour of the garrison. Recent experience had shown that people were not always what they seemed. In this, his work context, the place and occupation which had formed his mature years, would her husband show a side of himself that she had never seen before? Would he be utterly different, a stranger whom she would have to learn to know all over again? And would she want to?

Would he be pleased to see her?

The long journey, like the road in her dreams, seemed to roll itself up behind her, leaving just the here and now. It was hard to accept that she would be staying here, that this would be her home. Her mind was behaving as her legs had done after the sea voyage, continuing to move restlessly to a different rhythm.

His quarters were in the very heart of the garrison. They passed the bath-house and the gymnasium and drove at one point along the side of a long, blind wall, which she took to be barracks or stabling for horses. She had got used to the relative quiet of the open road, and the bustle and din of the narrow streets overwhelmed her.

The driver was more cheerful by the second. 'This is more like it, eh?'

'It's busy!' she shouted.

'Course it is! Frontier town, isn't it? Edge of the Empire. It's all happening here!'

Ubi tu Publius, ego Publia sum.

She'd imagined naïvely that he'd be waiting for her, but of course he wasn't. At the door of the residence a couple of slaves met them and helped the driver unload her baggage before disappearing with it.

She pulled herself together. 'Will you wait here? I'll see you are paid.'

'Don't worry, lady.' He pushed his hood back and there

was the shock-headed, ruddy-faced roisterer of last night, the severely bloodshot eyes attesting to the good time had by all. 'It's taken care of. My boss gets the money and I get my money from him.'

'If you're sure.'

'I'm sure.' He climbed back on to the driving-board. 'Cheerio, lady. Good luck.'

'Thank you,' she said, with feeling. 'And you.'

One of the slaves, a middle-aged woman, had returned to her side.

'I'll show you to the commandant's room.'

The house was recognisably Roman in design, but again there was that indefinable something. On the walls of the atrium Claudia noticed that the frescoes dealt with subjects which would have seemed outdated in Rome, scenes based on nostalgia, an idealised picture of the old country, full of picnics and frolicking animals and improbably overflowing amphorae of dark purple wine. It was the old urban-Roman obsession with country squiredom, with getting back to nature and leading a wholesome outdoor life. Whereas now – she didn't want to dwell on it – the great chilly outdoors stretched in all directions, there for the taking, calling their southerners' bluff.

The slave tapped on a door and for the first time in months Claudia heard his voice, rising peremptorily: 'Come!'

The woman pushed open the door and nodded her through, closing it behind her.

She was met by what seemed a sea of faces, all male. For a second she couldn't even make out Publius – her eyes scanned them all and her heart pattered uncertainly. She was wrongfooted and in response her mouth set and her chin rose haughtily. Two of the men who were seated pushed their chairs back with a scraping sound and got to their feet. As they did so Publius came forward.

She wanted to fall against him like a child, but it was out of the question. He seemed smaller than she remembered, shorter than the other men, but still more of a presence. She felt the bound strength of him thud against her even before he took

her hand in both of his and said her name. 'Welcome, Claudia.'
He lowered his voice. 'Darling wife.'

She found herself unable to speak. Over his shoulder she saw that the other men had turned away discreetly and were consulting papers on the table, although the room vibrated with their curiosity. In the narrow private space between them, the tiny distance that still remained for her to travel, he lifted her hand to his mouth and pressed it there, warm and open as his eyes momentarily closed.

She still hadn't spoken as he stepped back.

'I've got to finish some business here – it won't take us long, will it, gentlemen?' They smiled and shook their heads understandingly. 'Severina will show you and Tasso to your rooms – what is it?'

'Tasso isn't with me.' She glanced quickly at the others to show him it was private. 'I'll tell you later.'

'As you wish. I shan't be long.'

The female slave, who'd been standing by the door during this exchange, opened it and beckoned her through. When it closed behind her she heard Publius' voice, continuing where it had left off, conducting the military business of the province, and she smarted with disappointment and jealousy.

Her room, adjoining his, was large and nicely furnished with comfortable, solid pieces. There was a reddish fur thrown over the bed, and a sconce with a rush light burning before the statuette of a broad-faced British Minerva with braided hair. Someone had put her clothes into a chest and thoughtfully left the lid open so she could see where they were. Her hairbrush and pewter mirror were on a table. Beside them was a tray with a jug, a beaker, and a plate with some some small cakes. And, oh, joy! There was a squat, black peat-burning brazier in one corner that gave a cosy red glow and the impression at least of warmth. She went to stand by it and opened her hands. She mustn't begin by being angry and resentful. She wouldn't let their first conversation be one of whining and complaint on her part. If she allowed the demands of his work to upset her on the very first evening, what sort of precedent would that set? She missed Tasso, who would have understood her without words.

'Madam?' Severina had laid hands on her cloak and was pulling it gently, inviting her to take it off. 'Would you like to change? I can have these washed for you by this time tomorrow.'

'Thank you.'

With an air of dignity she did not feel she submitted to being undressed, and dressed again. Exhaustedly she craved the warm and thoughtless intimacy of Publius' embrace. Responding to a light pressure on her shoulder she sat down for her hair to be brushed.

'Not long,' said Severina.

The woman's eyes were downcast as she teased out tangles. Claudia wasn't sure what had been meant but heard the kindness in her voice.

With an effort she kept her own voice under control. 'Thank you.'

'It's my job.'

'I'm not usually so helpless.'

'You don't have to be helpless to be helped.'

'No.'

'You've come a great distance, haven't you?' It was a reflection rather than a question. 'We expected you to have a servant with you.'

'I did – he was taken ill and we had to leave him at a village in the south.'

'There.' Severina lowered the brush. 'Can I put it up for you?'

'No. Thank you. It's nice to feel it loose for once.'

'I'll take you to the bath-house tomorrow.'

'That would be wonderful.'

Severina put the brush down and ran her palms over the long hair. Claudia could feel the calloused skin of her palms catching on curls.

'And perhaps – if my husband's busy – you'll show me around the house, introduce me, so I can be of use.'

'Course I will. Here,' she picked up the jug and poured some brownish liquid into the beaker, 'have some of this. And these.' She gave the plate of cakes a push and said again, 'Not long.'

*   *   *

203

It wasn't that long. Probably no more than half an hour. But when the door opened and Publius came in she realised that it had been just exactly as long as she could bear.

This time he didn't come straight to her. She rose from where she'd been sitting and he opened his arms, wide and strong, like the eagle. It was a gesture both of offering and invitation. Here I am. Come to me.

She went, and was enfolded. Their heads, blinded with love, sought and found a kiss. I'm home, she thought. This is my home now.

CHAPTER NINE

————◆◆◆————

Bobby, 1992

Weeks passed, and months. If my life had been one of those old black-and-white films newspaper headlines would have whirled and flashed. House takes shape! Stranger gets acquainted with locals! Lone woman finds job!

And I started occasionally to 'see' Daniel Mather.

Interesting expression, that. Are you seeing each other? I suppose people mean what used to be called dating, but it could mean something else, too: that you're getting past the social smokescreen, the fencing, the showing-off or the reserve, and becoming attuned to one another. Or, conversely, that the scales are falling from your eyes and it's going to be over before it's begun.

With me and Daniel it was the former. It was all very circumspect – a neighbourly visit here, a drink there, week-end walks, lunch at the pub. For our respective different reasons neither of us had many friends in the village, he I suspected through inclination, I because I hadn't yet had the time or energy to cultivate them. We got on well, his reticence dovetailing with my polite sociability. We respected each other's space, is what my sister-in-law would have said.

And while we're on 'seeing', he had never uttered those words made famous on page and screen, 'I'd really like to see you again', which we all understand to mean, 'I fancy you rotten and want to sleep with you at the first available opportunity.' That sort of seeing hadn't really come into it.

Which was fine, as far as I was concerned. In fact, I was relieved. The years of being on my own and not having to pay much attention to appearances had taken their toll on the fine detail of self-presentation. I was in no hurry to expose my untoned, forty-something flesh to close male scrutiny. I was going to have to be very drunk, I told myself – that or completely overwhelmed – to get into bed with anyone. I vaguely hoped it would be the latter, without really asking myself whether *I* fancied *him*. In spite of my so-called independent ways I was light years away from being what Sally would have called 'in touch with my own needs'. Mine was a good old-fashioned pre-feminist sensibility.

Daniel rarely commented on my appearance. Whether this was because he didn't notice, or didn't care, or because he belonged to the say-nice-or-say-nothing school of observation, I didn't know. It was certainly restful. He took me as he found me.

The first time I went to his house I got a shock. It was half of a converted mill, but only in the sense that a loft in Wapping is a warehouse. It was empty, and monochrome. The living room was on the first floor, to accommodate the mill wheel, which could be seen through a glass panel in the blond wood floor. A rush mat here, a stainless-steel lamp there, beautiful, simple beechwood chairs and table that he'd made himself. The gas fireplace (no messy fuel) was a great black cast-iron wok, like the dish that holds the Olympic flame. There were no mirrors – not only was this a space that needed no artificial opening up but its occupant was without personal vanity. There were two enormous pictures, if you could call them that, mind-blowing expanses of minute wavy lines, black on white. It was also a controlled environment, insulated, draught-free, a giant pod: not lavish or luxurious, but high-concept.

Even his ground-floor workshop, built into the space next to the mill wheel, was relatively empty, containing only his tools and the single piece he was working on, a bookcase.

'Not tidiness,' he explained, as if excusing himself. 'I can only focus on one thing at a time.'

I suggested that maybe it was the other way round, that this might explain his lack of acquisitiveness.

He agreed. 'And my overdraft.'

He had, he told me, done most of the conversion himself. But it was still odd to see him in it, he of the scruffy clothes and ramshackle Mini. Dan Mather might have had the house but he didn't walk the walk, or talk the talk. There wasn't a pretentious bone in his body.

'Gosh,' I said, like the up-country hick in Manhattan, clasping her straw hat to the back of her head, 'it's not what I expected.'

'No?' He was making instant coffee in the white and Scandinavian slate kitchen. 'Why's that?'

I sidestepped the question. 'It makes me realise I don't know you at all.'

He put the coffee mugs on a tray and carried it through. 'There's no mystery. It isn't complicated. This is what I like.'

'You're so tidy.'

'I don't own much.'

I sighed. 'I envy you that, in a way. The lack of clutter. But I suspect that even if I wanted this more than anything in the world I could never achieve it.'

'There's no trick,' he said. 'You just leave things out.'

There was no point in arguing: he'd pinpointed one of the things that divides the human race in two.

'And anyway,' he added matter-of-factly, 'you don't particularly like it.'

Rumbled, I hesitated. 'I admire it.'

'Perhaps . . .' he began, though I was beginning to know that his diffidence was in manner only, not mind. 'Perhaps we envy things we want, that we feel we could have, and admire those we're happy to let go.'

This sounded so perfect that I very nearly didn't argue with him. But something prompted me to say, 'What about beauty?'

'You mean, in people?'

'Yes. We can't make ourselves beautiful, we have to make do with what we are. But women envy beautiful women.'

'They shouldn't.'

'What, because it's such a burden being gorgeous, no one likes you for who you are, no one falls for your mind, everyone's too bowled over to see the real you?' I realised I sounded sour, and laughed to show it was a joke. 'Too frightful!'

He didn't join in with my laugh. In fact, he wore his blushing look as he said, 'Just because that point's become a cliché doesn't mean it's not true.'

Soon after that, when we were taking a Sunday walk along the bustling, icy stream that was the eponymous Wither, I asked him how he knew Miranda.

'Everyone here knows the Montcleres. Like they know the pub.'

'But you were at the funeral,' I said.

'So was everyone,' he pointed out. 'So were you, and you'd only just arrived.'

There was something slightly defensive in his manner as if I'd accused him of something. 'That's true.'

'And you were at school with her,' he added.

'Yes.'

'Is she amazed at the coincidence?'

My turn to blush. 'I still haven't said hallo.'

To my relief he expressed no surprise at this, but frowned in agreement. 'It's difficult, isn't it?'

I appreciated his understanding, but did not then realise why he understood.

I might have given a false impression to Daniel. I had never envied Miranda, though others did. I envied those few who were close to her; and those who had been, and who might be. I wanted to be one of them. And now, after all this time and in only the simplest geographical sense, I was.

In the weeks following the funeral I often considered ringing, or even driving up to Ladycross and introducing myself, expressing my sympathy in person as any normal old acquaintance would. But I didn't, and the longer I left it the harder it became. I saw her a few times, fleetingly, either barrelling along in a four-wheel drive or in circumstances where, I told myself, it would have been inappropriate to approach her – having a drink with friends in the pub, or going into church.

This last surprised me, rather, and I wondered whether church attendance was a concomitant of marrying into the aristocracy: that it went – literally since the church was on Ladycross land – with the territory. She had never struck me as the religious sort. I certainly wasn't, and I had sufficient scruples not to manufacture a personal Road to Damascus in order to bump into her. In the end, I didn't need to. The opportunity was handed to me on a plate.

The job came my way via my neighbours, the ones I'd heard dining in their garden on my first evening. The Hobdays were an extremely nice, very sorted couple who, following Chris's redundancy, had set up their own independent desktop publishing company. This had started, they told me, in their conservatory, but had become sufficiently successful a year ago for them to rent an office unit in one of the converted barns on the Ladycross estate. Their expansion had persuaded them that they could now do with 'a third leg', as Kirsty put it. She wasn't sure of the job description but something that required the skills of an office manager with the sympathies of an agony aunt.

I'd been invited round to supper with them early on, and was returning the compliment. The Greek lamb had been one of my better ones, and we'd all had a few, so I was emboldened to say, 'I could do that for you.'

To their credit they didn't appear in the least taken aback. 'But, Bobby,' said Kirsty, 'you hardly know us.'

'Snap her up quick before she does,' suggested Chris. 'Though I must warn you that we have nothing to offer but blood, sweat and tears.'

'And the money's pathetic,' added his wife.

'I have simple tastes.'

'The woman's not right,' said Chris. 'Sign her.'

Though the Hobdays might have been a bit pissed that evening, they were shrewd enough when sober not to be bounced into any rash decisions. They sent me a nice note thanking me for dinner and didn't mention the job again for three weeks, by which time they'd had a chance to discuss me, and it, properly. Then they invited me into the office, questioned me discreetly about my experience and qualifications (which didn't take long), showed me what was involved, and suggested I start the following Monday. We agreed on a trial period of six weeks and no hard feelings if it didn't work out – we were neighbours, after all.

I was getting closer.

In theory I worked for the Hobdays at Smart Cards Monday to Friday from nine to five. But the reality was an informal flexitime, negotiable on a daily basis. We were lucky in each other, because their loose, democratic style of management would have sent many people up the wall, and at this stage in my life I couldn't have stood dictatorial employers. There were days when I was in the office at eight, glued to the computer and the phone till the same time at night; others where I would be deputed to drive late orders to Carlisle, Newcastle or Hull; and some where Kirsty would simply ask me to stay in for the plumber, or proof-read, or mind their elderly dog, Mutley, when he was indisposed. But the unpredictability of the work was what I liked about it. 'Multi-tasking', I suppose it would now be called: what women are supposed to be good at, and which Peggy Lee extolled in her immortal song. And the money, Chris's comments notwithstanding, was perfectly okay.

Jim and Sally, when I rang to tell them, were massively impressed.

'Quick work or what!' my brother exclaimed. 'You don't waste any time, sis.'

'I can't take any credit, it fell into my lap.'

'So can we come up and see you? There's a housewarming present in it.'

'Soon,' I said. 'I'm not straight yet.'

The house was fine, but I allowed him to think that was what I meant. The truth was that, fond though I was of my relations, I wanted to keep my new life to myself for a while. Once Jim and Sally had invaded and inspected it, it would no longer be entirely mine, but one more outpost of the family empire, an occasional weekend destination, a place that existed in their minds too, however peripherally: colonised and appropriated.

It was odd that in putting a physical distance between myself and the area where I'd always lived I gained a perspective on the past, too. One of the many uses of the job at Smart Cards was that it enabled me to sidestep the snug but stifling embrace of village life. I had somewhere to go, a routine of my own. And plenty of time to think.

One of the things I thought about was Alan. We were still on reasonable terms (so far as I knew, we didn't have much contact) and I'd debated whether to send him and Louise a change-of-address card. In the end I hadn't. After all, why would he want to know where I was? It was all done and dusted between us, and there were no children to be considered. Alan was fine: he'd moved on before we even separated! It was my own guilt that prodded me from time to time. Guilt over something that hadn't been in my power to avoid — that I'd never been in love.

It's all very well to say that what you've never had you don't miss, but you can still yearn for it. Some women who can't have children are sick with longing for a baby. It's primal, biological. And as the years had gone by and I realised that I had never loved, not properly, I was desolate. That was why I couldn't blame Alan the way my feistier girlfriends, such as Spud, urged me to do. 'Throw your toys about!' she'd urged. 'Get angry, you're entitled!' But I wasn't angry, that was the trouble. If the price of love was jealousy, my heart was cheap to run.

Maybe it didn't matter. Maybe, I told myself, contentment and self-sufficiency were just as well worth having as the capacity for passion. I had friends, and family (both at a safe distance), and a new life to go with my new house. But then I'd looked at that picture of Miranda and her husband, and seen her face as she walked in the woods, and as she returned to the shelter of the house from the sunlit celebrations of his lost life – and I knew, beyond all doubt, that I was missing something.

And underlying all this was the stark, brutal fact: that I was the woman who'd given her baby away.

I'd been in my last year at college and wanted only to be shot of it. Her. I didn't even look. She went from between my legs to another woman's arms without a touch or a glance. It had been a copybook delivery, swift and stitchless, but they kept me in for the obligatory five days because they said I needed rest. Needed, but didn't get. I wanted to escape. I couldn't stand the idea that she might still be in the hospital somewhere, that the adoptive parents might change their minds and send her back. For months afterwards I had a recurring nightmare in which the baby returned, still blood- and mucus-stained, whimpering and slithering like the son in *The Monkey's Paw*, to scrabble at my door and demand my care . . .

Not a soul knew, or found out. I went to a great deal of trouble to ensure that they wouldn't, and I was also lucky that she was born in the summer. I dieted and wore disguising but non-maternity clothes and told my parents I was going travelling with a girlfriend for a month as soon as finals were over. You can do anything, I discovered, if you're highly motivated enough.

The hardest part was just afterwards when I was back, alone, at the house I had shared during term with other students. The objective had been achieved, but my body wilfully refused to celebrate. It moved to a different and more visceral drum. It mourned and bled and cramped and produced milk, determined to punish me. But I didn't give in to it. I stuck it out. Within a fortnight I was back to normal.

And was I ever normal! I embraced normality with the fervour of the born-again. The relief was balm, the ordinariness of life as a non-pregnant student was very heaven. That, I thought now, was when I lost the love-gene. It was a messy old thing and I'd successfully excised it. The baby had never been mine, but his, the lustful lab assistant who'd put it there. I never felt anything but invaded and only went to term because, in spite of everything else, I chose priggishly to see abortion as murder.

No wonder I was so easily pleased in marriage. I just wanted to be part of the mainstream, to swim with the tide, not to shoot any scary emotional rapids. And in that I'd succeeded triumphantly, even to the point of letting my husband go without a murmur.

I was becalmed. But the white water was out there.

What happened was that Miranda came into the office. Smart Cards produced a line of blank-for-your-own-message cards using old photographs – family groups, lowlife studies and studio engagement portraits, that kind of thing, from before the Great War – and Ladycross stocked some of these in the tourist shop.

I was on my own there – the Hobdays had gone to a trade fair in Leeds – and she just walked in in her flat cap and wellies, leaving some dogs outside, and came up to the desk. 'Good morning, I'm sorry to disturb you but Kirsty said she had a new brochure I could look at?'

'Yes, we do – hang on, I'll get it for you.'

I fetched the brochure and handed it over. Her long hands were immaculately french-manicured; the left wore a plain wedding ring, the right a rough-cut diamond the size of a small walnut. This hand she now held out. 'I do apologise, I'm Miranda Montclere.' She narrowed her eyes, smiling speculatively, sensing something. 'We haven't *met*, have we?'

The moment of truth. 'Actually,' I said, 'we have. You won't remember me, but we were at school together, years ago.'

'Lord, no, really?' She removed the cap as if to see me better. Everything she did had a natural grace, was how things ought to be done in a perfect world. Her face, now so well known to so many, had scarcely changed except for a softening of the eyes, a light gauze of wisdom. As far as I could tell she wore no makeup apart from the high gloss of her own beauty and fame.

'I'm sorry,' she said, still smiling. 'You're going to have to help me out.'

'Roberta Govan. I was a few years below you—'

'Yes!' Her face lit up, she snapped her fingers. 'Bobby – didn't they used to call you that?'

My cup ran over. 'That's right.'

'How extraordinary! A fellow survivor of the salt mines!' She leaned across the desk, clasped my shoulders and kissed me on either cheek, laughing. 'God, how I hated that place.'

'Me too,' I lied. I hadn't hated it, I'd fitted in fine. 'Our parents had no idea.'

'You were in the sick room that very day . . .' She was still gazing at me, smiling, shaking her head in disbelief. 'I left under what they used to call a cloud. Do you remember that? Or perhaps you didn't even know.'

Didn't know? Didn't *know*? 'I think we all knew. It was terribly exciting.'

'That nasty, sad old woman was simply waiting for her opportunity, and didn't I just give it to her, in spades!'

'You did, rather. But look what happened,' I added. 'You made her eat crow.'

She seemed genuinely puzzled. 'How do you mean?'

'Well – fame, glamour, riches. Expulsion from Queen's and exposure in *Harper's*. The Lady Stratton – she must have been spitting feathers.'

Miranda considered this, although I couldn't believe it hadn't occurred to her before. 'Yes, I suppose so. Certain things did happen as a result . . . And if they hadn't, I might not have met Fred.'

She hadn't meant it as a reminder, but I was stricken at my own levity. 'I'm so terribly sorry about that, Miranda. The funeral was the day after I moved here.'

'Really?' She gave me a sweet, absent smile, distracted momentarily by what was in her mind's eye, and then refocused. 'So where are you?' she asked, and when I told her: 'I think that was the one Dan Mather did up, wasn't it?'

'Yes, he knocked on my door to tell me.'

'Pleased as punch, I bet. Do you like it?

'I love it, it suits me perfectly.'

'Look, Bobby.' She slapped the rolled-up brochure briskly in her palm. 'It would be so nice to catch up. Are you in the book?'

'Not yet.'

'Well, anyway, what the hell? I know where you are. Let's arrange something, soon.'

'We must.'

'Nothing more certain. Give my love to Kirsty and Peter. *Au revoir.*'

''Bye.'

She put the hat back on and left. Through the window I saw her striding away with a couple of black and white springer spaniels exuberantly orbiting her boots. I sat there, feeling as though some exotic foreign wind, strong but warm and benign, had picked me up, spun me round and left me dizzy in its wake.

There were two consequences of this that surprised me. One was an omission: she didn't tell anyone. Neither the Hobdays nor Dan, when I next saw him, mentioned it, so I didn't either. From this I deduced that Miranda's silence was not, like mine, an indication of the importance of this meeting, but quite the reverse: it had been a small and pleasing coincidence, not specially noteworthy in her high-octane life.

So the other surprise was especially pleasant. She rang up. I hadn't really expected her to, and she must have known that I wouldn't make the call myself.

'I got your number from the Hobnobs, I hope you don't mind.'

'No – no, not at all.'

'I'd have rung sooner only I've been a bit low.'

'Of course . . .'

'I've realised grief's like malaria, Bobby, it's in your system long after you think you've come to terms with it, ready to ambush you. But heaps better now, so I thought, I'll ring Bobby and we can chew over old times, spit them out and catch up on the rest. How about it? Would you like to come in for a drink one evening this week – you could come straight from work, save fannying about?'

'Sounds lovely.'

'Tuesday? Five-ish, or whenever you knock off.'

'Fine.'

'Magic. Back door, and don't mind the dogs.'

'I'm so glad,' said Kirsty to me. 'That girl needs all the nice women friends she can get.'

'Because the blue bloods,' added Peter darkly, 'will be circling like vultures.'

There was a bottle of *cava* and Waterford flutes on the kitchen table, and that was where we stayed. For the first few minutes we were joined by a nice Sloaney girl called Phyllida, a sort of housekeeper-about-town. I inferred that she performed roughly the same function, on a grander scale, at Ladycross as I did at Smart Cards. She called her employer 'milady' in a way that sounded like 'mate'.

Miranda put a packet of tortilla chips on the table, expertly opening the bag four ways so it formed a plate.

'When Fred was on his last legs,' she observed, 'and barely swallowing soup, he could always manage one of these. I used to worry it would choke him, and then think, Who cares? Death by chip could be a merciful release.'

I laughed nervously, but Phyllida remained stony-faced. One of the spaniels, Mark, rested his head mournfully on my knee.

'Is he allowed one?' I asked, to change the subject as much as anything.

'Sure. Now the master's gone they're allowed anything.'

'Oy,' said Phyllida.

'What?'

'Stop it.'

'Am I doing it? Sorry.'

Ignoring this little sub-plot, I gave Mark the chip and ploughed on. 'You have a greyhound as well, don't you?'

Miranda shook her head. 'I expect you saw the wanderer. I haven't yet found out who he belongs to, but they want to be careful. He doesn't wear a collar and he roams around all over the place.'

'What about your dogs? Don't they see him off?'

'Actually they take no notice, they ignore him completely, which is unusual in itself. He's not at all aggressive, and he does seem to like it here. He was even sniffing around on the night of the concert – do you remember, Philly? We had a rock concert here just before – a few months ago, and I saw him on the hill while it was still in full swing.'

Phyllida rose and rinsed out her glass under the tap. 'There must have been rich pickings for an enterprising pooch that night.'

'True. Dope, chilli, burgers, used johnnies, who could resist?'

'I'll away, then.' Phyllida dried her hands. ''Bye, Bobby. Nice to meet you, see you again, I hope.'

'Hot date?' asked Miranda.

'I wish.'

When she'd gone, I said, 'She's nice.'

'She is, very, but she'll be off soon.'

'Why's that?'

'She just will.' Miranda poured us both another one. 'They come, they're bowled over, they get chummy, then bored, then they go and work for oil sheikhs so they can get engaged to their dull boyfriends.'

'But you get on so well.'

'We do, but in the end she's not doing it for love. We're not friends, we're just friendly. We both know the score. I give it . . .' she mused '. . . another – three months? before she hands in her notice. She's a nice girl, she won't want to hit me with it too soon after what's happened, and then I'll probably persuade her to hang on over Christmas. Which brings us to January. Mid-February top whack.'

'And how easy will it be to replace her?'

'Not too bad. The money isn't brilliant, but there is all this,' she waved a hand, 'to make up for it. And we do a little car, you couldn't be without one here.'

'And what about "all this"?' I asked. 'It has to pay its way, I suppose.'

'I swear, Bobby,' she said, as though about to tell me something she had never vouchsafed to another soul, 'I *swear* I had no idea what work was till I came here. The worry alone's worth danger money. People like Fred who are born to it don't agonise quite so much because all those centuries of living on the edge are in their blood. They have this sense of continuity – they'll strut and fret their little hour but the house will go on somehow. That doesn't mean they don't take their responsibilities seriously, but they're more philosophical.'

I remembered the smiling man with the straw hat in the photo.

'And you?' I asked.

'I married this when I married Fred. I took it on, or at least my share of it. So, rightly or wrongly, I felt I had something to prove. I wanted to be the one wife who made a difference.' She must have sensed the question I was too polite to ask. 'There were two previous Mrs Freds, one dead and one divorced. And I have a grown-up step-son and two step-grandchildren, courtesy of the deceased. Fred and I, as they say, are without issue.'

'Me too,' I said, feeling I should offer something in return.

'You were married, then?'

'For a while, some time ago. To be honest, I don't think I was cut out for it.'

She fetched a box of small cigars from the side. 'Do you mind? Thanks. You?' She lit up with the unashamed and practised panache of a thirties film star and spread her right hand with its magnificent rock on the table. 'Look. I wasn't, or didn't think I was. That's why I came to it so late. But it's not marriage you have to be cut out for, it's a particular other person. The other bit of the jigsaw, the one who completes you, who goes out where you go in and vice versa. When you find that person, marrying them is neither here nor there, but you might as well. Marrying Fred was an act of sheer bloody bravado on my part, I wanted to show everyone I loved him enough to take on the whole Ladycross shebang. And I did.' She blew smoke as if it were own trumpet. 'I have!'

'And what happens now?' I ventured.

'It's Miles's. The Dower House and a dignified retirement beckon for the Dowager Lady Stratton.'

Dowager . . . it was ridiculous. 'Will you miss it?'

'Not the responsibility and the graft and the always being on duty, no. But the place, like hell. I mean, wouldn't you?'

'I'm not sure.'

'Of course you would, if you'd ever lived here. I guarantee it. A house like this isn't just bricks and stones and timber, it has a soul. It's a star.'

'Is that what Miles thinks?'

'Now you're asking. Who knows what Miles thinks?'

'You don't like him.'

'I don't *dis*like him, but it's a tricky one. I'm only ten years older, I was the ex-model who moved in and took over. It must have annoyed the hell out of him and the fact that I buckled down and made a go of it annoyed him even more. But his children are the light of my life so I'll forgive him anything.'

'What about Mrs Miles?'

'Penny's a nice Christian woman without a mean bone in her body. Loyalty is her middle name. Fred and I were a team, but in that outfit Penny goes where she's put.'

I noticed that the bottle was empty and that Miranda was drinking at twice the rate I was. It occurred to me that the confidences were coming thick and fast and that she might regret some of them in the morning.

'Well,' I said, 'I'd better be going. You must have things to do, always.'

She ignored this. 'Would you like to look round?'

'If it's no trouble, I'd love to.'

She pushed her chair back and stood with a flourish. 'It's not, and I adore showing her off.'

'So houses are feminine, like ships?'

'This one is.' She flashed me her sudden, brilliant smile, which conferred instant intimacy. 'You'll see – a woman knows.'

I did see. That, and much more.

I don't remember all the details she told me about the history and construction of the house and its occupants – she'd done her homework – but through her I experienced the allure of the place, its rich, old glamour, its secrecy and sophistication. And I sensed how proudly and profoundly she identified with this place, how she really had married Ladycross with her beloved Fred and shared him with it. And how painful must be the prospect of leaving.

'If you have a rival for a man's affections,' she observed, reading my thoughts again, you know this, Bobby, the best thing is to befriend her. Disarm her with attention. Draw her sting. That's what I set out to do. And I was almost too successful, because I really fell in love. Which is different from what Fred felt – Ladycross is family to him, but a big romance to me.'

I felt ridiculously honoured. She was so open. I had not even been her friend before, I was the merest acquaintance – not even that, a face in the crowd – and yet all this charm, all these confidences were being lavished on me, an embarrassment of riches.

But when Kirsty asked me how it had gone, I was reticent. 'We had a nice evening – but it's been a long time. We've both changed.'

'So lots of catching up?'

I realised we hadn't done any. 'Not really.'

I knew I should explain that we'd scarcely known each other before, that this wasn't a picking up of the threads of some long-ago friendship. The gulf between my perspective and Miranda's, between her confident generosity and my uncertainty was wider than they could possibly have imagined. The weird dynamics imposed by Queen's, and its culture of fierce but unexpressed feelings, were another world that they could not be expected to understand.

'She showed me round the house,' I said. 'I was blown away.'

'Quite lovely, isn't it? But she's the one who really brought it to life, she's a complete star. We all adore her. I feel sorry for the son, she'll be a hard act to follow.'

'Yes – what's he like?'

Kirsty gave a little sigh, as if to ensure she gave a fair reply. 'Perfectly all right. Nothing if not dutiful, he'll discharge his responsibilities to the letter. Pleasant Sloaney wife, sweet children. Understandably wary of Miranda.' She beamed, as if the answer had just occurred to her: 'Nice, but not naughty. Unlike his father.'

It was a quiet day and Chris wasn't in, so I seized my opportunity.

'And Miles's mother died – when?'

'Ages ago, long before we were here. Appallingly young, a long illness bravely borne, it must have been quite terrible for all of them . . . And then there was Polly, who we do remember, just, before she bolted.'

'A scandal?'

'Not that we know of, she simply couldn't deal with any of it. She had all the qualifications on paper – scion of a noble house, right age, forever pictured in *Tatler* but never falling out of her dress – but perhaps she'd had enough. Anyway, it ended in tears. Whereas Rags, bless her, arrived out of left field straight from the cover of American *Vogue* to much tongue-clicking and muttering, and took to it like a duck to water – hell's bells, look at the time!'

I told Daniel I'd been to the house, too. I still couldn't quite make out how well he knew Miranda personally, or if he knew her at all except in the general sense.

'How was she?' he asked, as if enquiring after a friend.

I thought for a moment, trying to sum it up. 'Fragile but gallant.'

'There must be a lot of stuff to see to.'

'She gave me that impression.'

We were sitting in the Mill House, by the fire. He touched my arm. 'She must have been so pleased to see you.'

'I believe she was,' I said, 'though I can't think why. We were never friends at school – she was far too exotic, and in a higher class.'

'A class of her own,' Daniel agreed. I felt a little hurt. I was allowed to say such things, but coming from him it had the effect of putting me in my place.

'Poor lady,' he said. 'Poor Miranda.'

I didn't see her again for weeks. The Hobdays said she'd gone on holiday to Italy with friends. We all agreed that a carefree spell in the sun was what she needed, but I missed her – or missed knowing she was there – and was childishly jealous of the friends. I imagined, entirely fancifully, that Ladycross pined without her.

It was October, autumn: the trees bronzed, the early mornings misted with frost. The cool breath of change was in the air. I had two chance encounters that were the outriders of that change.

The first happened one day after work. I'd been to Asda in Stoneybridge, five miles away, and was coming back into Witherburn from the north. It was a beautiful late afternoon. That golden, elegiac light that goes with the turn of the year struck fire from Ladycross on her hill, and I slowed down, caught as always by her spell. I was reminded that the evenings would soon be drawing in, and that what with work and being busy in the house I'd allowed precious little time to stand and stare like this. On an impulse I pulled over at a farm gateway, locked the car and crossed the lane for a walk.

Miranda had said I could go where I wanted, but I considered there might well be some fiercely conscientious gamekeeper out there who had not been informed, so I stuck to the footpath, the same one I'd taken on my first evening.

This time, when I emerged from the woods on to the long shoulder of the hill I turned right, north-westwards, following a sign that said 'Folly'. The path curved round the hill, with Ladycross to the left, to a point only a few hundred yards from where I worked – there was actually a stretch of unmade road leading from the barns to a clump of woodland further down the slope. I'd seen it from the Hobdays' window but never bothered going down.

As I set off along the path I was rather put out to be passed by a car going in the same direction. I'd wanted to be alone, but it was a free country, so I maintained the objective. I arrived to find the car parked but no sign of its owner.

The folly was lovely. I'd been prepared for a whimsically distressed Victorian Gothic tower with leaded windows, arrow-slits and miniature battlements through which Rapunzel might let down her hair. Instead it was a simple and beautiful pavilion made of the local stone, with slender pillars, and a roof of silvery slate. The floor was tiled, inlaid with a design of dog-roses and birds. In the centre was a round plinth on which stood a statue of a boy. The statue was simple, impressionistic almost. I walked right round it before I saw that there was a hound sitting pressed against the boy's legs, its muzzle resting on his hand, its eyes gazing up at him expectantly.

There was one of those visitor-information boards at one side, and I went to read it. It said that the folly had been built in 1816 by Richard Montclere, Third Baron Stratton, to a design by his wife, Amelia Rose. The pattern on the floor was said to be both a tribute to her, and to the famous ceiling of the pink drawing room at Ladycross, but there was no record of the inspiration for the charming naïve statue of the young hunter. The folly had been used by generations of the family for picnics, parties and even intimate concerts. To preserve its special sequestered atmosphere there was no official supervision of the building, and visitors were asked to treat it with respect.

It was quite lovely, an enchanted place. The westering sun filtered through the trees and bathed the statue in a drifting, dusty light. I half expected the boy to step down and walk away through the woods with his dog at his heels . . .

'Gorgeous, isn't it?'

I'd forgotten there was someone else about, and I jumped.

'My apologies,' said the man. 'I should have coughed or something.'

'No – I was daydreaming.'

'Right place for it. I'll leave you to it.'

It was no good, though. He was here now and the spell was broken. It would have been hard to imagine a figure more calculated to ruin the atmosphere. He was a big, untidy man whose dark city suit, the trousers tucked into wellies, only made him look untidier. His tie was not loosened but was askew, the knot a bit too small – probably left ready-tied on a hook overnight. He wore glasses and carried, for heaven's sake, a clipboard. There was a camera round his neck and a mobile phone stuck out of his jacket pocket.

Not wanting my distaste to be too obvious I hung around for a while longer but it was impossible to ignore the rustle of heavy-handed activity. He made notes, put the board on the ground, took photographs with much sidling and backing-up for the right angle, picked up the board and made further notes.

I was heading back the way I'd come when he said, 'I do hope I'm not driving you away?'

'No, no, I just wanted to see. I have to get back anyway.'

'Bloody infuriating for you,' he observed cheerfully, 'to come all this way for a spot of P and Q and find the likes of me barging about.'

'Not at all,' I said, but his teasing good-humour was disarming and my half-smile had already given me away. 'Well – yes.'

'I shan't be long.'

'It's okay, really. I can come another time.'

'I'm doing a sort of private recce,' he told me chattily, as though I'd asked, wandering over, but with his eyes still on the folly. The wellie-clad feet were huge; I was sure he'd catch one on a tree-trunk. But he reached my side without incident, and went on, 'I don't know quite what I expected, but this exceeds expectation.'

I agreed that it did.

'So, are you a local,' he asked, 'or just passing?'

'Local.'

'Can you tell me if the pub's any good?'

'It is, yes. But they don't do food before six thirty.'

'It makes no never mind since I shall be going there anyway and will sit over a pint till they're prepared to activate the microwave.'

I was thinking he might be hard to get away from and was about to utter a platitude and escape, when he outflanked me by saying, 'Cheerio!' and resuming his note-taking.

By the time I reached the top of the hill my humour was restored, and I rather wished I'd asked him what the recce was for. The thought crossed my mind that he might have had some criminal intention – one did hear, these days, of architectural thieves who simply walked off with tons of valuable masonry – but I put the notion aside: he hadn't appeared savvy enough for that.

I emerged below the wood, where I'd first seen Miranda, and there was my car parked in the gateway on the other side of the road. I experienced one of those inconsequential bursts of happiness, which don't mean a thing – a brief, blissed-out awareness of uncounted blessings.

As I got into the car I saw the dog, the one Miranda called the wanderer, come out of the wood and pause for a moment, looking my way, before racing like the wind over the hill towards Ladycross.

The second encounter happened the day after that. It was Saturday, and the Witherburn Harvest Fair – a village event with knobs on. As a newcomer I refrained from asking why they couldn't have a midsummer fête like everyone else, and was curious enough to put in an appearance and, anyway, it seemed like good manners to do so. The Hobdays had a little stand advertising their wares, especially their line in personalised cards, so I had a base camp from which to conduct forays.

Daniel was there with his catalogues rather apologetically displayed in the open boot of the Mini. I did ask him about the timing and he explained that the origins of the Harvest Fair were way back in the mists of time. 'It's a Witherburn thing,' he said, as one might say, 'It's a boy thing.' 'Traditional. They do have a May Queen celebration as well, but you weren't here for that.' He folded his arms and hopped from foot to foot. 'It's not always like this. Sometimes we have Indian summer.'

The show was held on a bumpy tract of common ground in the middle of the village called the sports field – one of the first-ever official FA pitches, it was pointed out to me, although there was no sign of any goalposts or white lines now. The weather was holding up but only just – it was one of those days when the sky ached with rain and the clouds ballooned over the hills like the roof of a tent sagging beneath a weight of water. It was cold, and most people were dressed in that most dispiriting of ensembles, the mac or anorak over smart clothes. Stall-holders were required to wear period dress of a generally Edwardian nature, which seemed to cover everything from *Charlie's Aunt* blazers and boaters, to bustles and whalebone, irrespective of gender. I contented myself with an Indian skirt teamed – as the fashionistas would say – with an ancient Laura Ashley blouse, which I'd been keeping against just such a rainy day, and my fringed car rug as a shawl. Kirsty and Chris adopted the token-gesture approach, with waistcoats.

'We're not exactly rushed off our feet,' said Kirsty. 'Bobby, do circulate.'

After ruining my put-together look with a waxed jacket, I bought four cheese scones at the cake stall, a strip of raffle tickets, and a Brenda Lee LP. I won a tin of pilchards (a food item I'd never thought to see again after Queen's) on the tombola, hazarded a guess at a doll's name and the number of sweets in a jar, and admired the entries in the show tent. I resisted the blandishments of the fortune-teller's barker, and of those running the slow bicycle race and the mixed tug o' war. It was increasingly dark and chilly and only three o'clock. I wondered how on earth I was going to last another hour and whether the Hobdays would think me a rat if I made my excuses and left.

I stood shivering near the coconut shy with my hands in my pockets and my collar up round my ears. A couple with young children were engaging in one of those exchanges, on the face of it purely domestic but in fact very audience-aware. The man had a particular kind of voice, strangulated yet penetrating, so it was him I noticed first. He had on perfectly nice moleskin trousers, but with a double-breasted blazer, firmly buttoned and a brown trilby.

'It's a bit too grown-up for you, Jem,' he said to his son, who looked about four.

'He can stand a bit closer,' suggested the coconut man. 'We got a kiddies' mark.'

The little girl, a few years older, announced that she wanted a go. 'And I don't need to be nearer.'

'If you're going to try you must throw properly,' said father to son. He pronounced it 'prop-ly'. 'Otherwise it's dangerous.'

The mother, who wore a blouse like mine, but new, and a Burberry, but old, was looking on with a fixed smile and anxious eyes.

'Millie, let Jem go first.'

'Okay.'

I was impressed with Millie's calm. She was a child with difficult straight hair, unsympathetically cut, and a nose she hadn't grown into, but she struck me as full of confidence and character.

Jem was the pretty one and his father wasn't handling him well.

'Stop making a fuss or you won't have a go at all. I'm sorry, is there a queue?'

'No problem, it's nice for the kids to get involved. Okay? Fifty p for the two of them. Take your time.'

The trouble was that the father couldn't let the boy get on with it. He stood behind him and guided his arm, and got testy when the child began to wriggle.

'No, no, calm down, Jem, you *must* throw it straight.'

'Let go!'

'I'll do it with you once, then you can do it on your own.'

'Leave me!'

'Miles,' said the woman, 'he'll be fine. He's not going to throw it very far.'

So this was Miles. On first acquaintance it appeared that both Miranda and Kirsty had been too charitable. He was awful. I watched with fascinated embarrassment as he struggled with his son while his wife and daughter looked on stoically. His knuckles were actually white with the effort of controlling the boy without being rough, and it was all so unnecessary! In the end the ball was thrown, about eighteen inches but straight, and then thrown again by Jem on his own, several feet but narrowly missing the stallholder's ear, which seemed to leave everyone vindicated. Then Millie had her go and did pretty well. The stallholder gave them their fifty pence back and Miles told them they could have an ice-cream.

I had a go, but only because I wanted to ask the coconut man a question. 'Was that Miles Montclere?'

'That's right, his brand-new lordship. Oops, have another one on me.'

Perhaps ice-cream in this weather made the air seem warmer, because I saw them walking away from the Mr Whippy van looking a lot more cheerful. No, I thought, he wasn't awful. He was as buttoned-up as his damn blazer – *and* tense, and doubtless nervous about taking over the title. *Le tout* Witherburn had its eye on him, poor sod. And he had to take over from Miranda.

Who, in God's name, I thought, would want to be in Miles Montclere's bespoke brogues at this moment?

On Sunday night, curled up in front of the telly in my plaid pyjamas, with a glass of shiraz for company, too lazy to get up, let alone get something to eat, I found myself gazing at an arts review programme. As well as the slow-spoken poet, the lady critic of colour and the ageing *über*feminist, there was a face I recognised.

'. . . Marco Torrence, theatre impresario, campaigner for the arts and all-round good egg or bally nuisance depending on your standpoint.'

What sort of a name was Marco Torrence? The sort owned by those who appeared on late-night review programmes. And, apparently, the klutz with the clipboard and wellies reconnoitring the folly.

CHAPTER TEN

Rags, 1979

It was a short distance, but a long journey for Miranda this afternoon. Visiting the past was like that.

She left the James Judd studio in Bethnal Green at two, called in at Face Value to see what they'd got that she wanted to do, and then, to set herself up before catching the bus to Parliament Hill, met Tom Worsley for tea on the House of Commons terrace.

She wore faded Ralph Lauren jeans, a man's white cotton shirt from M&S and a striped schoolboy belt; no makeup; non-prescription specs; hair in a ponytail; what Tom called her Rags-bag over her shoulder. It was a low-key, off-duty look in which she felt comfortable and that he particularly liked.

He made an appreciative sound in his throat as he greeted her. No kiss – a kiss on the mouth in this context would have been too showy, and he wasn't one for cheek-bumping. Instead, he held her chair for her, a mixture of gaucheness and gallantry. 'Look at you,' he said, 'it's criminal.'

'Low maintenance, too.'

'Been working?'

'I have, and I'm dying for a brew.'

'And you shall have it.'

He'd positioned her so she was opposite him, looking at the river, but as they waited for tea to arrive he moved his chair alongside hers.

'So I can see the view, too.' He glanced over his shoulder.

'Get a load of them, all pretending they haven't noticed and all ears as usual.'

'I doubt it.' She rummaged in her bag for her cigarettes and lit one. He didn't smoke and wished, more in sorrow than in anger, that she didn't, which slightly tarnished the pleasure of the first drag.

'So,' she said, 'tell me about affairs of state.'

'You don't want to hear.'

Tom was Labour, but with a sceptical attitude to what he called 'the management'. An apolitical animal herself, and not knowing him or the system well enough, she couldn't tell whether this attitude was the cause or the result of his never having been in the shadow cabinet. But even she could see that he was custom-made for the role of back-bench voice of conscience: a serious man with a keen sense of the ridiculous.

Their tea came and he poured while she munched on a smoked-salmon sandwich.

'What I can tell you is that it's going to be a late one, so no chance of dinner.'

'That's all right, I'm visiting an old friend. We're going out and we may be some time.'

'Male or female?' He was needlessly jealous, but philosophical: he liked to know so he could deal with it.

'Female. Actually you'd love her.'

Now it was his turn to say: 'I doubt it.'

'No, Tom, you would. She's a one-off. On her gravestone they'll write, "She didn't care."'

He raised an eyebrow. 'That's good?'

'Don't be po-faced, you know what I mean. She's an idealist in her way. It's the world's opinion she doesn't care for.'

'Right, well, I hope you have fun. When can I see you?'

'Afterwards? I could come to the flat.'

'I don't know when I'll get back.'

'Neither do I.' Before he could take evasive action she stuck a quick kiss on his temple. 'So that's all right.'

'You're a good woman, Ragsy.'

He often said this, or something like it, jokingly, and she'd play along and pretend to be annoyed, that it ran counter to her image. But one of the reasons she loved Tom was because he made her feel like a good person. Not virtuous exactly, but honourable. Sound, as he was. He was cantankerous when tired, was certainly ambitious and occasionally vain, but his instinct for the right thing was rock-solid.

After tea he accompanied her down to the lobby. 'Enjoy your evening. I'll see you later.'

'I can't wait.'

He pointed at the Rags-bag. 'Do you want to leave that with me?'

'Of course not!' She clasped it protectively. 'You might be tempted to dip into it. Try a makeover.'

'I'll go to the – that'll be the day.'

She walked up to Trafalgar Square, and crossed over to the bottom of Charing Cross Road to catch the number twenty-four. She chose the bus not only for the lofty perspective and the light but because bus travellers themselves were a more content and gentle breed than those on the tube, and conductors, unlike cabbies, didn't feel compelled to inform you that you weren't the most famous person they'd ever had on board.

Better still, this time the bus was two-thirds empty and there was a seat right at the front on the top deck. She took a childish pleasure in this position: it was like riding an elephant, cutting a path through the lesser traffic and with a view on all sides.

The other thing about the bus journey was that it gave her time to prepare. As the twenty-four bumbled north, via Tottenham Court Road, Camden and Islington, she rewound the tape of recent years until the past came into focus.

It was James Judd, whose studio she'd just left, who'd discovered not Miranda but Rags. It was in 1964, nearly two years after she moved to Khartoum Road, a year into her relationship with Nicky Traves. Judd was already making waves as a photographer with a fresh style, but he had a lousy memory for names and gave everyone simple, associative nicknames for his own benefit. It caught on. And then he took what became known as the 'rags-to-riches' pictures of Miranda for *Harper's*: her dream pictures, which told a story and defined a persona as well as selling clobber. The clothes were fabulous, fantastic evening dresses by young RCA designers with a couple of regal Hardy Amies numbers thrown in. Miranda was shown as a louche, smudge-eyed, rumpled rebel at a society ball – or, at least, on the fringes of a society ball. In the background was a marquee, a big house, a blur of posh guests; it was raining; in the foreground Miranda, wearing the dresses with wellies, un-done black lace-ups or barefoot; in one a chevalier in black-tie held an umbrella over her head; in another he shivered in shirtsleeves as she stood with his dinner jacket over her shoulders, her face turned to the sky and her mouth open, drinking the raindrops; in a third she balanced on one leg, hair dripping, examining the sole of her foot with a scowl; in the most famous one she capered, her voluminous tulle skirt bunched in her arms, her long white legs at bizarre angles, water spurting up from the grass beneath her feet.

The pictures were, in every sense of the word, fabulous.

To describe them as a high-risk exercise was an understatement. Only Judd had the balls and the clout to have tried it, and only designers who were very hungry or untouchably famous could have trusted him. Most of the dresses were spoiled, if not ruined, and she herself caught a chesty cough that put her out of circulation for two weeks. But the pictures were a *succès fou*. Two of them were still in the top-ten-selling posters, pinned on the walls of teenagers who couldn't remember the original. And they'd marked the magic moment when she went from model to role-model. From Miranda Tattersall to Rags. A brand-name.

She'd bought a flat in Bayswater, and a purple Mini Cooper. She partied, smoked dope and went on the pill. She was to remain quixotically faithful to Nicky Traves of the Road-runners, who regarded it as his duty and prerogative to spread his seed from Madrid to Manchester and who one morning, not long after her rebirth as Rags, failed to wake up while lying in bed next to her, his throat stopped by his own vomit. That morning, standing cold and shocked in the hotel bathroom as the police muttered in the bedroom beyond, she stared mercilessly at her own reflection, and did not blink.

Neither did she blink at Nicky's funeral. She took control, armouring her torn heart in elegance: a black Courrèges suit, black boots, dark glasses, giant *faux* pearls, her hair in a chignon. The Roadrunners were in disarray and, for old times' sake, she stood with them to talk to the press about Nicky's irreplaceable talent and charm. She was the same age as the band, but felt suddenly ten years older. At three the next morning she slipped away unnoticed from Nicky's send-off, and left the Roadrunners for good.

Since Nicky, she'd been more careful: of her heart, her life, her looks. The face in the mirror was her livelihood. It might be advantageous to be photographed looking pale and wan, even a bit dissolute, following the untimely death of one's rock-star lover. But to become an ongoing and gradually declining press story was the kiss of death. She wanted a status and success that was all her own, not linked to a dwindling past.

She went first to stay with Noah, who had given up modelling and launched a line of belts, ties and hats on the proceeds. He and his 'colleague' Paul, a choreographer, had a seaside retreat in Suffolk, a tall house shielded from the fury of the North Sea by nothing more than a narrow promenade and a rampart of shingle. Paul was away, up to his ears rehearsing a new musical for its pre-West-End run in Plymouth so it was, as Noah said, the perfect moment.

'Why didn't you get somewhere in the South of France?' she shouted, as they ploughed along the prom to the Lighter for fish and chips, heads down into the gale. 'Or Spain? Or Italy?'

'Don't think we're not going to!' Noah yelled back. 'This was Paul's mother's. Why? Don't you like it?'

'Is sunshine against your religion?'

'This will do you more good, Mand, blow away the cob-webs.'

'Perhaps it'll grow on me.'

'That's the spirit!'

But it was impossible for her not to respond to Noah's cheerful and unashamed pragmatism. He had few conversational scruples.

'Come on now, if you won't talk to the press, you must talk to me. Gimme some kiss-and-tell. Nicky was by far the prettiest in that lot, but was he any good in bed?'

'He was adorable.'

'That's no answer. *I* could see that. Spill the beans, girl.'

'No.'

'Too spaced-out.'

'I mean, no, I shan't spill the beans.'

'Nothing you say can hurt him now, he's gone to a better place.' Noah rolled his eyes upward. 'The great gig in the sky.'

This was true, and she knew that Noah was more discreet than he appeared. All the same she was adamant. It was too complex, too dark and intimate and secret.

'I was his friend, more than anything.'

'Ah-ah, *not* good!'

'It's true. He was a nice boy in a big mess. There.'

'And you were a part of the mess, is that it? That's why you're here, to forget . . .'

'Chance'd be a fine thing, with you wanting all the fruity details.'

'Darling, I'm sorry.' He clasped her hand, eyes closed remorsefully. 'I stand rebuked.'

Having let go this line of enquiry, Noah moved seamlessly to the question of her future plans.

'I don't have any,' she confessed. 'Except that I need to make some.'

'"Rags – The Lost Years".' He described a banner headline with his hand. 'But the work's still rolling in, surely. I saw you doing your denim-and-diamonds thing in *Paris-Match*.'

'That was months ago.'

'Well, you've been tied up. Everyone knows that. I saw the funeral snaps by the way. Very nicely done, if I may say so. Jackie Kennedy meets Audrey Hepburn. Rags Redux. Not to be tasteless, but it suited you.'

'You think so?'

'I do,' said Noah. 'Take my word for it, elegance is the way forward.'

Noah had been right in the past, so she was prepared to give him the benefit of the doubt. She needed a change, and one which declared unequivocally that her professionally misspent Roadrunner days were over. Because she was still — just — in a position to be choosy she selected a shoot for American *Vogue* that focused on classic English style. It was generally acknowledged that it was rarely to be found in its home country, and the editor's inclination was to be mildly ironic. But she persuaded him to use James Judd (their combined reputations managed to rise above recent falls from grace), and to allow him a free hand.

The result was six pages of ravishing black-and-white photographs, taken in and around Stowe School, photographs that defined a dream of Englishness, with Rags the apotheosis of sleek, velvet-skinned elegance, the polar opposite of the Judd pictures that had made her name. No edge, no irony. Just beauty, pure and simple.

Those shots were her passport to the future, they gave her *carte blanche* to reinvent herself as often as she wanted, and be — before the camera at least — whoever she wanted to be. Over the next few years there followed other shots that became classics, including the sexually ambivalent 'Scoop'. In the mid-seventies a collectable calendar was marketed using the most famous pictures. It was at a signing session for the calendar, in the foyer of the RCA, that she'd met Tom Worsley.

He'd been the very last in the queue. The last of several hundred over the course of the afternoon. Buyers had ranged from little girls, their mothers and their grannies to schoolboys pretending it was all a laugh, sheepish youths and nice grown-up men of a sort she wished she met more often. Tom came into the last category.

'Got the energy for just one more?'

'Of course.' She smiled up at him. 'You've been incredibly patient.'

'Put "Tom from Rags", can you?' He watched as she wrote,

and added casually, 'As a matter of fact I've been demoting myself all afternoon. Moving to the back.'

She handed the calendar to Janine, handmaiden from the publisher, to put in its cardboard sleeve. 'Why would you do that?'

'I wanted to be last.'

'You did?'

'So I could offer to buy you dinner.'

She could have sworn she heard Janine's creep-alarm activating. The man before them was fortyish, and stocky, with grey hair and brown eyes beneath bushy brows. He wore a blue suit with a hint of shine, and carried a briefcase and a frayed beige mac. It was hard to say why she reacted to him as she did, unless it was simply that both his directness and his appearance were diametrically different from her urbane escorts of recent years.

'That's a nice idea,' she said, and put Janine on the spot by turning to her. 'I think this gentleman and I both deserve a reward, don't you?'

'You've got Smith's in Birmingham tomorrow at eleven,' said Janine, in a tight, meaningful voice.

'But a girl has to eat.' She looked up at him. 'I'd love to.'

'Good. Tom Worsley, by the way.' He took his calendar. 'No rush, I'll hang around and we can jump in a taxi when you're ready.'

'I shan't be long. I just have to thank the staff and so on.'

He addressed Janine, who was doing everything bar actually sigh and suck her teeth: 'Would you like to join us?'

This, Rags conceded, was masterly. What could the poor girl do but decline?

'I hope you don't mind,' he said, in the taxi. 'I knew you were lovely, but I hadn't realised you were so nice with it.'

That was the moment Miranda felt herself relax, for the first time in years.

Her relationship with Tom had produced an uncharacteristic flash of jealousy in Dale, something other boyfriends, even Nicky, had failed to do.

'What's the big attraction?' he asked truculently, when she was next down there. 'I've seen him on TV. He's old.'

'He's forty-one.'

'That's what I said.'

'I really like him, Dale.'

'You could have anyone you wanted.'

'And I have.'

'I don't get it, Mandy.'

He sulked, but not for long. Dale was engaged now, to Kaye Fuller, with a deposit on a house in the Meadowview development, and a four-door saloon. In view of all this his jealousy was baffling, until Miranda realised that, for the first time, she was consorting with someone whom Dale saw as more like himself. Photographers, actors and rock musicians went with the modelling territory, but a nice, downright, average-looking middle-aged bloke, even if he was an MP, was altogether too close for comfort.

Kaye was a doctor's receptionist, with the gimlet eye and steely smile of her calling. 'You must come to the wedding,' she said, 'if you're not off in some exotic foreign location.'

'Nothing could stop me,' replied Miranda, inferring that an appropriately timed foreign location, actual or fabricated, might be welcomed.

Staying a couple of nights with her mother three times a year was now no more than a duty. There was no longer any pretence at intimacy, which saddened Miranda but not, apparently, Marjorie. She accepted what came her way – new carpets, curtains and three-piece suite, a refitted kitchen and bathroom – as her maternal due, while still reserving the right to disapprove of the career that paid for them. Pinned to the cork board in the kitchen was a copy of the only published photograph of herself that Miranda had ever seen here, a *Daily Mail* shot of her with the band members at Nicky's funeral. Marjorie had wasted no time in voicing her relief that Nicky had died – 'I can't say I'm sorry' were her exact words at the time – and had expressed only token interest in Tom Worsley ('Socialist, isn't he?') before blurting out, with an unmistakable gleam of excitement over the first evening's gin and tonic, 'Did you know your father was ill?'

'No, but why would I?'

'He's in the Royal Free. Isn't that near where you were before?'

'Yes.' Miranda didn't like the turn this was taking. 'A long way from Bayswater, though.'

'I don't suppose,' said Marjorie, prodding her lemon slice with her finger, 'that you'd consider dropping in on him, then.'

The question seemed to turn into a statement somewhere along the way, but Miranda was not about to let her mother sit on the fence.

'What? Mum!'

'No, I mean he's all on his own, and very poorly. Dying, probably, but there you are . . .' She glanced away with a wistful if-you-won't-you-won't expression.

It took a superhuman effort not to rise to the bait. 'Who told you, anyway?'

'Fran Shepherd. Remember, his secretary Fran?'

'She must be long retired.'

'Oh, from the business, yes, several years ago, like him. But I understand she's been keeping house for him and she thought we ought to know about this. I thought it was nice of her.'

Miranda didn't want to know anything about Gerald Tattersall, or to be discussing him at all, but curiosity proved too much for her.

'How do you mean, keeping house?'

Marjorie shrugged, not prepared to be curious at all. 'That's what she said.'

'But are they living together?'

'I think she does live with him at Godolphin Court, but I wouldn't know about the exact arrangement. Anyway, she was kind enough to ring, and she did sound upset.'

Miranda called to mind Fran ('Mrs Shepherd to you,' her father had pompously instructed), a smily, unflappable woman with a coiffure as symmetrical and unchanging as the Queen's. Even then it had struck her as odd that such a person should be working for the vile Gerald without complaint or, apparently, difficulty. She had once heard her father say to someone he was with: 'That woman may not have the face to launch a

thousand ships but she helps keep Tattersall's Barges afloat' –
a compliment, if a backhanded one.

'I'm sorry for her,' she said now, 'but it's not our problem.'

'He is your father, Mandy.'

'Please don't remind me.'

Marjorie shook her head. 'It's a shame to be so bitter at
your age.'

Miranda lit a cigarette to buy time. Her hands trembled. Stay
separate, she told herself. Don't let yourself get sucked in. Keep
the focus elsewhere.

'Let's hope –' she had a frog in her throat and cleared it –
'let's hope she's taken care of.'

But her mother seemed to take this as a softening of attitude.
'I'm sure it would mean a lot to him to see you.'

'I'm quite sure it wouldn't, Mum. And, anyway, I don't want
to.' She drew a deep breath and threw down a gauntlet of her
own. 'But I'll take you, if you like.'

Marjorie looked genuinely startled. 'Good heavens, no, it's
out of the question, completely out of the question. But you're
his daughter, Mandy.'

'You were his wife,' Miranda reminded her.

'A very long time ago. Never mind, if that's how you feel.
I'll tell Fran, it can't be helped.'

'No, it can't. And there's no need to tell anyone. It's not as
if he wants or expects me to visit. There's no disappointment
involved.'

Marjorie murmured something, and Miranda fell into the
trap of saying, 'I beg your pardon?'

'I said *I*'m disappointed.'

'Then *you* bloody well go!'

It had not gone well. Not only had she made the mistake of
losing her temper, but the remorse over shouting at her mother
somehow spilled over into the issue of Gerald's illness so that
she began to feel guilty about that, too. She did, however, feel
genuinely sympathetic towards Fran Shepherd, and a couple
of days later she rang her. She did so from Paris, as though
physical distance would prove a barrier to getting too involved.

She had to go through Directory Enquiries because she only had her father's name and that of the building. A woman's voice answered almost at once.

'Is that . . . Mrs Shepherd?'

'Speaking.'

'Mrs Shepherd – Fran – it's Miranda Tattersall here.'

'Oh! Miranda – my dear, how lovely!' There was no mistaking the unalloyed delight at the other end of the line. 'And congratulations on your wonderful success. I've been following it all along.'

'Thanks. I've been very lucky.'

'Lucky nothing, you may have had the looks but I bet staying at the top like you is jolly hard work.'

'Harder than people think,' conceded Miranda.

'Oh, my dear, I can quite believe it . . . And you've been through some sad times, I'm so sorry.'

After her mother's reaction it took Miranda a moment to realise that Fran Shepherd was referring to Nicky. 'It was a tragedy waiting to happen, I'm afraid.'

'A very dangerous world you were both living in,' agreed Fran.

There was a pause, as if they were both giving this exchange its due weight. Then Miranda said, 'I rang to say how sorry I was to hear about what's happening in *your* life.' She was going to great lengths to avoid mentioning Gerald, but Fran was having none of it.

'Your poor father, yes. I expect your mother told you I called her the other day. I'm afraid he's in a very bad way. I don't expect it to be long.'

'It must be awful for you.'

'It's awful for him. He was always such a go-getter, so full of fight—' She stopped, checked by emotion, but quickly regained control. 'And it doesn't help that he probably brought it on himself with the way he lived.'

The good-hearted honesty of this needed acknowledgement, so Miranda agreed.

'He was never a man to be told,' went on Fran, 'though I did try. When all this became inevitable I tried to prepare myself but it's torture, it really is, to see someone you love brought so low . . .'

Miranda seized the moment. 'Fran, I hadn't realised you and he were so close.'

'Yes, well, no reason why you should have done. You were estranged, after all.' She paused again; this time, Miranda thought, deliberately. 'He did regret that, you know.'

'Really?'

'Oh, yes. Not the divorce, that was unfortunate but these things happen and it was old history. But being cut off from you.'

'He cut himself off.'

'That's not how he sees it.'

'It's true.'

There was a wavering exhalation on the other end, a sort of sad but exasperated sigh. 'Miranda, would you go and see him? No – don't answer, I don't need to know, you're an adult and you'll make your own decision. I'll just leave it with you. Think about it. But not for too long. And why don't you give me your number in London so I can give you a ring if anything happens?'

'Of course.' Miranda knew she'd been let off the hook, freed from having to respond to anything more sensitive than the request for her number.

Tom, when she told him, said, 'I can understand how you feel, but there's no harm in turning up, is there? If it'll send the old boy off happy?'

He didn't understand – how could he? That Gerald could never be an 'old boy', or happy to see her, in the way Tom meant. She let it pass, and didn't tell him she had no intention of going.

Now, a week later, she turned up at the house in Khartoum Road at half past five, and rang the top-floor bell. A man's voice answered. 'Yup?'

'I've come to see Crystal.'

'She's not here.'

'That's okay, she's expecting me, I'll wait.'

'No, I mean, she's not around . . . Look, do you wanna come in?'

The buzzer went and she stepped into the hall, and back more than a decade. Nothing had changed. Al was still getting away with it. As she trudged up the stairs she encountered a skinny young man in a Che Guevara T-shirt coming down. 'Hi. You wanted Crystal.'

'That's right, we're going out.'

He frowned anxiously. 'Come up a minute.'

She followed him. The door to Crystal's room was closed. The other room was largely unchanged but for one thing: 'You've got a new kitchen!'

'Yup – you've been here before?'

'I used to live here years ago . . .' She stroked the gas cooker, smiling in wonderment. 'I never thought I'd see the day!'

'I believe Al had to do something,' said the young man. 'There was a catastrophe of some sort.'

'Why doesn't that surprise me? I'm Miranda, by the way.'

'Ed.' He shook hands, frowned again, thoroughly uncomfortable with the whole thing. 'Look, I'm afraid I don't know where Crystal is, none of us do.'

'But I only spoke to her last week.'

'She hasn't been here since the weekend. She does go off now and again but she usually tells someone. You're about the sixth person asking after her.'

'I've known her for donkey's years,' said Miranda. 'She was looking forward to this evening. I bet she shows up. I'll go into her room and wait for a bit. See if I can pick up some clues.'

'I ought to warn you, I don't think it'll be too good in there. I haven't liked to go in just in case . . .'

'It's all right.' She smiled reassuringly. 'I know her habits of old. I won't hold you responsible.'

Nothing could have prepared Miranda for what she found. She opened the door to the hum of small flies, and a smell so awful that she waded to the window with her hand over her face, and retched as she hauled it open, top and bottom. One curtain was missing and the other, heavily soiled, drooped from its two remaining hooks. The outer windowsill was encrusted with pigeon droppings. It looked like years since the window had been opened. The room was not merely disarrayed: it was filthy and in turmoil like a place that had been ransacked. The floor was hidden beneath dirty clothes, scummy china, much of it green with mould, old tinfoil takeaway cartons, used sanitary towels and tampons, cigarette ends, bottles and cans. Mouse droppings were everywhere. On the bed, the sheets and pillow were grey and stained with, among other things, blood, and the coverlet was burned in several places. In one corner was a large saucepan that had been used as a toilet, a special draw for the flies.

Shocked and sickened she came out again, closing the door behind her. Ed was standing in his own doorway, having anticipated her flight.

'Jesus!' She felt suddenly faint and grabbed the banister rail with both hands.

'Are you okay?'

She shook her head. Her face was cold and her legs seemed to be melting beneath her. 'Could I sit down for a second?'

He took her arm and guided her to the sofa, sweeping off books with one arm before lowering her on to it. 'I'll get you some water.'

She must have blacked out for a few seconds because the next thing she knew a china mug was bumping against her teeth and a trickle of cold water ran down her neck. She gulped, and took the mug from him.

'Thanks.'

As she dipped her fingers in the mug and wet her forehead he sat down next to her, cracking his knuckles nervously. 'It's not just me, no one's wanted to go in because we don't know when she's coming back. It is her room, after all . . .'

'But you – someone must have had some idea what was going on.'

'No. She didn't like Shirley to go in. We knew she was a bit of a wild child – a bit messy—'

'A bit messy? Have you actually looked?'

'Only a glimpse, you know, in passing.'

Miranda closed her eyes. 'She could have been dead in there and you wouldn't have known.'

'But she isn't, so—' He whitened. 'Is she?'

Miranda handed him the mug. 'Thanks for that. I'm going to see Al.'

'If it's really the plague pit you say it is,' said Al, producing an emollient bottle of chianti, 'I'll get Shirley on to it right away.'

'I didn't do it justice, and she'll want danger money,' Miranda told him. 'Al, believe me, that's the room of a person in a completely desperate state, out of control. I can't bear to think of it.'

He handed her a glass. 'Here, drink this, as they say in the films. She was all right when I last encountered her.'

'Did you talk to her?'

'We passed the time of day. You know her, a law unto herself, not one for the social niceties. I never pushed it with Crystal. She was a bit behind with the rent but I've never been a tartar about that. What's money, after all? She's been here for years, and a good tenant in lots of ways. Achieved local-character status — every house needs one of those.'

'I think we should try to find her.'

'Darling heart, it's been less than a week!'

'She may have been gone less than a week, but something's been happening in that room for months, longer.'

'So, what do you suggest?'

'What about the studio, the one where she helped out?'

'You know she only cleaned there, don't you?' said Al, superciliously. 'Not exactly on the creative team. And, anyway, they called because she hadn't been in and they needed to get someone else.'

'And that club she liked . . . I went there with her once.'

'If you mean the Kleek, it closed a year ago and I couldn't tell you what her haunts have been since then.' He leaned forward, eyebrows raised meaningfully. 'It wasn't my business.'

'But it will be,' said Miranda, responding in kind, 'if you need a new tenant.'

'That time is not yet come. If there's been no word of her by the end of next week, I'll make some enquiries.'

'Thanks, Al.' She put down her glass, rose and kissed him.

'Angel . . .' He caught her hand. 'Stay awhile.'

'Not this time.'

'As long as there's a next.'

As she crossed the hall, Ed pattered down the stairs, carrying a yellow notepad. 'Excuse me – um – Miranda – am I right in thinking I recognise you?'

'That depends who you think I am.' She tried to smile but her face felt numb.

'Rags – you are Rags, aren't you?'

'Yes.'

'Can I have your autograph? Timing's not great, I know, but I'd be so—'

'That's okay.' She abandoned the attempt at smiling, and wrote, 'Good luck Ed. Rags.'

Not, she thought as she escaped, that you're the one who needs it.

She trudged up Khartoum Road with as much speed as she could muster, then fled, panting, down Parliament Hill. She knew she was running away, leaving the mess not just of Crystal's room but her life, for Al to clear up, just as Ed, and initially Crystal, had left it for her. But she would be back, she told herself. When Crystal turned up, or was found, she'd be a good friend to her again.

At the bottom of the hill was a gloomy pub and she went in and ordered a glass of red wine, taking it to a table in the corner. She wished she could call Tom, but he'd be in the Chamber. She thought of Noah but hadn't got his number on her. Nicky . . . Nicky would have understood, and might even have known where Crystal was or been able to guess. She leaned her elbows on the table, put her hands on either side of her face like blinkers, and cried silently.

There was a number twenty-four already waiting at the South End Green terminus. It was empty, the driver was sitting on a bench in the sun, reading the *Evening Standard*. She got on and went to the front of the top deck. It was six o'clock. The no man's land of early evening stretched in front of her. She wished she could have seen Tom sooner. As it was she'd go home, have a shower, watch television, battle to stay awake until ten when it would be worth getting a cab to Spitalfields.

Another bus rolled up behind the one she was in, and disgorged its load of commuters. There were very few times when she wished she were part of the regular work-tide, but this was one of them. A nine-to-five life had a rhythm, like walking. At this moment she felt out of step.

There was still no one else on the bus and both drivers were deep in conversation. She went back down the stairs, stepped out of the bus and walked over to them.

'Excuse me, what time does the first one go?'

One of the men glanced at his watch. 'Ten minutes, love.'

'And the second?'

'Half an hour.'

'Thanks.'

She didn't return to the bus, but walked fast, head up, across the road towards the Royal Free.

She'd thought he'd be lying on a high bed, like a corpse, with his nose in the air and his mouth open. But he was sitting in a padded plastic armchair next to his locker, in the middle of a six-bedded bay. He wore green pyjamas, a paisley dressing-gown and brown leather slippers. His still-wavy hair was combed in thin, wrinkly streaks across his head. A folded newspaper was about to slide off his knee. He was asleep.

She told herself to keep walking. She'd come this far, she could manage a few more steps, a few platitudes, and her duty would be done. She didn't have to like him, let alone love him, just do the right thing, and she could get away at any time.

'Are you for me?' shouted an old man on the opposite side of the bay. 'Are you one of mine?'

'Belt up,' grumbled another. 'They're never for you.'

She reached his side and sat on the edge of the bed next to

Gerald, taking a moment to observe him unobserved. He was still identifiably himself but shrunk, deflated. What was the word Fran had used? Reduced. The purplish colour was still there on his nose, cheeks and neck, mixed with a yellowish pallor. His hands were particularly pathetic: those beefy hands that had squeezed the steering-wheel so terrifyingly were now bony claws curved over the arms of the chair. His skin was dotted with small lesions and sores, and on his ankles the skin itself had a scaly, reptilian appearance. His lower lip sagged, revealing a puddle of saliva about to overflow.

She didn't know what to say to wake him up. Her mother had referred to him as 'your father' but she herself had never called him that, or Dad, or anything for as long as she could remember. But if she couldn't find a form of address, she didn't want to touch him either. She compromised by giving his shoulder a small shake and saying, 'Hallo? It's me, Miranda. Hallo?'

She thought, I sound like someone on a poor telephone line, but he was fully awake immediately.

'What are you doing here?'

His voice was surprisingly strong, but every vibration was visible in his sinewy stalk of neck with its wobbling Adam's apple. She was reminded that he was not so very old, but very, very ill.

'I came to see you.'

'Why?'

Good question, she thought, and paid him the compliment of honesty. 'Fran told me to.'

'Well, now you have,' he said.

She didn't blink. 'How are you?'

'Never better, how does it look? Frigging awful. Can't eat, can't crap, can't walk, can't have a drink – can't wait to move on.'

'Have they said when that'll be?'

'I meant shuffle it off. Croak. Die.'

'Yes,' she said, as though she'd understood the first time. 'Have they said when that will be?'

'Soon. Can't be soon enough for me.' His skinny hands did

247

a pale imitation of the angry squeeze on the arms of the chair. 'So, what are you doing with yourself?'

'Still modelling.'

'Money good?'

'Very good.'

He looked her up and down disparagingly, taking in the jeans and shirt. 'What do you spend it on?'

'I've got my own flat, a nice car, I can pick and choose what work I do, go pretty much where I want when I want—'

'Did all right for yourself in the end, then.'

He seemed, in some gruesome way, to be trying to take credit for her success. 'I've worked hard.'

'Tell that to a coal miner.'

She wished she was allowed to smoke. 'I'm popping out for a fag. Is there anything I can get for you?'

'That was quick. Still, you can tell Fran and your mother you did it.'

'I'm coming back,' she said icily.

'Get some chocolate, I'm allowed that.'

She retraced her steps to the main concourse, telling herself she could always go now if she wanted to, he didn't give a damn either way, and as he'd pointed out she'd have done as she was told.

To calm her nerves she went outside the sliding glass doors, lit a cigarette and smoked half of it. Then she went back in, bought a bar of milk chocolate and one of plain, and returned to the ward.

A nurse met her as she went in. 'Are you Miranda? He's been asking for you.'

'I told him I was coming back.'

The nurse cast a fond smile over her shoulder at him. 'He's such a character, your dad. Must have been a real ladies' man once. Still is, on his good days.'

Miranda put down the chocolate on the locker. 'There you are. Would you like a bit now?'

'No, tell you what I would like, though.'

'What?'

'A little daughterly duty you could perform.'

Her skin crawled. 'What?'

He caught her hand in his chickeny one. 'You could finish me off.'

'*What?*'

'Record got stuck.'

She extricated herself. 'I'll get the nurse.'

He clutched her, his fingers digging in. 'Don't do that. They don't give a stuff anyway. NHS is run off its feet, they could do with the bed. I'm only hanging on because they're not allowed to put me out of my misery.'

She prised his fingers off. 'You look okay to me,' she said. 'Better than I expected.'

'You'd love to, wouldn't you?' His voice was gloating. 'It's what you've always dreamed about. We'd both be as happy as Larry.'

'How would I do it, anyway?' she asked, simultaneously realising she'd fallen into his trap.

'See?' He grinned. He'd always had big teeth and now they appeared long and yellow and skull-like, his strongest remaining feature. 'See?'

As she walked out he was still laughing, having the last laugh and coughing disgustingly, and the old man on the other side wailed, 'Don't go! Are you for me?'

Usually she loved her flat, but tonight it didn't welcome her. Its snug, casual luxury, the comfort and colour she'd lavished on herself with success, was like a reproof. She felt foolish, empty and alone. She couldn't wait to get out of it again, and to be in Tom's shoebox-sized Spitalfields apartment, the base camp of a busy, driven man, on which nothing had been lavished.

By the time she'd grabbed a sandwich and driven over there, she was trembling with fatigue. Tom still wasn't back. She had a soak in his narrow bath, put on his dressing-gown and sat up for an hour, nodding in front of the television, before giving up the unequal struggle and going to bed. She cried again, and then slept.

It was the small hours before he slipped in beside her and

hauled her hungrily into his arms. She buried her face in his chest.

'What's the matter?' He tried to lift her face to his but she resisted. 'Ragsy?'

She shook her head.

'How was your evening?'

'Stood me up.'

'Silly cow.' He kissed her hair. 'Calls herself a friend?'

CHAPTER ELEVEN

———————

Claudia, 137

There were some things Claudia never asked. Not because of Publius' reaction to the questions, but because of what her own might be to the answers. She preferred to remain curious, than to ask directly: How dangerous is this place? When will we go home?

And she did not ask about the night horrors.

Over the first five years of their marriage these occurred no more than half a dozen times, but on each occasion they shocked her so deeply that she could not even have found the words to frame a question.

Through all this turmoil, he never woke up, though she always did. Long before the crisis her eyes would snap open, alerted by some change in him, as though she could hear the quickening pace of his heart as it tried to escape what was bearing down on it. The third time that this happened she surrendered to her own prescience, slipping her arm around him from behind and pressing her lips to his shoulders, saying his name, trying to coax him back from the dark. His body was rigid, lost to her. She was scared to wake him forcibly unless, like a sleepwalker, the shock was too great. It was the only time when she feared his physical strength. She could only do her best to accompany him, clinging on and praying while the storm lasted.

He scarcely made a sound. She found it eerie that he could be going through so much and not emit the smallest cry, when his mouth gaped and his whole body seemed to scream, and

251

while he writhed and pressed his clenched, whitened fists to his face. She recalled seeing, as a child, the newborn baby of one of her father's slaves, and now she was reminded of the infant's involuntary convulsing.

Once, his flailing arm caught her a sledgehammer blow in the face and she yelped in pain. Her husband's arms had only ever been a source of sensual pleasure and protection, and she tried to catch his wrist and hold it fast but he was much too strong for her. All she could do was keep her own arms around his trunk, fingers linked tight.

The horrors could last for as long as twenty minutes. When they ended, they did so abruptly. Publius would fall away into an exhausted sleep, barely breathing: the sleep of the dead. It was she who lay awake until dawn, tortured by anxiety.

The day after one of these terrible nights he was always a little remote, but he never mentioned a nightmare and she sometimes wondered if he even remembered them. This, too, disturbed her. Unacknowledged troubles, she sensed, had more power to injure and estrange than fierce arguments.

When she'd had a swelling across the bridge of her nose from his involuntary blow, his puzzlement was genuine. 'What have you been doing to yourself in the night?'

It was her opportunity, but she chose not to take it. 'I tripped in the dark and cracked my nose on the edge of the table.'

Gently, he touched the place, which was tender and sore. 'Why didn't you wake me up?'

'Because it wasn't serious and I felt foolish.'

'It gives you a brigandly look. I rather care for it – so long as other people don't think I knock you about.'

Months would pass without a repetition of the horrors. With each lengthening interval she persuaded herself that it was nothing to worry about, a random occurrence. And then one night she'd wake with a start, her skin prickling with dread, knowing there was a third presence in their bed, an unknowable entity, hunting her husband down in the darkness of his head.

For a while she was haunted by the idea that these events had to do with their lost babies. Twice in one year she had failed to carry to term, and once, a year after that, a tiny girl was born two months early and died within minutes. Over the miscarriages Publius had appeared philosophical, his concern all for her and her return to health and happiness. He'd been strong, and calm. At the time of their daughter's birth he had been away on a week's scouting north of the Wall and it had not been possible in the mild summer weather to keep the tiny body for him to see.

By the time he returned Claudia had recovered some of her strength and was determined to put a brave face on it. She was not prepared for the tempest of his distress.

When he gasped, 'Oh, my poor girl, my poor darling,' and slumped, white-faced, into her arms, she had thought at first that he meant her.

'It's all right,' she said. 'I'm well, and the doctor says there's no reason—'

'Where is she?'

'Publius, we had to bury her.'

He was furious. 'You couldn't just have waited a little while so her father could see her?'

'We had to. I'm so, so sorry . . .'

'Did you name her? Did you give my daughter a name?'

'I did. Fabia.' She searched desperately for the right words. 'I thought you'd want me to do that.'

He didn't reply. His clenched fists hid his face as they did in the night horrors.

For the rest of that day she left him alone, and she went to bed in her own room at night. In the small hours he came in to her and folded her in his arms, bundling her into his embrace like a child, holding her tight. She was still sore and bleeding a little from the birth, so there could be no lovemaking. But closeness brought the relief of a few tears, and he kissed them and wiped her cheeks with his fingers. 'I'm sorry. It was such a shock.'

'And I'm sorry there was no way to soften it.'

'You went through all that, and I behaved like a bully.'

'I understood.'

He held her tightly and she thought she heard him murmur, 'Did you?' before they drifted into sleep.

These black moments apart, their privacy was precious to Claudia. Time spent alone with Publius was what enabled her to maintain her dignity and composure in the wider world of the garrison.

She treated her role of commanding-officer's wife as a job. It wasn't necessary, she told herself, to be suited to the role or feel at home in it, simply to play it effectively. She told Publius this, adding, 'Let's hope I'm never exposed as a sham.'

'No point in worrying,' he said. 'Most of us are, sooner or later. It's the effort that counts.'

The garrison was one of the most northerly in Britain, and one of the largest outside the three permanent legionary bases. The fort stood massive, brutal and confident on its lovely green hill. Its attendant native *vicus* and more disreputable shanty-town were spread all around but achieved greatest density on the south-eastern flank of the hill, in the lee of the fort's wall and sheltered from the prevailing wind. The road from the south, the one by which Claudia had arrived five years before, sliced authoritatively and straight as a sword from the fort's main gate to the horizon. She had a fondness for that road because she knew where it led. It was the escape route: the way home. To the north the road led further into the unknown, where she hoped never to go.

The garrison itself was nothing less than a complete, compact Roman town, with all of a town's vices, virtues and amenities enclosed within its walls. The only buildings outside the fortification were the men's bath-house and latrines, and – at a suitable distance from these practical facilities – the temple of Mithras. In the commandant's quarters they had their own bath-house, for which Claudia was grateful, and the food had been a pleasant surprise. Almost anything would have been after the stodgy sameness of the meals *en route*, but here the cosmopolitan tastes of the legionaries, and the need to keep them happy on this least-sought-after of postings, meant that there were a number of welcome imports – olive and fish oils, wine, some non-indigenous herbs, fruits and vegetables (and a creditable attempt to grow many of the latter locally), and there was always plenty of good meat.

Severina recommended a dressmaker to Claudia, and every so often she had a new outfit made, especially if there was news of a change of fashion in Rome, although she realised that by the time she'd caught up with it the fashion would probably be out of date. To present even a faint echo of Roman style was a source of satisfaction, although when she'd lived there it had meant little to her. Far more necessary, these days, was the need to adapt to the weather – you couldn't hope to look your best if you were chilled and sniffling, your skin chapped, your joints stiff, your feet tortured by chilblains and your nose and eyes running. Comfort and dryness were essential. In the *vicus* there were literally dozens of craftsmen and small manufacturers, either entrepreneurial locals or retired soldiers putting their army trade to use, and with Severina's help she got to know the shoemakers, the metalworkers, the weavers and the tanners who made the best foul-weather kit. She acquired several thick cloaks with hoods, leather boots and overshoes, gloves made of hide and fur, and big, dramatic brooches to use as fastenings.

She did not, however, find it easy to make friends. Her relative youth, her position in the garrison, and her concealment of her own insecurities behind an air of hauteur, all set her somewhat apart.

In the end Severina took it upon herself to broker a friendship. She made no bones about it. 'I was talking to the cook from over the way. Do you know the lady Flavia Marcella?'

'She was kind enough to give a dinner party when I first arrived.'

'A very nice lady,' declared Severina, as she straightened the bed. 'But she's got a daughter who's a real worry to her.'

'I knew she had children.'

'There's a little boy too, younger than Helena, but he's no bother. Obsessed with the army, like his father. No, Helena's the one the poor lady worries about – she's a clever girl all right, but a temper to curdle milk.'

'How old is she?'

'Thirteen. Old enough to be betrothed, but there's no chance of that.'

'Poor child.'

'Grumpy madam.' Severina blew on Claudia's hand mirror and polished it on her sleeve. 'She needs cheering up a bit.'

Claudia was alerted by the deliberately casual tone of this remark. 'Severina, you're organising me again.'

'Only trying to help the girl.'

Claudia had to laugh. 'But I'm at a loss to know how I could.'

'You could ask the mother and the daughter round!' Severina waggled the mirror to emphasise her point. 'Flavia would be delighted, the girl would be flattered, you might even like them.'

The process of acquaintance didn't follow the pattern Severina might have envisaged, but it did take place. When Flavia and her daughter visited the house, Claudia realised that she had seen the girl before, and made a note of her. She was big for her age, not only tall but heavy, with black hair, thick brows, and deep-set eyes: looks that in a confident, mature woman could be wonderfully striking, but were nothing but a burden to a gauche and unhappy girl of thirteen. Her mouth turned down discontentedly at the corners, and her eyes had a way of flicking sideways when she was spoken to, to avoid more contact than was necessary.

It was spring and they sat in the garden. Conversation was sticky at first. Flavia was a nice, sociable woman at least ten years older than Claudia and inhibited by the surly presence of her daughter. Claudia realised she had better justify including the girl so they all knew where they were. She had decided on a line. 'Helena, you could help me.'

'Could I?'

'It would be more polite to ask, "In what way?"' said Flavia, flashing a frown in her daughter's direction and an apologetic smile in Claudia's. She was caught in the cross-fire, poor woman.

Claudia soldiered on: 'How long have you lived here?'

'Lived where?'

'Helena!'

'I meant,' said Helena witheringly, 'did she mean in Britain, or in this place?'

'Both,' Claudia answered quickly, before Flavia could take issue with her daughter again.

'In Britain, all my life – I was born in Erboricum. Here, three years.'

'So you're an old hand. A true daughter of Empire.' Claudia continued gamely: 'I expect you could give me some tips.'

It wasn't working. The girl glanced at her mother with a what-is-she-on-about? expression, which was duly ignored.

'It must all feel very strange,' said Flavia. 'I do sympathise. I remember only too well what it was like when I first arrived, and we were in the south to begin with so I had a chance to acclimatise.'

'The journey helped. It was so awful that anything afterwards would have seemed pleasant. And, anyway, I'd hardly seen my husband since we were married.'

Helena fidgeted restlessly, a dark and unsettling presence. Claudia turned to her again. 'How well do you remember Erboricum? I'd like to go there some time. Is there a theatre?'

She realised as she spoke that these were stupid questions because the girl had been only a child when she left the city, but it would still have been better if Flavia hadn't rushed to answer for her.

'There is. I miss that, but we do go back from time to time. We still have friends there. The husband left the legion and they built a nice house—'

'Mother,' said Helena furiously, 'she asked *me*.'

'Yes, but you were very little at the time, so I thought—'

'I could have explained that.'

'It's done now.' Flavia gave the girl a look intended to quell, but it was too late.

'Yes, it is. May I go?'

'That would be impolite.'

'Please – may I go?'

'You must ask your hostess.'

Helena turned her face, though not her eyes, to Claudia. Her pursed mouth said: If I must. 'May I go?'

'Of course.'

Claudia sensed at once that this was the most popular she'd been all afternoon.

'Thank you.'

Helena rose and stumped towards the house, passing on the way the young German girl carrying a plate of cakes.

'Take a cake!' called Claudia, but Helena either ignored or didn't hear her.

Flavia was mortified. 'I can't apologise enough. She's so rude. It's like having a cantankerous animal in the house.'

'I'm sure she can't help it.'

'Or won't!' Flavia helped herself to a cake. 'All the more for us.'

'I know very little about children,' ventured Claudia, 'but I do remember what it was like to be thirteen and to feel different.'

Flavia laughed ruefully, catching crumbs in her palm. 'I forget, thirteen's not so far away for you.'

'And I don't blame her for not wanting to stay. I was doing my best but I was patronising her. You must tell her she can come round whenever she likes. I shan't interrogate her.'

'You're very forbearing.'

'No, I'd like it.'

It was months before Helena took her up on this offer, but in the meantime she and Flavia became friends. She reminded Claudia of someone, and one day she realised who it was – the redoubtable officer's wife on board ship. Was it, she wondered, that soldiers attracted a certain type of woman? Or that they went out looking for them? Or that all kinds of women became the same once they married into the army?

Would it happen to her?

Flavia was practical. She listened sympathetically when Claudia told her about poor little Fabia and the earlier miscarriages, and made some suggestions.

'Early on I couldn't even fall pregnant, and I was only sixteen! But listen, when next you do – and you will – I recommend an excellent man in the *vicus* who specialises in herbal supplements.

You don't need to creep about like an invalid, but take normal care, eat well and take a couple of these British specialities – your woman will bear me out.'

'Thank you. But there's no sign of anything at the moment.'

'How old are you?'

'Twenty-seven.'

'Plenty of time.'

A couple of weeks later Flavia asked, 'I don't suppose you'd like a puppy?'

It was the wording that made Claudia realise this was a request rather than an offer. She smiled, hesitated and in that moment was, effectively, lost.

'Come round and see. Marcus told me the dog belonging to the brewer has had an unwanted litter. The men have found homes for three of them but there's one left and once Didius gets wind of it we shall never hear the end of it.'

'Don't you want it?'

Flavia sighed. 'I suppose I wouldn't mind, but we already have Max, who we're all very fond of, and he's old and grumpy, it wouldn't be fair on him. Or the puppy. One way and another there'd be no peace and a lot of mess. Not that that lasts long,' she added hastily, 'and it's an outdoor dog that won't need pampering.'

'I'll see.'

'You can't tell without looking,' said Flavia firmly. 'Come round tomorrow morning while the children are with their tutor and I'll show you.'

She mentioned this to Publius while they were eating supper.

'I've no objection. In fact it's a good idea, I've been meaning to get a dog to train up myself.'

She wondered in that case why he hadn't got one already. 'I don't know much about them,' she said. 'Do you want to take a look at it as well?'

'No, there isn't time. We've got a fresh batch of men coming in tomorrow from basic training, all wide-eyed and ready to go. I shall be overseeing toughening-up fatigues all day. Don't look so worried. If the beast's friendly and has no obvious bad habits or diseases, take it. It's only a cur,' he added. 'If it doesn't suit we'll get rid of it.'

She murmured agreement, but such a course of action was, to her, unthinkable. Better not to have a dog at all than have to dispense with it so casually. By the time she and Flavia arrived at the brewer's premises the following day, she'd convinced herself that this would have to be a canine paragon for her to take it home.

The puppy was no paragon, but it was still love at first sight. He was lithe, slender and bright-eyed as a faun, with a honey-coloured coat streaked with brown, and white socks. He leaped and pranced ecstatically on their arrival, but when Claudia picked him up he folded into her arms and laid his pointed muzzle against her shoulder, quivering with devotion, his warm tongue occasionally darting out to kiss her cheek. The puppy's mother, with a greyer brindle coat, lay on sacking in the corner of the yard watching the proceedings with a soulful expression, her ears laid down.

The brewery had a strong, sweet-sour smell, which the puppy's coat had absorbed. Claudia could never again smell beer without thinking of this happy day.

'Nice little dog that,' said the brewer offhandedly, in the manner of a man who couldn't care less. He retrieved the pup from Claudia and held him in the air one-handed, turning him this way and that. The puppy drooped miserably, its long legs rigid with apprehension. 'Mother's a lovely bitch,' went on the brewer. He jerked a thumb in her direction. 'You can tell. But she's out of milk now and doesn't want to know.'

Claudia was affected by this tale of rejection, but Flavia recognised a sob-story, and ignored it. 'Any idea about the father?'

'Now, is that likely? You've seen what it's like around here. But one look, you can tell it's not a bad mix. That's a proper hunting dog.'

'Hmm.' Flavia folded her arms and surveyed the puppy. 'You'll be glad to get rid of him, I expect, with the bitch not interested.'

'Lady,' said the man, cannily handing the trembling pup back to Claudia, 'I'm not wasting any sleep. If he gets a home, so be it. If he doesn't he'll be out there fending for himself.'

That did it. 'I'm taking him,' said Claudia. 'What do you want for him?'

Flavia laid a restraining hand on her arm. 'My understanding,' she said, 'is that this gentleman would happily pay us to take him away.'

The brewer grinned incredulously, shaking his head. 'You're joking, aren't you?'

'We'll take him off your hands,' said Flavia. 'And we'd like some sort of lead.'

The brewer shook his head some more, then retreated into his premises, sucking his teeth, and produced a length of twine. 'Go on, then.' He spread his arms and shrugged eloquently, as if to say some people would stop at nothing to avoid paying.

'Thank you,' said Claudia. 'Very much. Does he have a name?'

'Down to you, lady. The bitch is called Kep.'

The moment they were on their way back, with the puppy bounding and tugging like a fish on a line, Flavia's manner changed. 'He's sweet!'

'I think so . . . but you didn't seem so sure in there.'

'Claudia, I was saving you from yourself. You were going to pay that fellow!'

'I would have done. It was the thought of him being abandoned, I couldn't bear it.'

'Of course you couldn't.' Flavia gave her arm a little shake. 'He knew that. And it wouldn't have happened. There's always a home for a nice hunting dog like this, but you had first refusal because he thought he could get cash out of you.'

'You're very confident.'

'Not really, it's all front. But I have lived in Britain a long time. And,' she added conspiratorially, 'I have an ulterior motive.'

Claudia named the puppy Tiki. The moment she got him home he went mad, haring from room to room, his skinny legs scissoring beneath him and his ears laid back, cornering on two feet, skidding on the tiles and bumping into pots and plants.

Severina took the dimmest possible view. 'Aah! What's all this?'

'Company, Severina. He's called Tiki.'

'He's a lunatic – ah! Where will you put it?'

Claudia had given no thought to this. The nights were drawing in and there was no kennel. 'In the kitchen?'

'The cook won't want that.'

'He'll eat up scraps.'

'And everything else too. They get big, you know, and they're shocking thieves.'

'Don't worry,' said Claudia. 'I'll take care of him.'

'It needs all this beating out of it. Get away!' Severina threw up her hands as the puppy ricocheted off her legs. 'It's not safe!'

Fortunately Publius was amused by the puppy's antics, though this might have been because by the time his new master returned he was tiring: after a wild airborne greeting, a couple of laps of honour and a large puddle the puppy collapsed into sleep.

'He's a terrific little chap,' said Publius, tickling the pup's ribs with one finger so that a hind leg pedalled convulsively. 'We'll soon lick him into shape.'

'Severina isn't keen.'

'She'll come round. A few weeks and she'll be eating out of his hand. And vice versa.'

This prediction proved correct. And in the event it was Severina who was most influential in civilising Tiki. Publius drew the line at having him in the bedroom, so Severina let him sleep in a box in hers, and got one of her useful *fabriciae* contacts to knock up a kennel and a run in the sheltered corner of the garden. Her mixture of sternness and bribery bore results, though she still affected the gravest disapproval.

'The sooner the animal's put to work the better,' she declared grimly. 'It'll get fat and smelly in no time.'

Publius agreed with this and expressed his intention to take Tiki hunting as soon as he was big enough to stand the pace. Secretly Claudia hoped that this time was some way off. The dog was an incalculable improvement to her life. When she took

262

him out on his red collar and lead (custom-made by another of Severina's little men and a slight embarrassment to Publius), people spoke to both of them with no consciousness of rank. The tradesmen gave him titbits. They thought Tiki a card, an opportunist. It amused them that this cur from outside should be the pampered pet of an officer's wife.

'One of the brewer's, is he?' they'd ask, laughing. 'He's fallen on his feet. There must be twenty of those a year.'

There were several of his kind, including a few of the pup's siblings, accommodated in a pen at the barracks, an informal pack kept just this side of peckish and already paying their way with rabbits. They set up a terrific noise if they smelt Tiki nearby and sometimes one of the men would come out to see who it was, and salute her informally.

Claudia took all this in good part. More, she liked it. The dog gave her an identity beyond that of her status as commandant's wife. And, more importantly, when she went back to the house, she no longer had to tell herself that it was home.

There was another consequence, too: evidence of Flavia's ulterior motive. Less than two weeks after Tiki's arrival, on a morning when Claudia was getting a headache over the accounts, Flavia's children were shown in. Helena was scowling as usual, but Claudia was glad of any excuse to escape the figures, and rose to greet them.

'Hallo! What a nice surprise. Is your mother with you?'

'No,' said Helena. 'I brought him round.' She nodded towards her brother.

This told her fair and square that the visit was an errand, and not of Helena's choosing.

'Fine,' said Claudia. 'Hallo, Didius. Would you like something to drink?'

Didius declined, and got to the point. 'Mother said you had a puppy, can we see it?'

Helena cuffed his shoulder with the back of her hand. 'Please.'

'Please.'

'Of course! Let's go and get him.' She paused and looked at Helena. 'Helena, do you want to go? Didius can stay here with me for a while, I'll make sure he gets back safely a bit later.'

'It's all right,' was the slightly graceless reply. 'Now I'm here I might as well stay.'

'Of course, that'd be nice.'

They stayed all morning. After the initial introductions, Claudia returned to her accounts, more from tact than conscientiousness. To begin with Helena sat on a chair nearby while Didius and Tiki careered about the small garden. But when the pace began to slow, and they came over and flopped down in the shade, she couldn't resist stroking the puppy's palpitating flank. Claudia paid no attention.

'Max isn't well,' Helena remarked, only just loud enough to hear, and without looking up.

'I'm so sorry, poor old chap. He's old, isn't he?'

'We've always had him.'

Claudia remembered that childhood meaning of 'always'.

'Much longer than Didius,' added Helena, with a slight edge.

'One year,' corrected her brother.

'Two.'

'He'll probably recover,' said Claudia.

Helena shook her head. 'He's in pain and being sick all the time. Father says if it goes on another day he'll have to do something about it.'

'That's probably for the best,' said Claudia, resorting to adult platitudes but without conviction.

Suddenly and unexpectedly Helena burst into tears – great, lurching, uninhibited sobs interspersed with racking intakes of breath that shook her large frame. Didius looked first aghast, then fiery with embarrassment.

'What's she doing that for?'

'She's upset,' said Claudia sharply, pulling her own chair next to Helena's and putting an arm round her shoulders.

He looked disgusted. 'I'm going!'

'No – where to?'

'Away from her.' He nodded towards his sister and went to sit some distance away and shy small stones at a flowerpot.

'Careful you don't break it.' Claudia stroked Helena's hair. 'It's horrible, poor Max. I'm so sorry . . .'

Happily Severina, who whatever her faults liked to save the day, came out and ushered Didius inside for a cold drink.

In a while Helena stopped crying and sat up, wiping her face with her sleeve. She looked very young and pathetic, but Claudia was wary: after what the girl would see as this public and humiliating lapse, things might go either way.

'I've known him all my life, you see,' explained Helena.

'I know.' In the interests of fairness, Claudia added, 'And so has your brother.'

'Yes, but when I was little, Max was little. We used to play.'

Claudia was swept a sudden sweet, strong thought of Tasso. 'Yes.'

'Once Didi wanted to play, Max was getting too old.'

This made perfect sense. An idea presented itself, as Flavia (she realised) had intended it should.

'Whatever happens, you can both come round here whenever you like.' She worded the next part of her suggestion carefully. 'I want to hear how Max is doing, and Tiki would appreciate the company.' Helena hesitated, and then, for the first time, looked her steadily in the eye. 'All right.'

Flavia had achieved her objective, and it was a success. Claudia knew she had been manipulated by an expert. All concerned had the satisfaction of feeling that they were doing someone else a good turn, with the added bonus of getting what they wanted.

In opening her doors to the children Claudia opened them to play, and noise, and mess and laughter, and conversation of the droll, enquiring, uncompromising sort that only the young could provide. The house felt warmer, lighter, smaller – more homely. Tiki was in heaven. Severina's nose was out of joint, but only temporarily. As the puppy had shown, she was essentially a pushover, especially where little boys were concerned, and Didius had only to show his face near the kitchen for Severina to appropriate some treat for him to the fury of the cook.

Publius was quiet on the subject. One night in bed she asked him if he minded the children coming round. 'Of course not. They're nice enough youngsters. Anyway, I'm never here, I hardly see them.'

She rolled on top of him and held his face between her hands. 'You do know that I love you?'

He hesitated. 'I hope that you do.'

'It's true.' She kissed him fiercely. 'This is a horrible place, why else would I be here?'

'Because you're a dutiful wife. A daughter of Rome.'

'Yes, I'd forgotten that! That must be it.'

'But,' he slipped sideways from beneath her so that they lay facing one another, 'I can see that you're happier now there are others in the house.'

'Yes.' As soon as she'd answered she realised the inference he would draw. 'I have a lot of time to fill without you.'

He smiled. 'I understand. You're young, you need other young things around you. It's natural.'

They made love and the moment passed. But she reflected on it, and a few days later it came to her. Publius was right. The puppy, the children, the sights and sounds of their play – they helped to fill the space left by Tasso. As a child she'd never owned a pet, or had a sibling. Tasso had unknowingly served in the office of both. With him she had been a mixture of parent, playmate and boss. She still clung to the passionate hope that he had not been responsible for the theft of her valuables. This had even prompted her to be less than completely truthful with Publius, allowing him to gain the impression that Tasso's disappearance and the loss of her possessions had been on separate occasions. They would never know, because they would never see Tasso again.

She still missed his refinement and gentleness, his singing, his playfulness; even his childish moods. For these, the exuberant antics of Didi and Tiki, and the gradual winning of Helena's confidence more than compensated. But what could never be replaced was Tasso's knowledge of her. He had learned his young mistress as he'd learned reading, writing and music. He had come to know her better than her father had, better even than Publius did, because he had witnessed the changes in her. And Claudia, in her turn, had learned him. All this mutual knowledge was implicit; unspoken between them. The many subtle shifts and accommodations that allowed for the alteration of their relationship were testament to it. She refused to believe that he had betrayed her.

Whatever special requests or offerings she might make daily to the *lares et penates*, their household gods, a few prayers were a constant.

Make this a happy home.

Protect my beloved husband.

Let us have a child.

Watch over those who are far away.

In this last she included Tasso as well as her father. She had heard from Marianus from time to time, though it was increasingly hard to decipher the words scrawled on papyrus (he disliked writing on wood) and blurred by weeks of travel. She was pleased that he seemed to be well and was no longer fretting, but a little guilty, too, that she thought of him less than she did of Tasso.

Claudia still found the winters hard to bear. There was a particular kind of bitter wind that came screaming from the north, bearing frozen rain that pierced clothing and skin like needles. In the middle of winter there could be scarcely any light for days on end. She even welcomed the luminous whiteness of snow, which until now she'd never seen before.

Tiki grew to maturity and was often out with Publius, hunting or simply trotting at his heels. Claudia knew it was the right thing for the dog – the discipline, the exercise and the natural focus for his energies – but she still missed him.

At fifteen Helena, a slimmer, calmer, but still painfully young Helena, was betrothed. Flavia was thrilled, and though Claudia was too, there was a sadness that she kept to herself.

'If you had told me two and half years ago that this would have happened, I should have laughed in your face!'

'It's wonderful news,' agreed Claudia.

'And so much of it is due to you. The day you became her friend was the day she began to change.'

'She would have changed anyway.'

As everything did. With no dog to visit, his sister soon to leave home and a more favoured grown-up existence beckoning as a result, Didi didn't come so often and when he did Claudia suspected the prompting of his mother. When Helena came it was to say goodbye, and there was more than a touch of the old Helena in her refusal – which Claudia recognised as embarrassment – to acknowledge any debt.

'I'm going to live at Corbridge,' she said. 'It's a bit more civilised than this.'

'And closer to Erboricum,' agreed Claudia. 'You'll like that. I'm so happy for you.'

'Do you remember saying how you were a newcomer, whereas I was born to army life?'

'I do.'

'Well,' said Helena, her eyes slipping away to the side and her cheeks pink, 'when I get there I'm going to be a newcomer too. Will you write to me?'

'Yes,' said Claudia. 'I will.'

No more than a month after Helena's wedding at the beginning of March, Flavia confided delightedly that she was to be a grandmother.

That was a low ebb for Claudia. It was early spring but still bitterly cold. The trees in the valley below the fort, beyond the British settlement, were dotted with a suggestion of new growth, their closed, hard buds disclosing the merest hint of green. But on the uplands there was precious little colour, the grass was a wind-whipped yellow, the off-road tracks either muddy or frozen, and the hills to the north grey and white with snow. Apart from the usual late-winter deaths among the very old and the young, there was illness about – a high fever and swollen throat accompanied by a rash – which took its toll of even the toughened legionaries, so the workforce was depleted.

Claudia had not been ill so far, and petitioned the gods

regularly for continued good health. But she was tired and dispirited. Publius had been involved in several skirmishes with the troublesome Scots, who seemed not to want to keep themselves to themselves, and for the first time she found she disliked being alone. His face seemed always to be grey and grooved with tiredness. Once he came back with a small wound – a piece cut from the side of his ear – and the injury shocked her, though it made him grunt with laughter. 'Now there's a bit of me that's part of Britain for ever.'

Then on a fine day in early April, Publius said he wanted to take her out, to show her something.

'A surprise?' she asked.

'Not a surprise so much as an idea . . . You'll see.'

They rode out, Publius on a rough-coated, thick-necked cavalry horse, Claudia on a mule whose ears stuck out like dragonfly-wings on either side of its head, Tiki trotting alongside. Riding through the great south gate she realised that she had scarcely been outside the garrison all winter and just to leave the walls behind and have the tang of the hills in her nostrils and the sharp fresh air in her lungs did a lot to raise her spirits. The moment they were out Tiki ran, flat out, for the sheer joy of it, then returned to mock their slower progress by bounding round them in circles, grinning and waving his whip of a tail.

'Where are we going?'

'Not far.'

About three-quarters of a mile from the fort, Publius turned off the road and followed a small track that travelled diagonally across the flank of the hill. Tiki shot ahead again and disappeared from view.

'We shan't see him again today,' she called against the wind.

'He'll be waiting for us, don't you worry . . .'

'So he's been here before?'

Publius jerked his head. 'He has.'

The dog was lying, panting, in the centre of a broad, shelf-like hollow on the hillside, about a quarter of a mile across. Because of its sheltered position, with the high ridge behind it and trees to the east and south, the spring seemed further advanced here, the smaller of the trees had a fine dusting of green and the grass showed patches of bright new growth and some small yellow and blue heath flowers. The high scudding clouds parted obligingly as they arrived and sunlight brought out the colours of the land. Here, out of the wind, Claudia felt real warmth on her skin for the first time in months.

'Like it?'

'It's lovely.'

'That's what I think.'

He dismounted and helped her to do the same, looping the reins over the necks of horse and mule. 'Come. Take a proper look.'

Quietly, arms linked, they walked around the tranquil space. They were still high enough to enjoy a magnificent view to the north and east.

'Look,' he held her shoulder with one hand and pointed with the other, 'the Wall.'

She could just make out the black line snaking across distant hills, a single mile-castle visible, like a thumbs-up.

'We would be safe and happy here, Claudia.'

'Yes.' She nodded before fully realising what he had said. 'I'm sorry, I don't understand.'

'I want to build us a house here.'

'You mean, live here?'

'I shan't be in command for ever,' he said, 'but I've been here too long to go back. Think of what we could do in a place like this, what we could make of it. There are wonderful houses being built all over the province now, the labour's cheap, we could have what we wanted.'

She smiled, moved by his enthusiasm, though her heart was racing with anxiety. While they were in the garrison they were birds of passage, the occupying army, likely one day to move on. But to move on *here*? The importance, the permanence of it, snatched her breath away.

'Claudia?'

She leaned her head sideways on his shoulder so that her face wouldn't betray her. 'Why not?' she murmured.

Publius couldn't know that it was a true question, and one

she asked not him but herself. His voice was bright and warm, more vital than she'd heard it in months.

'I'm getting the plans drawn up.'

Not wishing to be left out, Tiki came over and thrust his head between them. She felt the dog's muzzle in her palm. She was so tired. And suddenly, unaccountably, on the edge of tears.

'Just think,' said Publius, 'what a wonderful place this will be for a child.'

It was April: full parade, for the rededication of the eagles. Raining, of course, the sort of dense rain that, when caught by the wind, formed swirling curtains. You could hear the creaking of stiff joints, the hawking, spitting and coughing of the ranks. Not much stoicism here, they were going to put their ills on parade. The wretched *aquilifers* had the worst of it: they'd been standing for half an hour already, holding their burdens aloft, and the eagles' wings conducted the rain and siphoned it nicely down their necks.

Publius rode out slowly, not to extend their suffering but to give the sense of occasion that this parade should have. He could almost feel the spines straightening, the heads lifting, all eyes upon him. Surrounded by this mixed and motley force that was the Roman army, he was an emblem of Empire just as much as the standards.

The civilians, wives, parents and children, were gathered to the west of the parade-ground with their backs to the wind. As he passed them he saw Claudia in her terracotta-red cloak, its folds held across her face in the secretive manner of an eastern woman, beaded silver with the rain. Only her eyes were visible, and his didn't rest on her for more than a second. But when he turned to face the troops his heart was huge with love for his wife, and the child inside her.

CHAPTER TWELVE

Bobby, 1992

Daniel and I were several months down the line when we finally went to bed together. For all that time we'd continued to see a lot of each other while preserving a distance. I had my job, and he his work. I had the cottage, which, though now nominally 'straight', conformed to the Govan standard of comfortable disorder; Daniel had the wide, white spaces of the mill. I'd made a few local friends with whom I occasionally shared drinks and meals; he remained, but for me, an elective loner.

We'd grown to love each other in our own way, but neither of us ever said, 'I love you,' because those were the words of people in love. Instead we developed a whole repertoire of phrases to get round it: very fond . . . think the world . . . such a difference . . . can't imagine . . . so dear . . . The ground gradually altered, but the earth didn't move. I didn't delude myself that this was a grand passion, but I did consider that it was the best – the very best – that I was capable of. I, who had always lacked the love gene, was giving and receiving love, and that'd do me. Daniel too, apparently.

Spud, whom I spoke to every so often on the phone, was sceptical. 'It's high time I came up and inspected this man.'

'You probably wouldn't like him – but, Spud, that's not the *point*.'

'I agree,' she said, 'it's not. The point is, whether you're bewitched, bothered and bewildered, and your best friend will be the judge of that.'

It was a kind of joke between us, my dull unworldliness and Spud's self-appointed stewardship; neither of us took it particularly seriously. Also, her own social life was so complex and intensive that I knew she would never come up to Witherburn uninvited, whatever her concerns on my behalf.

She was, though, intrigued by the age difference. Though he looked even younger Daniel was still only thirty-five, nearly ten years younger than me. Spud inevitably turned this into further grounds for suspicion. 'What's he doing on his own?'

'He's not gay, if that's what you're driving at.'

'How do you know?'

'How does one know? Just because. Spud, this isn't very flattering!'

'Sorry, Bobby, but it's my duty to play devil's advocate.'

Daniel's gayness or otherwise was not so much something of which I was certain, as something that did not concern me. I would not have been shocked, or devastated, to discover there had been both sexes in his life. I put this down to a grown-up seam of discretion and tolerance in our relationship, but perhaps it should have told me something more.

I remember how, and why, it happened. I went round to the mill one afternoon, and he was busy. It wasn't the first time I'd turned up when he was working, but before he'd always noticed my arrival and come to the door to meet me: we never hung about there, it was his private place and he liked to be in it on his own.

That day he had music playing, Sibelius' *Finlandia*, which must have been why he didn't hear the car. Out of respect for his privacy I knocked on the open door, but he was oblivious; deafened not so much by the music as by concentration.

I felt what I was, an intruder, standing in the doorway, and was on the verge of leaving him to it when he looked up. And it was the oddest thing: his eyes and his calm, focused expression didn't change; it was as though I'd been somewhere in his mind as he worked, so seeing me was no surprise. He straightened up and turned off the music, then came over and put his arms round me in an intense, but abstracted way: he had stopped working, but was still under the spell of the work. The clean, dusty smell of the wood was on his hair and skin, and there was wood-dust on his clothes.

'I'm sorry,' I began, but he just took me by the wrist and led me into the house and up to the bedroom. I remember thinking, This is it, or making myself think it, but that wasn't how it felt. How it felt was calm, ordered, inevitable. We each took off our clothes separately, not touching, then curled into one another's arms on the smooth, pale bed. We made love as though we'd known each other's bodies for years. His was thin but strong, physically confident. Still there was no sense of the power, or the desire, resting more with one than the other: we were equal. In fact, looking back, power and desire did not come into it at all. At the time it was so wonderful that this was happening at all, after so many years, and with Daniel, that I could have wept for happiness.

I did not come but, then, I never had. That was just me.

Afterwards, we spoke and went about our evening together not as though something had changed, but as though something had been recognised. We were both reticent people, but our reticence on this occasion had different sources – I could not have known how different.

One advantage of 2 Church Cottages was that it was not big enough to accommodate Jim and Sally's offspring when their parents eventually came to stay. I liked my nephews and nieces, but as a fully paid-up member of the child-free persuasion I found our different agendas clashed when we tried living together under one roof, especially when that roof was mine. So the older two were to be left at home (an exercise in trust that made me tremble), and the younger ones bestowed on friends.

Even with just my brother and sister-in-law, and for only thirty-six hours, from Friday night to after lunch on Sunday, I decided to keep them busy. A structure was needed if they were not to quiz me ceaselessly on my life, my plans, my state of mind and how I *really* was. I decided to take them for a brisk all-day outing to the Wall on Saturday, including a pub lunch – which, given a following wind, they would pay for – followed by the Hobdays for the recommended easy but delicious dinner. On Sunday morning I could envisage a local walk to show them where I worked – and to show off Ladycross – followed by a pint at the pub, a roast, and a fond farewell followed by the bliss of a solitary evening in the glow of duty done.

They were early, of course – a classic case of weekend without the kids so let's get going! – with no thought whatever of circumstances at my end. When I had breezily told them 'any time after about five' I emphatically hadn't meant five past. But that was when they showed up, greeting my flustered appearance with great cries of how the last thing they wanted was to be a nuisance, and they'd just take themselves off and explore until such time as I was ready for them. But I gritted my teeth in the time-honoured manner, told them I'd *meant* what I said (why does one do that?), and of course they must come in, unwind, have a cup of tea, or was it too early for a drink?

A glass of wine would have sorted me out, but they opted for tea and I didn't want them to think me a solitary boozer, so tea it was.

'But this is *lovely*, Bobby,' said Sally. 'Your own space at last. And you've made it so nice already.'

'I haven't had to do anything much,' I confessed. 'It was in good nick when I moved here. There are a few things I want to change, but—'

'All the time in the world!' she declared, as if cheering me up, when actually she'd taken the words out of my mouth. I did wish she wouldn't do that. Jim was peering out of the window, chewing a mini-florentine as though it were a toffee, and staring this way and that as though half expecting a stagecoach to gallop past.

'Smashing village,' he commented moistly, prising florentine off his back teeth with his index finger. 'Is it a hotbed of gossip?'

'Not that I know of.'

'In that case they're all gossiping about you! How's the property developer?'

'Fine,' I said guardedly, thinking, Here we go.

'No romance, then?'

'Jim,' said Sally, 'give it a rest. It's not even funny, it's just boring. Poor Bobby.' She smiled sympathetically at me; she was dying to know.

I didn't oblige either of them. I hadn't invited Daniel to join us at any point, knowing how uncomfortable it would make him.

'So, are you wheeling out any locals for us while we're here?' asked Jim.

'My nice neighbours, who also happen to be friends and my employers.'

'That'll never last.' He was disappointed about the lack of titbits on my social life.

'Kirsty and Chris Hobday, you'll like them.'

'How *is* the job?' asked Sally, her brow furrowed with changing-the-subject earnestness.

'It suits me beautifully. Very flexible, interesting, nice bosses – wonderful surroundings. I'll show you.'

'Gosh,' said Sally, with a hint of disbelief that only I could have detected, 'what a woman. You are just so sorted!'

I was a good deal less sorted the next day. Rather against my better judgement I'd agreed to let Jim do the driving – 'least I can do' – but this arrangement jiggled the chain of command. In the passenger seat with my map I felt responsible, but not in charge, and this uneasy state of affairs was not helped by Sally, who wasn't used to travelling in the back and spent her whole time leaning forward with her face on a level with my shoulder, alternating family chat with uninformed suggestions about the route.

Locating the Wall was no problem since it was simply a case of point north and keep going. But I wanted to find a place where the walking was good, and where we could have as our objective a site of particular interest. I was not someone whose pulse quickened at the thought of wandering round a scattering of old stones with the aid of an explanatory text and an artist's impression – and neither, if we were both truthful, was Jim – but Sally certainly liked to think she was, and this was a holiday for Sally more than anyone.

Jim drove a tad too fast, making me feel that I wouldn't be able to direct him without causing danger to all concerned. Our surroundings brought out the Mr Toad in my brother, making him more than usually reckless, and noisy.

'This is glorious!' he bellowed. 'I could drive all day in conditions like these!'

I hoped this wouldn't turn out to be prophetic. Phrases like 'going to the Wall', 'backs to the Wall' and 'through the Wall' popped unbidden into my head.

In the end it wasn't the Wall or its accompanying historical sites, all well signed and with parking, that proved the problem, but the finding of a suitable pub. I chastised myself for not having done a recce beforehand: I had been so sure that there would be benign hostelries all along our route, over-flowing with bangers and mash and local beer. Our quest began late, because with typical greenhorn enthusiasm we overshot ourselves on our walk, exclaiming with delight over every fresh, dramatic vista, and only turned back at a point where we were already flagging and had a long way to go. The site we were aiming for was, I knew, just beyond the next couple of hills, but that was two hills too far for my unfit and thirsty brother. Added to which the weather had changed and heavy rain was swirling in from the north-west. Through three hundred and sixty degrees the sky was a dark grey, alleviated by darker patches here and there. Within five minutes of the rain starting you could make out the road in the middle distance because the cars had their headlights on.

'We could try for the bus!' I yelled. 'I don't know how often the stops are, but I expect we could flag it down in this weather.'

'On the other hand,' replied Sally, who to her great credit was still being a good sport, 'we could walk several extra miles and not see one at all. Better the devil we know!'

Jim said nothing. The dripping hood of his anorak obscured the whole upper part of his face, but his mouth was set.

'All right, love?' Sally asked him, though it was hard to express tender solicitude above the roar of the rain. 'Soon have you outside a pint.'

Though I warmed to Sally for trying, I wished I could share her optimism. Because of the rain, and our tiredness, the return walk took us almost twice as long and I realised I was going to be the pathfinder-general again, this time dealing with a damp driver in a bad mood. As the layby with our car in it hove into view, I decided to put down a marker. The other two had fallen slightly behind because Sally had loyally opted to keep her husband company. For a shrink who was a spirited advocate of women's autonomy and self-esteem, and the non-symbiotic relationship, she was a surprisingly supportive wife. I paused to allow them to catch up.

'Once we get going,' I said, 'I suggest we stop at the first reasonable place we see.'

'Absolutely,' said Sally. 'I don't think any of us is fussy at this stage.'

Jim broke his silence to announce: 'Forget the pint, I shall be having a large Scotch.'

He was beginning seriously to annoy me, and I was glad Sally was there to act as a buffer zone, or there might have been an undignified passage of arms.

Predictably enough, as we reached the car the rain eased off. By the time we were back on the road a pale, invalid sun was doing its best. Inside the car we steamed gently.

'Well,' said Sally, 'that was absolutely wonderful. What a feat of engineering! So dramatic. In fact, even more dramatic in the rain – when you think of what those wretched legionaries had to put up with!'

'At least they had shelter,' pointed out Jim, who was feeling a bit better, 'and all that famous Roman efficiency to see them right. Lived like kings compared with what we've just been through.'

'Regular attacks from maddened bloodthirsty Scots apart.'

'All in a day's work for Bibulus and Ravenous.'

I could take a hint. 'Keep going,' I said. 'There's bound to be something soon.'

There was, but we were pickier than we thought. The first pub had three coaches outside, and the next had net curtains and no lights on.

'I foresee pickled eggs and Cold Comfort regulars,' said Jim, driving past.

After that there was nothing till the coaching inn at the junction with the Witherburn Road, and we decided to cut our losses and go to the Burnside Inn, where I knew Dave would stretch a point about food after two p.m.

We all ordered the ham and leek suet-crust pie, a speciality of the house so readily available, plus a double portion of chips to share between us. Sally had a glass of red wine, mine was a Guinness, and Jim tossed back the first Scotch and ordered another before sitting down by the gas-fired logs.

'Perks of returning to base camp,' he told us. 'By Jove, I needed this.'

We all felt a lot better for having achieved this objective, but I was still fretting about the failure to achieve our earlier one. When Dave brought the food over, I asked his advice. 'Surely there's some Roman stuff in Witherburn?'

'There is, up the top. Couple of miles or so from Ladycross.'

'Is it worth a look?'

'There's not an awful lot there, but if you like that sort of thing . . . It'd make a nice walk.'

'We've already had one of those,' said Jim. 'It's wheels or nothing.'

'You don't have to come,' pointed out Sally. 'You could stay and have another, or go back to Bobby's and put your feet up.'

But if she was hoping to get rid of him for a bit it didn't work. 'I'd *like* to come, might as well do the full Roman monty now we're here – I just don't want to do any more walking. Immediately.'

'No, you can take the motor,' said Dave. 'Go back up out of the village and take the unmade road about a mile on your left. Keep on going till you get to the farm entrance. You can park there—'

'Farmer's unarmed, is he?'

'He's a pussy-cat – and then you want to hang a left, it's a signed footpath.'

'I knew it . . .' Jim put a hand over his eyes and shook his head.

'Fort's only a few hundred yards from there.'

'One in three? Loose scree? Flash floods?'

'All downhill on the way back.'

'Sounds perfect,' said Sally, 'I'm up for that.'

'But as I say, don't get too excited,' warned Dave. 'There isn't that much to see.'

The sun had his hat back on by the time we left the pub, and the warmth of the short drive after lunch made us sleepy. Jim was grumpy, and he was certainly over the limit, so it was a relief when we turned off the main road.

'Your poor suspension,' I said sympathetically, as we bumped up the track. I thought I should compensate a little for some of the mean thoughts I'd had earlier.

'Nothing to what mine will be by the time we get back,' he said. I revoked the glimmer of remorse.

The afternoon had turned so nice that we decided to risk it and leave our sodden macs in the boot, all agreeing that this was tempting fate and that every thundercloud within a fifty-mile radius would be moving in on us as we spoke. But by the time we'd trudged up the footpath to the fort we were sweating profusely beneath a cloudless sky.

Dave had been right, there wasn't that much there, but this had the priceless advantage that there was no visitor-pleasing either. No kiosk, no café, no shop, no informative maps and charts. No visitors. Just a flat-topped hill, very still in the sunshine, commanding a breathtaking view. The broken network of moss and lichen-covered stone foundations was like a giant board-game on the grass. A hawk shimmered above us, drawing a bead on some hapless vole. The only sounds were the plaintive whistle of curlews and the distant baa-ing of sheep.

It was a relief to have the space and the sunshine to enjoy it, to fan out and be quiet. Sally, who had brought a guidebook, sat on a rock and consulted it, glancing around from time to time to orientate herself and verify the information. Jim went straight to the southern end of the fort and lay down on his front with his arms at his sides, his head in the recovery position. I guessed he would be asleep within seconds.

I walked slowly round the perimeter. I did my best, but it was hard to imagine these low, weathered lines of stone on which flowers grew and butterflies settled as the tough modern army camp it must once have been. I was aware that my perspective was inevitably unrealistic and sentimental. Just as photography makes us see the late nineteenth and early twentieth centuries as a sepia, then a black-and-white period, in which people either stared fixedly or scuttled like puppets, so the sheer beauty of this place as it now was lent it a romance it could never have possessed in its heyday. The choice of this glorious position was a military one, the stone lines were the last remaining bones of a noisy garrison.

Sally came alongside, book in hand.

'Don't worry,' she said, 'I'm not going to swamp you with information.'

'Not at all. What does it say?'

'Not a lot, you'll be glad to hear. "Still visible are the commandant's house, C,"' she cast round and pointed, 'that must be that, "and the barrack blocks, B1 and B2," way over there, "with between them the remains of the central drainage system still visible." They were big on their plumbing, weren't they? Blah-di-blah. "The large parade ground was situated to the west of the camp with its commanding aspect over the valley. The north-eastern corner of the parade-ground is marked by the base of a turret, T . . . site of Temple of Mithras." That sounds intriguing.'

She paused to read further, and I continued walking slowly. I was at the southern end of the camp now. Jim was dead to the world, snoring gently with his mouth open. A ladybird was clambering doggedly through his hair. From where I was standing I could trace the line of the Roman road, sometimes clearly visible as a farm track, sometimes a mere thread, occasionally disappearing only to resurface. How forcefully, and with what robust practicality these people had stamped their identity and intentions on the land. After nearly two thousand years even the insidious tide of nature hadn't obliterated their efforts. On the contrary, I thought, remembering the Wall, their constructions had become as much part of this landscape as the woods and rivers.

'Look at him.' Sally, who had caught up again, looked affectionately down at her husband. 'What is he like?'

'A man taking a well-earned rest?'

'He doesn't get enough exercise, that's his trouble.'

She went on to explain why this was, the rigours of being the hardworking parents of four lively children. It was a familiar riff and I partially switched off. As we came round to the eastern side of the camp I caught sight of the dog, the wanderer, trotting purposefully from left to right on the hillside below us. He was beginning to be familiar, and seemed like a nice dog, so just for fun I whistled. He took no notice whatever, but Sally said, 'What was that for?'

'That dog – he's always roaming around but no one knows who he belongs to.'

'Which dog?'

He'd gone. It struck me that he always seemed to know where he was going: a dog with a mission.

'I'm going to rouse the Sleeping Beauty,' said Sally, taking charge. 'By the way, when are the guests due?'

The evening was a success. It could scarcely have failed, given the rather sweet determination of all concerned to give a good account not just of themselves but of me. Relaxed by a day in the fresh air and generous infusions of Chilean merlot, my brother and sister-in-law came through like the social troupers they essentially were, impressing upon the Hobdays their good fortune in having me as a neighbour, not to mention as an employee. Jim, though, couldn't resist a dig on the subject.

'What happens,' he asked, leaning towards Chris but for the benefit of us all, 'when you want to sack her? As a dispute between neighbours it beats easement of light into a cocked hat.'

We all laughed but I couldn't pretend I wasn't interested in the answer. Fortunately it was almost impossible to wrongfoot the Hobdays, who conducted their lives on the basis that if you assumed the right stuff in others they'd probably provide it.

'For one thing, it's not going to happen,' said Chris amiably. 'And for another if the business folds we'll all go down together.'

'Very diplomatically spoken,' said Sally, making applauding motions. 'Remind me where your premises are. Bobby did tell us, but I've forgotten . . .'

While Kirsty explained, Chris turned to me. 'Have you heard about the plans?'

'No. Which plans?'

'They're building a theatre up at Ladycross.'

That was news, and I said so.

'I say "they",' went on Chris, 'but it was essentially a long-term project of Fred Montclere's which he entrusted in his will to Miranda to carry out. Not Miles, you understand. I've heard Miles on the subject and he's frankly not keen.'

I couldn't help wondering why anyone would want to leave such an obviously divisive instruction in his will. 'Won't that cause the most awful ructions? Even Miranda said she and Miles don't see eye to eye.'

'But they're both in their way the soul of diplomacy and, more importantly, they both thought the world of Fred.' Chris paused reflectively. 'He could be a bit mischievous, it's true.'

That, I thought, was putting it mildly, but it seemed best not to criticise from a position of ignorance.

'Where will the theatre be? Are we safe in the barns?'

'Completely, don't worry. It's all essentially investment on behalf of the house, remember. This project will generate revenue just as the office units do. They're not going to rob Peter to pay Paul. No, the idea Fred had – and I believe he's had the planning permission for years – is to build something down by the folly. Do you know it?'

'What a coincidence. I walked down there for the first time the other afternoon.'

'Lovely spot, isn't it?'

283

'It is . . . I can't imagine this theatre, though.'

'It'll only be a small one. Bijou, one might say, not more than a hundred seats. I gather the idea is to put on a summer season, a sort of festival, and then to have special events all through the year. Make it a destination as well as a local resource. A sort of mini-Glyndebourne.'

Put like that, I could envisage it. Soft lighting along the path and among the trees . . . Music, laughter . . . Strolling figures in evening dress . . . Ladycross presiding, all aglow on her hill . . . Miranda would get it right. 'It could be lovely,' I agreed.

'And keep the prices reasonable so that we locals get a look in.'

'That's so important, don't you reckon?' put in Kirsty, who had been listening. She turned to Jim and Sally. 'We're talking about the local stately home and its very unstately chatelaine.'

'Oh, that's the model.' Sally was up to speed on the situation. 'Didn't Lord Stratton die a few months back? I knew the house was here, which was why I noticed.'

'Yes, and the rather dull son's taking over,' said Kirsty, adding swiftly, 'but I'm sure he'll do a good job.'

Peter said, 'You must get Bobby to take you up there tomorrow and show you around. Miranda's back but she won't mind.'

I told him I was going to, but Jim was on the scent now. 'Which model was that, then? Anyone I'm likely to have ogled?'

'That won't narrow the field,' said Sally.

'Probably,' I said. 'Have you heard of Rags?'

It was the first time I'd ever seen someone's jaw drop. 'What? Rags? No! Her with the posh frock and the bovver boots? You're joking.'

'That's the one.'

'Jesus!' gasped Jim. 'One of my all-time fantasies living just up the road! You'd better keep my bed made up, sis.'

We all laughed, Sally most of all. She had the generosity of a woman who, having never had pretensions to beauty, felt no need to compete. 'Watch out, folks, he's come over all unnecessary.'

'Are we likely to run into her?' asked Jim.

'Most unlikely.' I decided against reminding him I'd been at school with Miranda, in case he had a seizure.

Naturally, we did run into her. We'd walked up through the wood the following morning and I'd shown them Ladycross's finer points from a discreet distance. It was a joy to see, in their faces, all the wonder and delight that I'd felt on first seeing the house. We'd just emerged from a brief tour of Smart Cards, when Miranda appeared from the direction of the house, accompanied by a man I didn't instantly recognise.

'You're in luck,' I told Jim. 'There she is.'

'God!' he murmured reverentially, and then, 'She must be knocking on a bit, I hope I won't be disappointed.'

Sally frowned and sucked her teeth. 'That's an awful, sexist thing to say, the poor woman.'

'Bobby!' Miranda waved an arm in the air. 'Lovely to see you! I'm back!'

Perhaps in honour of her companion she'd abandoned the cords and rat-catcher's cap in favour of narrow cream jeans, sneakers, and a pink shirt, sleeves rolled up and unbuttoned, over a white singlet. Her hair was cut short and she had a tan. She looked like an unusually striking twenty-five-year-old.

'So nice . . .' She gave me a kiss, touched with Dune by Dior. I recognised the man now, but she introduced us anyway. 'This is Marco.'

'We've met.'

He took my hand, pinching his brow with the other forefinger and thumb. 'Oh, God, have we?'

I wasn't going to remind him, it was of so little importance. 'This is my brother Jim, and my sister-in-law Sally. Lady Stratton – Miranda.'

'How do you do? Miranda definitely.' She shone her smile on them, and I could already hear how Jim would describe this meeting to friends and colleagues. Marco said his name again and there was another round of handshaking.

We exchanged a few pleasantries of the had-a-good-holiday?,

down-for-the-weekend variety, and then she said she and Marco had better get on.

'Murky business down at the folly,' she explained.

'Sounds like a comic melodrama!' blurted out Jim – the first words he'd uttered in her presence.

She laid her hand briefly on his arm. 'Jim – hush! It could well be just that before we're through!'

As they made their way along the path, their heads were down as if they were deep in conversation. I'd wanted to show Jim and Sally the folly but that wasn't on now, and we set off for home.

Jim was *bouleversé*. 'Now I can die a happy man!'

'How old is she?' asked Sally, a touch wistfully.

'Late forties?'

'It's not fair.'

'Actually,' said Jim, trying to be emollient and not getting it quite right, 'she's not the most beautiful woman I've ever seen. She just has more charm and sex appeal than any person, of either gender, is entitled to.'

'Yes,' said Sally. 'I can see that.'

'It's like being exposed to gamma rays of the stuff. I bet it's not just blokes, either,' he added. 'Sal, hand on heart, not the tiniest frisson?'

'No!'

'Bobby? Honest injun?'

'She's a very compelling person—'

'That'll do. That's a yes,' he declared triumphantly.

'Jim,' said Sally, 'what exactly are you trying to prove?'

'That some attractions are universal. Don't worry, I'm not suggesting you two engage in anything indecent.' Sally was more tight-lipped by the second, but he sighed happily. 'Did I make a complete fool of myself?'

'Close shave,' I said. 'Now then, pub?'

They set off at about three, full of what a wonderful time they'd had. I was genuinely sorry to see them go. As I waved them goodbye I reflected that although one might find too much proximity to one's relations a trial, mutual understanding was not served by seeing each other barely three times a year.

Parting was a sweet sorrow, however. It was nice to have the cottage to myself again and I took pleasure in tidying it up, loading the dishwasher, stripping the spare beds and deciding which of the many appetising leftovers I'd have for supper.

When I'd done all this, and was still on a post-visitor wave of domestic energy, I went up to the second bedroom and brought down one of the remaining packed boxes, marked 'Miscellaneous'. I was in the mood for a miscellany. I dumped the box on the living room floor, put on some Billie Holiday, and poured myself a glass of wine. I left the curtains only half drawn because as the evenings drew in you could make out the glow of Ladycross from behind the trees on the hill, like a candle in a lantern.

Miscellaneous was right. It was like delving into a bran tub. I found, among other things: a small lamp for scented oil; two corkscrews; an old-fashioned steel mincer salvaged from the Beacon (though when on earth I'd thought I was going to mince my own meat, who could say); a Crown Derby table lighter without a lid; some – more! – padded hangers; a collection of town and city maps in an elastic band; and a carrier-bag full of photographs. The photographs exerted their usual magnetic pull, and I tipped them out on to the floor.

They were all from the same period, that of middle childhood, between about six and twelve, when the gappy teeth, pudding-basin haircuts and Clarks sandals tell you that it was a long time ago but seems like yesterday. In the way that the old feel they are still the same person inside that they were at twenty, so I felt, looking at the chubby-faced me in a pinafore dress and Viyella blouse, that I had not changed. I might have known less then, but I was exactly the same. I could slip back into that moment, relive that feeling, not as if it were yesterday but as if it were now. I peered at and pored over them, even got up at one point and gazed at myself in the mirror – my coarsened, scrubbed-up, more knowledgeable adult self, only another version of the self in the photographs. People weren't old or young for their age, I thought, but always the same. There we were, about to play garden cricket at the Beacon under the auspices of my father who'd taken the photo, me holding the bat and Jim the ball. I used to quite like cricket but for the constant exhortations to be a good sport and not to make a fuss. No concessions were made. If I dropped a catch or was out first ball I was expected to tolerate the jeering and put up with the consequences. There was another of me with my mother – she was leaning over, clasping me round the shoulders from behind with both arms, laughing, jollying me along. I looked as if I'd been crying and had been told to snap out of it.

There were the inevitable beach-shots: me and Jim with shrimping nets, our mother with her skirt tucked into her knickers, making a sandcastle, me standing in the surf eating a cornet (I was getting in such a mess with it and there were so many wasps gathering that my father had driven me to the edge of the sea for safety and his sanity's sake). I found a large, cardboard-mounted, tissue-covered studio shot of the two of us sitting side by side, with Jim pretending to show me a Dinky car. Gosh, I remembered that . . . the smell of the studio, the feel of the smocking on my dress, the man's light, irritable touch as he adjusted our positions, the torture by boredom – why had photographs taken so long in those days?

I resolved, as I did every couple of years or so, that I would do something with the photographs, make an amusing collage, get a couple of the better ones computer-enlarged, throw away the duds, put the others into an album.

Lining the bottom of the box was a yellow, brittle copy of the *Daily Sketch*. Beneath the main headline was a box containing a come-on: 'Page 5 – Today's Winner of Our Sensational B.B. Competition!' Spud had gone to unimaginable and undignified lengths to get me a copy, rummaging through the shoe-cleaning box of the old couple over the road for whom she occasionally ran errands. I opened the paper and gazed, for the first time in over thirty years, at the picture that had caused all the fuss. It was a nice picture – rather sweet, even – of Miranda pouting prettily in a gingham dress, with her hair in the approved tousled topknot. By way of a prop, the photographer had given her a basket of washing, which she carried on one hip beneath her arm. The other arm was across her body, the fingers resting lightly on the edge of the basket, an attitude that pushed her breasts together invitingly. But Miranda was no Bardot-clone: the photo's appeal (whether the picture editor of the *Sketch* realised it or not) lay in the tension between one beautiful but distinctive girl imitating another. A double-sexiness, an *hommage* between equals. An innocent irony. At fifteen, I realised, Miranda had known instinctively what it was like to be Brigitte.

I closed the paper and put it aside with the photographs. Beneath it was a blue envelope, opened, stamped and addressed to me at the Beacon. Inside was a note from Juliet, my college roommate: 'Thought you'd like this, in memory of a mad, bad evening!'

There were four of us girls sitting on the edge of a bed, our heads together, grinning wildly, waving cigarettes. Our skirts were so short you couldn't even see them, just a forest of legs, some in boots. The trendiest among us – I couldn't remember her name, but it wasn't me – wore a crochet top and op-art earrings. I was wearing a polo-neck jumper. My grin was the wildest; my eyes stared out in a kind of panic of assumed frivolity.

I remembered the jumper, and the occasion – a hop at the art college. The tickets were expensive because they'd got the Roadrunners playing in the second half, a group of the sort art colleges always managed to get hold of, who'd actually had a hit. Just my luck to go to the art college and wind up with a lab technician in a pullover. He must have seen the desperation in my eyes, the determination to have a good time, get sloshed, get groped – certainly not get pregnant, though that's what happened.

I don't think the phrase 'peer-pressure' had been invented then, but I'd definitely been susceptible to it. The pressure hadn't been overt, it was more something I applied to myself. I wanted 'fun' of the sort everyone else seemed to like, and to have. I didn't realise that fun was in the mind of the individual – that if you didn't find something fun, then it wasn't. That fun was not an objective fact, but a subjective experience.

In other words, I wasn't listening to myself. Least of all when the lab technician with the pully and the pimple (only one, but it was a biggie) asked me to dance a second dance, a slow one. The first dance didn't count because in spite of his unpromising appearance he might have been an embryonic Warhol, Dylan or Woody Allen; or a lecturer – always considered a coup, provided you chucked them immediately. But by the end of a disastrously inept jive (and no one was jiving in those days that saw the birth of the free-form dance) I had realised that he was nothing more than the weed he seemed, had damp palms, dandruff and an ego that, in spite of these disadvantages, flourished like the green bay tree.

That was the chief and, it turned out, the crucial difference between us. What would now be called his self-esteem was in excellent nick whereas mine was non-existent. The evening wore on. I got drunk, he got excited, I went to his horrible hall of residence for a coffee, put up with what followed – it didn't take long – and returned to the flat with a love-bite and a tall story.

'You're joking,' I said. 'Him? After you left I got off with his friend at the pub.'

'Nice?' asked Juliet.

'Very nice,' I'd replied.

My subsequent decision not to have an abortion but to have the baby adopted might have had something to do with shame over the whole incident. If I'm truthful I wasn't thinking of the child, but of myself – I needed to put myself through it, to suffer, to punish myself for the shabbiness of my behaviour that night. With hindsight, that seems like the shabbiest behaviour of all. I suffered all right, and probably put kinks in my emotional make-up, which have been causing it pain ever since. These days, I might have kept the baby, but I don't know . . . What if I hadn't fallen in love with my child either? An adopted child is chosen and favoured, always loved.

I didn't tell a soul, especially the baby's father. His name was Derek. I saw him about the place, but intimacy did not recur.

That photo I tore in half and put into the bin.

To take my mind off it I started sorting the others, and was still doing that, with the television on, at nine thirty when Jim called.

'Got back safely and just wanted to thank you for a marvellous weekend.'

'I certainly enjoyed it.'

'We were just saying how well and happy you looked. Nice job, nice house – amazing friends!' He chuckled salaciously. 'You seem really to have fallen on your feet.'

'Yes.' It's so hard, when you have the blues and someone else is busy counting blessings on your behalf, to summon the right reaction. 'Was all well at home?'

'Oh, fine, fine . . . No wrecks and nobody drownded. Picked up the younger two and found the others watching the box as though their lives depended on it in a strangely tidy house. Machines whirring. Sure sign of something having gone on, but what we don't know we won't fret over.'

'Good.'

There was an awkward pause. 'Bobby?'

'Still here.'

'You okay?'

'Yes, I've been rummaging through old photographs.'

'Sorry if I was intrusive about your love life. Sal's been ticking me off.'

'That's okay . . .' I yawned.

'Bed!' Jim declared, relieved. 'Now. We're tending that way ourselves. Night-night, speak soon.'

Daniel called when I was in bed. 'How was the family weekend?'

'Nice, actually. We had our ups and downs, but it was good to see them.'

'Something good happened to me, too,' he said. His voice was light, and animated. 'I've got some new work, proper work. A project.'

'Dan, that's great.'

'I don't know if you know, but they're going to build a small theatre up at Ladycross.'

I felt the lightest spider-touch of apprehension. 'I just found out about it last night, from the Hobdays.'

'Well, the chap in charge of it, Marco Torrence, has given me the job of making some outdoor furniture for it – so people can sit outside with their drinks. He wants to make the place feel like part of its surroundings – I can really have some fun.'

'Good,' I said. 'I'm so glad.'

He chuckled with delight. 'So maybe I shan't have to do up another slum property, after all.'

'That's great.'

'Night, Bobby, sleep well.'

'Good-night.'

That week Miles and his family moved into Ladycross, and Miranda moved out, or at least into what was called the Dower House but was actually the Victorian part of the house, a spur running at right angles to the south wing, overlooking the folly.

Although both moves were managed with a minimum of fuss, rather like a prime ministerial handover at 10 Downing Street, the changes were apparent at once. The spaniels, Trigger and Mark, moved to what (with Miranda's encouragement) came to be known as the Dire House, and in their place came an affable young Labrador, Frodo, and two hyperactive Jack Russell bitches, Mitzi and Heidi. The girl, Millie, rode up and down the drive and round the rear courtyard on a pink and purple bike. The little boy sometimes teetered about after her with stabilisers, but more often went in and out with a tall nanny in combats. We saw almost nothing of Miles and Penny – our first encounter was when they came over to the barns just before lunch one day to introduce themselves.

Apart from the rent we ran a completely independent operation at Smart Cards, but it was still impossible not to feel as though we were deserving peasantry receiving a visit from our betters. Kirsty said, 'Look who's coming!' and we instinctively adjusted ourselves and our desks. We might have been grovelling tenant farmers instead of successful business people.

'Morning!' said Miles, putting his head round the door. 'May we come and say hello?'

We chorused that of course they could.

Without their children in tow they both seemed more relaxed. He was rather more impressive and she prettier than I remembered from my brief first glimpse of them. He did most of the talking, saying how wonderful it was to be living in the house he'd always loved, but that there was still a lot to learn, and that his step-mother – by which, incredibly, he meant Miranda – had been 'amazing'.

'And she's still very much around,' said Penny. 'So this is a team effort.'

His smile became a bit fixed at this intervention. I sensed that for all his generous remarks he didn't see it quite like that. The subject was duly changed, and by him.

'I can't go without saying how much we like your product, by the way.'

Chris beamed. 'That's always nice to hear, thank you.'

'You know, don't you, that plans are under way for a little theatre in the grounds?'

I thought it best to keep my mouth shut but the Hobdays confirmed that they did, and Kirsty added, 'It's a wonderful idea. When will all that start happening?'

'It's started. Plans have been approved.' He slapped his pockets in the manner of a chap who had places to go. 'A long-held ambition of my father's, so nice to be able to make it a reality.' One had the impression that this was a rehearsed formula, designed to convey a sense of filial duty but no personal enthusiasm.

'You know Marco Torrence is helping us?' enquired Penny, with a hint of pride. 'Miranda persuaded him.'

This was definitely my turn. 'Yes,' I said. 'I met him one afternoon without knowing who he was, and just after that I saw him on telly.'

'He's absolutely marvellous,' she rhapsodised. 'Such an enthusiast. You need someone like that to keep the wind in your sails on a project like this.'

Once again Miles had nothing to add, or if he had he kept it to himself. And on this one I must say I sympathised with him.

For the rest of that day I felt a little uncomfortable, as though by not having taken a violent dislike to Miles and Penny I had somehow let Miranda down, although I knew she was the last person to see it like that. She was simply staying tactfully out of the way, keeping her head down as befitted the retiring incumbent.

On Friday evening after work I took some long overdue housewarming flowers over to the Dire House. I hadn't wanted to be *too* prompt. There was a pecking order in these matters, and in spite of her warmth towards me I had no illusions about the place in it of our friendship.

The front door was opened by, of all people, Millie, in her new school uniform of a red skirt and white polo-shirt. I wondered, did today's children know how lucky they were?

'Hallo,' I said. 'Is Lady Stratton in?'

This sounded dreadfully prim and formal, and I realised too late that Millie's mother was also Lady Stratton and there might be confusion. But this was a very composed child. 'Yes, come in.' She closed the door after me. 'Who is it?'

'Bobby Govan.'

There was a tremendous burst of laughter from another room. Millie looked at me gravely. 'Can you stay there a minute?'

I waited obediently in the hall. When Millie came back, Miranda was with her, her face still shiny with whatever had been so funny.

'Fantastic! I've been thinking about you such a lot but not getting round to doing anything about it.' Her candour was disarming, as it was intended to be. 'And look at these . . . oh!'

She kissed me, then laid her hand on Millie's shoulder. 'This is my right-hand main woman, and did quite right to check your credentials, don't you think?' She raised a collusive eyebrow.

'Absolutely.'

'Come and have a glass of wine. Marco's here but we're only gossiping.'

I thought, Damn! But it was too late, we were already on our way. The drawing room was uncluttered and bright, with mellow lighting – a couple of tulip-shaped amber standard lamps and a log fire. Marco Torrence sat on a sofa in front of which was a low table covered in sheets of paper – the plans. Miranda descended on the papers and swept them away, folding them with a series of brisk snaps.

'Enough already! You two have met, I gather . . . Millie, would you very kindly run to the kitchen and bring another glass? And some crisps from the left-hand cupboard?'

She sat down on a chair on the far side of the hearth leaving me no alternative but to sit next to Marco on the sofa. They caught each other's eye and there was another ripple of laughter, for which she at once apologised. 'It's so rude to giggle in front of someone else – very silly. It's not private, it would just take too long to explain.'

Marco turned to me. 'Nice to see you again. I'm still castigating myself for driving you away from the folly the other afternoon.'

'You didn't, not at all,' I said briskly.

'There's nothing worse than walking miles off the beaten track to some beauty spot and finding someone already there. Particularly,' he gave me a quizzical look over his specs, 'a bloke with a briefcase.'

Millie returned with the glass and the crisps and Marco poured me some wine. He seemed extraordinarily at home here.

'Cheers!' said Miranda.

'*Prost!*'

'With hindsight,' I said, 'I imagine you were there in connection with the theatre.'

'That's what he's here for now,' said Miranda. 'At least, that's his pretext . . .'

They nearly laughed again, but Millie was sitting on a blow-up armchair, munching crisps and taking in every word, so their self-censorship was obvious. We were an oddly assorted little gathering.

The conversation took a general turn – the village, the government, the theatre, builders. Fifteen minutes later, Millie was sent home. To my surprise she gave Marco a kiss before leaving. I thought there might be a communicating door, but Miranda saw her out of the front door and we could hear their voices as she saw her across the courtyard.

'How well do you know everyone?' I asked him, while they were out of the room.

'Miranda, pretty well. Their new lord- and ladyships hardly at all, although that is due to change. They have a sweet daughter. You?'

'Miranda and I were at school together.'

'Blimey,' he said, laughing. 'Respect!'

He laughed easily. It was quite hard to go on disliking him.

Miranda came back in. 'What's so funny?'

'We were talking about you,' he said. 'Bobby's just told me how far you and she go back.'

I was suddenly embarrassed in case she thought I'd been presuming on what had been the merest acquaintance, but if she did she didn't show it.

'I tell you Marco, it was hell there. Hell! You are in the company of two women of iron. Bobby even more than me. I got out. They sacked me.' She looked at me for confirmation. 'Didn't they?'

I nodded. 'What for?' he asked.

'Being Britain's Brigitte Bardot. Or one of them.' She pushed one hand into her hair and pouted outrageously.

'Ha!' He tipped his head back, slapping his knees with delight. 'Brilliant – you don't look a bit like her!'

'A padded bra, a friendly photographer, *et voilà*!'

'Shameless,' he remarked, shaking his head, and then leaned back as if this exchange hadn't happened and addressed me. 'So, Bobby, from your position of interested objectivity, what do you think of this little theatre idea?'

'It sounds a very exciting project,' I said cautiously.

'Exciting . . . great word, useful. A good portmanteau term. I believe you're right, though. Whatever else it may or may not be it certainly won't be dull.'

What the hell? I thought, and asked the obvious question. 'What about the economics? How many people will it have to attract – in a year, say?'

Neither of them batted an eyelid. He said, 'To pay for itself, a lot, in the first couple of year. Every spadeful of earth needs planning permission. Say twenty thousand? And that's while bedding in. After that we're flying.'

'Realistically,' said Miranda, 'it won't be in profit for some time. But the money's secondary. Fred allowed for it, and all the other projects, like you and the Hobdays, for instance, will help fund it. It was his dream.'

'And you gotta have one,' said Marco, putting 'Happy Talk' hands on either side of his face.

'We could put on *South Pacific*!'

'What, all those sailors?'

'The Witherburn Players.'

They laughed again, and Miranda put down her glass. 'Bobby, we've got a table booked, do you want to join us?'

'That's a good idea,' he said. 'Why don't you?'

They meant it, and I was tempted, but only for a second. 'It's so kind of you, but I must go.'

As she accompanied me into the hall he collected up the glasses, and called after us, 'I insist you come back very soon and spill the beans on doings in the dorm!'

'It'll cost you!'

She opened the door and leaned her cheek on it, gazing at me. 'Thanks for the beautiful flowers. I appreciate it.'

I said, truthfully, that it was my pleasure.

She seemed loath to let me go. 'What do you think of the Dire House?'

'Not dire at all. I've never been in before but I think it's lovely.'

'It'll do . . .' She stepped outside with me and looked up at the stars. 'I'm going to stay here till the theatre's finished and then take myself off, out of their hair . . .'

I was beginning to realise that I could be direct. 'They don't see it like that. I'm sure.'

She continued to stargaze. 'Miles is well brought-up. We both loved Fred. But he doesn't need me hanging about on the sidelines, and it's not where I want to be . . .' She lowered her gaze and smiled at me. 'France, I think.'

Driving down the hill I found myself hoping that the theatre would take a very long time.

CHAPTER THIRTEEN

<hr>

Rags, 1980

It was on occasions like these that Miranda knew Rags was worth every last penny of the five thousand they were paying her.

At nine a.m. it was already thirty-five degrees in the shade. A degree for every year. She knew because someone had put a thermometer in the tent. An electric fan, run from one of the jeeps, churned the stifling air. Outside, it was well over forty degrees. The yellow Mara plain trembled in the furnace. The rest of the crew were sitting under the trees; she could hear their desultory, heat-flattened voices.

She envied them, but they were only waiting for her. Everything was set up, the clock was ticking. Hers to submit to the process no matter how long it took, theirs not to count the cost. She was earning her money just sitting here, they were using up theirs. That was why, from the moment she stepped out of the tent, she had to be perfect. Not only perfect to look at but perfectly behaved, perfectly co-operative, perfectly professional.

Gerry Moynihan was her favourite makeup artist. An unflappable Ulster woman who did the best work and would not be hurried. She sympathised with everyone, but since she was here she was going to produce the goods. Rags – bare-faced in the African sun.

'Look at the light out there,' she commented. 'Brutal.'

'Let's hope they get what they want.'

'They will, my precious, because we'll give it to them.'

'This is . . .' Miranda paused while the dabbing sponge moved over her mouth '. . . one of those days that reminds me what a vulgar waste of money it all is.'

'None of that!' said Gerry. 'Hear me? Don't. It's the heat talking. You're a product to shift another product and there's no shame in that. Last drink before lips?'

Half an hour later Gerry said that was that and the stylist, Caitlin, took over. The theme of today's shoot, for Whitefeather, a stratospherically upmarket American catalogue, was Edwardian-style evening wear. They'd come to Kenya with the intention of shooting the evening wear at assorted emblematic sites – the Blixen House, Norfolk Hotel and Muthaiga Club, none of which would be recognisable except in the small-print footnote – and the day and casual wear in the game park. But once they'd got out here Africa had gone to the head of the excitable Australian photographer who had realised that the whole thing should be stood on its head. The woman from the catalogue company demurred and a noisy but good-tempered debate took place over after-dinner drinks at the poolside bar.

Miranda, lightheaded on mineral water, short commons and jetlag, got tired of listening and absented herself. It was half an hour before they'd calmed down sufficiently to wonder where she was, by which time she was getting out of the pool.

'I'm for bed,' she said, 'or no one's going to want the clothes. So what did we decide?'

'He won,' said Donna, the woman from Whitefeather. 'He's irresistible when roused.'

'And so?' Miranda looked at Con.

'One day's acclimatisation – in the shade – and a four a.m. start for the bush day after tomorrow.'

'For evening wear.' She was getting her head round it and this must have shown on her face, for he put his forefinger and thumb together to indicate utter exquisiteness of the concept.

'Darl, it's going to blow them away.'

'I'm sure you're right. Night, then.'

As she walked away they began talking again, but this time mutedly, with that mixture of admiration and sympathy with which she was all too familiar. Everyone had avoided mentioning, and she had refrained from reminding them, that she was to model menswear as well.

So it was that she emerged from the tent in full masher's garb, frock coat, waistcoat and stock, her hair slicked back except for a single kiss-curl, carrying white gloves and a topper. The sheet-metal heat banged down on her head. Sweat seeped out all over her. Con and the rest of the crew, holding their bottles of Evian, applauded.

'Absolutely fucking stunning . . . fuckinamazing!'

Con came over to her, fanning himself with his hat. 'You okay in there?'

'Fine.'

'Good on yer, girl. Right, ready to rumble!'

She was indeed fine, because she'd learned how to achieve the state of fineness. Gerry was right to describe her as a product, to remind her of her role in the mix. Whitefeather were paying, and Whitefeather would get what they paid for. She had perfected the ability to get out of her own head and be as objective about herself as they all were. There were those who privately considered that she had learned how to seal her pores so that not a drop of sweat appeared on camera and whatever else in the way of blisters, headaches and general discomfort Miranda might be enduring, Rags was the epitome of cool, androgynous chic.

After the frock-coat outfit there was another man's suit, this time with the jacket slung over her shoulder, the waistcoat open and a bow-tie hanging undone beneath a wing collar. It was cooler, but trickier because the dress-shirt had to stay looking crisp and white. They photographed her in full sunlight with nothing but the yellow plain behind her, a single thorn tree on the horizon.

'What's that on the tree?' asked Con. 'Don't tell me it's a fucking vulture.'

'Great touch,' said Donna, not joking.

They wanted to get the men's stuff done by midday, then have lunch and a siesta and shoot the dresses from four o'clock. Apart from the necessity of avoiding the worst of the heat, this allowed Caitlin time to transform Miranda, wash her hair, disguise any marks and clean off one bare face so it could be replaced with another. There was a buffet laid on by the Kenyan cook but Miranda stayed away from it in favour of several pints of water and a can of spaghetti hoops. She rested but didn't sleep, because she didn't want to be puffy-eyed. Tom had given her a book about Shackleton for the trip, 'to cool you down and remind you there's always someone worse off than yourself', and she leafed through it, peering in fascination at the snow-white desert, the black-clothed men, their eyes caked with ice in pinched, frostbitten faces.

At three Gerry, then Caitlin did their stuff. By four o'clock the temperature was no lower than it had been at midday, but was at least on the way down and they began the shoot. There were six dresses, three of them the full whale-boned, high-necked monty. She wore a carefully disarrayed hairpiece for two of these, but for the rest they decided to leave her *au naturelle*, since the tone of the piece was magic realism anyway. In one Con had her sitting beneath the canvas awning on an upturned bucket, legs apart, whittling a stick. For another they carted the whole operation three-quarters of a mile to the lone thorn tree – now mercifully vulture-free – and she stood with one hand on a branch, staring out over the plain. The bodice was tight, the lace was scratchy and the whalebones pinched but she kept her mind firmly on the trials of Shackleton, and did not blink.

'What would be great,' said Con, 'would be a dead lion – hush my mouth, a tranquillised lion – and Rags standing over him with a smoking gun. In the white dress.'

Donna tinkled with laughter. 'Now, don't get greedy!'

There wasn't time to shoot all the dresses and it was decided to do the daywear tomorrow and take another morning in the Mara, or the garden of the Norfolk, after that.

Miranda fell asleep on the drive back to the hotel, left a

message on Tom's answering-machine and went for a swim. The hotel had two pools, the larger one with a water-bar and music, linked by a waterfall over steps to a round lagoon, darker and more peaceful, with uplighters among the greenery.

Most of the crew were sitting on stools at the water-bar. Caitlin and Donna were in deep conversation at a poolside table. Miranda did a few lengths, then went down the steps into the lagoon. There was only one other person there. It was peaceful. She surrendered to the simple bliss of cool water and soft light. She chastised herself, though not very severely, for being so spoilt. Poor old Shackleton . . .

The man swam slowly past her towards the steps. Long, pale limbs in the dark water. 'Heaven, isn't it?' he said quietly.

'Yes,' she said, 'it is.'

At dinner she sat with Gerry and Con. The restaurant was open on all sides, a glass canopy supported by wooden pillars shrouded in bougainvillaea, the air sweet and heavy with its scent. Even here in Nairobi the night-garden pullulated with sound, muffling the blare and drone of the streets beyond.

Con became mellow. 'Question is,' he asked, 'shall we bother going back?'

'You suit yourself,' said Gerry. 'I miss my family.'

'You, Rags?'

'Gerry's right, it depends what there is to go back to. That you want to go back to.'

'That's the criterion. What's the answer?'

She felt suddenly bleak. 'I don't know, to be honest.'

'There's your answer, then. Go bush with me. We could do a photo-diary, it'd be fucking sensational. Gerry, what do you reckon?'

Gerry picked up the menu. 'I reckon I'm having the trio of tropical ice-creams.'

'Trio, bullshit,' said Con. 'They used to call that Neapolitan.'

When they were having coffee the bellhop came to the table and said there was a call for her. He offered to bring the phone to her but she excused herself and went to take it in the foyer. It was Tom.

'How's it going?'

'A lovely evening after a very long, hot day.'

'Good pictures?'

'I think so. They were uncomfortable enough, that's usually a reliable test.'

'I miss you.'

'Me too.'

'Right *now* I miss you. If I wasn't an honourable member I'd ask what you were wearing.'

'A long silk dress, with the necklace you gave me.'

'Underneath?'

'Nothing.'

'Jezebel.'

They didn't talk for long. When she returned to the table, Gerry said, 'Someone nice?'

'Yes.'

'Thought so, it's written all over you.'

'Buggeration,' said Con. 'Bang goes Plan A for the grass hut.'

Later on there was dancing, to a little combo playing near the pool. The crew split into bar-flies and dancers, along lines of age. Miranda stuck with the bar contingent whose conversation, with Con in the chair, grew steadily noisier and more scatalogical. At around eleven, when she was about to leave them to it, a man crossed the room to her side and said, 'Excuse me. This is impertinent I know.'

The others glanced at him only briefly. They had serious drinking to do. She was an experienced hand, she could sort it out.

It was the man from the pool. 'It is Rags, isn't it? I recognised you last night.'

'That's right.'

'Fred Montclere. Would you care to dance?'

'Thank you.'

She got up, conscious of a swift, supplementary nip of curiosity from the bar-flies, and followed him on to the floor. The band was playing fusion music, a guest-friendly *kwela* that lent itself to pretty much anything. She found herself hoping that it wouldn't be a hideous embarrassment. But he was a good

303

dancer, taking her at once by the hand and giving her a twirl, doing a gangly, customised jive with grace and pizazz. It was wholly enjoyable and they got more adventurous, laughing at their own inventiveness and winding up slightly out of breath. As the music ended a couple of people clapped.

'I think that was for us,' he said, producing an enormous hankie and mopping his brow, smiling and frowning at the same time. 'I must thank you for making me look good.'

'We were a good team for first time out.'

'Care for a second?'

'Practice makes perfect.'

They did a second, and a third, the band catching their mood and playing around, changing rhythms to see how they'd cope, inserting all kinds of crafty *glissando*s and syncopations. She noticed that the bar-flies were turned their way.

With the fourth number, 'Night And Day', the tempo changed to the gentlest of rumbas, and he slipped his arm round her, her hand, folded in his, against his chest. She was both relaxed and exhilarated. Until she remembered, with a horrible jolt, that she had no underwear on.

'I think—' she began, but he swung her away from him and then back into his encircling arm.

'Don't, I implore you. Thinking and dancing don't mix.'

She was hot with confusion.

'And anyway,' he added softly, but without looking into her face, 'it's a tremendous bonus for a fellow.'

After that, he thanked her again and returned her to the bar-flies, holding her chair for her and saying how decent it was of them to let her be dragged off by a total stranger. They mumbled that that was okay.

'Good-night, then.'

The moment he was out of earshot Con leaned across. 'Hey! You know who your toffish dancing partner was?'

'Fred Montclere, I think he said.'

'That's it. The Right Hon of that ilk. Lord Stratton. Just got dumped by his missus.'

'I wouldn't know.'

'I do. I read the diary columns.'

'We hardly talked at all . . .' This puzzled her.

'We noticed,' commented Gerry. 'Too busy clearing the dance floor.'

In bed that night she ran over him with her mind's eye: the intelligent, charming face with its long nose and humorous mouth; the tall figure, loose-jointed as a marionette but with such grace of movement; the engaging combination of gentleness and confidence; the simplicity and elegance with which he'd brushed aside her embarrassment.

She had to get up early again, but she was shivering with adrenaline and couldn't sleep. This was a wonderful man. Like Eliza, she could have danced all night. They had barely exchanged two sentences.

And she knew – she *knew* – that she had met him before.

Con had a very clear idea of how he wanted the day-clothes to look.

'Back from the bush,' he explained. 'The hunter home from the hill.'

It was a positive pleasure, after the rigours of the day before, to be photographed on the veranda of the Norfolk, and in the air-conditioned lounge of the Muthaiga Club, with plenty of drink to hand and comfortable conditions in which to prepare. The clothes were fun, too – men's brogues and baggy trousers held up by a tie, shirts and waistcoats that went either with the trousers or with a woman's high-waisted skirt and dusty boots (Caitlin dusted them specially); enveloping cotton coats, broad-brimmed hats, safari jackets, a cartridge belt.

She was leaning on the cocktail bar of the Muthaiga, with one hand hooked in her trouser pocket, the other grasping a bottle of Bollinger, and a cheroot drooping from her lips, when Fred Montclere walked past the door. She glimpsed his tall figure go by, and then return on a double-take. He was there for only a second, long enough to tip his hand to his forehead and smile at her. But it was enough to bring it all back.

It had been a long, long time ago: years since she'd even thought about it. That day in London with her mother . . . her little escape into the world of the rich and grand . . . the society wedding. And the man she'd stood next to opposite the church, the wedding guest that the bride had jilted, quite willing to confide in a teenage rubbernecker . . .

At the time, she'd been astonished. Now that she'd danced with him, none of that seemed at all surprising.

'Rags!' From Con's voice it was apparent this wasn't the first time he'd called. 'Rags, could we give a tad more attitude, please?'

Next day they were due to leave the hotel at five a.m. for a former colonial farmhouse fifty miles outside town, for the final session of the day-clothes shoot.

Dread of being thought a prima donna had made Miranda almost pathologically punctual, and she was in the lobby at ten to. But he was there before her.

'Good morning.'

'Fred – you're up early.'

'After I saw you at the Tiger I took the liberty of asking one of your lot what the plan was for today. I'm afraid this is a pre-planned ambush.'

'Goodness.' She thought, I'm tongue-tied, fifteen again, like the songs.

'It's just that my friends and I are leaving tomorrow and I'd very much like to see you when you get back to England. You are going back to England?'

'Yes.'

'In that case, may I have your telephone number?'

He was polite and direct, smiling the gentle smile that charmed her heart and turned her tongue into a lump of Plasticine.

'Or I could give you mine?' he suggested. 'If that would be easier.'

'Yes,' she said. 'Why don't we do that?'

'Let's.' He took out his wallet and produced a card. 'There we are.'

'Thank you.'

She was conscious of Gerry emerging from the lift, and stuffed the card into the outer pocket of her kit-bag.

'Will it be safe in there?' he asked doubtfully.

'Don't worry.'

'In that case I'll say *au revoir*.' He held out his hand, took hers and kissed her on either cheek. 'It's been an absolute delight.'

He passed Gerry with a cheerful 'Morning!' and went into the lift.

'What was all that about?' she asked. 'As if I couldn't guess.'

'We may get in touch back in England.'

'You amaze me. Good!' Gerry tilted her head. 'You want to, yes?'

'I do, as a matter of fact.' She couldn't help smiling. 'I really do.'

'Uh-oh, smitten, the pair of you!'

'Afraid so.'

'Poor old Mr Long-Distance, is all I can say.'

She waited till a week later, when they were in the departure lounge for the flight home, before taking a proper look at his card. The writing was embossed, but there was no mention of a title: 'Frederick Montclere, Ladycross, Witherburn, Northumbria' and two phone numbers, business and private, at the same exchange. On the plane, Caitlin leaned over from the row behind and dropped a two-day-old English paper on her lap.

'Take a look. Isn't that the bloke you danced with at the hotel?'

It was a diary piece. 'Spotted supporting children's charities at the True Blue Ball at the Dorchester, Lord Stratton accompanied by glamorous divorcée Mrs Angela Forbes Cortez, an old friend who is said to be comforting him following the break-up of his marriage. "I've been very saddened by all that's happened," "Fred" Montclere told Insider. "But now it's on with the dance, in an excellent cause."'

The photograph showed him in black tie, standing next to a striking middle-aged woman with a daring *décolletage*, her arm through his.

Miranda held up the paper and Caitlin took it back. 'That is him, isn't it?'

'Yes.'

'He's rather gorgeous,' observed Caitlin. 'For his age.'

Miranda did not, of course, take the newspaper piece to mean any more than it said – that Fred Montclere was not a man to feel sorry for himself. Not really. And yet she was utterly cast down, devastated would not have been too strong a word, to discover that he had this *soignée* and delightful comforter. She considered herself a sophisticate in matters of the heart: she had been around, knew the score, was a good judge of character, intentions and her own responses. The magic of this new acquaintance lay in the sudden loss of that sophistication, the complete ascendancy of heart over head. Her feelings still had the power to surprise her, they'd rolled her over and spun her round. Now, just as suddenly, with a few words in a popular newspaper, she had been put in her place.

For this reason, but not this alone, she did not contact Fred Montclere in the first week after her return. There was a message from Fran on her answering-machine.

'Miranda, I'm afraid it's bad news . . . Your mother said you were away, can you call me when you get back?'

There was another from her mother. 'Mandy, sorry to do this to you when you've just walked in the door from a lovely trip, but Fran Shepherd called, and your father's died. For the best, she seemed to be saying. Did you go to see him in the end? I shan't be going to the funeral, but maybe one of us should. Call me when you've had a chance to think.'

For herself, Miranda felt only relief. But she did feel sympathy for Fran, whose sturdy affection went some way to redeeming Gerald by association.

She called her mother first, to sort out the practicalities.

'Don't worry, I'll go to the funeral.'

'It's tomorrow afternoon at Golders Green crem – she put it in the *Telegraph*.'

'I'll be there. I'm going to speak to her anyway.' There was a pause. 'Are you all right, Mum?'

'Oh, yes, it's sad, of course, but it makes no difference after all this time.'

'I'll come down to see you very soon.'

'That'd be nice. You know it's Dale's wedding in a few weeks? I expect you got an invitation. I did, heaven knows why.'

'I haven't checked the post.'

'I'll let you get on, then. Perhaps you'll give me a ring after the funeral. Let me know how it went.'

The conversation with Fran was very different.

'Fran? It's Miranda. I just talked to my mother.'

'Oh, my dear, so you know.'

'I'm terribly sorry. You've been so close to him for so long. You must be devastated.'

'You think you're prepared, but nothing quite prepares you—' Her voice cracked, but she got control of it again. 'It's horrible. Quite horrible. But, Miranda, your father was so thrilled that you'd been to see him, I do want to thank you from the bottom of my heart. It can't have been easy for you but it made a big difference to him.'

She didn't know what to say, except 'I'm glad. And I shall be at the funeral.'

'That's marvellous, it would mean a lot to him, and it certainly will to me. Three o'clock at the crematorium, then down to Swiss Cottage for tea and drinks at the Maybury Hotel.' Her voice wavered again. 'I don't know how many people will be there. He could be so difficult . . .'

'Don't worry,' said Miranda, 'it'll be all right.'

When she spoke to Tom, he said at once, 'Want me to come?'

'Tom, you couldn't.'

'I couldn't come for him, but I could come for you. And if

mourners are going to be a bit thin on the ground I could help boost the numbers.'

'Thanks. If you've got the time, I'd appreciate the moral support.'

'You're on.'

In the event, it could have been worse. There were twenty-odd in the congregation, most of them besides herself and Fran former business associates of one kind or another. They sang (Tom with great gusto) 'Abide With Me' and 'The Day Thou Gavest, Lord, Is Ended', and the vicar did his best to honour the deceased with the aid of the workmanlike CV provided by Fran. She did well, smart in a pale blue suit, maintaining her composure and walking out of the chapel dignified and alone. Afterwards the congregation was channelled out to the garden of remembrance to admire the flowers. These made a fine show, because nearly all those connected with Gerald were the sort of people who believed expenditure should be conspicuous.

'I wonder what happens to them all,' said Miranda, 'these heavenly flowers.'

'They stay here, I suppose,' said Tom. 'I was about to suggest they'd be taken to an old folks' home but I can see that'd be a tad tactless under the circumstances.'

Miranda was glad to have him there, and afterwards at the Maybury, where his politician's ability to circulate and make common cause was a great asset. Having him as an escort also made things easier for her in a more direct way, by displaying the 'spoken for' sign. She was using him, but hadn't he asked to be used?

Fran was much taken with him. 'I do like your gentleman friend.'

'You didn't mind him coming?'

'Of course not! He's a delight, and just the person to have around.' She glanced quizzically at Miranda. 'How long have you known him?'

'Ages.' This wasn't quite accurate but conveyed the appropriate message. 'He's a very great friend.'

'That's nice,' said Fran. 'Someone in your position needs a man like that.'

When everyone had left, they offered Fran a lift home.

'No, no, thank you, I brought my little car.'

'Will you be all right, getting back on your own?' asked Miranda. 'Would you like me to to come back with you?'

'No. I've been on my own, remember, for weeks. I'll have a stiff drink, a good cry and an early bed.' She kissed them both, warmly. There were already tears in her eyes. 'Goodbye, my dear, and you, Tom, thank you for being here.'

'Lovely lady,' he said. 'Your old man must have been doing something right.'

'That's what I keep telling myself.'

They were in Miranda's car, and she dropped him back at the House.

'This has been a nice occasion in its way,' he said. 'But I fancy something a bit cheerier. How about tomorrow night? It'll have to be late, I've got meetings.'

'Tom, I've hardly caught up with myself, what with one thing and another. Can I ring you?'

'You can do that anyway.'

'I know.'

'Soon, okay?'

She nodded. Ten minutes after she'd left him she pulled over on to a double yellow, and burst into tears.

Her next job, a studio shoot for the cover of French *Cosmopolitan*, wasn't for almost a week, so the following day, as good as her word, she went down to Haywards Heath. She took with her presents from Kenya – a carved African chess-set for Dale and Kaye, and a bottle of the most conspicuously luxurious duty-free scent she had been able to find for her mother.

'You shouldn't have,' said Marjorie, 'I shan't know myself.'

'That's the idea,' Miranda told her. 'Don't be sparing, use it every day.'

'Good Lord, I couldn't! This has to be for best.'

Miranda would have given more credence to this position if

she had believed there was a 'best' for which the scent should be saved. She had a horrible idea that her mother had no social life and, which was almost worse, that she liked it that way.

'The funeral went well,' she said. 'He had a good send-off.' It was funny the way one slipped into these clichés, the argot of death, coming out with expressions one would never normally use.

'I'm pleased about that, because you never know,' was her mother's cryptic response. 'Many people?'

'Quite a few.'

She didn't really know what to add to this, but Marjorie asked, 'How was he that time when you last saw him?'

Miranda had been dreading this question but was also ready for it. 'Looking old and ill as you'd expect, but as bloody-minded as ever.' This, she thought, both covered it and covered it up.

'What did he say to you?'

'He asked me about modelling, about the money . . . Said how fed up he was in hospital.'

'He would be,' said Marjorie grimly. 'Those poor nurses – can you imagine?'

'He seemed very well looked after. But it was obvious he hadn't got long.'

'I wouldn't be surprised,' said Marjorie, 'if once he knew, he'd found some way of hurrying things along.'

Miranda agreed that such a thing would not have been out of character.

She took the chess-set along to Dale's office at lunchtime. He had a lunch appointment but they sat for a few minutes in the reception area, the receptionist all agog in the background.

'Do you want me to open it now?' he asked.

'Certainly not, you must open it together – it's not from your list, I do hope you like it.'

'We're bound to.'

'I'm so sorry I can't be at the wedding,' she said. 'I've got a non-negotiable job that weekend.'

'That's all right, Mandy, I know what your life's like.' His eyes softened. 'You look as incredible as ever, by the way. More incredible. Have you had something done?'

She laughed. 'What *are* you suggesting?'

'No, no, don't get me wrong, but we men are so unobservant. I thought maybe you'd got a new hairdo or something . . .'

'Nothing like that.' So it shows, she thought.

'I'm sorry about your dad, by the way. I saw it in the paper. I know how you felt about him but, still, it must be difficult.'

'Thanks, Dale.' She couldn't bring herself to tell him how easy it was. 'Look, I mustn't hold you up. Give my love to Kaye, won't you, and have a wonderful, wonderful day.'

They bumped cheeks. At the door, he said, 'Mandy . . .'

'What?' He was frowning, so she smiled.

'I really love Kaye.'

'I know.'

She also knew, as she walked away, that she had just heard a declaration of Dale's love for herself.

Her life was in a state of suspension. For a short while, at least, she had no work, and no man. She had not yet called Tom and his natural discretion meant that he would not ring her. She was still working out what to do about Fred Montclere. Half a dozen times a day she picked up the phone, only to put it down again, unsure of herself.

It wasn't that she doubted the sincerity of his wish to see her again, let alone hers to see him – she longed to, indeed thought of little else. Nor had the diary piece turned him at a stroke into some ageing Lothario dancing with indecent haste – and flair – on the grave of his marriage. No, the reason for her uncertainty was to do with herself. If she were once again to lay herself open to that heady, thoughtless onslaught of desire and emotion, she ought to know in advance what she wished for, in case she got it; and what she would be giving up, in case she lost it for ever.

So she held back. And while she did so, something happened, and Al rang.

'You've been away,' he said, a touch accusingly.

'Yes, on a job.'

'I kept getting your machine, but I didn't want to leave a message, it didn't seem right.'

Slowly, she sat down, and closed her eyes in order to hear him better. 'It's Crystal, isn't it?'

'I'm afraid so. She was found by a security guard, been dead for a few days at the time.'

'God almighty . . .'

'I'm sorry, angel, but there's no easy way.'

'What happened?' she whispered. 'Do we know?'

'Nothing sinister, apparently. Or not involving anyone else. Just living rough and lost it, I'm afraid. Lost it some time ago, by the look of that room.'

It was her turn to sound accusing. 'Someone should have checked.'

'Sooner or later we would have done. She was an independent old cow.'

'Don't talk about her like that!'

'Sorry, no, I'm sorry.' Al was contrite. 'I guess I do feel guilty and it makes me touchy.'

'Me, too.' She was crying now. 'I couldn't wait to escape that day, I didn't want to clear up any more than anyone else. I didn't want to find out. We're all to blame.'

'All – and none. This sort of thing was always in her stars, wasn't it? There's going to be a party for people who knew her, down at the Duke of Clarence, next to the recording studios – angel, you will come? We can all get pissed and purge the guilt.'

When she could cry no more she thought of what Al had said about 'this sort of thing' being in Crystal's stars. What sort of thing, exactly? Death by hypothermia in some derelict building, wrecked by drugs and booze, howling lonely at the moon while one's so-called friends got on with their lives? If such an end had been written anywhere, it was they who were left who had written it.

She put the party in her diary, telling herself she'd see how she felt on the day. Scruple – or it may simply have been fear – said that a febrile, over-stimulated gathering (she knew the sort from her Nicky days) would be an insult to Crystal's desolate death. And yet she wanted to talk about her, to know more, so that she could make her private goodbyes. In the end she did go, telling herself that the first moment she felt uncomfortable she could leave. How could she not have gone when Crystal had been the start of so much, the beneficent bad fairy with the power to grant wishes Miranda never knew she had?

It had been a stifling, starless summer night, but in that Bayswater basement of the early sixties it was Christmas. A louche, pagan Christmas, red, purple and gold, blurry with smoke, booze and hash, lit by joss-scented fireflies and candles with gnarled roots of wax. The room had no edges, no corners: it was an exotic tent, a womb lined with drapes and cushions and rugs, the ceiling sagging with dark blue velvet, scattered with tiny mirrors, a man-made heaven; the floor thick with brilliantly clothed people like a carpet of flowers; the music a hot tangle of guitars . . . Gorgeous, sickly sweet, seductive.

'My friends,' Crystal had said. 'Your friends.'

To this day Miranda didn't know whose room that had been. Then, as now, it existed outside everyday time and place, a room of the imagination. She could not have found it again if she'd wanted to, because the dark vividness of the room had wiped away the memory of how she'd got there, and how she'd returned.

Nicky she remembered. She hadn't even known his name, but lain alongside him on a fur-covered mattress. He was like an emaciated angel, white-faced and golden-haired, with heavy-lidded eyes and a broad, sculpted mouth. They had been in a dream, their own and each other's, too spaced-out for sex, but suspended in sensuality, inhaling each other's breath, stroking each other's faces, murmuring. Each thought they had never seen anyone, man or woman, as beautiful as the other. For a time, Crystal had come and lain with them, stretched alongside Nicky's back, her face resting on his shoulder so that Miranda seemed to see a two-headed creature smiling at her.

'I told you,' said Crystal, to one or both of them. 'I told you, didn't I?'

When she climbed the basement steps it was morning, but she couldn't tell, because the sky was black with summer thunder, the streets were dark and wet, and people hurried and ran beneath the roaring rain. She was alone, but not lonely. Blissed out. She fell into a taxi and, outside the house in Khartoum Road, gave the driver all the money she had on her. Had he really looked at it and handed it back? Yes – 'Have this one on me, darling, sleep well,' he said, and she'd gone up the steps to her front door shedding coins and notes like confetti, laughing, floating, knowing he was watching her.

She fell asleep on her narrow bed under the eaves with the rustle and flutter of pigeon feathers in her ears, like the sound of angel's wings, and a pale sun breaking through like an angel's face.

She woke in the afternoon to find Crystal sitting on the floor next to the bed, her chin resting on the edge of the pillow. Her eyes were luminous, but smudged with black, and she smelt of the basement.

'He wants to see you,' she said.

The next day Nicky came to collect her in a black Rolls with tinted windows, driven by a black chauffeur. She came down to find him leaning on the Rolls, dressed in white, an open bottle of champagne dangling from one hand. His only greeting was to open the car door. The seats were dark red leather, the interior like a gaping mouth. They'd made love as the Roller glided through London, his golden head like honey between her legs, his white, scarred arms reaching up to clasp her.

The start of the dream-time: the start of its ending.

She'd had to come.

The party – billed on a hand-written notice on the door as 'The Crystal Gazers Ball' – was in an upstairs room at the pub. There was a bar, a rhythm-and-blues band, and upwards of fifty people. She saw the flitter of recognition in some faces, the swiftly stifled registering in others as they were told who she was; and she was conscious of that deliberate slight turning away that was in some cases politeness and in others jealousy.

She cast around for a face she knew and caught sight of Al at the far end of the room talking to a portly grey-haired man in a diamond-patterned jumper. When she got to his side it was clear Al had been there some time.

He flung an arm round her shoulders. 'Angel-heart – you came!'

'Yes . . . But, Al, who *are* all these people?'

He shrugged, extravagantly baffled. 'She had a lot of friends?'

'Not enough, apparently.' She couldn't keep the disgust out of her voice.

'We did our best, we didn't know . . .' He tailed away, casting around for something more manageable to focus on. 'This is Carl, by the way. Carl, Miranda. Let me get you a drink.'

He headed for the bar. She and Carl looked at each other. They were at the opposite end from the band but the noise was still loud enough to preclude all but the most determined and clear-cut conversation. She took a deep breath. 'How did you know Crystal?'

'Pardon?

'Crystal! How did you—'

'I'm her brother!'

She didn't blink. 'God, I'm sorry!'

'Terrible business – but we hadn't seen each other for years.'

I bet you hadn't, she thought. The band announced a break, and she was able to ask, at a more reasonable level and quite sharply, 'Why was that?'

'Hard to say, really,' he mused. She was getting to dislike him more with each second. 'We were always chalk and cheese. She had a terrible temper, you know, she bullied me something rotten.' He shook his head and chuckled, but she didn't crack a smile so he rearranged his pudgy face into a more serious expression. 'She was always going to go her own way, and that's what she did. Sad, really, when these rifts occur in families, isn't it? But it does happen, I fear.'

'What does?' asked Al, returning with three glasses of white wine. 'There you are. Carl, I take it you were going to have another. Have you been chatting? Has she said who she is?'

'She doesn't have to,' said Carl, with a knowing smile. 'She's Rags. Aren't you?'

'Only when I'm working.'

'So tonight it's Miranda,' explained Al. His eyes drifted over the assembled company; evidently he couldn't wait to escape from the appalling Carl, which was understandable, but not if it meant leaving her with him.

'Al,' she said, 'there's a couple of people I want you to meet. Carl, will you excuse us?'

'Couldn't I meet them too?' He was unbelievable.

'It's a bit – personal.'

'Uh-oh! Say no more. I shall amuse myself and have a piece of that very tasty quiche.'

Towing Al to the other side of the room she said, through clenched teeth, 'He's her brother! Can you believe that?'

'Cunt, wasn't he?' agreed Al cheerfully. 'Who are we going to talk to?'

'Nobody, we both needed to get away.' They reached the safety of the far wall. 'Just stay with me till I've calmed down.'

'Stick with me, I shall repel all boarders.' He put a hand on her shoulder and turned her to face the wall. 'Have you seen the gallery?'

Along the whole of the wall, from bar to door at eye level, were photographs of Crystal. Laughing, drinking, smoking, dancing; sooty-eyed and tousled; vamping with a joint; jaunty in butcher-boy cap; romantic, as a somewhat lived-in Biba shepherdess; outrageous in nothing but a feather boa; older, spoiled and exotic, as Miranda remembered her . . . In two of the pictures Nicky, forever young and androgynously beautiful . . .

She moved slowly along the parade of pictures, transfixed by its furious, captured torrent of hedonistic life.

'I can't bear it.' The words were murmured, and so exactly expressed what she was thinking that for a second she thought she'd spoken her thoughts out loud: 'I just – can't – bear it.'

She looked at the person next to her. 'Fred?'

In the second that followed Miranda saw for herself the meaning of the phrase 'His face lit up'.

'Hallo.' He put his arms round her and folded her to his chest. His voice was still quiet. 'Hallo, hallo, hallo . . . Jesus, it's a miracle!'

She nodded against him.

'Can we go?' he asked, against her hair. 'This seemed like a good idea, but I can't bear it.'

She nodded again. As they left, she heard Al call, '*Au revoir*, angel-heart! See you found someone you know, then.'

They walked along the wide, tree-lined street, quiet with respectable wealth. Walked side by side, close, but not touching. Not heading anywhere.

'I loved her,' he said. 'I adored her. You could see from those pictures how lovely she was, but it wasn't just that. She was – magical. Fairy but feisty.'

'I can imagine.'

'Of course, you knew her as well, but – forgive me – you're so much younger.'

'She still had that quality,' she said. 'She hadn't lost it. She still cast the spell.'

'I can't believe—' He stopped abruptly and banged his fist against his brow. 'I can't *believe* it all ended as it has.'

'No.' She was silenced by his strength of feeling.

He turned to her. 'May I say something?'

'Of course.'

'You might find it a bit alarming.'

She gave a small smile. 'Tonight, that would take a lot.'

'It's because of Crystal that I know how it feels. Real, glorious love. The thunderbolt. Would you ever have got in touch with me if we hadn't met tonight?'

'I don't know. I didn't think you wanted me to.'

'But I'm in love with you!'

She stepped forward and put her arms round his neck.

'Oh!' he gasped. 'Thank you, Crystal.'

CHAPTER FOURTEEN

Claudia, 137

Publius, though he respected her wish to go to Rome, still tried to dissuade her.

Pressing her hand tight over his heart, he said, 'It's sad, but it's over now. Your father's no longer there. What difference can it make?'

'To me, all the difference in the world.'

'And me. I'm still here, and I shall miss you.' He placed his hand on her stomach. 'Both of you.'

'We'll come back,' she said. 'I need to go for my own sake, more than for his, to salve my conscience.'

'For what?' He stepped back, arms thrown wide, exasperated.

'For all the years that I haven't been with him.'

'Because you've been here! With me – your husband!'

'Publius.'

'I'm sorry. I apologise.'

Too late, she'd heard the fear in his voice. The fear that she might lose this baby too, and be far from home when it happened. She knew it was a possibility. Severina was irritable on the subject already. But Claudia herself was calm. So far, this had been a charmed pregnancy, a source not of sickness and anxiety but of well-being.

'Am I forgiven?' he asked.

She hated him to be humble. 'Don't say that. But please trust us. If anything should happen it will be the gods and not the journey to Rome that causes it. Severina's coming with me.'

He smiled ruefully. 'Who's going to keep the dog in order?'

'You will. She'll be concentrating her energies on me. I shan't have a moment's peace.'

'No,' he said, 'nor me.'

She'd heard the news of her father's death in mid-May. Three weeks later she was to leave for Rome with the disapproving Severina in attendance. She had agreed with Publius that she would be back by the end of October, in good time for the baby's birth the following month. They both knew that she would be travelling almost the whole time, that on that time scale she would be in Rome barely a week before she would have to head back. But there had been no further discussion. Her mind was made up.

The evening before she left Publius drove her out to see the start of their new house. It was no longer a peaceful, sylvan scene but an unlovely building site, surrounded by workers' shacks. She was a little shocked to see the first deep gouges marking out the foundations, and the great heaps of displaced soil. In high summer, work had only just ended for the day; tools, scaffolding and all sorts of site hardware were scattered about and the men were cooking over open fires and stoves.

'Not so beautiful at the moment, is it?' she said. 'We're tearing it up. It's hard to imagine how it will be.'

'We're going to make it *more* beautiful,' he promised. 'A superb family house with gardens, and water, and a temple. Light and warm ... We shall sit out here and command the best view in Britain. I know it looks a brutal business now, but the more brutal the process the more elegant the outcome.'

The site manager, Helvenus, spotted them at once and came over. 'It's going well, sir. If this weather lasts we'll have the footings up by next week.'

'What about all the materials we ordered?'

'Scheduled to arrive on time,' said Helvenus, which all three of them knew meant nothing. He turned to Claudia. 'I've sent those designs of yours to the mosaic chaps. Give them time to get their heads round the ideas.'

'They'll be able to do them, won't they.' She was careful not to make this a question. The floor designs weren't difficult, but they were out of the ordinary – asymmetrical and flowing.

'Course they will. I admit they're a bit change-shy some of these local craftsmen. They think they've got the Roman style sorted, and then someone like yourself comes along and shakes them up. But they'll adapt – it'll do them good.'

'We'll have a look round, if we may,' said Publius. 'Anywhere we shouldn't go?'

'No, it's all yours. As you know!' He chortled at his unconscious pun. 'Where the dugouts are, stick to the boards. Chap jumped over the other day and landed up with a broken ankle and no job. Want the plans with you? They're in the office.'

'It's all right, this isn't official.'

'Makes no difference to me,' declared Helvenus spiritedly. 'There's good work going on here.'

They began at what would be the front door, and followed the outlines of the peristyle, atrium, bedrooms, dining room and bath-house. The bare rectangles of ground appeared small, diminished by the scale of their surroundings. It took a considerable leap of imagination – and faith – to picture the finished house, a leap that Publius found easier to make than her.

'When you come back,' he said enthusiastically, 'you'll really notice a difference. And when the walls are up you'll see how spacious it is.'

She knew now what this latest visit was – not merely a progress report, but a hostage to fortune.

As they walked around, the groups of builders glanced up incuriously from their food. Claudia thought how strange it was that these men – roughnecks and hard cases as well as skilled craftsmen and experts from all over the Empire – were in the process of turning a dream into reality, without the least knowledge of what the dream was. By mixing concrete, digging foundations, laying one stone on another as they were told to do, they were making it come true, just as the legionaries up on the hills had built the Wall, which seemed always to have been there.

This house would be built, and with it her future.

Next day at dawn, she left. Her parting from Publius was muted. This time it was she who placed her hand on his heart. 'We shall be back in the autumn.'

He looked hard into her eyes. 'Till then. Look after yourself.'

As the carriage moved away, Claudia's eyes brimmed with tears, but they remained unshed. And by the time they reached the main gate her fickle, homing heart had flown ahead, to Rome.

Perhaps because she was retracing her steps and not travelling into the unknown, the journey south seemed shorter. It still took them the best part of six weeks, but the northern weather was kind, and as they got nearer to their destination she found she'd almost forgotten the intense heat of an Italian summer.

While she basked in the open, face lifted to the sun, sometimes even walking alongside the carriage, risking freckles and burning, Severina, scandalised, lurked beneath the awning, complaining bitterly: 'I don't know how you tolerate it, I wouldn't want to raise a baby in this climate!'

'Then it's as well we shan't be.'

'You mind you don't swell up.'

'Don't worry, I'm swollen enough already.'

Claudia had learned that the way to deal with Severina's grousing was to appear not to take it too seriously. Claudia understood, and sympathised – she had been a strong young woman going to meet her new husband when she had come to Britain, and yet she had been scared, shocked and homesick. Severina was no spring chicken, and had only the call of duty and loyalty to sustain her: she would sooner have cut off a hand than allowed Claudia to come with anyone else, but she was simply overwhelmed. The *mansios* they had stayed in on this side of the water had horrified her even more than the travelling. She saw, or imagined she saw, vermin in every room, stomach ailments on every plate of food, and cut-throats everywhere. She was astonished at Claudia's forwardness in striking up conversations with other travellers.

'After what happened last time, I should think you'd want to keep yourself to yourself,' she muttered, after one convivial evening, and Claudia's attempts to reassure her, by pointing out that on this trip she had brought very little worth stealing, failed utterly.

Rome itself took what was left of the wind out of Severina's sails. She couldn't even manage to be grumpy – it was all simply too much. Claudia sat with her arm around the older woman's shoulders, pointing out this and that with childish delight, in the futile hope that her own pleasure would communicate itself. The heat, the smell, the noise and the bustle lifted her spirits like warm wine.

The door of her father's house stood open – someone had been set to look out for them. The whole household was waiting, including some new faces she did not recognise, and some older ones, freedmen who had come back in order to welcome her and honour Marianus' memory before the house was sold. There were two young children as well, staring shyly at her round the adults' legs. These people had been her family, and like a family they greeted her – there were smiles, and a few tears, a pressing of hands, and expressions of respectful but heartfelt sympathy. She was moved, not just by the slaves' loyalty to her father, who had deserved it, but their loyalty to her, who had been away so long.

She handed over Severina, who was by now weaving with exhaustion, into the care of the housekeeper, and the others discreetly dispersed. Now, suddenly and forcefully, the reality of her father's death struck Claudia, and she mourned. She had never once been in this house when he had not been here, or nearby, about his business or his social ventures, charitable or otherwise. His expansive, sentimental, fussy, kindly nature had informed the very walls, the very air, of the place. Everything in it was his choice, or that of Claudia's mother whom he had loved so much. Now the process of packing up had begun, the less sensitive items had been put to one side for the sale room or the auctioneer, the precious ones and the papers left for her to deal with. The garden where she had played, first with her father, then with Tasso, and where Publius had proposed marriage, was neat and bare, ready for new occupants with new ideas. This place was withdrawing from her, awaiting its new life.

It was if a whole layer of the fabric of the house had been removed – the layer laid down by those who had lived in it for so many years: the patina of long usage, their scent, their breath, their movement, even their thoughts, now stripped away.

She wasn't quite a stranger, but she felt like a ghost. The memories she had of living in this place were not here, but in her head. Her brief stay couldn't bring them back to life. If before there had been not enough for the servants to do, now there was virtually nothing. Eusebor, now a very old man, swept the paths and colonnade with slow, trembling strokes, a young girl she didn't know watered the plants.

Severina would sleep the clock round. Claudia found herself dreading the moment she must have supper alone, and waited on by too many people. But as she sat at the table with meat, pastries and fruit enough for three, she felt a nudge inside her. Then another. The first movements of her unborn child, whose only home she was.

Marianus' affairs were in good order. Paperwork had been a hobby with him, so although there was a great deal of it, the correspondence, lists, inventories and contracts were painstakingly executed and filed. The only things she arranged to take back with her were her father's desk and chair. These plain pieces of furniture, the only undecorated items in the house, had been such a feature of his life – as work, a place to doze during the heat of the day, and a vantage-point from which to observe contentedly the daily routine of his household.

Sitting there sorting through his papers she felt his presence at her shoulder, guiding her hand, and took comfort from it. For a man so hectically emotional in life, Marianus' legacy was one of kindliness and order.

She had several visitors, of whom the first was Catia, her quondam bridesmaid, now a smart Roman *matrona*, and herself a wife and mother. The pretty coquettish girl had grown into a crisply elegant woman, anxious to impress upon Claudia how successful her husband was as an architect, and how free her own life was from constraints.

'I'm a businesswoman myself,' she said, in case Claudia should be under any illusion as to her independence. 'I import fabrics for sale, and Petrus recommends them to his clients. We're a very successful partnership.'

'It sounds like it,' agreed Claudia.

Catia looked at her coolly. 'And how about you, Claudia? How is life on the wild frontier?'

'Not so very wild. Remarkably civilised, in fact.'

'Not even the tiniest hankering for home?' Catia smiled a catlike, close-lipped smile, which implied that she already knew the answer.

'Only occasionally,' said Claudia.

'And when is the baby due?'

'In three months.'

'And you have that appalling journey ahead of you, when you've only just got here – couldn't you persuade Publius to let you stay on for a while?'

'No,' replied Claudia. 'I couldn't.'

'If you simply *told* him, surely—'

'No,' said Claudia. 'We will be going back.'

When Catia left, with many insincere comments on how wonderfully well she looked, considering, Claudia felt shaken. It seemed that these days she belonged nowhere.

Another visitor was Cotta, who ostensibly came to pay his respects but actually to gossip as usual. Not wishing to let her father down by being less open-handed than he would have been, Claudia overcame her misgivings about encouraging Cotta and asked for wine and cakes to be served. The years had done nothing to diminish his greed: jowls quivering and eyes bright, he tucked in and waxed emotional.

'And so, my dear, you've come back to us. What a pity it has to be for such a sad reason. Marianus is sadly missed, sadly missed . . . His hospitality was second to none.' He smacked his lips appreciatively, and raised his glass. 'Here's to a good friend, a fine scholar and a stalwart citizen!'

'To my father.'

'Now, is there anything I can do? In the way of transporting items, clearing up, ensuring a fair price?'

'I think it's all in hand. But thank you, and I shan't hesitate to be in touch with you if I need help.'

'Good, good. A very fine house this, always liked it. Gentleman's residence, lavish but not gaudy, every comfort, and spacious for a town house. You'll get a good sum.'

'I believe so.'

Seeing that this particular line of oblique enquiry was getting him nowhere, Cotta tried a more direct approach. 'So how's married life? Eh?' He ogled her. 'Publius looking after you?'

'We're very happy.' She decided there was no harm in feeding the poor man some news. 'We're building our own house, outside the garrison.'

'Are you now?' Cotta's face lit up. 'Bully for you. What's it like contracting the work up there, can you get what you want at the price that you want it?'

'We've not encountered any serious problems yet.'

'Honest men, in the main?'

'I believe so. Though, of course, it's the skill of a really talented cheat that he cheats you without your noticing, until it's too late.'

'Very good, absolutely!' Cotta guffawed. 'If something looks good enough but is jerry-built what can you do? Still, I'm pleased to hear of all these plans, this domestic stability. It's just a pity,' and here he wiped a tear, originally of mirth but now miraculously of sadness, from his cheek, 'that your father is no longer with us to hear of it.'

'Yes. And he was to be a grandfather, too.'

She thought Cotta would melt before her eyes. 'My dear,

my dear . . . I thought that extra radiance must be due to something, considering the journey and everything else you've endured. This is wonderful, wonderful news!'

'Thank you.' She let her hands rest in his moist, warm ones for a second, then withdrew them. 'The baby is another reason why I shan't be staying in Rome for long.'

'Indeed! You must be back with Publius for the great day,' agreed Cotta, still mopping and sniffing. 'And tell me, how is that husband of yours? Overjoyed, I hope, at the prospect of fatherhood?'

'Yes, he is . . .' The question, an echo of something Cotta had said to her before, prompted Claudia to say tentatively, 'I wonder if I might ask you something?'

'But of course!' He brightened up, all ears. 'Anything, anything at all.'

'I seem to remember, though I may be wrong, that when you and I were talking at my betrothal party, you mentioned that Publius' first wife had lost a child.'

'That's right, a tragedy!' He assumed an appropriately melancholy expression again. 'A little girl.'

Claudia knew she must word her next question exquisitely carefully: otherwise it would be all round her late father's social circle, and beyond, that there were secrets between her and her husband, which boded ill for the marriage.

'I just wondered if you were in a position to tell me a little more about the poor lady. I know that she was very young, and at the moment, in this condition, I feel so much sympathy for her – call it a pregnant woman's fancy. I don't want to bother Publius with it, but to be able to have her in my thoughts from time to time.'

Cotta's pudgy features puckered in ecstasy. 'Dearest girl, that's a sweet, charming idea. Of course I'll tell you what I know, though it isn't a great deal . . .'

Claudia braced herself for the torrent, from which she would have to sieve the facts.

It was many months since Publius had had the nightmare. But longer, years, since he'd had to endure it without Claudia next to him. Though she said nothing he could always see, next day, the shadow of the horror he'd been through in his wife's eyes. He hated the thought that she had been there with him and he had not known, that she'd suffered without understanding why, and that she was too sensitive to his feelings to mention it. He hated his own stubborn pride, which stopped him bridging the distance between them.

Most of all he hated the secret, which, imprisoned by his fear, grew darker with the years.

He always knew when the nightmare was coming. A small, warning shadow would flit across the back of his mind, playing with his nerves, taunting him. Today, all day, he'd been battling with an intractable tangle of administration. His head ached with it. Publius had rather engage hand to hand with an enemy's biggest, maddest killer than sort out a supply chain that had got bogged down in weather and red tape. In battle or on exercise he was ice-cool, but give him half an hour with a whining quartermaster and his temper was on the loose. Then there was the damage-limitation, the regrouping so that the desired result was achieved. In this province, he'd learned long since, bluster didn't work. A loud voice and a Roman officer's uniform were not enough, and a towering rage would reduce the civilians on whom the garrison depended to a state of dumb insolence amounting to sabotage. Roman rules did not apply, and the first and only British rule was that there were none. Habits, yes. Customs, yes. Unspoken understandings, hundreds of them. But rules? Not a chance. The two qualities most required in dealing with the native Brits – pragmatism and patience – were not his strong suit.

Added to which there had been an incident in a town twenty miles to the south and, subject to status, he would have to take a cohort down there to sort things out. It was only a civil disturbance, but the sort that could easily turn nasty if allowed to run on. After admin this was the type of job he liked least – neither one thing nor another, with a delicate line to be trodden between restoring quiet and being heavy-handed with the citizenry. It was always something trivial that started these things – a squabble between shop-owners, or some minor legal grievance about property, or a daughter's marriage – but in no time it would have exposed some real or imagined grudge about the administration, and escalated into trouble. Publius knew these civic disruptions to be a necessary evil in such a polyglot province, and certainly not life-threatening, like events beyond the Wall, but the required combination of firmness and restraint didn't come easily to him.

And now he knew that he was going to set out sick and exhausted. The night ahead would leave him feeling he'd done ten rounds with a German wrestler.

Usually Tiki slept outside their door, but in Claudia's absence Publius had got into the habit of letting him come into the room, not for the dog's sake but his own. The dog was a reminder of his wife. Tonight he hoped that Tiki, lacking Claudia's caution, might be disturbed by the nocturnal commotion, and wake him up before the worst part came.

The nightmare's familiarity only made it worse. The gods knew that it had been familiar the very first time he'd had it. Its horror lay in him being obliged to relive a single, terrible event, step after step, detail upon detail, the endless reopening of a wound that never healed.

He was standing in a hot, dark room, thick with the visceral smell of fresh death. His little wife lay on the bed, a neat bundle next to her. An elderly woman was tidying up. The only sound was the woman's breathing and her small grunts of effort as she did her job. He didn't move. Neither of them spoke. When the woman had finished she gathered up the soiled linen and left the room. As she passed him she ducked her head in the direction of the bed. When she'd gone he went over and looked down at his wife. Her child-face was white and blank, there were tear-trails on her cheeks. He didn't touch her. He picked up the bundle. It felt all cloth, the baby lost inside its wrappings. His skin crawled at how small she was, a thing not of this world. But when he looked, her eyes were open, fierce and accusing, a silent scream of hate. He was terrified. Sweat poured off him.

Then, he was walking fast through the streets, the bundle beneath his cloak. Hundreds of people thronged the pavements, going about their nocturnal business, but he could hear nothing. He was in a pocket of silence. The infant's mute, half-stifled hatred scalded him.

He reached the black mountain of the city's refuse-dump. Rats, and people like rats, crept and scuttled over it, sifting, depositing, taking. He walked around the mountain to the far side where it was darkest, and thrust the bundle into the side of it, pushing hard so that it wouldn't become dislodged. It was always then that he heard the first and only sound of his dream: the squeak of rats. As he walked away, he glanced back to see the infant emerge from her hiding place, her bright eyes fixed on him as she came crawling, pattering, after him.

Then he ran and ran. Ran like a madman out of the city into a featureless darkness, and kept on running till he fell.

When he woke, the room was grey with dawn. A little more than arm's length from his bed the dog sat staring at him, its head tilted to one side.

'This is only what I've heard, you understand,' said Cotta. 'And it's certainly not my business, but you can imagine how much it must mean to your husband that you're expecting his child.'

'Thank you for telling me,' said Claudia. She rose to show him it was time to go, but her legs shook. 'It sounds like a nasty, colourful rumour to me.'

'Maybe . . .' Cotta hauled himself to his feet. 'Probably. Who knows? It's history now, and the present and the future are what matters.'

When he'd gone, for the first time in her pregnancy she was very sick. Severina, invigorated by rest and by this welcome and long-overdue sign of weakness in her employer, ordered her to bed and took the opportunity to assume authority over the household. 'You stay there for once,' she said. 'If not for yourself, do it for the baby.'

Claudia did stay there, but not to sleep. New and terrible images tyrannised her.

She had heard of the practice of 'exposing' unwanted, usually female, infants – leaving them on the outskirts of town for the elements or urban predators to deal with. It was distasteful but accepted, though not among the equestrian and upper classes; perhaps it happened more than she knew but wasn't spoken of.

She did not know, until now, of anyone who had done such a thing, and she could not even now bring herself to believe it of Publius. Feverishly, she made allowances for this and that – Cotta's relish for gossip and exaggeration, people's dislike of reserve and their need to supply a reason for it, the fact (and this in itself denoted acceptance) that the motherless, sickly baby would have died anyway . . . But always she came back to the same thing. The night horrors. Some dreadful experience was stalking her husband, something so bad that even in his sleep, in the full agony of it, he didn't cry out, and next day his mind's door slammed shut, concealing it not just from her but from himself. Never in a thousand years would she have given stupid Cotta the satisfaction of thinking he had shocked her. It had taken all her resources to remain controlled and dismiss the story as hearsay. But now it was torture to her to be ignorant, and have no way of knowing, or even of asking, what was the truth.

Lying in the room she had slept in as a child, with the sounds of the hot, empty afternoon beyond her door, she recalled an incident she had kept buried for over twenty years.

She had been about six years old, walking back with her father from an informal concert party at the house of friends in the Via Sabara. The party had been dull for her, but pleasantly so – those were the days when Marianus was still intermittently melancholy over the loss of his wife, her mother, and she liked to see him happy, and to be spoiled herself by his friends. They seemed to think she was unhappy too, poor little motherless thing that she was, forgetting that Claudia had never known her mother and therefore didn't miss her. The music had tinkled and chirruped interminably. She'd played five-stones in a corner of the garden, studied a lizard with a malformed foot, shared sweets with a scabby-eyed cat, and longed to get home to play with Tasso. Her father had recited one of his poems and she could tell, although she'd been embarrassed to look, that he'd cried at the end of it and the lady of the house had fussed over him.

It was unusual for them to walk, especially in the summer heat, but in the late afternoon the sky had clouded over and the air became suddenly cool, so that was what they did. She enjoyed it, skipping along holding her father's hand, jerking and jumping on the end of it like a monkey on a string, trying his patience a little, but never enough for him to lose it altogether. Indeed, she could not remember that he had ever lost his patience, or his temper, with her. His love might have been too yielding and unconditional, but it was without limit. After Lucilla, she had been quite simply his life.

The walk took only a short while. Claudia was pleased to be going home, but Marianus didn't hurry. It wasn't the same for him. On one corner there was a speechmaker standing on his upturned box, spouting a torrent of rhetorical devices on the theme of family values. The strong paterfamilias, the dutiful matron, the ambitious son and industrious daughter all featured in his tirade. Marianus slowed down, murmured, 'Amusing fellow,' and paused for a moment to listen. Claudia tugged his hand, and he picked her up, kissing her absentmindedly, and leaning her over his shoulder.

Behind them on the pavement two mongrels were squabbling over a cloth doll. Claudia had one like it at home; she didn't care for it as much as her beautiful hand-painted Egyptian princess but she still felt sorry for this doll, being torn apart. She wriggled and her father let her slide down.

She took only one step towards the dogs – that was as close as she needed to be to see that it was not a doll. She shrieked and when Marianus patiently picked her up again she buried her face in his neck. A moment later the speechmaker ended on the approved clarion note, to good-humoured cheers. She kept her face hidden until they were well out of the way, but something about the way her father patted her back told her that he had seen it too.

'What was that?' she asked, against his neck.

'I don't know.'

'What the dogs were growling about? What was it?'

'Some sort of dead animal. There we are, our street. Are you going to hold my hand now?'

She had accepted his account – or his refusal to give one – gratefully. That, then, was how you dealt with such things in the grown-up world. You denied the evidence of your own eyes, and that made it all right.

Except that it was no longer all right. It had been a dead baby that she had seen, being pulled apart by the street mongrels. There were babies in Rome that no one wanted, that were left out for the dogs.

Tonight, Claudia lay still, one hand on her belly, waiting for her own baby to move. But her shock must have transmitted itself to the child, for it gave not the smallest sign of life.

Claudia remained in Rome for six weeks, during which time she was strictly practical. She made the slaves her top priority, ensuring that each had a decent job lined up, with security and the prospect of manumission in the medium term. She called in favours from her father's associates to retrieve some small sums that were owed to him, and she finalised the sale of the house and its spring-cleaning. She arranged for memorials to him on the wall of his favourite public garden, and outside the house. She kept busy and she kept her own counsel.

Severina, after all her rebellious grumbling about the trip, was now predictably loath to return. 'It hardly seems worth our having come all this way, I'm just getting used to the place.'

'I came for a reason,' Claudia reminded her sharply, 'and a purpose, to honour my father and put his affairs in order. Now it's time to go back.'

Severina was an old hand. Her over-familiarity was within accepted bounds, and she knew when she'd exceeded them. From that point on she was good as gold. She also, in spite of her abrasive manner, was beginning to understand Claudia's moods. The girl was expecting, she'd lost her father, she'd sold her family home, and something – something marital, Severina suspected – was on her mind.

The journey was supportable. This time it was Severina who

played the hardened traveller in the inns and *mansios* and Claudia who sat smiling quietly on the sidelines or went early to bed. Thankfully, she was still healthy and fit. She was now well into the middle third of the pregnancy and there had been no blood-spotting, no swellings or pains: the baby stretched and kicked inside her. She still walked when she could, because the bumpy transports made her stiff and gave her backache, but it was nothing much, and the walking helped her to sleep well at night, even when it was necessary to do so on the wagon benches.

Their only major delay came when they reached the northern coast of Gaul and were told by the galley master that sailing was postponed indefinitely because of adverse conditions. No, he couldn't say how long, that was why he'd said indefinitely; and no, he wasn't able to give a long-term weather forecast. All he knew was that it was a shit-storm out there at present and no sign of clearing up.

Their driver on this leg of the journey had been a cheerful, gabby youth who told them he couldn't hang about because of other commitments. But for these two ladies – and, it was implied, for a consideration – he would stretch a point and use his network of contacts to find them reasonable accommodation. Severina took the opportunity to display a few of her old neuroses: this was a sea-port, full of undesirables, the inns would be clip-joints and the beds damp.

Claudia grew short with her. 'We'll be very lucky if we get a bed at all, and I for one don't mind paying for it, so stop complaining. If you'd prefer the floor, that's fine.'

In the end (and due solely, if the youth was to be believed, to his good offices) they found hard but dry beds in a long shared dormitory over a beer-house. The landlord's policy was no-frills, no negotiation. He kept the place free of vermin, cooked plain food twice a day and kept his charges low. Any arrangements his customers wanted over and above what he provided they were entitled to make, at their own risk and cost.

The first night they were tired, and went to bed early, taking the two beds furthest from the dormitory door, Severina near the wall and Claudia, who was less apprehensive, between her and the other occupants. They were a mixed bag, all of whom kept different hours, but Claudia still managed to sleep, with Severina's agitated whisperings ringing in her ears.

The following day the storm reached new heights of ferocity. There was no chance of going out, let alone setting sail, and the inn lanterns swung and wavered crazily all day. Some of the patrons, those who'd staggered to bed in the small hours, remained in bed until the landlord turned them out; others started drinking early; the more respectable, like Claudia and Severina, sat near the brazier. Severina had brought some sewing with her which she had not touched for nearly three months, but now both she and Claudia made use of it, keeping their hands busy and their eyes down.

In the evening the rain eased off, and the wind dropped. It was still wretched outside, gusty and awash, but the two women went for a short walk. When they came back, Severina went up to the dormitory alone, though not without protest.

'Aren't you coming, madam?'

'Not yet. I'll never sleep if I go up now.'

'But I'll be on my own up there.'

'You prefer that, surely.'

On reflection, Severina did, and went off grumbling. Claudia tucked herself into a corner with some warm wine. She would rather sit here and watch the world go by than lie down before she was tired and be plagued by her thoughts.

For quite some time she was the only woman in the room, but she felt curiously protected, both by her condition and by the presence of the burly landlord who, for all his brusque abrogation of responsibility, was a decent man, disrespectful (she sensed) towards Rome but with a soft spot for a lady.

After an hour or so, when she had finished her wine and was thinking of retiring, the door opened and two more women entered. From the way they were greeted by some of the customers Claudia guessed they were prostitutes. One was no longer young, but voluptuous, dark, vivacious, a woman at ease with herself and her work, full of teasing and laughter. The younger woman was fair, and very tall and slender. She

336

was neither so forward nor, Claudia thought, so happy as her friend. Her beauty had a fineness and delicacy that didn't sit well with the men's boisterous caresses, although she did her best to respond, smiling and letting herself be squeezed and patted.

Claudia was unable to take her eyes off her. The girl had elegant clothes, an exquisitely painted face and stylishly curled hair; she put Claudia's own travel-stained appearance to shame. She must be doing well out of her clients. And yet Claudia's heart ached for her.

A stumpy, red-faced middle-aged fellow took the girl's hand and drew her to one side, to a table at Claudia's end of the room. Cheers and barracking accompanied this manoeuvre, but he must have been a regular admirer for the girl went docilely enough. He pulled her down on the bench next to him and began greedily nuzzling her neck, the other hand pawing at her lap. The girl's face rested on his shoulder, expressionless, eyes patiently closed.

Claudia took this as her cue to go. But as she was about to get up the girl's eyes opened and looked directly, pleadingly, into hers. They were blue eyes, as familiar to Claudia as her own reflection, and yet the shock was that of seeing a ghost.

'Tasso?'

The blue eyes closed again momentarily as the man's hand found its objective . . . Then opened again, swimming with tears.

'Tasso,' she whispered. 'It is you?'

The painted lips moved. Soundlessly, but Claudia could read the words.

'I'm sorry –'

The phrase was repeated, still silently but rhythmically, as though wrung out by the man's urgent, rooting movements.

'I'm sorry . . . sorry . . . sorry . . .'

Claudia would have waited all night, but after an hour or so the man, by now very drunk, staggered out to relieve himself.

He must have had some prior claim on Tasso, for no one else came over to bother him. Claudia knew that they had minutes at most, and wanted to say only one thing.

'Tasso, my dear, dear friend – I don't blame you for anything.'

Tears were pouring down his face. 'There is nothing to blame me for. I took nothing, did nothing. The driver stole your things and left me out there.'

'Tasso.' She put out her hand but he flinched. It was worse than a blow.

'Don't! How could you bear to? I'm disgusting . . .'

'No, never. *Never.*'

'He left one thing of yours, your necklace. It wasn't kindness, it was to make me look like a thief.'

Claudia saw the man returning, holding the sides of the door as he entered, unsteady on his feet, his big head dripping with rain.

'Tasso, come back with me, we're sailing back to Britain. You mustn't live like this.'

'Yes,' he said. 'I must. It's who I am.'

As the man staggered over and collapsed heavily on the bench, throwing his arm around Tasso's shoulders, Claudia, unable to bear it, got up to leave.

As she went, she heard her friend's old, sweet, familiar voice: 'Good-night, my lady.'

The next day was dull but calm. They would sail.

As they stood on the quay, watching their baggage being manhandled aboard, a boy tugged at Claudia's sleeve. 'Oy, lady!' He handed her a small cloth-wrapped parcel. 'I've got to give this to you.'

'Who from?'

He nodded over his shoulder, then shrugged. 'She's gone.'

He ran away. The fine twine that the parcel was tied with was human hair. She held it tight in her hand as she picked open the cloth. Feeling Severina's curious stare she closed

338

it again and put it, with the strands of silvery hair, into her bag.

'Something returned that I lost,' she explained. 'People are more honest than you'd think.'

CHAPTER FIFTEEN

Bobby, 1993

A person's world can change in seconds. There's nothing momentous about the day it happens; it starts out as just another bread-and-butter day, full of inconsequential detail. It's only when you look back that you realise those inconsequential details were in fact the stuff of calm and contentment. The big things, the things that are Out There, you get used to: they've become the background to your smaller concerns. Like wild animals, left undisturbed they won't disturb you. Or so you think.

As Mondays go, the one in question was pretty unremarkable. I'd been on my own in the office because the Hobdays had taken advantage of a trade fair in the Lake District to have a long weekend. They'd felt able to do this because things were quiet, so I had only the most undemanding paperwork to attend to, and a few routine calls to deal with. For the rest of the time I took the opportunity to do some office housework – tidying, rationalising, watering plants, clearing the dead wood out of the files and off the hard disk. Soothing, undemanding tasks.

It was February, grey and raw. Work was now well under way on the folly theatre and at lunchtime I pulled on my coat and walked down to take a look. The first cut was the deepest, and I'd got over the initial shock of tree-clearance and the sense that the ground was sustaining an injury from which it might never recover. Miranda had shown me the plans, and her enthusiasm had painted a vivid picture of how the building would look, and how it would not just suit but enhance its setting. The idea was that it would be like an echo, or perhaps a ripple, radiating out from the existing folly, the same shape as the smaller building, but embracing it.

'But not a copy,' she'd told me. 'It's got to be in harmony, but of its time – the next tree ring, do you see?'

I did, though the vision initially had been less clear in my head than in hers. There was another reason why I followed the progress of the building with mixed feelings: it charted a decline in my relationship with Daniel. It wasn't just that he was busier so we saw less of each other, there was a qualitative difference too. His physical and mental energies were taken up with this challenging new project. He was absorbed by and obsessed with it. And, crucially, he was under the spell of Ladycross, and of Miranda.

He didn't say this in so many words. He didn't have to. The light in his eyes and voice said it all. But I missed the sense of our – our what? friendship? affair? being something particular. It might never have been exactly central to either of our lives, but it had had, I believed, a specialness and importance as a way for each of us to define ourselves. That had, quite simply, gone. The Hobdays had sweetly invited us both round on Christmas Day, but I'd been conscious all the time of his discomfiture with the whole situation. These days we met, we talked, we sometimes, much less frequently, had sex, but our relationship was marginalised by the magic of the house on the hill.

How could I blame him? I was the same. But, unlike me, Daniel couldn't disguise it. He often came into the office straight from the Dire House, almost luminous with pleasure and enthusiasm for what he was doing, the sense of being part of a great and romantic enterprise. Whatever more humdrum connection existed between us was now no more than the background to that. I should, could, have inferred more, but I was (as Sally might have said) in denial.

Of course, I told myself rather small-mindedly, it was obvious that Miranda was involved with Marco Torrence, so she could never be more than a *princesse lointaine* where Daniel was concerned. His admiration, his crush, whatever you liked to call it, was something he had in common with most of the men who came into contact with her, my own safely married brother included. But even if it was just a phase, a bloke thing, it still hurt.

Once I was walking down to the site and I saw them – Miranda and Daniel – down there, and it stopped me in my tracks, because I couldn't face being buffeted by all that they now shared, and from which, no matter how they tried, I was excluded. I turned back, but not before I'd seen Miranda's face as she listened to Daniel. I didn't stop to define her expression, I only knew it was different from anything I'd seen there before.

To reach the site today, I had to circumnavigate Miles Montclere's Range Rover, which was parked with proprietorial insouciance in the middle of the muddy track. One of the back passenger doors was open and Jem was sitting on the seat playing with a Diving Action Man in a frogman's suit and aqualung. As I passed he pointed Action Man at me and made squirty laser-gun noises.

At the site itself, now marked out with warning tape to protect the unwary, Miles was in a huddle with two of the workmen. The others were standing around as if waiting for the outcome of these deliberations. A JCB stood to one side and a digger to the other, like a couple of prehistoric beasts about to join combat. Not wanting to appear nosy I kept my distance, but I'd been down here a couple of times before and the man nearest me gave me a nod.

'Afternoon.'

'Hallo.'

'Taking five, got a bit of a find.'

'What sort of find?'

'Little, like, statue? More like an ornament.' He held his thumb and fingers about four inches apart. 'Just trying to work out what it is.'

I nodded. 'I suppose in a place like this there must be all kinds of bits and pieces in the ground.'

'That's right. One job I was on we turned up an Anglo-Saxon

dagger. Didn't look anything much to begin with but it scrubbed up super in the museum. Ceremonial, apparently, not supposed to do any damage . . .'

'That must have been quite a thrill.'

'It was a thrill, it was. Bones, too, human bones, we get a lot of those. Old ones,' he added, to reassure me. 'Burial grounds, that kind of thing.'

At this point Miles detached himself from the group, spotted me and began to walk over, saying over his shoulder, 'Just keep your eyes peeled and let me know if anything else turns up.'

'Good afternoon,' I said, 'I was just taking a breather.'

'Was my son behaving himself as you passed?'

'He was. Action Man subjected me to withering fire.'

'Sorry about that. I don't like him careering about on the site, and I only intended to be a couple of minutes,' he explained. 'Nanny's day off and Penny's got a charity do. I'd better get back to him. Want a lift up the hill?'

'No thanks, this is a constitutional, but it's time I started back myself.'

'Hang on,' he took something out of his pocket, wrapped in a handkerchief, 'I must show you something. Look at that, will you?'

'Oh – may I?'

I held out my hand and he placed the object on it. It was the ornament the builder had mentioned, a small representation of a dog in what I guessed might be bronze. What was unusual and captivating about it was the dog's attitude: it sat with its front feet apart, head on one side, ears pricked, long tongue – the workmanship! – hanging out. Somehow the craftsman had managed to convey the animal's expression, even the brightness of its eyes.

'Charming, isn't it?' Miles's voice was shiny with pleasure. I warmed to him.

'It's absolutely enchanting,' I agreed, handing it back to him. We started walking towards the car. 'Where did you find it?'

'The digger turned it up over there. It was pure luck that it missed the lip of the shovel and dropped back, and the driver noticed it.'

'They must develop sharp eyes for this sort of thing,' I agreed, thinking of the dagger and the skeletons. 'Do you know what age it is?'

'Not the foggiest, I'm completely ignorant in these matters, but Miranda will doubtless know a man who does.'

We reached the Range Rover and were duly sprayed with another prolonged burst of fire from Action Man.

'That'll do, Jem. Anyway, jolly nice to see you.' Miles waved me off. 'Hey, old man, look what we found . . .'

Millie came in to see me when she got back from school. I guessed that Miles was busy in the office, Jem was installed in front of junior TV and Penny had not returned from the fundraiser, so homework could be safely postponed.

'Is there a job I can do?' she asked. She liked to be useful, but I knew this was also a pretext for hanging around for a while, and her defence against parental accusations of being a nuisance.

'Do people know where you are?'

'I told Daddy I was coming to say hallo.'

I gave her a stack of cards and a sheet of price stickers. 'There you go. Do that and there's a KitKat in it.'

'Cool.'

She stuck prices, I assembled material for the VAT return, to the accompaniment of chill-out classics on CD. While we worked we didn't talk much: it was companionable. I really liked Millie. She was one of the few children I knew – and admittedly I knew only a few – who made me wish I was a godparent. Not a parent, that was something I'd set aside a long time ago, but a kind of honorary relative who could advise, indulge, listen and sympathise. But then, I reminded myself, Millie would certainly have a fleet of well-heeled godmothers. Not to mention Miranda, the *ne ultima* of step-grans . . .

'Miranda and Marco are in the States,' she remarked, explaining albeit unintentionally why she was seeking diversion here instead of at the Dire House.

'Having a holiday?'

'Sort of – Marco's being an angel for a show,' she tossed out the term with the grand casualness of someone who'd just found out what it meant, 'and they're going to the first night. It's a musical – there are *sixty* people in it.'

'That sounds fun.' There was no pleasing me – I found myself hoping that I would not meet Daniel, missing her. 'Fancy that KitKat now?'

'Yes, please.'

'Cuppa? I'm having one.'

'No, thanks.'

I switched on the kettle and handed her the biscuit tin. 'Did Daddy show you what they found on the building site today?'

'The little tiny lurcher – it's so sweet!'

'Is that what he is, a lurcher?'

She nodded, and said, round a mouthful of water, 'Mm.'

I remembered something. 'There's another one of those round here, isn't there? That one that runs around loose.'

'M-hm . . .' she swallowed. 'The wanderer. Miranda worries Daddy'll shoot him but I think he's much too clever. He'll stay out of the way. Daddy's never going to see him.'

Something about the way she phrased this made me ask: 'You've seen him, though?'

'Yes, often. He sits at the edge of the wood really cheekily – like that statue – as if he's waiting for someone.' She imitated, head cocked, tongue hanging out, and I laughed because she got it just right.

'He's much more wary of me,' I said, 'he keeps his distance.'

Millie agreed. 'Yes, it's Miranda he likes. He's kind of adopted her.'

At this moment Penny's Volvo drove into the yard and Millie thanked me hastily for the biscuit and left. A moment later Penny put her head round the door. 'I hope my daughter hasn't been a nuisance.'

'On the contrary, she's been a great help.'

'I hope so,' said Penny doubtfully. 'She's a bit prone to latch on.'

'Don't worry,' I said. 'For one thing I've been on my own here today and I enjoy her company, and for another I'd always say if it wasn't convenient.'

'You're very patient, Bobby.'

When she'd gone I found myself thinking that Miles would do well to keep the day's little excitement up his sleeve because for once he was going to get a ticking-off.

At five thirty I locked up. It was a soft, clear evening and I paused, as I often did, by the west-facing window to gaze at the swathe of rolling countryside in the late-afternoon sun. Now that some of the trees were gone you could see the folly from here. The clearance gave it the air of a new building. But the upraised shovel of the digger next to it was like the head of a dinosaur. I was swept by a powerful sense of the sliding of time, the present always moving, the future rushing headlong to meet the past . . . My head spun, and I moved away from the window.

From a perverse, self-torturing curiosity, I drove down the lane to the mill, but his house was closed up, and the Mini wasn't outside.

I'd only been home ten minutes when the doorbell rang. I was still in that period of mild domestic reorientation, opening windows, checking for messages, putting the milk in the fridge, and thought, for an instant, Damn! before it occurred to me that it might be Daniel.

I opened the door to a young woman in head-to-toe biker black, with Ribena-coloured hair, carrying the sort of saggy sports bag that usually contains an array of overpriced household items for sale. I'd already arranged my face in a not-today-thank-you expression, when she said: 'Are you Roberta Govan?'

'Yes.'

'Can I come in?'

Her manner was so direct that I very nearly admitted her

without question, but the sports bag provided the necessary check. 'I'm sorry – who are you?'

'I'm your daughter.'

The world whirled a couple of times before bouncing, with sickening slowness, back into place, and stopping dead.

She said again, 'Okay if I come in? Only—'

I stepped back.

She hauled the bag past me into my tiny hall and dumped it heavily. I had one of those token chairs just inside the door, too uncomfortable for the living room, good only for visitors to put coats on. Now I sat down on it, grasping the arms tight, trying to push the blood through my veins.

She asked, 'Are you okay?'

'I don't know. Give me a second . . .'

She stood there watching me, giving me as many seconds as I wanted. Idling in neutral as I fought the sensation of drowning.

'Do you want a glass of water or something?'

I shook my head. When I stood up I staggered for a moment but she made no move to help, simply waited for me to recover my balance.

'Go through,' I said. 'Take a seat.'

In the living room she sat on the sofa, and I in the armchair. She was still utterly composed, but not relaxed – she sat on the edge of the sofa with her hands laced between her legs. I saw that she bit her nails. Through the shockwaves, small, simple questions filtered like drops of water.

'How do I know?' I asked.

She shrugged. 'Why would I lie about it?'

'How did you find out?'

'By accident. Someone let the cat out of the bag.'

'That's impossible,' I said. She continued gazing at me as if I hadn't spoken. I thought I'd never come across anyone so detached, and yet this was a person who had been, literally, attached to me. 'It's not possible,' I repeated. 'Nobody knew.'

'Of course they did. My parents, nurses at the hospital – think about it.'

Her parents – right. In spite of myself, I was stung. 'But it was years ago, and confidentiality, surely—'

'Is fine till it slips someone's mind. And by the way,' she added, 'it was over twenty years ago.'

'I know that!' I shouted, and she flinched, her head twitching to one side as if I'd slapped her. 'Don't you dare speak like that to me!'

She kept her face turned towards the window. 'How would you like me to speak?'

'What are you doing here? What on earth are you playing at? What do you want?'

'I wanted to meet you.' She turned back, but looked down at her hands, not at me. 'And now I have.'

'What's that supposed to mean?'

'Nothing. Exactly what it says.'

I was trembling with shock, and rage – at her and at myself.

'You must have expected *something*.'

'Actually,' she said, almost brightly as if she'd hit on something, 'I didn't. I had an open mind, but now I realise I did expect something because I'm disappointed.'

'I'd say I told you so, only I was never given the opportunity. You should never have come.'

'Supposing I had got in touch with you first, and asked, what would you have said?'

'I'd have said no. You can see why – it's pointless and painful.'

'Weren't you ever curious?'

'No. Never.' This wasn't wholly true but I wasn't going to open even the smallest chink in my guard.

'I was,' she said evenly. 'From the moment my mother told me. She did it the day after I began my first period, like some kind of tribal introduction to womanhood. But it was pretty stupid of her because from then on I knew I wasn't one of them, and I've been using it ever since.'

This new and alarming angle slewed my picture of the contented elective family walking hand in hand in the sunshine – the

348

picture that, no matter how unwelcome, would have absolved me from guilt.

'That's your problem,' I said. 'It's nothing to do with me.'

'Did I say it was a problem? I couldn't have done without it, it was my weapon against everything.'

I wasn't going to ask what 'everything' was. From the corner of my eye I could see her bag in the hall. I determined to ask nothing, for fear of what the answer might be. I longed for a drink, but didn't want to offer her one. We sat in a silence that writhed on my part with assumptions, resentments, misunderstanding, and most of all fear. Her own silence was unreadable.

There was a tap on the kitchen window and I looked round to see Kirsty Hobday waving cheerily from the shared path. By the time I was in the kitchen she'd come in through the back door.

'Don't worry, I can see you've got a visitor, I only popped round to say we're back.'

'Did you have a good time?'

'Absolutely smashing. Tell you all about it in due course. All well at the coalface?'

'Fine, nothing to report.'

'Okay, well, I'll just . . .' Before I could stop her she'd stepped into the living room. 'Sorry to disturb, I'm the neighbour.'

'Hallo.'

'Kirsty Hobday.'

'Fleur Wakeley.' I hadn't even asked her name.

'Right, I'm off. Thanks for holding the fort, Bobby. See you tomorrow.'

When I went back into the living room, she asked, 'Do people call you Bobby, then?'

'Some of them.'

She looked at me – not with the calm, unconcerned gaze this time, but more penetratingly, pinning me down with her fierce curiosity.

'I'll go if you want me to.'

The truth was I didn't want her to, not immediately. But I needed to know that the moment I did want her to go, she would.

I nodded towards the bag. 'Where are you off to?'

'Well, obviously I was coming here. But that can be changed.'

She was relentless. I was not to be let off the hook. It seemed I was being presented with a case of put up or chuck out. Out of the blue, I asked myself what Sally, in her professional capacity, would advise. Give yourself time. Don't be rushed. Don't add your own stress to the one being inflicted on you. If it's that important it'll still be there when you've made your mind up . . . Only in this case I sensed that I was being offered an ultimatum, and the decision was not so clear as it might have seemed only a few minutes ago, before the world changed.

'Where's home?' I asked, meaning: not here.

'Good question.'

'Where do your parents live?' I wielded the word 'parents' like a weapon.

'Bromley.'

'So what do you do?'

She fixed me with the look again. 'You really want to know?'

'I wouldn't ask otherwise.'

'People do, though, don't they, just to be polite?' she said.

'Well, I'm not. Being polite.'

'No,' she agreed pointedly, but then went on before I could retaliate. 'I've been waiting tables in Thessalonika for the past few months. I really like Greece. It's an accepting place. The work's hard and the pay's crap but the climate and the people are fantastic, so I keep going back.' She must have caught my look. 'I'm not brown because I don't want skin cancer.'

'Why did you come back?' I asked. 'Not for this, I hope.'

She shook her head. 'I'm expecting a baby in September and I had this daft urge to get back to base.'

It took me a second to absorb, and then I only really did so when I heard my own voice saying the words: 'You're pregnant.'

'That's right.'

'The father?'

'Is over there. He's a lovely, lovely man but I couldn't stand

350

to be married to him. Or any Greek male, actually. He cried when I left. We'll always be friends.'

'So,' I said, 'you're intending to go it alone.'

'More or less.'

I stood up. 'I'm going to have a glass of wine, would you like one?'

'Have you got any juice?'

I poured shiraz for me and orange for her. My hands were no longer shaking – I'd gone through the shock barrier.

She thanked me, and then said, 'I'm not asking you for anything.' She sounded like a replacement-window salesman. 'I'm solvent at the moment, and Spiro will send money, to begin with anyway. But my parents didn't exactly crack open the bubbly and you are this baby's grandmother.'

'No, I'm not. You quite rightly call your adoptive parents your parents, so how do I suddenly qualify as a grandparent?'

'Biology. The gene pool.'

'No.' I shook my head. 'No, sorry, not in this day and age.'

'All right.' She shrugged, and my heart flickered. 'Anyway, words, they don't change anything. Once I knew who you were, and found out where you were, I had to come and see you. It was all part of the process.'

I noted, with relief, the past tense, and relaxed just enough to look at her objectively. Hers was the sort of appearance that in another context might have seemed threatening. Dark puce hair that made not the smallest nod to naturalness; a creased and cracked black leather jacket and heavily studded denim waistcoat; one ear pierced so many times that its outer edge resembled a spiral notebook; a long dark skirt with (an intriguing practical touch, this) thick socks and walking boots. It all amounted to a statement that sat oddly with her unmade-up face, which was as calm as that of a Flemish portrait, and round and symmetrical as a clock.

'Please,' I said, in a businesslike voice, 'don't misunderstand me.' One eyebrow lifted, not quite imperceptibly. 'I wish you well. You've made a brave decision – about the baby and about coming here. But it's *your* decision. I made mine over twenty years ago. You should respect that.'

'I do.' She had a habit of responding in such a way that I was left with nowhere to go. I couldn't tell whether this was a strategy aimed at discomforting me, or whether it came naturally to her. Whatever her intentions I was beginning to think there was no reason why I shouldn't, for the duration of her visit, be equally plain with her.

'I was around your age,' I said. 'A few years younger. I wanted never to see you or think of you again, because I believed that would be best for both of us.' I had her complete attention now, and it was frightening. 'Or at least it would certainly be best for me, and what you didn't know you wouldn't miss. I can't blame you for coming here, but as you said yourself, it doesn't change anything.' What was I saying? In these few minutes the tectonic plates of my life had shifted, to create whole new seas and continents – a different planet.

She shook her head. She was not to be fobbed off, and what's more she thought like me. 'What I said was that *words* didn't change anything. I'm your daughter, this is your grandchild. And meeting you will make a big difference to us both.'

'Please,' I said, 'don't let's pretend it makes any difference to an eight-week-old foetus.'

She didn't reply. Her silence was not hostile, but it strongly conveyed her unshakeable self-belief. I didn't know where she got it from – certainly not from me. Perhaps there had been more to the lab technician than met the eye.

'I'm really sorry you've fallen out with your family,' I said. 'You should try to heal the rift, for the baby's sake.'

'I have tried. They just don't like me very much.'

'That's not uncommon, is it? People can love someone without liking them all the time. It's not insuperable.'

'But it is crap. If you care about someone you make the effort. Go the extra mile.'

I heard the double standard creeping in here and reminded myself that she was, after all, barely out of her teens. As if to emphasise this, she went on, 'I was pretty horrible, I know that. But parents are supposed to hang in there. They seemed to . . .' she looked away for a moment '. . . they seemed to decide I wasn't what they wanted, after all, and once they'd decided they made everything fit. Especially this.' She laid her hand on her stomach. 'This was just the evidence they needed that you can take the child from the feckless single mother but you can't take the feckless single mother out of the child.'

I was cut to the quick, insulted on my behalf as well as hers. 'Did they say that?'

'He did, my father.'

'It's a lousy, rotten thing to say.'

'I thought so.'

'*And* not true.' I moved on quickly to avoid the inner voice saying that patterns of behaviour repeated themselves. 'And where does it leave free will?'

'Right . . . But they didn't see it like that. I'd spent years using you as my get-out clause, my excuse for being a pretty bog-standard teenage nightmare. When I really needed their support they turned the tables on me and said I'd better go back to you.'

This beggared belief. 'They told you my name?'

'My mother positively threw it at me. I could tell from their faces they both knew she'd gone too far. Anyway, it's surprisingly easy to find someone if you know their name. Plus yours is quite unusual and you hadn't changed it.'

'I was married,' I said, a touch defensively, 'but after the divorce I went back to my own surname.'

I could see that something had suddenly occurred to her. 'Have you got other children?'

I shook my head. 'I never wanted them.'

'So it wasn't only me, then,' she murmured as if to herself, but loud enough for me to hear. She put her glass down and stood up. 'Better get going.'

'Where are you spending the night?'

'I'll pull over and have a kip in the car.'

'Isn't that dangerous?'

'Better than driving when you're half asleep. Especially in my old heap.'

She went into the hall and picked up her bag. I opened the front door. Once again I was aware of her composure, my turmoil.

'Goodbye,' she said. 'Thanks for the juice.'

'You're welcome.' It was surreal.

On the step she said, without turning round, 'The name's Fleur, by the way.'

'I know,' I said. 'I heard, when you— Goodbye, then.'

I'd like to say I watched as she walked to her car, but I didn't. I couldn't. I didn't want to see the old heap, or her getting into it, or which way she went. When I'd closed the door I even put my arms round my head and hurried to the kitchen so I couldn't hear the engine starting up. If I could have wiped out the last hour completely, I would have done.

What I needed more than anything was to tell someone. Speak it and lose it. Share it and halve it. Throw it to the winds. Dump. The trouble was, no one knew about that part of my past. So whoever I spoke to was first going to have to be told the whole story, and the prospect of going through all that was too much for me. The one person I could have confided in was Miranda, and she wasn't there.

There was no chance of sleep that night. I rode out the shockwaves of dismay, and anger, and resentment and loss. Loss at last, after all this time, because now I'd always be able to see her. She was real, and tall, and in her twenties. And pregnant. Her face and her voice would be an absence in my life. No matter that I didn't want her now any more than I had then. I'd been given no option: she'd left her mark.

'Who was your exotic young visitor?' asked Kirsty, in the office next day.

'Just a young a friend . . . She was in the area.'

'Cadging a bed, like they do?'

'No, no, just dropping in. She didn't stay for long.'

'You got off lightly,' said Kirsty. 'I remember when Chris goddaughter was here for the rock concert, she was still here three weeks later.'

She'd never know just how lightly. Nor how heavily it weighed on me. It was just as well I'd cleared the office backlog yesterday because I was strung out with tiredness. At around ten thirty I made us all a coffee and took mine outside in the fresh air. While I was standing there Penny's Volvo drew up in the yard. I could see a passenger in the front seat. It was Fleur.

Penny got out, smiling brightly. 'Morning! This poor girl's car's broken down on the Corbridge road and the chaps from the garage have towed it away for tests, so she's come back for a cup of tea and to make some calls.'

'Hi,' said Fleur.

'Good Lord,' said Penny, 'do you two know each other?'

'We met yesterday evening,' I said. 'Sorry about the break-down. What a nightmare.'

'Not really, I'm used to it.'

'Come on, then, let's get you sorted,' said Penny, taking charge.

'Let me know what happens,' I called after them, and my daughter raised a hand as she disappeared into the back door of Ladycross.

Half an hour later she reappeared. Kirsty saw her first, saying *sotto voce*, 'I told you they were hard to get rid of . . .' before going to the door and beckoning enthusiastically. 'Come on, come in! Hallo again, yes, she's here.'

Chris, the perfect gentleman, got to his feet.

'This is Fleur, a young friend of Bobby's,' explained his wife.

'Christopher Hobday, how do you do?'

'Hi.'

They returned discreetly to their work and Fleur perched on the windowsill next to my desk.

'This wasn't intentional,' she said, 'but I was absolutely miles from anywhere and when your friend pitched up with her mobile phone I was really grateful.'

'Lady Stratton,' I said. 'I hardly know her.'

'Well, she's the good Samaritan as far as I'm concerned, and she's like *that* with the local garage.'

'What's the diagnosis?'

'Apart from old age, rust and extreme decrepitude it's a burst radiator. Perfectly fixable, only as usual they're advising me never to drive the car again.'

'And will you?'

She shrugged. 'I've got to get back.'

It was awkward talking in lowered voices but knowing we could still be heard by the Hobdays. I felt that at any moment something might inadvertently be said that I would feel compelled at some later date to explain.

'Look, I've got a suggestion – let's pop out here for a moment.' I slipped Kirsty a woman-to-woman look as I opened the door. Once outside, I said, 'When will it be ready?'

'By tea-time, they said. I was going to go down to the pub.'

'You can use my house, if you'd like.'

'That's all right. I'm fine.'

'I dare say, but you can't sit around at the pub all day. Here, borrow my key.' I prised it off the ring and handed it to her. 'If you go before I get back, leave the back door unlocked and slip this one through the letter-box.'

She took it warily. 'And if I don't?'

'Then I'll see you later.'

'Okay. Thanks. I appreciate it.' She pocketed the key. 'I'll just go over and say thanks to your friend.'

I went back into the office, asking myself what on earth I was doing. This was an act of blind trust bordering on the insane.

'Aha,' said Kirsty, smiling but not looking up. 'Room at the inn?'

At about three my resolve – and my trust – wavered, and I rang the house. The answering-machine cut in, but she picked up half-way through. There was music in the background.

'Hallo?'

'Is that you?'

'Hi.'

'Everything all right?'

'Yes, thanks. I've had some orange juice and a sandwich, hope that's all right. And I'm lying on the sofa listening to your Bob Dylan album.'

'Fine.'

'Have to get the baby into the right music early.'

'I'll be back around five thirty.'

'Okay, I'll have them all out by then.'

I was alarmed. 'Who?'

'Joke.'

I realised, as I put the phone down, that we had both made the assumption that we would see each other again.

It's strange the way that having another person around slightly alters the character of one's house. Fleur hadn't made a mess – well, there'd scarcely been time – and yet I felt the change as soon as I opened my front door. She had a distinctive scent, rather like cloves – I'd noticed it on the cushions after she'd gone last night. Now it hung in the air like an invisible signature.

The music had changed to Ry Cooder and she was curled up on the sofa reading, wouldn't you know it? my hardback copy of Germaine Greer's *Daddy I Hardly Knew You*. Her walking boots lay on the floor. When I came in she used the remote to turn down the volume.

'Still here, then,' I said. I hovered between confirmation, which could be taken as endorsement, and a question, which might seem aggressive.

''Fraid so. I walked round to the garage but they'd found something else.'

'They always do. It's going to cost you.'

'So it costs. I have to be mobile. By the way, the pub has rooms so I'll go along there tonight.'

'Don't be silly, you certainly couldn't afford that.' I managed to make my invitation sound like a complaint. 'You can have the spare room.'

She gave me a sidelong look. 'Do you mind? If the pub means no hassle for either of us it's cheap at the price.'

I heard what she was saying – do it with a good grace or not at all. I did my best. 'I'd be much happier if you did.'

'Then thanks, I will.'

Suddenly the whole evening stretched ahead of us, heavy

with all that might be said, or left unsaid. I got a headache thinking about it and drank two glasses of wine quickly, which only made things worse. But Fleur was, as ever, calm. She asked where the sheets were and made up her own bed. Then asked if she could have a bath. All that took quite a while and when she came down and was told there was nothing she could help with she tuned to Jazz FM and curled up with Germaine again. It was actually quite nice to be perched on my stool with the *Telegraph* crossword, alongside the pasta sauce and the bubbling penne, jazz in the background and Fleur reading concentratedly, her fingers thrust into her blackcurrant hair. Following the bath she'd appeared in a weird Andy-Pandy suit, dark green and navy stripes, and slippers with cat faces. The effect of this ensemble, with the hair and the earrings, was striking, but it also made her seem younger. I felt something perilously like tenderness for her.

'I hope you don't mind me in my Babygro,' she said.

'Not at all. It looks really cosy.'

'You should get one. I'd wear this all the time, given half a chance. It's frustrating because I don't show at all, but everything feels a bit tight.'

'Yes,' I said, and was about to add, 'I remember,' but thought better of it. 'I can imagine.'

When it was time for supper and we sat down at the kitchen table, conversation couldn't be avoided, but she jumped straight in with 'I like your house.'

'Me too. I haven't been here that long.'

'It's homely. All the books and the music . . . I can't wait to have a place like this.'

'Where were you living in Greece?'

'I rented an apartment with a couple of blokes and another girl. It got seriously gross. I hate things to be like that, but you get so if nobody else cares you don't either.'

'And what about back here?'

'I was in Bromley at my parents' for about a week until the excrement hit the air-conditioning. I slept in the car on the way up. I'm going to doss down on a friend's floor in Kilburn till I find somewhere. Or maybe,' she gave a sidelong smile, 'I can find a way of driving her flatmate out.'

'How would you do that?'

'Make a pass at her.'

'She might be delighted.'

'In that case I won't mind going.'

I said nothing, but as she cleared plates and I put out the cheese and apples, I thought how I should loathe being in that position. This wasn't a sign of age – I had always liked a base, and roots, to know where I was. I remembered all too clearly the time of the baby's – Fleur's – birth. The loneliness, the placelessness, the feeling (entirely self-inflicted) of not belonging. For me then, and ever since, that feeling had been how I imagined hell, or purgatory anyway. I wondered whether she felt the same and was putting a brave face on it, or whether she had pulled a rogue nomadic gene out of the Govan pool.

'Thanks for supper,' she said. 'That pasta sauce is amazing.'

'A tried and tested part of my limited repertoire. Coffee?'

'No, thanks, but can I make myself some tea?'

'Sit down, I'll do it.'

Jesus, I thought, I'd be telling her to put her feet up next. But she was easy to look after, appreciative and unfussy. She cleared her plate, liked Bob Dylan and had taken to Germaine Greer (of whom she'd never heard before). If there was nothing she could do she didn't do it. On the other hand I had the impression that if I'd asked her to paint the living-room ceiling she'd have done so perfectly cheerfully.

Over her cup of tea she asked, 'Hope you don't mind me asking, but do you have a man?'

'I live on my own, if that's what you mean.'

'No, I meant is there anyone in your life?'

'Sort of,' I said, and then added, 'but it's nothing serious.'

Having tried the phrase on for size, I found it fitted, and that made me sad.

'Best way,' said Fleur.

Soon after nine o'clock she fell asleep. I'd switched on the news and, with the slight self-consciousness you feel when someone else is watching with you, turned to comment on the latest embarrassment of the party in government. She'd made herself comfortable, resting her head on the arm of the sofa and putting a cushion under her cheek, with her knees drawn up and her hands tucked, squirrel-like, under her chin. She looked about twelve years old in her striped Babygro.

I wanted to wake her, to encourage her gently to go up to bed. But I couldn't resist studying her as she slept. It was extraordinary – awesome – that this tall, unusual young woman had sprung from my body. Microscopic skeins of my DNA floated in there, causing her eyebrows to grow in the way mine did, and her mouth in repose to have the same downward curve that used to prompt kindly strangers to say, 'Cheer up, it'll never happen.'

Only now, it had. Those traces of me, in her, had made the pattern repeat itself in other more strange and powerful ways. Whatever bold words I'd spoken about independence and self-determination, I *was* responsible. The tyranny of biology had seen to that.

I touched one of her hands. The message, scrambled by sleep, caused the other hand to twitch. I shook her shoulder gently. 'Fleur?' It was the first time I'd addressed her by name, and hearing it made my eyes prickle. 'Hey . . . bed-time.'

She unfurled in a slow, sensual spasm like one of those stop-frame films of a flower coming into bloom. Scrubbed at her hair with both hands. Colour and consciousness made her face once more completely her own. 'Sorry . . . was I snoring?'

'No, but you might as well go upstairs and sleep in comfort.'

'Would that be all right?'

'Essential, I think.'

She got up. 'Night, then. Thanks for everything.'

'Good-night.'

'I'll check with the garage first thing.'

'Whatever. Sleep well.'

There was a split fraction of a second when we might, without thinking, have exchanged a kiss, as friends do. But we were both too strange, and too close, for that.

I sat gazing at the news, using it as my cover, listening to her footsteps upstairs, the tap running as she cleaned her teeth, the loo flushing, the creak of the bed in the spare room. Tomorrow, if the mechanics had done their stuff, she'd go. We'd part on friendly terms. For Fleur, mission accomplished. For me – I'd said it – whatever.

Next day she came downstairs, bag packed, as I was making coffee.

'I made the bed,' she said, 'as it was only one night.' Rain rattled on the kitchen window. 'Yuk.'

'You can give the garage a ring – they open at eight. Their number's on the board.'

She went into the living room and made the call. I heard her enquire about 'the beat-up Micra' and then, a minute later, about the cost of the repairs. Whatever the answer was she made no comment, but signed off with 'Okay, I'll come about ten.'

'No more problems uncovered?' I asked, as she helped herself to orange juice from the fridge.

'No, it'll be ready in a couple of hours.' She took a swig, leaving a faint moustache. 'As ready as she'll ever be, is how they put it.'

'The car will be safe, won't it?'

'Oh, sure – the speed it goes you couldn't have a crash if you wanted to. As long as it gets me back to London without packing up, then I can ditch it. Who needs a car in London?'

I thought, Only someone with a reason to get out.

At a quarter to nine I had to leave for work. She asked what she should do about locking up. I told her to turn the key in the back door, and simply close the front door after her. We stood awkwardly in the hall. At least I was awkward.

'Bye-bye, then,' I said, as though she were just anyone. 'And good luck.'

'Thanks. And thanks for having me.'

I shook my head, dismissing the thanks as unnecessary.

'Should we . . .' She frowned. 'Would you like to know about the baby?'

'Yes,' I said. 'I'd like to know that you're all right. You know where I am.'

'Sure. 'Bye . . . I still don't know what to call you.'

'Bobby.'

''Bye, Bobby.' Before I had a chance to think she stepped forward and dropped a light kiss on my cheek. Then she turned and went upstairs.

Half-way up the drive of Ladycross I pulled over to get a grip. The world might have changed, I told myself, but it was not a smoking ruin. I had begun to like Fleur, but I had stuck to my guns without, I believed, being cruel. I'd left open the possibility of further contact. For her part, she had levelled no accusations and made no demands. There was some comfort to be derived from the fact that we'd both behaved well. It had been as all right as it could be, in all the circumstances: a long, stifled cry of loneliness.

CHAPTER SIXTEEN

Rags, 1982

There had been one teacher at Queen's whom Miranda remembered with affection. In fact, apart from the head – and Matron, a special case – she was the only staff member she remembered at all.

Miss Drago had taught English. It was inevitable that she be called 'Dragon', but unfair. She was a skinny, scruffy, passionate woman in her thirties, in whom Miranda had at once recognised a kindred spirit. It was well known that the Dragon was keen on feelings. 'So what do we think the *feeling* is behind this?' she would ask, scanning the class with an intense, narrowed look. 'What *feeling* prompted the writer to write about this in these words, in this particular way?'

A lot of the girls giggled about this, and tried it on, with answers like 'lust' and 'indigestion', but for an outwardly spinsterish woman the Dragon was surprisingly hard to faze, and her reward was that she won over most of them in the end. She had the cast-iron confidence that came from complete mastery of, and passion for, her chosen subject. Those who laughed at her soon realised they were wasting their time because she simply didn't notice. And those like Miranda, who respected her, went on to be captivated.

Miss Drago had a line on love stories, from *Antony and Cleopatra* to *The End of the Affair*. 'A love story,' she would say, 'derives its dramatic tension from the obstacles placed in the path of the lovers.'

When Miranda had been with Nicky, she'd received a letter

from Miss Drago, sent care of the newspaper in which they'd last been photographed. It was a brief letter but it had brought her up short.

'You look happy,' Miss Drago had written. 'And I do hope you are. Do also remember that life is not a fiction, and *doesn't* need difficulties to make it interesting.' Recalling Miss Drago's stricture on underlining, that it showed a paucity of vocabulary, Miranda could appreciate the warmth of feeling here. 'There is no reason why you should take the least notice of this advice from an old stick from the past, which is why I don't hesitate to give it. It might interest you to know that, like you, I have left Queen's College under a small cloud; but quite unlike you I'm living a contented and respectable life in Peacehaven with a dear friend, and have a collection of poetry coming out next year, doubtless to general apathy, though it has been a great joy to write . . .' She signed herself, 'Yours, Elizabeth Drago (the Dragon as was)'.

Miranda had been touched by the letter, but did not reply. For one thing it did not seem to require a reply, and for another she was in a period of her life when responding to anything but the demands of the moment was beyond her.

She'd kept it, though, and a couple of years later came across *Life Lines* by E. A. Drago, a volume as slim and austere as its author and equally bursting with feeling. In a poem entitled 'What's It Worth?' there were a few lines that stayed with her.

> *This thing we think we have: is it worth fighting for?*
> *Or does the fighting make it worth the while?*
> *Or make us think it is?*

With Nicky, there had been something in that. The fraught and hectic nature of the relationship had been part of its potency, one of the many drugs on which it depended. They'd fought each other, their selves and (they liked to think) the world. And in doing so had left simple happiness bleeding in the gutter.

With Fred, happiness – joy – was there for the taking. She had no alternative but to tell Tom directly how she felt. As she did so the contours of his face seemed to implode with pain before her eyes, although when he spoke his voice was matter-of-fact. 'I knew it was too good to last.'

She felt completely helpless. 'I'm so sorry.'

'Come on, Ragsy, don't give me that flannel. You're in love. Over the moon, on cloud nine, walking on air. It's written all over you. Nothing to be sorry about.'

'The fact is I'm selfish. I don't want to lose you.'

'You won't.' He took her hand in both his. 'I'm the cake you can eat and have. I'm yours, me, whenever you want.'

'You mustn't say that!'

'Why not? I just did.'

She took her hand away in order to think more clearly. 'Because sooner or later, sooner probably, there'll be someone else in your life—'

'I certainly hope so.'

'– and she's going to deserve all of you. And you'll want to give her all of you.'

'That'd be nice,' he conceded. 'We'll see.'

Perversely, Miranda didn't know what she wanted, but it wasn't this: this stolid declaration that he was always hers, happy to be there in the background, on hold, ready to return at a moment's notice.

She confessed, 'I'm not sure I can handle the responsibility.'

'Tough. Anyroad, you're not responsible. It's my business how I choose to behave.'

Close to tears, she had to turn away. He put his hand on her cheek and turned her back to face him. 'Hey. Now, then, am I overdoing the I'll-be-your-rock routine?'

She gave a watery smile. 'A bit.'

'It's all a front, lass, don't you worry. What's the betting I piss off in a pet like we all do? But if you ever feel down you can always try my number, just in case I'm washing my hair.'

It was after midnight and he'd walked her to her car, her arm tucked through his. He waited while she got in and fastened her seat-belt, then tapped the roof and said, '*Au revoir*, Ragsy. Don't ask me to the wedding. I get drunk at weddings.'

She'd nodded, unable to speak. But by the time she reached the end of the road her tears had dried and her heart had wings.

In her case it was the things she loved that proved obstacles. Two of them — Tom, her work — proved not insurmountable and, anyway, were not lost to her. But from the first moment she saw Ladycross she was in the grip of a helpless, unrequited passion.

Three weeks after the Crystal Gazers Ball Fred drove her up there. They zoomed north in his white Morgan, with the top down most of the way. She wore a turquoise silk headscarf and aviator shades, and he said, 'Trust you to be every ageing bloke's fantasy passenger.'

'Just practical,' she told him.

'No . . .' He shook his head, smiling lecherously. 'Take my word for it – no.'

Cruising up the A1, he remarked, 'Contrary to what you may think this is not a menopausal toy. Well, a toy maybe, but nothing to do with advancing years. I've always had sports cars. She has to go in the garage all winter so I play while I can.'

'It's gorgeous.'

'Not too undignified?'

'Who cares about dignified?'

'What a woman.'

About ten miles from Witherburn the weather changed. It was cooler and they began to move in and out of patchy fog. Fred got out and put the top back up. 'Pity,' he said, 'but pretty typical I'm afraid.'

She didn't know the area and this, combined with the poor visibility, meant she had no idea how close they were to the house until he said, 'You'll see her in a minute.'

They were driving up a hill, and the mist was thinning. When the house first appeared it seemed to be floating on drifting skeins of vapour, the many facets of its roof and chimneys lit by a pale, diffused sun.

Fred slowed, and stopped. 'There she is.'

She was silent, but she felt him glance at her, and then away again, giving her a moment.

It was not, she now realised, the first time she had seen the house, but on this occasion, with Fred beside her, it was even more breathtaking. She was lost for words.

'You like?'

'Fred . . . you didn't tell me you lived in a fairy house.'

'Oh, yes.' He was perfectly serious. 'Good fairy or bad, it all depends.'

'On what?'

He started up the car. 'On who's living there.'

When they reached the top of the hill, there was a courtyard ahead of them and they could hear dogs barking, but he swung round to the left. 'As it's your first visit, we'll go in at the front door like proper nobs.'

He jumped out and opened the car door for her, remarking, 'One of the many advantages of a sports car, the reward for behaving like a gent is a fantastic leg show . . . By crikey, that was neat, you've been practising.'

She laughed. 'I did a whole series of ads for tights, getting in and out of an MG.'

'I might have known.'

'Oh, Fred . . !' She walked away from the car, and the house, and stood gazing. Now they, too, were floating. Here and there the sun had teased the mist apart to reveal treetops, a distant stone wall, the tower of a church far below them.

He came to her side and put a hand on her shoulder. 'There's a view on every side of the house. That's Witherburn in the valley. Church of St Brides, on our land as a matter of fact . . . To the north-east on a clear day you can see Hadrian's Wall, and there's an old Roman fort a couple of miles away.' He made a north-south signpost of his arms. 'Stratton country.'

'And west?'

'The same, for about three miles. And empty. I can trundle over there for half a day in the jeep and never see another living soul.'

He took her inside. She was always to remember the scent

of the house – roses and history – and the soft, dense quality of the atmosphere, as though even that had acquired a patina from the touch of so many lives down the centuries. She seemed to feel the air move over her, acquainting itself with her, caressing and exploring her.

The initial introduction made, Fred was all energy and enthusiasm, pacing ahead, opening doors, striding into rooms, pointing things out, giving potted histories of this and that. She couldn't take it all in, and wandered in the slipstream of his enthusiasm, wrapped in awed delight. The drawing room in pink and silver, the dining room gold and brown, the snug autumnal library, the priest's hideaway—

'What do you use this for?' she asked.

'Nothing except to show to visitors. It's a bit dark and gloomy. Both my wives thought it was haunted.'

'It's not haunted, it's neglected.' She ran her fingers along the panelling: it was warm and smooth to the touch, like skin. 'Sad and neglected.'

'So what should I do? I'm not a concept man. It's too small for most things, and I can't really see it tricked out in black leather. Now you, on the other hand . . .' He put his arms round her, so she felt lit like a lantern from the inside. 'Ever been a biker's moll?'

Upstairs there were eight bedrooms. His – the one they made love in – was the Red Room, suitable for a scarlet woman he pointed out afterwards, as they got dressed. 'It's where I retreat between marriages.'

'I see. The Playing-around Suite.'

'I never said that, did I say that?'

There were three huge, chilly bathrooms, and separate lavatories in rooms as long as tunnels, with dangling chains and distant, cobwebby cisterns.

'Must do something about these,' he confessed. 'There are a couple of nice *en-suite* ones, but that's no comfort to the wretched guests along here. Plenty of hot water, though,' he added. 'An army of blackened trolls toils ceaselessly below ground so that we Montcleres may wallow in scented steam.'

'You must introduce me.'

As they went back downstairs he asked casually, 'Ablutions notwithstanding, you still like the place?'

'I adore it.'

He caught her hand and kissed it. 'You don't know how much that means to me. Maybe you're ready for the kitchen.'

She wasn't, as it turned out. For a start the term 'kitchen' turned out to be a collective noun, covering half a dozen rooms – utility, scullery, pantry, still-room and walk-in larder as well as the kitchen itself, which was cavernous. Modern equipment – microwave, food-processor, an espresso coffee machine, an eye-level oven and ceramic hob – looked small and *déclassé* like arrivistes at a society wedding. Wooden drying rails on pulleys hung from the ceiling, with shirts, jeans and socks draped over them. Another rail carried a phalanx of saucepans of every size from one-egg to cannibal-cauldron. In the centre of the room was a monumental deal table, white with use, and an iron stove the size of a sarcophagus crouched in a brick alcove.

Catching her look, he said, 'Don't ask me, it's Norwegian. At the cutting edge of food-heating, so I'm reliably informed. And so it bloody well should be at the price: when it comes right down to it it's only a jumped-up Aga.'

The other rooms contained the same exotic mix of old and new. The utility room had two stone sinks and uneven flagstones, as well as a pair of washing-machines, another of tumble-dryers and a walk-in cupboard crammed with cleaning equipment.

'Who one earth does it all?' she asked.

'Seven mums with seven mops come up from Witherburn every day. Three, actually. And we have a closed week in spring and autumn for repairs, – no shooting, no meetings, no American weekends, nothing – refurbishment and general sprucing up.'

'You always say "we".'

'Force of habit. Me and the house. I beg your pardon, the house and I.'

The pantry was almost completely taken up with tall cupboards full of china and glass, a table, 'for cleaning silver on', and a fleet of trolleys. The scullery contained another huge old sink, plus a modern stainless-steel one and two dishwashers.

'And out here's the door I usually use,' he said. 'Do you mind dogs? They're penned up but they're noisy.'

The scullery was linked to the outer back door by a wide stone passage with windows to one side and a double row of pegs on the other. The pegs were heaped with jackets, macs, coats, scarves and hats of every size, colour and persuasion, and a similarly polyglot assortment of boots and shoes lay on the floor beneath. Beyond the window she could see the wire dog pen, with the heads of its madly barking occupants, ears flying, bobbing up and down at their approach. Fred took a handful of biscuits out of a bin before opening the door.

'These three are working dogs, believe it or not,' he explained, raising his voice above the crescendo. 'Given the job they're trained for they can be models of propriety. Shut up, shut up, enough!'

They gobbled up the biscuits, tails waving.

'Do they ever come into the house?' she asked.

'Only the old one. He shuffles in and kips in the kitchen in the winter. But Doris'll be waddling about somewhere – have we seen Doris?'

'I wouldn't know.'

'Yes, you would. She'll turn up. And that,' he went on, pointing across the corner of the yard, 'is the Dower House. It's our modern extension, only about a hundred and thirty years old. Mr and Mrs Bird, our live-ins, have the top floor. During my married periods it's been useful for in-laws, grannies, rackety chums, that sort of thing.'

'What about at the moment?'

'I'm thinking of letting it. The brutal truth is that when it comes to money the house is a *bad* fairy. She eats the stuff. We only open to visitors for a few days each year, and we have some shooting weekends, which do well. But we're always strapped for cash. We've got plans for the barns over there to be converted and we're going to let them as office units. And around twenty years ago we began hosting a rock concert, which has proved a success.'

Miranda put her hand to her brow. 'Northern Rock?'

'There you are – you've heard of us.'

'Not just heard,' she said, 'I've been here. It must have been only your first or second one. I never saw the house, which is why I didn't remember straight away.'

'Also, it was the sixties.'

She smiled ruefully. '*And* that. Top of the bill was the Roadrunners. They were absolutely fantastic.'

'Am I right in thinking . . . ?'

'Yes,' she said, 'you are. I came here with Nicky Traves.'

'Strange how circular everything is . . .' Fred put his arm round her and began walking across the courtyard in the direction of the outbuildings. 'There's one other thing I want to show you before I pour you a drink.'

They went between two of the barns, between scaffolding poles. On the far side was a rough expanse of hard standing, and then a gentle slope down to a wood.

'Down there,' he said, 'is the folly. It's early Victorian, put there by the father of the chap who built the Dower House. My brother and I used to spend whole days down there, happy as kings. I bet you'll absolutely love it. We'll walk down there later on or tomorrow.'

'What does your brother do?' she asked, as they went back.

'Alex died. He wrapped his motorbike round a tree at the bottom of the drive when he was nineteen. Perfect way to go, at speed, on a high, didn't know a thing.'

'A tragedy, though. Awful.'

'Not for him.' He opened the inner back door. 'On my life, it's Mrs Bird! And Doris!' A stout dachshund scuttled over and began turning round and round in ecstasy by his ankles. He bent down to pet it, gesturing with one hand at Miranda.

'Mrs Bird, meet my new friend Miranda Tattersall. Miranda, this is Mrs Bird, to whom all things are known . . . Yes, yes, you're a good dog . . .'

'Hallo.' Miranda held out her hand.

'How do you do? I hope you don't mind, your lordship, she was looking so down in the mouth I've had her over at the flat for an hour or two this morning.'

'If she's happy I'm happy, you know that.' He picked up the

dog and held it like a baby, its four oversized paws flopping foolishly.

Mrs Bird got back to chopping celery. She was a sturdy woman of about forty, with a decided jaw – now jutting in concentration – and the sort of thin hair that should never have been subjected to a perm. 'Been having a look round?' she asked.

'Yes, I'm completely overwhelmed. It's such a beautiful house – but I can't imagine what it must be like to run.'

'We manage, don't we?'

'*You* manage, Mrs Bird.' Fred put the dog back on the ground. 'The rest of us do as we're told, if we know what's good for us.'

Miranda laughed, 'That's what I like to hear!' and was rewarded with a hint of a grim smile.

'She's perfectly okay,' said Fred over G-and-Ts in the library. 'But she has a pash on me. Mind you, who can blame her?'

Miranda cuffed him. 'What's her husband like?'

'Wonderful chap – salt of the earth, hardworking, handsome, honest as the day. Completely silent. And you'll have gathered she's no chatterbox, so imagine evenings *chez* Bird! Never can telly have been so welcome.'

Miranda was there for twenty-four hours. She had a job on Monday, and Fred had to remain, so on Sunday afternoon he drove her to Newcastle and put her in a first-class compartment. In the minutes to spare before the train's departure he came in and sat opposite her, with his arms folded. 'So, what do you think?'

'You know what I think. I'm in love with Ladycross.'

'More than me?'

'Oh, much more.'

'Enough to take me on as part of the package?'

'What?' She laughed, not sure she understood him.

'I wondered if you'd consider marrying me.'

'Yes.'

'When the time is right.'

'Yes.'

'Along with all my worldly goods.'

'I don't want you without them.'

'Not forgetting the catatonic Birds.'

'Naturally.'

'Good. Well, I think that about wraps it up. Date of next meeting?'

They began to laugh, and laughed so much she had to shoo him off the train when it began to move.

It was eighteen months before they tied the knot. Eighteen months during which Dale and Kaye had twins, and Tom got married. When he rang to tell her about it she was wholeheartedly delighted. 'That's fantastic, Tom! Tell me all about her. Who is she, where did you meet, distinguishing features?'

'Pauline, she works in the constituency office. I knew her before you, and after you she came back into my life – no, back into focus. She's a bit of a stunner in her way, but we're a couple of patient, steady so-and-sos, ideally suited. You want an invitation to the do? The Three Awls at Tudbury. Near Doncaster.'

'Please.'

'What's your fella's name again?'

She told him. 'But he may not come.'

'I can live with that.'

They talked for a few more minutes, keeping it light. As she was about to say goodbye he said, 'Ragsy, something you should know.'

'Tell me.'

'I love Pauline. Really love her. We make each other happy. We're a team, built to last.'

'I'm *so* pleased.'

'But it doesn't change anything. I meant what I said.'

'What's this?' said Fred. 'A wedding? I love weddings, had a couple of my own and contemplating another.'

'Shut up. He's a very old friend. I must go if I possibly can, but it's up to you what you want to do.'

'Is that a polite way of saying this is your gig?'

'No, no, nothing like that . . . But it's not a three-line whip as far as you're concerned.'

Fred consulted his diary. 'As a matter of fact I can't, damn, it sounds fun too. I've got a trustees' meeting in London that day. Have a brown ale for me, my darling, and don't go rekindling any old flames.'

Long before that she had taken Fred to meet her mother. She gave great consideration as to how to play this, and settled for the obvious advantages of neutral ground and a treat. They went down in her car and took Marjorie to lunch at Hawsley Manor, a local country-house hotel with five stars and Continental waiters. Marjorie was understandably stiff at first, torn between a snobbish but perfectly justifiable maternal delight, and not wanting to appear a pushover. Miranda sat back and watched Fred work.

'This is the life!' he said, as a napkin the size of a main-sail was swished across his knees. 'I do love a restaurant where you can swing a cat – it's what you pay for, don't you reckon, Marjorie – OK if I call you that? – a bit of ambience, a bit of class? Some places, these days, are so uncomfortable, especially for tall people like us. You feel the customers as well as the food are subject to portion control . . . I bet there's châteaubriand on this menu and if there is I bet I'm having it . . . Now, what do we think? Champagne?'

It was a pleasure to witness her mother unfurl beneath this warm onslaught of affability. And to observe that although Marjorie had expressed reservations about 'the age difference' there were certain definite advantages to Fred's being of the same generation.

'Your stunning daughter is also the most wonderful dancer,' he said at one point, leaning towards her to indicate confiden-tiality. 'Does she get that from you as well?'

The 'as well' was a masterly touch, allowing Marjorie to be flattered but without embarrassment or the need to respond.

'She might do. I was very keen when I was younger. It was how I met my husband.'

'I didn't know that,' said Miranda.

'Well, it was. He was a show-off on the dance floor, and a very good leader – he could make any partner look good. But in all modesty I was a quick study and I did love it, I must say.' She had gone quite pink at the memory.

'Can you mambo?' asked Fred.

'I could then.'

'Terrific. I must say, I miss proper dancing. Gyrating and cavorting is okay, but it can never take the place of contact. I had to go all the way to Nairobi for an excuse to put my arm round the most beautiful and graceful woman in the room . . .' He kissed Miranda's hand.

This was the signal. They had decided beforehand that nothing short of unqualified success would merit the big news.

'Mum,' said Miranda, 'Fred and I are going to get married.'

Marjorie turned several shades pinker. 'Mandy! Oh, my giddy aunt!'

'Does that constitute your maternal blessing?' asked Fred. 'I do hope so.'

'I can't believe it!'

'Are you pleased?'

'If you're happy, Mandy – if you're both happy – it's absolutely wonderful.'

'Speaking for myself alone here,' said Fred, 'you don't expect to experience the *coup de foudre* at my age, and it makes a chap feel like a teenager, though I suspect it reduces his life expectancy somewhat. Anyway, Marjorie, I want to thank you for your part in giving me a second summer.'

They clinked glasses. Marjorie shook her head. 'You'll be Lady Stratton!'

Miranda cringed, but Fred was wiser. 'She will. Incredibly, that hasn't put her off. Yes, your daughter will be The Lady Stratton, mistress of Ladycross, and of its priceless contents, its dodgy plumbing, its draughts and its dogs. You

375

must come up and see it, Marjorie, you might have some ideas.'

After lunch they went for a walk in the manor grounds, and it was four thirty before they dropped her mother at the house. Fred said his farewells by the car, then got in to wait while Miranda accompanied her inside.

The moment they were in the hall Marjorie burst into tears.

'Mum, don't! What's the matter?'

'I wish Gerald was alive to see this . . .'

'Oh, *Mum* . . .' Miranda put her arm round her mother's heaving shoulders.

'He'd have been so pleased and proud.'

'Surprised, anyway,' she said thinly, 'since he never thought I'd amount to anything.'

'Nonsense, Mandy, he was thrilled with your success!'

Miranda could see that the longer this exchange went on the more contentious it would become, and there would be the risk of the whole day being spoilt. 'Come on,' she said firmly. 'Cheer up. I must go now but I'll ring you this evening when we get back. There's such a lot to talk about.' She hugged her mother and planted a kiss on either cheek. 'Hm? Speak to you soon.'

Fred read her face the moment she got back to the car. 'Tears?'

'Yes.'

'Very natural, I imagine.'

Miranda pulled away at speed. 'No, Fred. No. She was being sentimental about my father, him not being here when the great day came and all that . . . It makes me want to throw up.'

'You didn't love him,' he said gently, 'but that doesn't mean she didn't.'

'Fred! You don't know – she was terrified of him.'

'I suspect the two aren't mutually exclusive.'

'She didn't even go to his funeral. *I* went, and I hated him.'

'That makes perfect sense.'

'Shut up, shut up!'

'Darling, careful!'

'You don't know what you're talking about!'

'I'm sorry, slow down.'

'Now, look, she's made us have a row!'

He laughed. 'It won't be the last.'

A few minutes later when she was calmer, he said, 'I do understand, darling. And I'm truly sorry I blundered in like an ignorant pig on your feelings. But remember one thing neither of us knew before today – they danced together. Your bastard of a father taught Marjorie to mambo.'

For her mother's sake, Miranda determined to bear this in mind, though it was of little consolation to Marjorie when they discovered that in his will he'd left everything to Fran. By the time of his death this didn't amount to a fortune. River haulage was on its way out and many of the barges had already been sold for conversion into floating homes and pleasure boats. Fran sold what was left of the business and sent Miranda a cheque for three thousand pounds.

'I thought it best to send this to you,' she wrote, 'and not your mother in case she were to take it the wrong way. Please do with it whatever you think is right or would make you happy. I'm sure Gerald would have wanted you both to have something.'

Miranda couldn't help thinking that if he'd wanted that he'd have arranged it himself, but in acknowledgement of Fran's kindness she consulted Fred over what to do.

'Lie, probably,' he advised. 'Your mother's in the process of rewriting the past, which is fine if that helps her in the present.'

She fumed. 'I can't stand to think of that vile bully of a man getting credit for something he didn't do and wouldn't even have thought of doing.'

'You don't know that for a fact. He's gone now, it makes no difference to you and him. Give him the benefit of the doubt for your mother's sake.'

'For you,' she said grimly 'I will. But only for you.'

She passed on a personal cheque to Marjorie, explaining that it was part of a sum paid out of Gerald's estate into her account for both of them. This apparent last-gasp generosity provoked more tears.

'In the end, he wanted to look after us . . .'

Miranda let this pass. 'Don't be sensible with all of it, will you, Mum? Go out and blue a thousand on something lovely for yourself.'

But her mother was disposed to wallow. 'I wish now I'd come with you to the hospital that time.'

'You didn't want to, though. Remember that. Remember *why*. I went for both of us. You've got nothing to reproach yourself with.'

'What must Fran think of me?'

This was a new and more complicated line of self-recrimination which Miranda thought it best to nip in the bud. 'Mum, why should she think anything? For one thing she's a nice woman and for another she did very well out of him.'

Marjorie heaved a shaky sigh and supposed that this was so.

Miranda decided in advance how she would tackle Tom's wedding party. For, after their phone conversation, she was in no doubt that it had to be tackled. She would go in all smiles with head high, work the room, make herself agreeable to as many people as possible, never be seen alone or wearing an expression that might be interpreted as wistful. She would not arrive late. She would dress smartly rather than strikingly. She would be one – albeit the most agreeable one – of the herd.

But this intended self-effacement was blown out of the water within seconds of her arrival in the functions room of the Three Awls. She stood in line with the other guests and could see Tom just inside the door greeting everyone and performing, where necessary, introductions to his wife who was on the far side of him. However, when Miranda reached the front of the queue, wearing what she hoped was a suitably unassuming expression, she was pounced on by the new Mrs Worsley.

'Here she is! It is you, isn't it? *Course* it is.'

Her hand was wrung and held fast, and she was pulled to one side while Tom, having vainly tried to plant a kiss on her cheek, moved on to the next person.

'Stay here, you,' said Pauline. 'Grab a glass – hey, love, there's a thirsty lady here – and I'll be right with you.'

Miranda, aware that she was in close contact with a force of nature, did as she was told. The atmosphere in the room was warm, smoky and loudly convivial. At the far end was a platform with a drum kit, speakers and microphones. A squad of sturdy barmaids was working flat out, while the younger colleagues circulated with trays. A passing elderly man winked at her, and said, 'Lovely!' It would have been hard to imagine an occasion less conducive to well-bred restraint.

The bride, whose blush owed less to maidenly modesty than the half-pint of gin and tonic in her hand, was blasting late arrivals with the full force of her personality. Pauline was a woman approaching six foot in her slingbacks, an apricot-blonde in a scarlet suit, with lips and nails to match, a smile as big as all outdoors and a laugh like a foghorn. A woman who, one suspected, could keep the red flag flying singlehanded if necessary.

When the last guest was in, Tom claimed his kiss. 'Ragsy . . . you met the wife.'

'I saw to that, didn't I?' said Pauline.

'You did,' agreed Miranda. 'Congratulations, both of you.'

'It's me needs congratulating,' said Pauline. 'I'm not big on patience but I've kept myself for this one.'

Tom rolled his eyes. 'And the rest! I'm off,' said Tom. 'Drinking to do.'

Pauline drew her aside. 'I'm so glad you could come. Except there was me hoping to be star for a day and now there's *no* chance.' This was said with the utmost good humour.

'The impression I get,' said Miranda, 'is that you're a star, full stop.'

Pauline patted her hair and primped, sending herself up. 'I aim to please. But I want you to know how much it means to both of us that you're here. I'm not daft and I know Tom, same as you do. If you're special in his life you're special in mine.'

'Thank you.'

'Now, let's see who I'm going to introduce you to . . . Which lucky chap's day shall we make?'

All through the wedding, Miranda found herself thinking, Fred would have loved this. His discretion and her scruples had both been misplaced. These people were family. They seemed to know, with easy and innate sophistication, what her role was in the mix. They attached to it, and to her, neither mystery nor baggage. They were openly admiring while sending up both her and themselves with the gentle implication that she was posh totty. She ate, she drank, she rocked and rolled, she felt fêted and cherished. She realised the truth of the line 'Everyone loves a lover'.

At one point she slipped away and called Fred, who was overnighting at the Travellers Club.

'It's me.'

'Darling, what a wonderful surprise . . .' He sounded sleepy, she could hear him rubbing his face. 'Where are you? Still boogying?'

'Yes. It's a fabulous party, I do wish you were here.'

'Don't say that, you'll make me even more jealous. I wish I was too. After a day being harried and hounded about the bloody books I could have done with a good bash.'

'It's not just that.' She wanted to convey her exact feeling. 'Tom and Pauline are so happy, all the people are so nice. I love you so much, and I know they would too.'

'Ah,' he said softly, 'yes. The more we have, the more we give, the more there is. Listen, my lovely, you get back in there and enjoy it for both of us.'

Tom was looking out for her. 'Fancy a dance? I'm treating every lady in the room and your number's come up.'

Also, she thought, the right music: an upbeat version of 'Till There Was You' that demanded neither fancy footwork nor particular intimacy.

'Having a good time?' he asked.

'Wonderful. Thank you for asking me, I wouldn't have missed it for the world.'

'I'm sorry your bloke couldn't make it.'

'I am too, we both are, but he had this meeting.'

'It's okay, I'm not that sorry.'

'Tom . . .'

He laughed and gave her a twirl. 'Relax. You've met Pauline.'

'She's sensational.'

'A whole lot of woman. I shan't be giving any bother.'

After the dance, he said, 'Come and meet my mother.'

Mrs Worsley senior was a small, sprightly widow with a lilac rinse and good legs. An attentive gentleman was shooed away from the seat next to her so that Miranda could sit down.

'Don't mind Percy, I can talk to him any time. It's pretty typical, isn't it? I've been dying to meet you for nigh on two years and when I finally do it's 'cause he's marrying someone else.'

'They're blissfully happy,' said Miranda.

'They are that. Perfect for each other. Pauline's one in a million and she's lucky to have my son.' She chuckled and batted Miranda's arm with the back of her hand. 'I wouldn't tell him that!'

'Your secret's safe with me.'

Mrs Worsley gave her a sharp look. 'He still loves you, you know.'

'And I love him.'

'That's got that out of the way, then . . . Anybody special in your life, isn't that what the magazines say?'

'There is, and I'm going to marry him.'

'Ever done it before?' Miranda shook her head. 'Oh, well. I did it twice before I got it right. Third time lucky and then he had to dash off. So who's it to be?'

'He's called Fred Montclere.'

'You never – Lord Fred from up the road?'

'That's right.'

'He's done it a few times himself. Still, practice makes perfect. Is he good to you?'

'Good to me, good for me. I adore him.'

'That's smashing. Smashing. Your bloke needs to be someone a bit special, bit out of the ordinary. It can't be easy taking up with a woman who's famous and beautiful and in all the papers.'

'I don't think he sees it like that. And I don't. It won't be easy for me either, being The Lady Stratton.'

Mrs Worsley pulled a face. 'Telling me! You'd have to be in love to take on that barn of a place. Still I dare say you're not scared of hard work.'

'I'm not, no, but this is different. It's not just a job, it's a way of life.'

'Listen.' Mrs Worsley beckoned her close. 'Scrub that. It's Fred you're marrying. You keep your mind on that. Take care of each other and the house'll take care of itself.'

She spent the night at the Three Awls and the next day she set off early. Nobody else was up. It was a fine, cool Sunday morning in May with nothing on the roads. But she did not drive south to London. Instead she turned north, over the hills to Ladycross.

Miranda felt that it was waiting for her. Because of Fred's absence there was no one about, except the silent Mr Bird, to whom she made herself known. She walked around the house and garden unaccompanied except for Doris, who trundled at her side. She was touched by the stout dog's unquestioning trust, and adjusted her pace so that she could keep up. Outside, the grass beyond the mown lawn was full of flowers – daisies, cowslips, dandelions and violets. The chestnut trees were laden with candelabra of blossoms, cream, white and pink, and the ground in the woods was misted with bluebells. Once, she saw what she thought was a small deer in a clearing, but as it trotted away unconcernedly she realised it was a dog from the village.

In the house she made herself a sandwich in the kitchen and wandered the rooms and corridors quietly, wanting to befriend this place that had known so many owners and had been witness to so much history, both grand and public and profoundly personal. Once again, but more powerfully, she felt its soft breath and heard its heartbeat. She stood in the window of the red bedroom and looked down towards the field where she and Nicky had lain together, blissed out among the weeds, all those years ago.

When Fred returned that afternoon, she went out to greet him in the yard.

'Miranda . . . darling.' His pleasure in seeing her was nothing short of radiant. 'How wonderful!'

'I hope you don't mind,' she said, as they went into the house, arms round one another. 'I reported to Mr Bird.'

'Mind?' Fred kissed her. 'No, I don't mind. When I saw you waiting it was as though you'd always been there.'

'I'm glad,' she said, 'because that's how it felt.'

CHAPTER SEVENTEEN

Claudia, 138–145

The baby, Gaius, was at the age of maximum concentration on minimal subject matter. He was eighteen months and walking now, but so close to the ground that the minutest object could catch his eye. A beetle, a stray bead, a coloured stone the size of a pinhead would stop him in his unsteady tracks and absorb, instantly, his close and undivided attention.

This early summer's evening it was a tiny snail, its pink and grey shell no bigger than his own thumbnail. It lay on the floor of the covered walk at the back of the house. There had been rain that afternoon and the westering sun made the damp paving stones shine and picked out the little snail like a jewel. Gaius crouched next to it, his head bowed between his round knees. He breathed heavily as he studied his find. Leaning forward he reached for the snail: another exciting discovery had been that of the opposable thumb. Slowly and deliberately his hand opened and closed, like the wings of a sunbathing butterfly. The snail eluded him but he persisted. A stub of tongue, shiny and pink, protruded from his mouth. Pushed along by his fingers the snail came up against a stone. Success! At last he trapped it between finger and thumb, and lifted it carefully, laboriously—

'Gaius!'

Seeing her son's hand heading for his mouth, Claudia jumped up. At the same time Tiki, alerted by her voice, burst from the house and reached the baby before her, cannoning into him at speed. Gaius pitched forward on his nose, and Claudia rushed to rescue him. The dog, chastened, retreated to a safe distance. There followed a split second of shocked silence before Gaius, now in the shelter of his mother's arms, rent the air with his screams.

Claudia put her finger in his gaping mouth that was square with outrage, and checked for the foreign body while making soothing noises. Tiki lay down with his head on his paws, ears flattened in remorse. He liked the baby, but something had gone wrong.

Finding nothing and banishing the thought that whatever it was had been swallowed, Claudia carried her yelling son out into the garden. The grass was damp from recent rain, but the evening sun was warm. There was a sharp, fresh smell, peculiar to this part of the world where the weather was always changing. The hem of her tunic was sodden in seconds, but she kept walking, to calm herself and the baby. The contrite Tiki fell in at her heels.

She went down the slope to where the temple stood, gleaming and new. It was almost ready, only the mosaicists were still at work – they'd gone home now, but their satchels full of tools and baskets of brightly coloured *tesserae* stood in the far corner. The building of the temple had been more enjoyable in many ways than that of the house, because not so much hinged on it: it was an indulgence, but with a serious purpose. She could see herself coming here on summer evenings simply to be alone, and dream. For she did still dream . . . She stroked the baby's head. He was quiet now, sucking his thumb and gazing over her shoulder at Tiki, their friendship unshaken.

It was the permanence of the house that had frightened her. Once so much had been done, so much time, trouble and expense undertaken, what likelihood was there that they would ever go back to Rome?

She had come to realise that, without either point of view being articulated, Publius never expected to return, whereas she kept the idea always, like a good-luck charm, at the periphery of her mind's eye. Rome was where they truly belonged, the centre of their world, not out here on the outskirts of the Empire, with the hostile Celtic fastness to the north. She was at ease here now, but not at home. She never told Publius this.

There were things, though, that she had said to him. And they had opened up a wound between them which was slow to heal. It no longer bled, but they both knew that it would do so again very easily, and they were careful with each other. The greater understanding and intimacy, which she had hoped for, had not come about. There were times, especially when her husband was away, that Claudia felt she had lost him completely. But nothing could wipe out the words. They were there now, and their weight had to be borne.

Publius seemed to feel the drop in temperature the moment they were past the Wall. One expected it to be colder the further north one travelled, but it was more immediate than that. Once they'd passed through the massive double gates and were hanging on to their formation as they descended the steep earthwork ramp that fell away on the far side, they were exposed to the northern wind – and something else. The professional soldier in him resisted the idea that it was any kind of apprehension about the barbarians. They were a rough, tribal, disorganised enemy, more of a nuisance than a real threat. When they had surprise on their side they could give the legions a run for their money, but during his time there had been no serious damage inflicted.

He wasn't alone in experiencing the chill. He was always aware of a quiet, a watchfulness, that fell on the troops, and tried to combat it by speeding up the pace, and bellowing orders. These were disciplined and highly trained men, but most had little experience of soldiering outside the Empire. They were used to operating surrounded by the machine of Rome, its hierarchy, its infrastructure, its laws and mores. They had not built the Empire, and were unaccustomed to being strangers. Between the great Wall and the Antonine wall a hundred miles to the north there was a scattering of forts and settlements. But this was still, to all intents and purposes, no man's land, and they knew it.

Theirs was a routine sortie of a few days' march, of a kind undertaken two or three times a year. Its purpose was threefold: reconnaissance, maintenance and display. The risks were obvious, but calculated. This was not an exercise: the men must be ready and willing not just to fight but to win. Hothead young tribunes were seldom allowed out on these forays: they were a job for safe hands and calm heads that would do what was needed without courting danger.

On this occasion they were to go north from Vercovicium, repairing and restoring the log-road behind them as they went; then across the river, and down the established paved highway south and back following the line of the Wall. This also enabled Publius and his officers to test the observation, alertness and signalling of the men manning the forts and mile-castles along the way.

For Publius there was no longer any excitement to be derived from these forays. His wife and son were waiting for him in the house on the hill. With less life in front of him he wished to preserve what there was. Retirement could not come soon enough. And yet he knew that what he wished for was in reality a challenge far greater than a brave and bloodthirsty physical enemy: that of domestic intimacy, with no escape.

Claudia had known she must speak to Publius at once, and before the baby was born. If she let what Cotta had told her settle unaired in her mind, it would take root there and flourish: she would come to accept it, and it would become increasingly difficult to mention. And it must be evening when she confronted him, because the machinery of garrison routine began turning in his head, driving him forward, from the moment he woke in the morning. From before dawn each day he was leaving her, always leaving – no longer in her world but in his.

So on only the second night after her return, lying in his arms, she had asked, 'Publius, what do you dream about?'

He didn't move, but she felt the flip of his heart beneath her cheek. 'I rarely dream.'

'I mean your bad dreams. Your nightmares.'

'I prefer to forget them,' he said, too quickly, too lightly, as if her question had been a general one, referring to nothing in particular.

'But you don't,' she persisted, 'because they come back.'

There was a pause. His fingertips moved back and forth on her shoulder. 'Why do you ask?'

'I heard a story about you when I was in Rome.'

'I see.' Now he pulled his arm from beneath her and turned on to his side, away from her. 'What did this story say?'

She did not hesitate or even take a deep breath for fear of losing her resolve.

'It said that you were married to a young girl – too young – and that she couldn't be a wife to you. Only as a duty, a wretched one. That she was sickly and sad and her misery was a source of pain to you both. And that she died bearing you a child before term, a tiny daughter born alive but bound to die. So you took the baby to the outskirts of the city and left her there. The story said you were haunted by all this.' She leaned her brow for a moment against his back. Whispered: 'Publius?'

There was no answer. No sound, but clamorous silence.

'That's what the story said.'

The silence extended and became stifling. Even the baby inside her – usually lively at night when she wanted to sleep – was heavy and still, as if it, too, was waiting.

When she spoke again it was hard to stop her voice from shaking. '*Is* that what you dream of?'

He rolled heavily on to his back, his forearms shielding his face. Beneath the scarred, weather-toughened skin of his arms his mouth appeared vulnerable.

'Yes.'

'And is it true?'

'Yes.'

Claudia bit down on the shock. 'Please, husband, will you tell me what happened? I want to hear it from you.'

Publius lowered his arms, but did not look at her. 'Why?' he asked thinly. 'When your information's perfectly correct.'

'I need more than information. I want to understand.'

'What you want,' he said, 'is to be told it's not true. But it is. I'm not the first man to have done such a thing and I won't be the last.'

She was ice-cold, shivering with shock. 'Publius, please, I can't believe it of you.'

'Anyone is capable of anything, given the right circumstances.' His voice stung like a whip. 'I've seen it all in the army. Cowards can be brave. Simpletons can be inspired. Honourable men can cheat. Believe, Claudia.'

'Please—' she said again. She felt for his hand, but it was clenched into a hard fist, and wouldn't receive her.

'Who told you?'

'It doesn't matter.'

'Cotta.' He grunted. 'Foolish, fat, poisonous toad.'

So understanding was denied her. And she had also to contend with her husband's bleak, silent fury. She took no comfort from the fact that it was directed at himself and at Cotta as much as at her. She was in breach of some unspoken contract, and must pay for it.

Even the joy of Gaius' birth a week later was shadowed by these events. The birth was easy and quick, she and the baby were both well, but there was a veil of introspection behind Publius' eyes. She would have given anything to put the clock back, to have asked no questions in Rome nor confronted him with her fears. It appeared she had torn away one layer of secrecy only to have another harden over it, like scar tissue.

She must have sat in the temple for half an hour or more, thinking of these things. Publius was away, there was plenty of time for thinking; too much. Tiki lay outside on the step in the late sun, dozing. Gaius' head had grown heavy on her shoulder. But when she transferred him gently to her lap, her son's eyes were wide open as though he, like her, were gazing into the recent past. The fresh, red graze on his nose was forgotten, by him if not by her. She kissed it and he twisted his head away and wriggled to be let down. The moment his feet touched the ground he staggered off precipitately, tottering and reeling in his haste to reach the dog. Tiki looked up, his tail brushing the step in a chastened greeting.

Claudia was the last to move. She rose and followed her son out into the low, slanting light and reaching shadows. It was that time in the evening when the countryside seemed to become still, to hold its breath before sinking with the sun into the secretive whisperings of night.

Now, Gaius was independent again. He did not wish to be carried, or to hold his mother's hand. Claudia was obliged to walk at a snail's pace, she on one side of him, the dog on the other, back to the new, echoing house on the hill.

Time passed, a different emperor ruled. And with the years, the house ceased to echo: its fresh new fabrics absorbed the texture of the lives lived in it. House and boy matured together. The concrete and stone mellowed, and the red roof tiles weathered. Swifts made their nests in the angle beneath the eaves. The garden grew: the herbs that Claudia had set in sheltered spots flourished and shot out long flowering stems, and had to be divided up; the red and gold roses overflowed their giant amphorae; and the climbing plants spread up the walls, wave on wave, their leaves overlapping like fish scales.

The temple, when finished, seemed always to have been there. On summer evenings birds and butterflies flew in and out. Luke, whose job it was to clean the temple, complained of the mess, but Claudia liked to see an ebullient robin perched on the head of one of the gods, and if there was a butterfly that she could catch she'd place it gently in Gaius' cupped hands to be carried out and released in the open air.

Tiki was Gaius' shadow as he grew. The dog's honey-coloured muzzle was becoming grizzled and Publius no longer took him hunting, but he was still full of life and had naturally transferred his allegiance to the boy, in a capacity that was both playful and protective. Gaius' parents would say with a smile that if their son ever went missing they had only to whistle for the dog, and that would show them where he was.

This was as well, because the boy was dreamy and liked to wander. By the time he was eight these walks could last for hours, and only the knowledge that Tiki was with him prevented his mother being mad with worry. It was some comfort to her, if not to his father, that their son was not physically adventurous and was unlikely to attempt anything rash on these solitary walks, such as scaling rocks, jumping waterfalls or attempting to catch wild animals. They took the view that the countryside was an altogether safer place than the sprawl of settlements south of the Wall, and they set limits by landmarks beyond which Gaius was forbidden to go.

There was no doubt that he was different from other boys his age. Claudia chose to think of him as unusual. Publius worried that he was odd. He loved his son with a fierce, proprietory and largely unspoken passion, an attachment fraught with contradictions, fears and yearnings. He saw, in the boy's detachment and moodiness, trouble; in his combination of timidity and stubbornness, danger; and was rebuffed by the deep secretiveness that lay beneath the behaviour. Most of all he was baffled and affronted that there seemed to be nothing of himself in this small, intense person. What he failed or chose not to see was that although the outward behaviour might be different, its source was a nature very much like his own – solitary and introverted.

When the boy was small there had been no awkwardness – a baby was a baby and Publius accepted that his own role would be secondary to that of Claudia, Severina, and the Gallic nursemaid Larissa. But as the years went by, instead of becoming closer as he'd hoped, he could do nothing to prevent them growing further apart. Once he could no longer hold his son – or once Gaius no longer wished to be held – and tickle and tousle him and carry him about on his shoulders, there seemed to be no common ground left. He allowed his discomfiture to show so that it infected the boy, who grew awkward in his presence and as often as not drifted away apologetically at his approach.

It was years since he'd had the dream, and he and Claudia

had never again discussed the terrible episode that was its source. And yet Publius found himself wondering if this increasing alienation from the son for whom he'd waited so long was a form of retribution.

Though Gaius was not a carefree child, he did not wish to be grown-up. He didn't care for the look of the adult world, its noise, its smell, the way it went about things. He didn't much care for its representatives, though he made an exception in the case of his parents: his smiling, energetic mother with her slightly distracted manner, and his puzzling father, always seeking him out for no apparent reason.

Of the two, Gaius felt closer to his father or, at any rate, more like him. His mother seemed to be the sort of person who would fit in anywhere: there was always the possibility of losing her. Not that she would wilfully abandon them, but there was the chance she might be taken up by some other crowd of people, in another place, and be simply spirited away. She had a friend, an older woman called Flavia, who sometimes came to call and to whom once he had actually heard his mother say: 'I shall never be at home here.'

He caught the casual, unconsidered truth of it in her voice and was shocked. His mother, not at home? If this was not her home, this house that he'd known all his life, the metallic green hills and the grey fort, and the wall with its higgledy-piggledy backwash of townships, then what, or where, was? He'd hoped for an explanation, but she had caught him staring at her, given a false, loud laugh and changed the subject.

Concerning his father, who was actually absent for long periods, and a more remote figure in every way, he had no such fears. Publius was solitary and thoughtful, as he was. Despite their mutual wariness, Gaius felt a profound kinship with him. Not that this bond was ever spoken of or demonstrated. From quite an early age Gaius had not wanted to be picked up or carried: no matter how tired he was, he felt safer with his feet on the ground. He mistrusted caresses, because they mostly had more to do with the moods of grown-ups than his own.

And although he thought ceaselessly – long, large thoughts and elaborate imaginings – he had difficulty articulating what was in his head. There was too much of it and it was too complicated, so he stayed silent.

For the past year he'd had a tutor, Madoc, who came to the house in the mornings. Madoc was a native Briton. He spoke Latin with an accent, and was all smiles with Claudia, less cheerful with his pupil. Gaius recognised disappointment and bafflement in his tutor's face, but couldn't help. He found his lessons paralysingly boring. Understanding almost nothing, he retreated into a kind of trance, which to begin with Madoc mistook for concentration. It was only when asked questions or directed to write things down with the horrible scratchy stylus on waxed wood that the full extent of his mental absence became clear.

Madoc was kindly and keen. One fine morning he suggested they leave the house. 'Perhaps we can find something to interest us outside,' he said. The note of desperation was not lost on Gaius, who determined for Madoc's sake to do his best.

His mother was all for it. She put her warm hand on the back of Gaius' neck, one finger ruffling his hair. There was more than a hint of agitation in that tickling finger. 'That's a good idea. Look, Tiki wants to go with you, you don't mind?'

'Of course not.'

Gaius knew that it would have made no difference if Madoc had minded: Tiki would have accompanied them anyway.

'Let's walk up towards the fort,' suggested Madoc.

After a sluggish, silent start, it was surprising how much they found to interest them on the way. The walking loosened Gaius' tongue and it was good not to be trapped in the schoolroom. He would have preferred to be on his own, but it was certainly an improvement. Madoc concentrated on natural history to begin with, identifying native plants, and one or two foreign ones that he said had been 'brought by the legions'. He pointed out hawks, which he didn't really need to do, but Gaius dutifully cricked his neck to look at them. And then there were deer droppings, and a fox's earth, which got Tiki very excited – Gaius, too.

'Let's let him dig! He might catch something!'

'I don't think a dog of his age would be any match for an angry vixen.'

'I bet he would. He'd kill it.'

'Well, we don't necessarily want that either,' Madoc said reprovingly, 'she might have young ones. Come on.'

They trudged, along the spine of the ridge towards the fort. The path was on a slight upward incline, barely noticeable on horseback or in a carriage, but enough to make Madoc breathe heavily. They were coming to the place where the strange stones were. Gaius regarded them as secret, but under these slightly unusual circumstances he decided to take Madoc into his confidence.

'Do you want to see something?'

'What sort of thing?' asked Madoc warily.

'I'll show you.'

He led the way down the bumpy slope to where there was a small platform made of turf. On the top of the platform lay the stones, with writing scratched and gouged on to them. There had been so many laid there over the years that scores of them had fallen or been pushed off, and lay scattered all around, many half embedded in the ground.

'Ah, yes,' said Madoc, the relief evident in his voice. 'Now, then, do you know what these are?'

Gaius nodded. He had his theories and had half hoped to venture them. It was rather disappointing therefore that Madoc did seem to know and that the question had been purely rhetorical.

'I think they're curses, don't you?' mused Madoc tactfully, turning one in his hands. 'Let's see . . . Ah. No.'

'What does it say?'

'I think we'll leave that one. Try another . . . Here we are. "May the gods turn on Paulus who took my horse, and may he rot."' He glanced at Gaius who was staring back, transfixed. 'Another? Um . . . "Die, plug-ugly Marius, for what you did."'

'What did he do?'

'It doesn't say.'

'Go on.'

'This is a long one – hang on, it's a bit worn . . . Looks like "Let the hateful cheat Gloccus know that he will never be safe and the dagger of Lucullus is itching to bury itself in his fat arse."' Gaius gave a shrill yelp of delight and Madoc smiled ruefully at this coarseness. 'Not very polite, is it?'

'More!'

'Just one.'

But the one turned into half a dozen and it was only when Tiki's scratching threatened to collapse the turf mound that they scrambled up and went on their way.

'I read one of those when I was here before,' said Gaius.

'Did you? What did it say?'

'"My dog is best, pig-face."'

'Very good,' said Madoc. 'Very succinct.'

They continued in silence, now an easy and companionable one, and walked all the way to the *vicus*. Gaius liked to walk. He didn't tire easily; he seemed to feel better – quieter – when he was moving steadily along with the fresh, warm air in his face. It was the thinking that he found tiring, his brain either rushing from one thing to another or ceaselessly worrying and picking at a particular notion. Walking out of doors, he didn't exactly stop thinking, but the thoughts were less overwhelming when there was space all around. And one good thing about his tutor was that Madoc was straightforward: he didn't require to be understood, so being with him was the next best thing to being alone.

As they approached the village, Tiki fell in close to them, his tail and muzzle low, his nose almost brushing Gaius' leg. There were a lot of loose dogs about who came trotting over to investigate, but they soon sauntered off again, rebuffed by his flattened ears and curled-back lip.

At the back of the huts there were other animals as well – pens full of lean, whiskery pigs rootling about on their funny tiptoe hoofs, and jaunty-eared piglets jostling for attention and food. Gaius stood on the lower bar of the fence to watch them, and Madoc leaned next to him. 'It's not such a bad thing to be compared to a pig,' he commented idly.

'No.' Gaius considered this, his gaze fixed on the animals. 'But it was *meant* to be.'

'That's perfectly true,' said Madoc. The boy might not be a quick or assiduous student, but he quite often displayed these surprise flashes of accurate, intuitive understanding.

There were plenty of chickens scratching about, clucking and burbling among themselves, their foolish heads poking forward with each step. Tiki took no notice of them: they were too common and too easy – chickens were beneath his dignity, these days, although in his youth there had been some embarrassing incidents.

Beside one hut there were a couple of hutches containing fighting cocks, a very different proposition. The dog's ears went up and he stretched a quivering nose towards them. Blood was in the air. The nearest cock was black, shot through with brilliant blue and green, his tail feathers shiny and sharp as a quiverful of arrows, his small eyes glaring with hate. Even without his metal spurs, his talons could tear an opponent apart. Cockfighting was a favourite sport in the *vicus* and men from the garrison got involved as well, betting and brawling over these fights to the death. When the cockerel screamed and flapped his wings Tiki sensibly withdrew, whining; but the second cock, a heavier bird with red and gold plumage, stretched his neck and screamed back, hurling himself at the bars of his prison and gouging them with his dagger-feet.

'They're fine fellows,' observed Madoc. 'Even Tiki wouldn't last five minutes with one of those.'

'He would,' said Gaius stoutly.

'How?'

'He's bigger, and he could run away.'

There was, Madoc conceded, some logic in this. He picked up a scarlet feather from the ground and stuck it through the shoulder-fabric of Gaius' tunic.

They continued on their way. Madoc had a friend who fancied himself as a charioteer: a proper one, who believed in the traditional Roman ethos of the games, and who spent a great deal of time and money on training and equipment. Privately Madoc thought that Brasca, though a nice enough fellow, was a bit of a fantasist. He seemed to believe that by precisely replicating the tackle and technique of the sport he could make himself into something he was not – a true Roman, instead of a slightly fussy and humourless wheelwright with an elaborate hobby.

However, the advantage of Brasca's obsession was that he was always willing to talk about it. When Madoc knocked on the door, his wife answered. She was a rather forbidding woman, devoted to her husband and chary of his privacy.

'Good day, Madoc,' she said. 'And who's this?'

'This is Gaius Publius, my pupil. We've walked all the way from the villa and wondered if we could talk to Brasca.'

'He's in the workshop,' said the woman flatly. 'He's got a lot on at the moment.'

'I wanted to ask if I could show Gaius the chariot and the horses.'

'Wait there.'

She disappeared, leaving the door ajar. Madoc gave Gaius an encouraging look. And in fact when the door was opened again it was by Brasca himself. He was a small, sinewy man in his late thirties, clean-shaven and wearing a leather apron.

'Madoc, you want to show the boy around the stables?'

'If that won't be too much of a disturbance.'

'Not at all. Come, I'll take you round the outside. Erica and the girl are cleaning like women possessed.' He removed the apron and hung it on a hook before closing the door. 'So – Gaius, isn't it? – you know anything about charioteering?'

Gaius shook his head, causing Brasca to shake his, too, and throw a despairing glance at Madoc. 'These youngsters know so little of their inheritance. It's left to us enthusiasts to preserve the old traditions.'

'You do race, though, don't you?' Madoc prompted, before Brasca could reduce the whole exercise to the level of a lecture on fabric-weaving.

'Only occasionally. In good company, for the finer points of the driving, not to win prizes. Most of these chariot-meets are nothing but cheap thrills and poor horsemanship, a lot of loudmouths going flat out for a bit of local glory and a night on the town. Nothing to do with the real thing. Now, then, do you mind tying the dog up out here?'

Gaius managed to look both blank and mutinous. Madoc said, 'He prefers to be with the boy. He's very well behaved.'

'No, I'm sorry, can't risk it. It only takes a second, something to startle him, and one of the team could be damaged, and your dog kicked to pieces. I'll get you a rope.'

He came back with a length of rope and Madoc tethered Tiki to a fence post while Gaius gazed the other way. In his attitude Madoc observed the same elective detachment, the ability to remove himself from what he didn't like, which the boy employed in lessons.

They went into the yard and Brasca closed the gate firmly. 'I'll show you the chariot first – I made her myself to traditional specifications but with all the up-to-date improvements . . .'

The man talked and talked, and pointed to things, but it was Madoc who nodded and murmured and asked intelligent questions. Gaius gazed past him, and reached his own conclusions. The chariot looked like a giant insect, a dragonfly, perhaps, with its yoke-pole like a long tail behind it. The driver's platform was slung between the wheels on leather straps, and the sides were made of basketwork. None of it seemed very substantial. It was so clean it might never have been used, the woodwork and leather gleaming and the metal studs and joints brightly polished. Instinctively Gaius stepped forward to touch and smell it.

He heard Brasca's hissing intake of breath before he felt the touch on his shoulder and heard the warning: 'Careful!'

Madoc said mildly: 'May he?'

'Well . . . but have a care, you don't want to pinch your fingers.'

This warning seemed too stupid to warrant an answer. Gaius certainly didn't *want* to pinch his fingers and it seemed very unlikely he'd do so by touching a stationary chariot. With his fingers resting on the edge of the wheel he closed his eyes for a moment. Through his fingertips he seemed to feel the whole chariot, its perfectly balanced weight, the sprung tension of its spokes and shafts, all that bound speed waiting to be released.

'Does it go fast?' he murmured to himself.

Brasca leaned forward. 'What's that?'

Startled, Gaius realised he'd spoken out loud. 'Does it go fast?'

'Like a bird! Swooping and gliding, but never leaves the ground. Would you like to see what helps her to do that?'

Gaius nodded.

'Come on, then.'

In the stable next door Madoc lifted Gaius up so he could see properly. He stiffened, but was too interested to object. Inside were four perfectly matched dark chestnut ponies. They were smaller than Gaius' father's horse, Nesta, and shaped differently. Although he could not have put it into words, Gaius could tell that the ponies' conformation was perfectly adapted for speed. Like the chariot, it was not size but design that gave them power. From the soft edges of their quivering nostrils to the end of their plume-like tails they seemed to vibrate with energy.

They came to the side of the stable and leaned their heads over the door, stretching and blowing. To his great relief, Madoc put him down, and he stroked their noses.

'Careful, they're pretty, but they've got big teeth.'

'Hallo, red horses.'

'Red?' Brasca laughed, pleased with his possessions. 'You could say that . . . I might remember that. Red horses!'

'Do you run the four together?' asked Madoc.

'Sometimes. Always in parallel, not tandem. But it's more of a showpiece these days. The drivers who are on the circuit prefer twos. More of a ding-dong, more manoeuvrable. But these four going flat out are a sight to see.'

Gaius picked up on this. 'Can I come and watch?'

'He's keen!' Brasca ruffled his hair irritatingly. 'You can, and there's nothing I'd like more but I've got work to do. If I don't meet my orders I don't get paid, and if I don't get paid I shan't be able to afford this lot.'

There was some man-to-man chuckling, which Gaius' next question cut across.

'When can I?'

'He's persistent!' Brasca folded his arms, pleased to have made such a hit with the boy. 'You know what you'd like? The Saturnalia games. Ever been to that?'

'No. I'll ask my father.'

'He's bound to be there. Get your mother to bring you along. Afterwards you can come round and see these in all their finery.'

'Well!' said Madoc. 'That's a good offer, eh?' Gaius nodded.

Brasca had a last flourish up his sleeve. 'Before you go, take a look at this.'

He opened the door next to the stable. Hanging on the walls, gleaming in the half-light, was row on row of burnished golden treasure.

'This is what they'll be wearing for the games.'

Brasca went on to explain that it was all made of brass, and to identify the different items – chest-guards, bridle medallions, blinkers, brow pieces, leg shields – and to outline their functions. He handed Gaius a decorative disc to hold: it was so bright he could see his face in it, distorted by the image of the emperor, like a reflection in ripples. And then there was Brasca's own equipment, a helmet not unlike that of a legionary, a breastplate and gauntlets. In the corner stood a tall black whip, its shaft as thick as Gaius' wrist, tapering along its sinuous length to a point smaller than his little finger.

'Do you hit them?'

'I don't need to. Just flick the lead horse sometimes –' Brasca demonstrated with a gesture like the throw used to make a stone hop on water '– to ask for a little something extra. But the whip makes a noise that helps the horses run.'

When they'd unhitched the whining Tiki and closed up the yard, Brasca said, 'So, young man, do you think you might like to be a charioteer one day?'

'I don't know,' he said. 'I haven't tried.'

'Sensible answer. Logical, isn't he, for a lad? When you're a bit bigger you'll have to have a ride. See what it feels like.'

'Perhaps,' said Gaius, but after they'd said goodbye and were walking away, he added, 'I don't want to.'

Madoc had come to know that a great many of his pupil's remarks were addressed mainly to himself, but this one prompted him to ask, 'Why is that?'

'There'd be too many people all staring.'

'And it's dangerous,' suggested Madoc. 'There can be terrible accidents.'

'That's why the people go.'

Sometimes Madoc thought there was nothing useful he could teach the boy.

It was an educational morning in only the broadest sense. They meandered through the settlement, stopping where something attracted the boy's interest or where Madoc could make some enlightening observations. They looked at the tanner, the leatherworker, the pot-maker and the blacksmith. What with the bustle, the noise and the smells, Gaius grew increasingly peaky, staring and silent. Madoc's suggestion that they buy some lamb rissoles from a hot-food salesman turned the boy almost green, and they decided to head for home.

Instead of retracing their steps, Madoc opted for the shortest route out of the *vicus*, and a slightly longer walk home round the outside, in the fresh air. On the very outskirts they passed a metalworker's shop. Arrayed on a bench outside were dozens of small models, everything from miniature standards to pigs, and comical people with jug-ears and pot-bellies. Gaius paused by this display, gazing at it with big, exhausted eyes.

Madoc felt quite tender towards the boy. 'Do you see something you like? Look, there's a four-horse chariot like Brasca's.'

'And a dog like Tiki!'

'Oh, yes. You're right, it does have a look of him. When he was waiting for us at the gate.'

The dog was tiny, less than a child's handspan in height and width. It sat with its front legs apart, head cocked and ears pricked, its tongue protruding. The model was roughly done, like all the ornaments a way of using up the offcuts from armaments and horseshoes, but it was, nonetheless, full of life.

'Would you like him? As a souvenir of our day out?'

Madoc was rewarded with the intense gratitude in his pupil's voice. 'Yes, please.'

Gaius went to bed early that night, without protest, but in spite of his tiredness he was still not asleep when his father came to say good-night an hour later.

Publius sat down on the side of the bed. It gave a little beneath his weight. 'Your mother tells me you went out today.'

'Madoc took me.'

'Tell me what you saw.'

'I showed him the cursing stones. And then we walked all the way to the fort, and saw the chariot and the horses that belong to Madoc's friend.'

'Brasca, I know him. He's keen as mustard.'

'Can I go to the games?'

'We'll see. If you work hard. A holiday has to be earned, Gaius.'

Gaius didn't reply. He hated this kind of conversation with his father: it was dull and meaningless, like one of those terrible games grown-ups thought were fun but which were only embarrassing. For one thing he already did his best and it *felt* like hard work, so what more could he do? For another, everyone had a holiday for the Saturnalia so it wasn't true that it had to be earned.

'What's this?' Publius leaned across to pick up the model of the dog, which Gaius had placed in the lamplit recess next to the statue of Jupiter. 'Something new?'

'Madoc got it for me.'

'Hm.' Publius turned it in his hands. 'It's amusing, though I'm not sure it deserves to be on an altar.'

'It's like Tiki.'

'I can see that.' He replaced it. 'Is that why you like it?'

Gaius sat up, staring into his father's face. He wanted a proper answer to his next question. 'Does iron last for ever?'

'A very long time.'

'But not for ever?'

'Nothing does that.'

Gaius lay down again, curled on his side. 'Night, Father.'

'Good-night, Gaius.'

Claudia was sitting in her father's old chair, writing. Perhaps it was due to the chair, but for the first time Publius caught a glimpse of her father in the tilt of her face, the set of her lips, and the way she held the pen – saw how she'd look when she was old. The impression lasted only a split second as he came into the room. When she looked up and smiled, it was gone.

'Still awake?' she asked, putting down the pen. 'He's over-tired, that's the trouble.'

'I'm not sure what I think of jaunts to the town when he's meant to be learning.'

'Well, I know what I think. It's a good thing and they should do more of it. Madoc's a nice man, he gets on with Gaius.'

Publius felt the crawl of jealousy. 'Lucky fellow.'

'And so do you. More than you allow.'

Publius gestured to the house slave, who poured wine and handed it to them.

'That's too subtle for me. I'm like any father – I want my son to do well, to earn respect, to live an industrious, honourable life.'

'And a happy one,' suggested Claudia.

'Such a life would be happy.'

She looked at him steadily. His wife had a way of doing that which made him feel uncomfortable, as though he were lying.

She said, 'He's an unusual boy, we must accept him as he is. Don't burden him, or yourself, with too much expectation.'

'That's not something over which I have much control.' She lifted an eyebrow. 'I'll do my best.'

A moment later he remarked, 'Did he show you that dog the tutor gave him?'

'I can see why he likes it so much.'

'He asked me if it would last for ever.'

'And what did you say?'

'No, of course. One must be truthful.'

Claudia didn't reply, and they sat in silence as the shy girl crept in, and moved softly round the edge of the room, lighting the lamps one by one.

CHAPTER EIGHTEEN

Bobby, 1993

I had no idea, when I went away on holiday in the late summer, that it would be so eventful. I spent the first week in Brittany with Ros Cotterill, who had acquired a house there a couple of years before.

'You must stop calling me Spud,' she said, over white wine on the ferry. 'You're the only person who still does. It puts both of us in a time warp.'

'I'm sorry,' I said, 'but that's the point. Once I stop we'll be admitting officially to being grown-up, and I'm not ready for that, even if you are.'

'I suppose, but why should it be me who suffers?' complained Spud. 'And why was I called that, anyway? Tell me I looked like a potato and you're toast.'

'You did a bit. But, then, so did most of us. And you don't now,' I added hastily. 'It's a kind of reverse compliment to have a funny nickname if you're glamorous.'

She gave me a dry look. 'Don't overdo it. That only works if you're someone like Miranda Tattersall. Remember her at school? Nobody called her Rags then.'

I explained, very briefly, about renewing acquaintance with Miranda. Spud was all ears.

'That's right! Lady Stratton . . . he was rather dishy. But didn't he die?'

'Just a couple of years ago.'

'I saw the pictures in the paper, so *sad*. She still looked disgustingly wonderful. Is she as good in the flesh?'

'Better. And awfully nice as well.'

'Christ, I hate her ...' Spud sloshed out more wine. 'It's not fair. Still, I suppose she's got plenty to be nice about, one of the most beautiful houses in the country and no money worries.'

'She loves the house,' I said, 'but she doesn't live in it any more. Her step-son Miles Montclere's the new Lord Stratton. She's in a sort of posh annexe.'

'Not an annexe as you or I would understand the word, I bet.'

'No,' I admitted. 'But it is one.' I wanted to say something that would convey what I saw as the magic of Ladycross, and of Miranda. 'She absolutely adored her husband. They're building a little theatre in the park in his memory.'

Spud snorted derisively. 'Bobby, listen to yourself, you *are* swep' away. Little theatre? Park? It's a parallel universe.'

I wasn't going to argue. She was right, in a way. I wasn't so swept away that I couldn't see it all, and myself, quite clearly through her eyes.

Once we'd fought our way out of St Malo in a series of acrimonious stops, starts, wrong turnings and near-misses and were bowling west along the coast road, Spud focused what was left of her attention on me.

'I want to know everything.'

'I've told you most of it. I've got a nice new house, a new job—'

'New man?'

'What do you mean "new"?'

'All right, any man.'

'I thought I had,' I said, 'but now I'm not so sure.'

'I don't think you're trying.'

'I'm not,' I agreed, 'and I never was. These things either happen or they don't, and I don't mind either way.' Only part of this was true.

'Sorry – arrgh, roundabout! Sorry, but I don't believe that,' said Spud, who liked others' view of the world to accord with her own.

'There's a lot to be said for the man-free life.'

'I'll look forward to hearing it – push off, Frog! So what did you do to the one you had?'

I considered this. What had I done to Daniel? The answer was nothing. But something had happened to him, something I understood only too well.

'We kind of drifted apart,' I said lamely.

She gave me a look. 'You're hopeless, what are you?'

I had been to Spud's *gîte* twice before. It was one half of a converted 1950s villa overlooking the bay at Mont St Michel. The other half was the *maison secondaire* of a whey-faced Parisian businessman, Maurice. During his and Spud's protracted absences the houses were lent, less frequently let, and were looked after by a local agent from Erquy, and Marie-Laure the cleaning lady. Spud, a social worker, was twice divorced, and had bought the house following the latest change in her domestic circumstances. I was used to thinking that she was electively childless, 'like me', but now I would have to rethink that comparison. Quite unlike me she had conducted a lively social life both in and out of marriage, and approached her many relationships with a cheery and untroubled consumerism.

It was true that she had been a bit potato-like at school, a sort of Maris Piper to my King Edward, but she had blossomed since into an attractive, earthy woman, generous in nature and in girth, always dressed in long, flowing clothes and draped in scarves and interesting necklaces. She had an explosion of frizzy dark hair, subject to token restraint by a collection of ethnic clips and combs, and a lazy eye, which in her first year at Queen's had obliged her to wear one lens of her National Health specs covered. The eye was still lazy, and its wanderings gave her face an amiably crazed look that suited her eccentric style.

As was traditional, we dumped our bags in the house and went out again at once to buy basic supplies at the supermarket and walk on the beach. Spud was a great believer in immediate reorientation, in 'getting the new air into your lungs'. We'd been up drinking for most of the overnight crossing, but the cool, blowy late summer's afternoon was refreshing. We parked the car with its bootload of Mammouth groceries at the bottom of the unmade road and set off round the bay on foot.

We strode over the silky, pewter-coloured sand, I in my serviceable jeans and trainers, Spud with her flowing draperies billowing around her and her hair springing in wild black corkscrews from its bonds. I realised that if I was going to unburden myself about Fleur to anyone then Spud was that person, but I had yet to find a way of placing this enormous burden on the conversational conveyor-belt. I just had to hope that a natural opportunity would present itself, so that I could say, insouciantly, 'Oh, and by the way . . .'

The fact was, the situation was still only half real to me. Months had elapsed since Fleur had turned up on my doorstep, and in that time I hadn't heard from her again. If I narrowed my mind's eye I could almost fancy I'd imagined or misinterpreted the events of that and the following day. I might mention them to Spud, thereby setting her energetically on my case, only for nothing further to happen. So I kept quiet on the subject, aware that my silence was a faultline in our relationship.

'Tell me to butt out,' she advised pointlessly, as we rounded the flat black rocks on the headland, 'but leaving this latest setback aside for the time being, I reckon you don't get enough out of being free. From my perspective, you always seem to go right out and create another set of restrictions for yourself.'

This was a recurring theme of hers and one I could neither deny nor defend myself against, because she would simply not have understood. It had long since ceased to bother me but we had to go through it each time.

'That's not how I see it,' I said. 'You know that. I'm not like you.'

'No, no, heaven forfend, but you should allow yourself to have some *fun*, for God's sake.'

'I do,' I protested amiably, 'but everyone's idea of fun is different.'

She stopped abruptly and placed her hands on my shoulders. 'Bobby. Don't let Miranda Tattersall cramp your style.'

'What?' She was so close to some sort of truth that I sounded jumpy even to myself, and she must have noticed, for she pressed her advantage. 'Don't start living through someone else. Your life is just as interesting as hers, and much more important to *you*.'

'You don't have to tell me that.' I was again reminded just how little everyone knew. 'And, anyway, I'm here, aren't I?'

'Good point!' Spud started walking again. 'We'll have to see what we can do.'

What we did was pretty much what we always did in Brittany. Rose late, breakfasted till lunchtime, went out in the afternoon, stopping on the way back for supplies, a glass of wine or both, depending on plans for the evening, dined in or out according to mood, and sat up talking and drinking until the small hours. I was keener on the beach than Spud, who was easily bored and who, despite her untrammelled lifestyle, didn't care to remove her clothes in public, let alone to swim in the Atlantic. On fine afternoons I'd let her take off to distant *marchés artisinales*, *foires*, *châteaux* and *musées*, while I walked down to the bay and spread my towel in the lee of the rocks.

The beach here reminded me of long-ago family holidays in Cornwall, I suppose because this coastline was the complementary piece of the geological jigsaw: the shiny grey sand patterned with whorls and ripples . . . the shoulders of black rock glossy with kelp and bladderwrack, and the inky, secret pools . . . the long, shallow breakers and the lacy surf hissing as it fanned out stealthily. Mont St Michel rose like an Arthurian sepulchre from the sea in the middle distance. On even the clearest, sunniest day there was a breeze, and you could see people's hair and clothes blowing as they ran in and out of the glittering sea, raced with dogs, flew kites or chased crazily hopping beachballs. The beach was so vast, especially at low tide, that it was never crowded, and there were no 'facilities' beyond the unmade-up parking area and the accompanying wooden café with its lean-to convenience at the back. The people who came here did so because this was what they wanted. Spud occasionally complained about the number of Brits in the area, but if that was a problem I was quite happy to be part of it.

Half-way through the week, on one of those afternoons when we'd gone our separate ways, I'd been in for a swift, breathless swim and was drying myself in the sheltered sunshine of my base camp in the lee of the rocks. I didn't even know the dog was there until it leaped over me from above, giving me the fright of my life. It was vast and black, one of those continental breeds with a coat of a thousand dreadlocks and a tail like a billhook.

The dog landed a metre away from my towel and shook vigorously, sending arcs of cold spray all over me. As I yelped, its owner arrived via the same route, hopping down from the rocks and grabbing the beast's collar.

'I'm very sorry,' he said, in the accentless tones of the perfect English-speaker. 'We didn't see you there.'

'That's all right.' I was standing swathed in my towel in what must have looked like an unnecessarily maidenly manner. 'I realise he didn't do it on purpose.'

'Too stupid,' he agreed. He was fortyish, big like his dog and with the same curly dark hair, in his case worn rather too long. He wore glasses, a checked shirt over an incipient gut, khaki shorts and threadbare deck shoes.

He produced a lead and clipped it on. 'A beautiful day for it.' He pronounced it 'byuddiful', a minor slip-up. 'You've been in?'

'Yes.'

'You're English, of course you have!' was his comment, which I thought a bit cheeky. 'You were wet already, so no harm is done.'

'I suppose so . . .'

'Enjoy the sunshine.'

He went some distance before once more releasing the dog, and throwing a stick for it, way ahead of him, just in case.

★   ★   ★

That evening I got my opportunity. We were officially eating in, although things being what they were we had still not done so at nine thirty and were well into the second bottle. Spud was full of a village she'd stumbled on where there had been a *marché fermier* at which she'd augmented our already plentiful supplies of cheese.

'We must go there for dinner tomorrow night,' she said, 'and treat ourselves. I had a pit stop in a joint off the *place* that would suit us beautifully – nice and crowded, no Brits and a menu at fifteen francs. What do you say?'

I said it sounded good to me. 'And no children,' she went on. 'I don't want to sound like W. C. Fields, but if I'd wanted a family atmosphere at mealtimes I'd have arranged it for myself. You too, I bet.'

I realised this was it. Or could be, if I let it.

'Actually,' I said, 'Spud – I've got something to tell you—'

She shrieked. 'Jesus, you're not, are you? That's obscene at your age!'

'Don't be daft. No, listen,' I cut across her spluttering, 'I already have a daughter.'

She shrieked again, from force of habit. Then the chuckling died away as she realised I was serious. 'You what?'

'When I was twenty I had a baby. The other day she turned up on my doorstep.'

'Je-sus!' This time it was whispered. 'Bobby! Tell me about it – only let's have another before you do.'

Spud topped us both up and sat back, her gaze fixed on me. For once there was no affectation in her manner. I had her undivided attention.

'Give.'

I told her, as simply and quickly as I could, about Fleur's visit, and the reason for it. She put her enormous beringed hand over her face for a moment. As she dragged it down slowly her eyes were wide with near-disbelief.

'So . . . let me get this straight. One moment you're this well-ordered singleton with a steady job and a nice quiet life. The next you're the parent of a grown-up daughter, and about to be a grandparent.'

'That's about it.'

'Now I know why those damn-fool TV reporters ask, "How does it feel?" How *does* it feel, for Chrissakes?'

I wanted to be honest about this, but in searching for the right words I was a little too long answering.

Spud sighed. 'That exciting, huh?'

'It's just that I only met her for the first time a few months ago and I haven't seen or heard from her since. So I'm used to the idea in one way – but only one way. Only the *idea* that I don't know what's going to happen.'

'You're going to be a grandmother, Bobby! I mean – she could have twins!'

'She'd have known, surely . . . I mean, she'd have told me – wouldn't she?'

Spud lowered her head on to her knees, shaking with near-hysterical laughter. 'Don't ask me, this is your gig. If she's anything like you she'll be giving it full and lengthy consideration.'

Suddenly I wanted to cry. I felt foolish, diminished, useless. I wished I had said nothing. I couldn't even trust myself to speak. My throat, mouth, eyes were full of tears, my chest bulged with sobs.

Spud noticed at once, and was crouching beside me with my hands folded in hers. She smelt of sandalwood and wisps of wayward hair tickled my face. On top of everything else I had the desire to sneeze.

'God, Bobby, I'm so sorry. I wasn't laughing at you – or if I was it was only because it's all so bloody serious I didn't know what else to do. Fuck, fuck, I'm a thoughtless bitch, please don't cry I can't bear it . . .'

It was no good her imploring me not to, there was no turning back. I sneezed, and the tears gushed, the sobs burst forth, my nose ran in sympathy, and it was my turn to say, 'Sorry . . . sorry . . .' as Spud rallied round with tissues. The storm was violent, but at last I hiccuped to a halt.

'Okay,' said Spud. 'Fuel. I reckon we're both suffering from low blood sugar.'

Like Ratty rustling up supper from a bare cupboard for the

lachrymose Mole, she bustled about and brought in bread, cheese, peaches and a jug of black coffee.

'Dig in.' She stole a look at me to check my recovery. 'Remember, you're eating for three now.'

I managed a watery laugh.

She was right, I did feel better after food. It was a pleasant relief to have told someone, and particularly Spud who, though gratifyingly astonished, was a true friend.

'Actually,' she remarked, as we sipped coffee shot with Calvados, 'I think it's great news. All this advice I've been dispensing, and your wild oats have been flourishing away out there.'

'Yes, but it doesn't mean I'm any different,' I pointed out. 'I'm still the dull person you took me for. Except that now I'm a dull person with issue.'

'I never said you were dull,' she protested, 'just that you owed yourself a good time. But it sounds as if you had one.'

'No,' I said, 'I didn't.'

'I forbid you to downplay all this, it's fantastically exotic. Enjoy, woman!'

I indulged myself to this extent: 'Fleur — my daughter — is lovely-looking.'

'That's the style. Is she like you?'

Out of an ingrained habit of self-deprecation I was going to say no, and then I remembered that thing she did with her mouth when she was listening to me . . . and her flyaway eyebrows . . . her fingers . . .

'A little,' I said. 'Enough. My genes are in there, doing their stuff. But mostly she's herself, unique. That's what's so interesting, Spud — her separateness, not her similarity.'

As I said this Spud was watching me with an almost tender expression. 'You really liked her, didn't you?'

'I did. Do.'

'And yet you don't know where she is.'

'No. I wanted to leave the decision about what to do next with her.'

'Have you any idea,' said Spud gently, 'how noble and selfless and bloody ridiculous that was?'

'Not to mention cowardly.' I was reminding myself as much as telling her. 'It left me with no responsibility in the matter.'

'So when's the baby due?'

'In about a month.'

She frowned, asked quietly, 'What will you do if you don't hear anything?'

'I don't know. What can I do? Accept it and carry on.'

Spud smiled. 'They'll put that on your gravestone. You're a true Stoic, Bobby, you know that? Out of your time. You should have been born a Roman.'

The next evening we went out for dinner. There was always one night when Spud liked to don her warpaint and her fuck-off frock and hit the town, no matter how one-horse that town was, in the hope of 'big fun'. It fell to me on these occasions to drive and be the sober sidekick, a role that suited me perfectly. This, it seemed, was to be that night.

She'd booked us a table at Lalli, the restaurant that had excited her interest the day before, and where there was to be music. I was ready first. Spud came downstairs at the appointed hour in a red cheesecloth dress that exposed much of her superabundant torso and more than hinted at the rest. I noticed with relief that she was at least carrying one of her Castilian shawls.

It took about half an hour to drive to the village in question and I could see at once why Spud liked it. Méribeau had a rough-edged *Clochemerle*-ish charm – the raffish air of a place where all sorts of people got up to all kinds of stuff, largely undisturbed by outsiders or the Gendarmerie, according to some ancient and unwritten lore. There were a few tourists other than ourselves in the restaurant, but for the most part the tables were full of locals. A space, marked with a couple of battered microphones, had been cleared for the band near the door to the street, where there was a narrow pavement seating area.

I was normally wary of Spud in Big Fun mode, but this evening I was still in the backwash of relief at having confided in her, and consequently more relaxed. Besides, very little usually came of her hopes, especially in this neighbourhood where natural Gallic sophistication was mixed with northern reserve. The people dining in Lalli were filling their faces and talking up a storm, but were paying no mind to this expansive Englishwoman and her more restrained companion. I had put on my loose print trousers and wraparound black top, and it was perfectly possible they considered us an item in the approved English manner.

The eponymous Lalli turned out to be a fierce Breton matron with iron-grey hair and a manner that indicated you were there by her leave and would be wise to remember it. As she ran through the *prix fixe* menu her eyes strafed Spud's quivering *embonpoint* with disfavour. But the food, when it came, and kept on coming, was wonderful – vegetable soup, *assiette de fruits de mer*, salad, pork chops, enough *frites* for a children's party, goat's cheese, and *galettes* with apricots and ice-cream. Large plain bottles of first white, then red wine were placed on the table, like a gauntlet being thrown down. Spud was well up to the challenge.

'I hope there'll be dancing,' she said, over coffee, as the band began to assemble and set up. 'I could do with a good boogy – and so could you.' She tended to prescribe partying as though it were an antibiotic. I knew I'd have no option but to form a threesome with her handbag, until she'd built up enough steam to drag an appreciative male onlooker on to the floor. Then it would be a case of sitting it out till I'd built up enough steam to cart her away.

During the course of dinner a lot more people had arrived at the restaurant. The tables outside were all full, and extra chairs had been supplied for late arrivals. The smoke and decibel levels had risen appreciably. Children in the square were playing around, jumping on and off the stone water-trough; moths flittered in the dim halos of the terrace lights; a fat, faded cat wafted among the tables and chairs, trailing its tail over people's legs, avoiding the impatient tapping of cigarettes; Madame mellowed and appeared with a purple velvet jacket over her black dress and a shiny clip in her hair. I was reminded of a catchphrase of my grandfather's: 'Let the atrocities commence.'

For a second I found myself thinking how perfectly Fleur would have fitted into these surroundings.

Spud nudged me. 'No prizes for guessing what sort of music we're in for. This lot could make us feel like teenagers and that's saying something.'

It was an exaggeration, but certainly the average age of the band was forty-something. This was unmistakably a group of friends realising a youthful shared ambition. The youngest was the man with the dog whom I'd met on the beach. I didn't mention this to Spud.

'Pity they're tied up for the evening,' she mused, 'they're rather tasty.'

'Let's guess,' I said. 'Accountant, social worker, computer nerd, gynaecologist?'

'Architect, salesman, dentist . . . landscape gardener. Someone's always a landscape gardener, these days, it's what people do when they're made redundant.'

'So which is which?'

She craned her neck for a better view. 'If there's a gynae it has to be the one with the Byronic hair and the specs. Nice beady brown eyes. He can study my bits any time.'

After several minutes of tantalising strumming, mike-testing and conferring, the set kicked off with 'Honky Tonk Women'. I knew it would be only a matter of minutes before the beat got the better of Spud and she was out there. To buy myself some time I retreated to the ladies'. When I came back she was honky-tonkying away with a man old enough to be her father, but in whom the sap was enjoying a late surge. He was having no truck with independent gyrations, and was alternately clasping her and casting her off to be admired – briefly – at arm's length: he was getting full value for money. His style was authentic 1930s lounge-lizard, knees slightly bent and an expression of rapt, lascivious concentration on his walnut face. His hair gleamed with what had to be brilliantine. If Spud had been proactive in their teaming up, he had certainly needed no dragging. This was a man in seventh heaven and his element.

I sat down at the table, content for the time being to watch not only Spud's cavortings, but those of my acquaintance from the beach. He was on bass guitar and, like Spud's partner, a happy man. I thought how nice it must be to have this outlet, this night-time other life in which one could indulge oneself, both having and providing fun, and receive a modest fee for doing so. He was wearing what looked like the same checked shirt, but had swapped the shorts for jeans. I reflected, with a kind of embarrassed pleasure, that I found him attractive. If I could have been said to have a type, he was it – solid, sensuous, intelligent-seeming; neither smooth nor cool; a man at ease with his pleasures, as perhaps I wasn't. Something in the cut of his jib reminded me of someone, but I couldn't for the moment think who. Not my ex-husband, which should have told me something; certainly not the lab technician . . . And not, I realised, Daniel.

They stuck with the Stones, moving seamlessly from 'Honky Tonk Women' to 'Little Red Rooster', which sent Spud and her partner into fresh paroxysms of inventiveness. The arrival of several more couples on the floor meant that they had to curtail their more abandoned struttings and posturings, and were obliged to replace it with ever tighter and more sinuous holds.

After 'Jumping Jack Flash' the band embarked on a Beatles set and Spud took a breather. She plumped down at the table, panting and perspiring, drained one glass of wine and poured another. 'Phew! Marvellous! Did you see that old guy? Wasn't he amazing?'

'Totally,' I agreed.

'You want a really great dancer, you have to look to the older generation.'

'He was certainly enjoying himself.'

'Oh, lecherous to die for.' She leaned forward and peered at me, all damp and glowing from her exertions. 'And how are *you*?'

'Fine. Having a good time in my funny old-fashioned way.'

'I'll believe you. Not getting mournful, I hope?'

'Far from it. Pensive, maybe. But not mournful.'

'I'm pleased to hear it.' She sat back, lifting her mountain of hair off her neck and blowing down her cleavage. 'Because you have absolutely nothing to be glum about.'

This reassurance had the inevitable consequence of making me feel melancholy, but Spud was on to the next thing. 'Great band. Are you going to come and keep me company in a minute?'

'I'm quite happy watching.'

'Because if you *don't*,' she went on, 'I'll be stuck with the sex-mad granddad all evening and, good value though he is, I need to come up for air.'

'Let's see what they play next.'

That turned out to be anthems, starting with 'I'm A Believer', and moving swiftly on to 'Hi Ho Silver Lining', and 'American Pie'. God knows what the locals made of it, but they took it in good part and fell in, as I did, with Spud's chorusing and arm-waving as if it had been part of their cultural heritage since the dawn of time. It was impossible not to be caught up in the occasion's bibulous good-humour. The combination of atmosphere, music, and Spud's rampant exhibitionism, with my own anonymity, loosened my inhibitions. At one point I became aware of being the focus of amused attention, to find a man behind me making appreciative squeezing gestures in the direction of my bottom.

'Go, Bobby!' shouted Spud, in my ear. 'You're really getting into it!'

I was, but not as anonymously as I'd thought. At the end of the anthems the band announced a break, and we went back to our table. I calculated that half an hour after the break would be the moment to start making leaving noises, in order to get Spud out of the door an hour after that.

She instructed me to order another bottle and went to the *Dames*. Almost at once, as if he'd been waiting for this opportunity, the bass guitarist sat down next to me.

'May I, while your friend's away?'

'Oh, hallo again,' I said, as if I hadn't noticed him before. 'What a coincidence.'

'That's life.' He smiled. His gynae-eyes twinkled merrily behind the specs. 'You're enjoying yourself?'

'You noticed.'

'It would be hard not to.'

'My friend's an arresting woman. It's impossible to lie low in her company.'

He didn't react to this. 'You're a great dancer, really. Great movements. A pleasure to watch.'

'Oh, well – thanks,' I muttered. I had always been hopeless with compliments.

'I can't dance,' he said, 'except the slow, shuffling sort.'

'But you play brilliantly,' I said.

He was gallant enough not to show that I'd just given myself away. 'Adequately. Enough to get the party going in any case.'

'Are you going to introduce me to this usurper?' This was Spud, returned freshly painted, brushed and scented from the *Dames*. The man got to his feet at once.

'I'm sorry,' I said, turning to him helplessly. 'I don't know your name.'

Spud sucked her teeth. 'Honestly. I can't take her any-where.'

He held out his hand. 'Peter Krieff.'

'Is that Dutch?'

'It is.' Trust her.

'Ros Cotterill.' I reminded myself to make it Ros from now on. He shook her hand and turned to me, quizzically.

'And this is Bobby Govan.'

'Hallo,' I said.

'Perhaps I can buy you a drink after the set?'

'Sounds great,' said Spud. 'You're working well, by the way.'

'And you.'

He rejoined the others. Spud could scarcely contain herself. 'You little devil, you pulled, all on your own!'

'Actually I met him on the beach yesterday afternoon.'

'You never said.'

'There was nothing to tell. His dog shook all over me and he apologised.'

'Well, you must have made an impression if he remembered you. Did you know it was him up there tonight?'

'Yes, but—'

'You didn't mention it to me.'

'No.'

Spud raised an eyebrow. 'I'd say you were keeping him to yourself, only that's not your style.'

'You don't know what my style is,' I said. 'And, anyway, he's met you now, so what chance do I have?'

She thought I was joking.

During the second set we danced some more – with each other, and separately: Spud with the ageing sex-beast and a couple of others; I with a gaggle of cheery women whom I suspected of clustering round me because their husbands preferred to drink and gossip. We stood in a circle: whatever I did they copied, adding a few flourishes of their own. It was like some bizarre musical version of 'Simon Says'. We smiled at each other and got on down. It was all rather sweet, but Spud chose to put a more disturbing spin on it. 'Are you quite sure,' she asked, as 'Mustang Sally' howled to a close, 'that there isn't something else you haven't told me?'

'*We* were dancing together,' I pointed out.

'Yes, but I moved on. Ay-ay, here comes Peter the Wolf.'

'Bobby and – Ros? What can I get for you?' he asked. I asked for a Coke and Spud a Calvados.

'The Dutch are so cool, aren't they?' she mused, as he went to the bar. 'It's all that dope and openness and euthanasia . . . I reckon the Dutch are the new French.'

'Don't make too much of it here,' I suggested.

'Something tells me our secrets are safe. This is the one place in France where they have the same approach to foreign tongues as us.'

He came back with the drinks, and pulled up a chair from the next table. 'Are you staying here?'

'No,' I began, but Spud was in like Flynn.

'I've got a house near Erquy. It's nice to be able to have friends with you on holiday. What about you?'

'I live in the next village. It makes this one look like Shanghai, I promise you.'

'And the rest of the band?' I asked.

'Here and there. There's a – squad? – squad of seven of

us, and whoever's available for the night gets to play. Only one drummer and one vocalist though, so if they're sick,' he shrugged, 'no show.'

'What we're dying to know,' said Spud, in her upfront way, irritatingly including me as though I were too retiring to ask, 'is what you all do when you're not wowing audiences.'

He pointed at the others who were at the bar. 'Policeman, care assistant, house-husband.' He laid his hand on his own chest. 'Formula One driver.'

'Get away!' said Spud. 'Really?'

'In my dreams. No, I fix clocks.'

'How intriguing.'

'Fascinating for me, useful for other people, lousy money. Two out of three isn't bad, I think. And I'm on my own,' he added, providing the answer to Spud's as-yet unasked question, 'so I can live a student life.' Before she could hit him with the next one he turned to me. 'But it should be much hotter before I swim.'

I laughed. 'It's wonderful once you're used to it. I didn't care so much for the cold shower.'

'I apologise for that.'

'Oh, yes, your dog,' said Spud. 'I heard all about it.'

My knuckles itched, but he didn't bat an eyelid. 'I do my best, but she's young and she has no boundaries.'

I found myself thinking how much I should like to tell him about Fleur.

'Okay,' he said, 'we have one more set. Will you be staying for that?'

'You bet—'

'I doubt it—'

We spoke together. He smiled. 'I may see you later, then. Oh,' he felt in his hip pocket and produced two cards, one of which he handed to me, 'in case you're giving a party. Cheap rates, cheerful music.'

'Thanks.'

He laid the second one face down on the table. 'Fair exchange.'

Spud dug out a biro and wrote our names and the number

of the house in Erquy. Once again I felt she was presumptuous, but to demur in front of him would have looked at best prissy, at worst rude. He put the card back into his pocket without a glance and stood up.

'It was good to see you again,' he said to me, 'the dancing queen. Nice to meet you, Ros. Enjoy the rest of the evening.'

In fact, we didn't stay long after that. We had one more dance round our handbags, because they played 'Spirit In The Sky', and all the game housewives trooped out to follow our lead. As we left I caught Peter's eye and he lifted his chin to say goodbye.

It was midnight and there was an incredible moon, sharp and bright as a ten pence piece in a clear sky. I made a loop to the south so we could drive along the coast road. Spud was subdued, her head tipped back and away from me, gazing out of the window.

'Thanks for suggesting that,' I said. 'It was a lovely evening.'

'Hmm.'

'Great people-watching. Beryl Cook would have had a field day.'

'Say again?'

'Beryl Cook – the artist? She does—'

'Fat people.'

This was said with a slight edge. I avoided digging a bigger hole for myself.

'I wonder,' I mused for her benefit, to cheer her up, 'why I attraced all those nice women? It is rather worrying.'

'I think I'm getting old,' she said. Her voice was thin and bleak.

'I *beg* your pardon?'

She rolled her head to look at me. 'Do I seem like a sad cow to you?'

'Spud—'

'Please don't call me that.'

I never did so again. 'You are the opposite of old and sad. I'd go so far as to say you'll *never* be old and sad. You've got more

422

vitality than anyone I know. Look at you back there, you were a complete star.'

'Or a figure of fun.'

It was dismaying to see her so low, as if one of the landmarks of my life had been suddenly knocked sideways.

'You're a fun person,' I said. 'You know how to enjoy yourself, you help other people do the same. It's a gift, it really is. I wouldn't have done anything like that on my own, but because you made me I had a fantastic time. It really did me good. *You* did me good.'

She laughed, thank God. A bit wanly, but a laugh nonetheless. 'Gosh, me – a do-gooder at last.'

'I speak as I find. Oh, look . . .'

We'd rounded the top of a headland and suddenly there, stretched below and before us, a great swathe of beach – white sand, coal-dark tumbling rocks, gleaming black water streaked with the racing white horses of the Atlantic. A shimmering moon-path stretching to the sky.

I pulled over and switched off the engine. Now we could hear the rumble of the waves and the sigh of the prowling surf. Around and above us, the sort of silence in which one might hear the music of the spheres. We might have been the first ever to see this beach.

For a moment we sat quietly, drinking it in. When Ros spoke, it was scarcely more than a whisper, not wanting to break the spell.

'This is what I need more of . . .'

'Peace,' I agreed. 'Yes.'

'Not just that. *I* need to be quieter. Like you.' She was still melancholy.

'I don't think so. I think you should be yourself.'

She ignored this. 'You do right to keep things to yourself. That way other people can't grab a piece of the action. Your life stays yours for longer.'

'I suppose. But if I'm reticent, that's not why.'

'I'm sorry I grilled you about your daughter.'

'Actually, it was a relief. I needed to talk about it with someone but it took you to prise it out of me. I'm glad.'

'I shan't badger you any more. But please,' she looked at me, 'if something's weighing on you, remember I'm here. Or at the end of the line.'

'I will, of course. But you must promise me that you won't go turning all pale and interesting on me.'

She laughed voicelessly, in her throat. 'You can't teach an old dog new tricks.'

Peter rang at eleven o'clock in the morning, our last full day.

'Bobby? I hoped I'd catch you. Rock guitarists and people on holiday get up late.'

'Hallo.'

'I wondered if you'd have dinner with me tomorrow night.'

'We go home tomorrow.'

'Tonight, then? I simply thought that would be too short notice.'

'That sounds very . . . I don't know – let me just check with Ros.'

'Sure. But the invitation is for you.'

'Me?' I said stupidly.

'Unless you'd feel safer bringing a friend.' There was a smile in his voice.

'No. Thank you. Well, that would be nice.'

'Tell me where your house is, and I'll pick you up at, what, seven?'

I returned somewhat shell-shocked to the patio where we'd been sitting over coffee and *pains au chocolat*.

'Who was that?'

'Peter – from last night.'

She didn't look up from her plate. 'That was quick.'

I took a deep breath, telling myself I was a free and independent woman and had no need to apologise. 'I'm going out for an early supper with him this evening.'

'Good.' Ros raised her coffee cup to me without a tremor. 'He's cute. And you deserve him.'

★   ★   ★

At the time I didn't think that deserving had anything to do with it. I was a little uncomfortable with this reversal of the usual roles – Ros waving me off as I left for an evening out. But later I was to think that I must somewhere, some time, have done something to deserve what happened.

I said that I'd never been in love. But I'd read about it, and heard the songs, and noted other people's inability to describe it, and seen the look in their eyes. Even now I couldn't say whether that evening was about falling in love, but it was enchanted all right. What I remember most about it was that I was more myself than I had ever been, but unrecognisable as the self I was used to. That was Peter Krieff's present to me.

A more experienced hand than I – Ros, for instance – might have raised a cynical eyebrow at the discovery that dinner was to be at his house, but all I can say is that it felt perfectly natural. I wasn't alarmed, though perhaps I should have been. And sitting at his kitchen table, patting his dog while he cooked, with John Coltrane in the background, felt not just fine but lovely. It might have been his own gentle confidence that made me relax, and the whole occasion so benign. In my head I could hear Ros saying, 'Why wouldn't he be confident? He's an old hand . . .' All I can say is, it worked.

His house was a terraced cottage, not unlike mine in Witherburn but a lot less tidy. The biggest room was a conservatory beyond the kitchen, full of clocks, with his workbench in it. The kitchen table was laid with a red oilcloth, and a bunch of purple and red anemones in a china mug. He'd made sublime onion soup and, while we had our first glass of wine, he cooked – in front of me! – steamed monkfish with a watercress sauce and boiled potatoes. 'Bachelor cuisine, tried and tested,' as he put it. It was delicious.

He told me why he liked clocks. 'They're like people – they have faces and hands, and a heartbeat. A clock has a presence, it keeps you company. That room's more of a hospital than a workshop.'

'It's very fine, painstaking work, though.'

'Self-taught. The fruit of an obsession. I like the detail of it. I was good at maths when I was at school. I was in music publishing before. Music and maths go together, it has something to do with logic and harmony. Or maybe I'm talking bullshit.'

'Why did you leave the music business?'

'Do you know, I got tired of helping other people, very mediocre talents, to do what I really wanted to do myself. Not that I was good enough, but I didn't want to be on the sidelines looking on. I'd rather play regularly, for fun, as I do now, and be occupied with something entirely different most of the time.'

He volunteered other information about himself, which I should probably have been too polite to elicit. He had a 'lady', Friede, with whom, though they no longer lived together, he was still good friends, and by whom he had a son, Nicholas, now nine. They lived in Antwerp, and he saw them regularly. Twice a year Nicholas came to stay with him in the school holidays.

'Friede's a wonderful mother,' he said, 'but she's strict. It's right that she is. When he comes here he's allowed to stay up late, eat at funny times, come to gigs . . . do boy stuff.'

'And she doesn't mind?' I asked.

'No. She has a holiday, we have a holiday, everybody knows where they stand. It's good for Nick to see that life can be lived in different ways and still be productive.'

'What does Friede do?'

'She's a doctor. An obstetrician.'

The ex-partner was fleshing out into something approaching superwoman, but as if he'd read my mind he changed the subject and asked me about myself. I told him about my house move, the new job, the coincidence of meeting Miranda again after so long. 'You might have heard of her,' I said. 'These days she's Lady Stratton, but she used to be a photographic model. She was called Rags.'

'Ah, yes. She was very beautiful.' Byuddiful.

'She still is.'

He was looking at me intently. 'You are an admirer of people, aren't you?'

'Of some people.'

'Me too,' he said. 'I admire you.'

'But you don't know me.'

'I admire what I know so far. You're calm and dignified. And yet you can get up and dance like that, so all the other ladies join in. You have traditional English good manners. You are modest and yet confident.' He grinned. 'You swim alone in the Atlantic.'

I was *bouleversée*. I might even have blushed. I'd never been good with compliments and I'd certainly never received so many in quick succession, and from one person.

'I don't know what to say . . .'

'Of course you don't.'

'But I'm glad you think that. And glad you asked me here this evening.'

'And now you're here?'

'Happy. Really happy.'

'Me too.' He got up and removed our plates to the sink. 'Would you like some coffee?'

'No thank you.'

'Another glass of wine? A cup of tea?'

I shook my head. He came and stood close to me, picking up my hand from where it lay on the table and looking down at it as he spoke: 'Would you come to bed with me?'

I knew what my answer was, but still had to ask: 'Is that the reason you invited me?'

'Not directly.' He stroked my hair, closing his eyes. 'But I wanted to get closer to you . . . And now we have, don't you think we'd be good together?'

We were. Oh, we were . . .

Like the rest of the evening it was both easy – so *easy* – and a revelation. It made me realise I had come to believe this was not for me. Not even with Daniel. Indeed, this evening showed my friendship with Daniel in its true, untruthful light. The real truth, it seemed, was that I had never wanted this enough, nor had anyone wanted *me* so much, to make me let go and surrender completely. This was different – this singing intimacy of his skin on my warm skin, and the shock of him too – the different texture of his body, the smell of him, the lovely, tentative exploration and the rapturous discovery. The wildness, and the peace.

Afterwards we lay face to face with our arms wrapped round each other, my forehead resting on his chest. We were quiet, but I could feel his fingers stroking my back, still communicating, not abandoning me. I thought that this was how it should feel – free, but safe.

At last he said softly, 'I was right, wasn't I?'

I nodded.

'And you go home tomorrow?'

'Yes.'

'So,' he said, kissing me, 'we were just in time.'

An hour later, he took me home. In the car he played Ella Fitzgerald. I kept looking at his hands on the steering-wheel – hands that could make clocks well again, and which had brought me back to life. When we reached the house he took a pen from his pocket, and wrote a number on the back of my hand.

'Washable ink,' he said, with a smile. 'Copy or forget.'

Inside, only the hall light was on although it was barely eleven.

'Ros is being discreet,' he remarked. 'Or is she always early to bed?'

'No. Nor discreet either, actually.'

'I wish you weren't going back. But that was a great evening. I'm so glad we had it.'

'And me.'

'Here's to your dreams, Bobby.' He lifted my hand and tapped the number gently with his forefinger before kissing it. 'Good-night.'

As I opened the front door I turned, and we waved to one another. I closed the door and stood there, every inch of me humming with contentment. I supposed that this had been a one-night stand, so why did I not feel dissatisfied, used, foolish, embarrassed?

As I tiptoed over the landing like a teenager, I heard Ros's sleepy voice.

'Dirty stop-out.'

428

'Night, Ros.'

In my room I washed my face, cleaned my teeth and got into bed. But I couldn't sleep. And an hour later I turned on the lamp, fetched a biro from my bag, and, deciphering the smudged figures as best I could, wrote his number on the band's business card. The Fabs, they were called. To make your occasion special.

It wasn't mentioned again. The next day was taken up with the practicalities of packing up for the journey home, and the drive to St Malo. But over drinks – vodka-tonics this time – on the ferry, my friend remarked: 'So. Roberta. Here's to you.'

We clinked glasses. 'Ros. Cheers.'

'I believe this trip has witnessed a rite of passage.'

I kept a poker face. 'In what way?'

'It will go down in history as the time you stopped calling me Spud.'

CHAPTER NINETEEN

―――――○○○○――――――

Miranda, 1985

Miranda and Fred were married in a civil ceremony at Chelsea Town Hall, with a small party afterwards at the White Tower. They kept it as quiet as they could, but to Marjorie's undisguised delight there were still plenty of press outside both register office and restaurant. Miranda wore a white trouser suit and Fred dark grey with a blue shirt. His gardenia was in his buttonhole, his wife's behind her ear. On Miranda's side, Dale and Kaye did not attend, although the remaining Roadrunners and the Worsleys did. Fred's guest list included his son and daughter in-law, and close friends from Oxford and Northumberland. They had decided, to the disappointment of Marjorie and the representatives of the press, that there would be no grace-and-favour invitees. This was a society wedding in name only.

They spent a week in a house lent to them by friends in the far north of Scotland where they passed the brief, bitterly cold, brilliant days walking on an empty silver beach, and the long, snuggling nights in a bedroom that had an open fire. During this time Miranda reminded him of their first meeting.

'Kensington,' she said. 'Now that *was* a society wedding.'

'And a very narrow escape.'

She teased him. 'You said the bridegroom should have been you!'

'I was wrong.'

'But it might have been you.'

'Yes, it might, but fortunately for both of us the young lady hitched her wagon to a more reliable star and a less demanding house.'

'Were you in love with her?' asked Miranda.

'Almost. But fortunately,' he added, kissing her, 'I'd known Crystal, so I was saved.'

The house and the people associated with it were on Miranda's side from the first, as if they could read her heart and knew its good intentions. The tolerance of the whole household to her first months – years – of ignorance and uncertainty and well-meaning errors of judgement was nothing short of miraculous. She was welcomed without reserve.

For her part, Miranda found that here was something for which she had a real talent, unconnected with her looks, though the experience of modelling helped her to capitalise on it. From the start her vision of Ladycross was a lodestar that enabled her to rise above what she couldn't do, and to show her what might be achieved. She determined not to be demoralised, to believe that she had as much right as any of her forebears, illustrious or otherwise, to follow her star and imprint her personality and dreams on the proceedings. She was in love, too, and that brought everything within her grasp.

What modelling had taught her was the ability to act a role in order to become it – to put on the appearance that would beguile and recruit others. She had learned to 'be herself' in a public way. She displayed a natural combination of humility, hard work and enthusiasm, and used glamour only when it was appropriate to do so. She went with Fred to the gun-and-gumboots shop and kitted herself out with warm, serviceable outdoor clothes, a couple of weatherproof hats and tough boots. Around the house she wore spotless jeans, sweaters or shirts and flat shoes; makeup only rarely. When a social occasion did require the full former-model monty she played it to the hilt, seeing it as part of her job to glitter, and to make Fred proud of her.

Which he was. In fact, his admiration in the early days bordered on astonishment.

'Are you sure you haven't done this before?'

'Am I doing all right?'

'Frighteningly well. I can see I shall have to raise my game to keep up with you.'

'I'm a complete beginner, but keen to learn. For you, as well as for myself.' They were in bed and she kissed his neck.

'It must be very odd for you,' he mused. 'So different from what you're used to. You would tell me, wouldn't you, if it was all driving you completely round the bend?'

'Probably – but it won't.'

He pulled his head back on the pillow to look at her. 'You wouldn't just bugger off?'

'You're forgetting something. I love you, and all your worldly goods, as you put it.'

'Love me, love my house.'

'That's right.'

'What about La Bird?'

'We understand each other.'

Miranda knew this wasn't strictly true – understanding in the usual sense of the term wasn't an option where she and Beryl Bird were concerned, but they had developed a mutual regard based on appreciation of their complementary natures. Miranda decided almost at once that she would present herself as the front-woman – and, if necessary, the fall-guy – for Beryl's sweated labour. This sense of collusion put them both firmly on the same side of the fence.

She knew she'd cracked it the day she was hosting a charity lunch and came into the kitchen in what she considered the perfect grey suit and pink shirt, calculated to convey an air of beneficent authority and give offence to no one.

After only the most cursory glance, Mrs Bird said, 'Is that what you're wearing for the lunch?'

Miranda's antennae picked up the note of censure. 'I was going to, yes – why, what do you think?'

432

'It's very smart, my lady. Very elegant.'

'But not quite right? In your opinion?'

'Oh, it's absolutely right,' observed Beryl, with the merest disparaging emphasis on the last word.

Miranda positioned herself firmly in the other woman's sightline. 'Tell me. Please, Mrs Bird, be frank.'

Beryl straightened up and looked her in the eye in what Miranda knew was a woman-to-woman moment, and possibly a crucial one.

'Why don't you wear those stripy trousers? With the jacket. The ones you wore for that committee meeting.'

'The trouser suit?'

'Yes.'

Miranda was curious, and wary. There was always the possibility that Beryl was engaging in some kind of sadistic character-test. 'Isn't it a bit – jazzy for the occasion?'

'A bit,' said Beryl, returning to her chopping. 'But they'll expect it from you. Brightens them up, I dare say . . .' she murmured, stopping short of an actual compliment.

'Thank you, Mrs Bird, I appreciate it. I think that's sound advice.'

It was a risk, but she took it. Of course, there was no scientific way by which to measure the result, but the lunch went well and she could tell from the warm, bright smiles and sparkling eyes that her small contribution in the way of venue and speech were a success. That she looked a little different from the other guests seemed not only appropriate but, as Mrs Bird had indicated, desirable, and over a cup of tea and the clearing up, she told her so. 'You were right, Mrs B. You've got an instinct for these things. I must consult you more often.'

The faintest stain of pink appeared on Mrs Bird's cheeks. 'We've got a top model running the place, we might as well make the most of it.'

Still, nothing had prepared Miranda for the sheer hard graft, and the learning – on the job, as it were – of many completely new skills for which she had no natural aptitude. For all her keenness, she had imagined a life with plenty of leisure, a role more supervisory than hands-on.

433

In fact, she and Fred worked hard seven days a week, and harder some days than others. They both got up at six, and their early-morning cup of tea – which soon assumed the status of nectar and without which she was unable to function – was the only time they had together until seven in the evening, except for those rare occasions when the taking of their lunchtime sandwiches happened to coincide. As well as the farm, the maintenance of the building, the finances, the shoots and his own business involvements, Fred was a JP, a governor of the local comprehensive school and regional chairman of the Country Landowners' Association; he attended the Lords about once a month, and there were trustees' meetings in London. Bills, correspondence and paperwork of every kind flowed into Ladycross in a steady tide, and whoever was passing the desk played Canute for as long as time and money allowed.

Fred made no bones about the cash-flow problem. 'Stage one, open but don't read. Stage two, read. Stage three, place in pile with the rest. Stage four, receive the red letter and cough. Never pay till the final demand – why should the other buggers have the interest? All stages to be spaced out at intervals of several days.'

The sums involved took Miranda's breath away. Ordinary domestic bills running into thousands, running repairs into tens of thousands, security, cleaning, vehicle maintenance, staff pay, insurance – insurance! – it was enormous, beyond her capacity, like gazing up at the side of a mountain whose peak was lost in the clouds. She had to keep her focus short, to concentrate on what could be managed in any particular day or week.

She was to discover that, in spite of her inexperience and her extreme trepidation, she was more inclined than Fred to face up to the finances. The alternative was too awful to contemplate. She began to see that, in spite of Tom's mother's encouraging words, the house would not take care of itself. Ladycross had been there for centuries, but for it to remain for further centuries each owner in turn had to do their bit to keep things going. She could not have borne to be the Lady Stratton under whose supervision the place fell into decline.

She generally approached the desk and its fearsome burden

in the morning, with the first fortifying cup of tea inside her and the second in her hand. As often as not Fred would already have left, or be cooking sausages and beans in the kitchen for himself and the farm manager, Mark Maguire. The solitariness and quiet of the early morning increased her sense of kinship with Ladycross. In those hours before most people's day had begun, dark and chilly in the winter, softly lit in summer, she felt that she and the house were engaged not in a struggle but in a co-operative, mutually dependent venture. She took comfort and pleasure in the knowledge that Fred was out there, doing his bit, while she was here doing hers. It was, for Miranda, an expression of their love.

The paperwork would be mostly concerned with finances, and she'd sort it into piles mentally headed Delay, Delegate and Do, according to sound Harvard principles. It was rare that delegation was an option, but once a fortnight their book-keeper, Maggie Findhorn, came up from the village and finessed the figures.

Like Fred, Maggie had a philosophy: 'Rationalisation. Move it about, tidy it up, see the pattern, and it becomes manageable.' Her soothing numeracy skills went some way towards proving this theory, but there still remained the great rump of paperwork for which there was no such easy solution.

Structural matters she left to Fred, but the day-to-day stuff – blockages, breakages, malfunctions and mess – fell to her. There were readily available support systems in place for these situations but they had to be contacted, chased up and rigorously supervised. The notion that Lord Stratton, though a good sort, must by definition be a rich bastard, was widespread. If corners were not to be cut and advantage taken, a keen eye had to be kept on the carrying out of repairs.

The area that was most daunting, but also the one where she felt qualified to make the most useful contribution, was that of Events, of which there were many. These ranged from hosting charity meetings and fundraisers, to events particular to the house, in aid of its upkeep. In the last category there were six open weekends a year, through the summer months. These were the bread and butter of the Ladycross income, though

Miranda sometimes wondered whether the costs in additional security and staff — even allowing for trusty volunteers from Witherburn — cancelled out the perceived benefits. Fred pointed out that it wasn't all about money.

'It's PR, too,' he told her. 'And a bit more than that. This house isn't ours, or not in the private sense: it's part of the local landscape and history. Everyone has a right to see and enjoy it.'

She knew this to be true. And in fact 'the public', as she came to think of them — though who were 'the public' if not oneself, or anyone at all, in a different context? — were almost universally a pleasure to have around. Perhaps because Ladycross had no external attractions, no adventure playground, astroglide, pets' corner, miniature railway or carousel, only itself and its special atmosphere, it was spared the less obliging aspects of open days. Litter, trespass and damage, either casual or wilful, were pretty much unknown. The organisation of these weekends was vested in a set of mechanisms, which simply needed updating and activating, but Miranda made it her business to be visible, to act as hostess and guide, not only for sound commercial reasons but to remind people that, as well as being customers, they were guests in the Strattons' home. She took enormous pleasure in picking up the comments not intended for her ears: 'Isn't it beautiful, fancy living in a place like this?'; 'Someone's been busy on that silver, I'm glad it wasn't me'; 'Look at her in that picture, what they had to wear, no wonder they always look so pale . . .'; 'Fancy tea, pet? They do lovely cakes, you won't need to be cooking tonight!'; 'Let's walk around outside, it's that pretty and peaceful . . .'

Open days reminded her of her own first encounter with the Ladycross magic. She knew that this, more than any commercial or practical reasons, was what drove her in the service of the house.

Then there were the staff parties at Christmas and midsummer, the shooting parties in the winter and the country-house breaks whenever they could be fitted in. It was a shock to find that three-quarters of the catering was done by Mrs Bird with the assistance of a peripatetic (and hotly resented) Cordon

Bleu graduate, and Miranda herself, whose lack of culinary skills to begin with equipped her to be nothing more than a scullery-maid, on pot-washing and veg-scrubbing fatigues. She aimed at least to be ahead of the game, to be always ready for the next catering marathon, but it was hard to be even one step ahead of Mrs Bird who had been on this particular treadmill for fifteen years and in that time had seen two former Lady Strattons come and go.

Cooking was only one of the areas where she had neither experience, training nor aptitude. She had never arranged flowers, done public speaking, been in charge of a fearsome budget, looked after dogs, sat on committees or employed other people. She had never wanted to run a hotel, let alone one where she and Fred were added-value, expected to entertain the guests as though they were personal friends. She had been a public figure, but always beyond the barrier of the camera lens, and with its collusion. The highly personal scrutiny to which she was now subjected, freighted with expectation and some suspicion, was something altogether different.

But she acted the part, kept her head high and seldom blinked.

Of all the events it was the rock concert that was closest to her heart. It took place every second or third year, so she'd been at Ladycross more than two before the issue of the next concert arose. Fred, as its instigator, had a love-hate relationship with Rock on the Manor. 'It makes us money, but I sometimes feel I've spawned a hydra, always putting out new and ever-more-monstrous heads.'

'You don't have to do it.'

'I like it. It's fun, it's democratic, it's profitable. But it's getting too big.'

Miranda remembered when she had come that first time, over twenty years ago, as the glamorous sidekick of the Roadrunners. They and the roadies had come up in a couple of blacked-out buses, which did London – Witherburn in three hours flat. What she remembered was chiefly the music, and the pervasive atmosphere of sex and substances. They slept in the bus. In the early morning she'd climbed out for some air and seen the

437

house, unknown to her then, rising out of the mist like an Edmund Dulac castle, or a vast, enchanted UFO hovering over the valley. In fact, in her exhausted, spaced-out state it might have been either of those things, or a figment of her imagination. The next night, after the Roadrunners' set, she and Nicky had walked away from the concert site, for what seemed miles into the fields, and made love under the stars. It was the starlight, the dark hills, and being high that had made it so great – without those, she could see now, it would have been just another casual fuck, and a pretty agricultural one at that. Instead it was magical, transcendent, the beginning of something extraordinary . . .

She said, 'I think you should make the concert bigger.'

Fred laughed. 'What?'

'Make it so big it takes on its own momentum. Stretch it over a whole weekend.'

'Steady on!'

'I'll help you. You could lay on a campsite, charge for all those peripheral services – food, loos, fortune-tellers—'

'Drug-dealers, clap clinics.'

'Don't be a Jeremiah, Fred, it doesn't suit you.'

'I'll think about it.'

'We can think about it. It could be fun. Ladycross could turn into the Glastonbury of the north.'

'That's what concerns me,' he said, but she could tell from his expression and his tone of voice that, sooner or later, it would happen.

Though she was by no means as confident as she sounded about the organisation, Miranda knew she was right. The experience of her second Rock on the Manor, with its diametrically different perspective, showed her that. The place was turned upside down for a single concert lasting from two p.m. till midnight. There still had to be AA signs, a police presence, a massive parking operation, additional security, medical facilities, mind-blowing public liability insurance, advance publicity stretching back a year, and hundreds of extra staff. The bands and their entourages – all of which had grown exponentially since her days with the Roadrunners – needed to arrive in advance and park their luxury battle buses, often for two nights. If all this had to be in place anyway, she asked herself and Fred, why not get full value from it?

Then there was the music. The concert was in a time warp: warhorse performers from the sixties and seventies, blasts from the past coasting on the glory days, along with a couple of more up-to-date solo artists who had somehow managed the tricky generational crossover. All of them fine in their way, but not calculated to bring in the newly rich young.

The relaunch of Rock on the Manor Miranda made her special responsibility. She used her name and contacts shame-lessly to attract bands, sponsorship and publicity; and having done so she delegated wherever possible, knowing that people would be only too happy to lend their efforts and expertise to what was obviously a class enterprise. Aware that local support would be crucial she held two meetings at Witherburn village hall, to keep everyone informed, to elicit opinion, consult and confer, and involve as many people as possible in the undertaking. She told them this was an occasion that would benefit not only Ladycross but, if they played their cards right, the whole community.

As she suspected, there was some initial local resistance to the idea. Like Fred, but with rather more seriousness, they invoked drugs, vandalism, petty theft and wild sex in funny places. She assured them that if there was any of that, it would be on Ladycross land, and the Strattons would take care of it. But, she told them, these things took their tone from the top – Rock on the Manor would be great music for discerning people of all ages, a gathering of fans who knew how to enjoy themselves without tearing the place apart . . . She carried the day, and her listeners, by sheer force of personality, the shameless exertion of sex appeal, and the skin of her teeth. She employed the time-honoured tactic, so beloved by Queen's College, of disarming protest with responsibility, enlisting villagers' help in setting up, and clearing up, as parking stewards, crèche-attendants and sandwich-makers. She knew all too well that a lot rode on the success or otherwise of the festival (a conveniently user-friendly term), and that in either case the buck would stop firmly with her.

Long before that, though, in her third year as Lady Stratton, there was one of those serendipitous happenings that brought her back into contact with her old life. On one of the rare evenings when their schedules synchronised and they were able to have a drink together, Fred handed her a letter. 'This came today – think it's more your bag than mine.'

Her eye skimmed over the request for a fashion shoot for one of the snootiest brands in London, and paused at the signature. 'It's Noah! Oh, we must!'

'I will if you will. Who's Noah?'

'Well!' She tapped the letter. '*Now* he's publicity director for Togs and Co. When I knew him he was like Terence Stamp's better-looking brother.'

'In that case,' said Fred, 'I'm not having him near the place.'

'Oh, go on, he'll fancy you rotten.'

'I demand danger money.'

'They won't pay anything, unless there's any accidental damage. But Ladycross will be in all the photographs, and credited in dozens of glossy mags all over the world. It's exactly what we need – beautiful house, beautiful people, beautiful clothes, you too can buy a beautiful life!'

'I bow to your knowledge of these things. Especially if the place is going to be awash with leggy lovelies.'

'It will be,' she said. 'Noah may not be interested, but he can pick 'em.'

The shoot was in mid-October, with the accent, as Noah put it over the phone, on mists, mellow fruitfulness and autumnal colours. 'And Labradors, of course,' he said. 'Us townies don't think we've seen rural posh unless there's a Labrador in the picture. You do have several, I take it? Or do I need to book a couple?'

'No,' said Miranda, 'we have springer spaniels just as good. And an ancient dachshund called Doris.'

'Please! Dachshunds I can do. There's more than you can poke a stick at in the Finchley Road . . . But it will be lovely to see you.'

The Togs team arrived in convoy on a Wednesday morning.

Fred had arranged himself a clear morning to welcome them, and it was odd for Miranda to be on the other side of this particular fence, standing there and watching the three somewhat rumpled – and terrifyingly young – models disembark. Introducing herself and Fred, she knew that she hadn't been much older than this when she had started out, but these girls were waifs – so young, so skinny they looked barely pubescent. It was impossible to imagine them modelling the kind of clothes Togs were known for. Fred made it his business to look after them.

They went into the library where Mrs Bird had laid on coffee, tea and homemade biscuits. All the girls wanted to smoke: Noah told them not to, Fred said it was okay. Noah himself had grown large and prosperous, in his townie's country kit of spotless desert boots, green cords and a sweater draped round the shoulders of his Paul Smith button-down shirt.

'This is wonderful . . . absolutely gorgeous,' he declared, gazing about in admiration. 'I can see our problem will be getting the clothes to come out ahead of the house.'

'You'll manage, I'm sure,' said Fred, 'with such a bevy of beauty at your disposal.'

Miranda was by no means sure how well this benign remark – intended as gallant but sounding a little patronising – would go down, but she hadn't bargained for the power of her husband's charm. She could also tell instantly that one of the models, a redhead with a body like a racing snake and a smug, sensuous cat's face, was setting her cap at him. At every stage and in every job there were women like that, who had to give it a try for no better reason than that they could. It made Miranda feel graciously, wickedly forgiving. Poor little thing.

After the coffee Fred went about his business. The photographer asked if he could take a look round 'to see what we've got'. Miranda showed the rest of them to the playroom, which they were to use as a dressing room. With the models firmly in the hands of the stylist and the fashion editor and the room resembling something between a jumble sale, a bottled-water factory and backstage at the London Palladium, she and Noah withdrew.

'I want a cig,' he confided, 'but unlike that rabble I will not have one in your beautiful house.'

'I'm afraid we do.'

'Shame on you. Anyway, I'm going outside the front door.'

They went and sat on the wooden seat overlooking the woods, and the rooftops of Witherburn.

'I shouldn't really be here,' said Noah, lighting his own cigarette, then hers, 'but this was an opportunity too good to miss, so I gave myself a freebie.'

'You're doing well for yourself, aren't you? If I didn't know you better I'd say you look positively respectable.'

'It's a job ... The girls are mostly sweet, even if they are jailbait, not that that bothers me. And Togs is full of the most nicey-nicey people you could wish to meet, real heart-of-England stuff, mouths chock full of plums and silver spoons and not a mean bone in their bodies. They're a traditional business that's taken on a new concept and run with it.'

'What new concept is that?'

'That they have a particular style, which is essentially upmarket and conservative, but it can be adapted, and be young and fun too without losing its elegance.' He pointed his cigarette at her. 'You used to do that.'

'I suppose so ... They look so tiny – and so *young*.'

'They catch 'em young, these days. They're pretty savvy, most of them. And the boys! It's nice work, I can tell you.' In the wake of a lecherous grin, he asked, 'And what about you? Lady Stratton, God help us. But his lordship seems a real sweetheart.'

'He is. Fred's my better half. I'm completely in love with him.'

'As much now as at the beginning?'

'More,' she said, and then, 'No, different. This is what I always wanted, Noah, and thought I'd be lucky to find. Real love, to last down all the days.'

'Well ...' Noah dropped his cigarette and ground it out on the grass with his foot '... I'm very glad for you. Not a lot of people can say what you just said. I envy you, I don't mind admitting. Paul and I are a great team but, I mean – true love, *and* all this?'

She picked up the butt and placed it carefully on the arm of the seat. 'All this has got nothing to do with it, I promise you.' Hearing herself, she added, 'Actually that's not true. I'd have loved Fred just the same, just as much without Ladycross. But since the house *is* part of him, I suppose I love him the more for it.'

'You don't have to justify yourself to me, my sweet.'

'I know, but I want to. Being Lady Stratton's no soft option, Noah. This place is a tough task-master. I swear I didn't know what work was till I came here. It's dawn till dark every day, and long after that on most. We have to make money just to keep the place running, and then more money to preserve it and have it looking good after we've gone. And *we* have to look good, and be nice to hundreds of people we don't know.'

'Poor Rags, you'll have me in tears – but you're so good at that!'

'Shut up, it's harder than it sounds. I'm just glad I had the training I did. If I'd been a lousy housekeeper with no domestic skills *and* shy as a mouse, I'd be stuffed!'

'That's my girl.'

'Still, it's time off for good behaviour while you're all here.'

Noah and the Togs stylist, Tasha, were staying at Ladycross; the models were in the Dower House. The photographer and the makeup artist, who were having, as Noah put, 'a thang', had opted for the Witherburn Arms. To Miranda they all seemed younger, more distrait, unfocused, scruffier, than similar people of her vintage, but she was prepared to accept that this was a sign of old age. The redhead was Lizzie Cloons, already something of a star. The dark-haired *gamine* was known only as Faith, capitalising perhaps on a certain fey other-worldliness. The third girl, by far the youngest, was Olivia Hanson, and she was the one who reminded Miranda of herself. She was the least pretty but the most striking, with a face that could seem too decided and bony, but which glowed with life in front of the camera, when every plane and curve was made to sing.

Tasha, though, was a type she recognised. She was a hand-some woman in her early thirties who, to show that she was not in competition with her charges, affected an unkempt appearance and a careworn manner. Her deep voice would not have been out of place at a hunt ball. She chain-smoked and nibbled the ends of her fingers, a curious mixture of booming confidence and restless unease.

By the end of the first day (casualwear on the front lawn) the models had emerged from behind their looks and become individuals, this in spite of having been transformed into toffish vamps with smoothly waved skullcaps of hair, skin like vellum, and juicy scarlet lips that screamed 'nil by mouth'. Seeing them being pushed and picked at and pinned and prettified Miranda remembered what bloody hard work it was. It was not demeaning, for the purposes of being photographed, to be an object: it was your job. You were a commodity, and it was your task to be the best commodity you could. She went into the house and found some Polo mints – boiled sweets, the model's friend – and took them out. It was, she thought, as she passed the tube round, rather like feeding thoroughbred horses with sugar lumps.

Lizzie watched her walk away. 'You know who she is, don't you?'

'Noah said she used to be a model?' ventured Faith.

'Rags,' said Olivia. 'Did you ever see pictures of her?'

'She was fucking amazing,' conceded Lizzie.

'Still is, don't you reckon? I mean she looks incredible anyway, but whatever it is she's still got it.'

'And married a lord as well. So she knew how to use it.'

They stared at Miranda's receding back-view. Faith sighed, murmured, 'We should be so lucky.'

That evening, only Noah and Tasha had dinner at Ladycross. The girls opted for takeaway pub pizza in the Dower House, and an early night ('Or they're toast,' as Tasha put it). Tasha herself appeared for dinner in a silver jacket and palazzo pants with silver high-heeled mules. The transformation astonished Fred, but not Miranda, who could have predicted it.

'It makes me feel I should have made more effort,' he muttered *sotto voce*, pouring the drinks.

'It's because the competition's safely out of the way.'

'If you weren't Rags I'd call that a miaow. And, anyway, what about you?'

'For these purposes I'm not Rags, I'm Miranda Montclere so I don't count.'

Noah was impeccably groomed in a dark suit with a cobalt shirt and tie, soft black loafers, silver cufflinks and a discreet whiff of Armani for men.

'Fred,' Miranda could detect the simple pleasure Noah took in this familiarity, 'Fred, may I just ask about our eveningwear shoot?'

Fred gave him a smile both charming and wary. 'You don't want me in it, do you?'

'No, no, never fear!' Noah positively chortled. 'Though we may want photos of the two of you in the catalogue somewhere ... No, Tash and I were wondering about a suitable outdoor location ...'

'Something not too obvious,' explained Tasha. She turned to Miranda. 'Lady Stratton—'

'Miranda.'

'Miranda, I remember those breakthrough pictures of you in the rain. In the big frock and the boots? Well, our customers aren't quite ready for that, but I would like to do at least some of the pictures outside – sophistication in the wild, you know?'

'I do.' She looked at Fred. 'The folly!'

He held up his hands in surrender. These esoteric choices amused and delighted him. 'I'm somewhat out of my depth here, this is your area. You must give our friends exactly what they want.'

'Dogs too?' enquired Noah.

The following day, with the shoot up and running and the team due to leave later that evening, it was business as usual. Fred had a Landowners' Association meeting in Newcastle. It fell to Miranda to confront the groaning desk in its lair, and work through a list of twenty or so telephone calls, many of them associated with Rock on the Manor. Noah, at something of a loose end, wanted her to play. 'Don't you have today off, too?'

'No. And you have to let me get on or I won't have this evening off either.'

'Oh dear, I'm sorry, you have all these responsibilities . . .'

She caught the hint of affectionate mockery. 'You'd better believe it.'

'I'm sorry. Tell me about them.'

'Noah – after I've *done* some of them, all right?'

'All right.'

He appeared to have got the message, for he absented himself so successfully that when she took Doris out in the late afternoon she still hadn't seen him.

It was a perfect, golden, smoky autumn afternoon with the low sun firing the trees and dazzling off the windows of Ladycross. It wasn't necessary to walk far with the little dog: she was stricken in years and arthritic, quite happy to waddle along in a leisurely way, pausing now and then to snuffle in the leaves.

Miranda took her down the slope beyond the barns – turned into business units – then tracked across the side of the hill towards the trees that surrounded the folly. She knew the shoot was continuing until four, but it was very quiet, and the vehicles were parked out of sight. As they approached the wood a large, rangy dog something like a greyhound appeared and stood watching them, its ears pricked attentively. If Doris saw the stranger at all she took no notice. Miranda had never seen it before. It was still for a second, observing them intently, then loped off down the hill with long, floating strides and out of sight.

A curious thing happened as they came into the wood. Miranda knew it was no more than a hundred yards from the edge of the trees to the folly, and yet this afternoon it seemed more. Perhaps the shadows after the bright sunlight created a false perspective, but the trees seemed to close behind them and to extend, mysterious and half lit, ahead. Doris, already quite tired, pottered at her heels, silent on the leaf mould.

It was almost eerie, but then to her relief she saw one of the girls – the redhead – coming towards her. She would have made a beautiful picture, exactly like that, with her long, flowing pale green dress and stole, and her hair elaborately piled up, like a wood nymph or a dryad drifting between the trees. She was walking with long, purposeful strides, and she didn't pass close to them. Miranda guessed she was taking a break, for a smoke or the call of nature, or simply to get away for a couple of minutes.

Almost the second the girl had passed she found she'd reached the folly. It was rather odd, like rising from deep water. The light, the sound, seemed to change. Noah, perched on a shooting stick, hailed her.

'Hi there, come to check up on us? We're nearly through here. Oh, you brought Doris . . . come and see Uncle Noah . . .'

He picked up the dog. Tasha and the others were conferring. Two of the spaniels, Trigger and Mark, were sitting patiently, tongues lolling, on the grass. The girls were standing like the three graces, posed artfully between the pillars of the folly.

Miranda gazed at them. Three graces. Three. And all of them in white.

CHAPTER TWENTY

Claudia, 145

Gaius thought that tonight – the night of his parents' party – was almost perfect. He didn't trouble his head as to why, it was just – everything.

He loved to lie in bed on these long summer evenings with the cheerful, uneven sounds of a party on the other side of the house, and the quiet of the garden outside. Although his window of pale green glass meant it was quite dark in his room, he could see out through his open bedroom door. Sometimes one of the slaves would go by, with a purposeful air, in the direction of the dining room, or less urgently if he or she were simply taking a stroll. Gaius felt safe, protected on all sides by his world, his home. To complete his sense of security Tiki lay in the doorway, his front paws stretched out before him and his head up, scanning the scene. When someone came by, his ears would go down and his long tail skim back and forth over the tiles in acknowledgement, but now that he was old it would take more than that to get him on to his feet at the end of a hot day.

The party was well into its noisier phase. The drone and warble of bagpipes provided a descant to the babel of people's voices. Gaius liked the sound of the pipes, which he thought of as the sound of this place, the part of Britain where he belonged – a mixture of the local dialect, and the wind in the stones, the cry of curlews and geese and the calling of sheep on the hills. It soothed and pleased him as it soothed and pleased his father, but he knew his mother didn't care for it. To her, bagpipes were nothing but a discordant racket.

And there she was, stepping out on to the terrace and pausing for a second to drink in the evening. She was tall and beautiful, like the statues of Venus, or Diana: Gaius liked to see her when she didn't know she could be seen. But there was that persistent small fear, too, that she might escape, as she was doing now, and simply never come back. There was something unrooted in his mother: she flew like a hunting hawk, attached to the rest of them by a fragile, invisible bond of trust and, he supposed, love.

She moved away, out of sight, and now Tiki did get to his feet and, with a brief apologetic look over his shoulder, followed his mistress. Gaius didn't mind him going, not if it meant he was keeping his mother company.

He dozed, as the light gradually softened, giving way to that in-between time when the day was suspended, hushed, mysterious. His father's singing prevented him falling asleep completely. It wasn't very good, but he liked to hear it because it meant his father was happy and enjoying himself. The spell of his own happiness, though, and the illusion of the evening's perfection, was fractured by his mother's absence. Gaius wished she was in there too, smiling and applauding with the others, instead of wandering away with her own thoughts for company.

Publius finished singing amid a general burble of appreciation. The bagpipe started up again, but relegated to the status of background music – Gaius guessed that his father had sent the piper outside, perhaps in deference to guests less enthusiastic than himself. He was beginning to feel really sleepy, but wanted to see his mother come back before he allowed himself to give in. To help him stay awake he reached across and picked up the little dog that Madoc had bought him. He'd handled it so much that it already felt warmer and smoother than when he'd first got it. He had the idea that the dog was a sort of extension of Tiki, that if he fondled its ears and rubbed its flanks and called it by name he would be making contact with the real dog.

It was his favourite thing. To him it was magic that someone could fashion metal into an animal that looked almost alive. Sometimes if he glanced at it, and then away, he fancied that it *did* move: he caught the lift of its head and the twitch of its tail from the corner of his eye.

He turned on to his side, and put the dog on the pillow where he could see it. He might have dozed for a while. The next thing was that Tiki trotted into the room and jumped on to the end of the bed, folding his long legs underneath him like a deer.

Claudia came in after him, her tall, dark figure silhouetted for a moment in the grey square of the doorway, and then a closer, rustling presence as she sat down on the side of the bed. He could smell the summer night on her clothes, and her hand and lips were cool when she kissed him.

Because he still wasn't properly asleep she lit the lamp for him. She always said it was better not to struggle when you felt wakeful.

'Father was singing,' he told her. 'It was *awful*.'

He said this not to be treacherous but to make her smile and protest: 'He's got a nice voice!' He loved to hear her stick up for his father like that, even if she was laughing at the same time.

'So why did he wait till you'd gone?'

'A very good point.'

She picked up the iron dog and turned it over in her hands while she told him about who was at the party. He asked if Flavia could come and say good-night, not because she was nice, which she was, but because he wanted his mother to return with her.

'I'll ask her ... Don't stay awake, though, if you feel sleepy.'

'I shan't.'

She replaced the dog and got up. 'We'll see.'

This time Tiki didn't follow Claudia. His tail stirred the sheet briefly, but by the time she reached the door he'd slithered up the bed and tucked his muzzle into the crook of Gaius' neck.

Much later, Claudia did bring Flavia to his room. Tiki

450

didn't stir. The lamp had almost burned out and though Gaius wasn't fully asleep, he foxed, because he wanted to hear what they said.

The two women stood by the bed, he could smell Flavia's sweet perfume, and feel a stray strand of hair tickle his cheek as she leaned over to gaze at him. She missed her married daughter, and grandchildren. As his mother arranged the sheet, she whispered,

'He's asleep . . . Claudia, he's getting so handsome! But who does he look like? Not you.'

'Only a little. And I catch a trace of his father now and then. But mostly he's just himself.'

'Which is how it should be. Look at this great foolish dog! Don't you worry that he'll get on top of him?'

'No. Tiki's his guardian.'

'Sweet!' The lamp was extinguished and Gaius felt the women move away. 'You have everything here, Claudia. You're so lucky.'

'I know . . .' He heard in his mother's voice the 'but', unspoken, like a drop of cold water that chilled him and made his spirits plummet. He wanted to call her back, and knew she would come if he did, but that would have exposed his deception. And, perhaps, hers.

Tiki snuggled against him, and the dog's long, warm tongue wiped his salty cheek.

'You kept him awake with your singing,' said Claudia afterwards.

'Didn't he like it?'

'"Awful" was the word he used.'

'Is that so?' Publius was rather pleased with this, as she had known he would be. 'Well, the boy's young and has an untrained ear.'

'Flavia thought he was getting very handsome.'

'Now, there he *is* like his father.'

Claudia put her hand over his heart. He used to do that for her, place her hand and hold it there, so she could feel the truth of what he was unable to say. It was a long time since he had done that, and she missed it.

'I think he's like you in many ways.'

'Hmm . . .' Publius was drifting. 'I'll take your word for it . . .'

She watched him fall asleep, as she so often did with both husband and and son. It always saddened her a little, because the peace that came down over his face was like a curtain, separating them. On occasions like this evening, with friends about them and the wine flowing, seeing them both with others' eyes, she had the illusion of bridging the small, black distance between herself and Publius. But it was only an illusion and with his disappearance into sleep the distance opened once more. It was still no more than a fault-line, like the ones in the new plaster on the temple walls, but she feared that it would widen with the years until it separated them completely. He had never again mentioned that terrible part of his past, and he had not dreamed of it either, as far as she knew. It shocked her that his need to keep her out operated like a metal vice, even when he was exhausted.

And in recent years a small, treacherous hope had somehow slipped into her mind and taken root there – a hope not just that they might all return to Rome, but that if Publius did not wish to (and he declared he did not), she and Gaius might go anyway. She would daydream about showing him the house where she had been brought up, and all the wonders and gaudy delights of the greatest city on earth . . . and about taking him to the farm at Brixia, and the seaside at Ostia, for warm, sandy holidays . . . and watching as he heard the sounds of Italy and tasted the fruit and wine of the warm southern country that was his true home . . .

Her fantasy never went beyond this, but disappeared in something like a heat-haze. If she was truthful she never saw Publius in these imaginings. She told herself this was because he no longer wished to visit Rome, but the truth, when she faced it, was that she didn't want him there. The fantasy was of herself and her young son, rediscovering their lives. The ending was uncertain, unimagined. So she never knew if it included a return to Britain, or a reunion with Publius.

And yet, lying with her cheek against his back as he slept, she could not imagine life without him.

They had made a track for the races on the open ground to the north of the parade ground, between the garrison and the Wall. The organisers had done their best to produce a scaled-down version of the Circus Maximus – or how they imagined it to be – but conditions were against them. There was no lack of space, but the ground was uneven and the thin turf pitted with holes where the largest and most treacherous chunks of rock had been prised out for safety's sake. There was only one stand of seats, for the legate and his party, and for the rest it was a case of establishing a base as close as possible to the double row of post-and-rail fencing that surrounded the long oval of the arena.

Claudia had asked Publius to invite Madoc to meet them there, since it was he who'd taken Gaius to visit the charioteer. She and Gaius went up to the meeting in the litter, and Publius rode alongside.

It wasn't just the ground that was against them. It was one of those brilliant but wild British days, with huge clouds streaming overhead, so that one moment you were shivering in shadow and the next shielding your eyes from the glare. The pennants at either end of the *spina* that ran down the centre of the arena strained taut, and the horses in the collecting areas were fretful and spooked, eyes rolling, manes and tails fluttering like banners in the wind. Their edginess infected those who weren't taking part – old nags between wagon shafts nodded their heads and pawed the ground, and usually quiet riding horses sidled and pranced.

Gaius was white-faced with an excitement that was close to dread. He couldn't eat or drink anything that was on offer, and he couldn't speak, either. The atmosphere around the racecourse was hectic, like the *vicus* only more so, everyone shouting their heads off, buying and selling, cooking, brewing, making bets, hailing old friends and trading insults with rivals. Dogs ran everywhere, but this time they'd left Tiki at home with Severina, who wasn't keen on being alone in the house, these days. The dog wasn't used to being left behind; they'd had to chain him up till they were out of sight to prevent him following.

As a former commanding officer, Publius had been allocated seats at the lower end of the stand. Madoc wasn't entitled to a place here, but he and Gauis perched on the shafts of the litter. He could see the boy was nearly sick with anticipation, and probably would be unless diverted.

'Shall we see if we can find Brasca, and wish him luck?'

Gaius nodded, big-eyed.

'With your permission, madam?'

Madoc had already established that Brasca, his groom and the *quadrigae* were on the far side of the arena where they had some protection from the buffeting north-west wind. There were two other teams in that area, one of greys with heavily dappled necks and hindquarters, and another of slightly bigger, heavier dark bays. Brasca's little red horses were the best-looking, but playing up, tossing their heads and skittering. Brasca himself looked splendid in his driver's gear, but his face was shiny with sweat and his expression harassed.

'The going's a bit hard for these,' he said to Madoc, over Gaius' head, 'and this weather doesn't suit them either. A nice, mild, damp northern day is what we were hoping for.'

'What are your chances?'

'Well, there are only the three teams . . . but I can't see us winning in these conditions. Our race is a showpiece as much as anything. I'll be happy to get round without a fall or damage to the vehicle.'

'The horses won't get hurt, will they?' asked Gaius.

'Listen to him. No, don't you worry, my boy, I'll look after them. They're my pride and joy. Here, you want to get up on the chariot?'

Gaius wasn't sure that he did but he'd already been lifted off his feet and was now set down on the driving plat-form, precariously suspended over the chariot's back axle. He felt the platform swing and give beneath his feet – and they weren't even moving! It also seemed higher than it had

454

appeared from the ground, a small, unstable and terrifyingly unprotected position from which to control those fiery red horses . . .

'Can I get down?'

'He wants to get down . . . Course you can. Now, when you see us come hell for leather down the straight you'll have some idea what it feels like to be me.'

They stroked and patted the horses, but they weren't the same gentle, greedy pets they'd met in the stable behind Brasca's house. Here they were keen to be gone, stamping and snorting, finding the attention tiresome.

'Good luck, then,' said Madoc, as they left.

'I'll need it!'

When they got back to the stand Gaius was shivering and Claudia made him wrap himself in a rug from the litter. He was embarrassed, but he put up with it for her sake. A couple of boys of his own age were tearing about among the spectators with a kind of mad, unfocused energy, not exactly fighting but rough-housing, ricocheting off people and wagons, making dogs bark and men curse and receiving the odd cuff on their way. As far as Gaius was concerned they might as well have been another species, as different from himself as the mythical beasts in pictures. He both feared and admired them. Perhaps this was how his father expected him to be. If so, there was no hope.

At one point the bigger of the two boys crashed into him, and in the split second that their eyes met he felt the cut of the other's scorn. He might not understand them but they, it seemed, thought they understood him.

Blushing, he muttered instinctively, 'Sorry . . .' But Madoc grabbed the boy by the shoulder of his tunic and gave him a shove.

'Get off and do that somewhere else. You've caused enough trouble for one day!'

The grab, the shout, the rough push would have terrified Gaius if he'd been subjected to them, but the boy just gave Madoc a hard, mocking look and careered off in pursuit of his friend, to create mayhem in another part of the crowd.

'Little devils,' said Madoc. 'And you can bet they'll be thieving as well. Are you all right?'

Gaius nodded brusquely but kept his face averted so Madoc wouldn't see his mouth trembling. The tutor's sympathy put the final, exquisite touch to his humiliation. Here, in this thrilling, noisy, tough place, with his parents sitting alongside, he didn't want to be the awkward boy wrapped in the rug, the sort who was jostled by other boys because they scarcely noticed him and when they did they didn't care. He didn't want to be the object of their contempt, or Madoc's concern. He knew that he was somebody: he felt it when he was out wandering in the hills with the dog, or sitting dreaming by the temple. He had big dreams and great, complicated thoughts, but because he could not charge about and shriek and trade blows and insults he was invisible, a nothing.

Madoc gave his arm a little shake. 'Hey . . . First race is starting.'

It was a relief to focus on the race, to be truly one of the crowd, relegated to anonymity by the action in the arena. A great roar of glee rose up on all sides, and sent a swirling squadron of small black birds into the air from the bent trees on the hilltop. The first was a race for civilian riders. They rode bareback with thin, loose bridles, and their mounts weren't gleaming and fired-up like the chariot teams. But when the horn sounded for the start of the race the horses sprang forward with their necks stretched out, consuming the rough ground with their small hoofs, the riders leaning forward and screaming encouragement, flailing their whips, their legs swinging loosely so it seemed impossible that they wouldn't fall off. When they came along the straight past the stand the ground trembled and Gaius had a swift, vivid impression of violent movement, the horses' coats already streaked with scummy foam and their gaping nostrils wet, the riders not heroes but tradesmen and farmers, rough, tough and dirty. They were so close that he was sprayed with sweat, saliva, and grit thrown up from the ground. It almost choked him, but no one else seemed bothered by it.

'Gaius!' Claudia leaned round from her seat, he could see her elation. 'Which one do you want to win?'

'I don't mind.'

'I want the little man with the bald head to win – he's so brave!'

He looked at the riders, now tearing up the far side on their second lap of five. The bald man was second from last. Why was he brave? Because he was small? Ugly? Older than the others? Perhaps, thought Gaius, he was brave just for being in the race, something he himself couldn't conceive of doing ever, in his life.

By the last lap two of the riders had fallen off, a third horse had stumbled, and there remained Claudia's favourite and a wild young man with shaggy black hair and a beard that grew down his neck so he looked like a bear. In his dark face his eye-whites gleamed and his wide, yelling mouth was red as though it were full of blood. Gaius thought he looked mad. He won, by a long margin, and for an encore went round the arena standing on his horse's back, waving his fist, while the little bald man cheekily followed in his wake, waving to the cheers as though he were the champion.

Claudia rose to her feet – Gaius wished she wouldn't – and applauded him. He responded with a humorous little bow. Publius laughed, a real, warm laugh, and there was no doubt that much of the applause was for the little man, for being composed, cheerful and impertinent in defeat. The legate gave the laurels to the bear, but rewarded the loser with a smile and a kind word that seemed to Gaius to be worth more.

There was a race for cavalrymen after that, a more disciplined affair but less fast. No one fell and it was a close-run thing until the very last straight, when one rider seemed to release his black horse like an arrow from a bow, to leave the others in his wake. Gaius was shuddering with cold, and tension, hunger and thirst; he wanted to see the *quadrigae* event, and that was all.

But there were two chariot races before that, for two-horse teams, five chariots in one race and four in the other. The second one was a shambles, with chariots crashing and colliding, wheels locking, and at the far end one pulling another over, the screaming horses piling on top of one another and one driver leaping high in the air to escape the mêlée of broken

457

machinery and thrashing hoofs. The other did not reappear. Publius absented himself with a grim look and a unit of legionaries ran on and swarmed over the wreckage, righting some horses, dragging others away, clearing the track just in time for the two remaining chariots to storm past, taking no prisoners.

When the race finished Publius came back and Gaius saw him give a little shake of his head in response to Claudia's unspoken question. He felt rather sick.

'Brasca next,' said Madoc. 'Be ready to cheer.'

'Would you like to sit with me?' asked Claudia.

'No.'

'You look frozen. Madoc, is there another—'

'I'm all right.'

'Come here. Come along.'

She took hold of his wrist and pulled him gently but firmly towards her, and then on to the seat between her and his father. It was good to be shielded by their combined warmth, but he hoped that the two boisterous local boys couldn't see him. His mother's arm was round him, a familiar, comforting feeling, but then, for an instant, he felt his father's hand touch the back of his neck in a cautious, half-realised gesture of manly affection, and Gaius was flooded with a sweet, reviving pleasure.

The three *quadrigae* came into the arena to tumultuous applause. Gaius' heart swelled with pride as though he, not Brasca, were the driver of the beautiful red team. And, indeed, Brasca himself was transformed – no longer the fussy, garrulous, perspiring, middle-aged hobbyist but a superbly commanding charioteer, mysterious and fearsome in his visored helmet. The contrast between the teams – the calm greys, the powerful blacks and the spirited reds – was striking and you could feel the crowd responding to it, choosing their favourites, pointing and arguing, coming to the boil. This was the final event, and the ground was pitted and furrowed by the previous races. The wind had dropped a little, but the clouds were gathering, threatening rain. The rumble of the spectators was like thunder in the distance, a warning of the storm to come.

At the sound of the horn the three teams leaped forward,

slowed for a second as they hit their stride with the weight of the chariot, and reached full speed by half-way down the first straight. At the turning post the black team were ahead, with the other two neck and neck close behind. Gaius could not believe that they could corner so fast, and yet they did, the drivers leaning into the bend, feet apart, knees slightly bent, legs braced on the shuddering platform. The inside horse turned almost within its own space, the one on the outside seeming to fly, the chariot's offside wheel lifted clear of the ground. This was where the light, nimble red team had a natural advantage. As they came off the bend and turned down the straight past the stand they had made up some ground on the greys. Madoc and Claudia shouted their encouragement, but Gaius couldn't: his throat was sealed shut with the terrible excitement of it. As the chariots went past he felt the seats judder and the spatter of sweat and soil on his face. Scarlet spots on his own and his mother's clothes showed there was blood, too. The wheels bounced and slewed crazily on the rutted track. As the teams hurtled to the far end, he heard his father say over his head to Claudia, 'This rough racing is more dangerous than anything you'd see in Rome.'

'The drivers are brave men.'

'And stupid. Foursomes on this kind of surface should be for display only, but they've already started taking unnecessary risks.' He lowered his mouth to talk into Gaius' ear. 'Let's hope your friend's got more sense.'

Gaius felt that this remark conferred some sort of responsibility. Was Brasca his friend and, if so, would he be sensible? He glanced at Madoc, who had moved, or been pushed, up close to the fence, and was craning his neck as the teams came off the bend at the top of the track. His knuckles were grey-white where he clutched the rail and his face was red and wore an expression entirely new to Gaius. He was shouting, although you couldn't hear him because everyone else was, too.

Publius leaned down again. 'For the reds to take the lead he'll have to overtake on the straight, and that's a tall order. The black horses are the most powerful out there. He'd be wise not to try.'

There were to be five laps, and for the next two the order didn't change. It began to look as though this was how it would be at the finish – the blacks marginally ahead, the reds close behind, and the greys trailing. And then as they rounded the right-hand turning post for the last time the reds suddenly put on a turn of speed. Gaius could feel the collective intake of breath before the huge roar of encouragement that carried all of them, his parents included, to their feet. His own legs shook, but the seat behind his knees and the press of his parents' bodies supported him. The noise was deafening, but from somewhere behind him he caught the words '– going to do it! The reds are going to do it!'

The reds drew level with the blacks, and sparks flew as the chariot wheels rasped against each other. The little horses' heads were up, they were the most glorious, courageous creatures that Gaius had ever seen, and Brasca the greatest hero. But he needed to be ahead at the bend, and turned in a fraction too soon, before he was completely clear of his opponent. They could all see what was going wrong, but it happened at such a savage speed that they were still cheering, there wasn't time for the horror to have registered. The driver of the bigger team saw it too, for he hauled on the reins to avoid the disaster that was about to explode ahead of him.

Brasca's chariot cut across and crashed into the heads of the black horses. The combined speed of the teams and the violence of the collision created an impetus that carried them to well beyond the stand before both teams went down, the blacks grinding into the *spina* and the reds glancing off it with a hideous cracking sound and crashing down, sending a great shower of debris into the crowd. The driver of the greys was upon them, but kept his head and steered through the space with a whisker to spare, and on round the track to the winning post, raising one arm high above his head in a victory salute. The roar that accompanied his triumph on the far side accentuated the stifling moment of shock. Gaius felt the hot, shaming sting of piss on the inside of his leg. His mother's arm was like a vice round his shoulders or he would have fallen. His father had sprung over the fence and was racing towards the wreckage, shouting at people to get out of the way so the legionaries could get through. Four of the horses were back on their feet, a fifth lay, quivering, beneath one of the chariots. The driver of the black team was lying on his back across the top of the *spina*, his eyes wide open.

There was no sign of Brasca, but one of his horses, horribly injured, was lurching and scrambling on three legs across the track, trying to free itself from the harness, its glorious red coat dark with sweat. Its flanks were heaving like a blacksmith's bellows. Its broken leg flapped sickeningly. Blood was dripping from its mouth and nostrils. Claudia tried to turn Gaius' face against her so that he couldn't see, but he fought free in time to see his father grab the horse's noseband and slit its throat with a single upward jerk of his dagger. It collapsed, its life flowing out of it in a thick, spreading lake. The legionaries got to work, stretchering off the dead driver, unharnessing and leading away the surviving horses and clearing the wreckage from the body of the dead animal, and that of Brasca, which looked like a cloth doll, crushed and formless.

They were efficient. The grey team were able to perform a lap of honour unobstructed, and by the time they'd come round to collect their laurels from the legate, the track was clear except for a few pieces of wood and the still-settling dust.

The crowd dispersed, some chattering with excitement, some quiet, others loud and angry over lost bets. Madoc and Claudia had one of those urgent, under-the-breath grown-up conversations over Gaius' head, Madoc said he ought to find Brasca's wife and see what he could do. Publius rejoined them and once they were in the litter he mounted Nesta and cleared a path for them, bellowing at people to get out of the way.

Once they were clear of the racetrack it began to rain. Gaius could hear the patter of the drops on the roof, swelling to a steady sound like a drum roll. Beneath his cheek, his mother's heartbeat stumbled unevenly. He pulled away from her.

'I'm sorry,' she said, 'that you had to see that.'

'It's all right.'

'Those poor, brave men . . .' she murmured, half to him, half to herself.

This time he didn't reply. It was not the men he kept thinking of, not even Brasca, whom he'd met and who had been kind to him. It was the beautiful red horse brought low, crawling and scrambling, still trying to gallop when it could not even stand, its poor useless leg bumping and dragging over the ground . . . He would never be able to get that picture out of his head, never. The driven look in the dying animal's eyes, the striving angle of its neck, its awful, innocent courage . . . And he would never be able to forgive his father for killing it so quickly and casually, like a butcher, stepping over its still-twitching legs to get to the next job . . .

Just as earlier he hadn't been able to cheer, or even speak, for excitement, now he couldn't cry, for sheer desolation. He was bereft. The red horses had been like a dream, or a wild hope – prouder, grander, swifter, more wonderful than his own life would ever be. The fact that he had touched them and stroked their velvet noses and smelt the warm, branny smell of their coats and seen close up how their eyelashes fringed their liquid brown eyes – all this had helped him understand them. He was sure that no one at the races – not even Brasca – knew their hearts as he did. When they galloped past he felt he was galloping with them.

Now, all that was over. Turned shabby and prosaic like the horse his father had butchered so offhandedly. One minute a dream; the next, dead meat to be dragged off and disposed of. He had heard his mother say that Brasca's wife Erica (who hadn't seemed very nice anyway) was a widow now, with no breadwinner in the house, and wouldn't want the trouble and expense of keeping the remaining three horses.

He found his buried voice, and forced it out. 'What will happen to them?'

'Don't worry,' said his mother, 'they'll be taken care of.'

He knew that tone of voice. It meant she didn't know. 'Who by?'

'Horses are always valuble. I'm sure there'll be no shortage of people with good homes.'

He thought about this, and the good homes that most horses had – pulling goods' carts over the hill roads, or wagons loaded with travellers, or being ridden hard and ruthlessly by men like the bear, who wanted only to win.

'Why did Father do it like that?'

'He was being kind, darling. Putting the horse out of its pain.'

'Yes, but—' He struggled to find the right words. 'He didn't care.'

'Of course he did. And there were those poor men to be seen to . . . not that it would have made any difference . . .'

It was hopeless. He couldn't begin to explain. He leaned his head on his hand and gazed out of the side of the litter. The rain was falling quite heavily, but being blown in swathes, like smoke, across the slope below them. His father was riding a few yards away, keeping pace, hunched in his cloak. The rain smeared his hair flat to his skull. For the first time, and only fleetingly, Gaius saw his father not as his father but as a separate individual, a man as he would be. A man who was growing old.

When they got back, Publius and Gaius went to the bath-house. This was a relatively new thing, it had only happened twice before. Until his last birthday he'd still used a bowl and cloth, under Severina's beady-eyed supervision.

There was no supervision with Publius. They went about their bathing in a manly and companionable silence, and Gaius simply copied what his father did. Today the silence seemed heavy with his own pent-up resentment and his father's lordly lack of understanding. He was so tired that the heat of the *calidarium* almost knocked him out. He wished his father would hurry, but Publius' eyes were closed. As always Gaius was somewhat intimidated by his father's body. It was so sinewy, and *used*-looking: covered in the stains and scars of a life hard-lived. On his temples, forearms and hands, and his legs, veins stood out like ropes. A streak of dark hair shaped like a fern grew up from the tangle around his private parts, between his ribs, and faded below his collar-bone. Next to it Gaius felt pathetically soft and pale, like a worm that spent its life away from the light. Would he ever look like his father? He doubted it. He couldn't even bear to think of the horrible things that his father must have undergone in a lifetime of being a soldier.

When eventually they were getting dressed again, Publius asked, 'So, accidents apart, did you enjoy the races?'

'Yes.'

'Some of the local men are incredible horsemen. They're not disciplined, but they're bred to it.' There was a short silence, which Gaius found awkward, before Publius added, 'It's about time you learned to ride. Would you like that?'

'Yes.' He wouldn't like it, he was sure of that, but he could hardly tell his father so when he was being kind and encouraging. He wouldn't like it, because he'd be no good at it – not strong enough, too nervous, afraid of hurting himself.

They emerged from the changing room and went up the short flight of stairs into the main house.

'We'll have to see about a pony . . .' said Publius. 'It was a pity about that little chestnut this afternoon, but it might easily have been more than one.'

'Why did you kill it?' said Gaius. As with so many of his remarks it wasn't exactly what he wanted to say, and had come out wrong. He wanted to know if his father had been sad that he had to kill the horse, if he felt, even in the smallest way, the same way as he did.

'Why?' Publius gave a short, disbelieving laugh and stopped in his tracks so that Gaius had to stop too. 'I'd have thought that was obvious. A horse with a broken leg is as good as dead anyway.'

'Were you sorry?' This was the crux of it, what he wanted to know.

'No! I was first on the scene and did what any sensible man would do.'

Gaius could hear that he was perilously close to the boundary of what was allowed, so he didn't answer and began to move on, but Publius laid a hand on his shoulder to stop him.

'Listen. Your friend Brasca, Madoc's friend, did something

very stupid and dangerous. It cost him his life, which is what he probably deserved, not to mention the life of the other fellow, and it should serve as a salutary lesson to people like yourself who feel sorry for the damned horse.'

People like himself . . . His father did not and could never understand. Gaius' eyes stung with miserable humiliation. He was aware that his mother, alerted by Publius' raised voice, had appeared, and was standing on the other side of the hall.

'I'm sorry, Father.'

'Don't apologise, listen! You wouldn't see real pros making a mistake like that. If it was a mistake. There's a strong possibility the man actually intended to drive the opposition off the track. You saw it at the Circus Maximus from time to time. At far greater speed and executed with far greater skill. The crowd love it. But Brasca wasn't clever enough. Simple as that.'

'I see.'

'Do you? I hope so. Don't waste your sympathy on him, or his wretched horse. He got what he deserved.'

Gaius kept his lips pressed together, containing the tears.

'Hm?' his father prompted him curtly.

'Yes,' he whispered.

'Run along.'

He fled. As he passed his mother she said, 'Gaius?' and he felt her hand brush his arm, but he didn't look at her, or stop.

He didn't go to his room, because he couldn't have borne either of his parents to follow him there and witness the full extent of his misery. Instead he ran through the house and went out on to the veranda. The evening was still after the rain, there was that bitter-sweet smell of damp ground and greenery. He could hear the sheep calling from the other side of the valley.

He went to the furthest corner of the veranda and sat down, curled tightly with his back against the wall. Behind him in the house he heard his parents' voices. He could only just hear them, and catch the odd word. He could tell from the timbre of the voices that they were trying to keep them down, because of him. The sound was like a knife being drawn over his skin.

'. . . no understanding!'

'He's only . . .'

'. . . someone has to . . .'

'. . . too hard . . .'

They were arguing about him. He could hear the note of fierce protest in his mother's voice, and the one of angry despair in his father's. Because of him. He pressed his arms over his ears.

Tiki trotted round the corner and greeted him, licking his arms and nudging him, trying to get at his face.

'Enough!' shouted his father.

There was a thick, dreadful silence. Now his mother would come looking for him. Gaius got up and ran down the path, through the gate and down the hill towards the temple. After a moment, Tiki followed, trotting easily alongside his head-long flight.

He caught his foot on the corner of the temple step and fell. The little dog flew out of his hand. Eyes smarting with tears, Gaius scrambled to his feet, left it, and ran on.

CHAPTER TWENTY-ONE

<hr />

Bobby, 1993

After I dropped off Ros, I was bound for a couple of nights at Sally and Jim's. To get to their place from Dover I had to drive within two miles of the Beacon, and I couldn't resist turning off, and taking a look for old times' sake. I parked the car in the lane and approached the house on foot, the better to snoop inconspicuously.

It was incredible how completely the new people had put their stamp on it. Just from the front I could see they'd painted the outside, tarmacked the drive, added a rather pretentious five-barred gate, and renamed the house 'Heron's Holt'. That stuck in my craw. Didn't they know this piece of land *was* the beacon? The bluff beyond the garden was where the fire had been lit to spread the message of great events since Elizabethan times. Ken didn't care, though. The great opportunist was sitting on the sun-warmed bonnet of a blue Ranchero, looking fluffy and prosperous, and didn't favour me with the slightest flicker of recognition.

I walked round the pine-needly footpath to the smaller back gate, from where you could see the back of the house, with the loggia and the mossy terrace. This was even more startlingly altered. It was extraordinary how a bit of glass and a lick of paint could make a house look like a provincial golf club. They'd also created a kind of sunken area below the repaved terrace, although a pile of sand and bricks testified to the fact that this refinement was still incomplete.

'Can I help you?'

I nearly jumped out of my skin. It was Rhona Vickery, the new owner. Recognising me she became all smiles. 'Oh, *hallo!*'

'Caught in the act, I'm afraid. I was driving past the end of the road, and I couldn't resist – but I didn't want to disturb you.'

'That's perfectly all right!' She opened the gate. 'Come on in and take a proper look. There's only me here.'

'Honestly, I don't want—'

'No, now you're here you must.' She led the way across the lawn to the house. 'Gosh, you're brown, have you been on holiday?'

'I got back today. I'm on my way to spend a couple of nights with my brother's family before going back up north.'

'And are you happy in your new home?'

'Very. What about you?'

'Oh, blissful. We knew this was for us the moment we walked in. You must have been sad to let it go out of the family, but we all have to move on, don't we?'

I didn't specially want the guided tour, but it was clear Rhona was going to give it anyway. They hadn't got round to making many structural alterations inside (yet – Rhona implied that there would be plenty more in due course), but the place was freshly carpeted and curtained throughout, and the Vickerys' pale, plump leather furniture and luxuriant plants made it seem altogether different. There was a new rose-red *en-suite* bathroom with a Jacuzzi tub, and the kitchen was unrecognisable. Gone were Jim and Sally's sturdy low-budget pine renovations, and in their place was a culinary *Starship Enterprise* with every conceivable state-of-the-art mod con, something like Daniel's, though I suspected more cooking took place in it. Like Ken, the house was comfortable, cared for and on the up. It had got over me.

'Glass of wine to speed you on your way?' asked Rhona. She couldn't have made it much clearer that her duty was done.

'I won't, thanks, but thank you so much for showing me round. It's absolutely lovely.'

'We think so.'

On the way out I paused to stroke Kev, but as my hand reached out he jumped down off the car with an affronted 'prrp!' and ran off.

'You couldn't call Simba a sociable cat,' said Rhona, 'but we rub along.'

As I started up the car I reflected that while I could just about live with 'Heron's Holt', 'Simba' was a pretention too far.

It was odd, but my feelings about visiting the family were quite different from what they would have been a week earlier. Underpinning my relationship with them there had always been that defensiveness, a determination not to let them in beyond a certain point. Sally was nosy both by inclination and profession, and Jim occasionally adopted an attitude of fraternal concern that irritated the hell out of me. They didn't know me, was what I told myself, and had no right to know any more than I cared to tell them. I was hugely fond of my brother and sister-in-law, but I'd always been prickly with them.

Not this time. As I drove to their house I felt nothing but an easy, warm affection. I looked forward to seeing them and even to being with the tribe, though as always this depended heavily on the limited duration of my stay. I knew I wouldn't tell them about Peter – what was there to tell, after all? – but the difference he had made was there. It would not have been overstating the case to say I was reborn. I could even – and this perhaps, was the measure of it – laugh at myself for being so altered and enlivened by what had been, by any reasonable standards, a one-night stand. But trying half-heartedly to reproach myself for being a saddo didn't work, because I was so clearly *not* sad, in any sense of the word. I felt buoyant, guiltless, and grown-up. Perhaps, I thought, this was what was meant by the self-esteem Sally and her kind so enthusiastically advocated.

Their house was in a street of more or less identical three-storey Victorian semis and I always had to slow down to check the numbers. But once within hailing distance you could spot it because it bore all the identifying marks of the Govan household: two bikes lying on their sides outside the gate; a rangy pied mongrel, Bullet, on the inside with his paws on top; the front door wide open with a couple of children just visible; and – good old Sally – a poster advertising an 'Assertiveness Training Day' at the Jubilee Hall, pinned to the fence.

As I approached the gate the child who was theirs (I think it was Barney, their youngest) bellowed into the house, 'She's here!' before coming out with the friend and greeting me with a brief 'Hi' while restraining Bullet, who had gone into welcome overdrive.

Sally appeared in the doorway, looking disarrayed with her glasses on, hair in a scrunchie and a tea-towel over her shoulder. 'Bobby – brilliant! Bullet, shut up! Shut up! Barney, put him in the back and close the gate, will you? No, now! Bobby . . .' She clasped me by the shoulders and kissed me on both cheeks. Her hair gave off a whiff of frying mince. She stood back. 'You look *wonderful*, have you had a great holiday?'

I outlined how great it had been as I dumped my bag in the hall and we went into the kitchen-dining room, where the mince was sizzling merrily. If there had not been one of Sally's formidable British pasta dishes on my first night I should have suspected some shift in the planetary system. The vibrantly red Bolognese with grated Cheddar cheese, or the lasagne like a slab of the primeval earth's molten crust were key features of the cuisine *chez* Govan.

As was the Oddbins winebox perched on the work surface within easy reach of the cook. Sally handed me a glass. 'Help yourself, take a pew. Jim's taken Fliss to a disco, he'll be back soon.'

'How are they all?' I asked.

'Oh, keeping us on a short leash as usual. Barney you saw – that was Aaron with him, he's staying the night – and Ade's in London this weekend for some horrible event I'd rather not know about.'

'What about . . .' I rummaged for the name of the fourth,

fifteen-year-old child, and came up with it in the nick of time
'. . . Zoë?'

'Chloë.'

'Sorry.'

'Don't worry about it, you're doing fine. She's upstairs, you'll see her in due course.'

Sally embarked on one of her familiar, only half-joking animadversions on family life, and, listening to her, I thought how astonished she would be if she knew about Fleur. It was part of the weave of our relationship: her life freighted with the demands of husband (I was always somehow made to feel responsible for Jim) and children, and mine free, untrammelled, essentially selfish, although that word was never used. I wouldn't have dared complain to Sally about anything short of bankruptcy, fire, flood or terminal illness. This evening, for the first time that I could remember, I felt some genuine sympathy for Sally. I *was* lucky, and in many respects she did have a harder row to hoe than I. She was lively, and plucky, and her children were pretty nice, considering. How would it affect our friendship if – when – I told her that I was not only a parent like her, but about to be a grandparent as well?

We had done considerable damage to the contents of the winebox by the time Jim got back, and the giant lasagne was seething and darkening in the oven. My brother kissed me absentmindedly. 'Good hols? I must say, there are times when I feel that as a parent I fall far short of the ideal.'

'Don't, for God's sake, let's start worrying about the ideal,' said Sally, 'or we'll all shoot ourselves.'

'No, but –' Jim took a swig of Good With Grub '– you should have seen this place I took Fliss to tonight.' He turned to me as being possibly the most receptive on this score. 'It's a former railway-goods depot in the absolute armpit of town. To say it has no frills would be the understatement of the decade. It's just a ruddy great shed full of ruddy great speakers.'

'Which is what they like,' pointed out Sally, shaking up salad dressing in a jam-jar.

'That doesn't mean they should have it. If I were a dad

471

instead of a doormat I'd have turned straight round and driven her back here to the comfort and the moral certitudes of family life.'

'Don't be ridiculous.'

'Remind me how old she is?' I asked, in an attempt to avert a domestic.

'Thirteen.'

'Going on thirty.'

'A *child*,' said Jim.

'I bet she'll have a wonderful time,' I suggested emolliently.

'That's what I'm afraid of.'

Sally opened the oven and fished out the lasagne with her eyes narrowed against the heat. 'Call Chloë, can you?'

I got up and went into the hall and half-way up the stairs.

'Chloë!' There was silence. 'Chloë?'

'Yeah?' The voice was distant.

'Hallo, it's Bobby!'

'Oh. Hi . . .'

'Supper's ready!'

'Okay . . .'

I went back down. Barney and Aaron were seated on one side of the table, Sally and Jim at either end. I'll say one thing for them, they had managed to keep family meals alive against all the current trends. I sat down on Jim's right and Sally began dishing up.

'Where's the dog?' asked Jim.

'Out the back,' replied Barney.

'Have you got a dog, Aaron?' I asked.

'Yeah,' said Aaron, 'we've got a shihtzu.' They both snorted with laughter.

Sally tried to pretend they were laughing about something else. 'You can't tell which end is which,' she remarked, 'until she starts moving. It's sweet.'

'No problem about ends with ours,' said Jim glumly. 'One takes it in, the other chucks it out, and they're both smelly.'

The boys exploded again. Chloë came in and sat down next to me. Since I'd last seen her she'd crossed the dividing line between puppy fat and the grown-up sort.

'Whoa,' she said to her mother, 'half that, I'm not hungry. Hallo, Bobby.'

'Leave what you don't want,' said Sally, plonking it in front of her. There was clearly a family agenda here that defied outside analysis.

'I like your hair,' I said truthfully – Chloë's hair was auburn and curly and she'd grown it long. 'You could be in a shampoo advertisement.'

One of the boys murmured 'The shihtzu look . . .' to more sniggering.

Chloe said, 'Fuck off,' to them, and 'Thanks,' to me. We started on the lasagne. Barney and Aaron apart, there was a discernible tension around the table that even Jim's interrogation about my holiday couldn't quite dispel. I joined in with a will, telling them far more than they could possibly have wanted to know about the house, Brittany, the weather, the food and the locals.

'And what about your friend?' asked Sally. 'We met her once. Pud?'

'You're joking,' said Chloë. She nudged her untouched plate and added, 'I shan't get through all this.'

'No, she had a funny nickname . . .'

'Spud,' I said, 'but not any more. She's Ros, these days.'

'A very handsome woman, I always thought,' mused Sally, with instinctive maternal tact. 'Agreeably self-confident.'

'She's that, all right,' I agreed.

'Big, though,' said Jim. 'She could have given me a couple of stone.'

A look of blistering disapproval flashed down the table from his wife. 'And she makes the most of every ounce of it!'

'She is a sexy lady,' I said cautiously, then attempted to inch the conversation not too obviously in another direction. 'And the only one from my schooldays that I've kept up with.'

'Apart from the sublime Rags,' Jim reminded me.

'Apart from her. But she's just someone I stumbled on again by chance. She was never a friend back then.'

'Your aunt's new neighbour up north is a former supermodel,'

Jim told his daughter. 'In the days before supermodels were called that.'

'Cool.'

I was beginning to see that we should stay off supermodels. 'And now she's the lady of the manor, literally.'

'Is she loaded?' asked Chloë.

'I suppose she is. I mean, she must have been a rich woman in her own right to begin with. But owning a stately home doesn't make you rich.'

'Just poor in comfort.'

'Yes,' I said. 'Absolutely that.'

The boys finished firsts and seconds and were allowed to get down and fetch Mars ice-creams from the freezer. The three of us finished, and moved on to salad while Chloë pushed cold lasagne round her plate and made patterns in the tomato sauce with her fork. I had more salad. Jim shredded a chunk of French bread and put the crumbs, one by one, into his mouth.

After ten minutes of this agony, relieved only by the most stilted conversation imaginable, Chloë stuck the fork vertically into her uneaten pasta. As if to prove her point, it remained upright. 'Can we stop, please? I don't want this.'

'Now, darling—' began Sally.

'Come on,' said Jim, 'none of that. You can manage a few mouthfuls at least.'

'No. I can't.'

'That's ridiculous. Your mother's been to all this trouble.'

'Oh, *please*,' said Sally.

'Quite,' agreed Chloë. 'Don't try that one, it's so patronising.'

Jim's face darkened. I had never seen my brother really angry before, and it was frightening. I seriously wondered if he was going to hit her. What actually happened was worse – much worse.

'I wouldn't mind you turning up your nose at a decent meal,' he said, 'if you weren't so obviously stuffing your face with rubbish at other times.'

'And what's that supposed to mean?' It was like a scripted exchange, there was a ghastly inevitability to each remark.

'Simply that you wouldn't be so atrociously overweight if you ate sensibly.'

Sally made a little yelping sound, and I felt my own face flood with heat. I couldn't look at either of them, but kept my eyes on Chloë's fork, which was just beginning to tilt. As it finally subsided, the handle meeting the side of the plate with a dull 'ping', Chloë got up, and pushed her chair back so that it crashed over. She heeled it out of the way, and left the room. I swear her exit was so violent it created a scorching draught that made us flinch. She didn't go upstairs. There was no slam – she had left the front door open.

We didn't need to say anything to Jim. His head was in his hands. I didn't know who to feel sorrier for. Sally went out into the hall and presumably out of the house, for it was a long couple of minutes before her return.

I put out my hand and clasped my brother's wrist. Where my fingers touched his cheek, it was damp.

He muttered hoarsely, 'I wish I was dead.'

I tried to think of what he'd most like to hear. 'You love her to bits, you want her to be all right. That's why you said what you did.'

'No Brownie points for good intentions.' He rummaged in his pocket for a handkerchief and mopped his face.

'She understands that, really. She pushed you beyond endurance, I expect she's quite satisfied in a way. You know, something to help justify all that unfocused turmoil she's suffering. It's only words. You'll say sorry, and in the end she'll accept that you are.'

He gave a long, trembling sigh. From outside we could hear Bullet barking, being wound up by the boys. For something to do, I began clearing the table. We heard the front door being closed and Sally came in. I dreaded to think what further domestic bloodshed there might be. But to my surprise she put her arms round Jim and held him for a moment, her cheek resting on the top of his head. Her eyes and his were closed, rather as people close their eyes during lovemaking, to shut out every sensation but the one of their togetherness. I looked away, and ran water in the sink.

After a moment Sally joined me and began putting plates in the dishwasher.

'There's Italian ice cream,' she said, 'if anybody feels like it.'

We both declined. In the last few minutes food had assumed a somewhat vexed status in the scheme of things. Coffee, however, seemed like a good idea.

'I'm sorry to expose you to all that,' said Sally, sitting down while the kettle boiled. 'There's nothing worse than someone else's family row.'

'You're my family too,' I pointed out. 'And it wasn't really a row, it was a – thing.'

'However it sounded,' said Jim, desperately, 'I don't honestly *care* if she's a bit fat. But I do want her to be happy, and she's not. She's getting a hard time from her friends, she can't wear the clothes she wants, which makes her stroppy when she's quite stroppy enough already, and the lads are frightened off – you can't honestly blame them – so she pretends she doesn't care and the whole thing becomes a self-fulfilling prophecy.'

I was confused. 'But she wasn't eating,' I said. 'You were telling her to eat.'

'Oh, she's eating all right – eating us out of house and home, but never with us. Her room's scary. Absolutely stuffed with sweet wrappers and crisp packets and biscuit crumbs. Bloody yoghurt cartons with half an inch of mould in them. She eats drinking chocolate straight out of the tub with a spoon. Processed cheese. Cakes . . .'

'When she's in she keeps the door locked,' explained Sally. 'I do have to go in there when she's out sometimes just to reclaim the crockery and open the window.' She sounded apologetic.

'We don't have to justify ourselves, Sal,' said Jim, exasperated. 'This is *our* house, and *our* fifteen-year-old daughter we're talking about.'

'It's still her space.'

'"Her space"!' His voice was warped with disdain. 'Jesus wept. These disgusting habits flourish on too much privacy.'

'Where do you think she's gone now?' I asked.

'To her friend's, I should think,' said Sally.

Jim blew his nose noisily. 'Thank Christ she still has one.'

'Leanne, she's a nice girl. I might ring in a few minutes and check.'

'Careful,' said Jim. 'The slightest attempt at concerned parenting could land us both even deeper in the shite than we are already.'

After supper we watched television while the boys racketed around. At nine Jim drove them up to bed and Sally rang Leanne's house and discovered, to the considerable relief of us all, that Chloë was there.

What with the journey, the drama, and several glasses of merlot, I'd hoped to sneak off to bed early, but Jim had to go out at ten to collect Fliss from the disco, so it seemed only polite to keep Sally company.

'What about Chloë?' I asked. 'Can she get back all right?'

'Yes, I outlined the situation to Leanne's mother, without going into too much detail, and she'll keep her there till Jim arrives.' She must have seen my doubtful look, for she added, 'If she won't come back with him now she can stay overnight. It's Sunday tomorrow and we'll sort something out.'

'Does she do this kind of thing often?'

Sally heaved a short, gusty sigh. 'Pretty often. And I'm more sick of the food issue than you can possibly imagine. It's made mealtimes a war zone, when they should be the opposite. It means the others don't like eating with her either, so they go to any lengths to get out of it. She uses food as a weapon. It's absolutely classic.'

'Is she bulimic?'

'Not yet. Not that we know of. And she's not grossly obese either, or turning into a skeleton. That's what we have to watch out for.'

'Of course.' I found myself wondering whether this wasn't an instance of being too close to a problem to see it clearly.

'I thought,' said Sally, 'that having you here would make a difference but, as you saw, not a hope.'

'It may have made it worse. Put her on her mettle.'

'That's where she always is, unfortunately.' The phone rang. 'Excuse me.'

In a moment she came back in and held out the phone. 'For you. Someone called – Fleur? Does that sound right?'

'How did she know I was here?' I blurted out stupidly.

Sally gave the phone a little shake in my direction. 'Haven't a clue, Bobby. I don't even know who she is.'

'No, of course not, sorry.' I took the phone gingerly.

'I'll just go and empty the machine.'

Sally absented herself, pulling the door to discreetly after her.

'Hallo?'

'Is that – you?'

'Fleur?'

'I hope you don't mind me tracking you down like this.'

'How did you do it?'

'I called your business number and the man said he thought you were coming back via your brother, so I went through Directory Enquiries.'

'You're very resourceful.'

'And you're a grandmother.'

'*What?*' I gasped. '*When?*'

'A boy, eight and a half pounds in the small hours of this morning, with no problems. He's got mad black hair and his name's Rowan.'

'Oh, Fleur . . . That's wonderful. Congratulations.'

'Thanks. Yes, I'm quite proud of myself.'

There was no doubt at all in my mind what I wanted to do. It was suddenly, blindingly simple. 'Can I come and see you? Both of you?'

'That'd be great. They're sending me home tomorrow morning.'

'What? Isn't that a bit soon?'

She laughed. 'They've only kept me in this long because he's a bit yellow. I'm fine.'

I realised I'd sounded fussy and old. 'Look,' I said, 'I'm here till the day after tomorrow. You'd better tell me where you're going to be.'

She gave me an address and phone number in Kilburn. 'My flatmate's called Jude.'

'She's going to be around, is she?'

'For a couple of days. She had some holiday owing anyway.'

It was quite clear that Fleur didn't wish to be characterised as needy or dependent, but, well, she was my daughter.

'Is there anything you want,' I asked, 'for the baby, or yourself? That I could bring when I come.' I tried to make it sound like no more than a means of transportation, that there would be no present-giving involved, but she still turned me down.

'I don't think so. I got some brilliant bargains second-hand, and I'm feeding him myself, so I think I'm okay.'

'You sound it.' It was almost daunting how okay she seemed to be. But, then, she and I both knew that I was not a natural for the role of concerned mother and grandmother.

'Well,' I said, 'congratulations, I'm delighted it all went so well. And I should be there around mid-morning the day after tomorrow.'

'See you.' She gave a little laugh. 'You're going to really, really love him, you know.'

'I'm sure I shall.'

'There's no option.'

I pressed the button and took the phone back to its place in the hall. I was wondering what to tell Sally if she asked, but I was spared the decision by the return of Jim, with both his daughters. Chloë went upstairs at once without speaking to either me or her mother, who'd come out of the kitchen. Fliss on the other hand actually said hallo, and gave Sally a glancing kiss.

We congregated in the kitchen as people are wont to do.

'Good disco?' I asked.

'Wicked. I'm starving.'

Sally drew her attention to the last portion of the lasagne, which could be microwaved, and the untouched Italian ice-cream.

'Any Mars ices?'

'Yes, if the boys haven't finished them, but the other—'

'I'll just have that. Which one has Barney got tonight?'

'Aaron.'

'Could be worse, I suppose. Could be Seth.' She pulled a face to indicate what a nightmare *that* would have been.

She found the Mars ice-creams, took two, and went to watch TV in the sitting room.

'We don't worry too much about bedtimes on Saturday night,' said Sally. 'There's no point, and the later they go to bed the longer the blessed peace and quiet in the morning. How's Chloë?'

Jim leaned heavily on the back of a chair. 'Thunderous.'

'But she came quietly.'

'Only because Leanne's mother said they had to go somewhere early tomorrow. Pretty fancy footwork on her part, I considered. Nice woman.'

'Did you tell Fliss?'

'I didn't have to. It was perfectly obvious Chloë was in the vilest possible humour, so everyone understood each other.'

'Well . . . !' Sally yawned and stretched. 'I'm plumb tuckered out. If there are going to be further ructions tomorrow I need to sleep now. Bobby, what was your call about? Everything all right at home?'

'Oh, fine,' I said. Now was not the moment. 'Just a neighbour in a flap about something.'

'Rags?' asked Jim, wistfully.

'Not Rags. We're honestly not that close.'

'You must try harder, sis.'

'Jim, change the record,' said Sally. 'And go and turf Bullet out of the boys' room, will you? He needn't think he's spending all night on the bottom bunk.'

I found it hard to sleep for excitement. I could scarcely believe it of myself. I was wholly, unequivocally thrilled about becoming a grandmother. That my daughter, my own flesh and blood, had borne a son, and that son would, if I wished, be a part of my life. I remained wide-eyed and wakeful till well into the small hours, when I finally gave in and went down to the kitchen to make myself a cup of tea.

The kitchen was dark except for a low light, the source of

which I couldn't at first identify until I made out Chloë, sitting at the kitchen table with the fridge door open. Unfortunately she saw me at the same time so there was no chance of a discreet and tactful withdrawal. I opted instead for a breezy lack of interest.

'Any milk in there? I was going to make a cup of tea.' She reached in and handed me a carton. 'Thanks. I couldn't sleep for some reason.'

'Tea won't help, all that caffeine.'

'I suppose so, but it's comforting.'

'I know what you mean.' She closed the fridge door, plunging us both into darkness.

'Oops. Could you turn the light on?'

'Just a sec.' I heard her scrabbling about, followed by the clunk of the swing-bin lid. Then the strip-light flickered and doused us in its flat, pale glare. I could see from Chloë's expression that I looked pretty terrible – two a.m. with no make-up and no sleep wasn't kind to me these days – but her appearance shocked me, too. There was grease on her giant T-shirt, and around her mouth, and her face was red and swollen. The table and the floor by the fridge was scattered with crumbs. The swing-bin was half closed on a pile of Cellophane, cardboard and kitchen towel.

'Snacking?' I asked. I couldn't help it.

'Don't you start.'

'I'm not starting, but I do care about you.'

'Yeah, yeah, yeah, I'm going to bed.'

'Night.'

She got as far as the foot of the stairs and then came back. 'Don't say anything to them, will you?'

'All right.'

This time she went up. I made my cup of tea – a good, brown, caffeine-and-tannin fix with two sugars – and followed. As I crossed the landing I could hear, very faint but unmistakable, the sound of retching.

The next day was somewhat burdened by all the things I couldn't say – one because I didn't know how, another because

I wished to keep it to myself and a third because I'd promised Chloë. But nothing could seriously dent my good humour. I kept thinking how much I'd like to have told Peter my news, and how he would have appreciated and relished it. I wished now, as I hadn't done in the immediate afterglow of that evening, that he had asked for my number, instead of finessing the initiative my way . . . I considered, rather wildly, whether to get in touch with him, but Ros's imagined voice haunted me with her motto: 'The rules don't change.'

We got up late, except for the boys who had been rousted out of bed for a football match, transport courtesy of Aaron's dad. Fliss and Chloë were still in bed as we prepared brunch at eleven thirty. I didn't mention my nocturnal meeting with Chloë, but I didn't need to: the depredations in the fridge-freezer said it all. In the interests of peace and harmony Sally waited till Jim had gone to get a paper before unburdening herself to me.

'Quite apart from her state of mind and well-being, there's the cost! It's phenomenal what she gets through with this bingeing.'

'Does she buy stuff herself?'

'What with? She has an allowance but it's not big compared with most of her friends. In fact, that's another grievance, but there's no way we're upping it while all this is going on. It would be like flushing it down the loo, literally.'

I realised Sally knew more than she had let on. And why wouldn't she? I'd read that a mother can hear her baby before it starts to cry, so there was no way she would miss that terrible small-hours heaving.

'. . . what worries me,' she was saying, 'is that she might be *nicking* food. I've seen the packaging, swanky individual cream cakes and whatnot. But quite frankly, Bobby, I've only got the energy for one thing at a time. And if this eating thing is the cause, then that's the one to worry about.'

'I'm sure you're right,' I said. 'As long as she doesn't get into trouble.'

'Hm.' Sally broke eggs into the pan with a flourish. 'I begin to wonder whether that wouldn't be the best thing . . .'

Ade returned as we were eating. 'Fry-up, wicked! Any left over?'

'There's sausages and bacon on a plate in the top oven. Pan's there, you can fry your own eggs.'

'Cheers.'

Aidan Govan was one of those youths about whom one didn't worry. He was scruffy, idle, handsome, amiable, born to surf through life without causing or experiencing much bother. Watching him shovel out three fried eggs on to an already groaning plate – Sally's adult/child portion control was based on long experience – I reflected on how unfair it was that one person, Ade, could be up to all sorts to all hours and attract no opprobrium whatever, while another, Chloë, clearly 'conflicted' to use one of Sally's words, was permanently in the eye of the storm.

He carried his plate to the table. 'Shove up, Dad.'

Jim shunted his chair to the side so that Ade could squeeze in another between him and me. 'Hiya, Bobby, how you doing?'

'Fine, thanks.' I've noticed that one's response to this formulaic question depends largely on the expectations of the person asking. One was always fine with Ade.

'Good.' He downed the first mouthful. 'Where is everybody?'

'Barney's playing soccer,' said Jim, 'and your sisters are still in their pits.'

'All right for some.'

'And where did you spend the night?' asked Sally.

'I didn't.'

'By that I suppose you mean you didn't go to sleep, not that you're on a different cosmic plane to the rest of us,' said Jim.

'Yeah, that one, that first one. Mm – shit, this is the business.'

He munched away and we retreated behind our various supplements. I was engrossed in an article about a twenty-something actress who, like every other actress, was completely un-actressy, when Ade said, 'So, Auntie, how's the love life?'

Sally reacted a lot quicker than me, with knee-jerk parental consternation. 'Aiden, don't be so rude!'

'I wasn't, I only asked.'

'Well, don't,' said Jim. 'It's nobody's business but Bobby's, least of all yours.'

'Okay, hands up, Bobby, sorry, mate.'

'It doesn't matter,' I said. 'And the answer to your question is, quiet.'

'There you are, you see,' said Ade, lifting an insouciant hand, palm upwards. 'Nothing to get excited about anyway . . .'

To our eternal shame, we laughed. But mine was definitely the last.

In the afternoon there was one of those population shifts that seem to happen in family households. Fliss came down, and she and Ade settled in to watch the *EastEnders* omnibus in the playroom. Barney rang to say that Aaron had invited him back to his for lunch, so that was what he was doing. Jim and Sally took Bullet to the beach for a walk. Naturally I was invited, but I sensed they might like some time to themselves, and since this accorded with my own laziness, I stayed at home and read the papers, full length on the sofa with *Celtic Heaven III* on the CD player. After a while Fliss wandered in and said Ade had fallen asleep and she was going next door to Jamahl and Rita's: their cat had had kittens.

'Don't come back with one, will you?' I said, playing the responsible aunt, and was duly blanked.

The house was quiet, the papers unsurprising and the fiddles soulful. I'd practically dozed off myself when I was aware of someone sitting down on the floor opposite me. It was Chloë, barefoot, in another jumbo T-shirt and combats. She'd washed her hair and looked scrubbed and pretty in spite of her size.

'Am I disturbing you?' she asked, in the tone of someone who knew she was, but with good reason.

'Not at all, I'm just being idle.'

'Yeah, well, it is Sunday.'

'That's what I tell myself. Your parents are out with the dog.'

There was a silence. She clasped her knees and rocked slightly, gazing down at her toes, which were immaculately painted with black nail polish.

After a couple of minutes she said, 'This is Dad's CD.'

'I like it.'

'I gave it to him for Christmas.'

'Very well chosen.'

'I guessed it would be his bag.' Another silence. Then she said, 'Thanks for not saying anything.'

'How do you know I haven't?'

She gave me a look of genuine bafflement. 'You said you wouldn't.'

I was touched, both by this compliment to myself and the evidence of a certain innocence in her.

'That's true.'

'I haven't always been fat,' she said defensively. 'I'm not naturally fat.'

'I remember,' I said, hastily adding, 'not that I'd call you fat now.'

'Most people would. I would.'

'If it bothers you,' I said, 'it's easy to lose at your age.'

She looked at me sceptically from beneath her eyebrows. 'You don't have to pretend. Everybody knows I binge and throw up – except Dad. He wouldn't believe it if I puked in his face.'

I struggled with this arresting image. 'He knows you binge.'

'It's the other bit he couldn't handle.'

I asked the simple, simplistic, obvious question. 'Can't you stop?'

'No. I have to eat, until I absolutely can't eat any more. Then I feel so vile and disgusting and guilty that I chuck it up.' She gave a sour little laugh. 'It works for me.'

'You're going to make yourself seriously ill,' I said.

She held her arms out from her sides. 'Do I look like someone who's wasting away?'

'Not yet. Give it time. Not very much, if you keep this up.'

'Revolting, isn't it?' she agreed. 'I am repulsive.'

'No, you're not, you're a lovely-looking girl. A real babe.' I hoped I wasn't overdoing it but I wanted, badly, to make her feel better. 'You have to start treating yourself properly.'

'I can't . . .' Her eyes filled with tears. 'I don't know how to.'

'Then you need help, there's no shame in that.'

She started to weep, choking and sobbing, shaking her head, her face pressed into her knees. Before I could go to her, Ade entered the room, looking rumpled, and she scrambled to her feet and rushed out, knocking him off-balance on the way.

'Hey, easy, tiger!' He slumped down on the sofa next to me. 'Who rattled her cage?'

'She's upset.'

'No change there, then.'

'That's not very kind.'

'She wants to sort herself out.'

'She does, as a matter of fact.' That wasn't what he meant, but I wasn't going to collude with him. 'And she needs all the help she can get.'

Ade treated me to his engaging grin. 'You must love coming here.'

'I do . . . Why?'

'It must remind you how smart you were not to have kids.'

That evening the whole family were at supper, and everyone pretended not to notice Chloë not eating anything. Later that night I woke instantly and completely when the retching began. Like a mother.

Next morning as she left for school she said quickly: "Bye. See you.'

And I saw that perhaps, given a following wind, I could be a friend.

I got to the house in Kilburn at eleven the next morning, bearing the fruits of a visit to Small World. It was Fleur's voice that answered the buzzer. 'Come on up.'

As I crossed the linoed hall, with its scattering of junk mail and free newspapers, she leaned over the banister and called: 'We're up here.'

When I reached the flat I was out of breath. Fleur, on the other hand was the picture of health. She was carrying a little maternal weight but it suited her, and her hair was longer and worn in a couple of stubby pigtails. She wore a long black skirt, a blue sweater with a black sheep on the front, and tartan slippers.

We didn't exchange a kiss, because a social cheek-bump would not have been enough, and we weren't quite ready for a familial embrace.

'Come on in,' she said. 'Excuse the mess.' The flat was tiny, cluttered and shabby, the hallway was piled with boxes, books and carrier-bags and such wall space as wasn't taken up by the laden row of coat hooks was filled by a noticeboard covered in overlapping layers of paper, like geological strata.

Fleur pushed open a door to reveal a tiny girl in Lennon specs sitting cross-legged on a bed, surrounded by files and notepads. 'Jude, this is Bobby – who I told you about.'

Jude stretched out a hand. 'How do you do?' I wondered what exactly Fleur had told her about me. 'Come to meet Rowan?'

'That's right.'

'He's great.'

The living room was about twice the size of the hall, which wasn't saying much, and an effort had obviously been made to impose some order, by means of pushing junk to the sides of the room and underneath the sofa and chair.

'Here he is.'

I didn't at once spot the baby because he was shrouded in an enormous loose-knit patchwork shawl – which I later saw was a jumper – and wedged between two cushions on the sofa. But when Fleur went to crouch next to him, her face luminous with pride, I went and leaned over to look at him.

He was wide awake, was Rowan. His opaque navy-blue eyes stared up at me. His mouth was thoughtfully pursed. His brow was furrowed beneath its crazy thatch of black hair. He reserved judgement on his strange grandmother.

Not me, though. Just one look, as the song went, and I was solid gone.

'What do you think of your grandson, then?' asked Fleur.

I fell into cliché as one falls into love, easily and headlong. 'He's the most beautiful baby I've ever seen.'

'What, ever?'

With one finger I was stroking my grandson's cheek. With my free hand I reached up and touched hers. My voice was unsteady. 'I never saw you.'

She turned her hand palm outwards so that we were holding hands, like children. It felt sweetly, powerfully intimate.

'It's all right,' she said. 'Really, Mum. It's going to be fine.'

Mum. Her use of the word gave me a shock of joy and shame. I was so utterly undeserving. I couldn't let the moment pass.

'Fleur – darling Fleur.' I kissed the back of her hand and then released it. 'You must get in touch with your parents.'

At once she became guarded, picking up the baby as though I'd tried to snatch him from her.

'No. Why should I? They don't want to know.'

'I'm sure they do.' I knew that having embarked on this course, nothing short of complete honesty and wholeheartedness would do. 'They need to have the chance. *I* didn't want to know. At all, ever. But you gave *me* the chance I didn't want or deserve and I'll be grateful to my dying day for that.'

She held Rowan close, glaring down into his face with a fierce, angry expression that couldn't conceal her essential goodness: her impulse, for all her proud individual morality, to do right. In a spirit of make or break, praying I wouldn't lose her, I pressed my case.

'Please, Fleur. Not for them. Certainly not for me. We all let you down, but they put in the time, and the care. They wanted to. I didn't. They brought you up and loved you. Everyone fights with their parents. This was big stuff for them, huge stuff. It's huge for me, for all of us. Please, Fleur, talk to them. For yourself. And for Rowan.'

She lifted Rowan and snuggled her face into him. Hiding her feelings from me but also, I sensed, trying to make sense of them herself. I wanted to put my arms round both of them, but that was a privilege I hadn't yet earned, and an indulgence I couldn't allow. Instead, I held my breath, and my peace, and waited.

CHAPTER TWENTY-TWO

Rags, 1988

Miranda never found out who the woman in green was, whom she had seen on the day of the folly shoot. And, oddly, she was not disturbed by the fact that no one else was able to cast any light on the subject. She had certainly seen her, and there was no question of her being a spectral or unsettling presence – on the contrary she had struck Miranda as the sort of woman with whom she would hit it off: glamorous, but unorthodox and purposeful. Ladycross was an unusual place, which attracted unusual people; some of them stumbled on to the land without intending to trespass, or realising that they were, and the likelihood was that the woman was one of them, perhaps on her way with some tuxedoed escort to a ball or a concert.

Whatever the possible, plausible answers, they didn't stop Miranda speculating about the woman's identity from time to time down the ensuing years.

Years of being mistress of Ladycross, and wife to its master. Years of unrelenting activity, exhilaration and exhaustion, when she and Fred made love wordlessly, with a blind, nuzzling intensity because it was so often the only time they had to communicate with each other and they had to make the most of it. But no matter how tired she was, Miranda knew that their love for one another was not eroded but enhanced by their shared passion for Ladycross. The life of the house was not just an overriding responsibility, but a source of profound delight to them both.

Fred had told her in so many words: 'I'd have loved you to distraction anyway, you know that. But it's beyond belief that you care about this place the way you do.'

'It's just as well. I can't imagine doing this job without one's heart being in it.'

'But people do. My first wife was utterly dutiful, God rest her. My second bolted under the strain.'

Perhaps it was because his loyal, dutiful mother had died, as it were, with her boots on, that Miles had been wary of Miranda. He was too well brought-up a young man to be openly hostile, but he was clearly shocked by his father's choice of bride, only a few years older than his own wife at the time of their marriage, and trailing silver clouds of international glamour.

Their first meeting had inevitably been awkward. Miles was obliged to welcome her as his father's wife while aligning himself firmly with the Stratton escutcheon. She in turn wanted to get on with her step-son, but not at any price. She was determined not to be cowed or put off her stroke when for the foreseeable future she was to be mistress of Ladycross, and was already closer than anyone to Fred's heart.

It was a few months before the wedding, and Miles had come north alone, leaving Penny at home with the baby. She remembered the set look on his face as he got out of the car, the look of a man preparing for the worst. He'd presented himself at the front door, and she'd wondered if he always did this, or whether it was a kind of courtesy, an observing of the formalities in her honour. She reciprocated by hanging back in the library while Fred went out to greet him. Then she worried that this might look as though she were too much at home, so emerged to hover a little self-consciously in the hall.

The moment Fred turned to introduce her she went forward with a big smile. 'Miles . . . It's so nice to meet you.'

'How do you do?'

'Was your journey all right? It was pretty horrible on the A1 yesterday.' By this she hoped to convey, by means of polite enquiry, that she still had merely visitor-status. But as the words passed her lips she realised it might sound as if she were conferring the same status on him, so added, 'But perhaps it's always like that.'

'Not always, no.'

'You must be tired, though.'

'I have a very comfortable car.'

'Time for a swift half, I think,' said Fred, leading the way into the library. 'Your usual, old boy?' The 'old boy' was no affectation, but fatherly. Miranda was in new territory, that of the other people her husband loved, but who were strangers to her and she to them. She saw that she must approach this occasion not in terms of herself, but of Fred. However stolid and obstructive Miles appeared, there must be something of Fred there, somewhere, and she determined to find it.

By the time they were half-way through dinner – at the kitchen table, and cooked by her – she'd reached the conclusion that he was making things deliberately difficult for her. Either that or he was a rare example of a Montclere born without the warmth-and-charm gene for which the family was known. Conversation was chiefly between him and his father and centred on business and the sort of gentry economics on which she had not yet been able to form an opinion and which intimidated her. There was the briefest reference to the wedding – the date, the guest list and arrangements, a mere need-to-know passing of information – and she had felt a little self-conscious about the family ring Fred had given her on their engagement and which Miles, apparently, had noticed.

'May I see?' he asked, as she stretched out a hand to clear the plates.

'Of course.'

He lifted his glasses up to peer at it, and then returned her hand to her. 'It's a beautiful piece, that. Did you know that it's in two of the family portraits?'

'I showed you, didn't I, darling?' said Fred.

'I feel very privileged,' she said humbly.

'No,' said Miles drily, as if convincing himself as much as her. 'It's absolutely right that you should have it.'

'Tell me,' she asked him confidingly, 'how often should I wear it? Fred says I should wear it all the time, but it's an enormous responsibility. It would be so dreadful to be the person who lost it after two hundred years.'

'Well, you'll look after it, naturally,' said Miles, without a shred of comfort in his voice. 'And, anyway, it's none of my business.'

As she took the plates to the machine she glanced at Fred but there was no sign of unease in his expression. He must be used to this. And she would have to get through it.

The phone rang while they were having coffee, and Fred took it in the office. She suggested they go through to the library, aware all the time that this was Miles's house, where he'd been brought up, and that she was an interloper.

They sat down in chairs on either side of the fireplace. For almost the first time since coming to Ladycross she wished she could have been anywhere in the world but here. The space between them was much more than a metre and half of priceless antique Turkish carpet – it was a yawning abyss of suspicion and incomprehension.

She took a deep breath and hurled herself recklessly across the void. 'This must have been a magical place to grow up, Miles. I'm longing to live here, but there's so much I don't know – and perhaps I never will.'

For the first time there was something – the suggestion of pink on his cheeks, a softening of the lines around his mouth. 'I'm quite sure you'll learn quickly.'

'I keep thinking, what must it have been like for your mother? She must have been very young when she came here.'

There was a tiny pause before Miles said, 'She was, yes. Only twenty-two.'

'It must have been quite overwhelming.'

'I don't know. She never said. But, then, by the time I was of an age for us to talk to each other she seemed to me to be completely on top of things. If she had her petrified moments I never knew about them.' He looked at her more directly than he had all evening. 'I realise now she was a very strong woman.'

Miranda cast her bread on the waters. 'You and your father are going to have to bear with me. I don't think I'm nearly so strong, and I probably have even more to learn than your mother because I've had such a different life.'

'Yes.' He dropped his eyes now – she recognised the expression. 'Of course we're all familiar with your pictures.'

She smiled. 'A long time ago now – history, in fact.'

'Believe me,' said Miles. 'You're still instantly recognisable.'

At the same time as she realised she had been given a compliment, Fred joined them. 'Sorry about that. It was the bloke from Chicago about the shooting weekend.'

Miles said, 'I was telling Miranda she looks exactly like her pictures.'

'Doesn't she?' Fred sat down next to her and lifted her hand briefly to his lips. 'Ladycross may be wearying her, but the years certainly haven't condemned.'

She laughed. 'It's all done with mirrors.'

'The only really good photo of Mama,' went on Miles, 'is that one of her as a débutante, that they put on the magazine cover.'

'That was enchanting,' agreed Fred. 'Have I shown you that?'

She shook her head. 'I'd love to see it.'

'You shall.'

She could not have said that with this exchange everything was suddenly all right between her and Miles. Outwardly at least he was as different from his father as it was possible to be – profoundly reserved, cautious, and so socially ill-at-ease as to seem stiff-necked. But in that moment she knew they had each caught a glimpse of emotional common ground, and it was just enough understanding to create a link that remained in place despite the pressures.

As for Penny and the children, Penny was a nice, uncomplicated young woman whose put-upon manner belied a breezily pragmatic approach to her husband's family circumstances. And the children, first Millie, then Jem, were sweet. As they grew up Miranda knew she must be careful not to over-indulge them, and so appear to undermine their parents' authority, but she soon got the hang of where the line was to be drawn. As Grandpa, Fred was a soft touch of the old school, with inexhaustible tolerance to being clambered on and dragged hither and thither, pockets always full of loose change and sweets, and an inability to utter a cross word. She loved him for it, but was careful to put herself in the role of parents' as well as children's friend. Inclination and expediency fitted nicely together. She made a point of diverting over-excitement, easing problems at mealtimes by having options available, reading aloud or going for walks to see the dogs when Penny and Miles were frazzled. She would – unlike Fred – occasionally say no. It was a delicate exercise in social calibration, and one she had to learn on the job, for she had no experience of children.

She succeeded almost too well. At three years old Millie, a saucer-eyed, tight-lipped little girl, became her shadow and even, occasionally, leaned confidingly against her knee if they were all sitting round having drinks.

'You know, she never does that with me,' said Penny. 'She's the most untactile child I know.'

'Perhaps it's like cats,' suggested Miranda. 'They know which people haven't a clue and fixate on them immediately.'

'It's not just that, she adores you.' Penny wasn't to be fobbed off. 'You have fairy princess status in our house.'

'Penny, don't – I can't take the responsibility. After all, where can a fairy princess go but down?'

Miles said, 'Darling, I'm sure Miranda won't mind me saying this, but fairy princess is one thing, and Mum quite another. One's an extra, the other's completely and utterly indispensable.'

Miranda wouldn't have minded anyway, but seeing Penny's face would have dispelled any amount of offence. She liked Miles for saying that – it was what Fred would have done.

The expanded rock concert, her special project, was an area about which she knew both Miles and Penny harboured the gravest doubts. Miles had taken the unprecedented step of voicing these doubts quite openly on a rare occasion when she and Fred visited them in Kensington.

'Tell me, why does it have to be bigger? What's the matter with the way it is?'

'It's already a success, and it's been going for years,' said Miranda. 'I came myself ages ago, and loved it then. But we do need more revenue, and I've done the sums with Hanif at the accountants' –'

'Who, I can testify, is mustard,' put in Fred.

'– and he agrees that for the outlay we already have to make we could put on a weekend of music and make two, three times the money.'

'But there are other considerations. I mean, have you thought of the effect of the sheer weight of numbers on the house and grounds, and the village? The public liability alone is going to be like the national debt.'

'It already is,' said Fred. 'And, quite honestly, bar a few token rumbles, Witherburn is raring to go.'

'Naturally,' said Miranda, 'if it turns out to be absolute hell and a year from now we're wringing our hands and saying never again, then that'll be that. But I think we owe it to Ladycross to give it a try.'

'Speaking personally,' said Penny, who'd been quiet till now, 'the very idea scares the life out of me. I think you're awfully brave, but I'm jolly glad I shan't be there.'

'She's not brave, she's barmy,' said Fred. 'But it's time a little token madness was reintroduced into the Montclere line. We've been without it for too long.'

Rock on the Manor was an unparalleled success. Scarcely a cross word, as Fred observed, and an atmosphere, prevailing over three rain-free days, of gloriously irresponsible euphoria. Even the commonsense diehards from St John's and the local constabulary were obliged to admit that their job had been an easy one. The mess on the morning after – like a battlefield but without the bodies – was daunting, but was at least the source of bonding among the long row of villagers and friends who moved across the hundred-acre site with their binbags and work gloves. There had to be a little suffering by which to gauge the extent of the success.

Let's do it again, they cried – but not next week!

They decided on another the next year, to consolidate their success, and alternate years from then on. It was Miranda's coming-of-age as Lady Stratton. She had put her celebrity to work in the service of Ladycross, taken full responsibility and put in superhuman amounts of effort and time to ensure a profitable – and enjoyable – outcome. She'd been mindful of the concerns of the locals and kept them informed and involved at every stage. She had made them feel that her cause was theirs, too. Rock on the Manor enabled the conversion of the outbuildings to begin, with the creation of a handful of local jobs. Improvements to the house were put under way, and there were plans to increase the number of open days as a result, with all the contingent benefits to Witherburn.

Fred was boyishly overjoyed by her triumph.

'Darling, I am so darn proud of you – you missed your vocation, you know. You have a genius for this sort of thing. Don't, for God's sake, start hiring out your services as an organiser, or I won't see you at all.'

It was his pleasure that meant most to her. She had conceived the idea and made a present of it to him. She had never needed to win her spurs as far as Fred was concerned, but Rock on the Manor was the exhausting, exhilarating proof of her love.

Miles had come up on the second night, out of filial duty rather than enthusiasm, leaving Penny at home with the children. She and Fred had taken him down to the site, to their privileged position at the side of the stage, for half an hour of the Urban Myth set. It was pretty clear the whole thing was an ordeal for him, and the music left him cold, but he was touchingly determined to give credit where credit was due.

'You've obviously done incredibly well,' he said, over late snifters, with the pounding pulse of the concert still audible even in the kitchen at the back of the house. 'I do congratulate you. The logistics of all this boggle the imagination.'

'I'm a good delegator. And one thing I do bring to this job is a blue-chip address book.'

'She's being modest,' said Fred. 'None of it would have happened without her, and the fact that, touch wood, the whole thing's going so well, is entirely due to her too.'

497

'I believe it,' said Miles. He raised his glass and bowed his head in her direction. 'Here's to a great achievement.'

The years slipped past. She began to appreciate the truth of the saying that time passed more quickly as you got older. She decided that, in her case, it had something to do with the tyranny of the diary. Since coming to Ladycross, this year's was always full for months in advance, and she had to buy next year's the moment it was available. There was rarely a chance for them simply to be in the moment. Even on holiday Fred had to remain in touch, contingency plans took up the preceding week, and the last few days would be a winding-up for what awaited them at home.

Tom and Pauline came to visit. Pauline was predictably and volubly knocked out by the house, the contents, the grounds and, most of all, Fred.

'You've got a real gem there,' she confided, when they were out for a walk, the men in conversation a little way ahead.

'I know.'

'Course you do. Like me. I love Tom to pieces. But that man of yours is a real charmer, like Nigel Havers. I've always liked Nigel Havers.'

Miranda laughed. 'Yes, he is rather. I'm very lucky.'

'So's he!' Pauline gave her a womanly nudge. 'He's a poppet but he's no spring chicken and look what he's got! His mates must be green at the gills.'

'I wouldn't know. He hasn't got all that many.'

'Well, men don't, do they?' She nodded towards their respective husbands. 'Pity they can't get to see more of each other. Tom could do with a bit of male bonding at the moment. Which way does your old man vote?'

Miranda reflected that there were sections of society where such a question would be considered in the worst possible taste, and to answer it even more so, but she was dealing with professionals here. 'Liberal. That's old money, not SDP.'

'So, nobody's perfect. What about you?'

'A fully paid-up Don't Know, I'm afraid.'

'That's a respectable position. To spoil a paper is to make a mark, but don't tell Tom I said so.'

Tom was tired, he said, of being in opposition. And just plain tired.

'I've done my stint in the salt mines, Ragsy,' he said. 'It's not what I came into politics for. If I thought we were ever going to make a difference, even to this bloody shower, it'd be worth it, but whatever we sling at them just bounces off their thick hides. We're right, but they win, same thing every time. Truth is, I've had enough.'

Miranda was shocked. Tom's stubborn, principled commitment to the cause was one of the givens of her adult life; something she could scarcely understand, but was glad was there. 'You're not going to stand down, are you?'

'If we don't make it next time I will. You start thinking, Maybe it's me – people like me – who are the trouble, who are stopping us winning.'

'That can't be the case. You're the backbone of the party.'

'Yes, and seventy-five per cent of the population suffers with back problems that render them ineffective for weeks every year.'

They were sitting over coffee in the dining room. Pauline, who had been deep in conversation with Fred, had nonetheless got her radar switched on.

'He's not on about packing it in, is he?'

'I'm afraid so.'

'Say something, Miranda, tell him. I couldn't stand it. What would he do with himself? It'd drive us all mad.'

'You watch me,' said Tom. 'I'll write my memoirs, be the scourge of that after-dinner circuit. There'll never be a dull moment.'

'I've only just made your acquaintance,' said Fred, 'but I have to say it doesn't sound like you.'

'You're not wrong, Fred.' Pauline gave her husband a didn't-I-tell-you? look. 'You tell him.'

*   *   *

When they were getting ready for bed on the night the Worsleys had left, Miranda voiced her fears. 'I think he'd die without politics.'

'With the redoubtable Pauline on his side? Never.'

'He loves politics and the Labour Party more than anything, including Pauline. She's a realist, she knows that. That's why she's so scared of him packing it in.'

She was standing in front of the bathroom mirror in her nightshirt, putting moisturiser on her face. Fred put his arms round her from behind and rested his chin on her shoulder. Their twin reflections, his smiling, hers serious, looked back at them.

'I bet he loved you more than politics.'

'No, he didn't. I was an aberration where Tom was concerned. Pauline's exactly right for him.'

'Hmm . . .' He nuzzled her neck. 'That's what passion is, an aberration. We are not ourselves.'

'And all that stuff about the after-dinner circuit is bollocks. He's far too honourable to do the dirty on anyone, and it's only by doing the dirty that ex-politicians make money, as far as I can see.'

Fred turned her to face him, and kissed her. 'That's what I like . . . a well-oiled woman at bedtime . . .'

'You don't believe I'm serious, do you?'

'I do, actually,' he said, adopting a more serious tone himself as he got into bed. 'But I don't see what purpose is served by worrying about something you can't do a thing about. Your friend Tom is an extremely sane fellow, married to a woman who is a veritable powerhouse of good sense. I'm sure that between them they'll see him right.'

'I hope so.'

'Besides,' he opened his arms for her, 'the truth is I'm a bit jealous.'

She laughed as she snuggled against him. 'That's ridiculous.'

'Don't think I'm serious, do you?' he mimicked.

'In this case, no.'

'Well, you should. Listen.' He drew back from her a little so he could see her face. 'When you married me you took on

500

Ladycross. A challenge to which you rose, heroically. But when I married you I took on your prime, your beauty, glamour, fame, and about a zillion other men's hearts. And I'm old, and . . .' he hesitated fractionally, as though he'd been about to say one thing and changed his mind '. . . neither famous nor glamorous. No, quiet. I can't stop men falling in love with you – soppy susceptible romantics that we are, they're always going to do that. But those men who've actually succeeded in borrowing *your* heart for a while – that's different. They're competition. Bound by definition to be nice, but they make me uneasy just the same, yes?'

She touched his cheek. 'Yes. All right. I understand. But there is absolutely nothing for you to be jealous of, or about.'

'Unfortunately there doesn't need to be . . .' Eyes closed, he turned his mouth into her palm and kissed it. 'They only have to be there. The fact that Tom is so obviously an excellent man in every respect doesn't help.'

'He's just an old friend I worry about,' she whispered. 'He doesn't compare to you.'

Suddenly, Fred clasped her tight. 'I don't want to clip your wings, my darling . . . It's the last thing I want. But I'm only human and I wish I could keep you to myself for ever.'

'You can,' she said, stroking his head. 'You can.'

There was no reply. He held her close till long after he fell asleep when, scarcely able to breathe, she gently extricated herself from his embrace. She had hardly ever seen him sad, he was naturally sanguine and buoyant, but tonight, even in sleep, his face looked drawn, and old.

Twice a year they had her mother to stay, and twice a year she went down to Haywards Heath. She always dreaded the Ladycross visits, and they always turned out far better than she expected. This was largely due to Fred's sureness of touch with his mother-in-law – a combination of flattery, directness and the mildest ageism that involved the two of them playing the seniority card against Miranda.

Warmed by a couple of bottles of claret, he got her to teach him the mambo. He was a better pupil than Marjorie was a teacher and the result by the end of the evening was a pretty stylish performance that moved from the library into the hall and left both of them short of breath.

During the day Miranda traded shamelessly on the fact of how much she had to do. Early on Marjorie had struck up a relationship with Mrs Bird, based, Miranda suspected, on their shared view that Miranda had no aptitude for matters domestic, but was making a commendable fist of it, considering. It was perfectly plain that neither her mother nor Mrs Bird would have believed her capable of the job she did. Sometimes it appeared that having once been a model precluded you, in many people's eyes, from achieving anything that required more than half a brain cell.

When she went home, the boot was on the other foot. Marjorie was anxious to show Miranda that she, too, had a life, and one that was not dependent on her daughter's status. Miranda welcomed this new feistiness, but nothing could have prepared her for her mother's greatest coup.

She went down to Haywards Heath in the lull between the second Rock on the Manor and the first of the year's shooting parties. It was dull, tired, late-summer weather and she herself felt jaded. Fred was staying in London at the Travellers Club, seeing his solicitor and obtaining some valuations from Sotheby's. Unusually, he'd opted not to join her for a night at her mother's.

'Will you forgive me if I don't this time? Give my love to your mama, and I'll hope to see her soon. And tell her to get warmed up, the lambada's next.'

Marjorie affected to be devastated. 'Oh, no, I am disappointed – I found *The Best of Edmundo Ross* on CD as well . . .'

'Never mind,' said Miranda. 'We're both a bit shattered after the rock festival. Just you and me will be cosy.'

'It would have been so nice, though, to have Fred along. I've invited some friends to dinner tomorrow night,' Marjorie told her. 'Who'd love to have met him.'

Miranda's heart sank. It was almost unprecedented for her

mother to have people round and, given that she'd done so, it was true that Fred's presence as a social solvent would have made all the difference. She on her own, an ex-model married-in, was not a trophy of the same lustre.

The following afternoon her mother retreated into feverish culinary activity and she took the opportunity to go and visit Dale and Kaye. She rang first, sensing that Kaye was not someone who'd welcome being dropped in on if things were, for some reason, not up to scratch.

She was wrong on two counts. 'Come and have a drink after Dale gets in,' said Kaye, 'and meet James – I let him stay up to see his dad. You'll have to take us as you find us, though – you won't mind that, will you?'

James was seven months old and already crawling about like a small steamroller. Miranda had never till now caught the full flavour of the American expression 'rugrat'. The immaculate taupe carpets were strewn with toys and there was a plastic crate containing disposable nappies and wet wipes in the downstairs cloakroom. A mesh playpen like a lobster pot, which Miranda thought might have come in handy, was being used as a dump for less-favoured toys. Over the random stone fireplace hung one of those multiple photo-frames, every space displaying James, on his own or attended by one or other of his adoring parents.

If, as Fred thought, there were men who were still in love with Miranda, Dale was no longer among them. She, and even the still immaculate Kaye, had now been usurped in Dale's affections. Miranda watched in astonishment as he lay full-length among the plastic litter, not noticing, let alone blenching when his son dribbled curds on his work suit, allowing his hair to be tugged and his glasses yanked. When an acrid smell began to make itself known he picked the baby up, sniffed the offending area and went off to deal with it with a smile and a song.

Miranda smiled in astonishment at Kaye. 'I have to ask, is he always like this?'

'James or Dale?'

'Oh, James is sweet. But Dale – it's as if he's been in training for this all his life.'

'He's completely besotted,' said Kaye. 'All the magazine articles warn against making your husband feel left out, but it's more likely to be me that's left out in this house. I swear if Dale didn't have the office to go to I'd never see the baby at all.'

'Still,' said Miranda, 'it must be great to be able to share everything.'

Dale put his head round the door. 'I think it's bathtime.'

'Fine,' said Kaye. 'Have fun.'

Dale's head popped back in. 'Mandy, why don't you come up and take a peep in a few minutes?'

'I'd love to.'

Dale's rendition of 'The Grand Old Duke of York' as he went up the stairs contrasted with the sudden silence in the living room. Kaye moved Dale's untouched wineglass and topped up hers and Miranda's. Her French manicure was a work of art. When her heel slipped on a foam rubber brick she kicked it aside but did not pick it up.

'How are you, Kaye?' asked Miranda.

The answer came after a pause, which seemed fraught rather than reflective. 'Doing my best.'

Miranda was shocked to see that she was holding back tears. 'Kaye?'

'I wasn't expecting to get pregnant so soon. Some time, of course, but . . . I've always worked, I had plans.'

'It must be the most tremendous shock to the system.'

'Yes. And I don't seem to be dealing with it very well—' She pressed her lips together.

'Thank goodness Dale's being supportive,' said Miranda. There followed another heaving silence. 'You can go back to work. When you're good and ready, I mean. It's not the end, surely, just different. And James is absolute heaven.'

'He is, he's lovely . . . But, Mandy, I don't know what I'm supposed to be doing.'

It was a *cri de coeur*. 'Tell me.'

'Suddenly the baby's the centre of everything. Dale's much better at all of it than I am, he's a natural and I'm not. I feel like some kind of hired help who keeps things going during the day till he gets home. And he doesn't want me going back to work

504

just yet because he can't bear the thought of James being in a day nursery. So I'm left with feeling inadequate, which isn't something I'm used to. And the weird thing is he was never that keen on a family. When it happened he wasn't over the moon, he just accepted it. But the moment James was born it was as though he'd had some kind of conversion. And I wasn't like that. I love James, but I can't compete.'

'Surely you don't have to,' said Miranda. 'If Dale's so good at it, indulge him. You're looking wonderful, by the way, I'd have thought that was a triumph in itself. I've never brought up a baby but I'm sure if I did the first thing to be let go would be me.'

Kaye managed a damp smile. 'I do try. It makes me feel a bit more in control, a bit more like someone with a purpose.'

'Girls!' called Dale from the landing. 'An audience is granted!'

When Miranda left, Kaye came out to the car with her while Dale began tidying up the living room. 'I'm sorry I got weepy on you.'

'Don't be so silly, you've every right. If talking helps, I was glad to listen.'

'I do love Dale. And James.'

'I can see that. And they love you.'

'I suppose so . . . They're so wrapped up in each other it's hard to tell.'

'Listen.' Miranda took Kaye's hands in hers and held them firmly. 'Here's what I think. As James gets older he's going to be so proud of his mother, who always looked great, and was different and independent. And Dale must be the envy of his friends, having a wife like you who looks so gorgeous when she's just had a baby. Play to your strengths, Kaye. For what it's worth from a standpoint of complete ignorance, I think you're all doing *brilliantly*.'

They embraced. Miranda felt the other woman's shoulders tighten over a sob.

'Thanks, Mandy. Come again, won't you?'

'Try and stop me.'

★　　★　　★

'How were they?' asked Marjorie, when she got back. 'And the little one?'

'Blooming,' said Miranda, with enough emphasis to close the subject.

'I'm not trying to rush you but they're invited for seven forty-five.'

From this Miranda inferred that a major effort was expected. She didn't have many options with her, so retained her black trousers, swapped her sweater for a grey silk shirt and put on amethyst earrings then makeup.

The first to arrive were Rod and Carol, a couple from Marjorie's Latin-American dance class. They were a tad younger than Marjorie and were so determinedly vivacious that they might have had 'We are wild and wacky' stamped on their foreheads. Disconcertingly, Carol opened the batting by putting her hands to her mouth and emitting a little shriek. 'Look at her, Rod! She's exactly like her pictures! Did you ever see anyone so stunning! Marje, do you have a paper bag I can put over my head?'

Rod stepped forward and held out his hand. 'How do you do? The wife's pleased to meet you, as you can probably tell.'

Carol soon rallied, however. She perched trimly on the sofa next to Miranda and subjected her to a rapid-fire interrogation. 'Is your husband not here?'

'I'm afraid he's tied up with meetings in London, he's so disappointed.'

'What a shame . . . But I still can't believe we're meeting *you*. Rags! Do you get sick of people saying that?'

'Not at all, it's very flattering, but it's years since I did any modelling.'

'But you're a legend. Legends are for ever.'

Miranda pulled a wry face. 'Legend sounds fearfully old.'

'For ever *young*! For ever *young* is what I meant!'

Carol's level of excitable adulation was rather exhausting, and it was something of a relief when the third guest arrived, and was greeted warmly by everyone.

'And this is my daughter Miranda Montclere,' said Marjorie,

adding with a nonchalance that fooled no-one: 'Lady Stratton. Mandy, this is my friend Brian Conroy.'

Miranda shook the hand of a dark, dapper man in his early fifties, in a blue suit and a red tie. 'So,' she said, when he'd been furnished with a drink by Rod and they were all sitting down, 'how do you all know each other?'

'From Taking Steps,' said Brian; he had the faintest Irish accent. 'The dance academy.'

'We're all *aficionados*,' said Rod. 'Latin-American freaks.'

Carol gave another little shriek. 'Who are you calling a freak? Let me hand round these delicious dips . . .'

Brian fixed Miranda with a peculiar, unblinking gaze, which she was sure he worked on. 'Your mother's a fine dancer.'

'So I believe. She and Fred – my husband – samba up a storm, given half a chance.'

'Do they now. What about the tango?'

'Brian's a taxi-partner,' said Rod. 'He can make anyone look good.'

'I wouldn't say that.'

'It's true, though,' said Marjorie. 'I find the tango very, very difficult but with Brian I'm away!'

Over dinner Miranda became certain of two things: that she did not care for Brian; and that her mother was infatuated with him. Miranda did not like his boot-black hair, his prissy Irish voice, his fixed stare or his unshakeable self-satisfaction. But there was no denying Marjorie's sparkle, the upward inflection in her voice, her readiness to laugh and her more assured and flirtatious body language. If Brian Conroy was responsible for these changes, Miranda conceded he must be doing something right.

At the end of the evening he stayed for nearly an hour after Rod and Carol had gone, and she was suddenly struck by the awful thought that perhaps he was going to spend the night, and that she should therefore absent herself tactfully as if she were the parent and Brian and her mother the youthful lovebirds needing time on their own. She wished she didn't find it so dismaying: her mother was surely more entitled than most to some romance and happiness at this late stage – yet she was appalled.

In the end she did announce that she was tired, and would they mind if she went up? At once he got to his feet.

'I've outstayed my welcome. Two gorgeous women and a brandy and I lose all sense of time, and decorum. Miranda,' he held out his hand, fixing her with that bright, crow-like stare, 'it's been a pleasure.'

'It was very nice to meet you, too.'

'Marjorie, another delightful dinner as always.'

'I'll see you out.'

'Will you be coming to the salsa workshop next Tuesday?'

Miranda didn't go up, but went into the kitchen and poured herself a glass of water. When she emerged her mother waylaid her in the hall. 'What do you think?'

'It was a really good evening, Mum, thanks so much. Lovely food.'

'No, what do you think? Of Brian?'

Oh, God, she thought. It's official. 'He seems like a nice man.'

'He is, he's absolutely charming.' Marjorie tilted her head. 'You probably guessed, we're an item.'

Miranda knew from the way this announcement had been made that she should have expressed joy and delight, but she couldn't: she simply could not. The most she could manage was a casual worldliness that bore equally little relation to her true feelings.

'Good for you, Mum, that's terrific. You're looking tremendous on it.' She kissed Marjorie's pink cheek. 'Night. Don't suppose I have to wish you sweet dreams . . .'

She went up the stairs briskly, and into her room, where she collapsed on her bed, hating herself.

But Marjorie was not going to let it rest there. At breakfast next morning, with Miranda due to leave in less than an hour, she broached the subject once more. 'I ought to tell you, Mandy, that he's asked me to marry him.'

'Has he?'

'About a week ago.'

'And what did you say?'

'I told him I'd think about it. I wanted you to meet him first.'

'Why?' said Miranda, sounding abrasive even to herself.

'Because I value your opinion. No, your judgement. Remember,' her voice trembled, and she cleared her throat, 'I've only known your father.'

Miranda was flooded with remorse. 'Mum, I'm sorry. I'm pleased for you, truly. But I don't know Brian, and I can't take responsibility for your future.'

'You must have had an instinct, though. Go <u>on</u>. Please, Mandy.'

'All right, then. Since you ask. He's quite a bit younger than you, and he's . . .' she sought the word '. . . a smoothie.'

'Yes,' said Marjorie, her face alight with satisfaction. 'He is, isn't he?'

'I can't believe she'll actually do it!' she wailed to Fred on the way home. 'That she'll marry that creep!'

'The cry of relations down the ages,' observed Fred.

'I want her to be *happy*, just not with him.'

'I hate to say this, my darling, but it doesn't matter what you think of him.'

'She asked my opinion!'

'That doesn't mean it's going to make any serious difference to what she does. If she's in love with him she'll hear what she wants to hear. Besides, she was in love with your father once. Maybe she's one of those women who genuinely prefer cads. I hear they're out there.'

'I don't know that he's a cad. He's just smug and vain.'

'One woman's vain is another woman's charming . . .' He pulled over, hazard lights flashing, on to the hard shoulder.

'What are you doing?'

'I'm a bit whacked – could you bear to take over?'

'Of course.' They were in the Morgan, and she noticed that

it took him longer than usual to extricate his long frame from the driving seat. When they rejoined the motorway, she asked, 'Are you all right, Freddie? I'm sorry I was banging on, you do look tired.'

'The bugger of it is I'm tired all the time at the moment. More tired than I should be.'

'You do too much.'

'Only what has to be done. Isn't there a song about it taking me all night to do what I used to do all night?'

'"The Oldest Swinger In Town." And that's *certainly* not true.'

'I'm getting old, my darling. Correction, I am old.'

'Never, never, never.'

'Sweet . . . Yes. I know it's in the mind but the poor old body can't always keep up, and it doesn't seem to at the moment.'

She was shocked: she wouldn't have it. 'We need a holiday.'

'Maybe. But we're not going to get one till the new year, so . . .'

They drove for a few miles in silence, very fast.

'How old did you say your mother's boyfriend was?'

'I don't know – fifty?'

'Younger than me, much. And she's, what, sixty?'

'Sixty-one.'

'Wish them well,' said Fred. 'Women being what they are, she'll probably outlive him anyway. And in the meantime she'll have the time of her life.'

Five minutes later, when she glanced his way, he was asleep.

CHAPTER TWENTY-THREE

Claudia, 145

Claudia hadn't been unduly alarmed to begin with. She herself was profoundly shocked by her disagreement with Publius, so how much more would Gaius be if he'd been aware of it? When she'd found he wasn't in his bed she'd called his name a couple of times, but there was no answer, she didn't panic. Their son often wandered off, and on this occasion had good reason to want them to suffer: that was only natural.

Publius was more worried than her, his concern fanned to anger by what Claudia hoped was a disturbed conscience. 'Hasn't he caused enough trouble already today? I'm at the end of my patience with the boy.'

'You've made that clear enough.'

'I suppose I'd better get together some of the slaves and go out looking for him. That's what he wants, to cause maximum disruption to the whole household.'

'You know it isn't. He was frightened, first by you, and then by us arguing. It's been a long, exciting day, and distressing enough without us adding to it. We should have known better.'

Publius stopped short of agreeing with her on this, but his grim silence spoke for him. Her own voice was softer when she next spoke. 'Don't turn out the search party just yet. It won't be dark for quite a while. Let me take a look in some of the places he likes to go. He'll probably be there, hiding from us.'

'Making us pay,' said Publius ruefully. 'A night in the open would probably sort out all this nonsense.'

'Is that what you want? For us to leave him out there?'

'He'd come creeping back – but no. You see if you can flush him out.'

'Thank you.'

As her husband walked away, Claudia knew from the set of his shoulders the expression on his face – furious, hurt, baffled.

She walked quietly down towards the temple, not calling this time. If Gaius was licking his wounds in some corner she didn't want to frighten him away.

There was no one in the temple. Her heart pattered like a captive mouse in the silence. She lit a candle and said a prayer to each of the gods, the most fervent she'd ever offered. Their smooth, calm faces and opaque eyes gave precious little in the way of comfort, but the ritual was calming.

Emerging from the temple her sandalled foot hit something, a stray stone, perhaps, which rattled on the stone surface. In her agitated state this small pain made tears spring to her eyes and she swept the object impatiently away with the side of her shoe, sending it skidding into the grass.

'Gaius?'

There was no response, only the soft British air, creaking and dripping with moisture. Her feet were soon wet as she took the path away from the house across the side of the hill, but it was anxiety, not cold, that made her shiver.

She lost track of time, but after a while she thought she heard the sound of other people, men's voices, Publius' search party setting out. They were probably worried about her too by now, and for a moment she considered turning back and joining them. But then, suddenly, she saw Tiki.

He emerged like a ghost from the long grass at the side of the path, about a hundred yards ahead of her, and sat in a characteristic position – front paws slightly apart, head cocked, waiting for her to catch up. As she drew closer his tail swished back and forth a few times in a subdued greeting.

'Hallo, boy.' She patted and stroked him. He submitted to the petting, but his coat was wet and he was trembling. 'Where have you been?'

In a moment he rose stiffly, and paced away from Claudia, and from the path. His head and tail hung low, he didn't once look back at her but seemed to trust her to follow. The hills were deceptive up here: within moments of leaving the track it was no longer visible, and neither was the villa, shielded by the rising ground behind her with its scattering of wind-bent trees. She might have been miles from anywhere.

Tiki looked an old gentleman this evening. There was no spring in his step; his shoulder blades poked as he walked. The bounding puppy who had saved her sanity and cheered her loneliness so many years ago was nearing the end of his life.

The evening hush settled on them. Tiki's footsteps were inaudible; she could only just make out the whispering heartbeat of her own tread and the rustle of her hem in the grass.

Suddenly unsure of herself she stopped and called softly: 'Tiki!'

He paused and looked at her over his shoulder.

'Tiki . . . here, boy. Come here.'

Laying his ears down apologetically, and with a slow wag of his tail, he turned, but did not come. Instead he sat, gazing across the small distance between them, the very image of patient, divided loyalty. The moment she began to move towards him he stood once more, with the utmost weariness, and continued on his way, as if he had simply been waiting for her signal to go on. It was impossible not to interpret his movements as intelligent, not to feel that he was leading her somewhere – to show her something she both desired and dreaded.

Not for long, though. In another few quiet moments the dog stopped and flopped down at the side of the path, his head on his paws, panting slightly. The message in his eyes now seemed to be one of exhausted responsibility, and a dull, pleading hope.

They had reached one of those rocky declivities, small but steep, which scored the sides of these northern hills. The narrow sheep track along which they'd walked wound round to the right before cutting diagonally across the flank of the hill, away from the tumble of scree that swooped almost vertically beneath Claudia's feet.

Gaius lay at the foot of the slope. Having fallen headlong, he had come to rest in an attitude Claudia had often seen him adopt when asleep – legs curled to one side, head leaning slightly to the other, arms spread wide. Now, though, something in the angle of the head and neck told her that her son was dead.

Without a second thought she stepped forward over the lip of the ledge, skidding and stumbling on the loose stones, falling, catching herself, tearing her clothes and cutting her feet, hands and face. She heard herself sob, but felt no pain: she was engaged only in reaching Gaius.

When she did so she was unable to stop, and had to clutch at his leg: his body slithered sideways against her, head lolling, she clutched it, they went on down together, as if engaged in some boisterous game, the gravelly surface shaving the skin off her arm and leg. When they reached the bottom – the whole distance was no more than twenty yards but felt like a hundred – she simply lay there, holding Gaius in her arms. There was still no physical pain, but with the cessation of movement came the return of feeling, a slow blooming of grief: the blood trickling on Claudia's skin was like her heart's tears, seeping from her. She rocked, murmured his name, not to recall him but to print it on his soul and hers. His head flopped on its broken stem of neck as it had when it was still pliant, when he was newborn. She cradled it against her shoulder with one hand as she had done then, feeling the still-warm imprint of his short span as she had then the fresh heat of the one just beginning. His thin child's limbs, so awkward and uncoordinated in life, were limply graceful as a faun's in death. She draped his arm about her neck, simulating the embrace he could not give. She held him so tightly that her own arms trembled with the force of it. If she could have taken him back into herself, to the safe, warm, nourishing secret place from which he had come, she would have done so.

In the distance, growing closer, she could hear the shouts of the search party to which she must reply.

But not yet.

*   *   *

She had kept that brief time to herself – those moments before she called to Publius and told him where they were. She indulged a private ecstasy of grief, as intimate and wholly hers as the first time she had put Gaius to the breast. Something in her said that the moment Publius and others – friends, slaves, colleagues – knew of his death, she would become strong and dignified, knowing her own particular grief was greater than theirs, a near-mortal wound that she would hide and guard jealously. For this brief space only she could give way to it, hugging the sweetness of her little boy to her, and herself alone, for the last time.

When she first cried out, she barely had a voice, only the merest scratch on the damp, dusky air. She had to gather all her forces and when her voice eventually came it brought with it all the physical sensations that had till now been numbed. Wounds and grazes opened, her wrist and knee throbbed with pain, tears coursed down her cheeks.

'Publius! Publius, we're here! We're here!'

There was a lull in the men's voices, she could picture him saying, 'Hush – did you hear something?'

'Publius!' She was weeping now, the sobs drowning out his name. 'Publius, can you hear me? We're here!'

Another tiny pause, and now she heard her husband's voice, saying harshly, commandingly, 'There's the dog! Follow the dog!'

Tiki would bring them, as he had brought her. She bowed her head over Gaius and closed her eyes. It was over. And the rest, all the rest, had just begun.

Publius and a couple of others climbed down to her. He said quietly, 'Here . . .' and took Gaius from her. He did not hold the boy close as she had done: the limp body lay draped like a discarded robe over his arms, the head hanging back. She had closed his eyes, but for some reason there remained a slit between the lids, like those of a cat in the sun, which mocked and marred the peace of death.

Publius said nothing, but passed Gaius to the slaves to carry, and himself helped her along the side of the hill to where they could rejoin the path and climb back up to the grassy ledge where the others were waiting. Below them on the bare slope rabbits were beginning to emerge and hop about, but tonight there was no danger that the aged and exhausted Tiki would go after them. The low sun sent a broad wedge of buttery light along the opposite flank of the valley but on this side it was becoming cooler and darker with each minute.

At the top of the hill were two more of the house slaves – Luke among them – and Publius' horse Nesta looking fresh and moving restlessly, its ears pricked. As they appeared, Tiki rose stiffly and stood staring towards them with his head low. He didn't wag his tail. Everything about him spoke of resignation and despair. Claudia saw the shock and distress on the faces of the others as they appeared, but no one spoke. Publius helped her on to the horse's back and indicated that Luke should lead her. He took Gaius back into his arms and walked alongside, still holding his son's body stiffly, as if in some formal rite. Tiki brought up the rear. In this small, quiet procession they made their way back to the house. Once there they laid Gaius in his room. Publius, evading Claudia's touch, withdrew into the still and whispering house.

Severina, her face like a bone, came to help wash Gaius and lay him out in clean clothes. They lit only one lamp. Neither of them wept, though the softly shadowed room ached with their unshed tears.

As they went about their tasks – fetching water and towels, removing his tunic, finding fresh clothes – it was Severina who spoke, her old woman's practicality and stoicism giving voice to thoughts that echoed Claudia's. Her remarks needed no response: they were no more than a gentle counterpoint to what had to be done.

'This takes me back to when he was a baby . . . Arms up, there we go . . . Let your mother hold you there while Severina does your back, there's a boy . . . Look at this hair, no easier now than it ever was . . . Where do you get this hair from, sticking out in all directions? And you could grow vegetables under these fingernails . . .'

She sighed, and clicked her tongue gently, but her little commentary was a comfort to them both. In a far part of the house they could hear one of the girls crying, with the healing spontaneity of youth – doubtless one of the same girls who'd looked askance at Gaius as a strange one, with his moodiness and awkwardness and his going off on his own all the time. But Claudia was touched to hear the crying. The young were like animals, instinctive, free of anticipation or dread or a sense of what was appropriate. It was good that the girl was unjustifiably profligate with her emotions, for she was weeping for two: Claudia's heart was bolted and barred.

When they'd finished, they left the lamp burning in the room, for company. Claudia noticed that the little dog was gone.

'He'll have had it with him,' said Severina. 'He always had it with him.'

'Tomorrow I'll go back and look for it. Luke could go down the mountainside.'

'If you must.'

Claudia had learned to overlook this slightly accusatory note but now, with Gaius lying there between them, it was too much to bear.

'It's not a question of whether I must, it's what I'd like to do, Severina.'

'Very well.'

'He'd want it to be – to be with him.'

'I dare say.'

'Thank you for your help.'

Severina raised a hand and shook her head. Her mouth was a thin line, her eyes fiercely bright. She began to move away. Claudia caught her hand, turned her gently towards her and folded her in her arms. For a short moment the two women were bound together physically, and by grief, but each was spared the onslaught of the other's distress, their privacy protected by the embrace. When they drew back they resumed the composure of mistress and servant. Any further tears would be shed in private. But the bond of a child's short lifetime had been sealed.

Severina left the room. Without the focus of a practical task her step was that of a very old woman, shaky and hesitant. Tiki was lying by the door: in the soft darkness his eyes gleamed as he rolled them up towards Severina. He would no longer run her ragged and she would never more rant and rail at him. Claudia crouched down and fondled his cool, satin-soft ears. He lay very still but was trembling slightly.

Publius appeared and walked slowly along the colonnade towards them. Claudia knew he would have been waiting for Severina to leave. She rose, but Tiki remained motionless, his head on his paws.

'Come and see him,' she said, and led the way back into the room. As she went she held out her hand but he did not take it. And if she had been expecting a moment of truth and intimacy such as they used to have, a crashing down of the barriers, it did not happen. Even the manner in which he walked past her to Gaius' bedside told her that he wished to do so alone. She went back to Tiki and crouched there, stroking the dog's quivering back, as lost and confused as he was.

Publius stood by the bed, his back to her. He looked massive, a much bigger man than he was, silhouetted by the small light of the lamp, his shadow spreading like a black cape across the floor behind him. He did not appear to touch Gaius, but she told herself that his fingertips must surely have brushed his son's hand without her being able to see . . .

'We must make arrangements.' His voice was firm and hard. 'I'll post an announcement at the barracks. And the funeral should be tomorrow, or the next day.'

'He'll want to be buried here.'

'I'm not so sure about that – in the garden, like a pet dog.'

She flinched at the disdain in his voice. 'By the temple, perhaps.'

'We'll see.' He turned. 'Claudia?'

She got to her feet. 'I'm here.'

'What are you doing on the floor?'

'I was – the dog—'

'Mm.' Publius looked down at Tiki. 'He'll go soon.'

She stood immediately before him, barring his way. 'My husband. Publius. How are we to bear this?'

'With strength. Calmly.'

'We waited so long for him . . . and he was with us for so short a time . . .' She crossed her arms tight over her heart, bowed her head, rocked, longed to lean on him or for him to draw her against him, but he did not. 'Our beautiful son,' she whispered.

'I've asked Luke to watch over him.' He laid a hand on her shoulder, the briefest of touches, before moving away. She thought she caught the words, 'He could never have lived . . .' drift in the air behind him like the vapour of a winter's breath.

She went to their room. Only Tiki remained – too old, too tired and too devoted to leave his post.

Publius did not join her. There was a double emptiness in the bed. She cried long past the point where it seemed possible to cry any more, until her eyes were burning cracks in her swollen face and her mouth felt like an open wound. Her chest ached, and her arms and legs would not be still, still searching, reaching, for her child.

Far into the sleepless night, when the weeping had exhausted her and the stillness was like black water filling the spaces of the house, Claudia crept out of bed, wrapped herself in her *stola* and made her way to Gaius' room. It was the darkest time and, like the stars, the little lamp had gone out. It was not until she was near the door that she realised Tiki was still there, now curled in a tight ball, acknowledging no one, and that Luke had gone. Her heart lurched. Leaning on the wall for support, lightheaded with fear, she entered the bedroom, and felt her way to the side of the bed.

Gaius was lying there, but her relief lasted no more than a second. When her hand brushed his cool, stiffening one, the devastating reality of his death swept over her again. His body was here, for now. But Gaius would not be here again.

Memories of all the night-time visits she had made to his bedside crowded in on her: visits to say good-night, to tell stories, to sing— inexpertly — songs that her father and Tasso had sung for her, to soothe him when he was ill, comfort him when he was sad, or had bad dreams; and sometimes, as now, simply to tiptoe in and gaze on him, rapt with love.

That one accidental brush of hands was enough – she did not dare touch him again for fear of how he would feel. All that – the hugs and kisses and caresses – was consigned to memory now. Again she wrapped her own arms around herself, her hands pressed tight into her armpits, in an attempt to fill the void and put a tourniquet on her torn heart.

Then she saw Publius.

She might not have done so at all, but he stirred slightly in his sleep and made a dreamer's half-formed sound, as though about to speak. He was lying on the floor, close to the bed but on the further side, wrapped in his cloak, as he must have done many times in his soldier's tent, his head pillowed on his wrist.

Not wanting to, but knowing that it would be his wish, she left the room.

The announcement that Publius posted up was brief.

'Publius Roscius Coventinus and his wife Claudia have lost their son Gaius Roscius on Saturday 9 August. He lived for eight years and seven months.'

Claudia hoped and trusted that its brevity would be under-stood as the natural style of a military man, and not as want of feeling. She found the publicising of the death hard to accept. She sensed that the external formalities were a source of support for Publius: for her, they were a cruel exposure. The delicate caul of scar tissue could not even begin to form until these rites and observances had been undergone. She became cool and aloof – a little forbidding, so that people's well-meaning torrent of condolences was stemmed at source. If this, too, made her seem unnatural, then so be it. It was the only way she could manage.

On the day after his death Gaius, shrouded in clean linen

but with his face uncovered, was placed in a simple coffin of slate, made by the same mason who would make his memorial stone. On the evening of the following day some twenty people, friends and household, formed a procession from the house to his burial place near the temple. It was a day like its predecessor, one of capricious British weather that made your skin sweat one moment, pucker with cold the next, and punctuated with showers. At the time of the funeral the early evening was wet and fresh, with a pale sun showing its face as it sank between clouds and horizon.

Publius had agreed to Gaius' last resting place being here, and not in a more formal burial ground, justifying it on the grounds that their family would be here for generations and that it was proper such a site should be established on the property. Though glad of the decision, Claudia did not care to hear this. For now, for this moment, she wished only to think of her little son, not as part of some great scheme but for the dear, strange creature that he had been. There was a deeper reason, too, but she did not yet have the courage to examine it.

They had neither of them wanted a great cacophony of flute-players and horn-blowers, but she had conceded to Publius' wish for a single bagpiper – a tumultuous sound not to everyone's taste, but typical of this wild country where their son had been born. Tiki accompanied them, keeping level with Publius and a few yards to the side, his ears laid back miserably at the warble of the bagpipe. Because of his master's predilection for the instrument he'd got used to it, but when younger, Claudia recalled, he used to yelp and whine agitatedly at the sound. His complaints would delight Gaius, who imagined the dog was singing.

Breaking with tradition and protocol she persuaded Severina to walk near the front of the procession, just behind her. In this way everyone moved at her pace, and she would not be left behind. There were wild flowers mixed with roses on top of the coffin. Madoc – pale and dull-eyed with shock – had borrowed a little chestnut pony, a red pony, for the day, to pull the funeral cart. It was no beauty, but a solid domestic animal suited to the task, undismayed by either pipes or people.

They buried Gaius on the level ground on the side of the temple nearest the house so that, in winter anyway, it might be possible to see where he was. Here he would get the morning sun, and be sheltered from the prevailing wind, though at this time of day the area was in shadow. Claudia was glad of the concealing shade for this final parting with her boy. But sad that they had never found the little iron dog among the stones on the mountainside.

The burial was an ending of one sort, but the beginning, too, of a process of rediscovery. With the dead Gaius gone, the living one flowered vividly in Claudia's heart and memory. In the days and weeks following the funeral this process was often quite unbearably painful, the reliving of an amputation, but at other times, when she could sift through the pictures calmly, she knew that in the end they were the means by which she would be healed.

Publius returned to her bed but there was no reunion. Their physical proximity, without intimacy, was torture to her. If she did reach out to him he did not so much reject or ignore her, as seem not to notice, which was infinitely worse. Her own assumed aloofness and froideur at the funeral had been a defence against the occasion, and the intrusive sympathy of others. His distance seemed to her to be instinctive, an animal shrinking and freezing in the face of threat. But what threat? And if now, of all times, they did not have one another, what did they have?

The place where Publius was now was one where she, Claudia, could not be.

It was during this hurt, half-lit time, as late summer glowed and fizzled like a recalcitrant fire before being doused by clammy autumn, that the idea first occurred to her of returning to Rome. It was nothing as definite as a decision, or even an intention, simply a recurring notion, a mental picture of herself *in* Rome, in the house where she had been born, and played with Tasso, and listened to his singing and her father's sentimental verse . . . sitting in the courtyard with the sun on her arms and face . . . the sound of the fountain trickling, the throaty voices and rustling feathers of pigeons on the hot stone flags . . . the smell of the sun-warmed herbs . . . the din of the city, near but muffled by protective walls . . . No matter that the house was no longer hers. She had friends. Even – especially, perhaps – Cotta would welcome her with open arms. She pictured herself at home.

However many times she brushed the thought aside and erased the picture from her mind it always returned, and always stronger, like a loving, insistent friend tugging at her sleeve. From being a dream, an imagining, it grew into a possibility, something she might do, if only for a while. And then to being close to a plan, for after all – she made herself think it – what was there for her here?

Oddly, this was a subject she found easier to broach with the new distance between them. Being practical, it showed her acceptance of their situation, her calm recognition of their differences.

He looked, as always, bigger than he was, massive and solid in his uniform. He did not have to go to the garrison so often now, but the soldiering was in his blood: his strength and skill and consolation.

'Publius, I want to go to Rome for a while. You're occupied, and I'm lonely. I think I should get over Gaius' death more quickly at home.' The last word slipped out before she could prevent it, but his face showed nothing and he made no comment.

'I should prefer you to be here.'

'I shall be back.'

'I can't stop you.' He sat down heavily.

She thought, He looks old. Said, more gently: 'You can give me your blessing.'

'Then I do.'

The bleakness of this exchange alone might have served as a justification for her going, yet Claudia felt cheated. Two days later there was an alarm raised north of the Wall and Publius left with the men. His last words to her were 'I hope I shall see you when I get back. If I do not, I wish you a safe journey.'

So, she thought when he had gone, You have your escape and I shall have mine. But she did not leave at once. The truth was that, with Publius away and not expected back for some weeks, she could relax, visit Gaius as often as she liked, sing and talk to him for hours if she wanted. Once, in the very early morning, when she had not yet opened her eyes, she found herself thinking: My reason for being here has become my reason to leave. And the thought was like a small, deep cut, leaking unhappiness in her mind.

And then Severina became ill. Or, at least, ceased to be well. One morning when she had not been seen Claudia went to her room to find she could not get out of bed. Her attempts to sit upright when her mistress entered were pathetic.

'Severina, no – don't. Lie still.'

'I must rise!'

'No! You must *not*.' Claudia was firm. She sat down and pushed the old woman gently back. 'You must stay there. I'll send Luke for the doctor.'

'I don't need a doctor,' grumbled Severina, 'I need young bones, and it's too late for that.'

'It may be, but it's not too late for a rest. You're to stay there.' She took Severina's hand, thin as a bunch of stalks. 'Please. For my sake. As your friend.'

This was too much for Severina to take in. Being on friendly terms with one's employer was one thing; to be declared a friend took some thinking about. Her expression was stunned, but she lay still – resigned if not willing.

'You should have something to drink and to eat.'

Severina shook her head.

'You have to. How can you get better with nothing inside you?'

'I could manage a little beer,' came the grudging reply.

'Beer?'

'Just a little, mind.'

Claudia bit down a demur, and went to see to it. The shy, pretty British girl was hovering in the passageway.

'Minna, she says she'd like some beer.' She couldn't keep the doubt out of her voice, any more than Minna could keep the hint of amusement out of hers.

'I'll fetch some, lady.'

524

'With perhaps a little water in it.'

'Yes, lady.' From this small exchange Claudia inferred that Severina's liking for the local brew was something known and accepted by everyone except her employers.

She went back into the room. Severina's head was tilted slightly away, her once quick, busy hands lay on the coverlet like things useless and discarded. But her voice surprised Claudia with its firmness. 'I should like to go to Rome again.'

Claudia sat at the foot of the bed. 'You liked it there, didn't you?'

'I'd like to see it again.'

'Then you shall.' It was so easy to say. So easy to tell this weak old woman what she wanted to hear.

But though Severina was frail she was no fool. With a visible effort she moved her head so that she could see Claudia, her eyes black and bright as a bird's. 'Don't leave without me, lady.'

At that moment Minna came in with the cup of beer. Claudia didn't have to ask how news of her plan had reached Severina: the conscientious quietness of the house slaves was to their advantage too, they picked up all manner of titbits as they went about their business. And, besides, Severina knew her too well.

She took the cup and went to sit where she could help Severina to drink, which she did with slurping relish, her hand guiding Claudia's, her lips reaching forward thirstily. The thick, brackish smell of the beer reminded Claudia of Tiki as a wriggling pup in the brewer's house.

Setting the cup down, she said gently, 'You can't travel while you're like this.'

'I shall be better.'

'Of course, but it takes time.'

Severina gave a sniff, a pale echo of her characteristic snort of contempt. 'I'll be back on my feet in no time, don't you worry.'

She did not get back on her feet, and neither did she recover. The old bones of which she'd complained were worn out. As the days dragged by and she remained in her bed, she began to wander in mind. Claudia found this more distressing than her physical deterioration. While Severina could still talk back, and hold her own, the world was in balance. As she drifted in other times and places, Claudia's equilibrium was shaken and she felt deserted.

There were whole days when Severina seemed to be back in her youth, not a babbling second childhood, but in real times, relived. She smiled and murmured softly, her poor hands moved to her hair and cheeks with a girl's unconscious airy grace, and once she laughed, a clear, youthful laugh that Claudia, before entering, took to be Minna's. Realising that it had come from Severina was to share the room with a ghost, and her scalp crept.

The moments of lucidity were equally unsettling. It was hard to know, when the old woman's eyes suddenly focused and her voice took on the old abrasive edge, how much credence to give to what she said. But there was no doubt that on these occasions she demanded attention.

'You're still here, then,' she said one morning.

Claudia had come in quietly, thinking she was still asleep, and the sound made her jump. 'Oh! No, I haven't been here all night, don't worry.'

'I mean you haven't gone off to Rome yet, without me.'

'No.'

'And what about your husband?'

This was vintage Severina, robustly taking advantage of age and infirmity to overstep the mark.

'I don't know what you mean,' said Claudia, fearing that she did.

'The master. Publius.'

'Severina, I know who you are talking about.'

'You surely won't be leaving while he's gone.'

'I might do. It has yet to be decided.'

Severina grunted. 'If you go on your own, you won't be coming back.'

'Of course I shall.'

'Does he know that, I wonder?'

Her voice dwindled as she spoke and she appeared to be dozing again. Or she might have been foxing. It was impossible to tell. She had made her point and retreated.

Claudia had been trying to occupy herself with household tasks during these past weeks, but after this exchange she couldn't apply herself. There were fruit and vegetables to be picked and preserved, linen to be sorted and mended, letters to be written, shopping to be undertaken or delegated, the dreadful business of Gaius' room and his possessions still waiting to be dealt with.

She could face none of these tasks, most of all the last. Instead she wrapped her cloak round her and walked down to where Gaius lay, near the temple. As always, Tiki appeared as if from nowhere and paced beside her. He no longer strayed far from the house, but he seemed to know when she was going to visit her son, and always accompanied her. It was a chilly, golden September morning and the sun shone on the grave and reflected brightly off the temple wall. The flat islands of scrub that dotted the shoulder of the hill beyond – which had blinded Gaius to the danger beyond – were tangled with blackberries and rosehips. They had been thinking of trying to grow some grapes at the southern end of the colonnade, but in this climate you could never tell.

Tiki went straight to his usual place by the wall and flopped down in the sunshine. Claudia went into the temple. If the gods had given her no reassurance on the night of Gaius' disappearance, their unchanging calm had provided it since. They had listened, and seen, and noted her unhappiness without judgement, pity or reproof. Now they looked on just as dispassionately, witnessing her slow recovery. All through the night they were here, watching over Gaius as the owl, and the little bats, and the insects and the mice went about their nocturnal business. Their stillness was like a benediction, rising above her turmoil and absolving her.

She lit a lamp for each of them, shivering in the temple's cool greenish air. Then she sat for a moment on the seat opposite the door. She remembered a previous occasion, not long ago when she had done this – when she had escaped from that lively dinner party for some fresh air and moments to herself. She had sat here on the warm summer's evening and an inquisitive Tiki had appeared in the doorway, checking up on her, seeing if there was a longer walk to be had. After a while, then as now, she had gone to see her son.

And something else she recalled: going back to the party and meeting Publius' eyes over the heads of their guests, experiencing that old, sharp dart of mutual recognition and desire, knowing that he would not stoop to ask and she would not tell where she'd been. When had that finally gone? How had they lost it?

Minerva gazed sightlessly down at her, the mute and tranquil witness to so much. Claudia had heard of another religion that was growing in popularity now. She knew little of it except that it had only one god, and had been spread by a group of poor but zealous men from the Middle East, on fire with stories of their 'messiah' – a man executed as a criminal but who, they said, was the son of this one god, and who had proved it by rising from the dead. The story on its own sounded like the product of hysteria and superstition, impressionable minds under the spell of a charismatic leader – but if that were so then the way of life advocated by its followers, the Christians, was not what one might have predicted. Flavia had become a Christian, and she'd told Claudia that it was a religion of tolerance, humility and forgiveness to the point of loving one's enemies, a concept Claudia could neither grasp nor understand.

'It's not necessary to hate the person because of what they do,' was how Flavia had tried to explain it to her.

'But how else do we know the person other than by their actions?'

'Have you never done anything wrong or harmful? Have you always behaved right?'

'No, of course not.'

'There, then.'

Somehow it had not been enough, yet Claudia could see that her friend shone with belief, that in aspiring to this selflessness she had somehow been freed of the demands and restrictions of the self. That was the difficulty: even had Christianity attracted her, Claudia was not ready to give up her self. Sometimes she thought it was all she had: her will, her independence – her selfhood.

She left the temple and went to the graveside. The morning sun had dried the dew and she sat down for a moment. For better or worse, Gaius seemed older than her now, as if death had dignified and elevated him, given him some kind of special, ultimate wisdom, the knowledge of what lay beyond life. But now, with hindsight, she could see that perhaps a certain kind of wisdom had always been there. Her son had known and understood his parents in a whole and instinctive way that they themselves could not. She had felt it in his clinging arms, his wide, wary eyes, his odd questions and observations, his lack of confidence, his passionate secrecy and quixotic enthusiasms. He had been a boy confused by his big, wild certainties. She could not tell him that, now, she understood. But Flavia believed in an afterlife, and that *was* something worth believing in. When she laid her hand on his memorial stone it was warmed by the sun.

As she returned through the garden Minna ran out to meet her. 'Lady!'

'Yes? Is it Severina?'

The girl nodded, her hand hovering over her mouth.

Claudia walked quickly past her, placing a firm hand on her shoulder as she did so. 'Don't follow,' she said.

Seeing Severina now, it was not hard to hear again that fresh girl's laughter. Death had wiped the map of hardworked decades from her face. There was also – what? – not contentment exactly . . . Claudia sat down by her and touched her hair, which looked wiry but felt fine and soft. Perhaps it was a look of completion, of the task done and the day over. She herself felt no sadness yet, but she did sit there for a while, letting the memories sift gently through her fingers.

'Goodbye, old friend.'

She came out to Minna, who had brought Luke and Alex along for moral support.

'Severina's gone. Do any of you know whether she had relations? Or close friends? People we should tell?'

There was a second's silence in which no one looked at her

before Alex said, in a small, strangulated voice: 'Yes, lady, she had a husband.'

The husband, Cinna, was himself far less shocking than the fact of his existence. One could have predicted this skinny, wavering person with swimming milky eyes and wispy hair, a cobweb of a man. How, asked Claudia, could either of them have borne it? And for so long, and secretly?

She was gentle and patient with his dithering, which was less to do with distress than dismay at what must now be done.

'I presume,' she said, 'that you would like to take her, and see to the arrangements yourself.'

'Oh, I must, of course, it is my place . . . Oh dear, oh, ye gods, my poor wife, what am I to do?' He wrung his hands helplessly.

'Please. I can help you. My husband's away but he would want me to. She looked after him long before I came here. If you need transport, money, you only have to say.'

'No!' He seemed aghast at the idea. 'No, no . . . well, perhaps if you have a cart . . .'

In the end she sent Alex with him, with poor Severina's old bones bumping around in the back of the wagon despite the pillows they'd wedged around her.

Now, she thought, now I will go to Rome.

But Severina, like Gaius, had a long reach. It was that very night, the night Cinna had taken his wife away, that Claudia woke with a sense of falling, her eyes crashing open in the dark and her skin prickling with apprehension.

'"If you go on your own, you won't be coming back. Does he know that, I wonder?"'

And now there was no alternative but to go alone. Shrewd to the end, Severina had kept her here this long and, before going, infected her with doubt.

It had been four weeks since the cohorts had gone north. Almost a month during which she had thought of her husband only in terms of how and when she would leave him. She had not, in fact, considered the matter of her return. It was being there, in Rome, that mattered to her, the place she had never really left, where she could catch her breath, and take a long look at this other life where she had never taken root.

There was no news of the troops. She told herself that she would wait for one more week. The house felt not empty, but unoccupied. The very stones and tiles, the plaster and the wood, seemed to know her heart was not here. The slaves drifted about their tasks lackadaisically, without purpose. Those things that it had pleased and amused her and Publius to choose – the wall paintings and mosaics, the hangings and the vases, the plants, the sundial – now mocked her. She had never wanted them, she had not wished to settle here. He had not cared about the things: it was the *place* to which he was so passionately attached. She had felt more secure and optimistic in the bustling impermanence of the garrison with its mutating population and its house that had been occupied by officers before them, and would be by those to come. This house had been for Publius, but it was tricked out with inducements for her.

She and Minna drove the wagon along the hilltop road to the settlement and the fort to buy food, wine and oil for the winter. She made herself consider Publius in the house, alone, in the long, dark, northern nights, but the thought did not move her. That was how it had been with him, for years. He would be picking up the old life that she had briefly interrupted.

Flavia, her most loving friend, was appalled by this suggestion. 'He'll miss you terribly, we all will. Go, if you must, but come back. Your place is here.'

'No.' This, the mildest hint of censure, nettled Claudia. 'No, Flavia, this is not my place and it never has been. I stayed while – because there was a reason to. But that reason is gone now.'

'Oh, my dear . . .' Flavia wrapped her arms round her and rocked her from side to side like a mother with a child. 'What will we do? Helena will be heartbroken.'

'That's not true. Helena's a wife and mother herself, and it must be two years or more since I saw her.'

'But she talks about you, often. She's never forgotten your kindness, and the puppy, and all you did. She was so unhappy till you became her friend.'

'I'm glad of that,' said Claudia. 'I needed a friend too. And you've been that friend all this time. But I am going to Rome.'

She went to call on Brasca's widow, a woman terrifyingly diminished by the untimely death of her husband. Gone was the formidable ramrod-straight battleaxe who ran the small house like a military operation and who regarded her husband's charioteering as an extravagant hobby. The fierce energy had gone from her tall, spare frame, and the combative light from her eyes.

'I was sorry to hear about your son,' she murmured. 'Terrible to lose a child, with their whole life before them.'

'Yes. You know when it happened – that it was on the day of the games?'

'Yes.'

'He was terribly shocked by the accident.'

Erica gave a curt nod. Claudia realised how important it was to spare her the humiliation of tears.

'The remaining horses, did you find homes for them?'

'For one. The other two I had dealt with. I was able to sell the harnesses for a good sum. And my neighbour is using the stables as a workshop.'

'What trade is he in?'

'He's a smith.' There was the wraith of a smile. 'So I haven't got away from horses altogether.'

She and Minna did most of the marketing in the *vicus*, then continued through the south gate into the garrison. Claudia instructed the girl to remain with the wagon and mind the purchases while she herself went for a walk through the forum, to find out any news of the troops that had gone north.

It was weeks – months – since she had been here and the jostle and clamour were a shock to her bruised sensibilities. She felt carried along like a twig on a fast-flowing river, buffeted by so much noise and movement. Like Rome, but completely unlike, too, because this was a place whose very reason for existence was the Roman army, and that army was not here.

At least, much of it wasn't. A token troop remained in the garrison, their voices echoed in the barracks. The house they had lived in was now occupied by the new commander, absent like Publius at present. She had met his wife once, a cheerful British woman with three boisterous children, all ideally suited to their life.

In the block next door she found Malius Firminus, the young officer left, chafing, in charge of administration. 'They're on their way back,' he told her. 'The communications say it's been rough up there. All the drilling and planning in the world can't prepare you for an enemy who's quick and clever and is born to the terrain.'

'But the expedition was a success?'

He pursed his lips, glad to be the expert. 'It depends how you look at it. They drove them back. But it's only a show of strength, till the next time. These northerners won't go away. Our chief asset is knowing our limitations so as not to risk defeat.'

'So when do you expect them?' she asked.

He shrugged. 'The men at the mile-castles are already looking out for them.'

Two weeks, she had told herself. And now she said, two days.

It was Minna who told her, early on the morning of the second day. Her apparent diffidence was a front, it seemed. She was a Severina in the making, shaking Claudia awake. 'Lady! Lady!'

'Whatever is it, Minna?'

'The men are coming back!'

'How do you know?'

'I do! It's five miles away.'

Claudia sat up and pushed her fingers into her tangled hair. 'Thank you, Minna.' She was out of bed now, and full of purpose. 'Will you bring me some water?'

She washed her face and hands, dressed, and went out of the house. It was late October now, true autumn, and this morning was one of those chill, raw, lightless days peculiar to Britain. Not even the sparkle of frost on the ground. The air pinched her to the bone and made her eyes water. Luke appeared around the corner of the house.

'Good morning, lady. Do you want to ride?'

'No.' He turned away. 'Yes! Luke, bring Juno.'

The speed with which the mare was brought made her think she had been ready all along, but she allowed them their little conspiracy. As she rode away from the house she sensed its occupants watching her.

She rode along the ridge and then east, away from the fort, cutting across towards the main gate of the Wall. The hinterland of the Wall was a sprawl of houses, small farms, stalls and temporary shelters, the teeming system of mutual support and exploitation generated by an army of occupation. Even at this hour in the morning there was plenty going on: sparks flew from smithy fires, wagons and carts were setting off on collections and deliveries, women and children were fetching water, cattle were being moved, travel-hardened couriers changed horses and set off on the last leg of their journey to the coast, or the second of the far longer journey over land to the west.

With the main gate in sight she followed the line of the Wall to the wooded hill between the gate and the next mile-castle. This was where Publius had brought her not long after her arrival to gaze out over the land beyond the Empire: the forbidding, empty, non-Roman north.

She was there for three-quarters of an hour, her hands and feet beginning to hurt with cold, when the shout went up, and echoed along the line of the Wall. At first she could see nothing and when she did it was suddenly, as if the advancing black line had simply materialised out of the grey-green land. She watched, her eyes narrowed against the cold wind, until the column was within a mile of the main gate, and then she rode down to watch them come in.

The far gate swung open, and now the near. Sentries yelled at one another, people ran to watch, horses squealed with excitement, dogs barked and ran about. But as the column approached all other sounds were drowned in the rhythmic crash of marching feet, the rumble of the supply wagons and the thud of horses' hoofs, stretching half a mile back.

Publius no longer rode at the head of the column, but to the side, and he passed no more than a few yards from where her horse stood. The sight of him shocked her. He was filthy and exhausted-looking with a stained bandage around his thigh and scabs on the side of his face that bit into his beard. But the life-force that emanated from him was undiminished; enhanced, even, as he came back after cheating death once more for a soldier's pay. His eyes were red-rimmed but glittering, and his back was straight. His breastplate, shield and helmet shone, though his horse was heavy-footed. He looked – proud. And she realised how long it was since she had seen her husband so.

Quietly she turned the mare's head and rode home to await his return.

'Claudia. I didn't expect to find you here.'

'I didn't know that I would be.'

'I'm glad.'

Outside, a wind was getting up, bumping against the walls of the house. But in here it was warm and the light was soft. All day she had waited. Now that he was here, in their house, she sensed his pride and vigour beginning to ebb, giving way to utter weariness and a sort of despair that clutched her heart. She hesitated for only a second, not long enough for him to notice, before going to him and leaning her palms and her forehead against him. She felt his little intake of breath and then, a moment later, the slow closing of his arms around her like the drawing of curtains around a lovers' bed.

'I'm glad,' he said again, his voice trembling. 'I could not easily have borne it.'

She nodded against his chest.

'Go to Rome if you want to, Claudia, if it will make you happy.'

'I shall,' she lifted her face to look into his, 'for a little while. But I shall come back.'

'You'd thought of not returning.'

She nodded again. 'But I know now. This is my place.' She pressed her hands against him. 'This.'

*   *   *

He slept like a dead man, while she lay awake, counting the new marks on him. Claudia had missed Severina's brisk practicality in changing the bandage on his leg, but she had managed, and if she had hurt him he hadn't let it show.

Just before dawn she felt the dream creeping up on him, and this time she took her courage in both hands and woke him. He let out a great shout and then sank, shaking violently, into her arms. 'Help me, Claudia. My wife, help me . . .'

'I will,' she said. 'We shall help each other.'

CHAPTER TWENTY-FOUR

Bobby, 1993

Circumstances alter, and they alter you. But you don't always notice, until one day a particular meeting or conversation acts as a mirror to your translated self.

The things that changed were these. Fleur embarked on her life of motherhood with a vigour I could never have predicted. Within weeks she had got a part-time job, found – fairly cheerfully – a day nursery place for Rowan and a studio flat (I read bedsit) for herself in Cricklewood. Apparently Jude had said she was welcome to stay, but not outstaying the welcome was crucial to everyone's peace of mind. We spoke on the phone about once a week. Occasionally she was exhausted and weepy, but she didn't take an apocalyptic view of her moods, they were just baby blues, a temporary thing to be got through, and over. Mostly she was positive, a doting mother and a determined self-improver. Where had she got it from? How had I, of the quiet-life-and-no-complications persuasion given birth to this force of nature? When she asked if she and Rowan could come to me for Christmas, I was overjoyed.

In the interim I did go down one weekend to visit her in the Cricklewood bedsit, expecting to come away depressed, but it was great. A mess, of course, but a cheerful mess, and a couple of her friends were there, a boy and a girl, cluttering up the place, drinking beer and passing my grandson back and forth between them. She made them go out on to the landing to smoke. The job was in a local supermarket, but one of the friends was teaching her computer skills (something they both enjoyed by the look of him) and she was approaching the whole thing in an admirable spirit of humility and determination.

'You know,' I said, as we sat on the bony and resistant charity-warehouse sofa – me holding Rowan and she pulling mounds of minute garments out of a launderette bag, 'I'm so proud of you, Fleur.'

'Really?' She gave me a look that combined hope and disbelief. 'You are?'

'Yes. I admire you. I couldn't have done what you're doing. I didn't have the courage or the energy.'

'Ach,' she flapped a Babygro absentmindedly, 'they were different times.'

'Maybe, but still . . .' I bent to kiss my grandson, from whose rosebud lips a trickle of curds and whey ran down on to his collar. 'I want to do anything I can to help. You will let me know, won't you, if there's anything?' I had never wanted to offer her money directly. Perhaps if I had been a mother to her always it might have felt different, natural, but in the circumstances it would have seemed like conscience-money.

'Don't worry,' she said. 'If there is, you'll be the first to know. Shit!' She sat back and gave the launderette bag a disaffected kick. 'It just keeps coming, doesn't it?'

'Looks like it,' I agreed dreamily, caught in the enchantment of the baby's falling asleep.

This time it was my foot she nudged gently. 'And look at you.'

'What?' I asked. Looked up. 'What?'

'We love you, Gran.'

Again that spurt of pleasure that she could call me that, but mixed with the pain of all the lost years. I lowered my eyes to Rowan's small, sealed, secret face. 'Is that what he's going to call me?' I asked.

'If you like. Whatever you like. Only not Grandma, because the other one's bagged that.' She nudged my foot again. 'I did it. You were right. Poor little fatherless kid, two grannies are better than one.'

My heart was like a cup, full to the brim. I stayed very still, not wanting to spill a single drop, or wake my grandson.

I kept Ros abreast of these family developments on the phone, but now the novelty had worn off her interest lay elsewhere.

'Has the Flying Dutchman been in touch?'

'No,' I said, 'why would he? It did me the power of good but it was a one-off.'

She wasn't interested in this. 'Why don't you get in touch with him?'

I laughed. 'What about the rules?'

'Sod them, for once. What's the worst that could happen?'

'I could be totally and utterly humiliated and then all the good would have been for nothing. I'd rather keep it as a nice thing that happened, and let it go at that.'

I was lying, and Ros knew that I was. 'Pull the other one. Be bold. *He* was – you both were. Just make the call.'

'But he's in France!'

'France, wow!' I could hear her rolling her eyes. 'So?'

'So, it's too far, it's ridiculous.'

'Okay, whatever . . .' Her voice changed slightly. 'I tell you one thing, though, Bobby.'

'What's that?'

'That man lit your flame. Don't be surprised if one or two moths come your way.'

Jim had a meeting in Newcastle and came to stay for the night. Tired after a long day and far from the tensions of home, the first drink went straight into the vein and by the second he was mellow. I took a deep breath. 'I've got something to tell you.'

'Sounds ominous,' he said cheerily.

'I'm a grandmother.'

He frowned. 'How do you mean?'

I decided against asking how many ways he thought there were. 'I've got a grandchild.'

His brow furrowed more deeply. 'How?'

I realised that since I had leapfrogged a whole chunk of information this was not such a silly question as it sounded. 'My daughter has had a baby.' I made a winding-back gesture. 'I've got a daughter.'

Jim blinked. 'I'm sorry, Bobs. You're going to have to come back in and start again.'

'A little while ago I discovered I had a daughter. She turned up on my doorstep.'

'Surely,' he said, 'you must have known of her existence.'

It was hard to believe he was being so pedantic in the face of my cataclysmic news, until I reminded myself that this was Jim, my brother, avoiding the main issue by asking picky questions, as he had every right to do.

This time it was I who closed my eyes, assembling my thoughts. When I opened them again I said, 'In my last year at college I had a baby. Nobody knew, and I gave her for adoption. Early this year she turned up out of the blue, pregnant herself. We got on. And now she's had a baby. His name's Rowan. So,' I shrugged, 'I'm a grandmother.'

'Congratulations.' But he was already shaking his head. 'I don't know what to say.'

'You just did,' I suggested.

His face took on an odd look: it seemed to blur. I realised that what I was witnessing was melt-down; that Jim, of all people, was almost in tears.

'I don't understand,' he said. It wasn't the abrasive, searching statement of an older brother, but the pitiful complaint of a child. 'You never said!'

'I didn't want anyone to know at the time. In fact, I never wanted to think about it again. When Fleur found me, I went into shock – but it was all right. More than all right. Now I'm more grateful than I can say that she did. And I hope you'll be glad too.'

'I'm sorry, Bobs,' Jim got out his hankie and mopped at his face, 'I'm sorry, you'll have to forgive me.'

'There's nothing to forgive,' I said gently. '*I'm* sorry to spring this on you. I'd have done it sooner but things were so fraught at your end when I came to stay. There was no easy way of doing it. It was sprung on me, too. Imagine how that felt.'

'I can't.'

'Anyway,' I said, getting up, 'come and eat. Remember what Mum used to say? It'll look better on a full stomach.'

I put the plates of pasta on the table, and as Jim was about to sit down I went and put my arms round him. 'Okay?'

He nodded. 'I'll digest it with this lot.'

Gradually, over the next couple of hours, Fleur's existence achieved a kind of mutually accepted status between us. Jim began to ask avuncular questions such as how was she going to manage, and where was the father, and I tried to answer in the manner of someone who was taking on only the degree of responsibility and involvement that was appropriate under the circumstances.

'What about her adoptive parents?'

'She fell out out with them, big time, over the pregnancy. Though things are better now, I understand.'

'How do you know she's not using you to get back at them, for money, anything?'

'I don't,' I admitted. 'She just doesn't strike me as scheming and manipulative. I know – I'm almost sure you'd like her, Jim.'

'I'm not saying I wouldn't, but I reserve the right to have your best interests at heart.'

By the time we were sitting down again with a cup of coffee I was emboldened to change the subject. 'How's Chloë?'

'Mm . . .' Poor Jim, crazed women on every side, it must have seemed. 'The same. Stroppy, self-destructive, worrying us all to death. She likes you, though.'

'Really?' I couldn't keep what must have been an annoying note of gratification out of my voice.

'It's no exaggeration to say you get thrown in our faces.'

'How ghastly.'

'Not your fault you made a hit.'

I left a beat to give the impression that I was reflecting,

although the idea was not a new one to me. 'You know, if we could turn that to all our advantage, I'd like to try. Maybe she'd come and visit or something.'

Jim grunted. 'So she could bend your ear about what pigs her parents are.'

'No.'

'Forgive me, Bobs, that was below the belt.'

'You never know,' I said, 'she might like the baby. He is completely adorable, though I say so myself. She could come at Christmas. Help out. I bet she and Fleur would get on like a house on fire.'

I was making all sorts of assumptions and positing all kinds of theories, but Jim, poor chap, on an any-port-in-a-storm basis, was prepared to entertain them.

'I suppose she might. I've never regarded her as a maternal sort of girl, but then I've reached the conclusion that being a parent is a positive bar to understanding one's children.'

'I bet you wouldn't mind her being out of the house for a while.' I was determined to lift Jim's mood, but it didn't work.

'Jesus,' he said, 'what must you think of me?'

'I think you're my dear brother, who is coping manfully but could do with a break.'

By the time we went to bed that night I felt closer to Jim than I had in years. We'd cried a bit, laughed at ourselves for doing so, got a bit philosophical, and wound up deciding that life was, if not exactly a bitch, then at least a tart with a heart. We left it that I would give Chloë a ring in about a week's time when everyone at their end had had time to digest the information.

Jim's last remark as he got in the car was 'The monstrous regiment is on the move.'

This being more like his old self, I forgave him.

The Hobdays, not being so close, took my news in their stride. I didn't even need to tell them, but decided that if they were aware of a baby in my house over the festive season they might think I'd taken the re-creation of the first Christmas a bit too seriously. I kept it low-key, told them my daughter and I had lost touch for a while but that now we'd affected a rapprochement.

'Great,' said Kirsty. 'I don't promise to get my knitting needles out but I shall take my credit card to Baby Gap.'

Chris embraced me warmly. 'We may have succeeded in avoiding children of our own, but we like to feel there are people out there doing it for us.'

As for Miranda, she performed a pre-emptive trumping manoeuvre.

'Bobby, you shall be the first outside the family to know. Marco and I are getting married.'

I was shocked without knowing why, and for a split second I must have been unable to stifle the shock, for she said: 'You don't approve.'

I was dismayed by her apparent need for my blessing. 'What? No! Congratulations, that's wonderful.'

We were sitting in the garden of the Dower House drinking coffee. It was too cold to be sitting out, really, we were hanging on to summer as only the British can, using one of those days when the temperature in a sheltered corner was bearable to pretend.

I might have known something was afoot for Miranda was looking different. She had put on a little weight, and her face, though it had lost some of its patrician sleekness, had a soft, fresh appearance.

'I'm so glad,' I said. 'I really am.'

'Some might say it was all too quick.'

'Not me.'

'What I couldn't bear,' she said, 'would be for people to think that –' She paused, pressing her lips together for a long moment. 'You know what they might think. That I didn't care enough for Fred.'

I now understood that she was rehearsing these things to herself. That it was not my or anyone else's approval that she sought, but her own permission.

'No one who knows you will think that.'

'I hope not.'

'And the others don't matter.'

'No.'

In the silence that followed I could sense that each of us was considering her position in relation to the other. We were recalibrating ourselves and our relationship: trying, perhaps, to decide to our own satisfaction whether what we had was a true friendship, one that could sustain more intimate truths. I would always be grateful to Miranda, and love her, for being the first to decide, and to take the plunge.

She turned her head to look at me and I could see in her eyes that she had come down in favour of trust. 'With Marco,' she said, 'it's not the same. It couldn't be. It's different because he's a different person and these are different times. But we love each other enough to be happy together.'

She'd said her piece. I had to say mine. 'And is "enough" enough, do you think?'

She gave an anxious little smile. 'That's what I ask myself. On his part, he's asking for nothing more. He says I'm all that he wants and I believe him.'

'And what about on yours?'

'I love him, so I'm sure it will be. I do so want to be happy away from here – not to cling on.'

'It will be a wrench.'

'Yes.' She picked up her cigarettes and lit one. 'Fred always said we were a threesome – him, me and the house – and he was right. All the more reason why I should make a clean break while I have the chance.'

'In that case,' I said, 'I wish you all the luck in the world.'

'Bobby,' she looked at me very directly, 'I've already had it. All that heaven will allow. You see, I don't think the sort of thing I had with Fred happens more than once, if at all. I was doubly blessed. And now I have a chance for something different, what I need isn't so much luck as good faith. I've made a positive choice. I could either stay here, where I lived with Fred, on the edge of a past life – or I can go with Marco to London, and New York, and all the other places he goes to, and put Fred in the safe-keeping part of my heart.'

'So long as you're doing what will make you happiest,' I said. 'Living the best life you can.'

'What a good way of putting it.' She reflected on this. 'Not compromise, but best shot.'

I felt a little sheepish with my role of wise woman. 'What do I know?'

'More than you think, Bobby. You're too modest.'

'It's easy to be wise about someone else's life.'

'And thank heavens for it.' She dropped her cigarette, and squashed it with her foot. 'Can I ask you something?'

'I can hardly refuse!'

'Keep an eye on Daniel, won't you?'

It was one of those moments when we might have said a hundred things: explained, confided, justified. But it was a measure of our mutual understanding that we didn't. I remembered the sound of Daniel's voice, and the light in his eyes; the look on Miranda's face when they were talking together. Nothing needed to be said. She was giving life her best shot. Choosing the most happiness for the most people. But something told me that this was the moment to step aside, not to take on this responsibility for a small part of her life, or anyone else's.

'Daniel will be fine,' I said.

'But you and he are friends. And he doesn't have many.'

'That's his choice. I haven't seen him for a while.'

'He's been away.'

'And so have I. He knows where to find me.'

She gave me a sidelong look, an acknowledgement of what I was telling her. 'You're right,' she said. 'It's up to him.'

Not long after that I left, without telling her my news. I didn't wish to be niggardly with confidences, but we both needed time to catch our balance, and for what she had told me to be given its proper weight: due respect, you might say. Also, I had no doubt that the news would filter through via the Hobdays. What I noticed most in myself, as I walked down to see the progress of the new building, was something that I couldn't at first put my finger on, but which I realised was a greater sense of equality with Miranda. She was not a charmed or golden person any more than I was an also-ran. She was beautiful, certainly, and she had had her golden periods, but now she was making deals and accommodations with life just as the rest of us had to do; and was equally uncertain about her own motives, and the outcome.

A couple of days later I went down to the Folly Theatre. It was almost complete. There were no more diggers and cement-mixers about. The ground around it was still a little raw, but the paved and gravelled areas had been laid, and some new trees planted. Some of Daniel's beautiful wooden furniture was in place, its smooth, solid shapes like something organic that had always been there, just as he'd promised. The only workmen on site now were a couple of decorators in the foyer, and the contractor, who emerged as if to greet me and then stopped, registering disappointment. 'Sorry, I thought you were Mr Torrence.'

'Is he expected?'

The man glanced at his watch. 'Ten minutes ago.'

Same old same old, I thought. I come down hoping for a quiet wander, and Mr T turns up.

'Do you mind if I look round?'

'Help yourself.' He looked at his watch again, then turned to me rather more warmly. 'A nice project this, the sort that makes my job worthwhile. Brought in on time and not much over budget.'

'It looks as if it's always been here.'

'That's the idea, with a building like this. Mr Torrence knows what he's doing. You see we've incorporated the original gazebo into the front . . .'

He pointed out the various features proudly, and then there was the sound of Marco's four-wheel-drive coming down the track, and he said, 'There he is – excuse me, help yourself.'

The theatre itself was tiny and perfect. There was an outer lobby created from the skeleton of the hexagonal gazebo, the columns set into the walls. The bar area was a round space leading off to the side of this, and the auditorium, seating sixty

(I knew because there was a plan on the wall), echoed the shape of the rest and was set out like an amphitheatre. I sat down and gazed around. It was an elegant, compact space that felt beautifully sequestered, like a glade in a wood. As I took in the detail I realised that some of this had been achieved by using a tree-motif in the design. Upward columns fanned out into branches that criss-crossed the roof, and the colour scheme was green, ranging from so dark it was almost black to pale willow-silver.

When I returned to the foyer, Marco Torrence was there, talking to the contractor. When he saw me his eyebrows shot up, and he removed his glasses with a gesture that was like doffing his cap. 'Hallo there!'

'Morning.'

'Taking a look? What do you reckon?'

'It's absolutely lovely,' I said truthfully.

'We believe so,' he agreed, adding, to the builder, 'I'll be right with you.'

As he approached me his smile widened, as though it had only with difficulty been kept in check till now.

'Have a good holiday?'

'Yes.' So much had happened in the past fortnight that the word 'holiday' scarcely seemed to apply. 'Yes, thanks, it was marvellous.'

'Good, great. Have you heard our news?'

'What news is that?' I asked carefully.

'Miranda and I are getting married.'

'Actually,' I said, 'I did know, but I wasn't sure whether I'd be breaking any confidences. Miranda told me.'

'I'm glad she did,' he said. 'That makes it official.'

I thought, He's still unsure of her. So the fact that she told me means she truly accepts him, that she's committed.

'And I'm pleased for both of you,' I said.

'Thank you.' Marco looked serious for almost the first time. 'He was a wonderful chap, Fred. One in several million. I could never replace him, but I hope I can fill at least some of the space he left.'

This, I felt, was a confidence too far, and one on which I

wasn't qualified to comment. I didn't know what to say so confined myself to the practical.

'Look what you've done.' I indicated the little theatre. 'It's magic.'

'Not half bad, is it? If you're interested in that kind of thing you ought to go and look at the finds we made. They're in the museum up the road in Stoneybridge.'

'I will do that,' I said.

'You won't regret it.' He put his glasses back on. It was a mannerism he had, whisking them on and off, as if by this small change in his appearance he could somehow alter his mood or manner. He was a nice, nice man. The one, I realised, of whom Peter reminded me. I felt I'd been unduly niggardly with my good wishes.

'Miranda's so happy,' I said. 'It was lovely to see that.'

He didn't actually stammer, though his manner was that of someone stammering. 'I adore her, you know, Bobby. I may not deserve her, but I'm hers to command. Also,' he added cheerfully, 'we have great laughs.'

'You both deserve happiness,' I said. 'I'll let you get back to your work.'

It was a Saturday so I decided on an impulse to go to the museum that afternoon. Boldly – I seemed bolder, these days – I knocked on the back door of Ladycross to see if Millie was there and would like to come too. Mrs Bird and Penny were in the kitchen in a near-palpable state of armed truce. Mrs Bird spared me only the briefest glance before continuing with the ferocious trussing of a pheasant, and Penny stared distractedly, wrist to brow, for a full second before registering me. 'Bobby! Do excuse me, we're going completely spare here. Can I make you some tea or something?'

'No, I didn't come to make work for you – I was going to the museum to see the Roman finds, and I wondered if Millie would like to come.'

'I'm sure she would! How perfectly sweet of you, hang on a tick.' Penny was off like a greyhound from the slips. Left alone with Mrs B I felt a little awkward, a person obscurely connected with the old dispensation, trespassing on the new, at home in neither. She was obviously a woman accustomed to transferring her loyalties when necessary, but I was not part of that particular contract.

She pulled hard on a bloodstained end of string and snipped it off with the kitchen scissors. This gesture caused me to wonder what she thought of Miranda's marriage plans.

'How are you?' she asked, as if what I deserved was at the very least a dose of dengue fever. 'Nice holiday?'

This was clearly what I *didn't* deserve. 'Yes, thank you.'

There was an awkward pause as she placed the pheasant in a roasting tin and began tying up another.

'You're obviously very busy,' I said.

'Rushed off our feet.' This was not an agreement but a correction. 'There's a lot going on just now,' she added, vouchsafing more information at one go than I'd ever heard her give before.

I felt a sudden, unprecedented pang of sympathy for Mrs Bird, no longer young, coping with the demands of new, brisk but inexperiencd employers and probably nursing a nostalgia for Miranda's charm and humility. 'I honestly can't think how you do it,' I said. 'From the first time I came here I realised that running a place like this is a massive undertaking.'

'It is.' The truculence had left her voice: this was a genuine agreement. The awkwardness had passed.

Millie came in, with Penny in her wake. Penny said, 'Here she is – she'd love to.'

I glanced at Millie to see if this was true or whether she was simply being required to go. The enthusiasm was real, all right.

'Are you sure it's okay?' she asked. I could tell that this was the token enquiry of someone who'd been told to be polite.

'I'd really like some company. And I expect you've been before.'

'She has,' said Penny, 'but that doesn't matter.'

'I want to go again.'

'Good,' I said. 'You can explain things to me.'

In the car on the way to Stoneybridge Millie talked up a storm. She was such a nice girl, innocently unsophisticated but confident, qualities for which I realised her parents should take full credit.

'Miranda's getting married,' she said. Adding, in case I should ask the inevitable question, 'But she's not having bridesmaids.'

'Perhaps it's not going to be a big wedding.'

'No, it's going to be just them, she said.'

'They're going to live somewhere else, I suppose.'

'I wish they weren't.'

'You'll see Miranda, I'm sure. She'll miss you terribly, she'll want to see you.'

Millie didn't answer, but when I glanced at her she was gazing out of the window with a small, unhappy frown that picked at my heart.

The Stoneybridge museum was in a large Edwardian house on the edge of a park. There was a row of houses and a pub, the Galleon, on one side, and on the opposite corner a Methodist chapel and more houses. The ladies in charge of the museum were as inefficient as they were fierce and proprietory, a peculiarly irritating combination. As they faffed and fannied around over change and special rates I became irritable, and Millie, embarrassed, clammed up.

'We close in an hour,' said one of the women, loving it.

'That's all right,' I said. 'We only came to see the Ladycross finds.'

'Oh, yes, they're quite wonderful. Do you need any explanation?'

'No, thank you. Actually we have a connection—'

'I live there,' said Millie, in a spirit of helpfulness rather than arrogance.

'Do you?' asked the woman indulgently, not believing a word of it.

'This is Millie Montclere,' I said sweetly. 'She's going to show me around.'

This time we didn't wait for the woman's reactions but swept in.

'Cow,' I said. 'That's told her.'

Miranda laughed shyly.

The Ladycross finds were housed in a special cabinet in the

Romano-British room. We stood and gazed, our noses almost pressed to the glass. It was odd to see here, in this sterile, still environment, things that had only recently been buried in the rich soil of Ladycross, in the place where they belonged. There were coins, two of them perforated to make necklaces; a huge assortment of *tesserae* in brilliant green, turquoise and blue; shards of amphorae and pottery painstakingly reassembled; some greenish glass jugs and ampules; earthenware lamps and red Samian ware.

The little dog had pride of place. The note confirmed what Miranda had said, that it was a popular hunting dog, similar to the present-day lurcher. Among the array of decorative and utilitarian artifacts its rough, quick vitality stood out. When Millie spoke, it was to say something that I myself was thinking. 'I wish he wasn't behind glass. He ought to be with people.'

'Well,' I said, 'at least here lots of people will come to see him, and see how great he is.'

'But they can't touch him.'

'No,' I agreed, 'they can't.'

There was one other thing that caught our eye and our imagination. At the far end of the cabinet, beyond the heap of jewel-like *tesserae*, was a collection of terracotta roof tiles. The accompanying note pointed out that several of these tiles, when left in the sun to dry, had been walked over by birds, and one carried the paw prints of a dog.

We couldn't tear ourselves away from this – its immediacy captivated us, like a two-thousand-year-old snapshot.

Millie said: 'Perhaps it was him – *that* dog.'

'It certainly could have been.'

When we left the museum, the women on the reception desk had adopted a conciliatory air: 'Aren't they marvellous? I suppose you've seen them before.'

'Some of them,' I said.

The larger and bossier of the two addressed herself to Millie: 'And which do you like best?'

'The dog.'

'He is enchanting,' agreed the woman.

'Do you think those are his footprints on the tile?' asked Millie, who was a forgiving child.

'We like to think so.' This seemed to me to be the right answer and I felt a bit more forgiving myself.

On the way back in the car I said something to Millie, to find out how it would feel to say it. 'I've got my daughter and her new baby coming for Christmas. You must come down and see us. The baby's lovely. He's called Rowan.'

'That's a tree.'

'It is, a rather pretty one.'

She looked at me with her plain, thoughtful stare. 'So you're a granny.'

'Yes.'

'Not a very old one,' she commented, as though this were something of a shortcoming on my part.

'No.'

'I'd like to see the baby.'

'My niece Chloë might be coming too.'

'How old is she?' asked Millie, warily.

'Fifteen. She hasn't been very happy. I think you'd like her.'

'I don't know,' said Millie, straightforwardly, 'until I've met her.'

We got back to Ladycross to find Penny in a state of nervous tension that you could have plucked with a bowstring. She was back in the kitchen having changed into a plum taffeta cocktail dress with a bow across the bust and a white smudge of deodorant under each arm, her hair newly Carmen-rollered.

'Bobby, bless you, did you have a good time, aren't they wonderful? They've done it so nicely. Millie, have you thanked Bobby?'

'She has,' I said truthfully. 'It was great to have her company. I've told her she must come down and visit my new grandson when he comes to visit at Christmas.'

'*Oh?*' The single syllable reverberated with a host of discreetly suppressed queries. 'Well! What do you say to that, Mills?'

'He's called Rowan,' explained Millie. 'I'd really like to go.'

'We'll see,' said Penny. 'Christmas is ages away.'

It wasn't, but I inferred that the 'we'll see' was a verbal pacifier, part of a whole repertoire of parental behaviour I'd never had to employ, or consciously to reject. Fleur owed all that she was – the very considerable woman she had become – to other people, no matter how great the falling-out between them, and I should always remember that. When it came to Rowan, he was her child. My role – not a hard one – would be to dote, and support, but not to inter-fere. I felt for the first time a pang of sisterly sympathy and admiration for Penny who, like Sally, was bringing up a family, giving wifely support to a tricky husband, running (and how!) a house and still managing to remain half-way sane and kind.

'Have a good evening,' I said, as she came with me to the door. 'You look absolutely lovely.'

'Goodness!' She frowned with well-bred modesty. 'How nice of you to say so.'

'And your daughter's an absolute sweetheart.'

Now she smiled warmly, becoming immediately and fleet-ingly as lovely as I'd said she was. 'She is, I know. I'm very lucky.'

'It's got nothing to do with luck.'

I don't think I imagined that I caught a hint of approval in Mrs Bird's eye as I went out of the door.

That evening my sister-in-law rang, thrilled to bits and playfully outraged. 'Bobby! Have you ever been holding out on us!'

'I was always going to tell you, it was a case of the right moment.'

'Jim's pretending there are inherent difficulties and you've got to be careful, but that is so like a man, if you'll pardon my saying so. *I* think it's absolutely bloody marvellous.'

'I'm so pleased. And Jim's only being solicitous.'

'I know, but it's all tosh. When can we see the little one?'

'I've only just met him myself. This is all new territory for me, Sally.'

'Well, don't expect any help from me. I'm not a grandmother – yet. And I'm praying not to be for many years to come. You're on your own, kid.'

I knew that this, coming from Sally, was both a concession and a generous compliment, her sworn bond not to interfere or to assume superior knowledge.

'I know,' I said. 'And I'm suitably terrified.'

'Hang on a mo, Chloë wants to talk to you.'

There was a muffled pause and then Chloë said, 'Cool about the baby, congratulations.'

'Thank you. He is lovely.'

There was an awkward silence, so I added, 'How are you?'

'So-so.'

'That good, huh?'

I detected the hint of a smile.

'Not bad.'

'Look after yourself, Chloë. Do you want to come and stay some time – just you, on your own?'

'Sure.'

I decided to interpret this verbal shrug as warm assent. 'Let's arrange something. Perhaps over the Christmas holidays.'

'Could do.'

'It's a date. 'Bye.'

''Bye.'

There was another pause and then Sally said, 'It's me again . . .' her voice fading a little on the last word as she watched her daughter leave the room, then returning again, muted but intense. 'Not much change there, you'll notice. Though actually she is a bit better in herself.'

'I asked her to come up for a couple of nights over Christmas.'

'God in heaven, Bobby, do you know what you'd be letting yourself in for?'

'Perhaps not.' I decided to take a leaf out of Millie's book. 'I shan't know till I try.'

Sally made a sound that was between a sigh and a laugh. 'You never cease to surprise me. Still, now you've got a family I suppose you might as well get acquainted with the down side.'

'She's great, Sally. All your kids are great.'

I was suddenly overflowing with fond admiration and respect. I knew it couldn't possibly last, all this sisterly empathy, but that was all the more reason why I should give expression to it now while the going was good.

'Blimey,' she said, 'you have got it bad. Listen, you, I want photographs, details, opinions, information. You've kept us all waiting quite long enough.'

Photographs? That was something else I hadn't got round to – I simply wasn't in the habit of carrying a camera. 'Next time I see them,' I said, 'I'll take pictures, I promise. And send a full report.'

'You'd better.'

It was not that Sunday but the following one that I encountered Miranda in the woods below the house, at almost the same spot where I'd seen her on the night I moved in. As usual, the first intimation that she might be near was the dog, who I suddenly saw trotting between the trees to one side of the path. Dogging my footsteps, I thought. I paused, and he went a little further before pausing too, and looking over his shoulder.

'Here, boy,' I leaned forward and held out my hand, 'here – come!'

He didn't react in any way. Indeed, the impression I had was that he had heard my voice but couldn't see me. When I repeated, 'Here, boy!' his ears pricked a little more, and after a few seconds he moved on, with his ears now pinned back as if half expecting another summons.

Miranda was some distance behind me but I heard her call my name. I turned and she caught up with me, panting.

'I saw you call him, but he won't come. He never does. I sometimes wonder if he's blind.'

'He doesn't look very old, though.'

'Forget that.' She put her hand on her breast, and caught her breath. 'Bobby, Kirsty told me your news.'

To my utter surprise she put her arms around me. It was an embrace whose exact character was hard to define – she almost clung to me as if resisting some force that was trying to drag her away. Cautiously, I responded.

She said, 'I'm all choked up.'

'It's all right. I was too, believe me.'

'Of course you were, I can't imagine . . .' She drew back, and I saw that she was quite openly weeping. Without apology or awkwardness she fished out a man's handkerchief (I could see the GFHM monogram) and blew her nose. 'Isn't it weird how things go?'

'Yes,' I agreed fervently.

'We think we know what the pattern is, the relationship between places and people, past and present, but we don't.'

'We do, but for some reason we think it will always be like that,' I said. 'We think, Now I've done such and such, this is how it will always be. And then of course it isn't.'

She had her head slightly turned away from me, and her eyes were still shining. There was a faint tracery of lines around the corners of her eyes and mouth, I noticed, but these first signs of ageing made her appear even more beautiful, as if the fine membrane between body and soul were becoming almost transparent.

'You're a philosopher, Bobby,' she said, respectfully.

'Scarcely. A realist, more like.'

'Yeah.' She gave a wistful little laugh. 'Me too.'

'It's the only way.' I felt as I had before, that there was something still waiting to be said, and I didn't want to get in its way.

'Just think,' she went on, in the same soft voice as if considering these things in her own mind and heart, 'just think, when we first met I was widowed, and you were alone. Now you have an entire family and I'm about to marry again, and we probably shan't see each other much.'

I was about to say that I was sure we would, but realised that it wasn't true. I was very far from sure. 'There'll be something,' I said. 'There's bound to be.'

'I hope so. Good luck, Bobby.'

'And you.'

We embraced again, holding on tight, swaying slightly like the branches in the autumn wind.

It was after that encounter, and because of it, that I decided that I would ring Peter. I sensed that there was no hurry, that whatever the result it would not be time-dependent. I just knew that I would make the call in good faith, and with high hopes. And that the outcome, whatever it was, would be for the best.

It was something I owed to myself.

CHAPTER TWENTY-FIVE

Miranda, 1992

They were on holiday when he told her. In Barbados, on the verandah of their lodge at the Reef Club. From beyond the brilliant green foliage of the garden they could hear the splash and chirrup of small children in the pool. Between the trunks of the palm trees that leaned confidingly towards each other were the brilliant turquoise and opal sea, and the white beach on which hardened sun-worshippers lay under thatched parasols, and beachboys constantly, philosophically, cruised for custom: hair beading, jewellery, aloe vera, straw hats, sarongs, trips to the wreck, to the turtles, to the castle, rides on jet-skis, waterskis, speedboats, motorised bananas . . .

They'd decided, Miranda and Fred, that they didn't care if it was a sign of advancing years – they preferred to spend the heat of the day in the seclusion of the garden, with only occasional forays to swim, and beachcomb. At least once on each holiday they'd hire a car and cross the island to Bathsheba, to walk along the beach, on the wild and booming beauty of the Atlantic coast, where the surf began at the horizon. They came each year after Christmas, and at Epiphany they'd attend the service at the Anglican church, where the flower arrangements seemed to breathe fire from their massed technicolour mouths and the clothes of the congregation would not have been out of place at Stringfellow's.

But it was the peace they savoured most. Even the sound of the waiters laying up for lunch in the Reef Club's shady Pavilion restaurant, was balm to their hard-pressed souls. It wasn't luxury for its own sake they relished, but the luxury of being looked after. And as Fred had told her before she came for the first time, everything about this island seemed designed for that purpose – the soft air, the lapping sea, the slow pace of everything, the geniality of people whose national character had been shaped by those things.

It was midday. They were reading. Or, at least, Fred appeared to be. Miranda was forming a relationship with a Bajan sparrow who had been drawing ever closer to the fruit in what remained of her punch, and was now perched on the edge of the table, inches from the glass in her hand. Other less forward sparrows twittered and rustled in the palms overhead, egging on their more adventurous colleague. The sparrow tilted his head speculatively. Miranda remained motionless. He hopped on to the arm of the lounger, no closer to the glass but now, greatly daring, on her territory. After a couple of trial hops, he fluttered on to the lip of the glass, teetered, tilted forward, within reach of the topmost slice of orange.

When Fred put his book down, the sparrow disappeared.

'Goodbye, Peter,' she said.

'What's that?'

'The little bird – he was conducting a raid on my glass.'

'He'll be back.'

Fred reached out his hand to her and she took it. He wore his straw beach-bum's hat, so his eyes were in shade. But he was a person suited to the sun, adapted by nature to a hot climate. He tanned easily, visibly blossoming in the heat; his slow, limber movements were in keeping with the pace of Bajan life, its rhythm. Each evening, they danced, and were reminded of their first meeting.

'Miranda,' he said now. 'Darling. This is boring, but there's something I've got to tell you.'

She swung his hand, squeezing it. 'Go on.'

'I'm not well.'

'Oh, no, that's not like you. The stomach-cement pills are in the bathroom.'

'No, I mean I've got this wretched thing.' He touched his solar plexus. 'Here.'

'What?' She released his hand. 'What sort of thing?'

'A fucking lump. A growth. Romping away, so the doc tells me.'

'Cancer.'

'That sort of thing.' He looked away. 'Yes.'

The birds still twittered, the children splashed and chattered in the pool, the jet-ski jockeys zoomed over the blue water. In the restaurant, someone dropped a piece of cutlery with a 'ping' on the floor. Here, where they sat, it was dead quiet.

'I'm so sorry,' he said, 'to do this to you.'

'That's all right. It's not me it's happening to.'

'No, but – just the same. Easier to deal with oneself than at one remove, I suspect.'

Miranda was cold. In the moist warmth of the garden the skin of her forearms was puckered with gooseflesh. She put her glass down on the table and swung her legs over the side of the lounger so that she was sitting hunched over, facing him.

She said almost crossly, 'But you look great.'

'Maddening, isn't it?'

'How long have you known?'

'Only a couple of weeks. I went for the dreaded biopsy that weekend when you were staying with your mother.'

'I see.'

'I haven't mentioned it until now because I've been too bloody scared,' he said, looking out towards the sea. 'To tell you was to make it official.'

'Right.'

'Sounds pretty lame, I know.'

'What about before? You must have been feeling terrible, surely.'

'Not really. Chronically tired, but I put that down to *anno domini*. Pride forbade that I made too much of it.'

'I love you!' She spat it at him in an angry whisper, like an accusation. 'I love you, dammit! couldn't you bring yourself to make something of it for my sake?'

'Miranda – I've said how sorry I am.'

He put his hand out again, but she didn't take it, shaking

her head, refusing him. 'You'd better tell me everything now. Everything. I want to know what rock bottom feels like.'

'That I *can* tell you,' he said, this time without any ameliorating gesture, or even gentleness. 'It feels peculiarly free. Horrible. Bleak. Lonely. But free.'

It was as though the slow shock-wave that had begun travelling from him a minute ago suddenly hit her, and she began to tremble.

'Free – of what?'

'Of the need to put on a show, my darling.' Himself again, Fred held out his arms and she collapsed, falling forward on to her knees and into his embrace. 'My chance to behave like a cantankerous, self-centred, bigoted old bastard at long last.'

She sobbed, shaking her head against his shoulder. 'No! No, no, no, no . . .'

'All right, I won't. But only because you insist.'

She was still weeping when a waiter came down the winding path between the trees, and Fred ordered them both a Planter's.

'Oh, God!' Miranda sat back on her heels and wiped her face. 'What must I look like?'

'Like the woman who loves me and whom I love – I'd say more than life itself, only just recently I've been forced to the conclusion that that's not true. If it was you or me I hope I'd have the courage to say, "You have it," but if it's a case of going on before, without you, then no.'

She pulled her lounger closer to his and lay next to him, on her side, as though they were in bed. He rested his wrist on the back of the lounger, stroking her hair with his fingers. Her eyes closed, drawing his touch into herself. She told herself to ask what she wanted to know. To come right out with it. It would take only seconds, and in seconds more she would have the answer.

Even so, the psychological effort was so great that he beat her to it.

'There isn't anything they can do. I enjoy such rude health most of the time that it was well advanced before I even went to the doc, and even then I thought I just needed a pick-me-up.'

'So when did they discover it was more than that you needed?'

'Young Murphy, the new chap at the health centre, prodded me about a bit and said my oesophagus was bumpy and I ought to go and be inspected more thoroughly. Which I did. As a matter of fact I almost wish I hadn't.'

'How can you say that?'

'Since the very best they can offer is a few extra months courtesy of chemo, which I'd rather do without, I'm opting for a life of unbridled pleasure – also highly recommended, by the way – and that would quite frankly be easier if I didn't know the worst.'

The world turned a couple of times. The waiter brought their drinks.

'And what is the worst?' she asked.

They had their few months, until the early summer. It may not have been the prescribed unbridled pleasure, but they managed a life that on the face of it was largely unchanged. Fred told Miles, who told Penny, who decided quite properly, and on Fred's advice, that the children should not be told. Miranda informed her mother, who somehow managed to turn it into evidence of a plot designed to spoil her and the odious Brian's wedding plans.

'What a terrible thing,' she said. 'First Gerald, now Fred.'

Miranda was white with fury. 'I don't see that there's any connection.'

'Two men not young exactly, but still vigorous, with so much to live for.'

That much was true and, oddly, Fred had taken a rather similar line. 'Not for the first time I have some retrospective sympathy with your father. One day the mambo, the next, this. It's a bugger.'

Through the spring, they made plans. They tried to be practical and to take pleasure in what they were doing, but there was no escaping the fact that these were plans that would come to fruition when Fred was no longer around – the gradual handing over of the reins to Miles, starting with the off-site business and financial matters. Then there was this year's Rock on the Manor, which Miranda hung on to as a kind of talisman. She would never have considered cancelling it, and while it was there, in the diary, up ahead of them, it was something to work towards.

And there was the folly theatre. They'd talked about it from time to time over the years, but now there was a sense of urgency, of a moment needing to be seized. As with the rock concerts, Miranda had swung into action with shameless and singleminded opportunism. She refused to accept that things couldn't be put in hand swiftly, that a date couldn't be set for completion. She parlayed the best architect in Newcastle into agreeing that the folly was a feasible site, and then brokered a meeting between him and Marco Torrence, as project manager, in which each saw the other as competition for her undying gratitude. Her motto, which she found on a magnet and stuck on the fridge door, was 'Don't tell me why we can't do what we can't; tell me how we can do what we can.' In this way plans were drawn up and the required permission slowly but surely squeezed through the minute holes in the planning department's sieve. The theatre became something that would happen

And just as well, because by the middle of June Fred was dying. She'd known it since January, but now, in the space of a few weeks, it became clear. He had lost weight. He was weak, not too often in pain but frequently exhausted. And on his bad days, distant, too, as though he were already moving ahead, into the no man's land that preceded death.

During the day, Miranda was herself, and more than herself. Playing out of her skin, focused on the moment, wringing every drop from every second, her head up and her eyes bright. Not blinking. At night, though, she was terrified, unable to give in to sleep in case Fred should slip away the moment her eyes closed, and waking with a shocked, guilty start every time he made a sound. And terrified, too, of the unknown, of what it would be like without him, and whether she would be able to live with the desolation. She knew that it was selfish, childish, even, to think this way, but it was the price she paid for her selfless, grown-up days. She would find herself thinking, when they did some small thing – made supper together, updated the children's photos – There won't be many more of these. The larger things were somehow more tolerable because they were part of the life of the house, and not just of their life. At the end of the summer open day as the last cars rolled down the hill to the Witherburn gate, and the foot-visitors, shepherded by stewards, dawdled down the footpath, she joined Fred in the library and they got quietly and determinedly sozzled.

'Ladycross!' he said, proposing a toast. 'A public sweetheart. Long may she turn tricks.'

Whatever the staff may have said in private, they continued to behave as though nothing was wrong until well after the point when it demonstrably was. In the autumn they'd employed Phyllida, the latest in a long line of nice, tough, privately educated girls to help out with secretarial work and the day-to-day running of the house. The ad in the *Lady* had specified no more than 'initiative, humour, computer skills and a liking for dogs', but the mention of the 'historic family-owned house' was usually enough to provide a good shortlist.

Phyllida was the archetype of her kind, pretty much at home in these exalted surroundings, nearly as well-bred as Fred, her steely competence and energy honed by work in ski-chalets, posh bars and restaurants and at least one well-known advertising agency. She was a treasure, of a sort. She could, as she told them at her interview, make a mean *crème brûlée*, give an injection to a horse, and create a file of all-purpose letters of gratitude, condolence, apology, complaint or congratulation, which could quickly be customised to suit the circumstances. Oh, and she had her advanced driver's licence and was familiar with four-wheel-drives and horse-boxes. Both Miranda and Fred felt that Phyllida might be interviewing them rather than the other way round, but Ladycross did its work, and she duly accepted a salary more modest than she would have received nannying in New York.

Fred professed to be awed by her. 'Do you think there's a farm somewhere that produces these young women?' he enquired rhetorically.

'Yes. It's called the home counties. And boarding-school.'

'But you're those things,' he said, 'and you're not like that.'

'I'm not typical.'

'Damn right.'

'And anyway,' she grabbed his collar, 'what are you saying? That I'm a wimp?'

'Led go, led go, you're hurtig be!' he cried, in the manner of the Elephant's Child. 'Of course I'm not saying any such thing. But that girl has balls of steel. Definitely first choice for up the Orinoco.'

The *crème brûlée* proved contentious. Mrs Bird did not like anyone messing about in her kitchen, with the possible exception of Miranda whom she had trained up singlehandedly and for whose small skills she took sole credit; but unfortunately Phyllida excelled at the one pudding for which Fred had a weakness, and that Mrs Bird herself had never properly mastered. Once a week without fail, as the summer trudged by, Phyllida was commanded to produce this treat under the cold gaze of the culinary *Sturmbannführer*. What infuriated Mrs Bird still more than being usurped was that the alternative to the offending dessert was no longer her extensive range of trifles, crumbles and cheesecakes but – horror of horrors – shop-bought ice-cream.

Miranda tried to explain that it was nothing to do with Mrs Bird's cooking. 'His lordship's not well. He can only manage a little of anything, and it has to slip down easily.'

This was met with a tight-lipped nod, which Miranda interpreted as anxiety. The nature of Fred's indisposition was never asked, and she didn't know how to broach it.

Phyllida, though, was on the case. One evening in early July when Miranda returned from a meeting of the area NSPCC in Stoneybridge, Phyllida came out of the back door before she had turned the engine off. 'Welcome.' They had dispensed with 'my lady' in all but the most formal situations. 'How was the meeting?'

'Okay, reasonably productive. Too long as usual. How is he?'

'Not good. He's been sleeping almost all day.'

'He gets tired these days,' she said, as they walked towards the house, but her stomach squirmed with dread. 'Perhaps he needed to.'

Phyllida held the door for her. 'It was actually quite hard to wake him up at lunchtime. In the end I managed it by switching on the ladies' singles and giving him his lunch on a tray. Actually I joined him, so we could debate the shorts-versus-skirts issue.

Mrs Bird didn't approve, but at least he got some of her pasta salad down.'

'Well done.'

'But then he went right back to sleep, Miss Sabatini notwithstanding.'

Miranda tried to smile. 'He must have been tired.'

'I thought he might need the loo – he drank quite a bit of water. So I took him, I hope that was all right.'

Miranda paused in the kitchen doorway. 'You took him?'

'He was too sleepy to manage. I didn't want anything to happen.'

'No. Thanks, Phyllida, that was good of you.'

'He's still in there. Expecting you.'

'Thanks.' She was half-way across the hall, and turned to say, 'You can drop out now, I do appreciate you waiting up.'

'I walked the dogs.'

'Thank you.' She wished the girl would go, instead of delivering this catalogue of virtuous activity. Which, she reminded herself, she was paid to do. 'Night, sleep well.'

The moment she entered the library she could feel the difference. Though the window was open on this fine summer's evening it felt slightly stuffy. The television, tuned to Wimbledon's match of the day, bip-bip-roared in the background. There were several lamps on. Fred sat on the sofa, his head sagging forward. It was his hands she noticed first. They rested on his knees like objects that had come to rest there randomly. She saw how loose and freckled the skin was, how the long bones shone through and the nails appeared colourless and unhealthy: the hands of a sick old man. Like Gerald's had been; like her father's. The shock of the sight, and of the realisation, brought a bitter taste into her mouth and she paused, leaning on the arm of a chair, collecting herself.

Her husband, her love, her life-force, was dying. Was moving away from her with every second that he slept, in this breathless room. Conquering her nausea she turned off the television and opened another window, gulping in the fresh air.

He sensed her there, and opened his eyes. At once the inner light, the essential Fred, overcame his wasted body. His solitary journey was halted. He was, for the moment, back in the present, with her.

'My darling . . . you're back.'

'Just.'

She sat down by him and he raised his hand – his once strong, beautiful hand – to guide her face to his. The skin of his palm on her neck felt cool and papery.

'Mm . . . How were the charitable ladies?'

'Working well, but slowly.'

'Whereas I haven't been working at all.'

'Phyllida said.'

'She's a great girl, came in here and ate pasta salad with me.'

'Did you manage some?'

'Oh, yes. I think so. One of Mrs B's tastier efforts.'

'I'll tell her.'

Fred turned his head away. 'I'd ask, "Whatever's the matter with me?" Only I know.'

'You're having an off-day,' she said. 'It doesn't mean anything.'

'But the off-days are getting closer together, aren't they?'

Softly, but with her heart beating in panic, she brushed an imaginary thread from his trousers.

He stopped her hand with his. 'Aren't they?' he repeated gently.

'I suppose they're bound to . . . Yes.'

'When's my next outing?' This was how he referred to hospital appointments.

'Next week.'

'Maybe they can gee me up a bit.'

'Yes – maybe.'

She knew he was looking at her: a look of rueful tenderness that invited a collusion in which this evening she would not, could not, engage.

Instead she stood up and asked, 'I'm going to have a nightcap, would you like one?'

'Good thinking. I'll have a shot of the Bushmills Miles brought.'

'You got it.'

Tears spilled down her cheeks as she crossed the darkened hall, and she was wiping them away as she entered the kitchen and found Phyllida still there, eating a biscuit while the kettle boiled. 'Making a cuppa, can I do you one?'

'No thanks, we're going to have something a little stronger.' She collected the cylindrical presentation box off the side.

'Good for you.'

'Night, then.'

'My lady, can I say something?'

Alerted by the form of address, Miranda stood a little defensively with the Bushmills clasped to her chest like a teddy bear, or a hot-water bottle.

'Of course.'

'Please don't take this the wrong way – but do you think that perhaps Lord Stratton might need some extra help?'

'You mean – a nurse?'

Phyllida nodded. 'It's just that he's quite a big man, even now – I mean, he's tall, and it's quite difficult to help him when he's not . . . you know, if he's having a down day.'

Miranda heard the unprecedented note of anxiety in the girl's voice. Yes, she told herself, this is it: the next – she tried not to think the final – phase.

'I understand. You obviously coped manfully today, Fred said so. But it's not right that you should have to.'

'Don't get me wrong, I don't mind, I'm happy to, I just—'

'It's all right, Phyllida. Really. I appreciate your concern, and so does he. I'll talk to him about it and we'll make a plan.'

Phyllida's voice was small and tense when she next spoke. 'How is he?'

'Very ill, I'm afraid.'

'Will he get better?'

Miranda chose her words carefully. 'He'll certainly have better days. And worse ones.'

'I see.'

'But don't worry,' said Miranda. 'We'll see him right.'

It was the sensible thing to do. But, even so, the docility with which Fred acceded to the nursing help almost broke her heart. She knew him too well, understood that his natural distaste for the idea was overcome by his desire to make things easier for her. But, then, that was the truth of the matter — someone who was trained, who could make light work of what increasingly needed to be done, would make life easier for both of them. So Miranda in her turn refrained from too much discussion of the issue. It was discussed, decided, and put in place. To begin with, a Macmillan nurse would come in twice a day, morning and evening, to help Fred wash and dress, deal with his medication and take what he liked to call his 'soundings'. A nurse would also come in if Miranda had for any reason to be gone all day, or overnight, although these days she strove to avoid such protracted absences. Most often, though not always, it was Pat Callender, a soft-spoken Scot whose natural tact and long experience in these matters eased her into the life of Ladycross so that she seemed always to have been there. Hers was the sort of perfect and perfected professionalism that enabled her to defer, without loss of authority, to the professionalism of others. There was never the least doubt that when Pat was in the house Lord Fred was getting the best care possible, and this had the effect of making everyone raise their game accordingly.

This went for Miranda, too. It was inevitable that at the outset she experienced some guilt, and even a little well-disguised resentment, at this calm stranger assisting Fred in all kinds of intimate ways. Less responsibility brought greater insecurity. So she was more grateful than she could say when Pat made the position clear.

'You know what it is, my lady,' she said one morning, as she put things into the washing-machine, and Miranda was refurbishing the week's flower arrangements. 'We're a good team.'

'I hope so. But you do most of the work now, Pat.'

'Not so.' Pat poured a cup of powder into the wash compartment and snapped the door shut. 'You're the heart and I'm the hands. That's how it should be, and that's how it is here. Not everywhere, I can tell you.'

'You're a very safe pair of hands.' Miranda fluffed roses, coral and white, in a Spode vase. 'I don't know what we'd do without you.'

'Manage very well. But you've a hundred other things to do,

you'd burn yourself out. And your husband would burn up worrying about you. Don't think me impertinent if I say that you and he have something special. Something you don't see every day. Take my word for it. There.' She pressed the start button. 'I'm off. I'll see you tonight.'

That evening Fred was feeling chipper, so they went for a stroll. They'd adapted their evenings to suit the new regime, having their drink and dinner earlier than before so that Pat could swing into action when she arrived at eight thirty. To avoid inclines, which made Fred breathless these days, their little walk described a circuit of Ladycross, which enabled him to enjoy different perspectives on the house.

'A plus, you see,' he remarked, as they armed it slowly along the brow of the hill overlooking Witherburn. 'When I did nothing but rush about I had no time to stand and stare. Or not enough. And no inclination to do so. I'm only just beginning to realise how long it is since I really looked at the old place, from all sides. My brother and I used to lark about behind the Dower House when we were younger because it was secluded. Not too cold in winter, and not overlooked. I smoked my first cigarette in the angle of that wall. My first fifty, probably.'

'Why there,' she laughed, 'when the two of you had all of this to escape into?'

'Because an illicit activity derives most of its pleasure from the possibility of being caught.' He squeezed her arm with his. 'I speak only of smoking, you understand.'

'I'm glad to hear it.'

They walked a little further, around the side of the house and across the back of the converted barns where they paused, leaning back on the wooden slats, and looking down towards the folly.

'I'm so glad,' he said, 'that we've got that under way.'

'Yes,' she replied. 'It's going to be wonderful.'

'More accurately, that *you* got it under way. My wonderwoman. Sometimes your energy simply takes my breath away. Not a difficult thing to do these days, but all the same.'

'I've enjoyed it. It's like Rock on the Manor, a project, something to get my teeth into and that will show results.'

'Unlike running a crumbling old pile.'

'That's not fair, I adore Ladycross.'

He touched her cheek. 'I wasn't talking about Ladycross.'

'I shall ignore that.'

'If you like, but it's true. From where I'm standing, anyway.'

'Not from here.' She kept her eyes to the front, gazing down the hill, maintaining a shared focus. 'And, anyway, I don't do much . . . We have Pat.'

'Indeed we do, and a sterling sort she is. And your greatest admirer, by the way.'

'I find that hard to believe.'

'Oh, yes. She considers me a very lucky man, in that respect at least.'

Miranda could feel his eyes on her, and turned to meet them. 'We've both been lucky. Far more lucky than two people have a right to expect.'

'Are lucky,' he said. 'Not have been. Are.'

He drew her into his arms and they stood like that, leaning together against the weathered wood of the barn, drifting, warmed by the setting sun.

For Fred's birthday in July she gave him a chair. For some time she'd noticed that there was a need for a portable, comfortable chair, made to measure for his tall and now almost unpadded frame: one that could easily be carried to where he wanted to be – a particular window, a place in the garden . . . even, she dared to hope, Rock on the Manor. They had a wheelchair, but he liked to walk from A to B where possible and a proper chair of his own would not make him so conspicuous, nor so much (as he put it) of a sad figure.

Also, it was her express intention to give him something lasting, something both handsome, elegant and practical that carried with it no hint of short-termism, that would be his for now, but always have a place at Ladycross in its own right.

Kirsty Hobday, the nice woman who with her husband ran a printing office and card shop in one of the barns, recommended a man in the village. 'You want Dan Mather at the mill,' she said. 'He's an absolute whizz with wood.'

Miranda knew him by sight, a wired, wary young man who seemed to define the phrase 'keeps himself to himself'.

'I know. Has he made something for you?'

'No, but he did up the cottage next door to ours and was our neighbour for a while. He's a little bit strange, a bit of a loner, but he's got a workshop at the mill now and even I can see his stuff is beautifully made.'

'I'll go and see him.'

It was the run-up to Rock on the Manor, when she would normally have been like a headless chicken, but this year, through some kindly, sympathetic conspiracy, those in charge of different aspects of the event got on with it and troubled her very little. Most systems remained in place from year to year. Phyllida took over a lot of the phone calls and discreetly spread the word of Fred's illness, for even the bands were no bother, falling in with existing arrangements with a minimum of fuss and making no excessive demands. Still, Miranda spent most of each morning on it, with Phyllida and, if he was around and could be co-opted, Marco Torrence, who was the sort of genial arts heavyweight perfectly suited to the task.

One early afternoon when Fred was napping she went down to the mill. From week to week, almost from day to day, their routine changed, adapting to the progress of the stealthy growth in his chest. Good days were a blessing, a bonus. Bad ones were endured. Today was one of those when he was sleeping a lot, when if she was in the house she found herself constantly checking on him, terrified that he might have slipped away without her noticing. She feared that more than anything – that she would not be near when it happened. But Phyllida was there, and had told her to go, that it would do her good, promising to call her on the mobile phone if needed.

'You'll only be five minutes away. If I've got even the minutest worry I'll call you.'

She rang Daniel first and his voice on the phone was as she could have predicted – light, a little distant, not exactly chilly but certainly lacking the warmth of the natural salesman. Yes, she could come down, he was usually around. No promises there, then.

But as she pulled into the shared driveway of the mill houses he must have been looking out for her, for he appeared in the doorway.

'Hallo, Daniel,' she said, holding out her hand. 'It's very good of you to make time for me.'

He looked down at her hand for a split second before taking it. 'That's okay.' He seemed to hesitate again before saying, 'Come in.'

She'd expected to meet him in his workshop, not in these horribly austere, whitewashed surroundings. The thought occurred to her that a man who lived in a place like this would have difficulty in interpreting her vague yet complex brief with all its emotional connotations. Still, she was here now and owed it to herself and him to try.

'Can I – ah – get you anything?' he asked.

'I'm fine, thanks.'

'So what were you thinking of?'

The wording of this enquiry was slightly odd, a little ambiguous, as though he were surprised she'd turned up at all.

'A chair,' she said, 'for my husband.'

'What sort of chair?'

'He's very ill, so it needs to be easily transportable and as comfortable as it can possibly be, but also—' she took a deep breath '—beautiful.'

He was listening to her, but with his head bowed, looking down at his laced fingers. 'Okay.'

She felt she should justify her use of such an extravagant word. 'We live in that great barn of a place and it's packed with priceless stuff as you can imagine. I want whatever I give Fred to be able to hold its own. New but timeless. So that he'll know something's been added – in his name, if you like.'

'Yes – um—' he nodded matter-of-factly '—got it.'

'Right!' Miranda laughed, slightly nonplussed by his brevity and the speed with which things were going. 'I'm glad you understand. I thought perhaps I was being a little too non-specific.'

'You are being,' he said, 'but that's okay. Specifics are my job.'

'I don't suppose I could see some of your work? Only to my shame I'm not familiar with it.'

'Nothing to be ashamed of, I'm no Lord Linley.'

'No, but a noted local craftsman . . .' Did that sound pompous? She tried to get things back on to a businesslike footing. 'Anyway, I wouldn't want to waste your time by asking you for something that wasn't to your taste.'

He cracked a smile, which completely revolutionised his face, but which was gone so quickly she felt she might have imagined it.

'It's not my taste that matters. I – um – my aim is to chime with yours.'

'Good point. But perhaps—'

'Why don't I come up with a few ideas and send them to you, and then we'll have something concrete to discuss?'

There was clearly something sacrosanct about the workshop. Miranda would have dismissed this as both affected and unhelpful, except that Daniel Mather himself seemed neither of these things. Reserved and of few words, but nothing if not focused. And she could find no fault with the idea of him presenting her with plans.

'All right. Thank you.'

'What – when is your husband's birthday?'

She told him, asking anxiously. 'Is that feasible? I'm approaching all this from a position of ignorance and I may be asking for the impossible.'

He lifted a finger. 'Nothing's impossible. No, if we can agree on a design, that'll be . . .' He got up, went and opened a drawer in the kitchen and took out a moleskin notebook and pencil. 'Just writing down . . . And do you know your husband's measurements?'

'He's six foot four, but only eleven stone at the moment.'

'How does he like to sit?'

She was about to say that she didn't know, but then a picture of Fred came into her mind. 'He used to lounge, but these days he's more comfortable sitting upright but with his arms resting.'

'Can you show me?'

She did so, her back against the back of the chair, her elbows

574

taking some of her weight so that her shoulders hunched slightly, her hands linked in front of her. He subjected her to a brief, intense scrutiny, and then got to his feet, closing the notebook.

'I see, thanks. I'll get something to you in the next day or so.'

Miranda rose too. 'I'll look forward to it. It's exciting.'

He gave another of his thrifty smiles in acknowledgement.

After the quiet, white interior of the mill, the lanes of Witherburn were clamorous with colour and activity.

When she got back she put her head round the door of Smart Cards.

'Thanks, Kirsty, it was interesting.'

'Oh, good, I'm sure he'll be able to do something.'

'I hope so. He's not easy, is he? Plays his cards extremely close to his chest.'

'He's no chatterbox,' agreed Kirsty, 'but, then, he's an artist.'

The following day a stiff brown envelope was delivered to Ladycross by hand. On the front were handwritten the words 'The Lady Stratton – enclosed is my suggestion.' Inside was a single sheet of foolscap paper with not a plan but an exquisite, elaborately detailed drawing of a chair. *The* chair. The only possible one. In the corner of the paper was a box containing details of the wood (oak), the carvings (oak leaves and feathers), the slung leather panels, and the dimensions

She rang him up at once. 'You are *so* clever,' she said.

'You like the look of it.'

'I love the look of it. You've completely – got it.'

'Conceptualised . . .'

She thought he might be smiling. 'I expect that's the word.'

'So, ah, do you want me to go ahead along those lines?'

'Yes, please.'

'It's a pleasure, actually,' he said, in his offhand way. 'The sort of thing I like doing.'

She asked tentatively. 'Shall I be able to see the work in progress?'

'It's up to you.'

He might as well have said, 'What do you think?' except there was no truculence in his voice. It was clear that if she felt strongly enough he could not stop her, as the customer, coming to take a look, but she had better feel pretty strongly.

'Fine. And do you need an advance – for the materials and so on?'

'Not necessary.'

She pressed him. 'But helpful, perhaps?'

There was a brief pause. 'On balance, I think – I'd rather you saw the completed chair before you hand over your money.'

'Whatever you say.'

Several times over the next few weeks she had to resist the temptation to visit the mill. Fred seemed to be entering a new phase, less fraught but weaker. These days she often saw in his eyes a desperation that clawed her heart. It was almost, *almost* true, she thought, that helplessness in the face of someone else's pain was as bad as suffering the pain itself. But then she'd go out for a walk in the lovely, cool evening when he'd gone to sleep – when he was still peaceful before the wakeful middle watches of the night – and realise that nothing was sweeter than life, and no sort of pain worse than the loss of it.

Two days before Fred's birthday Daniel Mather rang to ask whether he could deliver the chair that afternoon.

'Normally I ask for commissions to be collected, but . . . ah, with this one I'd like you to see it for the first time *in situ*.'

'Two o'clockish would be good, Fred generally takes a nap then.' Miranda remembered the Mini she'd seen parked outside the mill. 'Are you all right for transport?'

'It's portable, remember.'

'Of course, how silly of me.'

'See you later.'

He came to the front of the house, carrying in one hand, a flat package swathed in cloth tied with string.

In the hall he asked, 'Where does your husband like to sit?'

'In the library.'

'Shall we . . . ?'

She led the way into the library, and he paused and looked round. 'Great room . . . What do you think? By the window, perhaps?'

Together they moved aside the table with the visitors' book, and the stiffly upholstered chair next to it, and Miranda watched as he unwrapped the parcel. Folded, the chair was sleek and slim, almost flat. When he opened it, and stood back, she gave a little gasp of sheer pleasure.

'Feel it,' he said. 'Sit in it.'

She did so. The golden brown wood felt like warm silk, the leather yielding, soft and buttery. The delicate tracery of leaves and feathers had been carved only on those surfaces that someone sitting in the chair would not touch – the sides and legs – so there was not the slightest roughness to the skin. The arms of the chair were broad enough to support her own arms comfortably, and the back and seat tilted, as if instinctively, to accommodate her position and the angles of her body. It was like sitting on air. There was even a small articulation at the top of the back, to form a head-rest that would adjust naturally, though Miranda had to pull herself up slightly to use it.

'It's made for your husband, remember,' he said.

'Of course it is . . .' The delight in her voice matched the quiet pride in his.

'One thing,' he said. 'I took a small liberty.'

There was none she wouldn't have granted him. 'What's that?'

'Let me show you. If you get up.' She did so, and he pointed to the rounded ends of the arms, on each of which was carved, so fluidly that it echoed the rippling line of oak leaves, an initial: F on the right, M on the left. 'I hope you don't mind. I got carried away.'

She shook her head. 'I'm so glad you did.'

'You see,' he sat in the chair himself, 'your husband, with his longer arms, will just be able to feel those, if he wants to, without reaching or effort. A little bit of sensory stimulation at his fingertips. And, of course, a reminder of you.'

The diffidence and reserve had gone from Daniel Mather's

manner and his voice. He was warmly confident and enthusiastic, a man in his element, alight with pride and pleasure in his work.

Miranda ran her own fingers lightly over the initials.

'He'll like that, Daniel. So much.' She looked up at him, not bothering to wipe away the tears in her eyes. 'And so do I. I can't thank you enough.'

'You already have. I just hope it will be of use. The basic design's that of the old Indian army chairs, made to be slung on the back of an elephant. You can put it anywhere you like, indoors or out, it's easy to carry.'

'It's quite wonderful.'

'As long as it suits.'

He began to move towards the door, but she found she didn't want to let him go, not yet. 'Daniel, can I offer you something? I know it's not the right time of day, but a glass of champagne, perhaps?'

He shook his head. 'It's a nice idea, but no, thanks. Thoughts to think, that sort of thing.'

'Well, then, I owe you.' She flew to her handbag. 'You haven't had a penny from me, all that work—'

'I'll bill you.' His voice cut in, sounding, for the first and only time, sharp; then softened again as he added, 'I quite like the feeling of – er – giving you something, so if you wouldn't mind indulging me for a few days . . . And I hope your husband enjoys the chair. You can fold it up and hide it till his birthday.'

'I will. I know he'll love it.'

Outside by the van they shook hands. It was the first time she'd touched him, she realised, and his hand felt warm and strong, enveloping hers decidedly.

'Perhaps,' she said, 'you'll come and see us again. So Fred can thank you in person.'

'Please.' He gave his gentle smile. 'But there's no need for more thanks. It's my job, and my pleasure.'

By the time of his birthday, Fred was very much worse. Miranda took the chair upstairs to his room and placed it where he could

578

see it without having too drastically to alter his position. Pat was just about to leave after her morning visit.

'Isn't that gorgeous? And the clever thing is it looks as if it's always been here.'

After she'd gone Fred, unable to speak, patted the edge of the bed for Miranda to sit there. She did so, placing her hand gently against the side of his face.

'You did all that . . .' he whispered.

'No, Daniel Mather did it.'

'But your idea, your thought, my darling. Your love.'

'Yes.' She remembered something Pat had said to her. 'I was the heart, but he was the hands.'

'Lucky man . . .' His voice snagged. 'Lucky bastard.'

To cheer him, she began describing the chair's practical features, the cunning and comfort of its design, but he stopped her. 'I'm frightened, Miranda – that I may never be able to use it.'

'Of course you will,' she began, but checked herself. 'It doesn't matter. You can look at it. And I'll put it where you can touch it. It feels lovely.'

'That's a good idea.'

'Besides,' she added, 'it's not only for you. It's for this place. For Ladycross.'

Now he held out his arms and she carefully, gently, leaned forward into his embrace that was now terrifyingly insubstantial. 'You know,' he said, 'don't you, how much I love you?'

She nodded.

He turned his face so that his lips were against her forehead when he next spoke. 'Well, my darling, it's more than that.'

Morning

On Christmas Eve we gathered to celebrate the theatre's completion. Just a few of us, because the formal opening and first night would be in the spring. We met at the folly at midday, on a cold day of such glittering perfection, gold, white and blue, that it dazzled the eyes and gladdened the heart. The frost had melted, leaving the merest silver glaze here and there under the shelter of the trees, and the rest of the ground gleamed with a moisture that would freeze again only hours from now. The broad, tranquil glade created for the theatre was itself like a stage, spotlit by the brief ascendancy of the winter sun shining through the tracery of branches. We'd started out in the theatre foyer, but after the toasts the lure of the sunshine was too much and we'd all moved outside.

It was for this reason that they'd chosen to have the party in the middle of the day. That, and for the benefit of the children, who larked about among the outdoor tables and chairs, and between the trees. And also because Christmas Eve was a busy time, fizzing with last-minute preparations.

Apart from the Montcleres, and myself with Fleur, Rowan and Chloë, there were Miranda and Marco; Miranda's mother, Mrs Tattersall, and her fiancé; Daniel Mather; Kirsty and Chris Hobday; a couple I hadn't met before called Tom and Pauline Worsley; Phyllida; Mr and Mrs Bird; the nice Macmillan nurse, Pat Callender; the building contractor and three of the men who'd worked on the project; and a handful of other people from the estate. A couple of old friends from Fred's university jazz-band days, whom I recognised from the funeral party, had brought along a keyboard and tenor sax and were playing in the theatre foyer. Penny had laid on mulled wine in Thermos jugs, and Miles had set up a barbecue and was serving hot dogs. A special chair – one that Daniel had made for Fred – had been brought down and the spaniel, Mark, lay on it, his head drooping over the side.

I thought, This is it – happiness! But quickly banished the thought as tempting fate. It was enough to know that even the appearance of such harmony, goodwill and grace could exist, on whatever pretext and no matter how fleetingly. The musicians were playing their part in this sweet alchemy with 'Blue Skies'. Fleur was dancing, swaying from side to side with Rowan clasped in front of her, facing outwards, the two of them swathed in her big black overcoat, his little head and arms in a Laplander hat and red mittens, sticking out over the top button. Chloë – better but not nearly better enough – was dancing too, after a fashion, hopping jerkily back and forth, her hands holding the baby's. Only Fleur, I thought, strong, cool, magical Fleur, *my daughter*, could have given that poor wounded child the confidence to dance.

Other people joined in. Miranda, with Marco: she was a natural dancer, he wasn't, but he bounced about gamely with a grin as big as all outdoors, she laughing, and having to bend slightly to twirl beneath his hand, and topple unsteadily back into his arms. Mrs Tattersall and her dapper boyfriend drew applause, gliding and reversing like professionals on the uneven surface. Millie and Jem jigged about with Penny.

Daniel approached me, glancing over his shoulder in that way he had, as though his attention were really elsewhere.

'Hallo,' I said. 'Do you want to dance?'

He shook his head. 'Not my bag. I've got two left feet and the right one's no good either.'

'Come whenever you like tomorrow.'

'It's so nice of you to include me.'

'It will make our day to have you, Dan. Rowan's in danger of being swamped by women.'

'I made him a present, but it's, ah, much too old for him. I haven't a clue about babies.'

'Babies don't need anything, that's the point. What is it?'

'It's an owl. Its head spins round.' He frowned sheepishly. 'You wouldn't call it hi-tech. I've never made a toy before.'

'That's so sweet of you, Dan. It'll be something for him to treasure.' I kissed his cheek, and felt his hand fleetingly on my waist, and heard a little sound he made – of acknowledgement, of pleasure. There was so much to be acknowledged, but it didn't need saying. Perhaps, in our odd-couple way, we understood each other.

'See you tomorrow.'

'See you.'

I went over to talk to Miles. 'This is a great day. You must be so pleased.'

'I am.' His hair was disarrayed and his face was pink from the barbecue. 'I don't mind admitting that I was a little . . . not sceptical exactly, but doubtful it would ever actually happen. Too many complications, too many imponderables.' He smiled. 'I reckoned without Miranda's inspirational arm-twisting qualities.'

'I expect,' I said carefully, 'that it meant a lot to her for all sorts of reasons.'

'To all of us. But, yes, to her most of all, I appreciate that.' He turned a couple of bangers before adding, 'And it's good to see her happy again.'

'Yes,' I agreed. 'I think it's a compliment, don't you, to the person who's gone, when the one who's left wants – not to re-create the relationship but rediscover happiness?'

'I hadn't looked at it like that. Maybe you're right. Marco seems an excellent chap, and he's mad about her so,' he shrugged, 'good luck to them.'

I took myself for a little walk, carrying my glass away from the party and wandering along one of the tracks through the trees. The voices, and the unamplified music, faded quickly. I might have been completely alone, except that I knew they were there, my family and my friends, dancing in the sunlight, just out of sight.

Breathless from dancing, Miranda slipped away and went inside the theatre. For today's celebration the auditorium had been lit as if for a performance: the stage bright, and the houselights dimmed but not extinguished completely. Centre stage she'd placed a microphone, with Fred's broad-brimmed straw hat – a yellow rose tucked into the crown – perched on top, and his walking-stick, highly polished, leaning against the stand. She went to a seat at the back, in the corner furthest from the entrance, and sat down. The musicians were playing the Nat King Cole classic 'When I Fall In Love'. She *had* fallen in love with Fred for ever, had given her heart completely, and yet his legacy to her was that there was more – still some of her heart to give – and for that she could never thank him enough. Sitting there in the soft, artificial twilight she felt him very close, could almost imagine his arm around her shoulders and his long fingers caressing her cheek . . . She closed her eyes for a second and was startled, a moment later, to find that someone was sitting next to her, and that it was not Fred.

'Penny for them, Ragsy,' said Tom.

'Nothing you couldn't guess.'

'It's a great do. A nice family feel. Fred would be chuffed.'

'He is.'

Tom put his glass down. 'Sticky stuff this, though. Not really my cuppa.' He looked at her as she gazed at the stage. 'What about you? Happy with your new fella?'

'Completely.'

'He seems a thoroughly good bloke. A surprise, mind. Total opposite to Fred.'

'Mmm . . .' She considered this before meeting his eyes. 'What they have in common is a gift for happiness.'

'Fair dos. When's the wedding?'

'In February.' She smiled at his raised eyebrow. '*Not* because of Valentine's Day, but because February's when everyone needs cheering up.'

'Can't argue with that. You're going to miss this place, though.'

'No.' She shook her head. 'No, I'm not. I'll always love it, and think about it and want to come to visit – when I'm invited. But I shan't pine for it. I'm going to live with Marco now. My memories of Ladycross are something that'll help launch me into my new life, not hold me back.'

'Good for you, girl.' Tom took her hand and squeezed it. 'Good luck, Ragsy. Go get 'em.'

As they left the auditorium, Marco was coming in.

'It's great,' said Tom, slapping him on the shoulder in passing. 'Really great. Congratulations.'

'Thanks. Yes, I think I can safely say, "We did it".'

He put his arms round Miranda. 'How's it going?'

'Very well.'

'Bit melancholy?'

'Just a little.'

'That's allowed,' said Marco, stroking her hair, rocking her from side to side. 'Everything's allowed. Let me be your buttress.'

She laughed, and drew long, deep breaths inside the solid warmth of his embrace, where there was always room to breathe.

Claudia wrapped her cloak around her as she set off back to the house. It was the middle of winter, which once she had found intolerable but which these days she no longer minded. Out of doors, she liked the sense of strength, of standing alone, that winter gave her: the knowledge that after these hard, bleak times, spring would come with sweet reliability, brushing the grey hills with green and gold and summoning back the swifts that nested under the roof of the temple. She had planted a rose where Gaius was buried, and as it grew it clambered lovingly around his headstone, obscuring the inscription with its clinging arms, and decorating the granite with white blooms.

At the gate that led into the garden of the villa, she paused. Even in the middle of the day at this time of year the sun was low, and the house looked burnished, its angles cast in shadow and its walls and roof glowing.

Publius was walking in the garden, slowly and methodically patrolling the paths, inspecting the bare soil, thinking as she was of all that it held in safekeeping – all that they had put there over the years and which in summer would reward them with fresh growth, scent and colour. Catching sight of him like this, when he was not aware of being seen, he still had the power to move and excite her. Her man, her heart's home – flawed like her, but also like her still hopeful, still eager in spite of everything.

'Publius!'

Not knowing where she was he looked up first towards the house. She opened the gate and the small sound made him turn his head. He stood waiting for her. As she reached him he frowned and glanced briefly away again.

'Did you hear music?'

'No,' she said.

'Something blown on the wind probably.' He took her hand and laid it over his heart. 'Where have you been?'

'Just walking.'

'For someone who hates Britain you walk a lot.' He could tease her now that it was no longer true. 'And is everything all right out there?'

She nodded. 'And here?'

'Oh, yes.' He looked towards the house. 'I'm proud of this place, Claudia.'

'I know.' They began to walk slowly back together. 'I get satisfaction from knowing that what we made will be here long after we're gone.'

'It has quite a while to go before that, I hope.'

On the terrace, on a patch of stone warmed by the unseasonal sun, the black puppy lay asleep. Claudia bent down and scooped him up, nursing him in her arms like a baby.

Publius said, 'You mollycoddle that dog.' But he still stood at her shoulder, scratching the blissful puppy's chin with his finger.

It was a moment of calm content. Soon, Flavia would be

here with Helena, and Helena's son, and the boy and the puppy would race around hectically, winding each other up until an accident or sheer over-excitement put a stop to things.

But for now, peace. Claudia leaned against her husband and felt his vexed, bound strength at her back. She his prop, he her support.

Today it would be dark early. But tomorrow, and the next day, the march would contine towards spring.

'*Ubi tu, Publius, ego Claudia sum,*' she said. Though so softly that Publius, moving away from her to return to the house, did not hear her.

As she followed, she too heard the music, faint and fleeting, wafted on the air from some distant, happy, gathering.

Not long after that, we left. The girls were ahead of me. Chloë first, trusted to carry Rowan, clasping him tight to her shoulder. Then Fleur, striding along, unconcerned, her black coat swinging. They were eager to be back at the cottage now, to finish the Christmas tree, to wrap things up, to light the fire and listen to music, and drink bottled beer, true celebrators of the winter solstice.

I brought up the rear, lagging further and further behind. Not because I didn't want to be with them, but because I wanted to stretch this moment, this in-between time, with the sun still high and the winter shadows short — this time when everything seemed possible.

By the time I emerged from the chill of the wood the girls, with Fleur now carrying Rowan, were walking together along the road towards Witherburn. I could hear their voices, a burst of laughter.

Ahead of me was home, Christmas, the talk I would have with Peter. And from way behind me, still, the last of the folly music.